THE FALL OF CELENE

THE GODDESS PROPHECIES

BOOK  TWO

ARAYA EVERMORE

THE FALL OF CELENE

Cover art by Deranged Doctor Designs

StarFire
Published by Starfire Epic Fantasy

Paperback Third Edition

ISBN-13: 978-99920-3-040-0

Also by Araya Evermore:

The Goddess Prophecies:

Night Goddess

The Fall of Celene

Storm Holt

Demon Spear

Dragons of the Dawn Bringer

War of the Raven

Acknowledgements

Thank you to Mollie, Sophia, Pauline, Jon and Angie for their excellent editorial work and advice and to everyone at The Writers Workshop and Corner Stones. Thanks to Jessica Allain for her wonderful cover art.

Thank you to my precious Reader Team who make this work that much more fun. A special thanks to Ian for his unending enthusiasm and help in spreading this story to other fantasy readers.

Thanks to the Cosmos for making this work possible. I would also like to thank you, the reader, for joining the adventure.

For Wisdom

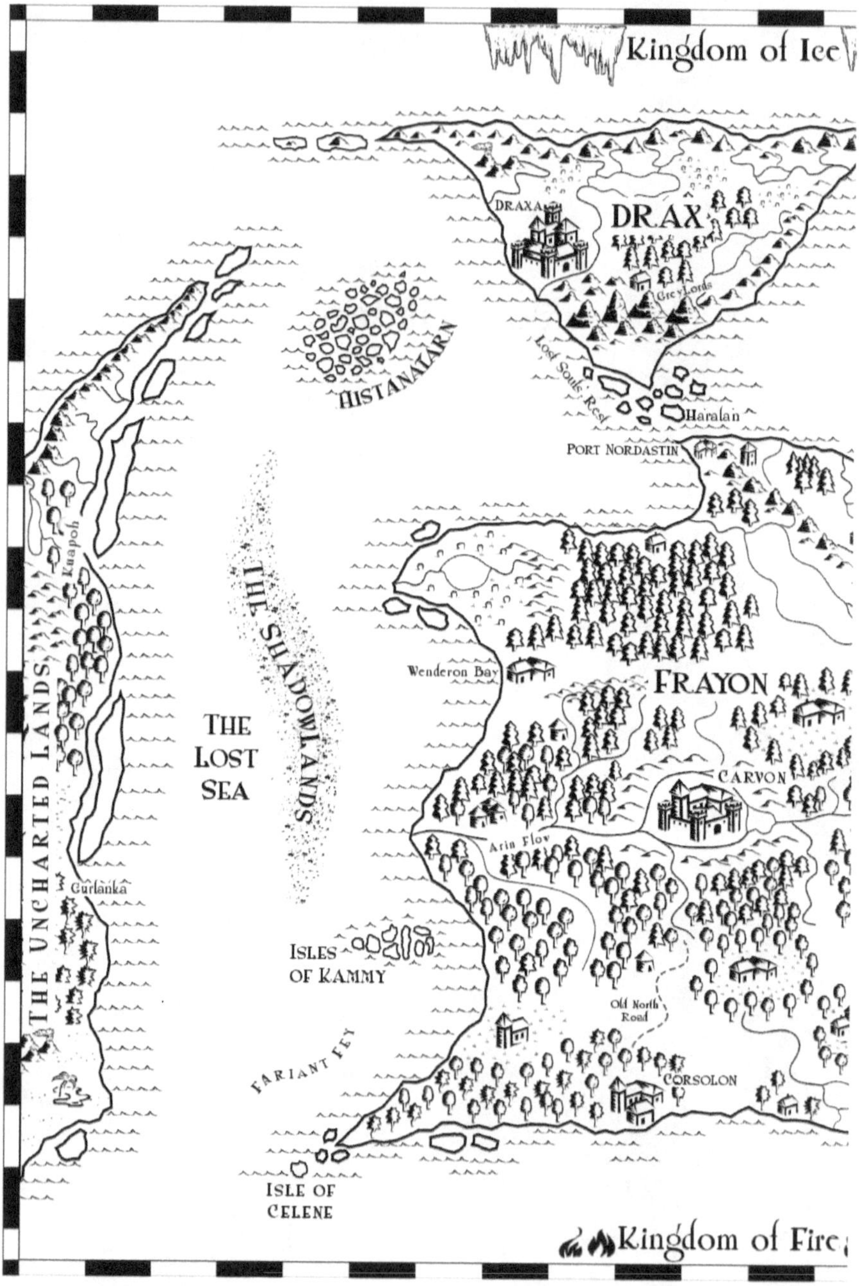
Kingdom of Ice
DRAXA
DRAX
Grey Lords
HISTANALARN
Lost Souls Rest
Haralan
PORT NORDASTIN
THE SHADOWLANDS
THE LOST SEA
THE UNCHARTED LANDS
Wenderon Bay
FRAYON
CARVON
Arin Flow
Gurlanka
ISLES OF KAMMY
FARIANT FEY
Old North Road
CORSOLON
ISLE OF CELENE
Kingdom of Fire

MAIORIA
THE KNOWN WORLD

N
W E
S

MUNLAND

Ocean Kingdom

LANS
HIMAY

TERAMIDES

INTOLANA

MAPHRAX

Mountians
of Maphrax

Excelline Mountains

ISLES
OF
TIRRY

Myrn

HALLANSTAR VK

OSTASIA

DAVONO REDMEN

TARVALASTONE

VENOSIA

JUROS

ATALANPH

CHAPTER 1

The Coming Darkness

JAGGED metal bit into rock with an ear-piercing screech, just missing Jinfrosthard's face as he fell back in the pitch black. Springing forwards he heaved down his axe, felt it slow, then crunch through bone. A scream of pain scoured his ears then fell silent. He wrenched his axe free.

The dark dwarven weapon that had missed him fell to the floor with a clang. The noise was lost in another scream of pain—his warriors or the enemy, he couldn't be sure. He swung his axe again. It slammed harmlessly into the wall of the narrow tunnel. He growled in disappointment. Again he swung and clanged against the armour of the enemy in front of him.

Something whistled through the air, and he instinctively dropped to his knees. The hurled blade of the dark dwarf scraped across the top of his helmet. Now kneeling, he could reach the knife in his boot. Jumping up, he sunk it into the dark dwarf's unprotected throat and stared into the burning yellow eyes of his hated opponent.

'Die you traitorous dark dwarf,' he roared. Those eyes gleamed in hatred and laughter before they turned dim. 'Curse them and their night vision,' he said.

The dark dwarves could see well in the dark. These cursed tunnels were their home. A place where evil flourished unreached and unchecked by the light. *No, no light could ever reach these forsaken depths*, he thought in disgust.

It came as a low hum at first, so low it was barely audible except for a subtle vibration, and he wondered if anyone else could hear it.

'Necromancer!' Someone screamed behind him.

He could do nothing now. It was the job of his wizards to protect them from evil magic. He couldn't feel magic, but the hands of the wizard beside him shimmered blue and a magic shield formed. The temperature dropped to freezing, and then rose so high sweat burst upon his brow. There came an explosive boom that shuddered through his body and sent his heart fluttering, and yet there was nothing to see. He glanced at the wizard's hands as magic flared and then went out.

'Shield shattered,' another wizard cried behind.

'Try again, and quickly,' said the one nearest him, but as he spoke the darkness moved—a cloud blacker than the tunnel around them.

'Duck,' he cried as a tendril snaked out toward him. But the warrior behind was not quick enough. The black cloud engulfed him just as the shield went up.

In the dim light cast by magic, Jinfrosthard fell back as the warrior fought something he could not see. The colour drained from the warrior's face and he screamed and tore past them. His screams echoed as he fled down the tunnel and disappeared.

'Leave him. He is lost. We must press on,' Jinfrosthard ordered, and yet his hands were shaking. He could only imagine what terror his warrior had witnessed. 'Find the source of the black magic and destroy it.'

'I have it,' a wizard replied, his voice strained in concentration. 'Left fork. There it is. IceFire, strike now.'

The other wizards obeyed. A white flare shot forwards then turned left into the tunnel. There came the briefest scream, and then silence. The heavy feeling of black magic went, and the temperature returned to cold.

Jinfrosthard sighed as silently as he could and wiped a trembling hand across his brow. He hated necromancers. He could deal with almost any form of Maphraxie, but the necromancers and their soul eating magic scared the hell out of him.

'Onwards,' he commanded, and led the line of warriors and wizards, all the while wondering how long he could keep moving. They were all exhausted, spooked, and hating the fact that they could not use magic to light the way so as to avoid detection.

For another hour they fought vicious skirmishes in the narrow, pitch-black corridors that wound on forever under the surface of Venosia. As hardy and battle seasoned as his warriors and wizards were, they were not as prepared for the strength of the necromancers' death magic. Many who had not fallen under enemy blades, were sent screaming from the tunnels with their sanity stripped from them.

Initially fifty, now only a solid fist of thirty light dwarf warriors pushed forwards in the dark. They had come to the deepest part of the dark dwarven tunnels.

'The barest light,' Jinfrosthard whispered as he slowed.

A dim orange glow formed above them. He stopped. Here the air was stale and frigid. He could see his breath in the gloom as faint puffs that rose before him then disappeared.

It had been a fair while, perhaps even half an hour, since they had last engaged the enemy, and the sound of the dead and dying had long disappeared behind them. The sudden lull made him nervous. The wizard beside him, which he could see now in the light, was Inklemak—a thin, long-bearded dwarf, pale-faced from fear and exertion. Inklemak whispered.

'The Flow tells me no necromantic wizard is near, and I sense no others here besides us.'

'So be it, Inklemak, your word has never failed me before,' Jinfrosthard rumbled, feeling grim despite the news. 'Let's have a little more warming light,' he shivered.

The wizard whispered a word and three torches held by warriors flared into life. At that moment, he wished with all his heart that he was sitting before his blazing hearth, in his favourite chair beside his wife, and in his home far away on the green hills west of Tarvalastone, the great city of the Dwarves of Light. He pushed the distracting thought aside. He must be getting old and tired of war, he thought with an inward chuckle.

Now here he was, deep in the stronghold of dark dwarven territory in eastern Venosia. Who knew how the battle above ground was going, or how the three thousand-strong army of light dwarves fared in yet another attempt to wipe out the dark dwarves. Most of the battles would be underground—the dark dwarves could not abide the daylight and had few holdings above ground. They would all be fighting, as was he, in the blackness of underground tunnels that were truly endless, and truly forsaken.

He pushed forwards, no longer leading, but following the flaming torch, glad of its light and what little warmth it offered down here in the cold. The band of warriors and wizards moved as a tight knot, blades and magic at the ready. All was horribly silent, and the world of light felt very far away.

They slowed as the torchlight fell upon a great slab of rock marking the end of the tunnel. Jinfrosthard pressed to the front, tugging on his braided beard with one hand and gripping his axe in the other.

'It's not an end, but a door,' he said, noting the obvious line around the rock that sealed the tunnel. He stared at the dark dwarven runes scrawled across it. They moved and danced like spiders in the flickering light. He bent closer, but then his eyes began to water, his chest constricted and he could not breathe. *Black magic.*

Magic shimmered, cast by his wizards trying to break the runic enchantment settling upon him. Whatever gripped his throat released, and he tore away from the evil symbols with a bellow.

'Damn them all to eternal torture,' he roared, hot-faced and gasping.

'We have less to fear, their wizards are all dead in this section,' Inklemak said. 'I cannot feel anything in the Flow besides our wizards. Without their necromancers nearby, the runes will weaken, and we might be able to break them.'

Jinfrosthard nodded once. Though his patience was wearing thin, and his body and mind weary, he could not force this. The wizard was right, as always. Unlike most dwarves who only trusted strength through iron and steel, he respected the power and wisdom of magic wielders.

'We shall wait.' With a motion of his hand, he set them all at ease. The warriors sat where they stood, and in the stale cold darkness, they waited for the runes to weaken.

A restless hour came and went as the dwarves fidgeted against the evil of the place, worried faces watching as the torches burned low.

Finally, Inklemak spoke. 'The runes weaken.'

The warriors jumped to their feet, and the five wizards entered the Flow. The warriors looked on, faces pensive, barely breathing. For another hour the wizards worked, the sweat rolling down their faces as they lay spell after spell upon the door trying to unlock the runes and open it. The pressure in the tunnel rose and fell, and magical sparks of orange and blue flickered around the dark runes. One wizard shuddered, turned white, and sunk to the floor. The other wizards did not break their concentration as the warriors pulled him aside.

The minutes rolled by, and seeing their sweat-soaked clothes and pale faces, Jinfrosthard knew that the wizards wouldn't last much longer. The air suddenly fizzled with red light, and a dull explosion rocked the tunnel. Another wizard collapsed as the enchantment upon the door broke. He was carried away and laid alongside the other. The two fallen wizards both breathed in ragged gasps, and their eyes fluttered feverishly bright, but otherwise were physically unharmed.

'The magic is broken, but the door must be opened manually now,'

Inklemak said, his voice and body trembling. 'We have some magical strength left, but not much.'

Jinfrosthard grunted as he laid a hand on the wizard's shoulder. Without a word he turned to the massive stone door, put his shoulder against it, and heaved. Others joined him, and together they hefted and pushed. The wizards spent what little magic they could draw from the Flow, and inch by inch the door slid to the left into the recess.

He squeezed into the chamber and the others followed. The light from their torches spilled into the gloom. The room was ten yards square with no other doors. At the far end, upon a stone pedestal, lay a thick dusty book.

'They fought to the death and cast their most powerful runic enchantments on this place just for a book?' He said. Inklemak gave him a look that suggested he thought otherwise.

Jinfrosthard shrugged. 'It's just a book.'

Nevertheless, he stepped carefully towards the leather-bound tome. His boot clanged against something metal. He looked down at a foot-square metal box chained to the pedestal. He glanced back at a warrior, motioned to him to free it, and turned back to the book. He was about to touch it, then hesitated, fearful of more enchantments. Inklemak gave him a reassuring nod.

Cracking his knuckles he reached and opened the cover. Symbols were scrawled in neat little rows filling the page. His skin crawled, and his sweat turned cold. He, blessedly, could not read dark dwarven runes, but Inklemak could, and he came to stand before the book, squashing his half-moon glasses onto his fat nose before peering down at the runes.

The warriors hacked at the chain holding the box until it finally broke. But try as they might, they could not break open the box by force. Setting it aside, the dwarves sat or stood and listened as Inklemak began to read from the book.

Over the next hour, until the torches began to splutter, they learned of the portended coming of the "Almighty Immortal Lord" from a dark and lifeless place beyond the boundaries of time. The victorious feeling of their recent battles was replaced with an all-encompassing dread.

' "Tusarza, the country most beloved of the foolish peoples of the Goddess, the place most blessed with pure magic and bountiful lands, will be where the Almighty Immortal Lord shall seed his being. Tusarza will be the first to fall to his might. Its purity will be his to consume and its magic his to conquer and wield. The fools upon Maioria know nothing of

the darkness that looks hungrily upon this planet. Our Almighty Immortal
Lord is the God to which we have prayed for millennia. When he comes
to us, true power will be ours, and none shall stand in our way." '
Inklemak paused to wipe the sweat from his forehead.

'Tusarza,' whispered Jinfrosthard. His voice echoed in the chamber
though he'd spoken quietly. He'd been there once and longed to stay for
the rest of his days, for it was a beautiful land of lakes, forests, rivers and
valleys. Mild winters allowed a myriad of plants and animals to thrive. It
was for all this goodness that Tusarza was named the "Orchard of
Maioria," supplying lands far and wide with food, even throughout the
winter months.

This haven was the only place in all Maioria where the Ancients, elves,
dwarves and humans lived in equal numbers, thriving peacefully alongside
each other. The land was everyone's, belonging to no one race in
particular. Those seeking refuge came to Tusarza, travellers and pilgrims,
and many were seduced by the land's beauty and never left. The magic
was strong in Tusarza for it was pure and untainted by greed.

'No one knows of this terrible thing coming from the skies. No one
knows what the murderous dark dwarves have been doing in their dark,
twisted lairs...' Jinfrosthard trailed off and looked at Inklemak, lips
pursed. Inklemak dropped his eyes and looked back at the dusty book,
tracing the letters as he muttered to himself and found where he'd left off.

' "...From life, he is not. From light, he is not. He is the darkness that
fills our minds and hearts; he is the death that needs not the life to be
forever. He is our King, our God, our Lord Eternal, for whom which we
have waited millennia to come and guide us. Hail the Immortal Lord. Hail
Baelthrom. Enter the Age of Oblivion..." ' Inklemak closed the book and
shook his head. 'I can read no more, and the torchlight dies.'

Jinfrosthard nodded. 'Let's leave. What about this?' He nudged the box
with his foot. A wizard reached over and placed a hand upon it.

'No axe can break this. No magic can open it. Only the key can unlock
it,' the wizard said and removed his hand.

Inklemak lifted the book from the pedestal, and there came a tinkling
sound of something dropped. A small black key gleamed on the floor.

'Why would they lock something and keep the key close?' Jinfrosthard
said. He looked at Inklemak who nodded, clearly thinking the same thing.

'They must have locked it for their own safety,' Inklemak said,
speaking Jinfrosthard's thoughts aloud.

Jinfrosthard took the key. 'Wizards, be ready for anything,' he said, preparing himself for any horror that might jump out of the box. He inserted the key and turned it. The box opened smoothly. Inside was a rag-bound object.

Inklemak reached inside. 'It's magical and heavy—too heavy for its size.' He let the cloth fall away and stared at the solid black object, about an inch thick and the size of a small plate. He held it back and squinted at it. 'It's shaped into a raven.'

They all clustered round to stare at it. Its wings were spread wide, and its head turned to the side. Every feather was perfectly detailed, its wedge-shaped tail fanned out, its eyes shining and lifelike.

'Dark dwarven black iron?' Jinfrosthard asked. Inklemak shook his head.

'No. It's more like marble or something, and yet it's a type I've never seen before. I don't know what it is or where it came from, but it's not evil, and it's not dark dwarven. Perhaps the Ancients will know. Its magic I cannot read. It feels locked away from me, somehow. It's not dangerous to us, as far as I can tell.'

'Well, whatever it is, the dark dwarves were clearly afraid of it,' Inklemak said, putting it back in the box and hefting the book under his arm again.

Jinfrosthard shook out the tension in his shoulders, wanting to relax, but the words Inklemak had translated from the book filled his soul like a dark secret.

'Let's get out of here and as far away as possible.'

No one disagreed with him, and they hurried out with the book and the raven object.

Jinfrosthard and Inklemak took the dark dwarven book to the king and queen of the light dwarves.

'We will not frighten the people with nonsense created by our most hated enemy,' said the king in response to Jinfrosthard's plea to warn the people of what they had learned. 'That's the last I will hear of it. If you so much as speak of this again, you will be beaten and hanged.'

Jinfrosthard stared at Inklemak, the wizard's face mirrored his shock. They had left the great hall in stunned silence. Only when they were alone did they dare to speak.

Inklemak shook his head. 'How can they not warn the people about the coming darkness? How can they not send warning to Tusarza?'

'They're afraid,' Jinfrosthard said. 'Fear stays their tongues. They are more afraid of the disruption and unrest that would spread through the kingdom than they fear the coming of an evil power. So it is easier for them to ignore it, to deny it.'

Inklemak nodded. 'Then we shall not tell them about the talisman.' That is what they had come to call the raven object.

'Take it, Inklemak. You should look after something that has magical powers. Keep it hidden and secret until we can find someone trustworthy who might know about it.'

Jinfrosthard decided to tell everyone, anyone who would listen, about the dark dwarves book and the coming Immortal Lord. His conscience made him. But when the king and queen heard, he was banished from Venosia under threat of death, and was forced to flee his homeland with his wife. He was thankful to make it to the peaceful Isle of Celene, but for the rest of his life, his soul was tortured with the knowledge of the coming darkness.

CHAPTER 2

Yisufalni

THE image of proud and noble Jinfrosthard, standing humble and pleading before the king and queen of the light dwarves, faded on the surface of Yisufalni's sacred pool in the Ethereal Planes. Yisufalni's eyes misted over as she lay beside the pool.

'So much is lost,' she breathed, curling her legs up. If they had known, perhaps they could have done something, but deep down she knew they could not have. The dark road Maioria would take when the Immortal Lord entered her lands seemed to be written in the stars, and no amount of pleading on Jinfrosthard's part, noble as it was, would ever change that.

He came to Tusarza, just as Jinfrosthard had warned. The sacred waters clouded over in response to her thoughts, and its surface filled with rain clouds.

A ball of flaming rock bigger than a mountain hurtled across the sky, trailing a scar of black smoke. It hit Tusarza, shuddering whole valleys, and flattening forests. The earth cracked and lakes boiled over, flooding entire villages. The sea slithered away only to resurge in a rage, smothering the land. Yisufalni knew the history, but she had never witnessed it, and she stared into the pool, wide-eyed at the destruction.

There came a moment of calm, then the ground began to shake. Valleys were torn apart as foreign black rock thrust through them, stabbing high into the sky. The three-peaked mountains of Maphrax were born, dominating the land and challenging the goddess herself.

She knew it didn't stop there. History said the earthquakes lasted for months, and great floods came and went without warning. The volcanoes of Maphrax, even thousands of years later, never stopped spewing lava, and volcanic ash poisoned the atmosphere, forever blotting out the sun over that land.

Those who survived the impact, the floods, the earthquakes, and the poison, soon fell to starvation when the crops failed and famine came. Change came quickly, and in less than a decade the place was a barren wasteland where not even the dead dared tread.

The image in the sacred waters showed how it looked today; ravaged, desolate, poisoned... A sky filled with magenta-tinged clouds, restless volcanoes and rivers of lava running like opened veins. Wind screamed as it tore across a land, unopposed by tree or house or valley. The life force of all things was ravaged and consumed by Baelthrom to feed his unholy essence and to ensure that nothing not of his design grew or lived.

Tusarza, and all that it had been was gone.

Maphrax. Yisufalni mouthed the name of the black mountains that would become the Immortal Lord's fortress but dared not speak it aloud.

"Maphrax" was the name joyfully whispered on the lips of the dark dwarves, the name of their holy land prophesized within their books. Eagerly they called for their Lord of Oblivion, as he, in turn, called to those who would be his followers. Long had the dark dwarves awaited their Immortal Lord. Long had they yearned for the power he would give them. Now he had come, now they had found their True God whom they could worship.

Under this new threat that came from beyond Maioria and time itself, the Light Dwarves and the Ancients, the Elves and the Humans, and all the beings of light formed the Feylint Halanoi.

'But it was not enough,' she breathed. Not nearly enough to stop the spread of darkness. Even splitting the magic life force of Maioria had not been enough to stop his rise to power.

Tears of joy mixed with sadness blurred her vision as she looked upon the tall, elegant frames of her ancestors holding the six orbs of power. 'We were so graceful, so beautiful, so... arrogant. We should never have underestimated Baelthrom's seething rage, and the retribution he would wreak if ever he broke free.'

She looked away from the waters, her heart fluttering in her chest. She did not need to see her people slaughtered again. None could touch Baelthrom's power, it was beyond the Flow of Maioria, it came from outside of it. The Under Flow they began to call it—a dark, unholy magic that flowed from the Dark Rift itself.

With the power of Maioria now split, we became weak. We didn't have a chance. It was our own undoing.

Such was their utter destruction at the hands of Baelthrom that the

Ancients created a myth to give those remaining strength and hope. In the myth, the fallen had not died but had fled to another dimension—a sacred holy land that they called Aralanastias, and it was hidden by mists and safe from harm.

'Nothing more than a myth,' she breathed, staring into the middle distance. Even the elven Land of Mists was more real than Aralanastias. But it would not keep the elves safe, nothing could. Baelthrom would find them in the end.

She rubbed her temples. Her energy was wasted from having spent too long in the physical world. Two days had passed since her last visit, and yet still she could barely stand. An hour at most in a small, weak form was all she had ever been able to manage before she had to return to the Ethereal Planes. All she could do was witness, impotent from afar, Issa battling Keteth.

Thinking of it now brought welcome tears of joy. Seeing the souls of her ancestors freed, after millennia bound in Keteth's prison, felt as if her own soul had been set free. They were free to return to the light of the One Source. Ah, the goddess had not left them to their dire fate, she never had.

The raven talisman. Yisufalni's thoughts turned to the raven sculpted object that the dark dwarves kept chained under lock and key deep within their underground cities. So little was known about it. Even the Ancients, with all their knowledge of the history of Maioria, knew little about it. Only that its magic was pure and old, older than the dragons, and not from Maioria. It may as well be as they said, that Zanufey herself crafted it and brought it to Maioria. It seemed the dark dwarves knew more about it than anyone, fearing it and locking it away like they had.

She had to find it. She couldn't help but think Issa would be able to unlock its powers. If it was as the prophecies said, that the Raven Queen would stand against the darkness, then surely the dark dwarves feared the talisman's power. Why indeed would they have locked it away? Why would she think of it now, and see it in the sacred pool? Was she meant to find it? Would the sacred pool show her where Inklemak had hidden it?

An orange glow drew her attention to the waters. The raven talisman lay upon black rock surrounded in flames, but it did not burn or melt and seemed impervious to fire.

'Where is this?' she asked. A cavern of solid rock materialised, glowing red in the lava light. The talisman was on an island surrounded by the rivers of lava. It was unguarded, from what she could see.

She sat back on her haunches trying to think. Inklemak and the dwarves of light lived in the great city of Tarvalastone in Venosia before Baelthrom came. Half the city lay within the mountain, and the other half sprawled across a land of hills, trees and rivers. Beneath the city ran the Red River, a river of lava carefully channelled and managed to assist the dwarves' mining, smelting and crafting of rock and ore.

Inklemak could have hidden it somewhere along the Red River. Could it still be there, forgotten? But how to reach it? Tarvalastone was controlled by dark dwarves and had been for a thousand years. If she went there, she risked capture and death.

Was the talisman even important? Why would the sacred pool show her it so easily if it wasn't? Too many questions. She closed her eyes. She couldn't return to Maioria until she'd regained her strength. Every time she went, she was sure Baelthrom could feel her, hunted for her. Going to Venosia was simply too dangerous.

But even as she thought it she knew she would try to find the talisman. It was either that, or live another millennium wondering what might have happened had she found it. Issa needed all the help in the world. Her own death would be nothing compared to the loss of life that would ensue if the Raven Queen failed.

Perhaps it was vanity that made her stay alive. Vanity that she was one of the last Ancients that still existed on Maioria. Did she foolishly hope the Ancients would return one day? She may as well wish her life away.

They all perished. All but two gone forever from the mortal plains, all but two to endure endless suffering. Unable to die, unable to ascend… Her heart ached with that old wound, it would never heal. She blinked back the tears and forced a smile. At least she could smile for those souls freed into the light by Issa.

Beloved Murlonius, I pray for the day when our curse is broken, that I might see you again before I too leave Maioria to join our ancestors.

At her thoughts, the dark waters brightened, and a pale blue sea was revealed. White light sparkled almost blindingly upon the waves. A dark shape came into focus, an ornately carved boat moving steadily upon the surface. Cloaked in a hooded robe, a man rowed. He had a tireless rhythm, for the sea was never ending, and he had been rowing his boat across it for thousands of years. Her breath caught in her throat.

'Murlonius,' she sighed and ached with longing. For one brief moment, the boatman paused and looked up. She strained to see his face in the folds of his cloak but could not. She never could. The man carried on rowing.

She had tried to reach Murlonius before, many times, thousands of times, but the curse proved true. She could not reach him. She could only see him from afar as he rowed his boat through eternity, doomed as she was to never walk upon Maioria again, and yet unable to leave its outer realms. They were trapped between the mortal and ethereal plains, but unable to ever meet in either.

Did he search for her or had he forgotten her? It was the one question that plagued her more than any other. He had heard her voice then, she was sure of it, why else would he stop rowing and look up? But did he recognise it? She lay back down again beside the pool, her eyes never leaving the boatman.

Baelthrom cursed them for his own pleasure. Murdered a whole race and spared them for a life of torture. Perhaps it would be his undoing. She prayed it would be his undoing. *I would have gone to Baelthrom millennia ago, and ended it all then, had I not seen a dark moon rising in the future.*

'Did you see the dark moon too, my love?' she whispered to the rowing man, even if he couldn't hear her. 'What is it that keeps you going? Helping those we can is a balm on the soul. We always do what we can. That's why I must find the talisman.

'How I remember your face, Murlonius, it is as clear in my memory as my own,' she smiled, remembering his deep violet eyes that always seemed to be laughing. He was the carefree, happy one, while she, a princess, was serious. His eyes were forever cloaked from her now, and she doubted whether they would be so happy.

'Do you remember our home? Do you remember our temples and our shining cities all made from marble and crystal? Even the elves speak of our grand dwellings and are unable to build them themselves.'

Murlonius's image wavered, and she reached for him, wanting to be with him, but the pool reflected her memory, and she looked down at the Ancient's city that had once been her home so long ago. White quartz crystal temples towered into the blue sky and gleamed in the sunlight. Below them a turquoise sea swayed, empty of dark and evil creatures.

There had never been anything so beautiful created again. Even if the people could remember how to shape crystal, there was no longer the power to do it. *Ahh Murlonius, our time ended here long ago.* The image faded back to the rowing boatman.

'I wish I could remember before the Dark Rift came. When there was no such thing as death, and only freedom and peace existed. What a place that must have been. Perhaps that is why we should stay alive, to remind others of what Maioria used to be, of what we all used to be.

'But I know the real reason why you and I remain,' her smile dropped, and her voice became hard. 'Not until the last breath leaves our bodies will we cease fighting the Immortal Lord. The goddess is with us, my love, and now we can all hope. One day I will see you again, and on that day Baelthrom will be destroyed.'

She bit her lip, worrying the hem of her robes. 'How we will defeat him, only the goddess knows. But I will help the Raven Queen, even if it costs me my life. You would understand, my love, you would do the same. With Zanufey's chosen we have a chance. Even if it's only a small one. There is hope in Issa,'

The image in the water changed to a dark ocean. Purple lights moved on the surface, and amongst them the pale form of Issa. The Wykiry were carrying her home. She was so tired she barely noticed the dark shapes moving fast upon the horizon as she drifted into a dreamless sleep.

CHAPTER 3

Dragon Flight

IN a feverish half-sleep, Asaph witnessed the final moments of the struggle between the one he loved and the one who had imprisoned him. It was through the flame ring she wore that he could see Issa now, and in his lucid dream state, with his soul somewhere trapped in Keteth's domain, he could actually see their bond as a silvery cord between them, stretching out across time and through space.

He followed that cord until he found her where the indigo light of Zanufey's dark moon fell upon the ocean. There she stood, suspended above the surface, bathed in powerful moonlight. He watched, somewhere between terror and awe, as a tall, slender figure materialised beside Issa. The Night Goddess hooded and cloaked in a robe made of stars.

Awesome power flooded from Issa as Zanufey stepped into her form. A wave of the strongest magic, the purest love, the feeling of absolute, unshakeable faith, and the power that such faith brings, flooded through him, and he knew it flooded through Issa and all that might be near her at that moment.

The white dagger flew of its own will from Issa's hand and pierced Keteth's twisted heart. Light engulfed all. There came a shattering tearing sound, and he felt his mind released. Relief washed over him with such intensity, he found himself groaning. Keteth was dead, now he was free. He felt as if he had been struggling in the twisted realities of Keteth's prison forever. His thoughts were suddenly clear, and his soul no longer felt wretched.

The light faded. Issa stood alone upon the blue moonlit ocean once more. Then he saw them, a vision so wonderful he thought his heart would break. The souls of the enslaved Dragon Lords, glimmering shining white lights, rose up from the depths of their prison. Their joyous songs were a melodic harmony such as only angels could sing. They were free too, and they moved as one shimmering ribbon up towards the light of Feygriene.

'Brothers and sisters,' he called to them in his mind. 'I shall eternally miss you. Be my guide in the Recollection, if you can. You are free, now and for forever.'

For a brief moment, he glimpsed Issa and the blue moonlight again before she faded. He tried to reach for her, but there came a pull, as of something drawing him backwards, and he could not resist.

Asaph opened his eyes. He tried to stretch. His body was weak, and he felt as if he had slept for an eternity. Though it was dark, he found his dragon sight adjusting swiftly. He peered through a gap in the curtains and did not recognise anything. He was in a large round room or hut with a conical thatched roof, and there was a hearth with a smouldering fire in the centre, giving the place a warm, dim glow.

Where in Maioria was he, and how did he get here? The soft snoring of two people came from nearby. One was the familiar sound of Coronos. He smiled in relief. His father was alive and close. He tried to sit up but fell back down with a gasp when his stomach muscles refused to obey. They had wasted from lack of use. How long had he been here?

He touched his side where Keteth had mauled and poisoned him. It was tender, but no longer burned in agony. He threw back the covers only to stare in shock. The wounds were healed—only thin white scars remained where once there had been jagged gashes. Someone had gone to great lengths to heal him. He reached for the flagon of water beside his bed and drank it all, feeling some strength return with the cool water.

He sat still for a long time, piecing together what he could remember, hoping to commit it to memory in case it faded like a dream upon waking. The last thing he remembered was staring down at Karalanths aiming arrows up at him. Everything after was a hellish nightmare. A croak made him jump. His looked to the window where a big raven now perched, its dark brown eyes looked at him questioningly. Issa's raven. He recognised it easily now. It always seemed to be the cause of all his troubles.

'Where is she?' he'd meant to whisper, but it came out a croak. Issa's face flashed in his mind, and with it came a desperate need to see her in the flesh, to know she was all right. He felt the raven press upon his mind, and a shadow passed over his eyes.

'All right,' he sighed, and closed his eyes to accept the raven's message.

The vision was hazy. Asaph flew low over an ocean. It was night. At first, there was only calm sea, and then he saw purple lights and a pale figure. Issa and the Wykiry. She was safe. He would have leapt out of bed for joy, had his body been able.

The vision moved fast. The raven flew higher, and he saw dark shapes speeding towards them. Ships, at least three of them. They were of a type he had never seen before, and they were big, even at this distance. The Recollection flickered in his mind. He *had* seen them before, but through another's eyes, and long ago in Drax. The same heavy black wood, the same curved wooden masts striking up towards the sky, bristling spikes upon the ocean's surface. His mouth went dry.

He turned as the raven turned and looked to the horizon. More dark ships loomed, and above them, black things flying. He shuddered, and the vision moved. Magic surged, and the sea churned under flares of fire. He looked down and saw Issa clinging to wreckage. His heart raced. The Wykiry circled close around her protectively. Though she lay motionless, her aura shimmered indigo blue, and he knew she was not dead. Yet.

Asaph broke his connection to the raven so swiftly the world spun. In a daze, he struggled out of bed only to stagger under his own weight. He had been bed bound so long, his body seemed to be made of lead.

'By Feygriene's fire, get me to her,' he gasped.

He grabbed the pile of clothes on a stool beside his bed, and with shaking hands yanked them on, uncaring if they were his or not. In the struggle to pull on his trousers, he lost his balance, fell through the curtains, and stumbled over Coronos.

The older man sat up with a gasp. Asaph was equally alarmed at the dark circles and weariness on Coronos' face. He looked as if he had aged ten years since he'd last seen him. He regained his balance, and reached out to squeeze the Coronos' shoulder, shocked to feel the bones beneath. He looked up at Asaph in disbelief.

'My son? Is this a dream? Is it you?' his voice was hoarse, then he pulled Asaph down into a fierce hug, tears falling down his cheeks. Asaph returned the embrace, and the worry he felt for him was replaced with joy. 'Praise Feygriene, I thought I'd lost you. I thought I'd lost you,' Coronos whispered.

'Me too, father. I have been to a dark place,' he said, his voice rough and weak from lack of use. They held each other for a moment, and then Asaph pulled away.

'Keteth is dead, father. I've seen it. You must have felt it in the Flow. Through Issa, the Night Goddess has freed him and all those he had imprisoned. That's why I was able to wake—Keteth's hold on me was broken when he was killed. Father, I have no time to explain more. Issa is in terrible danger. Keteth's gone, but now the Maphraxies come for her. I must go to her.'

A hundred thoughts and denials seemed to flicker across Coronos' face as he opened his mouth to speak, then frowned. He looked at the raven perched patiently on the windowsill, seeing it for the first time.

'The raven... always Zanufey's messenger,' Coronos breathed. His eyes glazed as if the raven too showed him a vision. 'Yes, Keteth is gone, I'm sure of it. I had a dream and saw his death on the blade of a white dagger, but now I know it was no dream. Thank the goddess you have been released from his clutches,' he smiled and closed his eyes for a moment.

'I *can* feel it in the Flow. There has been a change as if darkness has been lifted from the world. The flow of magic is stronger too.' Coronos opened his eyes and focused upon Asaph. 'And now, in the blink of an eye, you are back only to go again. Yet I know you must go to her. My son, you have been terribly sick. You are not strong enough and may yet still die if you go to her now.' Coronos wrapped his cloak around his shoulders despite the warmth of the room. The worry on his face caused a pang of guilt in Asaph's stomach.

'Believe me, father, I wouldn't go if I didn't have to. By the love of Feygriene, I'm the only one who can help her now.'

'The Dragon Lord returns to us,' a man said, and appeared from behind a curtain.

Asaph blinked at the deer man smiling at him. He remembered the Karalanth attack on the shore, but it seemed such a long time ago. He smiled and frowned at the same time, hadn't they tried to kill them? Coronos spoke as if reading his mind.

'Don't be angry, there is much you have missed. Without their help, and the seer they brought to you, you would be long dead.'

'Seer?' Asaph raised his eyebrows. He had never seen one except at a distance in the Recollection. She had worn pale blue robes, held an air of wisdom and humility about her, and seemed to command powerful magic. Coronos had told him about seers years ago when he was a boy, but he had never thought much about them.

'I vaguely remember a young-faced, white-haired woman,' Asaph nodded. 'Though I thought it was a dream.'

'That was her. Seer Naksu,' Triest'anth said.

Asaph frowned and shook his head, he didn't have time to think about seers.

'Thank you all for everything you've done for me,' Asaph said, hating the weakness and fatigue in his voice. 'I'm only sorry that I won't have time to repay you. I must leave immediately,' As soon as he had spoken his vision wobbled and Triest'anth reached to steady him.

'A dark cloud has been lifted from the world, but Coronos is right; I too feel danger growing…' Triest'anth said glancing at the raven still perched upon the window ledge. 'But the raven of Zanufey never lies, so you must hurry and help the slayer of the White Beast. None can travel as fast as a dragon, but first you must eat something. Otherwise you shall definitely die,' he said with finality.

'I don't have time to eat,' Asaph protested, struggling into his shirt.

Coronos went to help him whilst trying to avoid his flailing arms. The Karalanth took a red leather pouch from a shelf and poured the contents into the pot hanging above the hearth. He added honey and water.

'The seer left this for you upon your awakening,' Triest'anth said, dangling the empty pouch before him. 'She said you would have much need of it. She saw some of the near future, that much I'm sure. Her magic was strong, even in these times.'

'You cannot go alone, you are not strong enough. Take me with you.' Coronos continued his protest as Asaph fumbled with his sword belt and dropped it.

'But I must go alone, I cannot carry another,' Asaph said.

He gave up with the belt and let Coronos put it on. He reached for the steaming cup Triest'anth passed him. He took a gulp, almost scalded his throat, but continued to splutter down the contents as quickly as he could. Whatever the liquid was it was sweet and heavily spiced, and for a moment he thought his stomach would throw it back up. The sickness subsided, and hot energy flowed through his body.

'That's powerful stuff,' he said, feeling his strength returning.

'The initial strength it brings will last only for a few hours, and then you will be weak as a newborn fawn. Make sure you are somewhere safe if you cannot make it back to us in time,' Triest'anth said, as Asaph reached for the door, Coronos trailing behind him.

'You have my thanks for all you've done. That and much more. I will return as soon as I can,' Asaph smiled. He didn't know the deer man, but after all they had done for him, his sincere thanks was all he could offer.

'My son, please reconsider this journey,' Coronos said, grabbing the lantern by the door as they left the hut.

'Father, you cannot come with me. It's too dangerous, and I don't know what I'll find.'

'Do you think I have not flown a fresh young dragon before? It was I that taught them how to carry humans on their backs,' he said, stubborn-faced. 'With the Orb of Air, I know how to create a strong favourable wind that will get us there in half the time or less. I'll not leave you again,' he crossed his arms over his chest.

Asaph groaned. He didn't have the energy to argue, and Coronos, once decided, would not be swayed. He actually wanted him to come along but felt sick at the thought of placing him in danger. He dropped his shoulders and sighed, beaten.

'All right, all right, but I'll take you to the shores of the mainland and no further. I daren't travel over the ocean with another on my back. Besides, it's easier for me to search for her alone like I did in the Shadowlands, and I may need help from afar.'

Coronos was silent, considering.

'Right then,' he said, clapping his hands together with a grin. 'From there I'll scry for her, and my magic might reach you, with the orb's help of course. What on earth have I just gotten myself into?' He frowned. Asaph grinned.

'We'll need the thickest rope you can find, and the strongest fabric,' Coronos said, turning to Triest'anth.

Asaph watched the two men disappear back into the hut, only to emerge a few moments later with rope that took them both to carry, and a thick woollen sheet. Coronos dumped them down in front of Asaph, put his hands on hips and smiled.

'Which way do we go?' he asked.

'The ocean lies due west. You can follow the river all the way,' Triest'anth said.

There came a squawk, and the raven landed nearby.

'The raven will lead us, as always,' Asaph grinned. Perhaps the bird was growing on him, though the memory of it stealing his mother's ring still irked him.

'Ah-hah,' Coronos said with a wink. 'Are you sure you are able to fly?'

'You wouldn't believe me if I told you where I have been, and what has happened to me. I did not walk in darkness all the time,' Asaph said, thinking of Faelsun and the Dragon Dream. He would talk to Coronos of it, but not yet.

'Let's go,' he said, urgency driving him. 'But not here,' he added, looking around. 'I don't want to cause dragon panic.'

They made their way to a small clearing just beyond sight of the village. Suddenly he was worried. What if the dragon form did not come? Keeping his face an unreadable mask, he coughed and pretended to tighten his sword belt. Triest'anth looked on with bated breath as if ready to run should the dragon fear take him. Coronos was looking into the distance, though Asaph could tell he was being politely disinterested.

Well, he had not done this in public before, so why not make a show of it? He smoothed his hair back, and reached both arms forward, flexing his wrists. He closed his eyes and took three big loud breaths then held in the fourth. He stilled his mind until it was flat and still like a pond. All thoughts fell away, and he calmly, confidently, turned towards the dragon within. The golden dragon lifted its massive head and opened its shining sapphire eyes. He was sucked towards those glowing orbs, and there came a flash of light.

His body was growing, skin thickened as it spread over muscles that massed and bulged. New limbs sprouted outwards from between his shoulder blades and felt as if they would grow forever. Claws pushed forth from fingers that had become enormous. His mouth and nose grew long and powerful. Huge fangs slipped down and up in his mouth. Ancient magic flooded his body and soul as if from some great hidden reservoir.

He continued to grow until he thought he would never stop, and then, all at once, there came stillness and quiet. With his eyes closed, he stretched out his wings and tail, feeling the power of his muscles awaken as if he had been asleep for a thousand years. Any fatigue and weakness he had felt in his human form were gone from his dragon self. He filled his lungs with the forest air and felt fire rumble in his belly.

This was what he was, this was all he wanted to be. *I am Dragon.*

Asaph opened his eyes and looked up at the starlit sky just beginning to brighten with the coming dawn. He breathed out and looked down. Far below him stood an open-mouthed Coronos and a trembling Triest'anth. Coronos clapped his hands, barked a laugh, and embraced the shaken Karalanth.

'I'm ready,' Asaph said. Though he spoke quietly, his voice rumbled like thunder.

Under Coronos' direction, they secured the ropes and blanket around Asaph's neck and back to fashion a crude but strong harness.

'It will be fine,' Coronos reassured. 'I have done this before,' he added indignantly under Asaph's bemused gaze. 'Though with much better materials,' he added with a frown.

Asaph gave a smoky snort and lay down upon the ground, making himself as flat as possible whilst Triest'anth pushed his father up onto his leg. Coronos grasped the ropes and hauled himself into his seat.

'Phew, it's been a while,' he puffed, wiping the sweat from his brow. He wiggled about for a bit, securing his staff and orb and arranging himself comfortably. After a moment, he stopped moving and said magnanimously. 'I am ready.'

'Finally,' Asaph snorted and stood up. He didn't like Coronos on his back at all. What if he fell off? He was far less excited about the whole thing than his father seemed to be and desperate to be gone from here.

'Good luck, friends,' Triest'anth called out. 'Woetala protect you.'

Asaph nodded, and Coronos waved. He stretched his wings and bunched his muscles. There was no room to run forwards and launch for trees blocked his path. He would have to jump into the still air and beat his wings hard for lift. He leapt, easily clearing the trees, and beat his wings as hard as he could, feeling them fill with air that pushed him into the sky.

Coronos yelped excitedly. Asaph laughed and circled once around an open-mouthed Triest'anth, gaining height before turning due west along the frothing Arin Flow.

He looked for the raven, and the tiny bird darted fearlessly under his belly with a squawk. He followed as it turned southwards, and soon they were speeding low over the forests of South West Frayon. In his dragon form he easily felt when the Orb of Air drew on the Flow, and soon a strong wind was pushing them forwards.

He flew faster now than he had ever done before, and it was glorious to feel the wind gushing under his wings. The forest below was a green blur. He glanced at the raven close beneath him, using his slipstream. The bird barely needed to flap its wings, and he could sense it was enjoying the speed as much as he was.

'That was very well done,' Coronos applauded, shouting over the wind.

Asaph tilted his head to glance back at him, wondering if he was pleased for his father's praise, or indignant that a human should offer such opinions on a dragon's performance.

'Now don't tilt too far. With me on your back you are less streamlined,' Coronos said.

All at once they came to a jolting stop, hanging suspended above the trees with barely a move of Asaph's great wings. Coronos fell forwards with a shriek, struggling against the rope of the harness.

'Who's flying?' Asaph said, his voice sweet for a dragon.

'Mmmph, yup, right you are,' Coronos squeaked. 'Just a thought, that's all,' he muttered, rearranging his robes and shifting himself back to his original position.

'Just focus on getting that orb to create a gale in our favour.' Asaph beat his wings and caught up with the raven, hoping Coronos would remain silent for the whole journey. But Coronos was far too excited and continued to chatter. Asaph was relieved when he didn't offer any more advice.

'You must tell me more of what happened,' Coronos shouted. 'Say we are moving fast. I hope the raven can manage.'

'I'm sure Issa speeds it on too,' Asaph said. He struggled not to think about her. In the exhilaration of flying, he found some solace from worry. Though it was wonderful to have another join him in the joy of flight, he wished he could focus on just the enjoyment.

'Hah. I'm remembering more and more the art of the Dragon Rider,' Coronos said. 'Although I'll never be young again. Still, this is a boon to an old man.'

As they sped west, away from the growing light of dawn, the sky remained the same colour, dark and with a tinge of blue. He knew the dark moon had not long set because he could feel its power just beyond the horizon.

'The dark moon has set,' Asaph said. 'I think her power comes from it.'

'If that is true, and I think you are right, her strength will wane when it does,' Coronos shouted back.

He had to reach her before then, or the Maphraxies would take her. He angled his wings to as keen an angle as he dared with Coronos on his back, and reached out with his mind, searching for the familiar feel of the flame ring. He found it—a tiny pinpoint of flame-red light in the Flow, far into the distance. It drew him on faster. Coronos gripped the rope about his neck.

There came the smell of salt and then the ocean loomed ahead, a dark blanket lying upon the land. With the slightest angle of his wings, Asaph curved down towards the shore where waves crashed upon the rocks. He slowed and made a smooth landing, pleasing himself immensely. He laid low and helped Coronos dismount and undo the ropes.

'I'll await your safe return,' Coronos said. All the joy of flying now gone from his face, and the creases of worry replacing it. The orb in his hand was bright white in the dark. The wind it had created still blew strong, whipping Coronos' hair about his face and tugging on his cloak.

Asaph regarded. 'No need to worry. I shall return soon like Triest'anth said. I'll find her and bring her back, that's all,' it sounded simple. He prayed that it would be.

He turned and leapt from the rocks, following the raven once more.

Coronos watched the young Dragon Lord go. He looked like a bright comet shooting across the sky and was soon lost from view. How amazing it felt to fly again on the back of a dragon. He settled himself upon the rough blanket, held the orb in his lap and closed his eyes, letting the orb carry him in the Flow as he searched for danger.

There, far out to sea, he could see the taint of the immortals like a black stain in the Flow. Within that stain, turquoise light shone, calling to the orb in his hands.

CHAPTER 4

Baelthrom

BAELTHROM stood between the altar and the great iron ring, deep within his three-peaked mountain fortress that had first been his birthplace, then his prison, and now his stronghold. The mountains themselves were as much a part of Baelthrom as his own mind was. He stood motionless for so long that Kilkarn wondered if he had fallen asleep. The dark dwarf knew better than to interrupt his lord and so he too stood silently and as motionlessly as he could beside the closed stone door.

Kilkarn stared out at the physically uninteresting, yet energetically fascinating, chamber. The dark energy of the Under Flow was always loaded in here, the heart of Baelthrom's domain, and while he could not easily see magic (he was not a magic wielder) even he could feel it. The hairs on his arms rose and fell, the darkness swirled in ribbons around him, and every now and then light flickered. He glanced at his lord.

Baelthrom's giant human hands rested on his reptilian hips, demon wings folded behind him, and his scaled tail, usually flicking back and forth, was still. His legs from mid-thigh down were unarmoured, and muscles bulged beneath dark green scales. His eyes were lights that constantly changed colour, and Kilkarn knew they saw not just physical forms and light, but energy and magic.

Right now his eyes glimmered gold from within the triangular slits of his helmet—a helmet moulded into the shape of the three mountains of Maphrax and forever hiding his face.

Baelthrom stood more than half again taller than a man, and twice as wide. His torso and arms were covered in the same thick black, dark dwarven armour that all Maphraxies wore. The metal was mined from the

Maphrax Mountains, was fire resistant and virtually indestructible. Like Baelthrom, this metal was not natural to Maioria, but came, as did he, from the Dark Rift.

The dark dwarves had named him "Baelthrom" in their own language, and it meant "Lord of Oblivion" in reference to the Dark Rift of Oblivion from whence he came.

Over many years, the dark dwarves had tunnelled deep into the mountains and crafted an immense network of stone corridors and vast halls. Rooms, prisons, torture chambers, banquet halls, kitchens, libraries filled with books on black magic and necromantic arts, Sirin Derenax laboratories, and everything in between, all existed within the black stone Mountains of Maphrax.

The main chamber in which they stood lay deep within the tallest central mountain and was where Baelthrom spent most of his time, directing the war that swept across Maioria through the iron ring. This chamber was exactly crafted at fifty-five feet square, and so high that the ceiling could not be seen. The black stone walls sloped inwards and upwards to the tip of the mountain hundreds of feet above.

A huge iron chain swung down from that blackness, and on its end hung an iron hoop some fifteen feet in diameter. At Baelthrom's bidding, the iron ring could show any event in time in the past or present of Maioria, so long as it had a dark dwarf or Maphraxie presence in it. The iron ring was also called the Shadow Master, for it was through the Shadow Master that Baelthrom could communicate to all Shadow Stones.

The powerful Shadow Stone was made from bloodstone—a blood-red stone found only in the lava chambers within the mountains. The bloodstone was not molten for it was impervious to heat—even dragon fire did not scald it. The roots of the Maphrax Mountains ran deep, so deep that Kilkarn had yet to hear reports that the miners had reached the bottom. Perhaps they stabbed into the core of Maioria herself.

Once polished to a shine, Kilkarn would bring the bloodstones to Lord Baelthrom. His lord then worked his otherworldly magic upon them, making them powerful. When "infused" the stone cast no shadow in the light as if it were its own shadow, and so the bloodstone came to be called a Shadow Stone. If you stared into one, really looked deep into its blood-red surface, it would come alive with a dark glow and draw you into it. The Shadow Stone could be used to trap the soul of any mortal. Kilkarn had almost lost himself in those fathomless depths, despite having more knowledge about Shadow Stones than any other dark dwarf. The power-filled stones were then set in black gold also mined in the Maphrax Mountains.

These Shadow Stone amulets were gifted to each Dromoorai, Baelthrom's most prized and powerful war machines. Each Shadow Stone was connected to the Shadow Master, and within the Shadow Master, Baelthrom could see through all the Shadow Stones worn by his Dromoorai. He could view his army and the Feylint Halanoi they fought from many angles—a valuable weapon in their war to dominate all Maioria.

Beside the iron ring stood a black stone altar, within which were six round hollows. In one of the hollows sat a crystal orb the size of Baelthrom's fist. It shone dully in the low light of the brazier. The Orb of Life had not always been dull, Kilkarn had seen the time of its taking in the iron ring. Back then, long ago now, the orb had been bright and shining all the colours of the rainbow. Kilkarn had hated it, it hurt his eyes and made his head throb. The magic it held was the magic of the Ancients, and he was positively allergic to it.

Now it was dull, he could look at it easily, scornfully. For all its supposed power, Baelthrom had simply picked it up when its Keeper, an Ancient High Priest, slipped dead off his lord's sword. As the life force of the Ancient dwindled, so too did the light of the orb. It was through understanding something of the Orb of Life that Baelthrom had managed to tap into the natural life energies of the planet, and reverse them to create immortal life.

Baelthrom had mentioned once that two Ancients still remained, but more than that he did not say, and Kilkarn always wondered if, when those last two died, would the orb itself turn dark and die? Perhaps that was why Baelthrom allowed two to remain, in case the power of the orb died, but he could not know for sure.

There were five other orbs, and soon they too would fill the empty hollows, and their power would become Baelthrom's. For whatever Baelthrom wanted, he got, and he wanted nothing more than the power of all the orbs.

'Maioria.'

Kilkarn jumped at the sound of his master's voice. It echoed around the chamber.

'Abundant, rich in magic... And soon, like the land they called Tusarza, it will all be under my control.' Baelthrom did not move as he spoke and his lips, if he had any, were hidden behind his mouthless helmet. Only his pupil-less eyes changed. At first, they glowed dark green, then to red and back again.

'Soon, my lord,' Kilkarn grinned.

'Long have I waited. In the beginning, when first I struck Tusarza and before I had form, I lay dormant, and yet I knew all that was happening around me. I knew myself as thought, as consciousness, that I had come from somewhere else, somewhere dark and powerful, but even now I cannot remember this place...' Baelthrom trailed off and shifted so that his back and folded wings were facing Kilkarn. Kilkarn sensed frustration.

'We had long awaited your glorious arrival,' Kilkarn offered. Baelthrom considered this.

'Yes,' he finally said. 'Under the nurture of your race, my consciousness grew, or collected itself, and formed into order.'

'You grew strong, fast,' Kilkarn nodded.

'And yet stronger I can grow,' Baelthrom said. 'I have yet to find the limits of my power and my being—always there is more. Over years that turned into centuries, I drew into me the life energy of Tusarza. Then I chose my form from the creatures on this planet. Even back then my necromancers had great skill when they created my body. When it was ready, I seeped my consciousness into it. I could look outwards for the first time with physical eyes, I could feel things I had never imagined. I had to have more of this energy, this magic, it gave me strength and power, it gave me my very existence.

'Tusarza had been bled dry, it offered me no more, and that is why all of Maioria must feed me until I am complete. Or perhaps I have no boundaries of being, and even the goddess, even that Source of All they speak of here, will one day be mine. I think nothing can stop me, even the mighty Ancients fell to me. I destroyed their lands that lay to the east, hundreds of islands lying like emeralds scattered in the ocean ready to be plucked.

'Their magic was strong, their essence shone like the purest light. I had to have their power, I *had* to take it for myself. True power cannot be learnt, it cannot be shared. No, I had to take it and consume it. And how I fought them, for so long... I thought even I would break.'

The iron ring flared into life. A battle scene was revealed. An image of Baelthrom stood within it, looking as he did now, encased within armour, his eyes glowing red. Thousands of dark dwarves spread before him, wielding their weapons and casting their black magic against tall, graceful beings shrouded in light.

They fought upon a land of green grass, forests and rivers. In the distance reached the elegant spires of crystal cities—far more advanced than could be found on Maioria today. There were no Maphraxies, they had yet to be created.

Kilkarn snickered. 'Yes, Lord Baelthrom, I see in the iron ring my ancestors at your side, as I have seen many times before. In your power they are fearless. The Ancient's blood ran like rivers through the necromancers' chambers…'

'They were strong,' Baelthrom nodded, 'but they showed me where I was weak. Only a fool would deny how close they came to destroying me utterly.'

Kilkarn chuckled and then fell silent as his lord's eyes dimmed to blackish-red, and the air grew chill and heavy.

'They crushed me and bound me deep beneath these very mountains. And all I could do was watch, powerless…' Baelthrom fell silent. When he spoke again, his voice was a rumbling whisper.

'They were powerful enough to sunder the very magic of the planet, and bind me with unbreakable magic. For eons I struggled in that prison, trapped in my own body, seething in hatred. All the while, I planned the demise of those that bound me. My body wasted away, and I moved back into consciousness. I watched the world, learnt its power, its gods and goddesses, its people, its weakness, and in the end I planned its eventual downfall.

'I learned that the light is nothing without the darkness, and freedom does not exist without first the chains. I know true freedom, the chains that bound me taught me that,' Baelthrom fell into a brooding silence once more.

It unnerved Kilkarn. His lord was the epitome of confidence, unshakeable will, and swift, direct action. But now he seemed unsure as if something had challenged his confidence. Indeed, it almost seemed as if his lord was *concerned* about something, and this feeling he did not like at all. Which is why he chose to stay silent.

His lord never talked of the past, so why now? He had mentioned many times recently the subtle change in the energies of Maioria, and that was the only thing Kilkarn could think of that could be the cause of his lord's disturbance. It was impossible to think that the Feylint Halanoi had any power to stop Baelthrom now. Their concentrated numbers on the northern shores of Frayon were putting up a strong resistance, but even they were dwindling. It was simply a waiting game. And with Sirin

Derenax flowing in their veins, the immortals had all the time in the world. Yet still, Baelthrom was disturbed, and that made Kilkarn disturbed.

'There is no power that can stop us now, Lord Baelthrom,' Kilkarn chanced with a laugh that portrayed his utter confidence in their victory.

Baelthrom nodded, 'Indeed, Kilkarn. It would seem no power is greater than ours. Each day I feel my power growing stronger, and yet...'

Kilkarn waited as the minutes went by, and when his lord did not speak, asked, 'And yet what, Lord Baelthrom, what is it you see?'

'This new power in the west... It's strange. I don't understand it, and that is very dangerous. No, it isn't new. It's as if it has always been there, within or beneath everything, like the thought that precedes the action. But now it's... focused... It's linked to that cursed blue moon and... something more.'

'The Dark Moon of Death has been with us before, eons ago, my lord. So long ago that few scriptures remain, and only myth perpetuates its memory. It heralds a time of great change, and, Lord Baelthrom, you are that change,' Kilkarn grinned and nodded as his lord cast him a glance.

'This power is nothing compared to ours, Lord Baelthrom. Our powers only grow stronger as we assimilate all. Soon this power of which you speak will also be ours. We *are* unstoppable, and any that stand in our way will be killed. Either way, living or dead, willingly or not, they *will* be assimilated.'

Killed.

The notion rolled around Baelthrom's mind for a long while. Killing did not bother him, but he did not revel in and relish it like his dark dwarves and necromancers. Killing meant death, and the notion disturbed him. Even in choosing his body, the hybrid form in which his consciousness now stood, he had found the death of those beings from whom his parts were created, disturbing. The very thought of death, of not existing, disturbed him. If he really thought hard about death, and all its consequences, he came close to feeling something very alien and very uncomfortable. Fear.

Death was a terrible thing. To live and exist, and then to die as nothing, to nothing—even the thought of it now made him shudder. Death; seeing the life disappear from a once animate being, as he had seen it disappear from the things that had created his body... he could not understand it.

There was something terribly wrong with death. But not pain, no. Pain was good. Pain, like any information, was useful, and it could be used to teach very effectively. He had killed a great many things, but it was only through the Black Drink of Immortality that he found a chance to capture that escaping life force, to make sure it wasn't lost and pointless.

No, he did not agree with death. He was here to give all things a great gift—immortality. It was a pitiful shame that the beings upon Maioria were too weak and stupid to understand that gift. They followed the teachings of the goddess; a being that made them die, a being that refused to help the very people who worshipped her.

'It's time for a new god, Kilkarn. One who delivers on promises and answers prayers. One who gives immortality to all life. Too long have the people of Maioria been denied the eternal by a greedy, selfish goddess. What's the point of a goddess if she cannot even stop death, or worse, choose not to? I'm here to give back to the people what she has so long denied them.'

Kilkarn nodded and rubbed his hands, pleased to hear the certainty again in his lord's voice.

'Death is a disease that should not be,' Baelthrom continued. 'Long ago in the days when I was trying to take form and did not understand death, I kept the dead close to me. I watched their limp forms decay, smelt the stench of putrefaction. I waited for months for them to move again, but they did not. They rotted, disintegrated, and eventually disappeared.

'The horror of it was beyond my comprehension. "How could this be?" I asked, and I feared then for my own demise. It was a terror that haunted me like no other. But I did not age. I did not die. For I'm not of Maioria, but from the place you call the Dark Rift. All I remember of this place is that there was no such thing as death there. My immortality would be a great gift to this world. I just had to find out what it was within me that could bring immortality to a being. I had to create the greatest cure the world has ever known, the cure for death.'

'That is what our prophets told us, Lord Baelthrom,' Kilkarn said. 'The True God would end death. So we came to you, with as much knowledge as our necromantic art had taught us. It had taught us its darkness, its deceit, its terrible strength, and its awesome power, but it was wildly unpredictable.

'Even in the beginning, we called ourselves Life Seekers, for we sought the eternal, we sought immortality. But without you, we could not reach it. You rewarded us for our devotion; you gave us our greatest desire—

immortality. You taught us how to capture the life force within a body and use it to create the blessed Elixir of Immortality. Through you, Lord Baelthrom, we unlocked powerful magic from the Dark Rift itself.'

'Yes. The Elixir of Immortality describes this wonderful gift better than what the elves call it,' Baelthrom nodded. 'Sirin Derenax, the Black Drink. But it does more than instil immortality into the imbiber, it binds their small and weak soul to me forever, connecting them to the greater divine.'

Baelthrom chuckled. 'How crude the first creations were. They required scores of lives to create but one immortal. And now it takes only one. It is the key to taking over this world. Millions of lives have been sacrificed to make this most wondrous thing. Every life has made it purer, stronger, and more powerful.

'But the Maphraxies' desire for the elixir can never be quenched. This desire is a weakness for which we still need a cure. Though immortal, my Maphraxies still need to consume it, albeit a weaker cruder version. It keeps their bodies strong and powerful. Otherwise, they wither. Though they cannot die, they become useless lumps of flesh,' Baelthrom's voice hardened.

'Anything can be made immortal, from the ants in the ground to the fish in the sea, all human kin and dragons, but it changes them forever,' Baelthrom said. 'Perhaps this change is why few come to me for the great gift I offer. If the fools do not want my gift, then they will not be spared. I cannot abide stupidity,' his voice dropped so low the ground rumbled. 'That is why we must enslave them, they must be forced to take the elixir. I'm sure it's this goddess who makes them foolish. Even under torture, they do not deny her. She must be destroyed!'

Kilkarn covered his ears from the booming sound of his Lord's voice. For several minutes his words echoed around them and red magic fizzled around his furious lord. When silence descended, he tentatively spoke.

'Lord Baelthrom. The Black Drink has been a great gift to us all,' he lusted for it even now.

'It can be better,' Baelthrom said. 'Yet despite all I offer, the people still worship this goddess, this being with many faces, the eternal Source of All. How can they pray to something without material form, something they cannot see? Do the people not see the life stolen from them? Do they not yearn for a life that never ends?

'For all those years in my prison, I tried and failed to understand the people. I detest this thing to which they give their energies, this thing which makes death acceptable,' Baelthrom's voice rolled around the chamber and his eyes turned from gold to copper. 'But I will find this thing and destroy it. I shall remove the chains the goddess has placed upon the people, and take her power. The people will then worship me, and I will give them something she does not. I will give them immortality, and I will be a flesh and blood god who walks among them.'

'Your mighty kingdom awaits you, my lord,' Kilkarn bowed. 'Like the Ancients who, in their arrogance, refused your immortal gift, those who refuse you shall be... *assimilated.*'

A laugh rumbled from Baelthrom. 'Indeed, the Ancients refused immortality as they refused to worship me. I hated them and pitied their short lives, though they lived far longer than any race alive today. Their arrogance was their downfall. It's not just power that feeds me, Kilkarn, I also hunger for knowledge. There is more to life than just a physical body, there is the essence that animates, that which they call the soul.

'I need to know where these *souls* go when they die when they aren't distilled into Sirin Derenax, or ensnared in Keteth's Shadowlands. Keteth knows where they go, and that was why I let him live. But his mind is insane and too difficult to read. This new... force, this dark moon and the Night Goddess of which the people now speak... The truth lies in there, and I must have it.'

'You needn't concern yourself about so small a thing,' Kilkarn crooned. 'Over centuries your army has amassed into vast numbers. None can withstand our might as we swarm across Maioria. Even great Drax, the place we thought would fall last, fell sooner. As they die fighting us, their bodies and souls are assimilated into our ranks. We can only grow stronger, an unstoppable force purging the planet of death.' Kilkarn laughed, but his lord stayed silent for a time.

'Yet still there is this change in Maioria,' Baelthrom whispered. 'A movement in the energies that entwine this world, and a presence I don't yet understand—like another power let loose upon the world, or an ancient power reawakened. Nothing more than a gentle breeze, and yet this magic feels as old as the sun, and it grows in the west.'

'What exactly is this power, Lord Baelthrom?' Kilkarn stepped closer, but Baelthrom did not hear him. Kilkarn frowned and looked around. Everything had become completely still. Not that anything was moving anyway, there was not even a breeze that could reach in here. Instead, it seemed as if time itself had stopped and they were suspended like frozen figures within it.

'Keteth–' Baelthrom's words were cut off as a tidal wave of raw magical power surged through the room, through the fabric of Maioria.

Kilkarn was knocked off his feet. The magical energy struck Baelthrom so hard he was forced to his knees. Kilkarn's mind spun, and his heart pounded. Lightning flashed all around them and danced off the iron ring. The Orb of Life flared into a myriad of colours.

No longer were they suspended in time but being thrown about by magical forces. The magic grew in a crescendo that ripped through everything. Kilkarn gripped onto the pedestal he was beside. The iron ring blazed into life, flames of pure white ignited the chamber, and rippled like water spilling out from the ring's centre. The force of it sent Kilkarn flying backwards into the wall, where he crumpled and lay winded. Baelthrom roared.

CHAPTER 5

Freydel

'HMPH? What was that?' Freydel sat bolt upright in his bed.

He dragged the blankets closer around him, struggling to work out where he was. He always awoke wondering where he was, such was the curse of a travelling wizard. The suspiciously familiar looking scrolls and maps littering his bed rustled around him as he moved. Some fell to the floor, but he barely noticed, just as he barely noticed sleeping on top of them.

There had been dark blue light pulsing everywhere, and then a loud boom so low it was barely audible. He could still feel the after-tremors of that sound shuddering around him. He entered the Flow. It was alive with energy; a swirling maelstrom of indigo magic, a roaring noise that was only just beginning to recede.

'How strange,' he breathed. His eyes adjusted out of the Flow and to the room he was in.

'Ah, my precious study,' he sighed and relaxed his grip on the bed covers. The familiar mess of scrolls, maps, books, jars and all manner of magical devices filled him with calm. He yawned, half wondering why he still had his day clothes on, but it had been late and sleep had descended swiftly. He yawned again and smacked his lips together.

'The Flow is… Just nothing…' he muttered and lay back down, pulling the covers around his shoulders.

'Keteth!' he shouted, and jumped out of bed straight into a pile of books.

'Ugh,' he gasped, and sprawled over them. 'For goodness sake. I need light. Light!'

A brilliant light flashed at his command, and every candle and gas lamp burst alight, blinding him so he still couldn't see.

'Curse it. Dimmer.'

The lights dimmed, and he groped along the table to the secret drawer that contained the orb. By the time he had prised it out of its black velvet pouch his vision had returned, but the orb was burning, or was it freezing?

'Yargh.' He almost dropped it, but thankfully it had a mind of its own, and instead fell forwards and rolled neatly onto its holder atop the desk. He rubbed his hand and scowled at the orb. It was either burning hot or freezing cold, he still wasn't sure.

'Reveal to me the origin of that magical surge,' he breathed holding his hands carefully above it.

But the orb would not respond, and all it showed was a constant swirling indigo light, just as he had seen in his dream before he had awoken, and just as he'd seen in the Flow after he'd awoken.

'It's... busy. Hmm. What are you seeing, I wonder. I hope you are recording it.' He pulled on his beard. 'Is Keteth dead? Is Issa dead?'

He turned cold at the last thought and prayed it wasn't so. Without the orb, he couldn't scry to be sure. Maybe Lady Eleny had seen or felt something. He grabbed his staff and pulled on his boots. With a click of his fingers, a ball of light lit up the doorway and the steps leading down. Forgetting his age, he took the steps two at a time, and all but jumped out of his turret. He ran breathlessly into the main building.

The halls were empty and dark, save for his ball of light, the servants were still asleep. He ran up the wooden staircase, again two at a time, only to nearly collapse at the top. Clinging to the bannisters sucked in air and tried to calm his racing heart.

'Goodness,' he gasped, pulling himself along towards Lady Eleny's room. He tapped on the door.

'Lady Eleny, it's me, Freydel, are you up?' he rasped.

There came a confused mumble from inside, and a warm orange glow spread under the door. Seconds later the door, opened and a dishevelled Lady Eleny stood there, wrapping her robe about her. On seeing Freydel, the sleep was swept from her face and replaced with worry.

'What's happened? What have you seen?' she opened the door wide. 'Come in before we wake everyone.' He stepped into the room and she shut the door gently.

'Ely,' he began, (she preferred her informal name amongst friends, and Freydel had known her since she was a babe), 'it's less about what I saw, and more about what I felt. A great surge of magic in the Flow, in my dream. It woke me up. And it wasn't a dream, everything was trembling. Did you feel it?'

'Uh, no. I dreamed the world was rocking, though,' Ely yawned. 'Perhaps that was why. Tremors are quite normal.'

'That was no tremor, the Flow itself was throbbing with magic.'

'What about the orb? What has it shown?' she sat down on the bed. Freydel took the stool by the dresser.

'I tried to access the orb, but it's… busy. I can't explain it, it has never happened before. It simply won't let me access it. It's as if it's busy doing something else.' Could it be sensing the other orb? Yes, it had to be. Keteth had had the Orb of Water for a long time, and now he was gone, it was free. He decided not to speak his thoughts aloud, he needed more time to think it through.

'Is she…' Ely's hand went to her throat.

'I don't know, I can't see. I can't scry. I came here to ask you the same.'

Ely shook her head and swallowed.

'The magic was blue, Ely. Indigo blue like the colour of the dark moon. And it was everywhere.' He could still feel the glorious power of it, and the Flow still hummed. He beamed. 'I think she is alive, Ely.'

Ely tried to smile. 'I wish we could be sure. I've no magical ability with which to sense such things…'

'I should inform Cirosa immediately. She might know more,' he said.

Ely scowled. 'I doubt very much that the High Priestess cares at all whether Issa lives. In fact, I should think she'd prefer her dead. If only we had a caring, functional, priestesshood here on Celene, or on the whole planet for that matter. As you know, I'm suspicious that this was all a set up to destroy Issa in the first place.'

'I doubt very much there is any maliciousness to Cirosa, she's just ambitious and over-worked,' he tried to placate her. While Cirosa was not his favourite person, she would still be the Oracle one day, and it wasn't worth making enemies with The Order of the Great Goddess.

'I understand you two have had your… differences, but she *will* be the Oracle, and we must try to keep the peace.' He could see from her scowl that he was doing a poor job of soothing her.

'You always were so forgiving of her. The Order of the Great Goddess… pah. What is that? It certainly is all about laws and orders placed upon the people like a chain about the neck. And who is the one who makes up all these laws? That *woman* sat here on the most sacred isle of the goddess. The Order was supposed to be about the soul and spirit, not the physical control of people,' Ely spat. 'I wish Issa had never met the woman.'

Freydel put his hands up for calm, wanting to return to the most important matter at hand. 'We're all tired and worried—'

'Do you know what the people think?' Ely cut him off. 'What they say in the taverns here and across Maioria? What mothers talk to each other about while their children are playing? What soldiers on leave tell their families about? What the farmers speak of as they till their fields? Well, I'll tell you what. They say the rites of the Temple are no longer sacred but mechanical and soulless. They don't believe that the Great Mother would ever expect Her children to act according to rigid laws and scriptures. They are beginning to believe the goddess has given up on them, left them to their fate at the hands of the Immortal Lord. Their faith is broken, and people without faith are weak indeed.'

Freydel tried to speak, but the issue had clearly been eating away at Ely for a while, possibly all night, and she carried on with barely a pause for breath.

'Now most don't visit their temples or gather in groups to give thanks to the One Source. You saw it yourself. The Midsummer Celebrations were a third less in number than it was last year, and it's been dwindling since Cirosa came here with all her laws. Everyone I spoke to mentioned the lack of recruits into the priestess ranks. Some temples have even been deserted on Frayon. The common folk think the Temple has become corrupt and rotten from within, and certainly does not serve the spiritual needs of the people.

'If only I'd tried harder to be High Priestess, perhaps I could have stopped this. You know my mother could have taken over after Mielan?' Freydel nodded and opened his mouth to speak, but Ely didn't pause. 'She was the preferred choice by far. We could have stopped this rot.'

'You could not have,' Freydel raised his voice to cut through her rant. Ely halted. 'Cirosa was already in the highest favour in the Temple of Frayon before she came here.'

'Wormed her way up, conniving and plotting and backstabbing,' Ely seethed.

'Don't drag up the past, Ely, it will bring only pain. Dargan is gone, and what is done is done. If it's any consolation, I think they treated you most poorly. Be glad you're out of their grasp now.' He desperately wanted to get away from this topic, it was nothing to do with him. Only the Wizards' Circle held his responsibility, and the events currently fast unfolding were of utmost importance. 'But please, perhaps a conversation for another time? We must consider Issa's safety.'

The anger drained from Ely's face, and she looked down at her hands. 'I'm sorry, you're right. I've been fraught with worry and suffering nightmares. I just don't understand how such a terrible task can have been chosen, even if the goddess spoke to Cirosa, which I doubt very much. This whole thing stinks. Why was another task not chosen? Any task. Issa has been through so much, and she is barely a woman,' Ely clenched the hem of her robe.

'I did try,' he sighed. 'I said, "to slay the White Beast is too great a risk." I tried to think of some other testing that would prove her worth, that would show to everyone the power I know she has inside. As you know, I even mentioned the Storm Holt.'

Ely frowned. 'A wizards' testing.'

He held up his hands. 'It was all I could think of. Cirosa said the same thing, and that a wizard's test could never be used for one guided by the goddess. You know how she feels about magic and wizards, she scoffs at anything she cannot understand or master. She would hear none of it, and who am I to dictate matters of religion to the High Priestess of Celene?'

Ely scowled but said nothing.

'She is right, Ely. If the prophecy is true, then the Raven Queen must be strong enough to stand against all the darkness. Keteth is just one small part of it. Like Cirosa said, if Issa truly is chosen by the Goddess to free us from the immortals, then surely slaying this monster will be easy for her. The tasks ahead will be but greater still. If she fails here, she will surely fail against the Maphraxies.'

'Yes, but not now, it's far too soon,' Ely hissed, trying to quieten the rising emotion in her voice.

'All the heroes and heroines of old have proved their worth through some great deed,' he reminded her.

'But the Storm Holt would have been better. You could have helped her more easily, rather than have us sitting here useless,' Ely shook her head. 'Cirosa really has you convinced with her poisonous tongue.'

'But, Cirosa pointed out the truth. That Issa, the Feylint Halanoi, and all of Maioria cannot win this war through magic and sorcery. She is right, the Scorching War between wizards is long over, and since Baelthrom came, the magic left within Maioria is a far cry from what it once was. Besides, the Storm Holt does not fulfil prophecies or prove the goddess's chosen one. She even said she hoped Issa would refuse this task, for her own safety.'

Ely snorted. 'Cirosa doesn't care about anything or anyone apart from her own ambitions. I would not ever trust that woman.' Ely's shoulders slumped then, and she rubbed her eyes. 'None of this matters now, anyway. What's done is done. All we can hope for is her return. How indeed will she return? How can we help her now?'

Freydel relaxed, relieved to have the subject get back to the issue at hand. 'The Wykiry brought her safely here to Celene in the past. I scryed for her through the orb when she left with the Wykiry. They took her back to the edge of the Shadowlands, as I guessed they might. They won't have left her, and I have absolutely no doubt that they will return her safely once more. It's the Wykiry's self-made responsibility, since their fall from grace, to always know where Keteth is, and to help any victims in his wake.'

Ely looked hopefully out of the open window. It was still pitch black out there.

'Regardless of our feelings, Cirosa knows all that has happened so far. In fact, I should go there immediately in case she has heard anything,' he said, jumping up off the stool. 'I can be there a little after dawn if I leave now. Please, get some rest for now. You look as exhausted as I feel.'

Ely nodded and gave a wan smile as he turned and left.

CHAPTER 6

Hameka

BAELTHROM roared. He reached deep into the Under Flow. It surged around him as a shield of red fire. He turned his attention to the other magic that assaulted him and focused upon the Flow. Ancient magic was at work, and yet it was also new because he had never felt it before.

He followed the magic's signature, searching for the source of the power. Much could be learned from the feel and essence of magic, for it, like all energy, held information. For thousands of miles, he projected his mind, until finally, he drew near to it out in the open ocean, far beyond the west coast of Frayon.

'Keteth is dead,' he breathed in a voice so deep, it was more vibration than sound as it echoed around the chamber.

Kilkarn dragged himself up from the corner of the room where he had been cowering.

'This is of some interest, but surely no concern, Lord Baelthrom,' Kilkarn puffed, and stepped towards him.

'His pitiful prison of souls is broken,' Baelthrom said, still decoding the magic. 'And all their magic, all their power, has been returned to the world... but not to me,' he hissed.

'There is no danger here, Lord Baelthrom,' Kilkarn's voice was barely a squeak, and he hesitated mid-footstep.

Baelthrom continued to immerse himself in the Flow of the new yet ancient magic. It flowed around him as thick mist. He moved close to the source but struck a wall of magic that prevented him from getting closer. He searched for a way through, but could not penetrate the mist. And then as if in response to his probing, two huge eyes formed upon its surface and opened.

Blue-green eyes looked straight at him, trapping him in their gaze. He stared, unable to pull away, and in their glassy surface, he saw himself reflected there. It was him, with his three-peaked helmet and black iron armoured body, only now his body was wilting and shrivelling, crumbling away to dust, just like he had seen the lifeless dead decay until they were nothing. In those eyes, he saw that which he feared most; his own death.

A choking fear swept over him, grabbed him by the throat and squeezed. Rolls of sweat ran down his body, and not for the first time he detested his physical form. Then the eyes snapped shut, releasing him, and he was flung back against the wall of his chamber. Kilkarn shrieked and ran to him.

'Lord Baelthrom,' the dark dwarf snivelled.

Baelthrom shoved him aside, sending him rolling back into the altar, but the dwarf only jumped up and ran back to his side. The choking fear retreated and became rage. Baelthrom clenched his fists until the dark veins stood out on his arms. With a shove of his tail, he flung himself to standing and roared. The chamber shook, Kilkarn cowered. The echo finally fell to silence. The magic trail was gone, and there was no way he could follow it again.

'There is no danger here, Lord Baelthrom,' Kilkarn repeated.

The dwarf was right, he was not under attack, there was no danger, and even if there was it should be no cause for worry, nothing could defeat him. He released his hold upon the Under Flow and let his shield of fire go out. He folded his wings and relaxed.

'Indeed. Who would dare come here?' Baelthrom said, finding confidence in his own power. Kilkarn always knew the right thing to say, which was why he was still alive and at his side. The dwarf came forward now, emboldened by his words.

'Nothing can brave the Immortal Lord's fortress deep within the wastelands of Maphrax,' he said and laughed, a short monkey-like chuckle he stopped abruptly when Baelthrom growled.

'We must act quickly...' Baelthrom turned to the iron ring. As he spoke, a metallic film spread within the ring as if a pool of water had formed vertically. The liquid stilled and a cluster of islands came into view, barely visible in the darkness of night.

'Our closest armies to the source of that magic are positioned upon the Isles of Kammy. The Feylint Halanoi don't know the islands are now ours, and soon we'll be ready to attack the unguarded West Frayon coast.'

'Find me Dromoorai,' he commanded. The image in the iron ring focused upon the largest island.

Flaming braziers lit up the main port, what was left of it after the Dread Dragons had destroyed it. Blackened earth and crumbled walls ringed the harbour. At the end of the harbour pier, a great black shadow of a sleeping Dread Dragon came into view. It looked like a statue; unmoving and sat back on massive haunches, tail curled around its front legs, head raised but still—a veritable mountain against a starlit sky.

The Dromoorai rider slept mounted upon its back, flaring red eyes now finally dark behind the three-peaked helmet. The reins of the Dread Dragon gripped in gauntleted fists. Dromoorai always slept ready for battle.

'Awaken,' Baelthrom commanded. The amulet around the Dromoorai's neck flared into red light. Its eyes opened and matched the red light of the amulet. The Dread Dragon also opened its eyes, but all that was detectable were gleaming pitch-black orbs.

'Take all the ships and all the Dromoorai to the edge of the Shadowlands immediately.' He forced into the Dromoorai's mind the location of where he had found her. 'Find the one who has destroyed Keteth. Use all magic for speed and spare none. Bring her alive.'

'Yes, Lord Baelthrom.' Its voice rumbled through the ring and around the chamber, and it launched into the air.

'Find me necromancers,' Baelthrom commanded.

The iron ring dutifully obeyed and drew inland towards the keep of a castle. All the ramparts had been destroyed and blackened by the fire of Dread Dragons, but some of the greater structures—the towers, the bailey, the castle itself—still remained relatively intact. Into the castle, the image focused. Down winding stone stairs lit by braziers, and into the dungeons below ground. Here the necromancers always worked, away from the painful light of day, busy with their death magic and the creation of the Elixir of Immortality.

The skinny, dirty arms of prisoners hung listlessly out through the bars of their prison. The image within the iron ring moved past them, through a thick wooden door and into a torch-lit room. There the image settled upon a tall, black-robed and hooded figure. Impossible to tell whether male or female. Pale white chin, nose, and long thin hands were all that was visible.

'Obey,' Baelthrom commanded.

With necromancers and dark dwarves Baelthrom needed no Shadow Stone amulet through which to communicate. The initiation into his service, the wilful imbibing of the Sirin Derenax and the mark of Maphrax at the base of their throat, was all that was necessary to find them in the iron ring.

'Yes, my great lord,' the voice was airy, pleased to hear Baelthrom's command, but also impossible to distinguish whether male or female.

'The Dromoorai are ready. Leave now, take all ships to the edge of the Shadowlands.' He placed an image of what he had seen in the necromancer's mind. 'Find the one who has defeated Keteth. Use all magic to get there, spare none. Go now.'

Baelthrom ended the communication without waiting for a reply, and the image blurred to grey. He released his clenched fist. They could get there in time. They could trap her, she could not outrun the Dromoorai and their ships sped on with the most powerful magic. All he had to do was wait. But he hated waiting… He considered what else could be done.

'I must reach all my spies,' Baelthrom said. 'The harpy witches have a Shadow Stone. Find me Harpy Dereever.'

Harpies were one of the few races in league with his plan, and they had their uses. They were easy to control with promises of fertile young men and they made good spies. They could fly anywhere, and not raise the alarm of the Feylint Halanoi. Darkness swirled, and then the glow of a smouldering fire revealed hundreds of dark shapes. Harpies sleeping, slick feathers gleaming in the light.

The pale face of one awake came into view. Long black hair framed a tanned face, and red lips smiled, revealing pointed dark teeth. The smile never reached her all-black eyes that seemed permanently set in a scowl. Three white scars clawed across each of her high cheekbones, and a shining onyx stone set atop her brow marked her as the Harpy Queen.

'My lord,' Dereever hissed and inclined her head ever so slightly.

'Keteth is dead. Where is your brood? What has occurred there?' Baelthrom asked.

The harpy hissed a low laugh. 'We are hidden in the cliff caves of south-west Frayon, Lord Baelthrom,' her voice was high-pitched and crooning. 'Nothing has occurred here, but there has been strange magic felt on Celene, which is why we spy on the goddess's isle. We smell unrest there, and our magic reveals one who might be… turned. But we haven't discovered how useful this High Priestess might be yet.

'Go there, now. Give this priestess your Shadow Stone. I shall see to the rest. You will receive another Shadow Stone when you have done this successfully,' Baelthrom commanded.

The Harpy Queen hesitated and scowled a little as if she would prefer to be doing other things, such as sleep, but he knew she would not dare disobey him.

'Time is of the essence, and you will be rewarded,' he added, his tone sharper.

Her scowl turned into a greedy smile. 'My lord,' she inclined her head.

Baelthrom ended the communication and stood staring into the empty ring.

'Hameka,' he commanded. Suddenly keen to see his second in command—a man that had, as yet, never failed him. Aside from the dark dwarves, few chose Baelthrom as their lord willingly, and only one sane human ever sought him out purposefully, only one with his mind clear and clever, and his will hard as iron. A thin gaunt face stared back at him. Hameka's hair was dark grey, and a deep widow's peak accentuated an already large forehead. Thick eyebrows shaded intelligent but cold grey eyes.

He looked to be in his early fifties, though Baelthrom knew he was several hundred years older. He would not have aged past the young man of twenty-five who Baelthrom had first met, if he had accepted immortality then. Exceptionally, he had not forced him, preferring to let the man feel those first signs of age creeping into his bones, his flesh slackening and wrinkling just a little, his muscles weakening. Only then had Hameka accepted a taste of the Elixir of Immortality, but only the tiniest amount, enough to significantly prolong his life and delay ageing, heal his wounds and ailments faster, but not enough for immortality.

Hameka knew the elixir would change him forever. He'd said he did not want to jeopardise their war efforts, and only when Frayon had fallen and the Feylint Halanoi defeated would he take it. Until then he needed his human anger, his human hatred of the Feylint Halanoi, it drove him on, gave him strength.

So Baelthrom forgave him for not taking the elixir, though he had bound him to his word. Besides, back then the Sirin Derenax still needed much work to create something that was not brain dead and deformed. They still kept the old stock for the prisoners. Always they needed the immensely strong, but otherwise stupid Maphraxies who formed the vast bulk of the Maphraxian army. The purer elixir was expensive to create, taking a score of young, untainted souls to form it, years to distil it, and was reserved only for the necromancers.

Even without the Elixir of Immortality, Hameka had quickly proven his worth. With a cunning, clever mind, he had led them to victory on the battlefield again and again, advancing Baelthrom's agenda far quicker than he had hoped. Indeed, before Hameka there had been none who had led the Maphraxies to so many a victory. The man was brilliant, a true master of the art of war.

'My Lord Baelthrom,' Hameka said, inclining his head in respect as he stared into the blood-red Shadow Stone. The tripartite helmet of his lord appeared, behind which his face was permanently sealed. His eyes glowed a dark and dangerous red that matched the colour of the stone.

Aside from Dereever, Hameka was the only non-Dromoorai to wear a Shadow Stone. But his was more than just a Shadow Stone, it was the Shadow Key—a unique and special gift bestowed upon him. It was a mark of trust and responsibility as Baelthrom's right-hand man, and he wore it with great pride. The Shadow Key was the only bloodstone that had the power to communicate back to the Shadow Master, and to all of the other Shadow Stones. He could see in any place at any time, and still command Baelthrom's orders as he received them.

The vast power that Baelthrom wielded—a being come from the Dark Rift and beyond time itself—all spoke of one who was far more than the mortals of Maioria. Because of this, Hameka believed deeply that Baelthrom was the one true god come to lead them, and give them the power that was rightfully theirs.

He could not wish for more in his lord; cold, logical, infinitely powerful, not given to bouts of irrational emotion or rage. Baelthrom had said many times that they were a great army delivering the peoples of Maioria from the terrible annihilation of death, and giving them back strength and power in an otherwise weak and decrepit world. They were angels bringing salvation from an inept, absent goddess. It didn't matter to Hameka what they were, as long as he could serve his lord, and enjoy such powers as only Baelthrom could give.

'It pleases me to see you, my lord. Only moments ago, a force of strange magic flared through the Necromantic Chambers.' He shivered. His skin still crawled and his stomach churned since that awful force had rippled through him. 'For a moment, the necromancers were forced out of the Under Flow. Something few have ever experienced.'

Baelthrom nodded thoughtfully, his helmeted face giving nothing away, but over the years Hameka had, to some degree, learnt to read his lord's thoughts depending on what colour his eyes were. They had turned mid-blue, and that was always deep thought.

'Indeed, that is interesting. Perhaps, then, it will be of no surprise to you to know that Keteth has been slain, but by what and whom I could not determine.'

Hameka raised his eyebrows in surprise, wondering what, if anything, the death of the white slug meant.

'The death of Keteth ultimately means nothing, but what killed him does,' he decided.

Baelthrom spoke of what he had seen, and where he had followed that strange magic to. Images of the sea and a location on a map flickered through the Shadow Stone. Hameka listened patiently, beads of sweat formed on his forehead. He should be used to speaking with Baelthrom after so long, but he was always filled with nervousness whenever he did. He wasn't sure if the anxiety came from within or was placed there deliberately by Baelthrom to instil obedience.

However, these days he rarely saw the Immortal Lord, and it was only through the iron ring that they communicated, being based as he was thousands of miles away from Maphrax in the cold northern province of Drax. And if this was summer then he dreaded winter. He shivered again despite the sweat on his forehead.

'I've already sent Dromoorai and our ships from the Isles of Kammy to investigate the situation. As we speak, harpies search Southwest Frayon,' Baelthrom said.

'Is this interesting event linked to the power you have felt growing in the West? The harpy witches have reported no more since we last spoke a week or so ago,' Hameka said, unable to conceal his scowl. The harpies were disgusting allies as far as he was concerned, but they had wings, and when sent as spies they were inconspicuous and far more expendable than Dromoorai. As such he was forced to concede they had their uses.

Harpies inhabited the cliff caves of Ostasia, a land long since ruled by Maphrax that was mostly uninhabitable swamp and chunks of grey rock. It was through the Shadow Key that Hameka had ordered the harpies to investigate Southern Frayon. Harpies did nothing without bargaining for their petty needs, and so in return they were promised a handful of young men from the Maphraxie prisons. That was all it took to send the whores skyward.

Harpies would not go unnoticed, hated as they were by pretty much everything, but they were not uncommon in the south, and they were closer to where this new power came from. One of them had reported sightings of a dark-haired girl on the shores of the Celene after the dark moon rose. She had "smelt different" to the others, and a strange magic collected around her. But that was all he could glean, and he had not thought much about it.

'You must go immediately to the borders of the Shadowlands,' Baelthrom commanded, ignoring his question. 'This force, this thing that destroyed Keteth, must be stopped before it gets any stronger. It's already too powerful, and the people will become hopeful. I trust you understand the gravity of the situation?'

'Yes, my lord,' Hameka gave a tight smile as he accepted his undesirable orders.

The death of Keteth meant nothing to him. The new magical power, that even he could feel blooming in the west, held no interest either. What bothered him most was sparing any part of his army to begin new and unplanned excursions for, as he saw it, pure folly. The fighting was proving quite difficult in the press into northern Frayon from southern Drax. Battles at sea were never easy, and here in the north the sea surged viciously between the continents, swelling around hundreds of jagged-rocked islands ready to rip apart the hull of any warship.

Adding to the surging sea, the wind was high and frigid, and seemingly blew in whichever way it fancied. But more than that, and he did not like to admit it, since the rising of that cursed blue moon, the Feylint Halanoi were putting up a vicious resistance. He chanced his thoughts.

'The war is in the north, Lord Baelthrom. The humans have already dared venture further north since our last major offensive that destroyed most of them. We have already lost an island or two since we moved our forces from Haralan to the Isles of Kammy. If anything, we need more forces pushing south into Frayon, not less, my lord.'

Baelthrom's eyes turned a darker blue. Hameka never liked it when they turned dark, no matter what colour they were. It always meant his lord was growing angry.

'You are my most prized commander, Hameka. You have proven your excellence in battle countless times. Have I not always rewarded you for your prowess?'

'Yes, my lord,' Hameka stood up straighter and smiled. His lord had always rewarded him with power, gold, jewels, exquisite earthly delights and all the pleasures women could bring. All enjoyable things, but never as enjoyable as winning battles. Despite being Baelthrom's most favoured commander, he always trod carefully with his lord. He would never be able to wield power such as Baelthrom could, and he did not want to lose his place as Baelthrom's right-hand man.

'It's just that… My greatest concern is that our battles are won with careful planning and the ability to foresee ahead,' he tried to phrase it well. 'This mission has had little or no planning, and the necromancers have not had time to see ahead.'

'My lord,' he continued after a brief pause, ignoring the sweat building on his brow. 'You know how intense the fighting has been the past few months now our enemy is pinned to the Frayon continent. Frayon is vast, and any move forward has become painfully slow. Sometimes it seems as if we have gained only inches. The cursed Feylint Halanoi refuse to know when they are beaten. They fight desperately now, like a cornered animal sensing its impending doom. We are so close, they know their end is near.' He could taste the inevitable victory even now, and it made him rush on.

'With a bigger push, with more resources all focused on the northern front, Frayon will at last be ours. It's only the visible end of their short pathetic lives that makes them fight harder—'

Baelthrom cut him off.

'We have been fighting the north for too long. It is time to attack where they least suspect it, where they are most vulnerable. I want them in shock, weak and grovelling. They must know I will stop at nothing, and nothing is beyond me. Take the most skilled necromancers and the fastest ships—take as many as you can spare. Go immediately,' Baelthrom pressed.

'Lord…' he began weakly.

'My decision is final, Hameka. As always, I'm quite certain you shall not fail me. I have my complete trust in you.'

'Yes–' the communication ended before he could finish '…Lord Baelthrom,' he sighed, shivered and slumped down onto his cushioned chair, pulling his double-layered fur coat closer around him. The Shadow Key turned dull.

CHAPTER 7

Ocean Battle

THE sea changed the farther from shore Asaph and the raven flew until it was no longer calm and flat, but stormy with lashing waves, wind and rain. It was not a natural storm but fuelled by magic and the air itself was charged with destructive energy.

As a dragon, it seemed he was always in the Flow, and he could see the energy of magic that flowed through and within all things. Like all dragons and Dragon Lords in dragon form, he could easily read the signature of magic and find its wielder if he were close enough. Only the most skilled wizards could read magic in this way.

Magic was all energy, but its source could be water, fire, air, wind, ether, or a complicated mix of either, which added an extra "signature" to it. What it was used for; destruction, equilibrium, protection, healing or creation added yet another dimension. Finally, who was directing the magic added the last signature; depending on race such as human or elf, and whether male or female.

What he sensed now was an old magic that he could not read easily. It seemed older than he was, and what on Maioria could be older than dragons? It also seemed to be flowing from the blue moon that had not long set. He could feel a female signature to it, and he assumed it was Issa, but it was more than human and so pure it was almost divine. He shied away from the concept, unable to fathom what it meant.

The magic was being used destructively and at the same time protectively, as if it was destroying something bad and then restoring it to its original good. Its source felt to be ether, itself a primordial force, and yet it was beyond it or before it. Then the power changed to come from wind, but then again it was before wind, pre-wind. As he drew closer, the magic became stronger and clearer, yet he struggled to understand it.

It was power before the base elements as if she drew upon the dark matter that exists before creation, the dark light before there is light. A hundred realisations seemed to hit Asaph at once, and were it not for the battle scene unfolding before him, he would have pondered upon what he had discovered a lot longer. The only thought that stuck in his mind was; *that was why she was called the Night Goddess, the Goddess of Dark Waters, the darkness before creation—the ultimate creative force.* Before creation, there was the darkness, but not an evil darkness, rather a loving sea of pre-creation, the force of intention before thought, before word, before action.

The thought was swept away as he tilted his wings and arced down, descending through the swirling mass of clouds. Driving wind tore at him, but his bulk fared much better than the raven below who was struggling to maintain course. He respected the bird immensely—nothing would stop it from reaching its master. There came surges of magic, felt as subsonic booms and seen as lightning that flashed and sizzled around him, the static flickering off his scales.

When the Flow was used, all magic users nearby could see, hear and feel the magic, to a lesser or greater degree depending on their own magical ability, as he could now. It was a light and sound display overlaid atop the ordinary world. All around, Issa's magic flashed and flared in blues and purples. The sound thundered from deep vibrational rumblings to high-pitched screeches as the magnetic and electrical properties of the magic surged.

There was feeling too—excitement coursed through his body. The chaos and stress of the magical forces filled him with utter exhilaration as if the magic itself fed him power and strength. The Flow was another world of wonder, for in his human form he could not use magic and could only feel a little of it.

There came another type of magic, not from the Flow, but from a dark place he could not read. Baelthrom's magic, the Under Flow from the Dark Rift. This magic sapped at the Flow, trying to steal its living force. He felt it sapping at his own life force and formed a protective shield against it. A clearing in the clouds passed beneath him, and through the lashing rain, he glimpsed five Maphraxian ships closing in on a tiny speck of pale floating in the sea.

The exhilaration and excitement he'd felt, turned to fury in one seamless motion, and he focused on a single-pointed objective: destroy the enemy. He dropped lower in the clouds and saw more clearly the black ships lumbering upon the ocean, each some fifty metres in length, with three curved masts hoisting aloft many sails that stretched from bow to stern. Swarming on the decks were hundreds of black-armoured Maphraxies.

He grimaced. Though they were only indistinct creatures at this height, he could feel their unholy essence, could even smell the stench of death they exuded, and something sickly beneath. Sirin Derenax. Of course. So that's what Coronos meant when he'd said, "The deathly sweet smell of the undead immortals." He had only ever seen the Maphraxies in the Recollection. They exuded wrongness. It made him angry. By Feygriene's fire, those abominations should not be, must not be.

He turned to his plan of attack and angled his body upwards to hide in the clouds again. Stealth was best. He drew the Flow to him, just a little so that no magic wielder would notice. Unlike humans he, like all dragons, needed no object or gesture or even a word to direct the Flow. The magic moved to his will and intention, with purely his directing thought.

There was no endless stream of complex spells of wizardry to learn. Indeed, magic was easy for a dragon, but then their magic was wilder than the sophisticated spells of wizards, and, though both were powerful, for a dragon it took less of a toll on the mind and body. Humans (and elves, dwarves, harpies and all other intelligent magic wielders) had to sleep deeply and frequently to recover. It was impossible for a dragon to overuse magic, and thus die from overusing it, but also a dragon could never overstretch its limits, limits that were set from birth. Humans could learn to use more, their abilities were not necessarily determined.

The barest coral-coloured shimmer around him told him his body was cloaked. Those who looked in his direction would see only a denser patch of rain or a slightly darker cloud. He could have used a powerful spell but he daren't alert Maphraxie necromancers to his presence and hoped they were too engrossed in the battle to sense his magic.

Asaph looked for the raven, angled a little towards another clearing, and nearly fell out of the sky. A dozen more ships appeared on the horizon, and they were closing in fast. The Immortal Lord must have felt her magic and the passing of Keteth—how else were they here so soon? There was surely a whole fleet, too many to fight... They looked built for speed, for their hulls were long and thin, and they sliced through the water with unnatural speed. With necromantic magic speeding them on, it would not be long before they were here.

He dropped down through the clouds like a stone, swooped low over a ship, and recoiled at the sight of the Maphraxies close up. No shared dragon memory could have ever prepared him for the reality of meeting the undead immortals in the flesh. He shuddered at their soulless eyes alight with a feverish madness, eager for the life force of living victims. In places, their grey skin was so taut across their unnaturally big bodies that it seemed about to split apart, while in other areas it sagged into folds. Their faces were wide and flat and their muscles bulged and contorted in abnormal places, as if the Sirin Derenax had made the body strong, but in a disorganised manner. It was these huge muscles that caused their lumbering gait. He looked away in disgust.

Scanning below he turned and flew towards where the battle raged thickest. In the sea between the circling ships were the bodies of Wykiry floating amongst the debris, their silvery light now dim in death. All around the ships were bodies drifting out upon the ocean. Amongst them were the dark forms of Maphraxies, their grey-white faces the same in death as they were in whatever form of life they had been. There were not many, but then few would float with their heavy dark dwarven armour. He hoped that for every Wykiry friend slain, two or more Maphraxies had died with them. The battle was not over, and his nostrils flared at the stench of death.

As he looked closer, he could see it was not just Wykiry who had joined the battle, but animals too. Dolphins, porpoises, even whales fought against the Maphraxies. *Zanufey's creatures of the water come to Issa's aid,* he marvelled in wonder. They must know this battle was important, that they fought for the future of Maioria herself. Some bobbed lifelessly on the surface, others darted amongst the dead and debris, the sound of their clicking and the burst of their blowholes filling the air.

If they had not come, she would have been captured. But where was she? He could see clearly high in the sky, but down low in the chaos of battle, the raging waves, wind and rain, he could not find her.

Flying as slow as he could without touching the water, he angled around the black hull of a Maphraxie ship and came to a tight knot of living creatures. Mainly Wykiry moved, but every now and then a burst of air and gasp of breath told him the cetaceans stayed close.

Many Maphraxies had taken to their raft boats and left the big ships. There were at least five small boats packed full with maybe twenty immortals in each. Their axes, swords and spears hacked and slashed into the waves spraying blood and sea-water as they fought towards their goal.

Blue-grey flukes slapped the water as the cetaceans tried to strike the boats. A boat titled alarmingly and dumped half the Maphraxies overboard before it righted itself again. Beaked jaws closed upon the fallen instantly, and dragged them under the surface to their deaths. Necromantic black fire flared across the surface, incinerating anything that did not dive deep enough, even killing the Maphraxies still struggling in the water. He felt disturbed at the ruthless actions of his opponents.

A huge tail erupted out of the ocean, barely missing his forelegs, and crashed back down upon two boats, splintering them apart. Many aboard were crushed under the whale's blow, and the rest fell screaming into the water. Two down, but more raft boats were being lowered off the big ships, and there seemed an endless stream of Maphraxies boarding them.

Magic, this time from the Wykiry, crackled in the air and blue fire flared over the boats and upon the Maphraxies. They tried to douse the flames with seawater, but the fire was immune and raged harder. Wykiry magic was water born, idiots, Asaph nearly laughed out loud. He wanted to join his fire with theirs, but he dared not drop his cloak until he found her. The Wykiry's victory was short lived as necromantic magic extinguished the flames.

The sky was brightening, and the dark moon moving further away, its power waning. In the growing light of dawn, it was clear they fought a losing battle against the Maphraxies. Asaph continued to scan the wreckage. Where was she? He could feel her, but teeth, fins, swords, axes, and magical fire created a chaotic scene.

And then he saw her; a pale, limp form clinging to a piece of wood, too exhausted to do anything else but command the storm that was draining her strength. In one hand she death-gripped a turquoise orb—Keteth's Orb of Water stolen from the Wykiry. The orb glowed like Coronos' orb did, and Asaph was suddenly afraid. Baelthrom sought the orb.

He must know Keteth was dead, but did he know who killed him? If he does not, then perhaps her identity is still concealed. The thought gave him some hope. Wykiry swam protectively around her, but they listed weakly onto their sides as they swam, as exhausted as she was.

'I'm here, friends,' he whispered to them with his mind, knowing they could not see him, but would feel the signature of his voice.

'Help us, brother,' they called back in unison. Even their mind voices were faint with fatigue. *We cannot escape them. The black wizards have created a net of death around us.'*

He understood then why they had not fled taking Issa to safety. In the air he was, he hoped, safe from whatever evil magic they had placed beneath the Wykiry. Part of him wanted to destroy the Maphraxies then and there, but the other part knew he had to save her first. Rage filled his belly with fire.

He turned to the nearest ship. To attack would mean his shield of invisibility would drop, but that mattered little now time was running out. He came close and spewed out the fury in his belly, feeling the shield drop as he did so. A plume of fire exploded from his mouth covering the ship's decks in raging destruction. The sails burst into flames, and Maphraxies scattered in all directions.

Asaph beat his wings and circled up and around, preparing to attack again. But the Maphraxies aboard the flaming ship were already recovering from dragon fear and dousing his fire with magic and water. He realised then that the dead did not feel fear like the living, they were truly formidable.

Guttural yells reached his ears above the howling wind, and the Maphraxies aboard the other ships scrambled to obey orders. Thick archer bows, taller than the Maphraxies themselves, were thrown on to the decks. The ships began to move out, spreading their numbers apart so it would not be possible to cover them all in flames at once.

Cunning, he thought, his plan had been anticipated. In their haste to spread, they ran over their own raft boats and any clinging to wreckage in the water. Once again their expendability made him wonder how many Maphraxies there were that they could let them die so easily. Whatever the number, it was too many. Archers lined the decks and drew back their bows. Hundreds of arrows were pointed at him, their tips dripping green slime and shimmering darkly. Enchanted *and* poisoned. He smiled inwardly. What a battle to be his first fought in dragon form. Coronos would not believe it.

A horn blew, and the dull thwonk of released bowstrings filled the air. Asaph arched his wings, and drove upwards hard, away from the cloud of poisoned tips. He blew a huge bout of fire as he did so, and flew fast through his own flames. The arrows following him were engulfed in the fire, and their dry wood caught light easily. They fell harmlessly into the sea. More would be coming, they were probably already notched.

Far below he sensed Issa pull on the Flow, felt her magic surge, and the Orb of Water she clung to somehow doubled the power of her intention. A circular wave some twelve feet high surged outwards from her in an ever-expanding ring. It smashed into the surrounding ships just as the horn blew.

He glanced down with a grin as the unsuspecting archers were knocked off balance and their arrows loosened harmlessly in all directions but up, many piercing other Maphraxies. The ships floundered upon the waves, making it difficult for the Maphraxies to reload, let alone aim. She was trying to help him, and though it helped to delay their next attack, it cost her. The smaller boats were still moving closer, soon they would reach her.

He roared. The thunderous sound rolled out of his mouth, and the Maphraxies froze. So, they can still fear a little, though they recover quickly. He climbed high into the clouds, stretching out his neck and tail into one long line so he could streak upwards fast. He closed his eyes and focused on the feeling of the air as it rushed past him, then pulled his wings in tight as his upwards motion slowed and the air went slack.

He opened his eyes as he came to a stop, and for one surreal moment, all was perfectly still. The air in his nostrils stopped moving, and the trickle of smoke that came from them hung perfectly motionless. Then he began to roll forwards. In a split-second, he had tilted to face straight down towards the ocean. He hurtled towards the hated black ships.

The Maphraxies scrambled for cover, but there was nowhere to go. He roared and bellowed fire upon them once more. In one breath he set ablaze two ships close to each other, then he was straining upwards in a tight arch to avoid their arrows, his muscles quivering against the forces.

He turned to look back but to his chagrin, the Maphraxies did not burn as normal living things made of flesh and blood would. Though they screamed and smouldered, many resisted his fire. Protective magic. Get rid of their necromancers and break the magic.

He scanned the ships. Aboard each, partially hidden by a magical mist that his dragon sight could penetrate, was a tight ring of four or five black-robed and hooded figures, their faces bent together in concentration. Necromancers. His skin crawled. Most were tall, but some were short. The servants of the Immortal Lord came in all shapes and sizes, and from all races.

'Traitors,' he growled.

Now he had found them he could feel and see their presence as a dark stain in the Flow. His fire could not penetrate their shield, but it was destroying the ships. They could not put out all the flames he had created. His fire had already destroyed the sails, despite their magical protection.

There came a thunderous, splintering sound, then one of the flaming masts crashed down. It swung in the rigging and swiped across the bow, taking a score of Maphraxies into the sea with it. They sank with the mast.

'Dragon brother, help us!'

The desperate plea cut through the roaring flames and splintering ships. So absorbed had he become in destroying his enemy, he had forgotten the reason he had come. He discovered one of the few weaknesses of a dragon; they were easily lost in their own fury.

Forgetting his enemy, he turned to where the call had come from. To his horror, the Maphraxies in the small boats were upon her. They had hooks and nets which they were throwing at Issa. The Wykiry and cetaceans still fought, but there were too many raft boats crowding together.

In his peripheral vision, he saw the archers drawing their bows, and glimpsed the signal sounder bring the horn to its lips. If those arrows hit him, it would all be over. He roared in frustration and beat his wings. The horn blasted, and the whistling of arrows came from behind. He was still in range. He dropped his right wing down and spun down to the right, spewing out what fire he had in his belly. The arrows missed him, but only just, and one skidded the length of his tail.

He turned towards the ships, filled his lungs, sprayed them with weaker fire. All now had their sails alight. He racked his brains as he watched the enemy swarm to put out the new flames. He could not breathe fire upon the smaller boats, it would kill Issa and all those who helped her. He dropped towards the boats closest to her. Ignoring the screams of those aboard, he gripped them in his claws and crushed them. Wheeling away he tossed the crushed boats and their contents into the ocean.

Movement in the Flow caught his attention, it was being sucked into the Under Flow. He glanced back at the necromancers. They were up to something, but what? They all began to glow with bright green auras, and their power joined as one. From each group a blast of green magic arced up into the sky towards each other until the five arcs met in the centre, directly above Issa.

Asaph searched the intention of the magic, but could not easily read the Under Flow and could only detect destruction. Though he could see it in the natural Flow, they drew upon the unnatural Under Flow of Baelthrom's magic. Did they intend to kill her now? He dropped towards her as the necromancers' flaring green magic boiled and grew.

No, they wouldn't kill their prize, would they? Surely they intended to destroy him trying to stop them. Bastards. He couldn't call their bluff, he'd seen what they did to their own kind, why wouldn't they kill her? They were necromancers, perhaps they had already bound her soul. He drew what he could of the Flow, trying to take it away from them, trying to stop its drain into the Under Flow, but they were strong, and they were over twenty in number. The Flow still surged towards him as the green mass of fire fell. Everything moved in sickeningly slow motion.

I may die, father, but I cannot let her go. He drew his wings close and moved faster towards her. The green flames were only forty feet above her. He dared not even twitch as he closed the gap. The green magic was dropping; thirty feet, twenty-five feet. He was fast, he would make it. He *must* make it. Twenty feet above her and he was still twenty-five feet away. He held a breath and through half-lids saw turquoise flare as a white light blasted from across the ocean.

Two forces beyond any physical power he had ever felt struck him, sending his body spinning. A sonic boom rang through his ears and shuddered his heart. There was a horrible ringing in the following silence and then he plunged deep into the ocean.

Asaph hung in the dark water, dazed. His muscles twitching from the magical, electrical disturbance, and his nerves throbbed from quivering magnetics as his body tried to balance itself. Even his thoughts were scattered and uncontrolled as if his brain had been sent rolling in his head. And then he was swimming. His muscles ached like hell, but miraculously he was swimming. How was he not dead?

He broke through the surface, and gasped air into his lungs. *Issa.* With great effort he kicked to get his wings out of the water, beat the aching limbs, and struggled into the air, his body shaking with exhaustion.

'The orbs, brother. Two united as one. Lucky for us all,' the Wykiry whispered.

'The Orb of Air. Coronos must have done something, and just in time too,' he replied in wonder.

'The net is broken, take her and flee,' they said.

The ships were still rocking and reeling from what had happened. The Maphraxies struggled to their feet,. The necromancers remained on their knees, heads in hands. Many lay unmoving on the decks. They could not organise themselves or form any control over magic. All the boats that had surrounded Issa were completely gone, there wasn't even any debris. It was as if they had never been. Anything above the water was destroyed except her. He glanced at the horizon and saw the other Maphraxie ships speeding towards them.

'No chance,' he growled. Facing anymore of those bastards was the last thing he wanted, no matter how hot the dragon rage burned within him. He had to let the desire to destroy his enemies go. The Immortal Lord was drawing close, and he could not possibly face that enemy. While the enemy was recovering, he had a chance to get her and get away unscathed.

He flew over the bodies of the dead to where Issa lay unmoving. She was no longer conscious, and the storms she had caused were dissipating, yet still she clung to the blue orb as if her life depended on it. Three Wykiry moved beside her, trying to keep her aboard the splintered wood as they struggled with exhaustion.

'*Take her, brother, far from here,*' they whispered.

'The goddess look after you,' he said, wondering what the voices of the Wykiry had been like when they could speak and walk on land. Coronos had said they were called the "Angels of Maioria" for the beauty of their voices.

He hovered low until his wing tips dipped into the sea, and as carefully as he could, grasped her. She felt so small and weak and human in his dragon claws as he lifted her from the ocean. Rags were all that remained of her clothes, and even to his cold-blooded flesh, he could feel she was frozen. He held her frigid body close to his belly where the fire burned hottest and beat his wings.

'We will meet again, brothers and sisters, our job is done here,' he said to the Wykiry. 'Run from them, and recover your numbers.'

He watched the remaining Wykiry sink into the darkness and then turned east to where the sky brightened with the coming dawn. His wings quivered with fatigue, and his eyes lost their focus now and again. He was fast losing his strength now the potion the old Karalanth had given him was waning. He did indeed feel like a newborn fawn.

He flew just above the surface where the wind rushed hard, moving his wings and body as little as possible as the wind pushed him forwards. He longed for the sun's heat to warm his cold blood, and for the first time, he understood why the Sun Goddess was so important to dragons and Dragon Lords. Feygriene was the source of their strength. He glimpsed a black speck flying ahead and smiled. The raven guided him on.

His heart leapt with joy when he spotted a ray of white light reaching out to him from the horizon, just to the west of where he was heading. He dipped his wing and adjusted his course towards the light of the Orb of Air.

CHAPTER 8

Orb of Water

'KETETH,' Baelthrom breathed, forcing his mind off the girl and remembering the day he felt the birth of a new potential. The iron ring, still vibrating from the magical assault, now flickered with blue light in response to its master's thoughts. An image of the young boy Keteth wavered within it.

'How long had I spent trying to affect your stubborn mind?' Baelthrom said. 'Then, finally, I broke through whilst you slept and sowed the seeds that would bring you to me; a hunger for power that you could never slake. Once I was in your mind, you could never push me out.'

The image changed from a boy to a skinny mousey-haired young man. His sleepless eyes were hollow, and there was a tortured look about him.

'The human fools could never understand you, Keteth...' Baelthrom said. 'Your wonderful gift, to wander in the land of the dead and return to the living, was what I needed. I had high hopes. Your mind was strong, but I know humans very well. Curiosity and greed, given time, will always overcome fear in a human heart. And I had time, all the time in the world...

'You would never have found me in that endless dark maze had I not whispered to you, leading you deeper into these mountains, until you stood before the doors of my prison.'

'He looks so weak and pathetic,' Kilkarn snorted, pointing out how pale and thin Keteth was as he crept through the dark tunnels in the black rock mountains of Maphrax. His eyes were wide and gleaming, eager for power, and that made him bold, for few dared enter the Mountains of Maphrax of their own will.

'Looks have ever been deceiving to those without the gift of magic,'

Baelthrom said. 'The darkness of the dead world to which he travels surrounds him, and powerful magic awaits his command.

'Just as I can see his magic, I can also see his twisted heart. It was always the Orb of Death that Keteth hungered for. That orb would give him power beyond his imagining when combined with his strange gift. I could not let him have it, such power can only be mine. And so I tricked him…'

Kilkarn squinted into the dark image, for only a small globe of magical light lit Keteth's passage through the tunnel.

'…Nothing more than a simple illusion to make the rune for the Orb of Water appear as if it were for the Orb of Death. A trick even a fool could see through, but Keteth was so eager in his excitement and so unsuspecting,' Baelthrom said.

Keteth came to a stop and whispered a word. His globe of light grew bigger. Kilkarn cackled as a large, twelve feet circular door was revealed in the light. The door was nothing more than the same black Maphraxian rock from which it was cut. It fitted flush with the walls, and there was no handle or hole opening.

With a whimper of delight, Keteth hurried towards the door, but for all his efforts to move quietly, his feet made crunching sounds. He looked down and stopped, mouth open in silent horror when he saw the piles of bones upon which he walked. The skeletons of all races rested atop the dust of other, older, bones.

'Those who had come before, and tried and failed to unlock the power of the orbs,' Baelthrom said. 'Only death awaited them, and death not of my doing, but from the power of the Ancient's magic they laid about the cursed place.'

Keteth looked even paler now and stepped uncertainly towards the runic door. Six complex symbols circled the edges of the door and shimmered white with deadly enchantments.

'The runes are the names of the orbs,' Baelthrom said.

'Oh my, here it is, here is my destiny.' Keteth shivered with excitement. He hissed a laugh, then slapped a hand over his mouth.

'No one is here, no. It's perfectly safe. Bael…' Keteth gulped the name back as if afraid to speak it, '…is bound forever. He cannot harm me, noooo,' he trailed off into a hiccupping laugh and bent to glare at each rune in turn.

'Utterly mad…' Baelthrom chuckled, as did Kilkarn.

With quivering lips and shaking fingers, barely containing his excitement, Keteth traced the lines of the runes until he found the one he sought.

'I showed him the wrong one in a dream,' Baelthrom said. 'This was the moment I had been painfully working on for an eternity. Keteth did not know the names of the runes and was far less able to pronounce them. He could not read or speak the Ancient's language so he could not command the power of the rune. Only I, and the Keepers of each orb know their names. Only when Keteth had chosen his orb and traced the symbol of its name, would he be connected to it. Only then could I speak its name through his lips.'

Kilkarn held his breath as Keteth spoke the orb's ancient name aloud. The deep rumbling voice that echoed around the dark tunnel was not Keteth's but Baelthrom's. The rune burst into blue light. Its name had been spoken, it was unlocked. The door of rock shuddered, then the other runes began to flare violet.

'The symbols have a conscience of their own,' Baelthrom said. 'They knew the one who had unlocked the orb was not its keeper. The Ancient's terrible magic was about to be unleashed upon him, but Keteth, in his wisdom, knew the symbols were cursed, and he was prepared.'

Just as he finished speaking, the flaring symbols exploded outwards. Six bolts of violet fire joined together and hurtled towards Keteth. But he was quicker. With a backwards motion of his hands, and a great exhale he fell backwards and disappeared.

'Where did he go?' Kilkarn gasped.

'Keteth went where even I couldn't follow,' Baelthrom said. 'As easy to him as stepping across a stream, he passed into the Realm of the Dead. When the symbols tried to destroy him, Keteth was not there, he was already dead to them. Death passed him by. Through Keteth, I broke the seal of the Orb of Water. My prison was finally weakened.'

In the empty tunnel, the flaming symbols began to dim as the curse was cast. Only the unlocked symbol stayed bright, turning from violet to blue until it spluttered and then turned dim as well. After the last flicker of light, Keteth materialised back into the world, and stood before the black door. He placed a hand over the unlocked symbol and spoke.

'Give to me the power of this orb, take me to its location.'

At first, the magic was small, nothing but faint ribbons of light that circled around him. Then wild, erratic lightning snaked and struck the walls.

Sparks flew where they hit, creating huge cracks and tumbling shards of stone.

'The power of the rune is being released to him,' Baelthrom explained.

With greedy grasping hands, Keteth reached for the power, seeking to control it, and began collecting those snaking ribbons like cords in his hand. Light spilled into him.

'Ahhh,' Keteth breathed a long sigh. 'So long have I sought you. I see you're hiding place, I have the keys to your location. I know your name, and now you belong to me. I am your Keeper.'

'Keteth's excitement clouded his underlying surprise. The Orb of Death, which he thought he had unlocked, was not held by human hands, but deep within the great ocean kingdom of the sea nymphs. He would not see this trickery until later.' Baelthrom laughed at the same time Keteth did.

A vortex of light appeared, forming a tunnel leading from the black mountains into an ocean kingdom. At the end of the tunnel, tall, spindly towers were just visible as they rose up from the seabed, and lights of all colours moved around and within them. Keteth jumped into the vortex. It carried him to the Orb of Water.

He stepped into a brilliantly lit round chamber of aqua quartz about a hundred feet in diameter. The walls, the floors and the ceilings were cut from the same semi-opaque aqua crystal. In the centre of the room was a raised pedestal, also hewn out of aqua quartz, and atop it sat a beautiful, clear turquoise orb.

'Air and shield,' Keteth commanded. A bubble of air formed protectively around him, and around the pedestal in the centre. The orb shone from deep azure blue to the palest aqua. Its power flowed around him, and his greed for that power overcame his growing confusion.

'I'd thought the Orb of Death black, but it's not. And now it's mine after all these years.' He lunged at the pedestal, but when his hand touched the orb, horror formed on his face.

'A trick. This is not the Orb of Death,' he shrieked. 'I haven't the knowledge, the desire or power to wield it.' Keteth howled, and he tried to tear his hand away, but could not. Chaotic light exploded from the orb.

'The orb is trying to bind itself to its new master, but it's still bound to its original Keeper,' Baelthrom said. 'A new master who is no master of the element from which it was formed.'

The waves of light became searing waves of agony. Destructive magical energy that licked and lashed at Keteth, charring his flesh until it cracked and turned white. The image within the iron ring became chaotic and difficult to see. The sea nymphs came then, water and air breathing humanoid beings, and descended upon Keteth. His protective bubble shattered and he thrashed in the surging water.

'They couldn't kill him,' Baelthrom said. 'The power of the orb would not let this impostor master die. So instead they cursed him.'

The sea nymphs circled Keteth, chanting. He howled in pain as his legs lengthened and began to mould themselves together into one long limb. The bones in his feet and toes cracked as they grew long, then splayed to form twisted flukes. His body bulged, his arms shortened, and as his fingers grew long and thick until each was a tentacle. His head sunk into his shoulders and his eyes turned back moved to the side. He wailed, made a strange flick with his tentacles and disappeared.

'Yet Keteth still retained his first gift, and he managed to slither into the Realm of the Dead,' Baelthrom said. 'But even there he could not escape the ocean, the curse was so strong it bound him beyond death, and he moved in a sea thick with strange dead creatures, and the many souls of sunken ships. In his deformed body, he crawled along the seabed and hid deep within an ocean abyss. Having released a prisoner, now Keteth himself became imprisoned. His hatred grew strong as he hid away from the world, taking the orb with him, keeping it from the Ancients who now hunted for it.

'But always I knew where he was, always I retained a hold on what would become the White Beast. But the world of the dead was forever barred to me, and there he hid the orb from me too.

'For all their efforts over the following years, the orb was truly lost to the sea nymphs. It belonged to a new master whose power was now far greater than theirs. The Ancients cursed them as the nymphs had cursed Keteth, and bound them forever to sea forms, never again able to leave the ocean. It left me with one less race to dominate,' Baelthrom laughed. The image in the ring disappeared.

'In the Shadowlands of his creation, Keteth hunted a strange spirit,' Baelthrom's voice was so low, the room vibrated faintly. 'It angers me to know that he was indeed searching for it, searching for something important that I did not yet feel. This thing he hunted he desired more than he had the Orb of Death.'

A shady, ghost-world appeared, wraiths moved in a forest. The image focused upon the thin frame of a pale-faced girl, more ghost than solid in the Land of Shadows. Long black hair flared out around her in the wind, and her blue-green eyes were almost luminous in the gloom. Those eyes drew him into them now as they had the first time he had seen them weeks ago. He tried to look away, but the face in the ring held him. He clenched his fists and felt his neck throb with his pulse.

'The time is coming, your end draws near,' she spoke to him without moving her lips.

He was aware of the dark dwarf talking beside him in urgent tones and knocked him flying as he spread his wings. Sweat rolled down his back. A strange emotion came over him and he hated it. It was like panic only more complete, like pain but worse because it affected not the body but the mind. It was so all encompassing he couldn't do anything to fight it as it consumed him.

For the first time in his existence, he was touched with terror. This girl-woman whispered to him of his own death. He did not understand, for he could not die, and yet she spoke to him of death, reminded him of the power that he could never possess, the one power he wanted more than the orbs could give him – power over the creation of eternal life.

'She must be destroyed,' he roared.

This woman, this spirit who threatened his existence, must be annihilated. He'd tried to find her as Keteth had done, but she evaded him, making him want her more. A burning, obsessive, desire ate away at him.

The image paled into grey. Now that her face had gone, his breathing calmed, and Kilkarn crawled out from behind the altar where he had been hiding.

'Nothing is beyond your power, Great One,' Kilkarn soothed.

'Now I shall hunt her myself,' Baelthrom whispered and laughed. 'Yes, nothing is beyond me. I will find the source of her power and take it. There is time. All it will take is time and a plan.'

CHAPTER 9

Immortal Gifts

SHE ruffled her feathers, they shone in the moonlight. There came a rustle in the leaves littering the forest floor below. She swivelled her head almost fully around to stare unblinkingly. Whatever moved had sensed her presence and now was still. A raucous caw cut through the silence and made her heart shiver. The caw was answered by another a little further away. Her heart beat louder in her chest as she glimpsed a black shape flittering through the trees towards her. It was trailed by another and then another.

She leapt off the branch and spread her wings, but the ravens were faster and already in full flight as they descended upon her. Sharp talons struck her back and together they fell. The world was a tumbling mess of black beaks stabbing and her white claws clawing. Too many to fight. The ravens' talons ripped into her wings. She wondered why her blood was a deep blackish red as it splashed over her white feathers. She screeched in pain as they tore her body apart.

Cirosa awoke to her own gasping screams and her arms flapping, still trying to beat the ravens away. She sat up panting and sweating. The damp bed sheets were twisted around her like snakes. Through the gap in the window drapes it was still dark, and the edge of Doon visible. She could only have been asleep an hour or two, but fear of more nightmares forced her out of bed. She slipped into her silk robe draped over the gold-gilded chair and stepped into her slippers. She tiptoed down the moonlit corridors of the priestesses' sleeping quarters, and out the front door.

The night was warm as she skittered across the pavement towards the Temple of Celene. It stood proudly, shining white in the moonlight, but she could never find any wonder for the building hewn out of a single rock by dwarven and elven hands over a thousand years ago. For her it stood hard and unyielding, almost accusing, telling her that she could never conquer it, that she would never be blessed by the Great Goddess.

She shivered under its shadow, but it was defiance that made her enter through the large oak door. She always entered with defiance. The door was decorated with metal swirls, and it swung open silently without needing her usual shove, almost mocking her with the ease with which it opened. Why had she come here? She pursed her lips. This was her temple, her domain.

She swept along the pristine walls lit only by moonlight, and came to a stop atop the marble black and white flower that decorated the floor at the end. At her command the flower would open, each petal descending down lower than the previous to form steps leading to the Mother's Chamber. She didn't give the command. She was not a magic wielder, and the will and word needed to form the simple magic always left her exhausted.

Besides, the thought of walking along those pitch-black tunnels to a stuffy ancient place after her nightmares sent a shiver down her back. Instead, she lit the candles in the wall sconce with a match. They cast their flickering light wide in the empty temple. There were no chairs for worshippers to rest. There had been once when Mielan, her predecessor, ran the temple—albeit only on the yearly festivals and special occasions. Fewer and fewer people came over the years, and as Mielan got sicker, she had less strength to do the tasks required of the temple's High Priestess.

When Cirosa took over, the majority of those pointless, money-wasting festivals and celebrations dwindled, then were stopped. Not that the people seemed to mind. The islanders preferred to celebrate in their own villages, and with crops failing so often these years (and everyone blamed Baelthrom for that) their hands were full trying to grow enough to eat.

It was a rare wedding that ever happened at the temple these days, for few could afford the necessary fees the Temple required to keep running. They were all weak unbelievers squandering their money on nothing. What on earth could peasants like Issa ever know of the Great Goddess? Cirosa snorted in disgust.

Still, without the festivals, it gave her more time to focus on what was required of her to be the Oracle; the High Priestess of Frayon, leader of the Temple and the Order of the Great Goddess. The current Oracle, Hykerri, could barely do anything these days. Indeed, Cirosa was already doing most of the old bag's work, she may as well take the Oracle's place now and get herself off this awful hot and stifling island.

She had respected Hykerri once, before she had met her, before she came to the Temple of Frayon, in the capital, Carvon. But respect dwindled to none over the years of her working there. Hykerri was given to dreams and trances, and, though kind, she was weak. Why the priests and priestesses doted on her, hanging on her every word, she could never understand.

The whole Order was riddled with outdated laws, outdated thinking, unnecessary overheads (including too many festivals), reckless money spending and terribly wasteful and inefficient practises. As a result, there was an endless list of tasks Cirosa had to sift through every day. She had become convinced that if it weren't for her, the entire Order of the Goddess would have collapsed years ago.

Once she was in control, she would command only educated people and the wealthy, rather than rely on dreams and fanciful visions to run things like every Oracle had done before. Some order and discipline were required. The entire Temple was falling apart because of the Oracle, and when she was gone there would be more than just a few changes. It was only a matter of time. Once Cirosa was in control and her laws enforced, they could focus on recruitment, which would be a simple task by then.

But until then she had this wretched Issa to be rid of. She chewed a fingernail. Curse that damnable woman. If she wasn't plaguing her in person, she was plaguing her dreams and thoughts. Her feet paced of their own accord, silk slippers making a soft slipping sound that echoed in the empty hall. She tasted blood and looked at her chewed finger. Blood oozed from the torn flesh, and she wrapped a tissue around it.

The wench came to Celene talking about the goddess as if she had spoken to Her directly. Immediately she'd won the ears and hearts of Freydel, Lady Eleny, even Rance. The very thought of her former lover made her angry. She pushed thoughts of him away, he confused her logic with emotion.

Even her priests and priestesses were talking about Issa and the rising of the dark moon. It was all too much to take. If anymore happened, they would be putting Issa in the Oracle's place instead of her. Any threat to her plans, however small, filled her with gut-wrenching fear. She would not let anyone take away the position she held no matter what the cost.

A foolish woman-girl dragged up from some backwater island comes to lead them all to victory and threaten her plans to rule the Temple. Indeed, the Oracle had been waiting for someone such as Issa to take her place, and the sodding dark moon only made it worse. The rumours of Issa had spread too quickly amongst the weak and desperate people. She bet Freydel had had a hand in that, the superstitious old fool, and that traitorous bitch, Ely.

Issa was nothing but a fool, a fraud. Shipwrecked and washed up on Celene. A clever liar indeed; "survivor of the Shadowlands," "communicates with animals," "visited by Wykiry." What a load of tosh. It made her sick to the stomach.

But her plan would work, it had worked already. She slowed her pacing and smoothed her gown with a half-smile. Whatever Issa claimed to be, no one could survive Keteth. Her smile widened. Send her to Keteth to prove she was chosen by the goddess, let her own pride and vainglory be her downfall. And the other fools had believed it too.

But why then was she so worried? She chewed her lip. Was she not the High Priestess of Celene? Chosen by the divine to soon rule as the head of the Order of the Great Goddess? Had she not excelled in the teachings of the Temple? Had she not proved herself worthy to the Great Goddess? Had she not proved her devotion through years upon years of dedicated, exhausting service? Though she had neither the Sight nor the ability to use magic, they were simply things desired and not required to be the High Priestess of Frayon. She had worked so hard to make up for her lack of these and made very sure her hard work was recognised.

Indeed, had she not given up her friends and family to get where she was today? The goddess should be proud of her most diligent student, for, unlike Lady Eleny, she was dedicated to the Temple, mind, body and soul. She had no time for a husband or family. She did not need such things. Even though priestesses and priests were allowed lovers—it was sometimes expected as part of the journey through life—they took second place, and marriage was not allowed. Only when planned for specific reasons were children allowed, and the reasons usually involved promising them into the Temple.

Her ambition was her pride, it kept her strong and driven. Many disliked her ambitious nature, but bend to her rule they always did. She had spent her entire existence working towards this, and finally, she was the next in line. With any luck, Hykerri would be fortuitous indeed to see the year out. Such a shame she couldn't speed things along like she had helped speed along Mielan's end. Well, she had only helped ease the old crone's suffering, who wanted to live as a cripple anyway?

No, the wench would fail, she had to. She had hoped Issa would refuse the task, falling at the first hurdle, but was mildly amused when she did not. In her naivety, she had defiantly, foolishly, accepted. But what if she actually slew the beast? Impossible, she was weak, a fool. Cirosa quickened her pace. Wild panic bordering madness gripped her as her thoughts flip-flopped between success and failure. Keteth will crush and devour her. Her smile became a grin.

It didn't matter how Issa was destroyed, only that it happened was of paramount importance. Cirosa bit her nails again. She had done the right thing, hadn't she? Though she dismissed all prophecies of the dark moon out of hand as the mutterings of mad old idiots, Cirosa did, in fact, know The Prophecies of Zanufey very well. Such was the result of her endless years of study. She had enjoyed them as fanciful fairy tales but did not believe any of them, and yet when the dark moon rose, fear struck her to the core.

"When the dark hand of Immortality stretches his cold fingers across the land, await the dark moon for your saviour. Born upon the waves and delivered upon the Goddess Isle will she be, and terrible will she become to crush the lie of immortality and free the souls of the enslaved. That is what we must strive for, or else all is lost."

Cirosa too clearly remembered the prophecies of Mother Urula written over eight hundred years ago. She came to realise that nothing got the people spooked more than a prophecy and its fulfilment. And so the prophecies were a marvellous opportunity begging to be used by her to prove that she was the one chosen by the goddess.

Had the Immortal Lord's hand not spread far and wide? Had she not willingly come to this hot and remote Goddess Isle, and run the Temple single-handedly for many years now? The "dark moon" had arisen to mark *her* as the next Oracle. No, Issa was not the one. Cirosa was the one, she would make it so. She stopped pacing and let go of her gown that she had been clutching. But so what, that prophecy was written by a leprous hag who didn't even know the difference between day and night. A yawn forced itself upon her, and she rubbed her sore eyes, but the thought of going back to bed when the raven-filled nightmare was still raw in her mind kept her from it.

There came a great rumbling as if the earth was growling, and the whole temple shuddered beneath her feet. She yelped, and her heart leapt into her throat. The candles clattered to the floor, spilling their wax everywhere and leaving her in complete darkness. The rumbles subsided.

Tremors were common on Celene, but deprived of sleep and within the dark and unfriendly temple, they sent chills up her spine. The trembling came again, harder. She fell towards the wall and clung to it for balance. Then everything stopped and fell horribly silent.

Cirosa ran out of the temple, her heart pounding in her head. She stood outside of its oppressive walls, shaking and gulping in the cool air. She hated earthquakes, even just the little tremors, but that had been a strong one.

Doon must have set, and the sky clouded over, for it was very dark. A dim light came from a window in the priest's quarters behind her. The temple itself was a blacker menacing shape looming before her. On shaking legs, she walked to a bench next to a yew tree and slumped down. It took some time to catch her breath and still her shaking body.

I hate this island.

She yawned again. Bed seemed like a good idea. She got up and went towards her quarters. The hairs on the back of her neck stood up and a shiver slithered down her spine. There was a dark shape five yards away where there should be no dark shape. It was just a bush, but she was certain she could feel eyes watching her.

The shape moved. She took a step back. She foolishly didn't have her lantern, thinking the moonlight would stay, thinking the temple candle light would be enough. It was just a forest leopard or Dinry's mutt. But it really was far too large to be either of those and it was shaped very differently.

Though squat it was full and dense. Like a big, big bird. The ravens of her nightmare swept through her mind, but this creature was bigger, and for all the horror of it, it seemed to have a round, human-shaped head. She couldn't feel magic even if there was any, but there was something about the black shape that made her shudder, and it went beyond that awful sour smell that wafted from it.

She took another step back. Eyes flashed before her, though there was no light they could reflect. They gleamed of their own accord, maybe from magic.

'I have nothing that you would want. Get away from here,' her voice was rasping. She slipped her hand into her gown where she kept her letter opener. It wasn't sharp, but it was pointy, and to the thing before her, it would look like a real blade. She chose not to draw it out yet.

The creature cackled, a sound half-way between an old crone's laugh and a crow's chatter. It made her shudder again, and she took another step back. The creature was between her and the temple and the other buildings of safety were even further away.

The creature shuffled towards her. Dim light from the window filtered through the leaves and slid over oily feathers, a clawed foot like that of an eagle only three times bigger, long fair hair, and the curve of a full round breast. The harpy waddled closer. Cirosa's breath caught in her throat, it was barely five feet away. She whipped out her knife.

'Keep back, or I'll kill you,' she snarled, her dagger trembling in her out-stretched hand. That horrid cackle came again, but the harpy stopped.

'You weak human females are of no use to us, or anything else,' the creatures voice was cracked, like that of an old woman yet full of timbre. Star light shone down through a break in the clouds and illuminated the creature's soft round face, full red lips and smooth, unblemished skin. The harpy grinned at her, black teeth sharp, eyes dark and deadly. Cirosa looked away and thought she might be sick.

'You tread on holy ground, vile beast,' she gasped. She had to get away, harpies were deadly, and they could wield magic. It should not be here, so far west. She was about to yell for help when the harpy spoke.

'Hold your tongue, stupid woman.'

Cirosa's mouth snapped shut forcefully. She held the letter opener higher, but the harpy only laughed and spoke.

'Your efforts may have gone unnoticed by the weak and impotent goddess, but there is another, greater, more powerful being who watches you. One who is not silent... You are very fortunate indeed to be watched.' The harpy threw a bundle at her feet. 'Use this as and when you see fit, and see all fit you will. I would not ignore the Immortal Lord's gifts if I were you.'

The hideous bird-woman cackled and shuffled backwards, her black eyes gleaming, never leaving Cirosa. Once she had enough space she turned, spread her wings and launched into the air. Only when she was gone did Cirosa's jaw begin to work again. She sighed and wiped her sweaty forehead with a shaking hand. The sour smell of the harpy lingered.

Her eyes came to rest on the bundle at her feet. She swallowed and picked it up. It was slightly larger than her fist but solid and heavy.

Though the harpy had gone, something still felt wrong, corrupt, and she wondered if it came from the bundle now in her hand. A door creaked, making her jump, and light spilled out through the door of the priestesses' quarters.

'Everything all right?' a novice priestess asked timidly.

Cirosa slipped the bundle in her pocket along with her letter opener.

'Yes, Efren, go back to bed. I couldn't sleep through the tremors and thought I heard something. All is well.'

The novice nodded and dutifully shut the door.

In the dark once more, free from prying eyes, Cirosa pulled out the bundle and turned it over in her hand.

'The Immortal Lord's gifts?' she breathed.

This was all wrong, very wrong indeed, and yet it was also… exciting. She should have run from the harpy, but she hadn't. Why hadn't it attacked her? It had meant her no harm… But what did it mean; she was "watched"? Could the Immortal Lord see her? She grasped the collar of her robe. Could he see her now? She had to get inside, but could he see her wherever she went? Maybe he could only see into her mind. They said he could reach anyone in their dreams. Well, it was lucky then, that sleep was far from her now.

In the dark, she could just make out the unimaginative square shape of her administrative building lurking behind the temple. She ran to it. It was a simple four walls and roof affair built to her specifications. A place where she could think and work through her administrative duties uninterrupted. It served as a good solid reminder to everyone as to who actually ran the place.

She unlocked the door, slipped inside and locked it again. She leant against the door with a sigh, then reached for the lantern and clicked it alight. With another sigh, she slumped into her high-backed, red chair beside her desk, and adjusted the cushions about her aching back. She plonked her feet onto the velvet stool and stared up at the plain ceiling, ignoring the foot-high pile of papers. She cradled the bundle on her lap, the strange feeling of corruption that had originally emanated from it now seemed intriguing and enchanting.

The Immortal Lord's gifts…

CHAPTER 10

Ravens and Dragons

ASAPH landed on the beach as the first rays of sun broke across a cloudless sky, turning it brilliant orange. He was exhausted but still awed by its beauty. The heat that came with those rays was magic energising his cold reptilian blood, filling him with strength.

He laid Issa down upon the sand and returned to his human form without even thinking about it. All the strength the sun had given his dragon form was suddenly gone and he felt weak and human once more.

The raven landed beside him and peered at Issa. She was deathly pale, and he feared she was dead until he saw the faint rising of her chest. He tore off his cloak and wrapped it around her, smoothed her hair back from her face. Coronos came running over.

'She lives, but barely,' Asaph said, emotion and exhaustion thick in his voice. 'We must return at once to the Karalanths where we can better help her, and… Where we can hide.' Coronos shot him a look.

'The Maphraxies are coming for us,' Asaph said. 'It's no secret that a Dragon Lord lives and Keteth has been slain. It's possible Baelthrom knows that Zanufey's chosen has finally come. He will certainly feel the power of the dark moon. We must warn Frayon and the rest of free Maioria. For Maphraxies to be so far south, yet not on Frayon… they must be planning an attack. The war is coming to us, father.'

'I tried to control it, the orb, but I couldn't. It had a will of its own,' Coronos shook his head. 'Baelthrom would have felt the call of the orb to its sister, and then the power of two combined.'

'Lucky it had, otherwise neither of us would be here now,' Asaph replied.

'You have the Orb of Water?' Coronos asked, wide-eyed.

Asaph nodded and pointed to Issa's white knuckles as she clutched the turquoise orb. 'Try to get her to release it, if you can.'

Coronos stared at it, eyes glistening in awe. 'The Orb of Air still pulses warm at my side. I think it's speaking to its sister,' Coronos said thoughtfully, then looked out across the ocean glistening orange in the rising sun.

'You are no longer a boy, but a man, a Dragon Lord,' Coronos said. Asaph wondered if he were talking to himself, he spoke so quietly. 'Now the war is coming... I always knew I wouldn't live through it to see peace. I would not live to see my son happy with his own family. Blessed Great Mother, my heart is heavy for all those years that will not be mine.'

They flew back towards the Karalanth village. Coronos' orb and the sun's rays once more gave Asaph in his dragon form the strength he desperately needed to make it home. He gave silent thanks to the Sun Goddess for her warmth and for helping him reach Issa in time. Coronos said nothing throughout the whole journey and instead held Issa tightly, wrapped in his own cloak as well. She did not stir at all.

He landed a little way off from the village, mindful of not spreading dragon fear amongst the Karalanths. Dawn had not long broken, but the sound of voices and the smell of cooking told him the deer-folk were already up and about their daily business. He carried Issa's limp body protectively in his arms. She was still deathly white and cold.

'Another casualty of Keteth?' Triest'anth bounded over. 'Though I can see it's not fatal... This one sleeps, exhausted from magic,' he added, arching his eyebrow.

'The final casualty,' Asaph said, surprised at Triest'anth's perception.

Other Karalanths bounded over and crowded around them, intrigued by yet another strange looking 'two-foot' in their midst.

'The raven and dragon return,' Cusap'anth said, coming to stand beside his father.

Coronos turned to see the big black bird land on a branch and look at them. Bright sunlight suddenly spilled over the treetops, blinding Asaph and bathing them all in warmth. Silence settled over the Karalanths as they stared at Asaph. He blinked and shifted his feet awkwardly, self-conscious under their gaze. Cusap'anth broke the silence, his voice loud for all to hear.

'Karalanths, hear me. Do you see the truth of our sacred scriptures, the

Reun Tualath? For there it is written:

"Look and listen when the dragon made of fire carries forth the Queen of Ravens. For know then that the darkness is fully upon you. But fear not this time of cleansing, and all who choose love and seek freedom will walk once again in the light. Pick up your sword and your bow, for now is a time of trial and tribulation, a time of cleansing of the dark, so that a greater, purer life may come forth."

Triest'anth looked at his son with pride. Asaph caught the half-smile on Coronos' face but looked away before he could meet the older man's eyes. His face grew hot as the Karalanths bowed before him. Did they really think that he and Issa were the ones talked about in their prophecies? It just seemed too much to bear. Already embarrassed, he was mortified when Cusap'anth cried out.

'Hail the Dawn Bringer. Hail the Raven Queen. The prophecy is in motion, the Great Battle is coming.'

His cheeks burned crimson as all the Karalanths erupted into cheering. He didn't know their prophecies, and certainly didn't feel like he had fulfilled anything. Issa stirred in his arms in the commotion, giving him a welcome excuse to leave.

'I must get her inside. I need fresh water and bandages,' he said meekly, his quiet voice somehow cutting through the cheering.

Triest'anth nodded and escorted him to his house that had now become a permanent nursing home. Coronos remained silent as he followed them, the half-smile still on his face.

Asaph sighed when the door shut behind him and the cheering dimmed, feeling the weight of the Karalanths' prophecies, and the responsibilities they had assumed upon him, also shut out.

'The Reun Tualath are our sacred scrolls, written long ago during the time of the Dark Run, when we fled in darkness from the light dwarves and dark dwarves,' Triest'anth said as he prepared towels and boiling water. 'They were written by Ull'anth, under the dictation of the blind seer Fay'ynth. Ull'anth wrote down her visions until the dark dwarves came for them.

'They and their followers were captured and tortured; forced to consume the Sirin Derenax. Their souls went to oblivion, and their bodies became Maphraxie,' Triest'anth sighed. 'And so the Forest Lord never came for them; Woetala's paradise they never reached. Such was the ultimate price they paid to bring us the knowledge we have today.'

'The scrolls were hidden and then found by the appointed Karalanths who, under oath, memorised the text and taught all other Karalanths their wisdom. The scrolls were destroyed to keep them from the dark dwarves. The Reun Tualath has been faithfully passed down, exactly as written, through the generations.'

Asaph washed Issa's face, arms and legs as he listened, cleaning the blood and sea salt off where he could whilst trying not to disturb her too much. She slept like the dead. She was covered in bruises and had many small wounds that were red raw, but thankfully no longer bleeding. She was in better shape than he had expected, and he suspected a little magic at work. He could faintly feel an enchantment upon the silver bracelet she wore, but without his dragon form, his magic sensing ability was far too weak.

'It's exhaustion born of magic use that makes her sleep so deep. Especially if she is new to the Flow,' Triest'anth said.

'You can use magic?' Asaph asked in surprise.

Triest'anth raised his eyebrows. 'Oh, a little. I'm far better at sensing it than wielding it, though.'

'I can sense only a little… in my human form,' Asaph said.

'From what I felt in the Flow back then, there was powerful magic moving. She would not have been able to use it had she not had another wizard train her,' Coronos said. 'I think Freydel must have helped her. But a novice with power is a dangerous thing. Magic takes years to master. She is lucky not to have destroyed herself, and I think the dark moon had something to do with it. Hmm.'

Asaph's own fatigue was gnawing at him, but he fought it a while longer. He touched Issa's cheek and was relieved to find some warmth there now. She looked like a marble statue in some goddess's temple; dark hair spread about her, skin gleaming white in the dim light, and fine eyebrows arching over long-lashed, eyes.

He somehow felt complete and at ease now he was with her as if throughout all his life there had been this underlying tension that now relaxed. They were safe, for now. He wished it were forever—wished no war threatened their happiness and their lives. The smell of food made his stomach rumble. He left her to sleep.

A tentative look outside the door told him the crowd had finally gone, and the three of them took their steaming bowls of food to sit and eat in the sun. They ate heartily of Triest'anth's forest root broth and warm, dark Karalanth bread as they sipped sweet Karalanthian berry wine. Asaph looked at the contemplative yet content faces of Triest'anth and

Coronos and decided that they too were enjoying the same peace he felt.

He found he had an insatiable appetite that only just felt slaked after a sheepish third portion. But then, he could not remember when he had last eaten anything substantial. Whilst they ate he told them in detail everything that had happened, especially about his strange living dreams and the battles fought against Keteth in his twisted world. He even decided to tell them about finding the dragon door—at first appearing in the real world and then within his mind—and the beautiful shared realm of dragons, the Dragon Dream.

Triest'anth listened in captivated silence, whilst Coronos' brow furrowed in concentration.

'So it seems to me,' Asaph concluded, 'that the Shadowlands where the lost souls go may have always existed, but Keteth took control of it as he took control of their souls. Within it he created his own undead world amongst the living, trapping souls and feeding off them. Issa was lucky to survive there, and I think we were lucky to get out at all.' He spooned up the last few morsels of food from his bowl as the others sipped thoughtfully on their wine.

'But what of the Maphraxies? I felt a surge of magic flood the Flow, and I've yet to understand why,' Triest'anth said.

Asaph told them of the recent battle, of the Wykiry and all the cetaceans that had come to her aid, of the despised necromancers that nearly were the end of him, and made sure he left no detail out.

'I really thought that was it, but when I managed to make it into the air, she was still there, and the Maphraxies closest had simply vanished, obliterated,' Asaph said, the wonder of it still vivid in his mind.

'I wish I could fly and been able to witness all this,' Triest'anth marvelled, 'but from afar, of course.'

Everyone laughed.

'The Orb of Air burned so hot in my pocket that I had to take it out,' Coronos said. 'Only, when I touched it, it was so cold I had to place it on the sand. Lucky for me I did, for no sooner had I done so, it flared into white light, like a flame only still and unmoving. Then the light surged out across the ocean where it met another light surging towards it, only this one was aqua blue.

'Together they made a rainbow of the most brilliant white and blue light, the pure essence and power of air and water combined. In unison, they flared and magic surged, knocking me to the ground. Then all was still, and I knew something amazing had just happened. The orbs, so long separated, were somehow communicating with each other, working together as once they had before the Ancients split the magic of Maioria. I wish I could understand more. Master Wizard Freydel would surely know more.'

They chatted until it was late in the afternoon, the smoke from Coronos' pipe rising in dense clouds to hang above him. There was a shared contentment in the air, and Asaph felt inner peace and a completeness he had not known in his entire life. There was only one thing that was missing right now, and that was home, Drax. But Drax could wait for now, he had Issa to look after.

He yawned, stretched his arms behind his head and lay back upon the grass. He watched the sun descend in the sky. It never hurt his eyes to look at it like it did other people. He could stare straight at it for a short while and not be blinded. He wondered if other reptiles besides dragons could do that as he drifted off to sleep.

Asaph awoke alone but covered in a blanket that someone had kindly draped over him. The sun was gone, and it was night. He wondered how long he had slept, above him now hung the small pale orange moon of Woetala.

He was pleased there was no dark moon tonight, he did not understand its power, did not understand its connection to Issa, and that made him a little afraid of it. He vaguely understood that it heralded great change and it made him nervous. It would change her, he knew that, but as long as he did not lose her. Having lost her so many times before, he could not bear the thought of losing her again.

He got up and winced from his sore, stiff muscles. He tiptoed into Triest'anth's house and closed the door quietly behind him. Coronos and Triest'anth slept in their beds beside the opposite wall to Issa. She shifted as if sensing his approach but did not wake. He smiled down at her.

'Rest deeply,' he whispered and went back outside, satisfied that she was well. Unable to sleep anymore, he wandered into the forest. The night was fresh and alive, and for the first time in a long time, there was joy and lightness in his heart.

CHAPTER 11

Karshur's Gift

SOMETHING was calling Issa from far away. It wasn't an urgent sound but still, she felt she had to go to it. Light accompanied the sound. All about was blackness, but the sound and light came from ahead, light at the end of a long dark tunnel.

Issa sat up blinking. It was pitch black like it had been in her dream and she could not make out anything or tell where she was. A light grew from somewhere then went dim. In the brief glow, she glimpsed that she was wrapped in blankets and sat on a bed pallet. Thinking did not bring back memories, even trying to remember where she had been last, before here was here, was blank.

The light glowed again, it was coming from beside her. She looked over the side of the bed. There was something long and thin wrapped in a rag—Karshur. At least she remembered the blade if nothing else. The memory of Keteth returned to her, and the task which the dagger had just performed.

I killed him… horrible guilt swept through her. *No, I set him free. We set them all free.* It was the dark moon that gave her the strength, that made her the Raven Queen. She couldn't be her without it. Thoughts of the fearless warrior woman that she became with the power of the moon made her anxious and her head swim.

She laid back down and shut her eyes. If she focused on memories of home hard enough, she could pretend that the rough blankets wrapped around her were smooth, and she was back in her bed on Little Kammy. Her work clothes were freshly pressed on the chair beside her bed ready to be worn. Ma was healthy and sleeping soundly in the next room.

She sighed contentedly. The images were so vivid she could even smell the scent of the ocean on the air. Soon she would get out of bed to find it was a glorious summer's day, and she would run free and wild through the woods before breakfast.

I'm not a warrior. I'm not the Raven Queen of prophecy. I am Issa, and I live on Little Kammy, far from the world of war and the awful immortals. She couldn't be her, the Raven Queen, and whatever was expected of her. She couldn't unite the world and lead it to war, and she could never defeat Baelthrom and his Maphraxies.

Karshur glowed again, seeming bright even through her closed lids. Why was it glowing? Would it not let her be? She had done what it required of her. Did the Goddess want to make her suffer more? But thoughts of the strange women robed in the stars only filled her with love, not anger.

Tears filled her eyes behind closed lids, and the warm feel of her home on Little Kammy began to slip away. Yet, had she not accepted this task to rid the world of the Maphraxies when Zanufey Herself had come to her? But it was always different when she was with her. When the dark moon was there, everything was different. Without the moon her powers were weak.

And what about living her own life? As soon as she thought it, she wondered what her own life would be. Was she really in service to Zanufey? She healed horses, she was not a warrior wielding swords and magic. But then Little Kammy and everyone there was gone. Could she ever be what she was once before?

Karshur pulsed faster, and it was like trying to ignore a baby crying. She groaned, let go of the memories of her soft, warm bed and grabbed Karshur. The dagger was warm beneath the cloth as she unravelled it. In its soft light, her anger lessened. There came a whisper, barely audible, and she wondered if she'd heard it in her head.

'Return us home.' It sounded as if many people spoke at once.

'But how and to where?' Issa whispered, feeling silly talking to the dagger.

'Remember the sacred mound. You can traverse the pathways, but only we know the way. Consent,' the voices whispered.

She frowned. 'I can traverse the pathways?'

The sacred mound certainly seemed to be a doorway to other worlds and dimensions, and Keteth had cryptically given her his power to step into the world of the dead. Perhaps that's what they meant. But it wasn't as if she could control it, she couldn't seem to go to those places at will.

She closed her eyes and imagined herself sitting before the sacred mound. She was surprised at how easily the image formed in her mind. The grassy mound surrounded by ancient stones appeared before her as if she were really there. The air was cool and damp, and all was completely still and quiet. She opened her eyes and looked down at Karshur in her lap, then touched its smooth white surface.

'I guess I consent,' she said.

Karshur burst into light so bright she slammed her eyes shut. For the briefest moment, she felt as if she were tilting to the right and there came the sound of whooshing air, but there was no wind to be felt. Then everything was still.

She peeked through her eyelids, then opened them wide. The darkness had gone, the bed pallet and blankets, gone. There was no sacred mound, and there was no dark room, either. The only things that remained were the far-too-large man's shirt she wore and Karshur in her hand. It pulsed gently now, a warm and mellow light as if contented. There had been no lurching, no backwards falling feeling. It was as if someone had just switched her reality seamlessly.

She looked around, mouth dropping at the beauty she saw. She was in a warm sunny glade surrounded by old horse chestnuts and willows, or they seemed to be, for these trees were more beautiful than the ones she remembered. The willow leaves had a silvery tinge, the horse chestnut shimmered golden, and the grass was rich and green and soft. The air also sparkled as if it were alive. A tinkling stream flowed on her left, and the sunlight danced upon its surface.

The place was beautiful, peaceful. Issa felt remarkably well, rested and healthy. Beside her sat the raven, making her jump. He was a stark contrast to the beauty around her, his black form vivid in a shimmering pastel world.

'Have you been waiting for me here? Where is here?' She asked. But he only cocked his head and took a step towards her. She ruffled his soft neck feathers, and he made a cooing sound that made her giggle.

'Did you bring me here?'

The raven looked at her and shook his head once. She smiled, no longer surprised that the raven understood her, and sometimes answered back.

'No, it was Karshur,' she breathed, cradling the long white undulating blade. 'Karshur's purpose has been fulfilled,' she whispered, remembering Keteth again, but in his human form, the young man he had once been.

'I'm really here, and this isn't a dream, is it?'

The raven did a short, sharp nod.

'Then we've been brought here for a reason. To return Karshur home, to his people.' As she spoke, she felt as if the spirit of Karshur the elf wizard was near, but there was nothing she could outwardly see.

'But this isn't the Shadowlands where the dagger was kept.' The life-filled glade was very different from the shadow world of wraiths. 'Could this be his home? The home of the elves? The Land of Mists…'

She stood up and noticed with a start faces amongst the trees. Had they always been there watching her? They became more distinct and real under her gaze, and she saw that the faces were attached to tall, graceful bodies. Elves. She noted their unmistakable pointed ears, pastel-coloured hair and eyes. Their hard gazes were hostile, making her feel like a trespasser.

She tried to stand tall and proud though her heart was pounding. There seemed to be a good many of them staring at her, at least a hundred all crowding back into the forest. The raven also seemed uncertain and stepped closer to her.

Above the treetops, nine majestic, shining silver spires reached into the sky. She marvelled at the tops of the elven city. In Freydel's books, she had seen wondrous pictures of the elven cities of Intolana, and this was similar. Though it was mostly hidden in the trees, she sensed it was far grander.

Freydel had said not many elves lived in cities, many preferring the natural habitat of the woodlands, but the cities served a functional purpose, and the elves didn't know how to build ugliness, so all things they created were beautiful. None of the elven cities survived in Maioria anymore, all were destroyed by the Maphraxies, except this one. But then they were not quite in Maioria anymore.

'Yes, we still reside in Maioria, but in a place where only elves can go,' a melodic male voice spoke from amongst the crowd.

She searched for who had spoken, but could not determine from whom it came.

'This is our sacred haven,' the voice continued. 'Our promised land, our Land of Mists—and you should not be here.'

The elves muttered in hushed tones, looking at her in concern. It was well known that elves alone knew how to get to the Land of Mists, and only through elven magic could they enter. Even then, not just any elf could enter; only those who had chosen to leave Maioria and all her woes many years ago. The elves who chose to stay and fight Baelthrom were forever banned from the Land of Mists—something she found quite unfair to those valiant souls.

'Er, and yet here I stand,' was all she could think to say. She was pleased her voice sounded strong, showing none of the nerves that danced in her belly.

The elves moved out from the trees but stopped before coming too close to her. They were beautiful, slender and tall compared to humans. Their hair was worn long and came in pale shades of yellow and brown, to hues of purple and blue. They had slightly slanting almond-shaped eyes, and were dressed in flowing robes or tunics.

She swallowed down a lump of jealously, feeling heavy and ugly compared to their beauty and grace. Even though she was as tall as the elven women and as slender, she seemed to waddle where they glided. She was hairy and dark, where they were smooth and made of light. Only Murlonius the Ancient was more beautiful and ethereal by comparison. A man came forwards out of the crowd. She assumed it was he who had spoken. He confirmed this when he spoke again.

'The Raven Queen has no place in our peaceful Land of Mists,' he spoke softly, but his eyes were hard.

Issa considered the man. His long silvery hair hung over his shoulders and down his chest. He was dressed in a long white shirt that was bound at the chest with a golden rope sash. White trousers flowed from beneath the shirt, and he wore no shoes, none of them did. He had an air of authority around him, and she assumed that he must be the one who led them. He stepped towards her, his face serious, but less hostile.

'How do you know who I am?' she asked, doubting herself who she really was. She felt too small and meek, too *normal*, to be this Raven Queen of prophecy. Especially here.

'We watch the world of war below us in sadness, and are glad that we are no longer a part of it,' the elf said, ignoring her question, much to her disappointment.

She racked her brains on what to say just as Karshur pulsed brighter, reminding her why she had come. She swallowed and chose her words.

'Karshur is vanquished. The White Beast Keteth is dead, and the once good man within, freed. The souls of those enslaved by him; your kin, my kin, and all the Ancients who had been imprisoned for millennia, have been set free to return to the One Source of All.' Her voice remained surprisingly strong, despite her fluttering heart and the hostile eyes of a large crowd focused upon her. She held Karshur up, it gleamed. The elf's eyes widened in recognition, but then he pursed his lips distrustfully.

'I do not lie,' she said, indignant. 'Karshur brought me here, how else could I have come?'

She offered the dagger to the elf and gave a slight bow. The elf-man met her eyes. There was deep sadness within them as he took the blade.

'Karshur,' he breathed. 'You do not tell human lies. This is indeed the one.'

He stared down at the dagger. His eyes glistened, and she felt tears form in her own eyes. The presence of Karshur seemed stronger than ever before as if he stood right beside her. It occurred to her that elves lived a long time, and though this elf-man could not have been alive when Karshur was, she felt compelled to ask.

'Did you know Karshur? Was he your ancestor?'

The elf-man looked at her sharply, measuring her up, then his face became guarded.

'Time moves slower here in our Land of Mists, our years are long, and our memory never fails with age...' He looked away into the distance, seeing into the past. He spoke softly, partly to himself.

'I would with all my heart undo the past; of what Keteth has done and Baelthrom, of our imperative withdrawal into the safety of the Land of Mists lest we are lost forever like the Ancients... But that is not the way of things. We must move forward with what has happened and carry our scars as reminders so that we never forget.' His eyes hardened, and he spoke loud enough for all to hear.

'Karshur made his choice long ago. He chose to remain in the darkness, chose war over peace, chose the human world of strife over the elven world of peace. This is not his home, he is not welcome here.'

The elves shuffled anxiously. Some faces seemed ashamed, others hard and resolute. They began whispering amongst themselves.

She stared at him, unable to fathom quite what he'd said. Anger, intense and passionate, came from Karshur's presence. It sparked her own fury.

'How can you say this? I doubt Karshur had much choice at all. For all that I know of him, for all that the dagger has shown me, Karshur gave the greatest sacrifice. He gave his life, bound to this dagger for millennia until a time came when he could free the souls of the enslaved. Many of your elven ancestors have spent eons imprisoned in the Shadowlands, never to be let out. Wandering a hell for so long that even they no longer remembered who they were.

'Karshur chose service to others over cowardice and selfishness. Karshur chose freedom over slavery. And believe it or not, you elves hiding here in your Land of Mists are also enslaved. Imprisoned.'

Her face grew hot as she spoke. This was not her land, she was a guest, and yet here she stood accusing the people of cowardice, but she could not stop her angry words.

'I could have died, many times, trying to free those souls. Keteth nearly enslaved me too, but still I fought, I had no choice,' the anger faded, and she felt tired.

'A great task you took upon yourself, and you did not falter,' the elf-man agreed. His teal-coloured eyes pierced hers. 'Only a strong spirit, a blessed spirit, could have survived. But what happens now, Raven Queen? We remember the prophecies and suspect that you have come here not only to return Karshur. I see a darker road before you, one that leads to war and bloodshed.'

Why had she come? Purely to return Karshur? That *had* been why, but now she was here she felt there was something more she had to do. The raven was looking up at her expectantly. For the briefest moment, she looked across a vast battle between soldiers and Maphraxies. All around were the dead and dying. Rivulets of blood trickled through the earth into pools between the hacked off limbs and lifeless faces. Terrible magic ripped through skies that were black and red and full of thunder. Her heart was hard as stone and her soul crushed into emptiness.

Then the vision was gone, and she thought she would faint as the blood drained from her face. Was that her? Was that the Raven Queen? Was that what she must become? She felt horrified, but nothing about her outward appearance must have changed for the elf-man spoke as if nothing had happened.

'I, Daranarta, leader of the Elves of the Mists, and my people and our ancestors whom you have freed, thank you for what you have done this day, Issa, Queen of Ravens.'

She felt awkward and confused under the elf's gaze. A horrible weight seemed to settle upon her. She wanted to be gone from here, to be alone where she could curl up and cry and dream of home as if it were still there. She tried to mask her feelings though the elf was not looking at her.

He held the dagger in front of him and whispered in elven. Even though she was not in the Flow, she felt the air tingle and saw tendrils of magic move in shimmering green hues. They began weaving together as they were drawn into Daranarta's hands.

A strong breeze came, and the flame ring upon her finger grew warm. She had not felt elven magic before, and here in their secret land, it was strong. Freydel's lessons came back to her, but she could not quite determine all this magic's qualities. It flowed through the trees and the ground—a balancing, earthy, nature-based magic, but not as dark and gritty as Edarna's.

Whether it was used for healing or destruction, she could not be sure. It seemed to be a mix or could be used for either. But feel it she could, and that was always the first step in becoming a master of magic, of becoming a Wizard, so Freydel had said.

Still, she had no idea what Daranarta was doing but knew better than to interrupt magic in mid-flow. It seemed as if he were communing with the dagger, reading it somehow. When he spoke, his voice was pitched low yet loud, loud enough for all to hear. He was looking so intently at the dagger that she wondered what he saw there.

'The vengeance of Karshur is spent. It was relinquished when it pierced Keteth's heart. But the voices of those within the dagger will not let me transmute the blade... They have a gift for the one who set them free.' Daranarta's voice was changing as he spoke, and becoming overlaid with other voices; male and female, all talking in unison in almost a singsong fashion.

'Dark places we both have been, into evil we have seen. Our journey now is done, yet yours has just begun. Have faith in the darkness, move through it, with it, but do not become it. In the Shadowlands we have come to understand many things. Remember that, when we walked there, between the darkness and the light, beyond the living and within the dead, the Immortal Lord could not find us. Keteth gave his powers to you, to walk amongst the dead, but our gift will take you there most easily. Accept our gift. Be as the raven, Raven Queen, and walk between two worlds. It shall be as the prophecy foretold.

'Speak three times the elven words; *A'farion, A'farion, A'farion*. They mean, "I walk in death," and touch the raven mark with the talisman.

Then will you find yourself far from the living, in a land of shadows not of Keteth's making. Never linger past the hour, and never enter more than once a day. Otherwise, your soul will begin to depart, and you will become as the Forsaken, never able to return.'

She frowned. 'I don't understand. What is the *talisman*? What is the raven mark?' But Daranarta was not listening, and she was forced to stop talking when he continued to speak, or rather the voices of Karshur spoke through him.

'The elves must return to Maioria, it is their destiny. Without them, Maioria is lost, and so too are they. You *must* get them to return. The dark moon rises even here, calling them home,' the voices fell silent.

'They won't listen to me,' she said and stared at Daranarta, wondering if he understood what he said, or if the words were intended only for her.

The voices said no more and Daranarta blinked as his eyes came into focus. The dagger shimmered in his hands until it was no longer solid but silver-white light.

'The magic has its own will,' he breathed in surprise as the light swirled above his palms.

The light contracted then exploded, casting everything in light. She yelped as a freezing burning pain seared her sternum.

The vortex of the heart is the portal between dimensions,' a voice whispered in her mind.

Issa gasped and clutched at her chest, but after a moment, the pain went. The presence of Karshur disappeared. She pulled down the hem of her top. There was a faint blue shimmer on the skin above her breasts, halfway between her clavicle and the end of her sternum. She rubbed it. It was tender, but not painful. Daranarta ignored all and continued to stare at his own hands in amazement.

The raven was still looking up at her expectantly, and her heart sank. Daranarta was right, there had always been more required of her than to simply return Karshur. She closed her eyes, suddenly feeling very weary.

'It seems you are right. There *is* another reason Karshur brought me here,' she spoke louder for all to hear. 'I didn't know it until now, but Karshur and those within the dagger have made it clear what is obvious. I only pass on to you what they told me through Daranarta's lips,' her voice was strong as it rang out in the glade. She felt sweat bead on her brow and Daranarta's eyes narrowed as if daring her to say it. Did she really have to say it?

'I'm just the messenger,' she could not stop the words falling from her mouth if she tried. 'Maioria is dying, and she needs your help, we all need your help. I ask you to leave your Land of Mists, to join us in Maioria and help fight against the Maphraxies that plague her. Zanufey's moon has risen, and I know it rises even here in your Land of Mists, calling you to help your world. We cannot win against the Maphraxies until all the races agree to stand at each other's side. If we don't fight the immortals, then we'll all be destroyed.'

She paused to see the effect of her words. Her pulse was racing. At first, there were hushed mutterings amongst the people. Some looked worried, maybe even guilty, others frowned as if in disbelief that she would ask such a thing. The crowd grew louder. Clearly, none of them were happy.

Daranarta looked at her sadly as he spoke, just loud enough for the crowd to hear.

'Pain me as it does, the answer is surely no. Our place, and our world is here in our sacred land. The affairs of humans and their enemies upon Maioria are not of our concern. We fought our battles and buried our dead long ago. Our old homeland Intolana, is nothing but a distant memory, lost to Baelthrom over four hundred years ago. I will not risk the lives of my people again.'

'But if you return to Maioria and fight, Intolana can be yours again,' she said. Surely they could see that? If *she* had half the chance to get Little Kammy back, she would. Anger flared within; anger for Karshur, and anger at Daranarta's stubbornness and the stupid belittling expression on his face.

'Don't you see? You have to return. Nobody wants to fight, but we have no choice. Baelthrom won't stop until the whole world is his. And after Maioria, where next?' She thought of that dark force hunting her in the Shadowlands, powerful and vast and ruthless. 'I have seen the darkness, and it has a thirst that is unquenchable.'

Daranarta's face was impassive, resolute, and she wondered if she was approaching this from the wrong angle.

'You are young,' Daranarta said, his voice commanding and imperious. 'You talk of a foe you have met only in your dark dreams. You have not suffered as we have suffered, and cannot begin to comprehend the decisions we have taken, and the terrible paths we have trodden to be where we are today.'

'I may be young, but I have seen much,' she retorted. The scorched earth where houses had once stood, the blackened remains of people she had once known…

'I've seen death and have felt the cold hand of desolation—the utter blackness of the heart falling in the Shadowlands. But still, I fight because I have to. Baelthrom will not stop until all we love is destroyed and ruled by Maphraxies.' She trembled with the fire she felt inside.

'You hide away in your haven, pretending this isn't your war. He will find a way into your world, just as he found his way into Maioria, just as he hunted me in the Shadowlands. Baelthrom is strong, and he wields a dark magic that comes from beyond Maioria. It will take all of us united to defeat his armies, but still we have a chance—' She stopped herself abruptly, she was going around in circles.

'His power comes from the Dark Rift torn into our skies,' Daranarta said.

The sad look in his eyes irritated her. Would these people not fight for their freedom? Did they really think they were free and safe?

'Daughter of Zanufey,' he spoke with a sense of finality, 'our answer remains the same. The risk of losing ourselves is too great. Our decision is final, we cannot aid you. Take your talk of wars and bloodshed and depart from our tranquil lands, never to return, for ours is a life of peace. Whatever gift you have received here, I hope it serves you well, but expect no more from us. I bid you safe journey back to Maioria. No further into our land may you step without harm coming to you.' With that, he turned away, and the elves began to disperse at his gesture.

'What about you other elves? I saw no discussion amongst you?' she cried.

Some turned and looked at her, but after a moment shook their heads and turned away.

'Damn you, man. You cannot hide from the world forever. Don't you see? Baelthrom will come for you.'

She stood speechless, breathing heavily and her head pounding. Daranarta did not turn back, and a swirling mist hid everything from view, even the grass beneath her feet. *I failed, Karshur.* Tears stung her eyes. She was supposed to be the Raven Queen, messenger of Zanufey, but she had failed, the people would not listen, they had even turned her away.

If they would not unite, how on Maioria could they ever expect to stand against Baelthrom? No wonder they hadn't been able to stand against him in the past. Could they not see? Did they not care? The questions echoed around her head. She was trying to force a broken people to war, a people who had suffered much and lost all. She felt terribly tired and longed for her bed.

CHAPTER 12

The Immortals are Coming

A loud rapping at the door jerked Cirosa awake in her chair. She winced. Her neck was so stiff it felt broken. The strange object from the harpy was still in her lap. She hadn't dared to unwrap it yet. She tightened her robe.

Damn it. She'd fallen asleep in her office, and now there were visitors. The light of the morning sun spilled through the small window to her left, illuminating the dust in the air. The raven nightmares seemed distant and foolish now.

The knock came again. She stuffed the object into a drawer and smoothed her hair back.

'Yes?' she said, driving the sleep from her voice. Who the hell was it? She hadn't arranged for any visitors this week. She remembered that she'd locked the door from the inside, dragged her aching back off the chair and went to unlock it.

A pale-faced sombre priestess peeked up at her. Tamany was her name. Her brown robes matched her eyes and marked her as an advanced novice. She curtsied and spoke quickly when Cirosa frowned.

'Master Freydel is here, High Priestess.'

Cirosa sighed but kept her face straight. 'Well, send him in then, I have at most half an hour.'

Tamany inclined her head and shut the door. Cirosa went back to her chair, trying to make herself as presentable as possible in her night robe. Moments later, there came a single wrap.

'Come in,' Cirosa smoothed her scowl as best she could.

Freydel entered. There were dark circles under his eyes, and his usually well-kept and neat beard was unkempt, as was his hair. He was dressed in his riding clothes; a white shirt and tan-coloured breaches, his cloak was draped over one arm, and his thick wooden staff in the other.

What did the old fool want now? She purposefully looked from the stack of papers on her desk awaiting her attention and back to the worried face of Freydel. He did not notice and instead sniffed the air, wrinkled his nose and looked around with a frown. Her stomach fluttered, could he feel the strange object the harpy had given her? He was a Master Wizard, the best in all Maioria, surely he could feel something. Her heart began to pound. So it *was* magical, whatever it was. Still, she had done nothing wrong, despite feeling guilty.

'What is it, Freydel,' she tried to sound exasperated.

Freydel shrugged and stepped towards her. 'She has been gone the whole night and still no word. Not even scrying shows me anything but an empty ocean.' He gripped and released his staff as he spoke.

'I assume you mean Issa. So we can also assume she's failed?' she barely managed to keep the excitement out of her voice.

Freydel shot her look, but she kept her gaze steady and her face blank. He looked away. 'It's too soon to tell.'

She huffed. 'Well, how long do we give it? A week? A month? Maybe when Keteth comes here and tells us himself?'

'You did not feel it then?' Freydel raised an eyebrow.

'Feel what?' She snapped. A horrible feeling was rising in her stomach.

'In the Flow, a surge of magic greater than any I've ever felt,' Freydel's voice was soft, and his amber eyes were wide with wonder.

She bit her lip and tasted the sour taste of blood just as that same blood drained from her face. It didn't mean anything, yet.

'Oh, *that,*' she smirked. 'There was a tremor, who didn't feel it, huh?' But he didn't seem to be listening.

'Unfortunately, at the time I was sleeping,' he said. 'I should call together the Wizards' Circle. It's dangerous, and it has been a long time, but this is too important. Maybe they'll know more.'

'Well, is Keteth dead or not?' she demanded, too tired for this nonsense, and her patience was slipping. The Wizards' Circle was a bunch of outdated old men waffling on about magic. She yawned at the thought.

Freydel looked at her. 'I don't know. Something has happened, something big, but what I don't know. It may be that someone has died, to release that amount of magic... But I cannot know who.'

Cirosa couldn't keep the smile from curling her lips. Issa was no trained magic wielder, not enough to match Keteth in any case.

Freydel smiled with her. 'Let us hope Keteth is dead.'

She smiled harder to hide the grimace.

'Well, we must never be too hasty to jump to conclusions,' Cirosa said. 'It's highly unlikely that Issa is "the Chosen One" she wants us all to believe she is. In these dark days, people are desperate for a saviour, a tipping of the balance of this war in our favour. You know what the commoners are like; they jump up and grab at anything vaguely fitting the prophecy. Don't forget there are many versions of "the prophecies," as well you know.'

'Oh?' Freydel raised an eyebrow. 'I don't recall *that* many versions.'

'Yes,' Cirosa said firmly as she racked her brain. 'For example, despite what Mother Urula may have said, let's not forget the Dark Prince of Davono. Now, what was it he said again... hmmm, "Beware the raven caller, for she has been sent to destroy us." '

Freydel's brow furrowed. 'Yes, that's true, but the Dark Prince is named aptly; he was a black magic delver, a traitor to his own race, and everyone suspected him to be a necromancer actually in league with Baelthrom.'

'It doesn't change or lessen what he said, and besides, any of the prophets could be proven to be mad, or traitorous for that matter,' she said. He continued to frown, but there was a hint of uncertainty in his eyes.

'And what about Keteth?' She grabbed hold of his uncertainty and pushed it further. All she had to do was sow the seeds of doubt. It was so easy to fool people, so easy to control them. Push a little this way or that, make them think what you want them to think...

'He was once a man and don't forget, he wrote in his unfinished works, The Pathway of the Dead; "I have seen the death of death, the death of us all in the eyes of Zanufey's chosen".' She kept her voice silken smooth, and leant forward on her desk, her eyes wide and innocent.

He nodded, sighed and melted into the chair opposite her desk. She scowled, she hadn't said he could sit, but he didn't notice.

'Keteth, the man, was mad, we all know that. Keteth, the beast, is insane,' Freydel said, rubbing his eyes with finger and thumb.

'Well, there are more examples I've talked about before,' she said. Did the stupid fool think he knew everything about the prophecies?

'There are endless reams of boring prophecies, and they contradict one another. You don't get into my position within the Temple without ceaseless study of these things,' she said confidently, reminding the wizard of her status. 'I can show you if you like. I still have my old books and notes. One thing they all prove is that nothing has been set and sealed in stone.'

Freydel fidgeted. 'It's well known you don't believe in the prophecies, you've stated publicly yourself. Still, Issa was adamant she had dreams and visions wherein a goddess spoke to her in the form of a woman robed in the stars. But, prophecies aside, what was this vision you had? You mentioned the goddess spoke to you too some time ago, about the testing of Zanufey's chosen one?'

Her heart leapt. Here was an opportunity to fly. In all her years the goddess had never spoken to her. Always her voice was silent, an absent deity in her cold and empty life. She had regrettably admitted it to Freydel once, in her darkest moments when she had first come to Celene. What a fool she had been. Never should she have let that truth be known.

The goddess had never spoken to her, not even in a dream, but many claimed they had been spoken to, and this wench claimed it too. It was a bitter pill to swallow. The goddess had given her beauty, ambition and endurance; it was more than most people had. But gratitude was not one of her traits, in fact, she scorned it. Gratitude kept you from striving, for reaching for more. For who wants more when they are content and grateful? And that is why she would survive where most people perished. She had cunning and foresight, and whatever the task ahead, no matter what the cost or how it was achieved, she always succeeded.

'Yes she did,' Cirosa smiled and indulged. 'It was one of those heavy prophetic dreams—the first of many more to come no doubt. A tall, beautiful figure with an air of mystery told me to send the young woman to Keteth to prove her strength. The woman-child I was shown had long black hair. I had not even met Issa yet.'

It wasn't a total lie, it was more an embellishment of the truth, a useful interpretation. After all, the priests and priestesses were taught in their first lessons to search within to find the true meaning of their dreams and visions? She *had* had a strange dream wherein she saw a dark-haired girl fighting a white monster, but no voice had she heard, and no direction given.

'And what did this goddess look like, her voice sound like?' Freydel asked.

Cirosa felt her face flush hot with anger. Didn't he believe her? A young grey-robed priestess, the mark of the beginning novice and lowest rank, knocked and entered the room without waiting for an answer. It was

Efren, and she was busy looking down at the mop and bucket she carried. Terror swept across her face as her eyes settled on Cirosa.

'I'm so sorry, High Priestess,' she stammered. 'I'm assigned to clean your office in the early hours. Always the rooms are empty.'

On seeing Cirosa's dark expression, she left, the door not so much as making a click as she shut it. The priests and priestesses were afraid of Cirosa, and she would not have it any other way. It was easy to rule people who feared you, things got done quicker and you got what you wanted most of the time.

Efren had given her an excuse to forget Freydel's question. She shoved herself up and began sorting through the papers, ignoring the obvious fact that she still wore her nightgown.

'I have to get on, look at all these papers. Come back to me when you know for definite what has transpired. Nothing of interest has happened here apart from the usual tremors.' She engrossed herself in a particular sheet signed with an illegible child-like signature, the signature of the Oracle.

'You know your own way out,' she said dismissively, pretending not to notice Freydel.

'The tremors were magical,' Freydel mumbled as he dragged himself up with his staff. But he did not say more, clearly being too tired to pursue matters further, much to her relief.

'There's something else you might like to know, or not,' he said when he reached the door

She raised an eyebrow, hoping it was quick.

'Rance somehow learned of where Issa was going before he understood fully what was going on. As you know, we tried to keep everything as close to our chests as possible, lest the enemy discover what we were trying to do. Maybe one of the priests or priestesses that were with us that day mentioned it to—'

'Oh? What of it?' she cut him off and tried to sound uninterested, but her heart was pounding. What had her buffoon of a former lover gone and done now? It was obvious Rance had taken a liking to the wench, the way he was falling all over her at the Midsummer Celebrations. Issa had bewitched everyone.

'Apparently he took a boat and went to find her, even before she left.'

Cirosa slammed the paper down. 'How do you know this?'

'Arla told me.'

'Curse the girl,' she said, but knew Arla never lied. Where was that feral child anyway? She always seemed to disappear when she was needed, and reappear when she was most unwelcome. 'Well, has he returned?'

'No,' Freydel shook his head. 'Keteth has been close to Celene recently, probably since Issa arrived. All fishermen and traders have been cautious, some choosing not to leave port. I worry.'

'Rance is an excellent sailor. I doubt he will be gone for much longer,' but despite her dismissive words, her stomach still twisted.

'Maybe,' Freydel said and opened the door. He paused, sniffed and frowned again, looking about the room. She held her breath. He shrugged and closed the door behind him.

Cirosa sighed, fell back in the chair, and closed her eyes. *Rance you complete idiot.* What on earth did he think he could do anyway? If Issa wanted to prove she was the chosen one, then no one should try and stop the wench. She opened her eyes. Her gaze was immediately drawn to the drawer where the object was. It drove all thoughts of Rance from her mind. She stared at the smooth varnished wood and black iron handle shaped into a scroll for a long time.

Was something given to her from so foul a beast as a harpy really worth looking at? It could be cursed or poisoned or worse. The Immortal Lord's Gifts… She should throw it into the sea immediately. She lunged for the drawer, then paused. She didn't want to touch it and yet somehow she had to. She grasped the handle and pulled open the drawer. The bundle was small, a harmless thing.

She sat back and stared at it. Slowly she reached down and grasped the bundle, lifting it into her lap gently as if it were a kitten. She couldn't really feel its power, other than an unsettling yet intriguing feeling. It was heavy and dense for its size.

This is foolishness.

She unceremoniously opened the cloth. The fist-sized bloodstone was set within a thick blackish-gold amulet attached to a heavy chain of the same metal. The bloodstone began to glow, and even without magical skills, she could still feel the unnatural and otherworldly magic that seeped from it. A heavy power that was both corrupt and alluring, like stolen gold. She gingerly stroked it and drew back with a gasp when it warmed to her touch. She covered it up and threw it back into the drawer, slamming it shut.

Hand over mouth she stared blankly at the book-filled shelves lining the walls. She hadn't been hurt, had she? Why did a harpy think she needed an amulet? But then it wasn't just an amulet, was it? That's what scared her. Having that powerful thing near... She was out of her depth. But when had she ever felt out of her depth where power was concerned? She was being foolish. It was just a stupid necklace, some harpy joke on her. But harpies were not known for foolery, only killing and stealing things. Not giving them.

"...there is another, greater, more powerful being who watches you...". Were they watching her now? Cirosa swallowed, her heart pounded as her gaze darted around the room. Did they know she had touched it?

She stood up, annoyed at her own paranoia. Whatever it was, it was most certainly evil. She would throw it into the sea, but later. She had to wash and dress before the other priests and priestesses were up. What would they think if they saw her still in her nightclothes? She left her office and went back to her room.

All the time Cirosa was away from the bloodstone amulet, her thoughts were upon it. The only break came when she thought of Rance. Like everything she did in life, she had spent a lot of time planning and trying to win the man. She wore her long blonde hair down, her lithe body cleverly dressed in loose yet clinging clothes, her blue eyes made large through the use of black eyeliner. She was no other than the High Priestess of Celene, attractive and clever—he would not be able to resist. She suspected he was afraid of her, but that only served to fuel her sense of power and allurement.

For all her efforts, in the end, he began to refuse further offers of her bed. The rejection had infuriated her. No one denies a priestess, and certainly not the High Priestess of Celene. The last time she had bothered to speak to Rance had been like the others since he had rejected her, strained and unpleasant. After watching him fooling around with Issa at the Midsummer Celebrations, she had approached him dressed in her High Priestess robes and flanked by her priests and priestesses.

'Found yet another wench to flirt with?' She had said. She had intended to humiliate him in front of everyone and was pleased when he flushed in anger. He had dared to ignore her and stalked off. Her dislike of Issa cemented into cold hard, bitter hatred. The bitch had ruined everything.

It was with that bitter taste in her mouth that she now swept back towards her office, not an hour since she had left. Once more she locked the door from the inside, slumped down at her desk and opened the drawer.

She lifted up the amulet and watched the light glint off its surface. This time she felt less afraid of it. The strange feeling of alluring corruption seeped into her again, stronger than before. The bloodstone began to glow once more with that odd dark light, and something moved within it. She brought the stone close to her face. It glowed brighter, filling her vision with red. She wanted to look away but found she couldn't. Pressure grew in her temples, and her heart began to pound. She suddenly knew without a doubt that she was not alone.

She wanted to be the commanding and imperious High Priestess, but in the end, she trembled and shivered under the weight of the power that exuded from the amulet. She was to be commanded, whether she wanted it or not.

'Cirosa...' the name slithered out of the amulet. Chains of magic wrapped around her shoulders. She could not let go of the amulet even if she wanted to.

'Who is this? I–' her voice was a quivering rasp that caught in her throat.

'Cirosa...' the voice breathed again. The unseen chains slipped around her neck and arms, firmly grasping her. Panic grew as the cords tightened on her throat and then released as if to tell her who was in control.

'Cirosa...' her name echoed, and the cords wound around her waist and legs. Her own name was being used to bind her. She could not move an inch, not even to talk or blink. Even the feeling of panic was not hers to command and it slowly seemed like a distant emotion. She felt like a fly trapped in a web, being bound by a spider who would consume her later.

'Who slew Keteth?' the demanding voice was so airy and deep, it could almost be mistaken for the wind. The bloodstone seemed to deepen, drawing her into it so that she floated in a blood red sea. Images flickered through her mind, her own memories being sorted through by whoever was ensnaring her.

'Who slew Keteth?' the voice whispered again.

An image of Issa came to the fore. She was dressed in grey robes and looking away as she stood beside Freydel. The last time Cirosa had seen her before she had gone to Keteth. Just the sight of her caused a surge of hatred. With her throat constricted the rising fury made her feel faint.

Laughter too deep to be from a human throat echoed around her and the cords around her throat loosened. Her breath came a little easier.

'Your hatred will be your undoing,' the voice said.

'I care nothing for her, whoever you are,' she rasped.

The effort to speak made her choke. The cords tightened. Her heart pounded with the lack of air. She had to sit extremely still and upright to get enough breath into her body and keep from passing out.

'Keteth is dead,' the voice was dangerous.

'She cannot have killed him. She is nothing, she is dead,' she croaked, and tried to choke in air.

The image of Issa rose in her mind. The cords constricted tighter. She could barely sip the air. Her head began to pound in time with her heart. Blood-red waters filled her vision, her mind. She was drifting away.

'Keteth is dead. I will have who has killed him. This girl must be found.'

She nodded, or at least she thought she did for she could not feel her body anymore. Her consciousness was drifting. *She will return to Celene.* The thought was read by whatever held her. The voice laughed again and the cords around her neck loosened completely.

Blood rushed through her body, filling her head. She quivered and gasped and dribbled, and would have fallen had the cords not held her. For the first time in her life, she was grateful to be alive.

'Thank you,' she gasped, 'thank you, thank you.'

'Feel the power I can give you,' the voice said, low and commanding.

There came a strange feeling then. Powerful energy moved and weaved through her body, and she suddenly knew how to speak the commands that would bend magic to her will. The room around her quivered and shook, or perhaps it was her vision that did so. Waves of reds, violets and blacks swirled around and through her.

Was this how Wizards felt? Was she really feeling magic? It could not easily be described, only felt. The power grew and grew within her. She closed her eyes in the ecstasy of it. Immense power over the elements and all things. She groaned in desire, willing for more. She was not denied, and more came, filling her until it felt like a hundred orgasms rolling through her one after the other and she lost all sense of herself. It was totally consuming, and yet not wild but controlled and directed. She could destroy the world and create a new one if she wanted, she only had to say the command.

The power stopped, and it flooded from her as quickly as it had come, leaving her weak and trembling.

'The Immortals are coming. Your information has been most useful. I will have need of you again, High Priestess Cirosa.'

The voice became faint as it spoke and the bloodstone seemed to be shrinking, or she was being pushed out of it. As soon as it became dull and cold, the cords constraining her vanished. She slumped forwards onto her desk, sending her papers flying. She lay there panting and sweating. Her rifled mind was a mess that could not organise itself. She felt raped—body, mind and soul—and yet no one had been here, and there was no mark upon her body. It took several minutes for her heart to calm itself, several more for her mind to settle, but she knew she would never get over the memory.

Finally, her breath came a little easier, but still her muscles could not move. All the while she lay there, she lay in paradox. The power she had felt she could only dream of. Yet the horror of utter domination, the ease with which her mind, body and soul had been taken, crushed and conquered, she had never felt before, not even in her darkest nightmare.

And yet still she would do it again, if only to feel the power once more, if only for a second. The harpy was right, the Immortal Lord was not silent and impotent like the goddess.

CHAPTER 13

Marakon the Half Elf

MARAKON the half-elf, commander of the second attack fleet stationed at Port Nordanstin on the coast of northern Frayon, leant against the metal railings and looked out over the calm blue sea. He rubbed his short beard impatiently. He could never relax when they were soon to engage the enemy. They were supposed to be given ample notice before any attack force was planned in order to prepare his ships and soldiers in time. But he had been told only an hour ago by his senior that they would be leaving tomorrow. The ships were barely checked from the last operation, and his soldiers were not recovered.

As if to rub it in, his senior was walking towards him now in his usual chest-forward striding fashion. His limp caused his scabbard to constantly clink against the studs of his high boots. An unmistakable sound that let everyone within earshot know the admiral was about, and a sound he was certain the older man deliberately tried to make for that intended purpose. He took a deep breath and let it out. Though he actually respected the older man, he wanted to be alone right now.

'Admiral Linker,' he said with a slight bow to the shorter fatter man.

The admiral wafted his hand dismissively. 'Enough of that. We trained together for six years, Marakon, bunked together for two. The only reason I have this rank is because you turned it down, and well you know it.'

Marakon smiled. 'Enjoying the paperwork then?'

The admiral snorted. 'You made the right decision, I was ever the fool.'

'My place is not behind a desk, never will be,' Marakon said. 'I don't have the brains or patience for it either.'

'You know if we had more time I would give you more time, Marakon,' Admiral Linker got to the point as he smoothed down what remained of his grey hair circling his otherwise shining bald head. 'You saw in the meeting how uptight everyone is. The dark moon has given people hope and spurred them on, but it's also made the enemy fight harder. The Maphraxies are moving quickly now, and we *must* move quickly to counter them if we are to keep them from the shores of Frayon.'

Marakon nodded and looked out across the glistening ocean. Though he tried to deny his feelings, knowing how psychologically important it was for a soldier to keep faith in himself and the Feylint Halanoi, deep down he knew this war was one they could not win. Not without some miracle. A miracle in the form of a hundred thousand of the most powerful wizards, or the goddess herself, coming to fight against the Maphraxies.

The dark moon filled him with foreboding, whereas it filled most others with hope-filled fervour. The goddess had not abandoned them after all, that's what they thought. But to Marakon's suspicious mind this moon was probably another trick of the Immortal Lord. He had been at war for too long to have any real hope that there would ever be a peaceful life left for him.

'We're outnumbered, as always, and that gap is widening. We can't find enough soldiers to replace the ones we lose each battle,' Marakon shook his head, wondering why he spoke his thoughts aloud, it's not like they would change anything. They couldn't out-breed Baelthrom's war machine. Those soldiers not killed were captured and turned Maphraxie before the day was through. 'I'm sure that each one of those bastard Maphraxies I meet is bigger, stronger, and quicker than the last.'

'Ah, I understand your concerns, Commander, but we have no choice; fight and die or die sooner,' Admiral Linker reasoned, completely unfazed. If he ever doubted they would win this war, he never showed it. But he was right, they couldn't surrender, they had to fight. Baelthrom did not do negotiations.

'Every day, new soldiers arrive to join the ranks of the Feylint Halanoi,' Admiral Linker continued and spread his arm back towards the camp.

Marakon glanced back to where the once green fields were now filled with soldiers' tents of all sizes. There were so many, they spread back into the line of trees and beyond them to the horizon. The morning mist was dissipating under the sun's rays, and he could see a short but growing queue of people outside the largest white tent. People eager to sign up.

Men and women of all ages, some old enough to need walking sticks and some very young. They carried simple weapons, old blunt swords of grandfathers long dead, notched and rusted axes that were now more useful as gardening tools, and, more often than not, no weapon at all. At least the weapon's smith could sharpen a nicked blade and possibly clean a rusted axe.

'I bet the young ones are barely past their sixteenth birthday,' Marakon murmured at the pitiful sight of skinny young girls and boys that would barely be able to lift a short sword. 'I'll bet again that they'll lie about their age too.'

'Just like you did, Commander,' Admiral Linker said with a tilted grin.

Marakon smiled wryly. Indeed he had, full of the glory of war. What a lie that had been. It seemed like such a long time ago.

'I remember the day well,' Admiral Linker said. 'Not only did you lie, you lied a lot. Said you were twenty-five when you were not long past your fifteenth birthday. Was sixteen not good enough for you?' he squinted at Marakon in the bright sunlight.

'Well, if you're going to lie, may as well make it a big one,' Marakon grinned.

'You had everyone fooled. Thanks to your elven heritage, you were already a foot or so taller than men of twenty-five, and now you're taller than most tall men. I think that was the only time you ever used your heritage as a positive.'

Admiral Linker was right, again. Marakon's mother had been an elf, his father human, much to both their parents' woe. He felt a confusing mix of shame and pride at the elven half of him. After his acceptance into the Feylint Halanoi, he tried to hide his elven looks, but he could not hide his height and his complexion was always smooth and unblemished – which was why he grew a very human beard.

He rubbed the thick black hair on his chin. He kept it short, mind, just enough to throw people off. Luckily his ears were only slightly pointed and his eyes barely almond shaped at all. Thankfully his hair was dark brown, so dark it was almost black, and thick and cut short like his beard. Very unlike elven hair that was glossy and fine and fairer.

As if reading his thoughts, Admiral Linker said, 'You do a good job of hiding it, but what will always give you away is the colour of your eyes, or should I say "eye"?' he jested.

Marakon smirked. His eyes were violet, just like his mother's.

'It's lucky, then, that I only have one of them now,' he said, and rubbed under his eyepatch.

It wasn't quite true, but his strange eye was another thing about him that he tried to keep secret. He still had his left eye, but not one he wanted others to see. It was pure white now, yet see with it, he could. It had been damaged in battle by a monster of a Maphraxie eight years ago. The brutal encounter happened on an uninhabited island many miles north of Frayon, closer to Drax than here. He was lucky to be alive. Out of a band of ten soldiers, only he survived, and so he always considered it a small price to pay.

'The training camps are full,' Admiral Linker said proudly, changing the subject.

He could hear the high-pitched twang of weapons clanging from the new people training. So many soldiers he saw, new and fresh to battle. All fought bravely, feverish battle lust in their eyes, their hearts brimming with retribution, and all died gallantly, painfully, yet still believing they were making a difference, that through their death they had somehow won. Just a little bit. He knew the bitter truth of it, knew that in the end they died in pain for nothing, in a war they couldn't hope to win.

'You are right, as always, Admiral. What else can we do? Let the bastards come without a fight?'

It was Marakon's job to command his soldiers, and so he did it as he had been trained to do. If he did not, then he had no job and no wages— no use when he had a family to support.

'But still, our numbers never seem enough.' *Not nearly enough.* Marakon breathed, hoping his morose mood would get rid of the optimistic admiral.

'You always were practical about such things, Marakon,' Admiral Linker seemed pleased. 'If only we had a hundred more like you.'

His superior's praise no longer fed his ego or confidence. *Words, that was all they were, words.* Action. It was action that changed things, not words. So, then, that was his reason to fight, it was always good to be reminded why he was here. There was nowhere else to go, except retire at home with Rasia. It would not put a meal on the table, and he had no clue how to farm. All he knew was how to fight, how to kill Maphraxies.

'Humans like us don't have the elven choice, Commander,' Admiral Linker's face became serious. 'We were never gifted with a special land to which we could flee. Always we had to stand and fight.'

'Cowards,' Marakon growled.

'Mind you, had I had the option of fleeing to a haven, I wonder if I would have taken it,' Admiral Linker mused. 'So don't take the Burden to heart.'

To the elves that remained in Maioria, the exodus of their people was seen as a sin, and their guilt they labelled the Burden.

'I never would have fled,' Marakon scowled, thinking about his cowardly elven half-kin.

The Ancients had their sacred land, Aralanastias, if it ever existed, and the elves had their Land of Mists. The rest of Maioria had to stand and fight when Baelthrom came out of Maphrax. The elves feared that they too would share the fate of their distant cousins if they did not flee. So nearly all departed for their hidden land. The few that refused to go were forbidden entry into the Land of Mists. The elven homeland of Intolana was now Maphraxie and had been for hundreds of years.

What an easy picking for the Immortal Lord when its inhabitants simply fled without a fight, he grimaced. Well, good riddance to the cowards. He snorted aloud and gave silent thanks to the goddess for the half of his blood that was human, the part that gave him the courage to stand and face the enemy.

'Still, you can't blame them,' Admiral Linker continued. 'After centuries of infighting against the greedy dwarves and us warring humans, why would they feel an allegiance to any race upon Maioria?' Marakon wondered if the admiral was trying to appeal to his half-elven heritage. 'Perhaps, after all, we are indeed the lesser race the elves think us.'

'Someone needs to stand up and fight the bastard,' Marakon said. 'What if the whole world turned and fled? The elves aren't up to the job. They would rather sing and dance and tend to their forests.'

'Isn't that what you would prefer, Commander?' Admiral Linker watched him closely. 'It's certainly what I would like to do.'

Marakon looked away. Yes, indeed that's what he wanted to do—today more than ever.

'It's our duty,' was all he could think to say. And it was, wasn't it? Their lives spent for the hope, the desperate longing hope, of freedom. What else was there to do in this life? 'And there's nowhere else to go… Unless we're cowardly elves.'

Admiral Linker laughed and slapped him on the back. 'Indeed, Marakon, indeed. We're stuck in this hell-hole of a war whether we like it or not. It's sink or swim, Commander, fight or die. Even the dwarves think they are safe beneath their mountains as if it's a different planet completely to the scourge that spreads on the surface above them.

'I think the dwarves hide in guilt, thinking that, by withdrawing from the world, it will undo the damage they caused by failing to destroy the dark dwarves before Baelthrom came. But perhaps I'm being unfair. Blaming the dwarves for Baelthrom would not have stopped his arrival in Maioria.'

'Probably not,' Marakon agreed, 'but the elves' refusal to aid Maioria in the fight against him, have made the Maphraxies stronger. Though I can never forgive them, I wonder, even if they fought alongside us, whether it would be enough to defeat him now. Not even the Ancients, with all their wisdom and magic, could stop Baelthrom's rise to power.'

'We can't change history, and so I guess there's no point in dwelling on what might have been,' Admiral Linker reasoned.

What might have been... they were thoughts for dreamers and poets, and Marakon was neither of those. He was a soldier and had been since he was fifteen years old.

'You always were this dour before a battle, Marakon, but when you're in it, I've never seen such a gifted fighter,' Admiral Linker regarded him seriously. 'No one could ever beat you in the field, and, for all your wounds, you are the last one of your original unit to still be active in battle. Which is why you are our most valued Commander. Though I'd hate to lose you on the field, why do you turn down every promotion offered to you?'

It was true, he should be at the top by now, but he had turned down every promotion and accepted just the reduced pay rise. Now he earned nearly as much as Admiral Linker. All that money and he was too busy fighting to spend it. He knew Rasia would be spoiling the boys with it, and that was good.

'It's more than just a sheer hatred of desks and paperwork isn't it?' Admiral Linker chanced.

Marakon smiled at his officer's insight. What would the coming battle bring? Was his death waiting for him on this mission? All of his battles against the Maphraxies had been different, but they were always brutal. His first encounter with them had been no different, the events were branded upon his mind.

'I told you I was only a boy when they slaughtered my family,' Marakon began. Oh, how many soldiers had the same story? Did they also have the same half-elf guilt mixed with the same vengeful hatred of the immortals? Probably not. That's what made him so viciously effective. 'Back then our home in southwestern Munland was far from the frontline.

'My father, also a soldier of the Feylint Halanoi as you know, was home for a short time. It was a surprise attack, as always from those honourless dogs. They arrived on the backs of Dromoorai,' and it was the first time he'd soiled himself in fear. He remembered the dragon fear with a shudder, it gripped hold of your spine and shook your body so hard even your soul trembled. You couldn't run, the fear immobilised you.

'They came with nets, magic, fire and blades. The village was essentially unarmed. Apart from my father and his friend, the village was filled with the old and young and mothers. The Maphraxies moved with organisation and devastating speed, we didn't stand a chance.' Even now he could hear their screams and smell the choking dragon smoke, feel the heat of his village as it burned.

'My mother, father and baby sister fled on horse and mule, but foltoy and death hounds gave chase. They wouldn't let anybody escape.'

The green-eyes of the foltoy were vivid in his mind. Massive, undead, cat-like beasts the size of bears. Furless and able walk on two feet, or run faster than a horse on four. They also had a terrible intelligence; a handful of soldiers who had confronted them recently said they could even speak.

'Of course, there was no escape. In the struggle, I fell from a cliff and landed on a ledge. There I lay unconscious as my parents and sister were left to the Maphraxies. I never saw their end, thankfully. I still pray they were killed rather than...' he trailed off.

'So you could say I have an insatiable desire for revenge,' he gave a hollow laugh. Admiral Linker's mouth was grim.

'How did you survive alone?' he asked.

'Well, I nearly didn't. It took me a day to inch down the cliff via nooks and crannies until I reached the ground. Nearly died of thirst. Then I met an older man, an elf named Falharlen fleeing from an elven village in the south. He gave me water, took me into his care. It seemed the Maphraxies were purging the whole area; we met many others fleeing to the port. We took whatever boats were available, and fled to Frayon. Falharlen cared for me until he died quite suddenly and without reason, ten years later. It was then that I joined the Feylint Halanoi because there was nowhere else to go. The rest is history,' Marakon smiled wryly.

'And now you have a lovely wife and children,' Admiral Linker leant on the railing. 'My wife ran off with the Smith, and now I'm too old and fat to find another,' he sighed. Marakon laughed.

'To be honest, I worry all the time for their safety,' Marakon admitted, 'and if I didn't have such a slave-driving officer, I'd be able to see them more often.'

'You'll have a full month of leave after this excursion. More than I get, you lucky bastard,' Admiral Linker scowled. He glanced at the sky, and his demeanour switched to his rank.

'I'd best be off,' he stood up and adjusted his sword belt. 'See to it you leave at dawn, Commander. The rest I shall leave in your capable hands.'

'Yes, Admiral,' Marakon too stood up straight and saluted.

With a curt bow, the admiral turned heels and strode back towards the officers' tents, his sword clanging against his boot. The noise faded into the distance, and Marakon turned back towards the sea.

Marakon hadn't been totally honest with the admiral. It wasn't just revenge for the death of his family and the loss of his home that drove him to battle against the enemy. He also harboured an unresolvable guilt on behalf of those elves who had abandoned Maioria and her peoples to the Maphraxies. Falharlen had felt that same guilt, and Marakon learned that all the elves who chose to stay felt the same. They all felt the Burden like a shameful sin. Each death he dealt to a Maphraxie was a salve upon his soul, a balm upon the Burden. But his guilt, like his revenge, seemed insatiable.

It wasn't just revenge and guilt that kept him fighting, either. He gripped the railings and clenched his jaw as that familiar, awful feeling of emptiness swept through him. He didn't know why it came or where it came from, but it was as if he'd done something awful, and yet he could not remember it. Like brutally murdering someone in a rage, but having the memory of it removed whilst the feeling still remained. He wanted to remember, and yet he didn't, he really didn't.

The feeling plagued him and left him in darkness. The darkness had been with him his whole life like a black hole, a void he could never fill. An empty loneliness that brought upon a desperate searching for something, but he didn't know what. If he could find that something, everything would make sense and his soul would find peace. He thought having a wife would fill the void, but it didn't, it only held the darkness at bay. He thought having children was what he sought, but though he loved his sons the dark emptiness still visited. Only when he was fighting Maphraxies was he free of the darkness and elven guilt. He shifted his weight onto the other foot.

'Rasia, I wish you were with me now,' he sighed, focusing on thoughts of his wife.

He wondered, as always before every battle, whether he would see her again. Her long copper curls falling to her voluptuous hips, her big brown eyes. An unlikely soldier but she had been a good one, though less driven by rage and revenge, and more driven by skilled archery. They had served together for many years before they'd married after she became pregnant. Twins now young boys whom he also missed.

He pushed thoughts of his family aside and scratched his eyepatch irritably. The black leather only served to absorb the sun's heat. He should get a tan one made, he thought, and not for the first time. The Maphraxie blade that took his eye had been enchanted, they always were, and the beast moved with a speed he'd never seen before. He remembered those dead eyes watching him with an unusual and unholy intelligence that made him hesitate. He fought with everything he had, and nearly lost it all.

There had been magic involved, he was sure of it. Blackness had surrounded him so completely that he couldn't see or breathe or think. The enemy struck and there came a searing pain in his eye. Attacking wildly in the blackness he had fallen backwards and fled, he'd never fled before or after.

Ever since that day, he always wondered why the Maphraxie didn't follow. It hurt like hell, but he hadn't actually lost his left eye, and it healed, kind of, but now was pure white with no iris or cornea and it gleamed brightly, embarrassingly. He covered it up, mostly to stop people staring, but there was another reason, one he had told no one, not even Rasia.

The change frightened him at first. The vision in his left eye had been replaced with what he could only call extreme far-sightedness. He could see a bird in a tree ten miles away and make out every detail, the colour of its eyes, the fine strands of its feathers. If he covered his good eye, he could look straight at the sun and it would not hurt.

Fear of this new sight had turned to wonder. He could see the enemy coming from miles away, and it had saved him and his unit many times. His soldiers and superiors just thought him an excellent commander; not suspecting the help his sight gave him. It was an asset as much as it was an embarrassment, and yet something deep within him recoiled from it, wanted it gone, this strange gift from his most hated enemy. Many a time he had held a knife to it, but for all his fearlessness in battle, he could not stomach putting his own eye out.

He arched and stretched his back. He couldn't stand here thinking of the past all day, there was work to be done. But when he looked at the sun it had moved only a little, and he had been stood here half an hour at most. The time always passed so painfully slow before the coming battle. He needed this battle, when he was fighting all thoughts apart from striking the enemy before him were blissfully gone from his mind.

CHAPTER 14

Forget all Else

THERE was no Land of Mists when Issa next opened her eyes, and she was far from whole and healthy because every muscle screamed in pain. It was light enough to see now, and she found herself alone in a large round hut where a fire burned low in the central hearth.

Her right arm ached the most, and her hand was thickly bandaged with a dark red spot on her palm where blood had worked its way through. Still, considering, her wounds were not nearly as bad as they should have been thanks to Ely's bracelet. A healer's bracelet worn by a healer. She traced the silver leaves, glad to find she had not lost it in Keteth's prison.

She drank from the pitcher beside her bed, noticing a round, cloth-covered object beside it. Relief washed over her, the Orb of Water was safe. She touched it and could feel its magic as a soft hum beneath her fingers. But what was she supposed to do with it? She couldn't lug it around with her, had no idea how to use it, and had no pocket large enough for it. Why had the Wykiry given it to her? Her power came from the dark moon.

There had been lots of magic. Wykiry died, along with many others. Her throat constricted at the memory, she could hear their crying voices. Zanufey had left her when the blue moon set, and with their leaving, so too did her power and strength. The Wykiry had come to take her back to Celene. It had been slow going for she could no longer breathe beneath the waves and was frigid with cold. A thick dark fog surrounded them, filled with the stench of immortals. They became lost in it and in the confusion the black ships came.

She had no power to fight, and without the moon, her magic was spent. But with the help of the Wykiry and the magic of the Orb of

Water, which they knew how to use, she found some power. Consciousness faded in and out, and in the spaces, she glimpsed a golden dragon before all turned black.

She fell back upon the bed. She prayed the Wykiry were safe now. Was she on Celene? Where were Freydel and Ely? Through a gap in the curtains surrounding her bed, she glimpsed a wall made of mud, not stone, a shelf littered with jars and vials, a simple wooden table and stool. Far simpler an abode than even Edarna's. Was this a hermit's house?

With a lot of effort, she pushed herself up and dragged her legs out of bed. The action sent her breathless, and she had to stop to catch it. There was a deep pain in her side, and her left leg was bandaged from her groin to her ankle. Cuts and grazes covered most of her body, and every one of them stung. She certainly felt like Cirosa saw her, not Zanufey's Chosen but a frail, weak girl.

She still wore the far-too-large man's shirt. Where she got it from and what had happened to her own clothes didn't bear thinking about. And she smelt bad, sweaty and sea-weedy. How wonderful a bath in Castle Elune would be.

People's voices came from outside. She struggled to her feet and slumped against the wall. She stayed there for a moment, willing her body to obey. Slowly, her legs began to give into the assault. Clinging to the wall, she shuffled to the door. By the time she got there, and it took a good while, she could almost stand up unsupported. The door was simply two planks of wood nailed together. Beyond it came muffled voices.

She opened the door and was immediately blinded by sunlight. The hut had been deceptively cool and dark, never letting on that it was mid-day outside. She stood there blinking, feeling the warmth of the sun fill her limbs with strength. Her eyes came into focus. She was surrounded by a forest of broadleaves and evergreens. Several rounds huts, much like the one she currently clung to, stretched off down a dusty road that was more of a worn path than anything constructed of stones. She stepped out of the hut and hung on to the door.

Her heart lurched when she saw Asaph. He had his back to her as he spoke to Coronos. His reddish-blond, shoulder-length hair was loose. He had a sword belted to his waist and was naked above it. His skin was tanned and smooth over broad, well-muscled, shoulders.

Shirtless... she fingered the collar of the shirt she wore, feeling the heat rising up her chest and throat and into her cheeks. All thoughts about whose shirt she wore were swept from her mind as her eyes came to rest upon the most bizarre creature she had ever seen. The man-beast was also shirtless, had the head and torso of a man, but the body and antlers of a deer. She blinked. If she hadn't been hanging onto something she would have fallen.

The deer man rested his gaze upon her, and she wondered if he had smelt her presence. She smelled bad for sure. Coronos and Asaph turned to see what the deer-man was looking at. She felt her cheeks grow hot as Asaph came striding over. The sunlight catching his fair hair, his lips were smiling and his sapphire blue eyes filled with concern.

Uh, he's alive and well... and here!

The worry for him that had lain like a dead weight in her stomach now lifted. She was so glad to see him, she smiled foolishly up at him as he towered above her looking concerned. And then, all at once, she was really angry.

Where had he been? Why had he brought her here? Where, in fact, *was* here? And why the hell had he not come to her on the Isle of Celene? If he could find her in the Shadowlands, he bloody well could have found her on Celene. She could have died. She nearly did die. The fury reached boiling point, and before she could stop herself, she slapped him.

He did not so much as flinch, but a look of complete shock covered his face as well as red marks where her hand had struck. The motion sent her over balance, and she staggered forward. He caught her, but her legs wouldn't work and she sagged against him as he held her, the world lurching violently. He took her arms gently but firmly and held her away from him.

'What are you doing?' he asked, stunned.

'Where have you been?' she demanded. Despite her anger, she felt quite ridiculous being unable to stand whilst she argued with the person holding her up. 'I thought you were dead. You could at least have come to find me.'

Her anger burned hot and fast and was quickly spent. She felt more exhausted than ever. The red marks upon his face looked quite sore, and her hand tingled. She looked down guiltily. She shouldn't have slapped him, even though he had got her into all this mess. Violence was not the way to deal with emotions, she reminded herself, resolving to somehow control her temper better. Over his shoulder, she glimpsed the smiles of amusement on the other men's faces.

Asaph grinned, making her blush again, and then embraced her.

'Thank Feygriene you're all right. I was so worried,' he said hugging her tightly. The smell of him filled her nostrils as she was crushed against his bare chest and made her pleasantly dizzy. She hoped he couldn't smell her too much.

'Uh huh,' she mumbled into his chest.

'I didn't know you had such fire within you, or have you changed since we were last together?' he asked, laughing softly and smoothing back her tangled hair. He stood back and held her shoulders. 'You look as beautiful as ever, despite your bruises and bandages, and obvious inability to stand up.'

'Oh really?' She was taken by surprise. She tried to take her own weight and look a bit more dignified.

'I guess that you either don't care or you must have forgotten that you are half-naked too?' he grinned impishly, pointing out that all she wore was his loose shirt that barely reached her knees.

She looked down in dismay at her white legs, noting that they could do with some sunshine. She tried to stand straighter and look proud.

'I clearly don't care,' she said, straight-faced, though she'd actually completely forgotten.

Asaph laughed and hugged her again. After a moment, she found it in herself to relax into his embrace and return the hug. As soon as she let her defences down the strain of the last few days, of the last few months, washed over her. Embarrassed by the tears that came up out of nowhere, she hid her face deeper into his chest, unable to stop the tremor that shook her.

She had defeated Keteth, but in returning Karshur she had failed to gain the elves as allies. There was so much to be done, and yet she didn't know how to do it, or really what she was supposed to do at all. So much seemed to be expected of her, of the Raven Queen. She needed time alone, to be herself and not the warrior that kept calling to her. And she wanted to be with Asaph most of all and forget all else.

Asaph could feel the wetness on his chest and simply held her and stroked her back. He felt like crying too; for all the agony and terror spent in Keteth's domain wishing that he would die to end the torment, for very nearly dying and never seeing her and Coronos again, for all the death and destruction he had witnessed and wrought himself. His dragon self knew no horror or guilt or fear, but when he came back to his human form it all rushed upon him.

And now she was here, again in his arms. After so much fighting and struggling, it seemed too much to cope with. How her long slender legs made his pulse quicken, the bandages only adding to her vulnerability. Though exhausted and weak, she was not as frail and timid as he first thought she was. He sensed that something had awoken within her just as it had awoken within him.

The war was coming. Baelthrom and his Maphraxies were certainly hunting them now. Whatever their future might be, it was going to be treacherous. He stroked her hair, so soft under his rough hand. They had time to be together, he told himself.

Yet, despite his reasoning, he could not shift that cursed nagging sense of urgency. He would have to live with it, for now at least, because at this very moment, all he wanted to do was hold her. He had longed for this moment. It had been her leading him through the darkness, her making him strong, her refusing to give up. The demands of the future could wait, just for a little while.

She did not resist as he gathered her into his arms and carried her back into the hut. He laid her down and pulled the covers up around her shoulders. She was already asleep.

Issa slept deeply and dreamlessly at first, but in the early morning hours, the nightmares came.

She stood on a hill on the Isle of Celene. The sky was filled with green-tinged clouds and anxiety bordering on panic gripped her. Something terrible was about to happen, and she should run away from this place as fast as she could, but her feet would not move, and there was nowhere to go.

Darkness smothered her. She was in a small, enclosed space, rough wood at her back. A snort and stamp of a hoofed foot came from close by. Her eyes adjusted to the dim light and she made out the silhouette of a horse.

'Duskar.' She smiled and went to him. He whinnied as she stroked his nose.

'Soon now, my friend. I'll be back soon,' she said, but then he backed away from her and the whites of his eyes showed.

'Duskar?' she whispered, a knot of fear forming in her belly. He began to quiver, sweat streaked down his neck, and he tossed his head wildly.

'Duskar, what's wrong? It's me, Issa,' she said, her voice shaking with fear.

He reared at the door, and she backed away from him. It wasn't her he was frightened of, but something outside. His eyes turned blood-red, and thick froth began to drip from his mouth. She sobbed and cowered in the corner of his stable.

He bucked and kicked and bared his teeth as he fought something in the darkness she couldn't see. Then he screamed, and she smelt blood in the air. She was frozen in terror, she couldn't move to help, she couldn't reach the Flow. She covered her ears and shut her eyes and screamed.

CHAPTER 15

An Old Soul

AFTER a hot roasted lunch with his soldiers, and an extra, hearty plate heaped full of North Frayon spiced potato, Marakon left his officers in charge of completing the final preparations and went for some exercise. The sun was high and warm in the clear blue skies, though a cold wind came from the north, reminding all that winter was not all that far away. He hugged his coat closer and walked through the encampment.

The northernmost post of the Feylint Halanoi had become a large, semi-permanent settlement nestled to west wall of the medium-sized harbour city of Port Nordanstin. There were far too many people, soldiers and refugees alike, to house even a quarter of them within the city walls.

Amongst the tents and carts, small wooden houses had been erected and, though easily moved, it was a testament to how long the soldiers had been there, and that people thought they were likely to be there a good deal longer. The locals welcomed the protection and trade the Feylint Halanoi brought them and, whilst most places across the free lands struggled, Port Nordanstin was booming. Construction work for permanent housing had begun in earnest, and the whole area around the outside of the city walls was a building site.

Despite his earlier mood, he found the sun and exercise lift his spirits, so he wandered further than intended, and his feet brought him to the bustling West Gate entrance into the port city. Being market day, it was packed full of people inside and outside the city walls. He kept no track of the days and had long ago learned that a soldier on duty had no day off, no special day to look forward to.

At the gate entrance, two bored guards stood chatting to each other completely ignoring everyone else as they moved through the gate.

Clearly, they felt they had little to do now the Feylint Halanoi surrounded the city. They didn't even glance at his sword as he stepped past them. He joined the bustle of people carrying baskets and pushing wheelbarrows, or pulling small carts filled with wares to sell, or wares just purchased. This was considered the trade gate, the city's main Southern Gate was for horses and larger carts.

He stood for a moment, in a quieter corner of the huge square courtyard that today was filled with the tents of traders. Fabric roofs crowded his view, all purples, reds and blues, some tall and rickety, others short and wide. The crowd were mainly fair, northern Frayonesse people. Amongst them, he spotted the odd short and strong-looking dwarf, a few dark skinned Atalanphian soldiers and several tall, broad reddish-blond Draxians. Quite a mix.

Even so, his gaze settled with some surprise upon a young elf girl in a tiny purple draped marquee. The metallic shimmer of the fabric was clearly of superior elven material and workmanship. Most things of elven design were superior, he conceded grudgingly.

He felt sorry for the girl. Despite his unfavourable feelings towards elves, she looked out of place, small and vulnerable in the busy market. She also looked very young, but Marakon knew to correctly guess the age of an elf was no easy feat. Though she looked to be in her teens, she may very well be past thirty. Her shy demeanour was probably why she was getting so many young men to her stall. She was quite beautiful compared to those around her, a gem hiding amongst rocks. Her long plaited hair hung over one shoulder like flowing silver, and her skin gleamed in the sunlight.

He made his way over to her stall.

The girl looked up with pale golden eyes and smiled shyly as he approached. He knew she would instantly recognise his elven heritage—elves could always tell from the colour of his eye and smooth skin hidden so well under his human beard. And, though it was obvious that he wasn't pure elven, her smile seemed genuine as if she was pleased to see one of her own kind, if only a half-elf at that. A testimony, he thought sourly, to how few of the elves remained to fight against the immortal scourge upon Maioria.

'There are not many elves this far north-west and so close to the battle front,' he said as he searched through various sized bags of hessel leaf. She was mostly selling herbs and incense, half of which he recognised, half he did not.

'My father and mother are dedicated to the Feylint Halanoi, sir,' her voice was melodic, like the low notes of a flute. He noted the pride in her voice and also something more, whether a touch of reproach or defensiveness he could not tell.

'My mother is half-elven too,' she added.

'Ah.' He moved to some other herbs and nodded slightly, making sense of everything in a second. 'Three-quarters elven,' he smiled.

Did she feel as confused and guilty as he did about having a mixed heritage? The girl seemed flustered and her face had reddened in embarrassment, instantly showing the part of her that was human, and suggesting that she did feel as he did.

'Then I'm honoured to serve alongside your parents, though I've yet to meet them,' he beamed.

'Oh, they are part of the Night Watch,' the girl added hastily, clearly thinking he didn't believe her. 'Which is why I run the herb stall alone. They're sleeping...' she trailed off awkwardly as if she felt she had said too much to this stranger.

'Elves have excellent eyes for the night. I shall sleep more soundly knowing they are watching over us,' he said sincerely, and the girl smiled again, her shoulders relaxing a little.

'Yes, we're not all bad are we?' she murmured in Elvish, and he saw the flicker of shame pass across her eyes. He spoke in elven, saying something he thought he would never say in defence of the elves who had fled.

'They had their reasons for hiding. Maybe they were right, and none would have survived Baelthrom had they not fled. I wish I'd had the choice to follow them,' he laughed at his own words, and she laughed too, though the guilt remained.

He didn't need anything, but wanting to purchase something from her, he picked up the biggest bag of hessel leaf he could find, and passed her a silver coin, refusing to take the eight copper ones she gave as change.

'We're not poor, sir,' she said in Frayonesse, blushing indignantly.

'And neither do you look it,' Marakon said. 'Still, keep it for yourself. I have too many coppers in my pouch anyway.'

She slowly took back the coins. 'Thank you, sir.'

She said nothing more but her eyes watched him. Not knowing what else to say, he turned to go, but then she spoke.

'I do not say such things to strangers,' she said in Elvish, maybe speaking in that language so others nearby would not understand. He turned to look at her. She squeezed the coins anxiously in her hand.

'My grandmother had the Sight; I have a little of it,' she chewed her bottom lip as if wondering whether to speak. 'It's known amongst those with the Sight, that long ago we lived forever. That there was always enough time to do all of the things we needed to do. But now one lifetime is not enough. After death a soul often chooses to reincarnate back into a body to continue what it came here to do. Some of us are old souls and have been around for a long time, though no one fully remembers their lives before.'

He frowned, but intrigue moved him back into the stall. 'I had a friend whose mother had the Sight. He died in battle a while back. After so long speaking with him, I never doubted we live again, but why do you tell me this?'

'You're an old soul, sir.'

He stroked his chin and smiled. 'Somehow that doesn't surprise me,' he laughed, but the girl only gave a half-smile.

'You have returned to fulfil a great deed.'

He shifted uneasily, wondering if the girl was angling for more coins, but the sincerity and sombreness of her tone told him otherwise.

'I can see it in the heaviness of your aura. You walk a double path, though you don't know it.' She looked far away, beyond the bustling market, and into another time and place entirely. 'There's darkness and sadness about you. Can you find and restore a long forgotten glory? Can you right a terrible wrong that was done unto you and your companions?'

The girl's questions were introspective, and they struck chords deep within him that made him suddenly afraid. She looked directly at him then, but seemed to see deeper as if into his soul.

'Despite its look and its nature, fear not the raven, Forgotten King. It's strong and loyal, as are you. It too walks a double path, between this world and the next.' She blinked and looked about herself as if she had just awoken. He stood staring at her, lost in thought.

'I'm sorry. I shouldn't tell people the things I see, so granny said, but it seemed important,' she said in Frayonesse, pulling her silver-threaded cloak closer.

He blinked and came back to himself. 'Did you see anymore?'

She paused, then shook her head, suddenly the shy young girl once more. He had a desperate need to walk in the sunshine and to be alone.

'Thank you for your thoughts, they mean something, though I don't know what... My name is Marakon,' he added but didn't know why. He stepped away.

'You're a good soul, Marakon. A strong and good soul,' she called after him.

He turned to look at her. She was smiling. and her eyes gleamed as if they were filled with tears. What was it she had seen? He forced a smile and left. The crowd engulfed him and for a brief moment, he stood still breathing deeply of the cool air, letting the sunlight fall upon his closed eyelids as the people bustled past. Then he was moving with the throng.

Marakon walked as fast as he could, wheedling his way past barrows filled with pumpkins twice the size of his head. He squeezed past families clinging to each other and so fearful of anyone becoming lost that they moved as one being in a long line or a tight bunch, making it impossible for anybody to get past or move quickly.

He headed for the West Gate thinking upon what the elf-girl had said. It was even slower going as he neared the narrow gate, it had become so busy it was single file in, single file out. He gave up pushing and relaxed into following the next person in front, letting his mind wander.

The girl had unlocked something within him, a memory or idea that he couldn't quite bring to mind, and yet he felt it to be true. It seemed as if his whole world had suddenly changed, but he didn't know how or why or what was different. He was so deep in thought that it took him a while to realise that the press of people had stopped along with the chattering and laughing. Everyone was quiet except for hushed whisperings. Everyone except for one person.

The cracked, strained voice of an old woman shouting somewhere behind him cut through the din of the market, bringing them all to silence. Looking over his shoulder, it took him a while to find the source of that trembling voice.

The crowd suddenly parted to let an old woman through. People fell back from her, afraid she was diseased or possessed by a demon. He could see she was not ill or infected, just a bent over old woman clinging to a walking stick. She wore a fraying patchwork shawl and a faded green dress that reached the dusty road. Her long grey hair hung around her shoulders in knotted strands. She shuffled unsteadily forwards.

'You!' she cried.

He did a double check around him, and found that the crowd had fallen back, as they had from the old woman, and he was suddenly horribly alone with her. It seemed as if he and the woman were on some kind of dusty stage, surrounded by an audience and about to enact a play. She pointed a finger towards him, making it dismally clear that it was indeed him to which she shouted.

'You have come again, but to serve us or destroy us?' She was forced to stop by a hacking cough that racked her body.

He sighed and slumped his shoulders. What was going on with the world today? Was it "get Marakon" day? He was about to turn away and leave this nonsense, but to his chagrin he saw some of his soldiers watching with interest. He knew better than to push his way through a now highly suspicious and superstitious crowd. Also, the guards who walked atop the city walls had stopped to watch the spectacle, all boredom gone from their faces.

He sighed again, this was the last thing he wanted right now, some superstitious nonsense coming from a half-mad old crone to set his nerves on edge before battle. Perhaps some good could come of this, though ideas failed him. Perhaps the woman needed a coin to shut her, up or a helping hand somewhere. He turned to face her.

'What can I help you with, wise lady?' he forced a smile. 'What is it you see?' he found himself asking before he could stop himself. He'd done it now, now there would be no easy getting away.

The woman's clear hazel eyes, looked up at him as she shuffled forwards. There was no madness in them, and this unnerved him all the more.

'The king has returned!' she said, and the crowd began to murmur more loudly amongst themselves. But as she neared him, her shouting dropped to talking. He realised that this was not intended to be a show for the people, and that the woman, like the young elf girl, probably had the Sight and was compelled to share it.

'Wise woman,' he said, loud for people to hear. 'I am no king. I am just a soldier of the Feylint Halanoi. You must be mistaken.' *And bloody well going to get me into a lot of treasonous trouble, usually rectified by hanging*, he thought miserably.

'I'm not mistaken!' the old woman shouted and he winced, holding up his hands for quiet, wishing for all the world that there was not an audience watching.

'I knew it was you,' she said, nodding her head and giving a tilted smile, her voice was just above a whisper, much to his relief. 'But you do not know yourself!' she cried. He flinched. The crowd was talking now, but still they looked eagerly on.

'I do not—' he began, but she talked over him.

'I can but show you, though it will drain me,' she said, and before he could move away she grasped his arm and clung with surprising strength. Her eyes flashed blue.

Before Marakon could prise off her bony fingers, pressure filled his mind and a cloud passed over his eyes. Suddenly he was looking up at a blue sky as fluffy white clouds swirled around him. A dull throbbing pounded in his head, and the air became thick and difficult to breathe. Something was on his head and he reached up. The cold metal of a helmet met his touch, but he had not put it there. He took it off and looked at the gold circlet adorning it. He recognised it and yet knew he had never seen it in his life.

He looked down and found the clouds surrounding him had become his mount, a gleaming white horse armoured in shining metal. The tabard he wore was familiar, but not Feylint Halanoi for it was white with a silver star embroidered in the centre. The crowd that stared at him were not market-goers and merchants, but townsfolk mixed with lords and ladies and all dressed smartly. They were smiling and cheering and for some reason he too felt the same elation.

Then he was galloping across green grass under a clear blue sky with other knights dressed as he and mounted upon white horses. The freedom was palpable. Their hearts were pure, they were knights of honour and protectors of righteousness, and he was their king. Dark clouds swept across the sun and the scene changed.

They were no longer mounted, but on foot and in the thick of battle on a cold and desolate plain. Between the clang and clash of steel, the wind howled. Before him lunged a warrior with an old notched and rusty sword. He thrust his own sword forwards, parried a blow and sliced hard right knocking his opponent's sword down as he punched upwards with his gauntleted fist.

His foe's helmet wobbled loosely back, and with a yelp of horror he saw he fought a skeleton. Armour hung off its bones, its sword held aloft in bony fingers. Under that loose fitting helmet, empty eye sockets bore into his own, and the stench of death filled his nostrils. He swung his sword fast in terror and scraped through the skeleton's ribcage and pelvis. It crumpled to the ground.

He gawped at his own sword arm—it had no flesh either, only gleaming white bone. His legs were not flesh and blood, but bones. He looked across the battlefield. They were *all* skeletons. And just as he realised, they stopped fighting and looked at him. They raised their fleshless arms and pointed at him accusingly, anger in their eyeless sockets. He fell back, choking in fear. He stumbled and fell, but the ground did not break his fall, and dark clouds and rushing air engulfed him.

A female face formed in the clouds, green eyes looked directly at him, pale lips spoke words he could not hear. His wounded eye began to burn. He felt as if something was very wrong with him but he didn't know what.

He looked down and found himself naked, cut and bleeding in a hundred places. He could not move but he could see, and he looked out across a plain covered in decaying bodies. They stretched outwards from where he lay, to the far hills on the horizon. The raucous caw of carrion birds filled his ears as they hopped upon and feasted on the rotting dead. The sight and smell made him retch.

A black shape fluttered in the corner of his eyes, and sharp claws landed on his head. He looked up at the huge, sleek form of a raven, the biggest bird in the field. He tried to move, to shake his head to be rid of the bird, but he could not move his useless body, it was paralysed or broken or both. He screamed as it stabbed at his white eye, trying to peck it out. The pain was like nothing he had felt before, it burned right down to the soles of his feet. Hot blood trickled down his face as it jabbed again and again. The pain made him senseless, and he was only dimly aware when something hot and slippery slithered down his face.

His eye was gone and the pain dulled, but then he felt as if a great burden had been lifted, so great a burden that he began to cry in the joy of its release.

The grip upon his arm released and he looked down through unshed tears at the old woman. His heart was pounding, and sweat covered his face, but he clung to that feeling of release.

'We cannot do all the things we came to do in one lifetime. Wrongs must be righted, the truth cannot hide,' the old woman whispered.

'A raven is always a messenger,' she added, and then became confused and looked about her as if she had lost something. She seemed weaker than before, and her walking stick trembled under her weight. He steadied her, wondering what on earth had happened. The market around them was in full swing again, and though people gave them a wider berth no one was watching anymore. The guards walked the walls and chatted amongst themselves, and the people went about their own business.

'Mother,' a woman's voice called out from somewhere in the crowd.

'Mother, there you are. I've been searching for you for ages,' a woman in her thirties with shoulder-length chestnut hair and big brown eyes pushed through the crowd towards them. The old woman looked up squinting, vaguely recognising the voice.

'Mother, where have you been? I've been looking for you everywhere.' The brown-eyed woman gave him an apologetic smile. 'I'm sorry, she gets a bit lost and confused because of all the people.'

Marakon smiled as much as he could and wondered what to say. 'It's no problem, she seemed, uh, a little upset and unsteady. I think she saw something with the Sight.'

'Oh, oh dear,' the younger woman said. 'I do apologise. She was a priestess once and now she's older, the Sight controls her more than she controls it.'

The old woman blew through her lips in disgust. 'I was a witch thereafter for much longer than I was priestess. Rotting, corrupt order that it is now,' the old woman scoffed.

He laughed and the younger woman gave him an exasperated smile. He let go of the woman as her daughter put a supportive arm round her.

'Come now let us get some hot tea,' she said. The old woman was muttering to herself as if she could not really hear.

'The Goddess bless you, both of you,' he added uncertainly, the brown-eyed woman looked up and smiled, then led her mother away.

That evening sleep was a long time in coming for Marakon, disturbed as he was after the strange experience with the old woman and the words of the elf girl. When sleep did come, it seemed his restless thoughts of the coming battle were determined to play themselves out in a half-sleep.

He stood in full armour upon a high rocky place surveying a treeless valley, when a mighty wind blew and he was cast in shadow. Terror froze the hairs on his neck as he turned to face the gusting wind. His eyes travelled upwards from the foot long black claws, up shining scales the colour of oil, to stare into the blood-red eyes of a monstrous Dread Dragon. Its snaking neck and horned head was the size of four oxen and was not ten feet from his own face.

The stench of rotting flesh and sulphur leaked from flared nostrils covered in brown stains and each the size of his head. On its back sat a black-iron clad Dromoorai with its three-pointed helmet. A heavy claymore held easily in one gauntleted hand, and in the other the clanking chains of the dragon's reins.

Instinctively he held up his puny sword. It shook as his body trembled and his teeth chattered. Sweat soaked him, but he could not move, he was rooted to the ground. The dragon opened its mouth and heaved. He cried out and fell back as a wall of fire engulfed him.

His own scream half awoke him, but the dream clung hard, not willing to let him escape, and dragged him away from the welcoming light of his tent in the real world.

Back into the flames he was drawn, but now a slender figure in dragon-scale armour and a crown of black feathers stood between him and the Dread Dragon, and the flames could not reach him. He couldn't see who it was for she had her back to him and the brightness of the fire was blinding. A shield of magic spread from her outstretched hands which the flames could not penetrate. He fell back, and an exhausted, dreamless sleep overcame him.

CHAPTER 16

Calling the Wizards' Circle

FREYDEL slumped into his chair in his study. The orb refused his mind, and now he was exhausted from trying to use it. His head thumped dully, and his eyes burned as if he'd rubbed Atalanph chillies into them. Sleep would help, but worry for Issa kept him from it. He felt ethereal and exhausted, but how could he rest when her life might depend upon his current actions?

Talking with Cirosa had drained him, as it always did, but this time it had been particularly bad. She wasn't alone in her study, and whatever else was there was sucking out the life of everything, even the Flow had been sluggish. He had been glad to leave.

He got up from his chair and set about making some spiced apple tea, purely to do something constructive rather than glare at the unresponsive orb.

With a steaming mug in his hand, he felt a little better. Cautiously he touched the orb's shining black surface. He gasped. Where it had been freezing before, now it was burning hot. He let his hand drop. The Orb of Death, a chilling name that always sent shivers down one's spine as they were forced to momentarily think upon their own eventual demise. He preferred to call it the Orb of Undoing. He knew more about the orbs than any of the other Keepers, and yet he knew only a fraction of their power, and even less how to use it.

If only the Ancients were still with us, we would at least know more.

The orb gave him twice as much power as he could wield alone, but it was a destructive power. It had been passed down to him from the wizards who lived on Celene over the ages. Celene the Sacred Isle, where the last light of sun leaves the Known World. It was the orb that had heralded the coming of Zanufey's dark moon—shining indigo blue not an hour before the moon first rose. A colour the orb had never shone before. Usually, the orb sucked all light into its blackness and swirled with tiny pricks of light, a miniature galaxy filled with stars.

'Do you remember when the blue moon of Zanufey rose and you shone the same colour?' He said to the orb. He often spoke to it; it was more than just a crystal ball and had an intelligence and consciousness all of its own. The orb remained unchanged, and he got the feeling it was still busy, for want of a better word.

'Do you remember Issa, Zanufey's chosen? Well, I need to know if she's all right.' He sighed and sipped his tea, he felt like he was pleading with the orb.

'For the sake of the goddess, am I your Keeper or not? At least let me know if Issa is alive!' He slammed his mug down and sloshed hot tea over his hand.

'Yargh, curse it.'

He clutched his burnt hand and began to clear up the mess. All at once the orb burst into indigo light that filled the room. He dropped the cloth and stared into the orb.

'Issa?' he stared closer, dragged a chair behind him and sat down. Within the orb, a calm sea formed beneath a dark indigo sky.

'It's dark. The blue moon has set. This must be a vision from the past,' he murmured. He saw her then, pale and weak and amongst the Wykiry.

'She lives!' He yelped and jumped up with a laugh. The vision changed, sweeping all happiness from his face.

'Maphraxie ships,' he breathed, horror forming a knot in his stomach as he looked upon the dark lumbering shapes.

Light flared, and interference made the images flicker nonsensically, forcing him to look away. The orb began to calm, and he saw her again, flying in the clutches of some great golden beast. A dragon? But not a Dread Dragon, that can only be a good thing. The orb turned dark, and he stroked his beard.

'A dragon… Maphraxies in The Lost Sea… I must call the Wizards' Circle at once.' But it had been years since he'd last called it, he could not even remember when. He did remember that it had been interrupted by Baelthrom, and they all had fled. No one could forget that. Maybe the last time had been before Coronos disappeared over twenty-five years ago. Since then it has been too dangerous. Perhaps now there was a chance.

The Immortal Lord's eyes would be drawn to Keteth… and this was too important. It had been so long, would Coronos even hear the call?

Freydel went over the spell to call the Wizards' Circle together. It had been so long he had forgotten how to do something he once knew so well. While he thought about it, he pulled on his purple wizard's cape and hat. He hated wearing hats, especially when it was hot in summer, but he enjoyed looking like a proper wizard.

With Baelthrom's ceaseless drain upon the Flow and his ever watching eyes upon the magic flowing through Maioria, it was becoming harder to communicate over distances, much less teleport places physically. It was hard for *him,* and he was probably one of the most adept wizards in the Circle.

Still, he needed counsel. There was danger close by, with the Maphraxies so far south, and that other niggling worry. Whatever was in Cirosa's study was wrong, very wrong indeed. Evil lurked there, and he had the awful feeling that she knew it was. Maybe it was Lady Eleny's words instilling doubt in his mind. Yes, Cirosa served the goddess, but he had never met one in the Order with so little faith.

He'd tried to teach Cirosa magic, but she had no ability, and that had been a source of bitter jealousy and anger on her part. He sighed and set about clearing a space on the floor free of books, maps and scrolls. It wasn't easy, there was nowhere else to put anything. In the end, he just piled them on top of each other.

'Right, what next? Time of day,' he looked out of the window. It was overcast, but he reckoned it to be about mid-afternoon.

"Spin to the right in daylight and then to the left." It was reversed if performing the translocation at night. Of course, there were quicker spells to call the council, but for bodily transportation this needed to be as secure and safe as possible, and he was prepared to take the time to make it so. He picked up the orb, now warm and easy to handle, and with the tip of his staff, he drew a circle around him, the sound of wood scraping on the floor boards as he drew.

'Earth,' he said as he completed the circle.

He dipped the tip of his staff into the water jug on his desk and drew a circle of water atop the previous one.

'Water.' He clicked his fingers and lit a candle. Dipping the staff into the flame, he then placed the hot end above the water circle and drew another.

'Fire.' He placed his staff just above the floorboards he drew another circle around him.

'Air.' He held his staff in his left hand and the orb in his right and closed his eyes. Slowly he began to turn to the right with his arms wide and chanted the Ancient's magic words followed by their translation in Frayonesse.

'A'nkahrin malfea dun; I command the elements,' he said slow and soft at first. He began to spin faster, and as he did so, he spoke the words louder and faster. The orb began to hum and the magic built around him as he reached his peak, then he slowed and brought the toning back down. He then spun to the left and repeated the process.

He stood there still and silent, feeling the energy of the Flow swirl in counter-rotations around him. He smiled with his eyes closed. Though time-consuming, this was his favourite spell, and he missed using it. When the silent roar of magic seemed at its peak, he spoke the word loud and commanding.

'Now.'

The ring of air burst into a swirling motion, two counter-rotating rings of gushing wind that moved swiftly up above his head. The ring of fire burst into flames, and the two counter-rotating rings moved upwards to the level of his shoulders. The ring of water gushed forth and appeared as a two counter-rotating rivers that rose to the level of his abdomen. The ring of earth burst into life, a slower moving counter-rotating flow of the deepest, richest earth that stayed at his feet.

'I call the Wizards' Circle,' he commanded, focusing hard on his memory of the meeting place and willing himself to be there.

He touched orb and staff together. White light grew from within the tube of circling elements, then the rings collapsed upwards from the bottom. There came a flare, and his study was gone.

The Flow gushed and pushed him, then he stood on a shining white cloud and all about him was bright light. In the distance, shooting closer, were the six stone chairs of the Orb Keepers and the six chairs of other wizards. Twelve chairs in total, one each for the twelve countries of the Known World.

Would they come? Could they come? They better had, he thought. If any had died since Grenahyme, he would have known. Grenahyme had been old, very old. Thankfully, it was old age that killed him and not the

Maphraxies. But since his death, they had been unable to replace him with another representative of Lans Himay. Grenahyme had been a learned and powerful wizard, and Freydel sorely missed his wise, kind counsel.

That was something else they had to do; find a replacement for Grenahyme on the Wizards' Circle, if one was to be found. Finding any wizard past a novice was proving harder and harder these days. If no wizard could be found, then usually it was the king of the country who was tutored in as much magic skill as they could master.

Lans Himay had no king since the royal family was wiped out by the people—sometime after Grenahyme died ten years ago. Freydel was sure it was Grenahyme who had managed to keep the peace between the king and his unhappy dukes. Once he was gone, the people rose up. No one could blame them. The king was mad, and the Royals were accused of black magic.

Freydel didn't think the royals were even capable of using magic, no matter what kind. Still, the place was a boiling pot of unrest, and until it settled down they would not be able to find a wizard or a leader to sit on the seat of Lans Himay. Hence no one, not even himself, ever fancied searching around Lans Himay while political unrest abounded.

The people of Lans Himay were renowned for their hardiness and aggression. It had taken Baelthrom to come and destroy every country around them before the three tribes would consider uniting. Once they had, they formed a formidable army that made sure no Maphraxie ever set foot upon their land. Now that army fought within itself for the power of the throne, and the three tribes were once more divided.

Refugees fleeing from Intolana, Munland and Drax, had created a confusing mix of races; elves, Draxians and humans thrust together and forming a mind-boggling set of allegiances that Freydel pitied anyone to try and unravel. Still, their hardy warrior spirits kept the Maphraxies from their shores, and thus from the shores of Frayon, and that, really, was all that mattered.

The circle of stone chairs was close now, and he breathed a sigh of relief. Although he travelled in the astral planes of Maioria, it still meant he had to travel over Maphrax, and that was where the danger lay. The journey was most dangerous for those who had to travel over Maphrax. So far it seemed his gamble had paid off, Baelthrom's eyes were looking elsewhere.

The tower was clearly visible. It was less a tower and more a high raised platform, for it had no inside, only solid stone with rough-hewn steps circling the outside. A huge round dome of magical glass surrounded the circle of chairs to protect the wizards from the elements. It was created by the Ancients of Maioria when Baelthrom had first made his entry into the world. A secret meeting place accessible only to those initiated into the Wizards' Circle. It was built on an uninhabited island beyond the eastern shores of Maphrax.

The wizards speculated that the island had once been a part of the land of the Ancients, but they hadn't been able to prove it. The island, though small, was beautiful, with a small inactive volcano, a single wide river winding through trees, and tiny coves. It lay at the farthest eastern point of the Known World, reaching to the very edge of the vast, unexplored expanse of the Ocean Kingdom. It was well beyond the sights and interests of the Maphraxies. Even if they decided to come here the Wizards' Tower would not be visible to them.

Like the elven Land of Mists and the Isle of Myrn where the seers lived, it was protected and veiled from view to all but the initiated, and the initiated kept its location and even its existence a closely guarded secret. Since Baelthrom's rise to power, he had destroyed many of these secret places veiled from view, but so far he had not discovered the Wizards' Circle because the wizards rarely met anymore in case he did. That was why it was so treacherous to call a meeting and make the journey.

He readied himself for solid ground, relieved to have made it across the astral plane undetected. His body began to re-solidify, letting him know he was leaving the astral planes.

Something felt wrong in the Flow. Everything lurched and then moved sluggishly as if he was suddenly moving through water, heavy and dragging. The white tunnel and the stone chairs ahead suddenly turned dark as if he'd shut his eyes. He blinked to make sure they were open and gripped his staff and orb.

'Take me to the Wizards' Circle,' he commanded firmly. Fear fluttered in his stomach.

The white tunnel tried to form around him again, but the Flow wobbled and flared. Erratic static energy made the hairs on his arms rise and fall as unstable magic surged. *Never mix fear and magic!* It created wild, unpredictable results.

He tried to control his thoughts, bring calm to his mind. He went over the words in his head, trying to decipher where he had gone wrong, but he had said them true. This disturbance had to be caused by more than just his fear. He tried to grasp the Flow more firmly, but it evaded him.

The Wizards' Circle blinked into view between the bouts of complete darkness, it was barely ten yards away. The bouts of darkness lengthened until no light came again.

He pushed down the rising panic and focused on all his senses and abilities to determine what was going on. Despite the blackness, it felt as if he was suspended in an enclosed space. He used the magic within his staff to create a ball of light but instead, fire exploded all around him, illuminating nothing but darkness, and then went out.

Freydel considered his situation gravely. He was stuck somewhere between his tower upon the Isle of Celene and the Wizards' Circle. Somewhere between the physical planes and the astral. Any magic he dared to use, when he could command it, was dangerously wild and unpredictable.

Stuck in a place without dimensions... Did time even exist here? He pondered in hope, time was what he needed most. Though he could feel no ground beneath his feet, he tried walking, but had no idea or any way to tell if he was moving forward or simply swinging his legs.

He couldn't even use the magic within his staff and orb. A ball of light had almost incinerated him. He stopped swinging his legs and solid ground formed beneath his feet. Gravity seemed to be working again, and he found he was no longer weightless, though he was still in pitch black darkness.

He reached down to touch the ground, it felt cold and smooth, like solid rock. His searching fingers discovered right angles. Large paving stones. He stood up and reached around, but could not feel any walls. He put the orb in his pocket, placed the tip of his staff firmly on the ground, out-stretched his arms and walked in a wide circle, his footsteps echoing in the eerie silence. The cold stone of a straight wall met his out-stretched hand.

He placed his back against the wall and walked forwards slowly, feeling out each step with his foot. Six steps later he found another wall. He lifted his staff up high, and it touched a solid stone ceiling. Slowly he began walking in one direction, but he did not find another wall. He was in a tunnel of sorts. A physical, solid place, but where? He desperately needed light.

If he never completed the journey to the Wizards' Circle, could he make it back to his tower instead? He hadn't tried to return to his starting point after a failed connection. Without touching solid ground, the other wizards may never have heard his call, or at least would think he cancelled it. They may never know he was stuck somewhere between the astral and the physical planes.

He grabbed the orb again, feeling its erratic power on his fingertips. The hairs on his neck stood up, and he hesitated before drawing it out. Something was watching him, or if not watching him aware of him. His mouth went dry, and sweat beaded his face. Wherever he was, he had a bad feeling about it and wanted to be gone as soon as possible.

He reached for the Flow, it was no longer as erratic, but was oddly unwilling as if he were a complete novice wizard trying to command it. It took all his effort to form a tiny orb of light, just enough to make out the dark, damp stones beneath him and the closest wall.

The footsteps started then, a heavy scraping sound of clawed feet on stone somewhere in the distance. He stared ahead, trying to see into the darkness unsuccessfully. He wanted to hide, but where? The footsteps were getting louder, echoing off the walls and filling his heart with dread. Something knew he was here, somehow, maybe the orb had alerted them. He had to get the orb to safety.

He turned in the opposite direction and ran. The footsteps quickened, still gaining. He trusted his magical skills, he was powerful, but magic was untrustworthy here, he could only use it as a last resort. He ran on, panting hard, but the awful sound of stone grinding upon stone came from ahead and made him slow. He slammed into a wall and gasped. He searched frantically, but there was no opening. He was trapped, and the footsteps were almost upon him.

He put his back against the wall and tried to calm himself. The footsteps pounded upon the floor making that strange clawing sound, and now he could hear the clinking of armour, the horrible sliding sound of a blade being drawn. His tiny orb of light spluttered as a dark figure formed, twice the height and width of a man. He lost his grasp on the Flow completely and shivered in terror.

The figure stopped ten feet away. Freydel gawped at the awesome sight of his enemy. He had never seen him in the flesh. A three-peaked helmet encased his face, black armour encased his body and hands. Only his bulging biceps and elbows were bare, revealing pale grey flesh. His legs were partially armoured to mid-thigh, beyond which green saurian scales glistened. Black metal greaves extended past the knee and beyond them were bare reptilian feet armed with claws. Claws that made a scraping sound as he walked.

Freydel could not make out any features, did not want to make any out, and tried to tear his eyes away. The awful realisation that he had not, in fact, made it past Maphrax in the astral planes undetected, dawned on him. Baelthrom had been scouring the astral planes, not turned away from them. He prayed to the goddess that he hadn't discovered the Wizards' Circle.

He cowered and hid the orb behind his back with shaking hands. Inside the black helmet, two eyes burst into flickering bolts of blue. The only sound in the deathly silence was the rasping of Freydel's breath.

'That which bound me in my prison now belongs to me,' Baelthrom thundered, and reached out a huge hand.

Terror flooded through Freydel, scattering all thought and reason. He tried to sink through the walls as he steeled himself against his fear, sought to climb the insurmountable mountain of his terror. He racked his brains for a spell, anything, but the words of power failed him.

'There's a mistake,' Freydel said, his voice shaking. 'I have nothing.'

'Pathetic wizard,' the walls shuddered as Baelthrom roared. 'You will be my necromancer.'

Freydel had to get the orb away, it didn't matter whether he survived or not. He could not make it to the Wizards' Tower, and he could not return the way he had come. There was only one other place he had a spell to get to, the Storm Holt.

Whether the spell worked or not was another matter. Whether he would even survive the journey with Baelthrom before him was debatable. No one had ever gone into the Storm Holt twice, not when the most powerful wizards barely survived their first trial there. Baelthrom could follow him there, but the spell was an immediate translocation, not a tunnel through which one travelled.

His legs went weak at the memory of the Wizards' Reckoning, as it was called. He would prefer to die at the hands of Baelthrom than suffer that again. But then he would not die, he would become a necromancer, his soul chained forever to the Immortal Lord, and he would lose the orb and Maioria would fall. It was losing the orb that sealed his decision.

Baelthrom's sword flashed, caught Freydel's cloak, and pinned him to the wall. The blade sliced into his shoulder, not deep but the searing pain of enchanted iron made him cry out. Hot blood trickled down his arm. He struggled to keep the orb behind him.

'Where is the one who has killed Keteth?' Baelthrom's voice dropped to rumbling.

The flickering blue eyes came close to his face. He tried to shut his eyes, but they locked onto his and flooded the flickering blue light into his brain. Images of Issa formed in his mind. He tried to shut them out, but his mind was being taken from his control.

'It's the same girl,' Baelthrom breathed, the sound of the wind blowing through autumn leaves. 'Tell me where she is, wizard, and I shall allow you to be a powerful necromancer.'

When he did not answer, invisible knives stabbed into his flesh. He cried out and writhed against the wall. Sweat soaked his clothes. The pain went, and he sagged.

'Thank you,' he gasped. To his horror thanking Baelthrom for ending the pain. 'Please. I don't know where she is.'

The pain came again but this time in his head. With all his effort he narrowed his consciousness into a ball trying to shut out all the physical pain he was suffering. Something he had not done since he had entered the Storm Holt. The one thing that kept him sane was focussing on Baelthrom's blue, flickering eyes. They reminded him so much of the entrance to the Storm Holt. Through the pain, he recalled the image of the oval entrance filled with swirling clouds and lightning. He spoke the Ancients' words for 'I enter the Storm Holt' silently in his head three times.

A'falee an Doth Any, a'falee an Doth Any, a'falee an Doth Any.

'Now,' he gasped.

The spell did not fail. Blue lightning filled his body, ripping Baelthrom's connection to his mind apart. Intolerable pain came as if a limb had been torn off. He was vaguely aware of dropping his staff, and then he was falling, clutching his throbbing head in one hand and the orb in the other. His body dematerialised, and wind gushed through every cell in his body.

CHAPTER 17

Bokaard

MARAKON awoke before dawn. Somehow his body always knew when he should awake; it just didn't always know when to sleep. He lay there for a moment, listening to the silence, trying to hold on to the stillness in his mind before thoughts of the coming day rushed in. But he was not able to stay there for long, and the thoughts came. He yawned and stretched and swung his legs out of bed.

How many would die in this next battle? Would he be one of them this time? He pulled on his trousers. How many would be captured by the Maphraxies to become the living dead, to become the enemy?

His left eye, uncovered for sleep, saw well in the dim light. He drained a cup of water from the pitcher beside the bed, and washed his face in the basin, shivering against the chill of the water as it trickled over his shoulders and his bare chest. A glimmer caught his eye and he glanced over at his clean and shiny armour propped against the tent pole, waiting to be worn.

'Sir. The regiment is up and eating, sir,' Avil's quiet voice came from outside the tent.

The observant man had heard him get up. He smiled. Avil was a trustworthy man and had been a good soldier, but his ability to fight ended when Maphraxian poisoned arrows pierced his right arm and left leg. He was lucky to survive, much like Marakon. Avil had recovered, over many years, and at least he was no longer bed bound. He now walked with a permanent lurching limp and a crutch under his good arm.

'Thank you, Avil,' he said, pulling on his boots. 'I look forward to seeing them.'

He stepped outside. Avil looked at him, saluted, and then anxiously looked at the ground. Silently cursing himself, Marakon turned back into his tent and snatched up his patch. His white eye always disturbed people because it was the first thing they looked at. They made their way to the food tent, each man's embarrassment fading in the growing light of dawn.

'You know other soldiers get paid for the work they do? Even if they aren't able to fight anymore,' Marakon said.

'No need, sir,' Avil said, lumbering along. 'I have everything I need provided for me in abundance. In truth, sir, I doubt they would be so generous if I received pay for my work.'

'Hmm, I guess not,' Marakon said.

Avil had no family left, all were killed or enslaved by the Maphraxies. He took no soldiers' wages but had abundant food and accommodation always provided for him by the Feylint Halanoi. In return, he readied the soldiers for battle, helped nurse them, cooked, cleaned armour, took weapons to the smith for mending, and various other small but invaluable tasks. He was actually more useful now than he had been as a soldier.

Maybe I should be doing his job, Marakon thought with a half smile.

'Still, I wish I could join you on the battle side, sir. Nothing can bring that back for me.'

Marakon looked sideways at the slender, tawny-haired man. 'In all fairness, Avil, I wish I had your job this morning,' he slapped him on the back. Avil grinned.

'Everyone feels the same before battle, sir.'

It was unusually quiet in the food quarters. Where Marakon's soldiers sat eating, there was none of the usual banter and laughter. Instead, they were pensive, quiet, and probably wondering if this breakfast would be their last on land ever again. The mood needed lifting, and it was always his job to do it.

'What a bunch of sour ugly faces greet me this mornin' eh?' he boomed.

They all turned, and, on seeing their commander, saluted before relaxing into nervous smiles.

A grin spread across his face. 'Don't you know this mission will be a victory, and we'll be rewarded as such? The goddess has foretold it.'

The tenseness in the air melted and one dark-haired bear of a man, Eran he believed his name was, spoke up in his thick South Frayon accent.

'I dunno which goddess you were with last night sir, but all I heard was a few farts from Tomant 'ere,' he slapped the shoulder of the short, plump man beside him.

Tomant snorted over a mouthful and dug Eran in the ribs. A ripple of laughter ran across the room.

Marakon grinned and took a seat next to a slender young man. Perhaps it was the elf-girl or the old woman yesterday, he couldn't be sure, but something about this morning felt different, like a sudden turn in the wind foretelling the changing of the seasons. There was a lightness in his heart, a feeling of hopeful anticipation that seemed to come from outside of him rather than from within. It could be nothing, he thought, stuffing bread and jam into his mouth and washing it down with cocoa so strong it could kill a horse.

'Is everything all right, sir?' the young soldier next to him asked, jerking him out of his reverie.

Marakon gave him a quizzical look.

'Uh,' the soldier blushed, 'you said something about this morning being different.'

'Ah,' Marakon hadn't realised he'd spoken aloud. 'Yes, victory will be ours,' he grinned, gripping the young man's shoulder reassuringly. It was all he could think to say. He didn't know this young man of average height, brown hair, blue eyes and tanned skin. He picked his chewed fingers nervously, and Marakon wondered if this would be his first battle. He liked to train his own soldiers himself, but these days they took whatever they could get and placed them in a unit quickly and mostly at random.

'New recruit?' Marakon asked.

The man smiled shyly. 'Yes, sir. The names' Lanac, sir.'

'Lanac, you picked the right battle,' he said, and they both laughed.

Marakon tucked into his porridge. Positive thinking was good, but he was thinking far too much lately, and needed to keep his mind clear, in the present, especially today. But he couldn't seem to shake the feeling that something important was going to happen. He only hoped he survived it.

'When will we arrive at Haralan?' Lanac asked.

Haralan was the largest island that lay almost exactly mid-way between Drax and Frayon. Recently it was a hotbed of battles as the Maphraxie army slowly but surely pushed southwards, drawing ever closer to the Frayon continent. Haralan had become synonymous with certain death to the Feylint Halanoi. Marakon spoke in between bites of food.

'In those new Atalanphian ships, we'll be there three nights from now. Sooner if we're lucky enough to gain a good wizard's hand. Ships from that hot desert of a continent are the fastest in all Maioria,' Marakon said.

'Then the battle will be on land, sir?' Lanac asked.

He glanced sideways at the young man. A quick and clever one, he thought.

'Ships from Atalanph,' Lanac said, thinking Marakon's look was to explain himself, 'though the fastest in the land because of their lightness, are somewhat delicate in nature, making them poor battleships.'

'You'll go far, Lanac,' he winked. 'You'll make commander if you can keep your head in battle.'

Lanac grinned, clearly pleased to have impressed his commander.

Marakon finished the remainder of his honey cake and slurped down the rest of his cocoa. It made tears come to his eyes, but it certainly slapped the brain awake.

'I'll see you all on the ships and sharp. Dawn is breaking,' he said loudly to his soldiers.

After he had collected his armour, sword and small pack of belongings, he strode down to the harbour where his ship was docked.

Many ships from all over the Known World filled the port. Long sleek Atalanphian ships contrasted with the wide Lans Himay ships that were more like floating battering rams. They were of dwarvish construction, and he thought it strange that the shortest race in Maioria, who liked to live deep within rock, would build such floating beasts. Maybe they were making up for their small stature.

In between the dwarvish ships nestled smaller but deadlier Frayon warships, and to their right beautiful elven ships decorated in gold paint, and sails made of elven cloth that shone silver in the sunlight. They were more fit for a parade than surging into battle. Yet, despite their beauty, each carried wicked elven harpoons, which would be operated by skilled archers to match. He fancied he could feel the elven enchantments upon those harpoons even from this distance.

The ships were the last of their kind, for there were few elves left to build them, and the blue oak trees from the great forests of Intolana, from which the ships were made, stood no more, having been so utterly destroyed by the Maphraxies that nothing new could grow in their place.

He came to his ship, the Sea Hare SM. The Atalanphian captain, Bokaard, swung down to greet him. SM stood for Sopho Morlin, the capital of Atalanph, where the ship was made and where the big captain was from.

Bokaard was a large man; tall, heavily muscled, barrel-chested, and with thick black hair and beard. Blue eyes glittered under heavy eyebrows, a striking contrast to his black skin, like sapphires glowing in the night. All Atalanphians had bright blue eyes. In their desert kingdom, they lived partially nocturnal lives to escape the burning heat. As a consequence, their bright blue eyes had adapted to the dark. Seeing in bright light hurt them, however, and sometimes they wore tinted glasses that they called "sunshields" to protect from the sun.

Bokaard looked tired and was possibly irritated at having to travel during the daytime when he should be sleeping like other Atalanphians. Even after eight years of service, he still couldn't get used to travelling in the light.

'Welcome aboard, sir,' Bokaard said in a heavy accent, slipping his sunshields into his shirt pocket. He bowed ever so slightly and touched his weather-beaten hat. He squinted at Marakon and pulled his hat lower.

'Captain,' Marakon replied and bowed.

He'd met Bokaard four years ago, and, after serving a year or so together, they had become good friends. He grinned and grasped his friend's right hand, laying the other on Bokaard's left shoulder, in the Atalanphian way of greeting friends. He felt his moodiness lift a little and stepped onto the ship with a lighter heart.

'We'll have victory this time, my friend,' Marakon said. 'Then you can sleep all day and party all night once more.'

Bokaard barked a laugh. 'That'll be a first. It was only last month when I saw you running for the decks with five of 'em dark devils on your tail. No doubt I'll be racing to save you again this time. And that's if you survive the trip there, you white belly.'

Bokaard's laugh was infectious. White belly was what the Atalanphians called anyone suffering from seasickness, and the mere mention of it churned his stomach. He hastily checked for his pouch of hessel leaf and relaxed when his fingers touched the coarse fabric. What kind of seasick soldier ever got promoted to commander, he didn't know. He spent half his time onboard every ship trying to mask his seasickness, and the other half trying to work out how he could ever get out of being a commander. Something that, despite his seasickness, his superiors would never allow him to do.

'Half of them are well-seasoned. The other half are new and barely able to swing a sword,' Bokaard noted as they watched the rest of the crew board.

'The Goddess help us,' Marakon sighed. 'And it's too soon between battles. All of us are tired.'

Bokaard snorted. 'I should be going to bed about now,' he looked up at the brightening sky. Marakon grinned.

Within the hour they pushed off from the dock and headed out into the open sea.

Marakon stood at the prow, breathing the cool, fresh air deeply as it rushed past him. Soon the wind was strong, and the sails billowed until taut. The calm sea of the coast became rougher out in the open ocean, and the waves splashed white and frothy against the bow of the ship.

After an hour, when they had lost sight of land, he looked behind. Bokaard was busy at the wheel, his eyes hidden behind sunshields, and the rest of the crew were busy manning the sails and ropes. Satisfied he was not being watched, he turned back to the ocean, lifted his eyepatch and closed his good eye.

All he could see was a blur at first. Slowly the focus came, but he could make nothing out other than endless an ocean. He could see at least twice as far as the captain's spyglass, and though Bokaard suspected something odd about his eyes because Marakon was always the first to spy land, the captain never much about it.

He looked down at the waves slapping the bow. What did the elf girl and the old woman mean? They were right, somehow, and the more he thought on it, the more he felt there was something he had to do, something important he had to remember. Something was missing in his life, and he had to find it but he couldn't for the life of him think what it was.

Perhaps he should find a witch or priestess who could see into another's past lives. No, priestesses scorned such things, and witches were a mixed bag. He'd be better off approaching a seer. They were light workers, they would be safer. Seers were as adept in magic as wizards, their male counterparts, were, but they were far more secretive, incredibly rare nowadays and hard to find.

The visions from the old woman were so strange and real. She'd said he was a king. The memory of the raven pecking out his eye made him shiver. She'd said they were good omens, but why did it attack him? A sharp pain stabbed him in the eye again, as it had when the raven pecked at it.

'Everything all right, sir?' One of the sailors frowned down at him from the rigging above.

He realised he had clamped his hand over his eye. The terrible stabbing pain receded. He dropped his eyepatch.

'Yes, thanks. Sometimes it pains me,' Marakon muttered.

'No doubt it does, sir,' the soldier nodded. 'I can still feel me fingers throbbing,' he held up his left hand to reveal two missing fingers. He grinned, revealing many missing teeth as well, then scampered up the high ropes and onto the mast like a squirrel.

He turned his thoughts to the mission ahead, mindful to keep his eyes on the horizon, the real reason he stood at the bow. The sea was choppier now, and he keenly felt the lurching of the ship in his stomach. He pulled out the hessel leaf pouch and held it to his nose, breathing in the pungent aroma. Then he pulled out a small handful of the dried leaves, unstoppered his water flask, and sprinkled them in. After shaking the flask for a few moments, he gulped it down quickly, trying not to taste the foul liquid.

He caught Bokaard's eye, who was standing at the wheel, sunshields low upon his nose. The big man smirked, shook his head and mouthed "white belly," his teeth flashing white against the smooth darkness of his skin.

Marakon sighed and grinned sheepishly.

An hour or so later, when the hessel leaf had started working, Marakon stood beside the captain at the wheel.

'It's an aggressive move,' Bokaard said. 'We haven't attacked so far to the north of the southern islands since we lost Haralan. I would have picked a smaller, less northerly island,' he shook his head and chewed on his Atalanphian cigar. The thick smoke smelled of the hot, dusty desert from which it was from.

'At least the enemy will be as surprised as we are,' Marakon said. Bokaard chuckled. 'It's good to attack, to keep the enemy on their toes. Hopefully it won't be well guarded because of our attacks further east. They won't think we would dare venture this far north yet.

'Those Maphraxie dogs have enough expendable bastards to set up camp in every corner of Maioria,' Bokaard growled, unconvinced. He squinted as he constantly adjusted the wheel to counteract the flow of the tide and the tilt of the ship in the swell.

'It's a bit of a gamble, I agree,' Marakon pressed on, 'but I think our commanders are right on this one. Less Maphraxies and caught off-guard could mean victory.'

Bokaard huffed. 'I'll believe it when I see it.'

'When we've anchored and made it to shore, we'll move over the island. Once we've successfully made the halfway point, runners will head back to the ship and give the orders for the fleet to sail round to the western side, ready to send in reserves if needed,' Marakon said.

It wasn't a bad plan, it just relied upon too many unknowns, all their plans did. How many Maphraxies there might be, where they were concentrated at any given time, where they were most likely to attack next, whether the Feylint Halanoi would be facing magic wielding necromancers or dark dwarves, deadly Dread Dragons or Maphraxie grunt soldiers—they never had much to go on. He didn't speak his thoughts aloud, he didn't need to add to the big man's scepticism.

'It's always so difficult,' Bokaard said, grimacing. 'Our spies cannot infiltrate Maphraxies, our wizards cannot penetrate the enemy's minds no matter how hard they try, for who can read a dead mind? And always, always, the Maphraxies seem to know what we, the Feylint Halanoi, are doing. I'll bet they have spies amongst us, or some evil wraith that we cannot see taking down our plans and reporting back to that immortal bastard. They make our plans of surprise attack mostly useless.'

'I know,' Marakon said sourly. 'It's as if Baelthrom himself watches and calculates our every move.'

'But still we have to try,' Bokaard's shoulders slumped. 'What else can we do? All we have against an enemy this large and this strong, are small attacks to nip at the beast's hooves and then flee. Chip away at them slowly.'

He joined Bokaard in silence for a while, both scanning the horizon for the familiar peaks of the southern islands, or the long black shapes of enemy ships. The wind was blowing cold now, and he pulled his scarf higher to cover his nose, his cheeks red and burning from the chill. Bokaard seemed not to notice and stood with collar down and gloveless, a grim expression set on his face.

'Remember in the old days when we took prisoners?' Bokaard said, his face breaking into a grin.

Marakon barked a laugh. 'Yeah, let's hope we never go back to that. Those abominations are best put out of their misery as quickly as possible.'

Bokaard chuckled. 'Ugh, they stank out the ships for days after,' he grimaced. 'But I'd prefer a stinking Maphraxie Grunt to one of those cursed necromancers. Pure undead evil. I could feel them draining my soul with their eyes. They didn't even flinch in torture. It was as if they enjoyed the pain.'

'You don't mess with black magic wielders,' Marakon nodded. 'Kill them straight off as quick as you can before they take your soul away. Not taking Maphraxie prisoners is the smartest move the Feylint Halanoi ever made.'

CHAPTER 18

You are my Goddess

ISSA yawned, stretched, then winced when her wounds complained. She was painful and stiff all over and needed a week of rest just to feel normal again. Karshur was gone, returned home, its task complete after millennia of waiting. It was Karshur and the power of the dark moon that had freed Keteth, not her. She couldn't bring herself to think that she had killed him.

She touched the mark upon her chest. It was tender. She undid a few buttons of her shirt. In the centre of her sternum, there was a silvery-blue mark, about the size of a copper coin, and it gleamed softly. *The vortex of the heart... the portal between dimensions.* She craned her neck to try and see it more clearly. *The raven mark...* There was indeed a faint outline of a raven flying, the familiar heavy beak pointed to her neck, wings stretched wide, the unmistakeable wedge-shaped tail. Would it ever go away? It shimmered, and she thought it was actually quite pretty.

A'farion... *touch the raven mark with the talisman. Then will you find yourself far from the living, in a land of shadows not of Keteth's making.*

Would the enchantment take her back to the Shadowlands? She shivered. Perhaps she wouldn't try it just yet. A strange gift, but one that might save her life. Or end it. She had not expected anything from Karshur the elf, had not really thought much about him at all. He'd given his life and bound it to the dagger, rather than flee and live peacefully in the Land of Mists. Still, the elves would not listen to her, and they would not fight. How would they ever be able to stand as one against the Maphraxies? How could they ever be free?

The morning came quiet and still. Even the birds were lazy today for they had not yet started to announce the dawn. She breathed in the fresh forest air that came in through the window, the smell of pine was rich and invigorating. She reached over, peeked through the curtain and smiled. Asaph lay on his side with his bare back to her and beyond him lay Coronos, both sound asleep. On the other side of the room was another curtained enclosure, which she assumed was where the elder Karalanth slept.

She wondered of what they all dreamed, and lay back down quietly, enjoying the peace and quiet and chance to think. She should get back to Celene as soon as possible. Ely and Freydel would be worried. She could send word before then, maybe. Freydel had taught her how to scry with a mirror and pool of water, but she had never tried it alone. Edarna would know the White Beast was gone for sure. She should scry for her too.

The Isle of Celene would be her home now. She felt good there, and it was an island like Little Kammy, albeit much hotter and humid. But Little Kammy would always hold her heart. Would she ever return? She didn't want to even if she could. She was so different now, and everyone she knew back there was dead. Poor Ma, poor Tarry, poor, poor Rance. She closed her eyes, the pain raw.

Ely had lost loved ones, and Asaph had lost both his parents, his whole country in fact. And what about all those enslaved by Keteth? The annihilation of the Ancients...? So many had died at the hands of the Maphraxies, she wasn't alone.

How little I knew of the world, Ma. I wish you'd told me. But even if Ma had, would she really have cared? To the islanders, the mainland was so far away it may as well have been another planet.

Fraya would always be her mother, but her blood mother could still be alive somewhere out there. Maybe she could find her. The thought had her pulse racing. Maybe she could help her understand who she was; why Zanufey spoke to her, and what it was she was supposed to be and do. Her real mother could tell her about her father too.

Ma had said she was a seer, but what exactly was one of those? She knew witches and fairies but had never met a seer. Freydel had said so little, only that they were magic wielders and lived on the Isle of Myrn, wherever that was. She closed her eyes and tried to recall that old map in the classroom, but still didn't remember where Myrn was. Somewhere east beyond Frayon, and probably completely over-run with Maphraxies.

She sighed and her mood sunk. It would be near impossible to find her mother, even if she was alive. Maybe Freydel could help her. Yes, she must get back to Ely and Freydel as soon as possible, and tell them all that had happened.

Sunlight spilled through the open window, and the air was warm and heady with the smells of late summer. She swung her legs out of bed just as Asaph peeked through the curtains. She squeaked and covered herself with a blanket.

'Can I have my shirt back clean, please?' he said quietly, grinning at her.

She half-grinned, half-scowled at him, feeling her cheeks redden. Who did he think he was walking in like that without announcing himself? But her scowl softened into a blush under his humorous gaze.

'It could do with a wash,' she agreed. *And so could I.* She smelt of seawater and sweat.

'It's good to see you looking better,' he said, still grinning. 'You even have some colour in your cheeks, though you could do with fattening up.'

'Hmph,' she grunted. A double insult. Didn't he have any manners? And yet she found herself beginning to smile as she looked up into his eyes. She had no idea that eyes really could be that deep and blue. She stood up, still hugging the blanket.

'Is there some place I can wash? And where in fact are we?' she asked.

'There's a stream with a small pool close-by, but it's cold. I can show you if you like,' he said. 'We're in a Karalanth village, deep within the western forests of Frayon.'

'Frayon,' Issa said in wonder. 'I tried so hard to get here for so long… and now I simply wake up and find myself here.' Now she was here, she wished she were on Celene.

'You and me both,' Asaph gave a wry smile.

She started to walk, refusing his proffered arm, only to stumble on unsteady legs. He caught her, and she felt her cheeks redden again. Gaining her balance, she walked unaided and tiptoed past a softly snoring Coronos. She made it outside and stumbled again.

'If you left the blanket, you might find it easier to walk,' he suggested. Issa hugged the blanket tighter. 'You didn't seem to want it last time you got out of bed,' he added.

She stopped and looked at him, the memories flooding back. His cheek was still blush-red from her slap. She grimaced, mortified.

'It's all right, though. You weren't very well,' he said quickly.

'I'm so sorry. I didn't mean to…' she began and then frowned. 'What happened to my clothes? And how did I get here? I don't remember anything after the Maphraxies attacked us.' She wanted to sit down. He took her arm, supporting her gently.

'When I found you, you were wearing nothing more than rags,' he said.

She felt her face just get hotter. He seemed startled by her look and added, 'I gave you my shirt. You were freezing to death.'

'Thank you,' she said tightly, and strode off, her legs wobbling and taking away any dignity she might have had.

'You don't have to be embarrassed,' he called out.

'Hmph,' was all she could think to say.

Asaph stood there confused at her actions as she stomped off. So much for saving someone. Why was she being so difficult? Had he done something wrong? Maybe she didn't like him. That last thought worried him. Maybe they just needed longer to get to know each other. Hopefully, then, their relationship would be easier. She had suffered a lot, more than he knew yet. Which was why they needed to have a good long chat about everything. Things would be fine then, he nodded to himself and ran to catch up with her.

They passed a Karalanth with her young son. Their fur was a rich red and her antlers tall and majestic, whilst her child's were small and only two-pronged. They both glanced at Issa and smiled before turning their eyes respectfully away. They looked so odd Issa had trouble trying not to stare at them. She nodded her head by way of greeting and hurried passed, feeling smelly and bedraggled, wondering how she must look; all dirty, dishevelled and wrapped in a blanket.

The pool was small but deep and fed by water trickling over rocks from above to create a miniature waterfall. Willow trees grew along the banks, dangling their leaves into the water. She turned to look at Asaph expectantly.

'Oh, er, I'll wait here by the trees and check no one is coming,' he said hurriedly, suddenly seeming flustered. 'Don't worry I'll, uh, respect your modesty,' he gave a weak smile and turned his back to her.

She decided against telling him to leave since she didn't feel all that strong, and the deer people were disconcerting, though they surely meant no harm. She sat down on the blanket on the bank and peeled off her bandages. The flesh had healed so well, barely any scars remained. They still ached and itched, though, and were tender when touched. Whoever had tended her wounds was clearly adept at healing. Perhaps it was more than that, she thought, touching the silver leaf bracelet.

Ely, Keteth is dead. We won. She smiled, wishing she could see her friend.

She slid into the cool water, feeling very much alive as she submerged her head, and delighting as the salt, dirt and dried blood washed away. She checked Asaph's back was still turned before she slipping off his shirt and her underwear. She set about scrubbing them against each other. They needed soap, but she had forgotten to ask for some. For now, the water would have to do.

From the pool she watched him. She should have been friendlier, but she felt too embarrassed. She hardly knew the man and already he had seen her mostly naked. She didn't really want anyone looking at her naked when she was unconscious, or conscious for that matter, even if she knew them.

Though she preferred dark-haired men like Rance and Tarry, Asaph was undeniably attractive; tall and broad-shouldered, chiselled chin and eyes so blue they were like the sky on a clear day. Perhaps that was why she was so embarrassed. When he was near she felt dizzy, and she ended up saying all the wrong things and feeling awkward. She chewed her lip as she tried to sort out her emotions.

There was so much she had to do, so much she had to be. The whole world was at war and losing… It seemed pointless, maybe even wrong, to imagine what a life with Asaph would be like. She almost laughed aloud. On Little Kammy she was begging Ma to be married, now the very thought of a husband seemed silly.

Tarry had been the closest to a boyfriend she'd had, and they probably would have married and lived out their lives on Kammy. How different her life had become, she could never have imagined. Rance had done no more than flirt with her, and now he was dead. Could she really risk anyone getting close to her? Could she bear it if they did and then died horribly? Perhaps to think of Asaph as any more than a friend would be a distraction and a worry she didn't need.

She tugged on a strand of hair, wrapping it around her finger as she tried to understand her feelings for him. She couldn't bear the thought of him being harmed. She sighed, feeling relieved through logic. Maybe in a different life, in a different time, they could be together, but not this one.

So much had happened since she had left the shores of Little Kammy. She had changed, it was almost as if she had become a different person. Now she had an inner strength and a hard resolve. Before, she had been naive and ignorant and very much afraid.

Even now she could feel the power of the Flow that surrounded her, whereas before she had never noticed it. She wondered what the Flow must have felt like when it was full and untainted before the orbs had been created. Maybe it felt like when the power of the dark moon filled her, exquisite, divine, omnipotent.

She opened herself to the Flow. Magic energy pooled within her; the energy of the plants and trees, the water, the rocks—all had their own magic that flowed around and through her. She felt something move in the Flow, a golden light that pulsed and then dimmed. She released the Flow and looked up at Asaph, startled.

'What's wrong? Is everything all right?' he asked worriedly.

'Yes, everything is fine. Why?' Issa folded her arms over her breasts. Had he sensed her in the Flow?

'I thought I felt magic, coming from you. I thought you were in danger,' he sighed in relief, and then looked at her wistfully. 'I didn't know you could use magic until I saw you and Keteth.'

'I didn't know you were a dragon,' the thought scared her. 'And you can use magic too.'

'No, well, yes, but only when I'm a dragon. I can still sense it, but it's greatly diminished.'

'Freydel the wizard taught me,' she said. 'Well, the ability was there, so he said, he just helped me open the door. I've been able to control more each day. How could you tell I was using it?'

'Freydel the wizard?' he was surprised she had met him. 'Coronos said that he was probably the most powerful wizard in the Known World.'

'Maybe,' she said. 'Freydel never really talked about himself. He found me after Keteth attacked us. Somehow I made it to Celene. I think the Wykiry helped. He saved my life.'

She realised then how little they had talked and how much had happened since they were last together. Why had he never bothered to come and find her? She remembered now why she had slapped him, feeling somewhat more justified for doing it.

'What happened to you, then? You found me in the Shadowlands, only to plunge us into the jaws of Keteth. Why didn't you come and find me on Celene?' anger tinged her voice.

'No, it wasn't my fault, and that's not how it was—' he began. 'We only just escaped Keteth, only just. If it weren't for Coronos and his orb, then we wouldn't be here. The Wykiry came and took you, and then the orb couldn't reach you. I fought Keteth and would have lost were it not for Coronos. After then, I would have died of my wounds if it weren't for these Karalanths and a travelling seer. For days I wandered a terrible place… They thought I would die. Don't you remember coming to me?'

She saw his anguish and felt guilty. 'Yes, I remember that dark place…' *Asaph within Keteth's death embrace…* she shuddered.

'You called to me,' she said, 'through the ring. I had to come, I couldn't leave you. Zanufey was with me, I'm sure. In a way, I think it was the Raven Queen who came to you and not I…'

'You and she are the same. One day you'll realise that,' he said. 'If you hadn't slain Keteth, we would both now be enslaved.'

'I'm thankful beyond measure that you're here, fit and well,' she said. 'I thought I would never see you again. You know I wouldn't have survived the Shadowlands.' The thought of that wraith-filled place made her shudder.

'Thank you for finding me there,' she said and smiled.

'A pleasure. Hopefully we can do it again sometime,' he chuckled, but then his face grew serious. 'I *have* dreamed of you my entire life. Don't be alarmed, I don't fully understand either. There's a lot we have to talk about, but maybe another time, before you go cold and wrinkly,' he grinned.

He was looking at her funny, and she felt her cheeks reddening. She remembered with a start that she was naked in the pool, and the water was only just covering her breasts. With a mortified gulp she submerged herself completely.

Asaph turned away before she could see his face turn red. The sight of her had his pulse racing. He found her beautiful, and it was hard not to stare, hard not to think about anything else, the way the water rippled around her pale shoulders and above her breasts. She looked so vulnerable, trembling in the water, that he wanted to jump in and hug her, tell her it was all right. She would probably slap him again if he did.

'Can you pass me the blanket?' a meek voice came from behind. 'Just put it on the rock by the water.'

'Sure,' he reached for the blanket and glanced at her, unable to stop himself, but she had her back turned. He left the blanket by the rocks and walked away.

When she was wrapped in the blanket, he took his dripping shirt from her outstretched hands and suppressed a smile when she held her head high and imperious as they walked back towards the village.

'It's the best I could do without soap. I'll need to find some new clothes,' she said, looking somewhat worried.

'Maybe we should go naked like the Karalanths,' he grinned.

Only some of the deer men and women wore short hunting-type tunics, and he doubted she would go bare-breasted. The look on her face confirmed it, much to his dismay.

'I'm sure we'll sort something out,' he said, but all he got was a "hmph."

There was something different about her, he thought. Something had changed, though for better or worse he could not tell. It was in the small things; the way she tossed her head, the way her eyes shone from within, the smile upon her face that spoke of untold secrets or an understanding of ancient knowledge. There was a subtle yet strong power that exuded from her. But it wasn't like he knew her before, anyway.

The girl he loved, who had called to him in his dreams all his life, was now a woman, a woman of untamed ability, and he was a little in awe and fear of her. Would he ever be a part of her life? When the world was at war, would their treacherous paths be by each other's side like he wanted? It was a question he could not answer.

She had stopped to return his stare.

'Asaph? Are you all right?' she said. 'You seem lost, or something.'

He took a while to respond. 'You're different to when we last met, somehow. Your demeanour, your eyes... It's like you have become alive, more alive, or discovered some great ancient mystery. Maybe it's the goddess in you. I'm not explaining it very well,' he shook his head, feeling like an idiot.

She was looking at him seriously, clearly not thinking him an idiot. Her gaze became far away.

'I can barely describe what I've seen in a sacred place,' she breathed. 'I saw the mind of divinity. I saw whole peoples upon many planets rise to wondrous heights and beyond, and some fall. I saw worlds created and destroyed, whilst others lived on eternally. I saw beings made of light and love who can never die, and I saw the darkest horrors and beings who know only to bring death. I saw it all, I was it all, I created it all and all in the blink of an eye.'

Emotion overwhelmed her, and a tear fell down her cheek. He reached up and touched it, felt the dragon within stir, and saw her eyes widen as she saw it too. His ancient, dragon-self understood more than his limited human mind and tears filled his eyes.

'I can only catch a glimpse of what you speak. You are my goddess,' he whispered, wanting nothing more than to touch this living goddess, and she did not resist. He drew her into an embrace.

Together they shared a moment in eternity, like a pearl of light held between them both as the world stood still. The moment passed, and they realised they stood in the village with Karalanths walking by them nodding knowing smiles.

Issa reluctantly drew away from his embrace. Would there ever be time for them? She gasped, remembering the Orb of Water. How in all Maioria could she forget a thing of such power and importance? What if it had been taken?

'Is everything all right?' Asaph asked.

But she was already running back to Triest'anth's house, struggling with the blanket. He ran to catch up. She burst into the now empty hut, and frantically searched around the bed, but there was no sign of the orb.

'If you're looking for the orb, Coronos is taking care of it for you. He wants to talk to you about it,' he said.

She sank down onto the bed with a sigh of relief, suddenly feeling dizzy and weak.

'You're pale again. You need food. I'll sort it,' said Asaph and scampered out the door. Yes, she definitely needed food.

Asaph had only been gone minutes but returned swiftly carrying a tray laden with bread and fruit and a mug of something hot with leaves floating in it. He set it down beside her and hurried off again. She sat cross-legged on her bed and tucked into the food. He was gone longer this time, but when he returned he held a bundle of clothes.

'I got what I could, but it wasn't easy,' he said sheepishly. 'They don't wear many clothes.'

'Thanks,' she smiled uncertainly. Reaching into the pile, she pulled out a hardened tunic like the Karalanth huntresses wore. 'Hard-wearing for sure, but there's not too much of it.'

'It'll look great on,' he said. She raised an eyebrow.

'It's a girl's size, apparently. The Karalanths are somewhat broader than us mere humans,' he said.

Next, she held up a finely woven square of mid-blue cloth and looked at him questioningly.

'Er, well, we can turn them into, er, riding trousers. They are surprisingly good with a needle, so Triest'anth said, and make all sorts things like, er… sacks, and er… blankets. Hah.'

She sighed. He was doing a poor job of convincing her, but he'd done his best and she was being ungrateful.

'Thank you. I'm sure we can make them fit,' she smiled weakly.

'I'll wait outside' he said and left.

She wrapped the blue blanket around her waist and tied it like a skirt. It would do for now. She slipped the top over her head. The strings that tied it, immediately entangled her arms. For such a small thing it was remarkably complicated.

After several minutes of breathless struggling, she wrenched it down and sat panting. She pulled the strings at the front closed. It exposed her midriff, making her feel vulnerable, but it was otherwise soft and comfortable against the skin. Luckily it was summer otherwise, she would be freezing. It would do until she could buy some other clothes.

Buy… The thought of money sent her to her bedside. Her blacksmith's belt was there beside her bed, and a quick search revealed her money pouch still inside one of the zips. At least she could buy clothes and food. She strapped it around her waist, feeling protected and warm now her midriff was covered.

She went outside. Asaph was sitting on the grass polishing his sword. It was not the sword she had given him to fight Keteth, the sword she had held at her anointing. This sword was plain and simple but looked solid and strong.

'Where is the other sword? The one with the red pommel?' she asked.

He stopped rubbing the blade and stared off into the forest. 'Coronos says it's somewhere hidden in Draxa, the capital of Drax. Or at least it should be. I long to go there, to see my birthplace and find the sword.'

He looked at her, then stared her up and down, bringing crimson to her cheeks. She smiled shyly, secretly enjoying the way he looked at her.

'I can sew them for you,' a timid voice came from behind, making her jump. She hadn't even heard the Karalanth woman arrive. The Karalanth had wrinkles around her hazel eyes and grey in her light brown fur and hair, hair that fell half way down her back.

'I'm Lys'ynth' she bowed.

'I'm Issa. Thank you for the clothes,' she said and held out her hand in greeting. The Karalanth looked at it quizzically and then embraced her. Taken by surprise, she returned the embrace.

'Right. I'll go find Coronos,' Asaph said, making his excuses to leave as

Lys'ynth busied herself adjusting Issa's clothes.

'It's an honour to welcome guests to our home, particularly one blessed by the goddess,' Lys'ynth said.

Issa felt uncomfortable at that. She felt powerful in her visions and dreams, and when the dark moon was with her, but when those things were absent she felt very different; indecisive, insignificant and very normal. A far cry from the dragon-scale armoured Raven Queen she was supposed to be. Did everyone really think she had jumped straight out of the scriptures?

Maybe it was enough that they believed in her, even if she doubted. After all, she *had* killed Keteth, and Zanufey *did* speak to her. An image of the Raven Queen flickered in her mind, face cold and hard, and dressed in dragon scale armour.

She suddenly wished she were someone else, someone normal. Someone who could spend a life with Asaph, someone who was not the Raven Queen. *If only someone else could be chosen.* She pushed her thoughts away, there was no comfort to be found in her own mind.

'We women have seen many things in the fires of our rituals,' Lys'ynth said as she folded and sewed the fabric. 'Take heart, Queen of Ravens, you have many friends. From the people at your side to the beasts of the wood. Woetala protects you too, child, for all aspects of the goddess pay homage to the Night Mother, who leads her children through the darkness into the light.'

Issa smiled, but because of the apprehension that had come over her the smile didn't reach her eyes. Something moved within her and made her speak.

'We all have to unite against the Maphraxies, from men and women of all races, to the beasts of the wood and birds of the air. The only question is, will they come? Will you come?' she asked.

'Of all the peoples on Maioria, Karalanths alone await the goddess's call,' there was fire and determination in Lys'nth's eyes. 'No matter how few we may be, we will fight and die to take our land back.'

Issa put a hand on the woman's shoulder. She wanted to cry. 'Daranarta, the leader of the elves, refused, but maybe there is hope in others.'

'I know nothing of the ways of elves,' Lys'nth said, 'but when the war comes to them, they will have no choice but to fight.'

'I pray your homeland will be restored to you, one day, and the Maphraxies and dark dwarves driven from it for good,' Issa said.

She remembered in her eternal state seeing the rise and fall of empires, the plight of many peoples. Somewhere in the future, there was a timeline in which they were free. All she had to do was reach for it, ask others to reach for it, and there would be the chance of freedom. Those lands laid waste by the Maphraxies would flourish again one day.

'We must always believe we can be free, we must always reach for freedom.'

'I can add nothing to that,' Lys'nth smiled, hope bright in her eyes.

Within the hour Issa was happy. She finally wore a pair of loose trousers. She prayed to Woetala that the Karalanth clothes would last longer than the others she had worn over the past few weeks.

CHAPTER 19

Ancient Land of Dragons

FOR Marakon and his soldiers, the hours passed uneventfully. The current was in their favour, and with the added help of two wizards' magic, a good wind spurred them on. The second day passed in the same way as the first, although the small southern islands had now been spotted.

Fortunately, so the crew seemed to feel, they had not seen a single Maphraxian ship the whole journey. But for Marakon, rather than relief, it made him tense. Where was the enemy? Where were they hiding? As the hours passed, the tension built until even the crew felt nervous.

To their left, the southern islands of Drax passed like shady lumbering beasts. Some islands were very small, mostly black and grey rock and only a few hundred feet wide or so. Others were massive, stretching so wide that they seemed like the mainland. They were covered in hardy tundra; thick, gnarly gorse and stunted evergreens growing in sparse, salty soil.

'There should be thousands of seabirds this far away from civilisation,' murmured Bokaard as he scanned the silent islands devoid of any life. 'This place is becoming more wasted every time I come here. I'll bet even the fish are dead.'

Marakon nodded. 'The immortals lay even the grass to waste. It's all blotched and diseased,' he noted how the gorse had patches of brown and grey.

The sea had turned unusually calm and a low wind blew just strong enough to fill the sails while the wizards rested. The calm silence only added to the tenseness of the crew. There was no sight of the enemy, no ship on the sea, no chimney smoke on the horizon. The Feylint Halanoi had never come so far north without coming under attack before.

Another hour passed with virtually no change in the weather or scenery. Then the shrill hail of a sailor at the top of the mast called out the sighting of Haralan. A few minutes later the familiar peaks of Haralan's rocky hills came into view.

The ten Atalanphian ships stayed out of range of Haralan as the captains surveyed the enemy-held lands, and awaiting Bokaard's direction. With spyglass to his eye, Bokaard spent so long staring at Haralan, it seemed to Marakon that he had become a statue. Unfortunately, there was nowhere he could stand to discretely pull up his eyepatch. He was just about to consider climbing a section of rigging when Bokaard spoke.

'I see nothing. No smoke, no movement, nothing.' His voice was grim, and Marakon wondered if he had been hoping for battle immediately. He too would prefer something rather than nothing.

'It appears dead and empty, like everything else around here,' Bokaard said, dropping the spyglass and slotting it shut.

'Get ready to anchor,' Bokaard shouted his orders and the crew scampered to ready the ship.

They anchored out to sea facing a large sandy cove. Twisted hardy sand pines dotted the island between the rocky hills.

'Once more we approach the ancient land of dragons,' Marakon murmured. 'They used to live on these islands and all the way up to the northern pole.'

'And I'm well pleased they are gone,' Bokaard grunted. 'I've never trusted lizards, not even flying ones.'

Marakon chuckled. 'Come now, under Draxian rule they had become quite tame.'

'And I don't trust humans that can turn into dragons either,' Bokaard glared as he hefted the wheel.

Raft boats were lowered over the side and boarded, leaving Bokaard and a skeleton crew to manage the ship. The other ships did the same so that thirty raft boats filled with soldiers approached the sheltered shore. Marakon eagerly watched the land, knowing that once he set his feet on it, his churning stomach would finally settle. The beach was deserted, or at least it appeared that way.

'It's better to suspect an ambush than not,' he spoke his mind aloud.

The soldiers shifted uneasily in their seats. He turned away, lifted his left eyepatch and scanned the shore looking for the tiniest movement, any sign of Maphraxies. A fern leaf moved, catching his attention. He stared at it, willing it to move again. It did not. Only the wind moved through the trees, creating a peaceful rustling belying their violent mission. It was as if the island was barren of all life except trees. He let his eyepatch drop and signalled to land ashore.

As soon as the bow scraped the sand, he jumped out with the other soldiers. A single rower remained to take the raft boats back to the ship.

'You four,' he whispered to those closest, 'take branches and cover our tracks.'

They moved up the beach into stunted foliage, the four soldiers whisking branches over the sand and mud behind them. Haralan, unlike most of the other islands, used to be more abundant in its flora, even supporting a few small evergreens before the Maphraxies came. The black sand was a testament to the volcanic activity that had created these islands several thousand years ago. The volcanic earth provided richer soil for a greater array of plants, and its relative abundance was the reason why it was once one of the few inhabited islands of Drax.

He looked at a few withered trees, spotting the familiar grey canker. Yes, only Maphraxies inhabited this place now, the original people slaughtered or captured years ago.

For a day and night, the Feylint Halanoi searched the island, taking only a few hours of rest amongst the bushes of stunted gorse. They saw and heard no one and nothing. The only thing of interest found was the burnt-out remains of an old fort and village nestled on the south of the island. Closer inspection revealed that it had been destroyed years ago. Only half a blackened human skull remained to prove that people had been here. It didn't take much to imagine what had happened to the rest of the population. There was no sign of the enemy, and all was silent.

Marakon, hand poised permanently above his sword, tried to reason it out as he and Lanac skirted their way around the village. The field they walked through was filled with dead crops and sickly-looking weeds that crunched under their boots. Though Lanac also looked ready to grab his sword at any moment, there were dark circles under his eyes, and he yawned frequently. The young man broke his brooding silence with a concerned question.

'I thought there had been reports of Maphraxies on Haralan a week or so past, but now there is no sign of them. Did they discover our attack plan and flee?'

'There had been reports,' Marakon confirmed, 'and no, they wouldn't have fled.'

'Is it a trap?' Lanac gripped his sword and looked behind.

'Relax,' Marakon said. 'I've been wondering about it since we arrived. If they had made a trap, we would be in it by now. Besides, the Maphraxies don't make traps. They've never needed to in the past so why should they now?'

'You mean they left this outpost of their own accord?' Lanac didn't sound convinced.

'Possibly,' Marakon nodded. 'Which leaves us only two questions. Why did they go and how long have they been gone?'

Lanac looked about him as if searching for a sign. 'But there's nothing to find because they leave nothing behind.'

'They held this island for a long time despite our most ferocious attacks. We'll find something,' Marakon said in certainty, his face grim as they neared the first blackened and burnt house.

The look on his face must have silenced Lanac for he said no more. Marakon glanced behind him and saw two more soldiers just breaking the brow of the hill. Beyond them were another two cresting the previous hill. He signalled that he was going inside the house. They nodded and dropped their hands to their pommels. They entered through the hole that had once been a doorway.

'I've never seen a Dread Dragon before,' Lanac said, inspecting the burnt stone closely.

'Lucky you,' Marakon said grimly.

'In fact, I've never seen a dragon at all. Look here, its fire has melted the stone,' Lanac said excitedly.

There was nothing except the stone structure of the house. The wooden beams and windowsills and all the furniture had been incinerated. The smell of soot and ash made them cough.

'Nothing here,' Marakon coughed. 'Move on.'

They walked the dusty path between the destroyed houses, checking each one, but there was no sign of Maphraxies.

'Perhaps there's something in there?' Lanac pointed to a structure at the end of the road.

It was so destroyed, it was difficult to tell whether it was a warehouse, a town hall or a farmer's barn. They peered into the dusty darkness, swords drawn. He didn't expect to see the enemy, but it never paid to be caught off-guard. His eyes had adjusted, and he stepped silently through the doorway. Lanac shuffled close behind him. Sunlight trickled through cracks in the wall, making it just about possible to see. Nevertheless, the younger soldier clattered into him when he stopped. Marakon shot him a look over his shoulder.

'Sorry,' Lanac whispered as their armour clanged.

He turned back to the gloom. He'd forgotten his half-elven sight helped him see in the dark. He padded over to a partitioning wall, peered around, and saw what he had been looking for.

'Goddess rest their souls,' he murmured.

'Great Mother,' Lanac said, the colour draining from his face.

Along the far wall were ten wooden platforms raised up and tilted at ninety degrees. On each platform, dressed in rags, was a child, hands and feet tied to each corner. A strap bound back their heads and their mouths were forced open with a piece of wood making them look like they were howling. Each child was pure white like chalk, even their eyes, lips and hair were white. They glistened in the dark as if crystallised. The oldest may have been eleven, the youngest only two.

He was dimly aware of Lanac retching behind him as he approached the bodies. This was what he had been looking for, this was what Lanac had to see. As much as he hated to show him, the young man and the new recruits had to see what the enemy did, how they went about making Sirin Derenax.

He looked down at the crystallised face of the closest child. The semi-translucent curls of the young girl's hair were like carved crystal. She could be ten, or younger. He reached to touch those shimmering curls but thought better of it.

'Like an angel,' he breathed.

Beside her was a boy with the same delicate little nose. Maybe her younger brother. He could not have been past five years old and reminded him of his own sons. He didn't know why, the boy didn't look like his children. Perhaps any young dead boy made him think it could have been his son. Anger seethed into his guts, and his head began to pound.

'They're so young,' Lanac said, wiping his mouth. His sword trembled in his hand as he came to stand beside Marakon.

'The Maphraxies have no need for child soldiers, they're small and weak. The Sirin Derenax can only make an adult body grow big and strong.' Marakon kept his voice matter-of-fact, in case he broke. He had seen this before, many times, but it always affected him the same.

'And children before puberty make the best Sirin Derenax,' he growled. 'Something to do with the purity of their soul, I…' he swallowed down the rising fury, 'I don't quite know why, but that's what they do.'

He stared at a crack where the light was falling through, wishing the Maphraxies were here so he could take his vengeance.

'No don't,' Marakon said too late as Lanac touched the girl's hair.

He snatched his hand back as the body crumbled into dust. Then the dust disappeared, and nothing remained of the girl.

'How the...' Lanac gasped, his voice trembling.

Marakon looked away to hide his glistening eyes.

'They have no soul, fool,' but his chiding held no real malice. 'The only thing that remains of them is in the memories of other people. Their life essence has been stolen from their bodies, from every single cell. They have been frozen, crystallised, into dead light. At least that's how our physicians and wizards explain it. Nothing can save them, nothing can bring them back. Their souls are gone.'

Lanac stared at the empty platform where the girl had been and swallowed. 'Children of the islanders?'

Marakon shrugged. 'Maybe. More likely brought here, caged alive like livestock. I guess the Sirin Derenax is best made fresh.'

'Sir, come look at this,' a woman's voice called.

Marakon grasped Lanac's shoulder as he passed. On the opposite side of the building was another partitioning wall. Two female soldiers were bent down and examining something on the floor.

A female dwarf soldier, Fren was her name, and an older human man named Darad, stood watching above them, faces frowning in morbid fascination. Fren was as fierce at fighting as she was at drinking. Marakon avoided the bar whenever he saw her there, which was often, so he didn't know her too well. Darad was a quiet man and had probably shot more arrows than he had spoken words. He was one of his most senior officers on this excursion and his best archer.

The woman who had spoken stood up. She was middle-aged, tall and heavily built. Erylin, her name came to him. She was a new officer, usually serving in the Feylint Halanoi ground armies, which was why he'd only briefly met her once or twice.

'This is where they made some of it,' she said, wiping the sweat from her cheek and leaving a smear of soot. She passed him a dark glass vial. He took it gingerly, more afraid of touching the foul stuff than she was.

'The top is cracked,' he said, noting the sharp fissure.

'There are four others, all broken,' the younger, smaller woman said, still kneeling down. Her light-brown hair was braided and hanging over one shoulder.

The vials lay scattered amongst burnt debris. Marakon could smell that strange sweet acrid smell of the Sirin Derenax and it made his soul shiver. He wondered if the others could feel the taint of black magic, of necromancy, that all elves could feel. Only Darad looked like he wanted to be gone as far away as possible from this place. The dwarf simply scowled, her gauntleted hand clenching and unclenching the haft of her axe. Marakon felt like them both; he wanted to flee this place and yet fight and kill every Maphraxie in the land.

'What did you find over there,' the dwarf jutted her chin towards where he had come.

'The victims,' was all he said.

Silence descended as they stared at the broken vials. Marakon broke the silence.

'To most of us, this is nothing new. We all know the enemy and what they do. To fight and die is the choice we made. To be taken alive by one of them is never an option. This we are all taught in the first training camps. Now we have a reminder why. How long have they been gone?'

'Not more than a week,' the younger woman said.

'You're a tracker?' he asked.

'Yes, sir.'

He nodded. 'Then our only question now is; will they return? If you ask me, I can't wait for revenge,' he muttered as he left the room.

Marakon licked his lips. He was annoyed at what was looking like a wasted trip. They all wanted to fight. Was this the only kind of victory they would be allowed to have? Maybe it was true what people whispered in the inns late at night, maybe the goddess did indeed favour the enemy. Maybe Baelthrom was there to cleanse the land of them. Maybe many things, he thought irritably. *I'll leave those thoughts to the priests and priestesses in their temples far away and safe from this bloody battle.*

They moved less cautiously now through the charred remains of the village and discovered nothing more. The stone walls of the houses still stood, predominantly, but the thatched roofs and wooden beams were all gone. An inn's sign still hung half-hinged, burnt and illegible, and its rusty hooks screeched in the bitterly cold wind. It wouldn't take much to fix the place and make it habitable again if crops could be grown.

They ate a simple lunch of dried fish, salted blue seaweed and dried apricots. Afterwards, Marakon walked alone until he came to stand at the edge of the village where the land fell away into the sea. Steep cliffs dropped down to an ocean swell that pounded on the rocks. He scanned the horizon with his left eye, looking for ships both friend and foe, as he tried to fathom what the enemy was up to.

They had left at most a week ago, and he suspected they were nowhere nearby either. Why they left was a mystery, they had never left any gained ground before, so why now? He sighed. It was becoming obvious there was no point staying here, but he was under orders to at least sight the enemy. He could not return until then, yet he had no orders to push further north towards Drax. It would be suicidal to go deep into enemy lands.

If he sent half his ships back to base, taking some of their supplies aboard the others, they would have enough food to last a month. With only half of his soldiers, they would probably travel quicker as well. Travel where though? There was no point going east for the same reason there was no point going north, it went straight into Maphraxie strongholds. There was only home or west.

Erylin and Darad came up to him. He dropped his eyepatch and turned to face them. Erylin carried her helmet under one arm. Her hair was mousey and slightly longer than shaved off completely. A scar ran from the top of her forehead, into her hairline and down to her ear. Darad also carried his helmet and also had a scar, a vivid red one that ran across his chest, just visible through the loosened collar of his chainmail. Marakon knew that that scar ran from his left shoulder down to his right nipple.

He grinned at them and under their querulous gazes he said, 'What a bunch of scarred bastards.'

They looked at each other and grinned. 'Perhaps that's why we're still here,' Erylin said in her sharp northern accent and rubbed her scar. 'There's nothin' like a Maphraxie blade to teach you a thing or two about survival.' Darad grinned at her.

'So, there are no Maphraxies. What do we do now, Commander?' she asked.

'There's still no sign of Bokaard and the other ships, though the runner will have reached them by now,' he said. 'I expect we'll see them in the next few hours. Our orders are to at least sight the enemy, which we have so far failed to do. If we turn back now, it will be a wasted mission, and yet we've been told not to go further north or east beyond Haralan.'

'It would be a suicide mission if we did,' Erylin said.

'My thoughts are to head due west and search the other islands.

Perhaps the frontline has moved,' he said.

'What about reforming a base here?' Darad asked.

'I would if we had the resources,' he agreed, 'but we were sent here as a war party, not a settlement party. I've no orders to reform a base here. However, the sooner our leaders know this island is free, the better. It's my thinking that we should send half our ships and soldiers back to base as quickly as possible to report on what we've found. They can then send a recolonisation party here if they want.

'We'll take the supplies that the returning ships won't need, and I'll lead the other half of our fleet west until we sight the enemy or our supplies run low.'

Darad and Erylin nodded.

'I'll take most of our experienced veterans, they won't be needed on the return party, and a few new recruits to learn from them.'

'The ships are here,' Darad said, nodding towards the horizon. He turned and saw the Atalanphian ships sliding into view.

'Erylin and Darad; choose your most experienced soldiers and a few new recruits. I'll brief everyone once the ships have dropped anchor and we're ready to board.'

'Yes sir,' the said in unison.

Once aboard, it took the rest of the day for the supplies to transfer between them to those that would be travelling west. The soldiers returning showed a mix of relief and disappointment in equal measure, whilst the others expressed only excitement.

That evening, Marakon stood watching the sun set. *Blessed Woetala, please don't let my boys end up like that.* He thought of the dead children in the warehouse, their crystal white faces and soulless eyes were burned into his mind. Seeing the atrocities committed by his enemy made him stronger, his resolve hard as iron. It was the fury that had kept him alive for so long, he was certain of it.

When it was fully dark, they set sail, five ships headed south back to Frayon and five headed west. The Atalanphian captains were happy too. Having rested most of the day and now travelling at night, they were in their element.

CHAPTER 20

Histanatarns

FOR three days they sailed west, following the islands south of Drax, but there was no sign of the enemy. By the fourth day, the islands curved north, signalling their approach to the vast expanse of the Lost Sea, and it was not without a feeling of dread that Marakon looked out across that endless blue. Somewhere out there he feared the White Beast still lurked.

The wizards had informed them that Keteth had been destroyed, something to do with the dark moon and a magic-wielding woman. But he found it hard to believe that the monster who had plagued the world for so long and destroyed their greatest heroes, could be killed just like that by some unknown person.

'A hundred years ago, this sea was teeming with merchant ships and fishermen,' Bokaard said. 'My grandfather said the trade between Drax and Frayon kept the whole of Maioria flourishing.'

'He came this far north?' he turned from the sea to look the big man in the eye.

'He was a Farsea Gold Trader,' Bokaard explained. Marakon nodded. Farsea was the official name given to long-distance merchant traders.

'Trading gold with dragons was the hardest and most dangerous trade of all. Dragons are not known for their bartering skills and have no ability to control their temper, much like Draxians,' Bokaard grinned. 'But if done well, and my grandfather was one of the best, one trade would set you and your family up for life.

'My father after him was also a Farsea Gold Trader, but only briefly before he became a captain of warships much like this one. We had so much gold in the family and yet no time to spend it. When this cursed war is over, maybe I'll be a Gold Trader too.'

Marakon barked a laugh. 'You and me both. We'd be the richest in the land. But don't worry, I'd always let you bargain with the dragons...'

Bokaard grinned, his white teeth gleaming in the light.

Marakon turned back to the ocean and his humour dissipated. Before him stretched the endless sea. Would the Maphraxies be so far out to sea away from the living, the source of their Sirin Derenax? He doubted it. There was no choice but to return to port. A failed, wasted, mission. If they were to head to Drax, they would need the whole Feylint Halanoi army and an extremely well-planned attack. It was highly unlikely the enemy would have left Drax as well. Something was up and not knowing what irritated the wits out of him.

'Damn it,' he sighed, slapping the rails. 'No sign, nothing. Captain, your thoughts?'

Bokaard lifted his sunshields and squinted across the glittering ocean. He was quiet for some time before he spoke.

'Not into the Lost Sea. Keteth or no, there is nothing there but endless ocean. Orders are "to sight the enemy." If it were up to me, Commander, I'd turn north and follow the islands as close as we can until we either see the enemy or spy the towers of Draxa.'

Marakon nodded. 'Yes, it's risky, but that's what I think. How far until we can expect to see the city?'

'Unless the wind picks up, five more days,' Bokaard replied. 'But then again, the wind always picks up this side of Drax, blowing in hard from across the Lost Sea. So I'd say four, maybe three.'

Marakon nodded. 'Sight the enemy... I've never failed an order before. What if they spot us?'

'They won't be expecting us,' Bokaard said, 'and being few in number, the wizards will be able to cloak us as we turn and run. These ships are the fastest ever made. It's risky, but I see no choice other than returning on a failed mission.'

Marakon rubbed his beard. 'Sight the enemy, mission accomplished. Let's do it.'

No sooner had he finished speaking, Bokaard was barking orders to the crew. The change, of course, was signalled to the other ships. All five ships turned northwest, and the wind filled their sails. He watched the islands slip past. Those dotting the south-west tip of Drax were treacherous and numerous. It was no surprise that the seas adjacent to this coast were named Lost Souls' Rest. The wind and waves were savage in winter, and only the toughest rocks seemed to be able to withstand the pounding. The ships kept well away from them as they moved past.

'When was the last time you sailed here?' Marakon asked. Personally, he had never been this close to the mainland of Drax. 'They can't have sent the Feylint Halanoi this far north for years.'

'I was a boy, and it was not a year before it fell to Baelthrom,' Bokaard said. 'I remember it to this day because I was so terrified and excited to see a dragon. When I saw the great green lizard, I wet myself,' he laughed.

'I did too. Though mine was black and stank of death,' Marakon grinned. 'I thought Draxa was not accessible by sea?'

'It isn't, except to the king and queen,' Bokaard smiled mysteriously. 'There are secret tunnels that lead from one or two tiny coves, and only the king and queen and other such special types are allowed to know. My grandfather, father, and I were once such "special types," because we were on an important journey to deliver a message from our then queen of Atalanph, and a gift of gold.

Drax's east coast was under attack, so we were given royal permission to approach the western coast. Do not ask me what the message was, none of us knew. For everyone else, Draxa was only accessible across land, from the bays along the southern tip, over the Ember Plains, and through the narrow passes of the Grey Lord.'

'A remarkably impenetrable place to anything that does not fly,' Marakon said. A thought occurred to him. 'Then you are one of those few who knows about the secret tunnels?'

'Possibly,' Bokaard shrugged. 'Though I couldn't tell you where they are, because we were blindfolded. And, anyway, the tunnels were hidden by magic and opened by magic.'

Marakon sighed in disappointment. His vision of attacking Draxa via the secret tunnels suddenly dashed.

'It's my hunch, Commander, that we *will* see Dread Dragon scouts long before we set eyes on Draxa. As soon as we so much as glimpse one of those devils, I recommend the wizards cloak our presence and we turn back the way we came as fast as possible. We'll need at least ten wizards to take on just one of those bastards.'

Marakon agreed. 'It always was a big risk, and one day our risks will get us killed. But every time we defend rather than attack, we miss an opportunity to push the enemy back. And I'm tired of defending.'

Bokaard said nothing for a while as he continued to man the helm. Then he took a deep breath.

'Just make sure you spot those bastards long before they see us.'

Marakon had an uneasy night trying to work out what the enemy was up to. The winds were strong and from the rocking of the ship he knew they were making good progress. The light coming through the porthole was growing, and with a sigh he got up to meet the coming dawn.

'We had to turn west to avoid the rocks,' Bokaard said. Dark rings under his eyes said he had not had much sleep either.

Marakon looked at the vicious black rocks breaking the surface to their right. Some lay treacherously just under the water.

'The only grave stones of the lost souls,' Marakon said. 'Sight the enemy, then back to port for a good night's rest and a settled stomach. That's what keeps me going.'

He couldn't wait. The queasiness had started early today, brought on by poor sleep. He was just about to leave the deck to get his hessel leaf pouch when a sailor cried out from above. He was high up the mast, dangling like a monkey, shouting and pointing to the western horizon.

Bokaard grabbed his spyglass and Marakon ran to the side of the helm. At least a dozen black specs dotted the horizon. While Bokaard was busy with his spyglass, Marakon lifted up his eyepatch and stared at the strange looking boats hurtling towards them.

Histanatarns, no mistake. Though they had human-like bodies, they somehow seemed closer in appearance to fish than people. He could see clearly their nutmeg-coloured skin with that unmistakable green gleam. They had scales rather than human flesh, and their ears fanned out from their heads like small fins. Their fingers and feet were webbed, and they had spikes for hair. They were smaller a than humans, and slender to the point of skinny, but wiry and strong. Some say they were the unholy alliance of human and fish, though no one could prove it. They were coming in fast.

'How come we didn't spot them sooner?' Bokaard said, peering through his spyglass.

'We didn't see them because they weren't there. What do you see, Captain?' Marakon said as he dropped his eyepatch, knowing full-well what the captain saw.

'If we weren't so far east of their cursed kingdom, I would have said Histanatarns, Commander. But they're moving too fast. Nothing moves at that speed on water.' Bokaard passed him the spyglass. 'It must be magic.'

'Not a magic that we know of,' Marakon growled, putting the spyglass to his good eye. He found it weak and hazy. 'Histanatarns, no doubt about it. Those bastards have come a long way east. Maybe even in league with Baelthrom, and without Drax to give them a beating, this ocean is their own.'

Bokaard spat in disgust. 'Everything on Maioria loathes those vicious, greedy bastards. Well, I'll never be a sacrifice to Ex, their god of death. Fight and die. None of us will end up in their blood rites, and nothing will be left for them to steal.'

'I've always wondered what happens to those captured, none have ever escaped alive to tell us,' Marakon said. 'All we have to go on are the accounts of those who can scry. They say the victims are sacrificed at the end of some strange ritual. No wonder we scare our children into behaving, otherwise the "sea devils" will get them.'

Bokaard grinned. 'Yep, my mother knew how to keep me in line.'

Marakon stared at the approaching boats. They were low and flat and had no sails, so how did they move so fast?

'We cannot outrun those boats,' Bokaard said.

'And why should we?' Marakon grinned. 'No Feylint Halanoi ever fled from Histanatarns, and we're all itching for a fight. Prepare for battle, Captain. It looks like fish for lunch.'

Bokaard laughed deep and loud as Marakon passed him back the spyglass.

'Prepare for battle,' Marakon yelled. 'Enemy to port.'

The crew scrambled to his orders, and Bokaard took the helm with a devilish grin.

In a matter of minutes, the Atalanphian harpoons were at the ready, their vicious tips shining in the sunlight as they pointed out from the gunwales. Those tips were set with explosive enchantments, which is why they shone so brightly.

The small Histanatarn boats numbered in their fifties, and despite the five large, menacing and fully armed Atalanphian warships now awaiting their approach, they did not slow. The Feylint Halanoi were outnumbered, but aboard each ship were some of the best and seasoned soldiers Marakon had, and they were hungry for battle. Like their name, the Feylint Halanoi, meant, "freedom or death," they were ready to fight and die.

He gripped the pommel of his sword. The thought of battle after so long at sea filled him with relief mixed with the usual knotting in his stomach. He had hoped for Maphraxie blood today, but it seemed these fish dogs would have to do.

The Histanatarns slowed and spread out, stopping just out of range of their arrows and harpoons. Their pale yellow boats were long, thin and shallow—not built for long journeys for they offered no shelter or place to sleep. Had they come all the way from Histanatarn?

He couldn't see any paddles or sails to explain how they travelled at such speed in the water. They seemed to be powered by something spinning on the stern. It looked like a long hollow drum on its side, like the wheel of a windmill. Just under the first wheel, he could see another submerged in the water. Maybe more ran on the underside of the boats, but he couldn't see. The faster they turned the faster the boats moved, churning up a large spray behind. Two rudders were attached either side of the wheels. He noticed a shimmer around them, the tell-tale signs of enchantments.

So they used magic to power the boats, and that suggested wizards aboard them. He scowled, he had only two magic wielders to counteract them, and neither of those were that experienced in combat magic. They were skilled in weather management; more wind, less wind, wind in a different direction type of thing, and in cloaking magic.

He discreetly half-lifted his eyepatch and continued his swift analysis of the enemies' vessels. If he survived this day, he would detail the ships to his superiors and wizards so they could copy the design and add them to their fleet.

Aboard each boat sat at least twenty Histanatarns. Snarling like animals, they brandished their long spears—spears complete with a barbed hook to make sure they stayed stuck in whatever they pierced. The spears shimmered with more enchantments.

He dropped his eyepatch. If there weren't so many of them, it would have been a fair fight. Bokaard turned to look at him, and the crew waited in silence for their orders, their eyes locked onto the enemy. Sweat beaded on their faces, though it was cold. His small band of five ships, each carrying fifty soldiers aboard, sat bobbing on the waves drifting further into the Lost Sea and further away from land.

Only seconds passed, but it felt like hours. It always seemed remarkably still and calm in those few moments before the violence—something that always struck Marakon as profound. He considered his options swiftly; the calm silence would not remain forever. The Histanatarns remained out of firing range, which at least showed they were wary. Their lances could easily sink through the enemy's small boats if they came within range.

A short high-pitched bark from one of the Histanatarns sent his adrenaline surging. In a blink half of the Histanatarns jumped ship and disappeared into the water, leaving their long spears aboard the boats.

So, they attack first and plan to board and fight on *our* ships. Though why they left their spears behind was a mystery. They would be armed with knives, though.

He barked orders and pulled his sword from its scabbard. Soldiers scuttled to obey, readying their weapons for close contact. Axes were lifted, ready to cut the hooks and ropes that would soon fly over the sides. He checked a dagger was still hidden under his shirt and another tied to his thigh. He bent to check another blade always stowed beneath the captain's wheel, but it wasn't there.

Bokaard winked at him and tapped under his thick coat. The big man carried lots of knives. They both knew the Histanatarns were dirty fighters. The enemy darted under the surface as quick as fish. They were soon in easy range.

At his orders, a shower of arrows cut through the water. Like a shoal of fish moving as one, the Histanatarns dived deeper to escape the arrows. Dark patches of red blotched the surface where some had not been quick enough. They surfaced under the ships, hugging the curve of the hull closely so the archers could not get the angle to shoot them.

Their thin metallic ropes with barbed hooks shot out of the sea and hooked onto the deck. Soldiers ran to cut them loose as the enemy started climbing. They hacked at the rope but it would not cut and instead left notches in their axes.

'Enchanted, sir, or something,' screamed the nearest soldier, who then fell back slashing his axe as a Histanatarn swung up in front of him. Rather than hacking the ropes, they were now forced to hack at the enemy. The Histanatarns were small and nimble, and swung adeptly on the ropes, dodging their blades. The decks soon teamed with them, and the bloody battle began.

Two green-scaled Histanatarns swung over the side and approached Marakon, each brandishing a curved, wickedly sharp blade. He swung his sword, forcing them back from him. Another high-pitched cry came from the enemy still aboard their boats. They had come closer now that the soldiers were too busy to fire the harpoons. At another scream, those spears left behind were now raised and aimed. They couldn't possibly be in range of those hand-held spears, but he dared not risk it. He yelled out an order as he slashed at his foe.

'Man the harpoons, open fire! Quickly now.'

Those able and nearest the harpoons jumped to do his bidding, and in seconds they sprang into action. The harpoons shot forwards. Hastily aimed, many fell short, but some hit their targets. They slammed into the wooden boats and exploded. Soldiers cheered. The enchantments had worked. Wood, sea and blood sprayed into the air as eight boats were obliterated and several more heavily damaged.

Dozens of spears fell from the sky. One struck inches into the wood, not a foot from where Marakon stood. The closest Histanatarn also narrowly missed it. Many spears found their targets; the enemy had had time to aim before firing at the exposed Feylint Halanoi.

A squat soldier in front of him—he recognised her as the female dwarf from the Haralan excursion—stopped swinging her sword and turned with a look of surprise on her face. She took one step forward, staggering against the spear that had struck through her neck and out of her ribs. He couldn't help her. All he could do was stare as she dropped her sword and toppled over the side of the ship, immediately sinking from the weight of her armour.

He growled, and he lunged forwards, his sword slicing into the belly of a Histanatarn. In a rage, he chopped down another and didn't slow until he came upon the one she had been fighting. It howled in battle-fury and came to meet him, its strange, glassy yellow eyes gleaming with hatred. He struck so hard and so fast his sword all but fell through the Histanatarn's flimsy armour. He whirled to face another as it fell gurgling to the floor.

Now he understood why they had left their spears aboard. The enemy now on deck yanked their spears free from their bloody targets and used them as weapons along with their knives.

In his peripheral vision, Marakon saw many of his soldiers fall in the onslaught, but the only emotion he was able to feel was an all-consuming battle fury as he, like everyone else, fought two Histanatarns at once. Everything was a blur. He had no idea where Bokaard was, but the man was a tough fighter. Another screaming order cut through the din of clashing blades and screams of pain. He glanced behind and saw the enemy taking aim once more.

'Take cover,' he screamed.

He lunged forwards, sinking his sword between ribs, and in one smooth motion hurled it sideways over the side, noticing absently how the sea was turning dark with blood. He whirled to face another who jumped before him, then slammed back against a mast as spears peppered the deck.

Despite his warning, many failed to find cover in time. Some were impaled to the deck, trapped by their own limbs. They made easy pickings for Histanatarn knives. It was some respite that, despite their speed and fearless ferocity, it still took two Histanatarns even to have a chance of bringing one of his soldiers down. It evened out their numbers somewhat. At least they would take many Histanatarns with them before they died.

'Fire. Fire at will!' He screamed, not even knowing if anyone was able to man the harpoons.

To his relief, harpoons blasted from the gunwales again, this time with deadly precision. The ship rocked sideways with the blast. Scores of enemy boats exploded in sparks and fire. The harpoons were being reloaded, but many Histanatarns now jumped from their boats as they fired again. More boats exploded, but most of the Histanatarns were underwater and heading to the Atalanph ships.

The enemy streamed over the sides, and the fighting became cramped and desperate. Screams, shouts and the clang of metal filled the air as the sun reached its zenith. Blood and gore slopped over the decks, and both Feylint Halanoi and Histanatarns slipped and fell, turning the battle into a savage kind of drunken brawl.

He nimbly dodged the blade of a Histanatarn who had jumped in front of him out of nowhere, only to find himself sliding the same distance. He staggered against the railing and steadied himself, barely striking back that flashing blade. He punched his pommel into its face. Blood sprayed. In the same motion, he grasped his second blade from his sword belt, and drove it upwards. It found home in the soft underside of the Histanatarn's chin. Surprise replaced the hatred in its eyes.

He twisted the knife and jerked it free. The Histanatarn shuddered and fell to the floor, blood spurting from its neck. Another set upon him immediately and another somersaulted over the side of the ship behind. He was forced to whirl around to keep them both in view. They approached him slowly, eyes glittering, webbed feet splayed, making them more stable than he was in the slippery blood.

He licked his lips, eye darting from one glistening blade to the other. He could take two at once, but they came from opposite sides. He lunged towards one and slashed as he passed, but the enemy dodged his blade, as he knew it would. He whirled around and had both before him. Slowly, with his sword raised ready, he backed away to buy some time and let them think he was afraid. They continued to advance until his back touched the mast. Not taking his eyes off them, he sheathed his second blade and wound his free hand above him around the rigging.

One lunged at him. He parried the long curved knife and shoved his boot into its chest flinging it back hard against his companion. At least he thought it was a he; it was impossible to tell. Perhaps if he'd had more time, he would be able to see what was male and what was female. Whatever they were, they recovered quickly and lunged at him.

At the last moment, he jumped and heaved himself up and away from their slashing blades. At the same time, he sliced his sword down and around with such speed and force he beheaded one and sliced through the skull of the other. Blood and grey matter spewed over the deck, and his stomach heaved. He landed back on his feet, but there was no rest as more came for him. He tried to pull his arm free from the rigging to reach his knife, but his hand was stuck. Cursing savagely he tried to yank it free.

Pain seared his right side as a tiny blade sunk between his lower ribs. It only just missed his lung, and his vision blurred in agony. He fought to control his senses as hot blood soaked down his clothes and pooled in his boot. He turned to anger to shut out the pain and swung his sword. The Histanatarn dodged it but slipped, giving him the second he needed to hit him on the shoulder with the pommel. He felt a crunch as the shoulder collapsed and the Histanatarn screamed. He drove down again with his pommel and the Histanatarn fell beside the others.

Panting hard, he wiggled his arm loose of the rigging and fumbled for the knife in his side. Grimacing, he eased it out. Hot blood spurted over his fingers and his vision swam sickeningly. His eyes stung from sweat and blood and he lifted his eyepatch to wipe it away. Ripping off part of his undershirt, he tied it firmly around his side to stem the flow. There was little he could do, the battle was nowhere near over and at this stage he couldn't tell if they were winning or losing.

For a moment, no Histanatarns approached. Leaving his eyepatch off in the hope that he would see more clearly without it, he ran to help the nearest soldier. In his haste, he stumbled over the body of a young soldier sprawled atop a dead Histanatarn. Lanac was gone. Anger and remorse hit him. His tanned skin was grey and blood smeared.

He wanted to reach down and close those blue eyes, but there was no time to do it. That made him more furious. His eyes rested upon another unmoving young soldier, the plaited hair of the young tracker woman all matted with blood. A spear still stuck out of her pinning her to the deck. Another young man's bloodied face he did not recognise lay beside her.

Many of the younger soldiers were dead, despite the efforts of his seasoned soldiers to protect them. Being outnumbered left them only able to protect themselves. It had been his decision to bring them along. The guilt was his to shoulder. If he survived this day, that guilt would come to him in his quiet moments and rip him apart. He let the relief of battle consume him. If he was busy fighting for his life, the guilt couldn't come. He could still feel rage though, and he nurtured it as he swung his sword.

In grim fury, he fought as savagely as he knew how. His wound bled heavily, and every move made him weaker. The Histanatarns had lost many, but still, they came on. A blinding headache was setting in too, just to make things worse. It hammered so hard his white eye ached. He didn't pray much, but the gravity of the situation was sinking in, and he found himself saying a silent prayer to Woetala, and to Rasia, as his blade flickered in front of him.

He glimpsed Bokaard in the distance, fighting with his heavy Atalanph axe. The big man crushed his enemy more than he sliced them, taking two out in just one swoop, but he too was struggling against the smaller, quicker, and more numerous foe. Sweat and blood poured down his face, but there was still fire in his eyes, and he lacked or hid any serious injury.

They had drifted out into open ocean, and the land was nowhere to be seen, even with his white eye. It was better than being swept back onto those black rocks, he thought, thanking the goddess for small mercies. But with the open water came rougher seas and the clear, sunny skies were now becoming overcast with rain clouds. The ships had also become separated, though all remained within sight.

He almost admired the enemies' stamina; they would fight and die just like the Feylint Halanoi. It was the perfect making of a long, bitter and bloody battle. The ships and all they contained would be a great prize for them, as were the skulls and bones of their enemies that they would use to decorate their temples and give as offerings to their war god.

He thrust and parried, slower and slower, his aching muscles turning to lead. The pounding in his head grew worse. The tiredness moved him past caring if he lived or died—a dangerous place to be. All he could focus on was hack, slash, kill and move on—which was why he didn't notice the black shadows passing overhead. Later he would wonder whether he'd assumed them to be seagulls. Not that it mattered. It was too late by then, too late by far.

When he glanced up, his heart lurched in his chest. His legs trembled, and he fell back against the mast, unable to breathe. They were not clouds or seagulls but gigantic black dragons, and what he felt in his trembling soul was dragon fear. Paralysed by fear, he watched the Dread Dragons swoop low. His headache reached its peak and he sagged. Histanatarns and Feylint Halanoi alike, succumbed to dragon fear, ceasing their fighting as they froze to the decks. So, the Histanatarns feared them too, he thought as his heart hammered in his chest.

The Dread Dragons circled lazily above them, their huge wings longer than the length of an Atalanphian ship. He could see clearly their long craggy heads, horns striking up along the snout and becoming great black spikes on the forehead.

Out of the clouds, seven more Dread Dragons dropped. Unlike other Maphraxies, the Dromoorai were not hunched and deformed, but upright. They did not act crazed but were controlled and cunning. Their faces hidden forever within thick three-pointed helmets, and their eyes, like their steeds, burned lava-red and alight with something that was not life.

The Dread Dragons came so close, their bone-raking cries drove Marakon to his knees and to his chagrin his bladder emptied itself. The clatter of armour told him he was not alone in his terror. He groaned, closing his eyes and stuffing his ears to be rid of the terrible sound, but it seemed to echo within him. Their screeches cut through his headache and became a shard of intense pain seemingly meant only for him. He clutched his head as if to stop it from splitting apart.

Screaming came from everywhere, and despite the agony, his eyes were forced open. He did not understand what he saw. All of the Histanatarns had fallen to the floor, but were writhing and howling in pain while the Feylint Halanoi were just frozen in dragon fear. There came a flash of red from each Dromoorai—he was sure it came from the blood red amulets they all wore—and then the Histanatarns exploded into fire. Some clawed their way off the decks and flopped over the sides.

What was happening? Were his soldiers to be taken as slaves? But the pain and fear scattered his reason. A Dread Dragon overhead was so close he could smell its stinking breath. It screamed, and pain seared into his mind. He sprawled as consciousness slipped away, but all the while his white eye remained open as if under a will of its own and watched all.

CHAPTER 21

Maphraxie Spy

HAMEKA tried to control the growing frustration. He stood within his cabin aboard the sickening swaying Maphraxian ship somewhere off the west coast of Frayon. He was not given over to emotions he had not allowed himself to have, but the frustration forced itself upon him anyway, irritating him further.

He smoothed his hair back and inhaled sharply, composing himself in front of a mirror. It wasn't that he disagreed with Lord Baelthrom's orders, it was more that, lately, they had changed too frequently and with too little notice. How could you maintain control of an army when you had to continually dictate new, and radically different, orders to your commanders?

His initial orders were, "Start a permanent settlement and Sirin Derenax production plant on Haralan." A day or so later it was, "leave Haralan and go south"—so far south, in fact, that they may as well be going to another planet. And by doing so, they were leaving to the Feylint Halanoi precious islands that they'd not long held.

That was just part of his irritation on this windy, rainy evening at sea. Most of his annoyance came from his lord's fixation with that dark haired girl causing a nuisance in the west. He had glimpsed a hazy image of a skinny pale wench—barely a woman—in the Key Stone. It was highly unlikely she was the cause of the trouble or the source of the new power, and even less likely that she had, in fact, killed that big slug. Regardless, Keteth was a buffoon and a hindrance as it was, and whoever *had* killed him had, in reality, done them all a favour.

However, trying to convince Lord Baelthrom that she was no threat to the might of Maphrax had fallen on deaf ears. His lord had instead pointed out that it was actually Hameka's limited human view of the world that was the problem. He conceded his view of the world was limited, especially when compared to his lord, but *human*? The very analogy of himself to one made his blood seethe. He hated humans, hated himself for being one.

But he would never disobey Baelthrom's orders, knowing that his lord saw and understood far more than he could possibly fathom. Something that always made him hold his tongue and dutifully accept his orders, even if he did not like them. So, following those orders, he had filled their fastest ships to brimming with Maphraxies, dark dwarves and necromancers, and immediately embarked on a ludicrous mission to find her. *Her,* a needle in a haystack, and their enemies' haystack at that. Less a needle in a haystack, more a thorn in his bloody side.

If she was strong enough and driven enough to even *try* to destroy Keteth, then she would never willingly join the Maphraxies, he was sure of it. They would have to destroy her. He rubbed his temples as the irritation grew. He had to be rid of her. If she was half as powerful as Baelthrom seemed to think, then extracting her elixir would be a joy. He might even take it himself.

Perhaps if Baelthrom really focused his energy on the Frayonesse continent, like he was currently focusing on the stupid girl, it would be theirs by now. He wisely kept those thoughts to himself. There were some positives, though. Even though he hated the sea almost as much as he hated humans, with their best necromancer wizards aboard, they had reached the southern Lost Sea in days and not weeks.

The Key Stone hanging on his chest was still warm from a recent communion with Baelthrom, a short communion detailing their whereabouts. It glowed a dull reddish hue, telling him that Baelthrom still watched silently through the Shadow Master. Hameka did not mind his lord's absent watching; it made him feel powerful and important.

He'd spent most of the day in his cabin, despite the rocking of the ship making his stomach churn. His cabin was small, but it was the largest onboard, and even had a desk and chair built into it. Three drawers on one side of the desk contained his few belongings. He fidgeted. It was too hot this far south; cramped and sweaty and suffocating. He was used to the cold frigid wind and snow of Drax. He had hated the cold when he was there, but now he could think of nothing better. At least he could think straight in the north, even if he was frozen. This damn heat dulled his brain.

He looked down at the map he had been studying. He had been studying the bloody thing the entire cursed journey down here. He now knew the west coast of Frayon, and all its inlets and outlets, as well as he knew the veins and creases on the back of his hand.

The only places left unstudied of the Known World there were no maps for; the Kingdom of Fire to the south, the Kingdom of Ice to the north, the Ocean Kingdom to the east, and the Uncharted Lands to the west. It was popular belief that no people inhabited these places and that the environments were so harsh only a few hardy animals could survive.

He believed little of what he heard, though, and planned to lead the Maphraxies to those undiscovered places, claim them himself, and set up bases. But that was a long-term plan, after Frayon had fallen, after he had become fully immortal. Yes, he had made a promise to himself that he would not become immortal until the last stronghold of the bloody Feylint Halanoi had fallen. Frayon must fall, and the quicker it was done, the better.

He opened the top drawer and picked up the tiny dark blue vial, his fingers trembling with desire as he did so. He tilted the bottle, the fluid itself was extremely viscous and black but glowed with an aura of brilliant white light. A star captured in a bottle. Baelthrom himself had captured that star. He laughed, even looking at the Elixir of Immortality was addictive. He actually didn't enjoy the feeling of addiction because it meant he was not in control. He fought and overcame the lure of the elixir. It was akin to winning a battle, triumphing over the enemy which was his desire.

How many souls had it taken to make just that amount? It was the most exquisite and expensive of all the elixirs ever made. Twenty souls? Fifty? Some might say a hundred. It took one hundred human lives to make just one worthy one.

The first time he had tasted just a drop of it was like tasting exquisite euphoria. It had taken iron will, and all the will he had, to tear away the bottle from his lips and thrust it back to the excited necromancer. At the time it had been the purest elixir made to date. The one he currently held was ten times purer, and they said it could be purer still. He would not take it all until it was the purest it could be.

Besides, he didn't feel quite ready for everlasting life. He chuckled at the thought; who in their right mind was not ready for immortality? But, if he was honest, he was afraid of losing himself to it. And then losing the battles, and then his position as the right-hand man of Baelthrom. The risk, whether real or imaginary, was simply too great. He needed a clear head, and the gift of immortality made him keener.

Yes, he could wait a little longer, but every time he tasted it, it grew infinitely harder to pull that liquid away from his lips. And his body was slowly weakening with age, his joints stiffening, his hair thinning. Time was running out, but he could wait a little longer.

The necromancers said they had a new batch for the Maphraxies ready for testing. One that had fewer side effects; less deformity but the same size and strength, and a far greater intelligence not previously seen. That was exciting. He was growing tired of ordering the lumbering numbskull Maphraxies around. He could do with a few dedicated and competent commanders at his side. The dark dwarves and necromancers were not specifically battlefield focused as he was.

For the whole journey he had railed silently against the decision to travel so far south, but when they had arrived at the Isles of Kammy, he understood Baelthrom's plan. What a great blow to the enemy it would be, to strike at the enemies' unprotected side so far from the front line.

He looked at the rough circular land of the Isle of Celene. The most westerly point in the Known World. To strike a place as sacred to them as the goddess's own Sacred Isle... It would shake their confidence to the core and could be the turning point in the war. He wondered why he had not thought of it before.

So now they headed to Celene, seeking a girl who had eluded them in the clutches of a golden dragon that the Maphraxies had failed to capture or kill. They would strike hard and fast and without remorse. Any hope sparked by the death of Keteth would be swiftly snuffed out. They would find the girl and bring her to Baelthrom, and the matter would be over quickly so he could get on with the war. The thought of finally being rid of her served to lessen his irritation somewhat.

He unstoppered a bottle of fine Davonian port, and topped up his glass, swaying with the ship as he did so. He sipped it and stared at Celene. They would surround the island before first light and attack at dawn. The necromancer wizards would create a fog to hide their approach, just as they had in Drax. Then they would kill the unsuspecting inhabitants, just like in Draxa, and spare only those deemed best for elixir extraction. It would be too late for any to escape, and too soon for soldiers of any note to aid the defence. They would move so quickly that they would not have time to even arm themselves. The Key Stone upon his chest flashed and then was dull.

Hameka whipped up straight. Dromoorai in battle? The amulet always flared like that when a Dromoorai engaged in a fight. But the ship still continued its monotonous swaying, and there was no sound of the guttural barking of Maphraxies. He took hold of the amulet and stared into it.

'Show me,' he breathed, and the bloodstone obeyed.

A clear image formed as he looked through the Dromoorai's Shadow Stone. The long snaking neck of the Dread Dragon, its black scales gleaming with a metallic-green tinge, sharp onyx horns along a massive head that moved up and down with the steady beat of its wings. A blue sky half-covered with white clouds filled the rest of his vision.

The gauntleted fist of the Dromoorai rider pulled on the clanking chains that served as reins. The dragon turned its head to the left, and its neck and body followed. The world tilted and spun, and he closed his eyes from the sudden vertigo. He blinked and looked down at an expanse of ocean and five ships engaged in a battle against many smaller boats. The ships were not Maphraxian, and they were heavily armed with harpoons sticking out of the gunwales. battleships.

'Name your position,' he ordered through the Key Stone.

A deep, airy sound returned, not unlike Baelthrom's voice, only lacking the timbre as if it was trying to speak through long dead vocal chords. An analogy, he realised, that was probably close to the truth.

'Southwest of Drax, northeast of the Lost Sea,' the Dromoorai replied without embellishments.

'Go lower,' he commanded. 'Stay out of range.'

The Dromoorai obeyed and angled the Dread Dragon lower.

'The Feylint Halanoi,' Hameka sneered, recognising the Atalanphian ships and the annoying Feylint Halanoi tabard of a golden shield on a red background. 'And what a pity the Histanatarn sea dogs are too numerous. An embarrassing loss if ever I saw one.'

The Histanatarns were no match for the Feylint Halanoi, but when outnumbered by three to one, as they seemed to be from his aerial vision, the odds were against the Feylint Halanoi. He felt about the Histanatarns as he did about harpies—disgusting creatures. Yet, watching them destroy his favourite enemy was good entertainment. Nothing was more fun than watching the destruction of humans. *Let them destroy each other. It means one less battle for us.*

The Histanatarns were not in league with Baelthrom but they never fought against the Immortal Lord or his armies, and so were considered no threat. They would be forced into submission when the Maphraxies extended their reach westwards to the Uncharted Lands. Something that would be a lot easier now without Keteth.

The Histanatarns were almost too feral, too animalistic, to be allies to the Maphraxies. It would be like trying to form an army out of ogres; they only answered to their leaders and did not have the brains to make deals with outsiders. They probably didn't even understand immortality. He snorted at the thought.

The Dread Dragon turned in circles out of reach of the harpoons, though there appeared to be no danger since the Feylint Halanoi were too involved in the battle to notice the dragons in the sky. The Dromoorai was clearly waiting for its next orders.

'Are the dragons hungry?' Hameka asked, rubbing his chin.

'Yes,' came the simple reply.

'Then feast,' he smiled. 'They're too busy and out-numbered to man the harpoons.'

The Dromoorai circled down, followed by the other Dread Dragons. Flames spewed forth from the Dread Dragon's mouth, and for a moment the bloodstone was filled with fire. Hameka could almost feel the searing heat in his cabin.

The masts of the enemies' ships exploded into pillars of flame, and the sails became sheets of fire. Dragon fear swept over Feylint Halanoi and Histanatarn alike, and the chaotic brawl stilled. He smiled. Even from here he could see big armoured men shaking. Their sharp and shiny swords looked small and pathetic in the face of a Dread Dragon. He wondered if their chain-mail jingled and rattled whilst they shook.

The Dromoorai circled up and around for another attack. An armed enemy had to be killed before they could be feasted upon. The world spun from sea to sky and back again. Hameka blinked and rocked in his seat, feeling sick. Flames filled the dragon's open mouth, vivid red-orange captured between black fangs as sharp and long as spears. But the flames flickered out, and the dragon faltered as if in confusion.

'What's happening?' he demanded. 'Kill them all now.'

'Spy, an Infected,' the Dromoorai breathed tonelessly.

'A Maphraxie spy? Where? Show me.'

The Dromoorai moved the Dread Dragon low beside one ship. There, sprawled face down on the deck, was a big man. He squinted into the bloodstone and saw the familiar red hue surrounding his body. An aura that was only visible to those who had imbibed the Elixir of Immortality. The aura of a human infected by enchanted Maphraxie blades to become the Immortal Lord's unwitting spy.

He could not believe his luck. So, their attempts at infiltrating the Feylint Halanoi had not failed completely. That was good news indeed. Baelthrom would be pleased. It had been Hameka's plan from the start, and it seemed to have some use. Though their victories were won faster through the brute force of numbers rather than spying, it was not without its merits. It was through the eyes of spies that the necromancers were able to see where the enemy was and outmanoeuvre them.

All Maphraxies were forbidden to kill their own spies. The Dread Dragon could not have destroyed the man even if it had wanted to. They would leave him alive and feast on the others. Perhaps it was time to create more spies, he mused.

'Finish the job,' he yawned. The entertainment was growing dull.

'Yes, Commander,' the Dromoorai wheezed.

He ended the communication through the Key Stone and let it dangle upon his chest. Lord Baelthrom would have seen everything through the Shadow Master. He got up and went to his hammock and settled down to sleep, the amulet still glowing faintly in the dark.

CHAPTER 22

King Marakazian

MARAKON wandered through a sea of mist. He could just make out the sandy ground beneath him, a few rocks scattered here and there, and not a blade of grass. He was shirtless, and his trousers were nothing but rags that flapped in the wind. His boots were in tatters. It was not cold, but he felt exposed and vulnerable without a shirt, or his sword and armour.

He neither knew where he was nor how he had gotten here. His memory of pretty much everything was blank. Had he died? Was this a dream? He stomped on the ground. It felt solid enough. It was too real to be a dream, and he didn't feel dead, but then what did being dead feel like? Was this one of those places between worlds? Though between Maioria and what else he didn't know.

He thought about the Shadowlands and shuddered. If only the mist would clear, he could see more. But it swirled around him and blanketed out the sky. If he kept walking, he would get somewhere, or the mist might clear. It could be worse; he could be stumbling through a baking hot desert or the frigid tundra of some Draxian island, or starving to death, or horribly wounded. *Praise the goddess for small mercies,* he thought sourly.

The mist did clear and became hazy swirls drifting upon an endless flat and dusty plain. He squinted into the distance. There seemed to be rocks ahead marking a change in the landscape. He went to lift up his eyepatch, but it was not there. Had he dropped it? No, he'd never had it on in the first place.

He covered his good eye and stared with his left. The rocks in the distance were still far away and blurry. He had his normal sight back, but he immediately missed his far-sightedness. At least he didn't have to worry with the bothersome patch anymore. An awful feeling stole over him. He had to be dead. But what had happened and how had he died? Why didn't he remember? Still, he felt pretty good and quite alive for someone dead. Maybe it wasn't so bad being dead after all, and wherever here was it had to be *somewhere*. He purposefully headed towards the rocks.

He felt he could walk for days, his legs were not weary, his throat was not parched, he was not even hungry. All those things only made him worry more that he might be dead. The flat, barren landscape became a path through terracotta-coloured rocks and into a craggy valley with steep cliffs rising up hundreds of yards on either side.

Dotted within the cliffs were crumbling doorways, windows and pillars. Intricate decorative carvings that looked like animals and people also adorned the rock here and there. People had lived here once, in this ancient landscape, carving out their homes in the rock. And judging by the hundreds of doorways, it seemed the people had positively thrived. Perhaps he walked the riverbed of a long dried up river, and everyone left when the water went. Whatever had happened, the people were gone now, how or why only the rocks themselves knew.

The valley led towards flatter land again and he came to the banks of a vast lake or sea—he couldn't see the horizon because of the mist that hung above it. He started in surprise when his eyes rested on the intricately carved boat beached and tilted on the sand. The prow was carved into the head of a sea serpent or dragon, and in its mouth, it held a lantern.

Within the boat sat a huddled, unmoving grey figure with his back to Marakon. Perhaps he was asleep. Thank the goddess there was someone else here in this cursed place. He trotted over.

'Hey there,' he called jovially.

He'd meant to say it quietly, but his voice echoed loudly. What if they were armed? His hand strayed to his side where his sword should have been. Well, he could still fight hand-to-hand if needed. The figure stirred at his approach but otherwise remained still and his face concealed within a deep grey hood. He stopped beside the boat.

'Hello?'

After a moment, the figure spoke in a slow old man's voice.

'Who is it that walks the Valley of Death?'

Marakon looked around him. The Valley of Death? The name sounded familiar. Had it always been called the Valley of Death? He looked back at the dwellings in the cliffs. Suddenly they too seemed familiar. He didn't want to know what happened here. He felt unnerved.

'Who is it that walks the Valley of Death?' the old man repeated.

'It is I, it is...' Marakon stuttered, and then found the words falling from his lips, 'I, Marakazian...' he frowned. That was not his name; he was Marakon, and yet Marakazian was also his name, his *real* name.

'Marakazian? Cursed King of the Banished Legion, the fallen Knights of the Shining Star?' the old man asked, surprise tinged his voice.

'Yes...' he began before he could stop himself. He shook his head. 'But I was not always called that. I was... I was King Marakazian, a Knight of the Shining Star...' He trailed off, wiped the sweat from his face. If he felt unnerved before, he felt positively scared now.

'I've spoken these words before, a thousand times before. But I don't remember when, I don't remember why... What is happening to me? What is this place?'

The hooded figure said nothing, only nodded slightly. Marakon realised then that he was waiting for the old man to say something important. *There was something this old man should say, I know it, I feel it!* He suddenly felt as if they were acting out some play, their lines rehearsed and remembered many times before.

'What is it you seek, Cursed King of the Banished Legion?' the old man asked.

He was keenly aware of the stillness; nothing moved, not the water upon the shore, or the wind, or the man before him. All was silent, waiting for his answer. It was as if a great burden was about to be lifted, the smell of freedom on the wind for a lifetime as a slave, redemption and forgiveness for a terrible crime committed. He knew the words he had to speak, *must* speak, had waited a thousand years and a thousand lifetimes to say.

'I seek a passage to my people. The sentence is served, the millennia have passed, and the time has come.'

The figure was still for a while. Marakon knew in the heart of his soul that the words he spoke had never been uttered before. Slowly the old man nodded.

'So quickly the time has passed in my realm. Very well, Marakazian, Cursed King of the Banished Legion, you must answer this question correctly to prove your right of passage to the Land of the Banished. Who is it that you serve?'

Marakon licked his dry lips. He did not know the answer to the question because the answer had never been known, could not be known, not until now. It seemed the silence deepened and the sun grew hotter, burning everything around him with a terrible oppressive heat. The heat spread over his skin and burned in his throat as he breathed.

A shadow passed overhead, and a memory flashed in his mind. He looked up and saw a raven flying, its black body in stark contrast to the brilliance of the sun. The sun turned from yellow to blue, casting all in cool, indigo light. The raven cawed. The answer was his.

'I serve the dark moon... I serve the Night Goddess Zanufey,' his words were loud in the stillness and fell like stones dropping into the stillest pond. The earth rippled beneath him and then was still.

The old man straightened his back in surprise. 'The answer is... different. You have not said those words before. The dark moon of Zanufey has indeed arisen upon Maioria. Perhaps, then, it is she who can cleanse the darkness from your soul, Cursed King Marakazian. The change has come. So be it, King Marakazian, leader of the Banished Legion.

'Perhaps the price has been paid, the sentence fulfilled. Now the hands of the clock turn once more and the hour is near. I will take you to the Banished Lands, but only you can find your people. You must find them and return to me before the time runs out. If you do not, you will be forever lost, doomed to walk as a Lost One in the endless Land of Shadows along with your Banished Legion. This is the final task to complete before you and your knights can be free. Do you accept it?'

'I accept it. I will return in time. Take me to my people,' the words caught in his throat as emotion rose and threatened to overwhelm him. *My people.* He felt as if a great weight had been pressing down upon him and was now lifting.

'What is this place?' Marakon asked.

'An ancient land. They called it Unafay. Once a place of life and beauty until the people made the Dark Rift and dark things came. Here the Demon Wars were fought, and the land desecrated. In the Valley of Death terrible things happened.'

'The Demon Wars? They were fought thousands of years ago, but no one knows where,' Marakon said.

'There's much you do not remember, King Marakazian, but you are an old soul. One of the oldest. And memory will come in time,' the old man said. 'You won't find this place within the mortal planes of Maioria anymore. It was flooded, it sank, and now it lies somewhere between the Murk and Maioria.'

'It's no surprise that Keteth created his Shadowlands where he did, between the Uncharted Lands and Frayon, where this land once existed. The place where thousands of souls died. Access to the world of the dead taught Keteth many things that had long been forgotten. Perhaps it can be made whole again. Perhaps it can rise back into Maioria. But until then it is a place where the cursed come. Cursed people to a cursed place.'

'Why are you here, then?' Marakon raised a suspicious eyebrow.

'You are not the only one who is cursed.'

Marakon considered that. He was cursed? How? What had he done and what was the curse?

'And besides, we have always met here, when death is close at hand. In fact, you are rather late,' the boatman said.

'Am I dead?'

The hooded face turned to look at him, but despite peering, Marakon couldn't make anything out within the hood apart from an ancient, wrinkled neck. The old man gave a low laugh. Though there was only humour there, Marakon felt irritated.

'Look, I don't remember anything. I just remember walking. I don't know how I got here, I don't know where I'm going, and I don't know what this curse is. I—'

The old man lifted up his wrinkled hand, motioning for peace.

'You got here because your spirit is linked to this place. You're not dead, not fully. But you are near death. It's always hard for people such as you to understand this. Better explained as a dream, only a real one, and you are your soul walking here. Just as in a dream.'

People such as me? 'Where, then, is my body?'

'Where you left it.'

Marakon gave an exasperated sigh.

'But don't worry,' the old man said. 'Where we go now, your body will also follow, for it's simply a vessel for the consciousness. And in reality, it is the soul, the consciousness, that leads the body, and not, as you have it in your world, the other way round. I know this because I am the boatman, and I traverse the oceans between worlds.'

Marakon frowned, confusion making him weary. The old man pulled out an hourglass from a sack in the bottom of the boat. His hands were shaking, and he noticed how old and shrivelled they were, older than old as if his body had died long ago but something inside still lived on. He set the hourglass in a holder at the bow of the boat. Tiny grains of golden sand began to trickle through the narrow centre into the empty bottom.

'Is that the time I have?' Marakon asked.

The boatman nodded once. He chewed his dry and cracking lips. The boatman raised a hand and pointed at him. Unseen hands gripped him and lifted him easily into the boat. Cautiously he sat down facing the figure. The boat righted itself and slid into the water of its own accord.

The boatman took up the oars and began to row. Marakon was about to offer to row instead, but the old man shook his head before he could speak, and so he let it pass. They moved out upon the water to where the mist became a thick.

'I am the boatman, and I traverse the ocean between worlds...' What did he mean? A great weariness he could not fight descended upon him, and he fell asleep.

Marakon awoke abruptly, choking. He spluttered and coughed out sand and salty water. Water rushed over him, and he coughed and spluttered again. He lifted his head higher, gasping and blinking through stinging salt. His whole body ached from the effort.

This was more like how being alive felt, he thought sourly. Pain, cold, wet and just plain hard work. But being alive, even in this state, brought with it a certain amount of relief.

He was lying face down on a small horseshoe-shaped beach. A large piece of wreckage that looked like half a keg thumped against his leg. His arm was draped over the other half in a rather painful position. Waves washed over him again, and he struggled to his elbows to get his head above them. Everything hurt like a demon and some parts of his body, especially below his ribs, burned with the fire of more serious wounds. He tried to ignore the pain and get his bearings.

The sea was somewhat warm, almost as warm as the seas surrounding the Atalanph desert continent. He had first met Bokaard there ten years or so ago. Bokaard... memory of the man's dark face, white teeth, and vivid blue eyes flashed before him. Where was Bokaard? He had been with him recently, but his mind was foggy.

He tried to lift himself higher and cried out from the pain in his side. His throat burned with thirst, and he ached in every place possible. He touched his side. There was a deep stab wound, and it oozed something foul. Ignoring the pain as best he could, he dragged himself up the beach away from the water's edge and collapsed in exhaustion on drier sand.

Water woke him once more. This time it was splashing on his back, his head, and dribbling into his mouth. *Not salty.* It took a good few moments to understand the strange pattering on his body. It was raining heavily. Thank the goddess. He flopped onto his back with his mouth open, letting the heavy drops fill it with the pure, life-giving water.

He inched his way onto his knees, the effort making him breathless, and then onto his feet. He staggered towards the dense woodland surrounding the cove, and leant against the smooth brown trunk of a tree with a sigh, relieved to be out of the torrential rain.

He fumbled for his sword and laughed when he found it still in its scabbard. It was covered in sand and took some wiggling to get loose, but finally, it came free with a satisfying ringing sound. He held it out and let the rain rinse the sand and salt and blood off. *Blood... Bokaard... we were fighting. Fighting Histanatarns...*

He sheathed the sword. *"Look after your sword, and it will look after you,"* so his sword master had told him once. He could not remember his face anymore. He looked up at the tree he rested against and did not recognise it at all. It was like no other he had seen before, for its smooth bark was pale brown, and it had huge green leaves wider than the span of his outstretched arms. He took in his surroundings. The forest was thick with trees and bushes of all shapes and sizes. Some were so tall he could not see their tops, others were no taller than he but had leaves half the height of his body.

Thick vines with long thin leaves draped themselves between the trees like ropes. They looked strong enough to climb and swing upon too. Despite the rain, it was positively hot and muggy. Dense clouds of moisture rose up from the forest floor. Brightly coloured birds of all shapes and sizes flittered through the treetops. He didn't recognise any of them.

His eyes came to rest on a small brown monkey. They had monkeys in southern Frayon. He had seen one once at a fair. It had a cord about its neck and wore a silly toy jacket. He remembered feeling sorry for it until it had thrown nuts at him. The monkey above was joined by four more, all twice the size of the one he had seen at the fair, and they stared down at him with big golden eyes.

'I'm a strange visitor,' he said to them, but his voice was all croaky and weak. They probably didn't speak Frayonesse, he thought, but then they chattered in laughter and scampered excitedly around each other. This most definitely was not Drax or Frayon or even the elven homeland, Intolana. He was in a jungle unknown to him.

He scratched his eyepatch as memory returned. He had been walking in a barren land, surrounded by mist. He had no eyepatch then. Before that? Yes, he'd been fighting with Bokaard and his soldiers aboard ships. Fighting against the Histanatarns. Then came the Dromoorai and the world went dark. But there had been that old man in the desert who had called him Marakazian, King Marakazian. That had happened after the fighting, he was sure of it.

He looked back at the beach, but there was no other wreckage save for that broken keg. He must have clung to it, floated here. There was no sign of any of his soldiers. He closed his eyes and leant his head against the tree. Rain dripping from the tree trickled down his face into his beard and onto his bare chest.

They were all dead. Probably even Bokaard. The whole mission had failed, and more than that for they had all been killed. Nothing gained, everything lost. If tears would come, it would help, but he was always denied tears, denied any release from the grief and guilt. The dead were dead, leaving him alone with a terrible soul-destroying regret.

He had ordered the mission. He should have returned instead. They would all be alive if he had. Bokaard, Erylin, young Lanac… Thank the goddess he sent some back. And now he was stuck in the middle of nowhere with no way of knowing where to go or how to get home. *Home to Rasia.*

"You'll have a full month of leave after this excursion. More than I get you lucky bastard." Admiral Linker's words echoed in his mind from an eternity ago. *Who's the lucky bastard now, eh?* It looked like more than a month of leave, he thought, glancing around at the jungle; it looked liked forever.

He stared through the leaves at the grey ocean, the pattering of rain drops dappling its surface. Maybe the sea would be blue in the sunshine and the sand golden, instead of this grey menagerie.

Golden sand trickling. *"Is that the time I have?"*

Time was running out. A feeling of urgency overcame him. He had to do something, but what? He shook his head, had he gone mad? He could not coherently piece together the past few days. The wound in his side wasn't helping, it hurt a lot and oozed infected dark blood. He remembered the Histanatarn throwing its tiny knife. Bastard. Hopefully they all got eaten. The wound needed treatment, it could kill him if it turned septic. The saltwater might have done it good, but not being submerged in it for so long.

On Frayon he would look for yarrow root or comfrey leaves, but he did not recognise any of the plants in this place. He let the rain wash it and grimaced when it stung like hell. He tore off the cleanest section of his ripped trousers and tied it around the wound. He would have to search the forest and look for food too. Staring up at the trees, fruits and nuts seemed to be falling off them. Some of it had to be edible.

He took a few paces and picked up a brown fruit covered in soft fur. Taking his knife from his belt, he sliced easily through the flesh. It was bruised and brown, and he let it drop. He headed deeper into the forest, hoping to find some plant he recognised. Every step caused a shooting pain in his side. He picked up a pinkish brown fruit twice the size of his fist and cut into it. Inside was soft pink watery flesh. He dabbed a bit on his tongue and waited. Nothing but a sweet taste. He took a bite and swallowed. Nothing happened, but it made him suddenly ravenous. He cut chunks out and swallowed them down. If it killed him, he didn't care.

He ate another one and was about to start on a third before deciding decided against it. Best see how he felt after the first two. Hopefully, he wouldn't start vomiting. He kept two more of the fruits for later and carried on through the trees, immediately feeling better now his hunger was gone. As he walked, he began to get the feeling that he was being watched. He glanced about, but there were only birds flittering through the trees and the monkeys. Could it be the monkeys watching him?

Pressure came upon his ankle and then a snapping noise. He was so intent upon the monkeys that he did not see the twine until his foot set off the trap. Decades of a soldier's training immediately told him he'd been had. He sighed in exasperation with himself and partially smiled at his easy ending after so long spent struggling.

Although everything seemed to happen in slow motion, he couldn't move any faster. The rock on the rope swung towards him through the tall trees. *That's a long rope, how did they tie it so high?* He thought as it smacked into him hurling him off his feet and the knocking the breath out of his lungs. The wound in his side flared into exquisite agony, then he was falling from consciousness.

CHAPTER 23

Dolphins and Harpies

EDARNA, the witch, sat on the rocks that ran from the shore and a little way into the sea, not far from where she, somewhat violently, stopped Issa from falling under Keteth's spell. She had her warm boots on and her thick shawl, the morning was clear but cold. Autumn was on its way, and she shivered in the early morning sun. The bucket of fish next to her stank and made her gag.

'Go on, hurry up, this stuff stinks,' she said with a grimace, picked up a fish and threw it to the dolphin. With a clicking sound and a whistle that was certainly laughter, the pale blue-grey dolphin caught it neatly in his pink mouth.

'I was here at dawn catching these fish. I've done myself out of dinner too. You'd better be grateful.' The dolphin clicked in reply.

Well, "catch" was a slightly loose term. A small explosion in the water from enchanted sand and a very rare root was what every amateur witch knew how to do. Then it was simply a matter of netting the stunned or dead fish and plonking them in the bucket.

The dolphin eyed her expectantly, his mouth set in that permanent dolphin smile. There was a bloody scar across his forehead and several scrapes down his side—a testament to the vicious battle it had had at sea against the Maphraxies after Keteth had been slain. The scar made Edarna guilty, a little, and so she gave all of her fish to the dolphin, keeping none back for herself.

'We sure showed 'em Maphraxies hey? Ha! Bloody immortals. I knew they'd come, like vultures to a carcass. They can't help 'emselves.'

The dolphin whistled.

She'd scryed for Issa when the death of Keteth rocked the world, and the souls of the enslaved were freed from their prison. That heart-stopping surge of magic bolted her out of bed, leaving her sprawled and shaking on the floor. As soon as she was able, she'd gone to her scrying mirror. The magic was wild, light and sound flickering in the Flow in a fantastic display. She followed the blaring signature under the light of the dark moon to where Issa was. It was easy to find her. Then she saw black ships on the horizon.

'I never doubted she would get rid of Keteth. Never. But I never thought *they* would come so quickly. You took half an hour to answer my call,' she waggled a fish at the open-mouthed dolphin. He snapped his mouth shut and angled his head indignantly.

'We could have all been doomed. That you were sleeping is not a good enough excuse when the fate of the world is at hand.'

After seeing the Maphraxie ships, she'd sprung into action and found the dolphin. One didn't live for decades on a remote island without making some sort of friends. Edarna was no Daluni, but all witches learned a thing or two about animal communication through their familiars. Having access to an earthier, natural magic, witches were able to read animals very well. And a little bit of 'mind-opening' potion made the task that much easier.

Unable to understand the grunts and squeaks that made up the dolphin's name, she decided it must mean "Fish Killer" and had called him that ever since they'd met a decade ago. A meeting that had occurred not on the best of terms. She still hadn't forgiven him for stealing her fish after a very special explosion of her own design. She'd had to go without supper that day, and that had made her very cross.

Nevertheless, seeing Fish Killer with his pod became a regular occurrence, and they got to know each other through fish favours. She taught him how to collect and bring to her mussels and oysters, and in return, she shared her fish explosions with him and his pod. Fish Killer gave an expectant moan, shaking her out of her thoughts.

'There's only three left,' she said, chucking him another fish. He gave a disapproving grunt. 'You're getting fat,' she added. He snapped his jaws.

She had asked (very firmly) if he and his pod would "assist" Issa and help her escape from the Maphraxies. After all, she had killed Keteth, and Keteth was a threat to the dolphins and all cetaceans too. Grudgingly he had taken every dolphin in the area to find her. When next she scryed, she was stunned to see whales and dolphins and all manner of sea creatures by Issa's side. She had not expected there to be a battle, but events had taken a turn for the worst, as they always did when the Maphraxies were involved.

When the two orbs joined their magic, the blast knocked her out of the Flow and sent her sprawling on the floor once more. Her scrying mirror luckily landed on the bed unharmed. She couldn't move for an hour after, even entering the Flow still made her feel frazzled. No longer able to scry, she had to wait for Fish Killer to tell her the rest of the story several days later. Now she was paying him back for his efforts as promised. Two buckets of fish and no back-chat.

'Well, I wish a great golden dragon would come and save us,' she huffed. Though the fish were gone, Fish Killer stayed to chat, or listen to Edarna talk at him. 'Now she's safe, it's us I'm worried about with those Maphraxies so near.'

She looked down at the grinning blue cat sat below her licking his whiskers after eating his fish. He blinked up at her with half-lidded eyes and wrapped his tail around his paws.

'So, you say the ships came from Kammy. That's how they got there so quick, hmm.'

Fish Killer clicked in agreement. He had told her a day ago there were Maphraxies swarming the Isles of Kammy. Looked like they were there permanently, though the dolphins couldn't get too close. Dolphins were not spared from Sirin Derenax extraction either, nor was any living thing.

'It's not safe here, not safe at all,' she shook her head and frowned. 'It seems my time here has come to an end. With Keteth gone, the Shadowlands have either shrunk or are no longer quite so connected to this world. I don't for a second doubt the Shadowlands still exist, but they are no longer easily accessible to me. Hmph, what on Maioria am I supposed to do now?'

It was Fish Killer's frantic train of clicks and whistles that roused her from her thoughts.

'What?' she scrunched up her nose trying to understand what the dolphin was saying. 'What? Danger? Why? Harpies? Where? Argh!' She almost fell off her rock as the big bird-like things appeared flying low above the ocean.

'Great Goddess.' It was too late to use magic, or at least much of it. She slipped down onto the rock the cat was on and in the same motion pulled her shawl over her head.

'Earth, conceal me,' she commanded. 'Mr Dubbins be scarce,' she hissed at the cat.

He hissed back and then crawled under the shallow ledge of the rock. It was a pitiful spell, but to anything looking down the witch would look like an odd-shaped rock amongst the other rocks. A closer inspection would reveal a hazy shimmer of black boots and a green skirt seemingly sticking out of the rock.

The dolphin squeaked laughter at her, uncaring of the five harpies that were approaching.

'I'll talk to you later, now shoo!' she growled.

Fish Killer snapped his jaws twice and then disappeared beneath the surface.

'I hate harpies, disgusting things.' She fell silent as they drew close, peering through a gap in her shawl. They shouldn't be this far west.

One had blonde hair and the others were black-haired. All were pale-skinned and similar looking, probably sisters from the same nest. If only their head and torsos were visible, they looked like pretty women with black eyes, the soft young skin of their breasts, their smooth faces and long shiny hair. But the rest of their bodies were a sharp contrast with razor sharp talons, greasy feathered legs, tail and stomach, and black-fanged mouths. Their feathers weren't soft but slick and shiny as if covered in oil. They smelt bad too. They were not known for washing and, unlike birds, they did not have beaks to preen themselves.

'Filthy creatures,' she hissed. Then her heart caught in her throat as they angled right and headed straight towards her. They circled once and landed in the spot where Issa's boat had been.

'Smells straaange,' one bird-woman screeched, looking around her.

Edarna's heart was pounding in her head and not in her chest where it ought to be. She ran through everything. Had she left the oven on? No. Had she left the washing out? *Damn, I can't remember.* Had she put the shield up? Yes. The shield would conceal the house from above but not from land. Bugger.

The bird women waddled awkwardly around the beach. They had an excellent sense of smell, but thankfully Issa had left a while ago. Perhaps they could feel Edarna's magic. They couldn't possibly be smelling *her*, she'd had a bath only last week.

'There's nothing here,' the blonde harpy said. 'No men, no nothing. Let's go. There are richer places to search, and my nest has been cold and empty for too long. Baelthrom doesn't reward us for finding nothing, fools.' The others scowled at her.

'But he does punish when we miss something important. Idiot. If you got your head out your nest for a second, you might think more clearly,' said a black-haired one.

'We're not looking for men, we're looking for that girl. When we find her, men will be the reward,' the other black-haired one said, and with a swipe of her wing hit the blonde one on the head.

The other black-haired one hit her on the head in return. 'Don't smack her. It was your fault for coming here anyway.'

'I smelt something funny, like human magic, didn't I,' said the first black-haired one.

Edarna couldn't quite make out what was said next as the harpies descended into a screeching wing bashing argument. Eventually, the sisters calmed down and stood there with ruffled feathers.

'Dereever will pull our tails out if she sees us fighting again,' the blonde one said indignantly. The others shuffled their feet and looked at the ground.

'Our Queen said the Shadow Stone has been delivered. We must not kill the High Priestess of Celene,' the second black-haired one said.

'Pfft, well, accidents happen,' said the blonde.

'Your execution won't be an accident though will it?' said the first black-haired one.

Edarna sighed and stuffed her fingers into her ears as the harpies began screeching again. *The High Priestess? A Shadow Stone delivered?* She knew the bloodstones the Dromoorai wore were called Shadow Stones and that they were powerful, linked to Baelthrom somehow. Why would the harpies be talking about a Shadow Stone, and delivered to where exactly? Something foul was afoot. Harpies spread foulness wherever they were found.

'The Immortal Lord has sent his ships and his finest Commander. The battle will be an easy win, so our Queen says. They don't even suspect we are coming. Then we can all fill our nests and our bellies with men,' said the second black-haired one. They all cackled and jumped about.

A loud screeching above made Edarna jump. The birds didn't notice the strange moving rock and instead stared up at the sky.

'Come on, fools, the ships will be there before we are,' an airborne harpy screeched down.

The three sisters scowled at each other and launched into the air to join the other harpy.

Edarna sighed a long low sigh of relief, but couldn't relax because more harpies filled the air. They were flying south, and she lost count of how many there were after thirty. Going south to Celene. Why were they going there? It was surely too dangerous for them.

Her magic was wearing thin, but she daren't drop her shawl just yet, even though the skies were now empty. Mr Dubbins was purring softly under the rock.

'I bet you slept right through all of that,' she rasped, but the cat made no response.

Edarna chewed her lip and waited longer before sitting up. She stayed there thinking. The Isles of Kammy were Maphraxie now, and they were a long, long way from Maphrax. She was probably the only person who knew that. She had to warn everyone. Why would the harpies care about the High Priestess of Celene? And what about the ships they mentioned? Were they all going to Celene?

'The harpies work for Baelthrom,' she said aloud. Mr Dubbins poked his head out from under the rock and meowed.

'You can't be hungry already,' she scowled at him. He began purring, letting her know she was correct. But instead, she fell back to her thoughts.

What did they want with the High Priestess? Edarna had no love for the Temple, but it seemed unlikely they were in league with the Maphraxies. The Oracle was soon to be replaced, or at least that was what the score was ten years ago. Somehow the woman clung to life even though her head was half in this world half in the next, the way she babbled on about her dreams and visions. Who knows, maybe she had already been replaced.

A personal trip to the main temple on Frayon would be a magnanimous gesture. The haughty priestesses should always be reminded to respect witches and their wisdom. They would want to know if a High Priestess has sparked the interest of the Maphraxies. Perhaps it was their plan to infiltrate the Order from within. Maphraxies were good at infiltrating bodies with their Life Seekers. The Temple must know the danger they are in.

The thought of helping the Temple left a bitter taste in her mouth. It was the Order of the Great Goddess that had disbanded the Coven over fifty years ago when Edarna was a young witch. And all because of the actions of one witch who delved into black magic. She had probably been infected by a Life Seeker anyway.

The witches were systematically stripped of their magic and imprisoned if they used it. What was worse was the disinformation and fear spread about them by the Temple to the common people. Once witches knew how to fix a broken bone, end a cold, and deliver babies, but ever since the Temple destroyed the Coven, the people were afraid to come to them.

'The Temple was afraid of us and our ancient magic,' Edarna nodded. 'We were a threat to them, their authority, their control of religion. We would not join their Temples of control, and so they threw us out, disbanded us. As bad as the bloody wizards are, Mr Dubbins. No, in fact, they're worse. Well, look at 'em now eh? No one believes in the goddess, not like they used to, anyway. Pah.'

Wherever a green robe (the colour of the robes witches wore) was seen, they were driven out of the villages and into the wilderness, sometimes they were hunted down and killed. So the witches hid their green robes away and hid themselves away too. How she missed wearing her lovely green robe. She chose instead to live her life alone on a remote island, keeping her earthy magic to herself. The witches were all still out there, somewhere, but now it was wizards and alchemists who helped the sick—all men! And they did a poor job at that.

'What's a village without a witch? What can men ever know about soothing menstrual pains or delivering babies?' she said. Mr Dubbins meowed louder, food was clearly more important. 'And all the seers do is hide away on the Isles of Tirry.'

Sure, the seers had taken witches in after the 'Derobing' as witches called it, but once a witch it was hard to move from their earthier magic into the adept wizardry of the seers.

'It's all fractious, Mr Dubbins. We should all be working together; witch, seer, wizard, priestess, but instead the men want all wizardry to themselves and the Order of the Great Goddess want religion to themselves. None of them are right, Mr Dubbins.'

'Issa could be a great witch, Mr Dubbins, but I think she may belong with the seers, communing as she does with the goddess n' all. Somehow I don't think she's going to be fulfilled just healing horses and fixing broken bones. After all, how many people actually have the sacred mound come to them? The sacred mound found *her*. Most of us spend a lifetime trying to find it. The wizards may have that awful Storm Holt to test their masculinity against, but I tell you, finding something sacred is far more a lesson. Finding the sacred mound has ever been the making of a witch.

'And that's another thing. The seers should be looking for *her* if they weren't so engrossed in whatever it is seers do. Which is not much as far as I can tell. Seers know all the prophecies, they bloody well created most of them, so why aren't they looking for her? And the Temple is far too corrupt, she'll find no wisdom there. Who'd ever of thought that religion could lose its spirituality, eh? Hah. Hmph. I think a few visits are on the agenda, Mr Dubbins, to give these people a piece of my mind!'

Mr Dubbins suddenly stopped purring and stared, golden eyes wide, at the horizon. A horrible prickling danced up her back. She glanced out at where the cat looked.

'Oh my,' she breathed.

Just past the horizon were several fast moving ships, their black masts splayed wide, making them look like giant spiders. She didn't think they were coming for her and Mr Dubbins.

'If my feelings serve me correctly, Celene is in terrible danger,' she whispered.

CHAPTER 24

Shrinking Potion

EDARNA rolled off the rock and ran all the way back to her house with Mr Dubbins trailing along behind her.

'I knew our time to leave would come,' she said to the blue cat. He sat purring and smiling up at her as she gathered clothes into a sack. 'I just never thought it would come so quickly. The Immortal Lord's noose is tightening around Frayon. First Kammy, now Celene. They have finally come to the west and now so far south. With the east gone, we are totally surrounded.'

She stopped to catch her breath. 'Oh, my. We must warn Celene, but it'll be too late by then. It'll take me half a day to make that bloody potion as it is. And that's another thing, Mr Dubbins; you'll be coming with me this time.' The cat meowed, hissed and ran out of the bedroom. She grinned wickedly.

'We must try to get to Celene,' she called after the cat. 'Lady Eleny I think her name is.'

She vaguely remembered a kind, fair-haired woman she had met briefly at the Midsummer Celebrations many years ago. 'I'll not go to the Temple *there*, that's for sure,' she shuddered, remembering the other cold-hearted, fair-haired woman who had been in charge of the Temple of Celene. 'What a great person to be in *control* of religion.'

She shook her head and went to a chest draped over with cloth and securely locked with a padlock as big as her fist. No key could unlock it. She whispered her witch's spell instead. It clicked open, and she heaved up the lid.

'Oh,' she smiled and reached inside, tenderly picking up her neatly folded moss-green witch's robe. She stroked it and reached into the folds, carefully drawing out her foot long hazel beam wand. She sighed forlornly and set them aside. There was another smaller chest inside, also locked, and she pulled it out. Whispering another word it opened and she pushed back the lid.

A waft of musty, rotting air greeted her, and she leaned back gagging. 'Great Goddess. At least they're still fresh,' she spluttered. She peered back inside. There were several glass jars and vials, ranging from no bigger than a thimble to about the size of an apple.

'It can take a lifetime to get all of these ingredients, Mr Dubbins, and a week to prepare them. Luckily I have done all the hard work already,' she smiled smugly at her own preparedness. 'We live in uncertain times,' she murmured picking up a vial.

'Eye of newt,' she peered through the dark magenta glass at the small black slimy thing.

She picked up the biggest jar and a blackish-green patch of tough leathery material shimmered within.

'Scale of dragon. Nearly cost me my life that did,' she set it down and picked up a smaller jar.

'Wing of bat, poor thing,' she sighed, set it aside and rummaged around in the case. 'Now let's see what else is in here.'

Dried lavender. Deven Star root. Cocoa leaves. Dried Mavy's kelp. Red and black lintel weed. So all she needed were the final ingredients that could only be used fresh. Feather of bird—it was always best to use the feather of a bird you would be travelling on, which meant her usual mode of transport, a gull. Sea salt and green grass. And what else... *ah yes, cat's whisker.*

'Mr Dubbins!' she shouted, but he did not appear.

After an hour of searching, she still couldn't find him.

'Sodding cat. Never here when you need him,' she sighed and got on with everything else.

By the time her cauldron was bubbling upon its stand, it was already past dinner time. Despite the worry that knotted her stomach, many years as a witch forced patience upon her. There was no rushing these things. She settled down to a huge bowl of pumpkin soup and brown bread.

The smell of food proved irresistible to the blue cat and, as she suspected, it wasn't long before a sheepish-looking Mr Dubbins peered around the kitchen door. They eyed each other cautiously. She didn't even blink as she chewed her bread and swallowed. Slowly her eyes dropped to the plate of fish beside her, the cat followed her gaze and seemed to freeze.

'That gull has more guts than you do, you wimp. He even pulled the feather out himself. One of your whiskers belongs in that pot there, otherwise, they'll be no fish for you, and no meal ever again when the Maphraxies land here.'

The cat meowed plaintively and poured himself through the door.

'I don't like it either. You know how sick this stuff makes me. But we've no choice, the world is in terrible danger. So if you can spare a whisker, we might actually survive to have another meal.'

After a plate of smoked fish and much convincing, Mr Dubbins suffered a whisker to be drawn from his face, but not without a lot of crying and meowing afterwards.

'Will you quit that racket,' she said and shoved another portion of fish his way. All pain and grievances were forgotten as he tucked in.

She dropped the whisker into the cauldron and stirred it with a wooden spoon. The sun had set, but the potion would not be ready until an hour or so after sunrise.

'There's is no rushing this, Mr Dubbins,' she sighed worriedly. 'We may well be too late. But these are the last of my ingredients, and if I mess this up there'll be no leaving this place ever again. I hope you've said your goodbyes to the mice, we won't be returning for a very long time. If ever.'

The thought made her sad. She would be homeless for a long time like she had been before. Perhaps she could seek out other witches, hidden as they were about the Known World. Maybe they could rekindle the Coven in secret.

'When I've visited the Oracle and the Seers of Myrn, maybe then I'll have a better idea about what to do next,' she stirred the pot absently. 'Issa needs our help. She needs everybody's help.'

In the next few hours before bedtime, she packed her few belongings into the smallest chest. A change of clothes, a bag of food enough for two meals (she was a witch and could forage from the forest, or pretty much anywhere, better than anyone else could), her witch's robe and wand. Lastly, she stuffed in her thick spell-book. She locked the chest and with a command it shrunk to half its original size. Now she could hold it under her arm easily.

She settled down to sleep, but thoughts came instead. She had planned to grow old and die here on her tiny island, but it seemed the goddess required more of her. And if the Night Goddess required a witch's skills and wisdom, then she wouldn't deny her. She would miss her bed, her oven, these four walls and roof she had built with her own hands—or rather witch's magic and a little help from the gulls.

When thoughts of her home turned to thoughts of Celene, she slipped into an uneasy sleep where Dread Dragons brought fire and necromancers stole souls.

The sun rose, and an exhausted Edarna rose with it. The cauldron was still warm, though the fire beneath it had gone out. She poured the tan coloured liquid into a pint-sized glass and tried not to vomit at the sight of black lumps floating in it.

'Don't look, Mr Dubbins,' she said. He meowed and scowled.

She cleaned the cauldron, and with a word it shrunk small enough to fit in her pocket.

'Right,' she said, picking up the pint of vomit-looking liquid, 'let's call the gull.'

With her chest of belongings under one arm, she left her house forever. She stood in the garden beside the washing line and made a strange crying sound that sounded uncannily like a gull.

'He'd better come,' she said, glaring up at the sky.

Eventually, a gull swooped low and landed beside her. It was a young male already as big as the cat was. Mr Dubbins did not like gulls, and he hissed at it. The gull made a deafening cry as if laughing at the pathetic cat.

'You know what we need,' she said to the gull who stared at her unblinking with fierce eyes. 'Safe transport to the Isle of Celene, or any safe ground before the potion wears off.'

The gull twisted its head and peered one-eyed at the pint of gloop.

'As you know, I'm very generous in my payments. You can have a free nesting spot in my now unused chimney,' she said magnanimously.

The gull looked up at the chimney, then back at the witch and cawed.

'All right! And fish. Fish when we get there, and only if we get there safely. Praise the goddess, gulls strike a hard bargain,' she grumbled, well aware of the nature of gulls. They were fickle and looked down upon the ridiculous looking humans, who were to be stolen from and laughed at at every opportunity.

'That's settled then,' she sighed and grimaced at the foul liquid.

She poured a small amount of it into Mr Dubbins' water bowl. He looked up at her with bared teeth.

'We'll drink it together, all right?' she smiled weakly. It was the worst potion she'd ever had to make, but possibly the most powerful one as well.

'I'm too old for this.' She remembered how ill it had made her before. Unable to use magic, not even to scry with. Unable to think at all, really. But it was drink it or watch the world die at the hands of the Maphraxies, and then watch yourself die too.

'All right, one, two, three!' She tipped the liquid to her mouth and swallowed. She tried to shut all else out, the foul taste, the lumps that clogged her throat, the feeling that maybe something wasn't quite dead in it. She dropped the glass on the grass and clamped her hands to her mouth to keep it from coming back up. Mr Dubbins had done his part but refused to look at anything but the ground in front of his feet.

The gull eyed them curiously. The potion worked quickly and there wasn't the gradual shrinking that would have been almost enjoyable, no. The house, the garden and the gull doubled in size. There was a brief pause. Mr Dubbins was now the size of a mouse. He looked up at her wide-eyed in terror and his meow came out a squeak.

'I know,' she squeaked back, getting ready for the next lurch. The gull cackled in laughter. She scowled, her head now level with its. The lurch came again and everything doubled in size once more. Now she looked up at the huge gull and Mr Dubbins huddled between her feet, shaking.

'Now you know how mice feel,' she scolded, although she too quivered at the sight of the gull towering above her. That orange beak looked enormous and very sharp.

'Right, that's it. Let's get on with it.'

She opened her sling for Mr Dubbins to jump in, tucked her travel chest under her arm, and walked uncertainly towards the tree-trunk sized orange leg of the gull. He eyed them with a gleam of hunger.

'I have my wand at the ready, so don't even think about it!' She squeaked at the gull.

It snapped its beak and sat down. Edarna clambered breathlessly up one extended wing and settled down as low as she could between the gull's wings.

'And if you drop us I shall come back to haunt you forever,' she warned. The gull ruffled its feathers.

'Now we understand each other, remember the deal; lots of fish and the best nest on all the islands put together. So let's go to the Isle of Celene.'

CHAPTER 25

The Sunless Dawn

HAMEKA awoke when the ship stopped rocking. Looking through the portal, it was not quite dawn. He dressed in a plain undershirt, toughened leather breeches and tunic. After second thoughts, he pulled the tunic off. He was already sweating and he still had to put on his uncomfortable, heavy chainmail vest. He secured a thin grey woollen cloak over his shoulders. Despite the heat, it protected against the sea spray and rain if there was any.

Next, he belted on his rapier. The sheath was made of a sheet of metal, decorated with a few simple scrolls and whorls. He pulled out the long thin blade, enjoying the low slithering sound it made followed by a ringing that lasted several seconds. The sword shone orange in the lamp light. The steel was of excellent quality, beautifully tempered and springy. The blade had, of course, been recently sharpened. The crossguard was the heaviest part of the blade and the most ornate. Intricate looping metal entwined together and created a basket shape for his hand.

Despite the intricate metalwork, the metal was extremely strong and did not bend when he tried to force it. Neither did the blade buckle, even when his whole weight was against it. Something he'd discovered when he had run a man through with such force that they'd fallen back against a stone wall, the blade never breaking.

With a twitch of his wrist he flicked the point down, and the blade swished in the air. The corner of the map upon his desk drifted to the floor without so much as disturbing the rest of it. The weight of the crossguard made swinging the comparatively light blade incredibly fast.

Unlike most weapons used by the Maphraxies, this sword was not made of black iron from within the Mountains of Maphrax, but was human-forged steel. His rapier was the only thing he admired that humans had made. He liked the idea of using human-made weapons to kill humans. Too bad he never really used it much. He slotted it back into its sheath with another slithering ring and picked up his most prized weapon instead.

His crossbow was not just any crossbow, it was probably the tiniest crossbow ever created. Certainly, he had never seen one as small, nor one so deadly. It was the length and width of his hand. Its thick wooden trunk was hollow, and inside were many darts the length of his finger and slightly thicker than a matchstick. Each dart was tipped with deadly Saran poison from Venosia. Just a nick from a dart would paralyse those it hit.

Once embedded, the dart was impossible to remove unless you knew how (and only Hameka knew how), for three tiny barbs shot out on impact, embedding themselves into the victim. If the poison was left untreated, within an hour the victim's veins would expand until they burst. Not only was it deadly, it was an excruciating way to die. Every cell exploding. The steel bow prod was stretched back and enchanted to ensure deadly accuracy. The metal twine had not broken in ten years and was still strong and unworn.

He sat there admiring his invention. It had been crafted according to his own design, and he had never been disappointed with it. He knew how to use many weapons—one didn't live for hundreds of years as a battle commander without learning everything you could about weapons. He was excellent with his rapier, it required skill, unlike the heavy brutish axes, maces and flails used by the numbskull Maphraxies. But then, with their lumbering size and incredible strength, perhaps it made more sense to hack, bludgeon and crush your way through the enemy.

However, over the years he had found his true skill lay in this tiny crossbow, and after so long at war, he preferred to fight from a distance. Close combat was boring, easy almost. But the mess the blood made of his clothes, the sweat and stench of the enemy's breath in his face, the festering wounds and other annoying sprains that were inevitable. No more. Fighting from a distance was much cleaner and ultimately more fun. His rapier was only for emergencies. Of course, he rarely joined in in the fighting now anyway and preferred to direct and observe the carnage.

He tucked his most-deadly-of-weapons into his belt and pulled on stiff gloves that made his hands sweat immediately. He headed out of his cabin, at once relieved to be away from the boring confining room, and walked the narrow corridor lined on either side with the closed doors of other cabins. His shiny black boots made an authoritative tap as he walked and the Maphraxies he passed hunkered their bulks into the walls with some difficulty to let their commander pass.

As soon as he opened the door to the deck, he was greeted with buffeting winds and rain that tried to drive him back in. Gripping the door frame he heaved his body out onto the deck and whipped his hand away as the door slammed viciously behind him. The deck was swarming with Maphraxies, dark dwarves dressed in waterproof oil-skins, and six necromancers bunched together at the prow; black robes whipping around them in the wind and their deathly white hands and faces seeming to glow in the gloom.

Hameka peered over the railing. The sea was still and grey under the green-tinged clouds that clambered around the ship. The wind was magical, but why did there always have to be rain as well? Even as he thought it, the wind began to drop and the rain turned from needles into a patter. At least the awful weather brought them here quickly, he thought, wringing out the hem of his already sodden cloak.

The wind became a gentle breeze, and he released his death grip on the rail. He smiled, the necromancers had done their job well. He made his way over to them; the Maphraxies and dark dwarves falling back to let him pass. The necromancers stood unmoving and looked so alien that they might as well have been standing on another world entirely. He barely recognised the white faces as elves and humans anymore, so long and thin did they seem. Their eyes had been turned black by the elixir.

They were watching the fog that billowed from them. Twelve white hands reached out in unison, then moved from right to left. The fog moved in the same direction and like a long thick gaseous snake, it slithered over the side of the boat. Hameka watched it move across the sea towards a dark expanse of land a mile or so away.

A dark dwarf shuffled to his side, yellow eyes gleaming. 'The Isle of Celene, Commander,' he snivelled and chuckled. 'They won't suspect a thing. The harpies have told us there aren't even any lights on.'

'Perfect.' Hameka allowed himself a small smile. He looked up at the sky. There was the barest amount of growing light, and the stars were getting harder to see. 'Dawn is coming, but for Celene, the sun will not rise today.' No light would be able to penetrate the fog that now darkened the land.

The dark dwarf cackled again and shuffled away. Around him dark dwarves readied themselves for the coming battle, their yellow eyes gleaming excitedly as they ordered about the lumbering Maphraxies. Their ashen skin was slick with sweat and salt water; their long grey beards with the barest tint of red were sodden and lank.

Despite their small stature—they barely reached his chest—they were vicious fighters. They always had that keen look in their eyes before any attack, for they had been promised the usual spoils of war and they were eager for a good choice of women. Likewise, the harpies had been offered the men. Neither species cared who had had the spoils before, nor in what state they got them in. They would happily rape a corpse. Foul creatures, both of them, he scowled.

He would certainly not wait around to witness their sordid acts, and he was long past participating in them himself. It was messy, made you dirty, and was horribly disease prone. It was also boring. When you could have who and what you wanted whenever you wanted, such types of revenge and sordid domination were no longer desired or needed. He held up the dull Key Stone hanging on his chest and stared into it.

'Dromoorai above,' he addressed the eight Dromoorai circling on their Dread Dragons above the ships. Their amulets flared blood-red as they obeyed. Their eyes were like fires in the dark and he wondered if they even looked human behind those helmets anymore.

'The one we seek must be taken alive.' He projected an image of the girl Baelthrom had shown him into the bloodstone. A slender young woman with long black hair, green eyes and pale skin. It wasn't the clearest picture.

'Capture anyone who might fit the description,' he spoke loudly for those around him to hear as well. 'There may be a wizard with her. The rest remains the same. Take alive all magic wielders, young or old. Capture the children for elixir production.'

Wizards were highly prized by Baelthrom. They would become necromancers. The more skilled and powerful the wizard, the greater his power after consumption of the elixir. It was raids like these on towns and villages that supplied them with children for the very best elixir production. Soldiers didn't tend to take their children to war.

'Stay out of sight until we attack,' he said into the Key Stone.

The six Maphraxie ships moved slowly and silently towards the hulking slab of land. The wind dropped and the slack sails were reeled in. The green fog continued to billow out from the space in front of the necromancers, thicker and wider than before, but the swell caused by their magical storm was gone, and the sea was eerily still and flat like a mirror.

The anchor slid down into the water silently, all noise and splashing concealed by necromancer magic. Unfortunately, without the magical wind, it was a remarkably still and quiet morning. They would have to rely on the thick fog and tread quietly to avoid raising alarm too soon.

The amulet on his chest grew warm and glowed in the gloom. Baelthrom watched from far away. Irritatingly he could sense his master's eagerness to find the girl. He was beginning to hate her. She could not possibly escape now, not even in death, he smiled. If there were a wizard with her, he would be taken for questioning before the elixir was administered. If she proved to be elusive, the wizard would be forced to lead them to her.

He looked up at the sky, but could no longer see the Dromoorai. They would strike from the air, sending terror through the people as they rained fire upon them and their villages. He used to be nervous before battle but not now, now he only felt a little excitement. Another victory, another blow to the enemy. One thing was for sure; he would put on a good show for his master. The goddess worshippers would be punished severely for their defiance against the Immortal Lord.

Hameka climbed down the rope ladder into the raft-boat beside the ship. The green fog blanketing thickly around them as they rowed towards the shore. Anyone outside of the green fog would not be able to see in, but for the Maphraxies within, it was easy to see out.

Each boat was packed full with dark dwarves and Maphraxies, and in the centre of each was a giant cage. The snarling slavering sound coming from within told him the deliberately starved death hounds were hungry. He peered through the bars, and two pairs of yellow eyes glimmered back. They fidgeted and snapped at each other, keen to be free.

The death hounds were half again as big as a wolf with black matted fur covering heavily muscled bodies. Their muzzles were stubby but heavy and powerful, and lined with inch long canines. A line of bony spines ran down their backs to the tail tip.

Not quite the cuddly pooch they started out as. He grinned at the thought.

The boat ground onto the sand and they jumped out. The death hounds led the way, picking up the scent of humans, straining against their steel collars and heavy chains held by Maphraxies that struggled to restrain them.

The day was brightening. He glimpsed the turret and chimneys of a large red-bricked mansion ahead. According to the map, this should be the Castle Elune. They moved swiftly through the trees towards it. The wood was empty and silent as if all the animals and birds had sensed the immortals and fled.

He hoped the clank of armour and the growling beasts would be muffled by the fog. But the closer they got the less of a worry being discovered became. Their attack was imminent and already deadly, for it was far too late for the unsuspecting islanders.

He glanced sideways at the deformed lumbering chunks of muscle. The Maphraxies were not creatures of stealth. *Numb-skulls...*

They paused where the trees ended. A sweep of landscaped gardens sloped up to their right, and flat ground and stables to their left. The horses in the stables began to whinny and neigh; they had smelled the death hounds.

'To the stables,' he growled. 'Kill the horses quickly before they make a racket.'

It took two Maphraxies to control each hound now they could smell fresh meat. As they neared, the horses whinnied and screamed louder, their stables becoming their prisons. He tapped his foot impatient with the noise.

The first death hound released ploughed through the door of a stable, wood splintering. The other death hounds found their own stables. The horses' screams stilled into the sound of snapping bone and tearing flesh. Now the screaming had stopped, he relaxed a little.

A large black bird darted past his face, and he ducked instinctively. Crossbow in hand, he whirled to see what it was. His eyes rested on a raven landing on a branch. It stared back with unnerving intelligence that made the back of his neck sweat. It opened its beak, rolled out its pinky-black tongue, and cawed raucously—a sound like laughter that echoed through the stables and across the lawns.

He aimed his crossbow but something cold sunk down his throat. It wrapped its cold tendrils around his heart, and he froze in fear. The only warmth in his whole body came from the burning amulet on his chest.

'Kill it.' Baelthrom's command echoed in his brain, cutting through the icy tentacles that bound him. He fought to lift his leaden arms, raised the crossbow once more and fired.

The dart flew too fast to see, but it never struck home. The raven jumped from its perch and dropped towards him like an arrow, sharp and deadly through the fog. He fell back too slowly. Claws scraped down his face and a razor sharp beak sliced across his forehead. As quick as it had come, the bird turned in mid-air and darted to the stables, out of sight before he could fire again.

'Bastard!' he cursed, blood trickling down his face.

'Find it. Kill it.' Baelthrom said.

Hameka tried to follow the bird, but couldn't see for the stinging blood in his eyes. Swearing profusely, he tore off a piece of his shirt and wrapped it around his head to stem the flow. The wounds weren't deep, but stung like hell and bled plenty too. The pain was nothing compared to the rage the bird had sparked in him. Filthy creatures of the goddess, they'd destroy them all. Maphraxies and dark dwarves came to his side.

'If you find that sodding bird, kill it. Kill any bird you find, kill them all,' he snarled, wiping a bloodied hand on his cloak.

Blinking through the blood, he lunged in the direction it had gone. He rounded a corner and came to a stop before two stables stood apart from the others. The door to the first was open, the other closed. He scanned the trees but the raven was nowhere to be seen.

At first, he thought a death hound was busy inside the closed stable, the way it was rocking. The wood groaned and cracked as if under strain, and there came the snorting of some furious beast. But the door was still whole and latched closed. He stepped cautiously forwards.

A frenzied scream was followed by splintering wood as the door exploded outwards. He froze as a huge black devil of a horse burst through the flying wood and headed straight towards him. The whites of its eyes were shining crescents and its mouth frothed with rage or terror or both. He hurled himself to the left, narrowly missing slashing hooves as the demon horse deliberately tried to strike him. It came back at him again. He rolled to his left, pounding hooves striking the ground barely inches away.

A hulking death hound lolloped around the corner, its growl so deep and loud it rumbled the ground. It lunged for the horse's throat but missed when it reared. The horse screamed in fury as the hound jumped on it. Together they fell, a tumbling mass of snapping teeth and slashing hooves.

The horse rolled to its feet, reared, and drove its front hooves down onto the hound's head. There came a sickening crack, and the death hound's skull collapsed, spilling its dark, bloody contents onto the grass. With another scream the horse reared into a gallop, hooves spraying up great clumps of earth as it tore away and disappeared into the trees.

Hameka stood up and brushed himself down, shaken but furious at this charade, especially with his master watching. He looked around, but the raven was nowhere to be seen and his smouldering fury deepened.

'Forget the bird,' Baelthrom said, there was no anger in his voice, only a subtle pondering.

The stench of butchery was rich in the windless fog and the sound of snapping bones soon overcame the remaining horses' death screams as the hounds devoured them.

He watched the bloodshed in grim detachment. It had not gone well so far. He would make sure the inhabitants would not be as troublesome as the animals had been. At his command the Maphraxies regrouped, barking their guttural orders back to each other, and moved as one dark mass towards the castle.

A cloud passed overhead, reminding him of the Dread Dragons' presence and that they also needed feeding. Beneath them now circled the smaller shapes of harpies. He grimaced in disgust.

The first person they came across was an old maid hanging out the washing in the servants' gardens. She was too deaf to have heard the commotion at the stables and did not see the death hound that jumped her from behind, severing her neck in a smooth fluid motion. She was dead before she hit the ground.

Hameka stepped over the feeding hounds and blood soaked sheets, vivid red on white, and into the rear of the castle. That would be all that was left of her. Everything would be devoured, not even her bones would remain.

They met only a few more servants who screamed and scurried away from the Maphraxies like terrified mice. Maphraxian blades cut down those who still slept in their bed. Even though he knew it would be easy, he was still surprised at how easy it was, these people were woefully unprepared for an attack and he'd yet to come across a guard or soldier.

Old and young were slaughtered alike and he wondered if the Maphraxies could tell the difference. They probably couldn't even tell the difference between day and night. Hopefully they would be careful not to kill a dark-haired girl, though any girl matching her description had yet to be found.

He moved from room to room with increasing speed, searching for her, the amulet burning brightly on his chest. Finally, he came to a large bedchamber more richly decorated than the others with its four poster bed, heavy velvet drapes and ornately carved dressing table. The chamber was empty.

'The lord and lady of the castle are not here, and what of that wizard the harpy mentioned?' he murmured, half to himself, half to Baelthrom. But the amulet was a silent glow. With a roar of frustration, he gripped the side of the dressing table and hurled it over. The contents of the table top and drawers spilled out onto the floor, silks and cottons tumbling together with gold and silver jewellery. Worthless and of no interest to him.

He whirled away and stalked out the door. He made sure all the rooms were ransacked, and the cellars crawling with Maphraxies, yet still nothing was found. She had to be somewhere. He made his way to the courtyard at the front of the house where a small collection of prisoners was forming.

'Magic wielders,' a dark dwarf motioned towards a smaller group of people separated from the rest. Three shaking and sobbing maids, and two beaten-unconscious young male guards.

Hameka snorted. Young untrained people couldn't wield much magic. But then the elixir worked its magic in mysterious ways, sometimes making the most useless novice in magic able to wield huge amounts of black magic. The dark dwarf eyed the maids with a loathsome lust.

'They are not for you, as well you know. Bind and gag them. Their snivelling is more than irritating,' Hameka commanded. The dark dwarf scuttled away.

There were ten other people, five men and five women ranging from late teens to early forties, and all in a similar state; snivelling, shaking, beaten and bloodied. They were once servants, cooks or soldiers, and now the unfortunate spoils of war. Half lay unmoving, the others stared in terror at the ground. *Yes, we do make quite an ugly sight,* he grinned at the thought.

There were four dark-haired women, but one was too old, one was too young, and the two obvious sisters were too short, barely taller than the dark dwarves themselves. He sighed. None of the women matched *her* description.

The dark dwarves looked as hungry as the death hounds, their eyes already devouring the terrified maids. The men would be fought over by the harpies, and if they survived that they would be taken back to their nests. Harpies had many ways to ensure no man denied them their offspring, it was the only way they could reproduce since all harpies were born female.

Once the act was done, the men, having served their purpose, would be eaten. The witch-birds were already circling low, and their eager cackles grated his ears. He almost felt sorry for the humans.

'Finish the job,' he sighed and walked away in disgust. He didn't want to hear, see or smell it. But not hearing it was hard when the harpies cackled so loudly.

CHAPTER 26

Enemy on the Doorstep

CIROSA'S neck prickled. Her attention whipped back to the present, and her gaze settled on Arla, the bothersome child that she was bound by oath to look after. She stood in the doorway of her office, looking pale and grubby as always.

'What is it Arla?' she snapped. 'Can't you see I'm busy?'

The girl raised her eyebrows as if to say that pacing the floor and clenching fists was not really what one would call busy. She glared at the child. Arla's robes were covered in grass stains, her knees muddy, and her white hair tangled with leaves. Filthy, feral child. Despite numerous scoldings, the child refused to take notice of her superiors, and moments after washing and donning clean clothes, she somehow managed to cover herself in all manner of forest matter.

She had changed little from the girl they found wandering the eastern shores of Celene in nothing but rags several years ago. The old High Priestess of Celene, Mielan, had found her and taken her in. Mielan claimed she had seen the child in a vision, though the girl's purpose had not been made clear to her. Mielan never found out what her vision meant, for she died six months later from a wasting sickness that had been eating away at her for years.

No one on the island claimed the child as theirs, and so she became one of the Temple novices. It was fairly common for the temples to take in abandoned or runaway children. Maybe Arla had been shipwrecked, but they never thought the child was their saviour, did they? Cirosa grimaced. Back then the girl didn't speak and didn't even know her own age. She remained small and frail and stunted, and both Cirosa and Mielan suspected she was much older than she looked, though she still showed no signs of adolescence. Maybe she was permanently stunted.

Mielan had always acted wary and distrustful of Cirosa; hiding away her notebooks in which she recorded her dreams and visions, speaking to others of her thoughts but never Cirosa. Yet, she conceded that there was no one more suitable to run the Temple of Celene when she was gone. The few trainees they received were far too young and unprepared— Cirosa had made sure of that because young girls could never pose a threat to her succession to the High Priestess of Celene.

Mielan would die soon, too. A few crushed roots here, a sprinkling of herbs there; the old priestess didn't even notice the poison in her dinner. It only served to speed up the death process and lessen her suffering, of course.

But unfortunately, Cirosa was forced to take care of the child by a binding oath Mielan made her take on her death bed. The girl was blessedly silent and absent most of the time, but despite her placid nature, she was wary of the girl to the point of being afraid. She had the feeling that Arla suspected her plans and knew her innermost thoughts and desires, even knew about the roots and herbs she had given Mielan to speed up her death. But the girl never said anything.

'Why do you stare so, child? Answer me,' Cirosa demanded irritably, but Arla said nothing and continued to stare up at her as if she were looking straight through her.

The girl was prone to trances. Mielan had thought it was important, but to Cirosa she was just a simple child given to daydreaming. The child still did not respond. Cirosa began to feel nervous.

'Arla, what is it?' she asked more gently, feeling the patience drain from her. The child's serene face turned to a mask of shock, her eyes opened wide with fear and her bottom lip quivered. Cirosa bent down, taking her firmly by the shoulders. 'Are you sick, child?'

In a female voice too old to be her own the child spoke. 'The beast is slain, retribution comes. Too late to flee, betrayer, too late!' Arla screamed and collapsed.

Cirosa trembled as she grabbed the girl and dragged her into the chair. The girl lay unconscious and floppy like a rag doll. Cirosa chewed her fingers, and her heart pounded. Her eyes came to rest on the bottom drawer of her desk. The girl was talking gibberish nonsense as always. She laughed aloud, hoping to rouse the girl and still her pounding heart, but the fear ate at her. How could she possibly know the beast was dead?

'Arla? Arla, wake up. It's safe now.'

The girl moaned and blinked as she came around. With both hands, she took the glass of water Cirosa passed to her and drank noisily, sweat shining on her pallid face.

'What did you see, Arla?' she asked, keeping her voice level.

'I don't remember it all, High Priestess,' the girl replied in her normal childish voice. 'There were many black shapes moving like insects. They moved in a green mist bringing terror and destruction before them. There were huge black dragons that brought fire. People were dying and screaming. I called to the goddess but she couldn't reach us, I... I don't know why,' she stammered.

Never before had she seen the girl exhibit any other behaviour than complete serenity, even in a trance, not since Issa arrived at least. The wench Issa had unsettled everything and everyone.

'But I saw another thing in my dreams last night,' the girl's worried look turned hopeful. 'I know that the White Beast has been slain, High Priestess. I'm sure the goddess has not abandoned us, and her Raven Queen comes to save us,' the girl gave a rapturous smile.

Cirosa's stomach lurched, and the room spun. The blood drained from her face, and she clung to the table to keep from falling. She closed her eyes against the spinning room. The girl was wrong, she had to be. But Arla was never wrong. The rage began to grow within her.

'Leave me child' she said hoarsely, her eyes clamped shut.

The girl made a small noise as if she were about to speak, but clearly thought better of it and left. Cirosa heard the door shut and stayed very still. Issa gnawed away at her like an infected sore. Could she trust the bloodstone, trust whoever or whatever had spoken to her through it? That Keteth had been slain by Issa was just too awful to believe. She needed some air to clear her head.

She stumbled outside struggling to breathe, for the air itself seemed thick and solid. To avoid being seen, she slipped around the back of her office building and ran towards the trees. She stumbled along the narrow path that wound through the trees to the cliff's edge, where it then zigzagged down ancient steps cut in the craggy rock to the beach far below.

She gripped the hand-rope as her feet carried her down the stone steps. Her legs were like jelly, and her breath came shallow and fast. The wench was like poison in her veins, threatening to ruin a lifetime of hard work and carefully laid plans. So, she had succeeded in destroying Keteth. It did not mean anything more than that.

The prophecies were still no more than the wistful gibbering of mad men and women, they did not dictate the truth, did not dictate the future and the lives and actions of people who did not yet live. The Maphraxies would come for Issa, the voice in the amulet said they would, and then Issa would simply disappear. Problem solved. There was nothing to worry about and everything to look forward to.

She smiled, feeling a certain amount of calm return to her as she stepped onto the white sand. She smoothed back her hair, took in a deep breath and walked to the shore where the waves lapped the sand. A mist covered the sea out upon the horizon, and it grew thicker and closer even as she watched. Bad weather heading this way. She slipped off her shoes and walked barefoot in the waves watching the white froth cover her neatly trimmed and polished toenails. She considered her future gains.

She would be the Oracle, nothing could change that. *Nothing*. She would tell the amulet everything about the foolish wench.

Lost deep in thought and staring at her feet, she did not notice the wreckage of a boat at the water's edge until she was almost upon it. She looked up in surprise at the sky blue painted bow. The world stopped turning as she traced with a finger the remaining painted letters;

...e Skies

'Blue Skies,' she said aloud the familiar name of the boat. Her breath caught in her throat, and her heart faltered. *Rance's boat!*

'Rance,' she gasped. 'No, it cannot be.' She shook her head as tears of denial filled her eyes. It could be someone else's boat, but his was the only one painted sky blue. She looked closer at where the wood was splintered and noticed the holes in the wood, about ten or so deep punctures forming a neat crescent the size of a small shield.

Keteth. Rance is dead... She knew it to be true.

Dimly she was aware of a high-pitched whistling. When she collapsed to her knees, the noise stopped, and she realise it had been her own screaming. She felt sick. Gasping for air, quivering with weakness, she gripped the splintered wood and pulled herself to standing. The place was as silent as the grave, even the waves seemed to be silent as she stared at the broken boat of the man she still loved.

She did this. The thought was a blank statement, free of emotion, pure as logic. *She did this. You knew where she had gone, you fool! You thought you could help her?* Anger flooded through the pain.

'You chose to go to her instead of me?' she shouted at the wreck. 'She has bewitched you. Now you are dead. Dead!' The sobs came in great shudders as she clung to the cold wood of the boat.

She did this.

Issa was to blame for his death, and she must be punished. She would pay in kind, a life for a life. Her face burned hot with a feverous hatred. She would kill the bitch herself. She stroked the sky blue paint of the bow and laid her forehead against it. Issa had destroyed the only thing that she had ever been able to love in all Maioria.

There came an intense burning sensation on her thigh. She frowned, reached into her pocket and pulled out the rag-bound amulet. She did not remember putting it there. She stared at it for a long time.

Cirosa would have stayed there for hours, uncaring of the changing weather, the thickening fog, the slow pattering of rain, but a shadow passed overhead bringing her back to the present. She looked up, but the shadow had gone, and a dense fog now surrounded her. The only sound to be heard was the gentle breaking of the waves upon the shore.

The fog was strange. It had a greenish tinge to it and something about it felt quite wrong and unnatural. The hairs rose on the back of her neck. She was being watched. She looked down at the amulet in her hand. What if that harpy was nearby? The thought made her sit up.

A loud cawing croak followed by a cackling laughter from several throats came from above. Not just one harpy, but several. Her heart began to pound. She got unsteadily to her feet and stared upwards into the impenetrable mist. Just because the harpy hadn't harmed her before, didn't mean she and her brood wouldn't now. Human women were considered competition when it came to men, so harpies killed them without a thought.

Cirosa turned and fled through the fog. It was so thick she would have lost her way had she not spied her own footprints leading back up the beach. She took the long, zigzagging steps up the cliff face as fast as she could and did not slow until she reached the top. Her breath was ragged in her throat and her legs heavy as lead.

She chanced a look back down at the beach and wished she hadn't. The fog had caught up with her, and there were things moving in it; scores of large black lumbering shapes. Flying ahead of them were many harpies. The light glinted off their slick feathers as they wheeled and cawed like seagulls following a farmer's plough. Her heart lurched into her throat.

The witch birds must have seen her, and they could have easily attacked her, so why hadn't they? She wasn't going to hang about until they did. She saw no one as she hurtled through the temple grounds and slammed into the oak door. It was stiff to open as if it didn't want her inside. She shoved it open aggressively and shut and bolted it from the inside, hoping it would provide protection from whatever was coming in that awful fog.

She should warn the priests and priestesses. They could run and warn the nearest villages that the island was under attack. But there was no way she was going back out there and risking her own life. Cold sweat ran down her back, and her pulse pounded deafeningly in her head.

The wench had not only murdered Rance but brought the wrath of the Maphraxies down upon them. Issa had brought the enemy to their very doorstep, the Goddess's Sacred Isle itself.

They couldn't get inside the temple, could they? She glanced at the huge arched windows lining the white walls, inlaid as they were with thin stained glass. This was no fortress. It was never built to keep anyone out, but rather let them in. It had been her idea to put the bolt on the inside of the temple door. Before then, it had been left open, and the weather used to make a terrible mess inside with rain, leaves and sand.

She peered through the corner of a window but saw only trees partially hidden in the rolling fog. The cawing of the harpies came louder—they had to be directly above. She clapped her hand to her mouth and felt her bladder go weak. She tore away from the window and ran to the black and white marble flower decorating the floor. Her voice shook so much she could barely formulate the magical opening command. She gasped it louder again. This time it worked, but the magical exertion gave her the usual splitting headache, leaving her swaying for balance.

The petals lowered one after the other into the dark tunnel. She stepped into the darkness, the lantern barely driving back the dark. The secret staircase closed behind her, and she stopped to steady herself. For some reason, the tunnel to the sacred Mother's Chamber felt foreboding, almost malicious, and her heart pounded so loudly she was sure it echoed. It was just fear of the harpies and those awful things in the fog.

'Blessed Mother, please protect me,' her voice trembled with the first prayer she had ever thought to speak.

Whatever the Immortal Lord had offered her, she did not want it. He would sooner kill her than have her join him. But what about the power she'd felt? No, she could not leave her temple. Her duty was here, to the goddess, whether or not she spoke to her.

'Please protect me,' she breathed again, hand gripping the cold rock. 'Whatever he has to offer, I don't want it.'

Of course, the goddess would save her, she was the High Priestess of Celene. She would be the Oracle. The goddess would not let her die at the hands of the Maphraxies. But what about the power? She would not be killed by the Maphraxies, she had the amulet after all.

Had the voice not said: "I will have need of you again…"? She would not be killed, what use was she dead? Maybe they would find her. Maybe she would be rewarded—rewarded with powers beyond anything the goddess could offer. That power, it was divine. She longed to feel it again.

She couldn't think such thoughts about Baelthrom in the sacred Mother's Chamber. She had committed a great crime; communing and dealing with the Maphraxies. For a moment, she could not breathe and slumped against the wall.

'Goddess save me and avenge us for Issa's foolishness,' she whispered, but her words were hollow and empty.

The goddess wasn't here, she never had been. The goddess didn't give a damn about her. The old bitterness welled up, and tears blurred her vision as the familiar loneliness descended upon her.

CHAPTER 27

The Elders

'URG,' Marakon swallowed, his head swum and pounded at the same time. He opened his eyes, and his stomach heaved as everything blurred and moved. He registered shards of light, sunlight, falling through palm leaves. Leaves like those found in southern Frayon. They were interleaved to form a roof held up by a wall of bamboo sticks.

Bamboo. Southern Frayon. He was home, or at least somewhere he recognised. He grinned. It had all been a terrible nightmare. He was wounded and delusional. The aches and pains that gripped his whole body reassured him that he wasn't dead too. His side burned. Hot wet fabric covered it.

'Leave it,' a woman's voice commanded from behind him, her voice was deep, and so heavily accented he didn't immediately understand what she said.

He tried to see who spoke, but the world spun again when he moved. He dropped his hand and closed his eyes. A restless sleep descended upon him.

When he came round again, he was covered in sweat. His hands and feet were now bound, albeit loosely. His sword was gone and probably all his knives. It was dark save for the light of a candle in a large jar. Voices came from nearby, a man and a woman talking; the same woman who had spoken before. They had a heavy, lilting accent and often they spoke words he did not understand. It was too exhausting trying to understand everything they said. He gave up and studied the ceiling instead. Whoever they were they did not trust him. Why would anyone trust an armed stranger wounded and bloodied from battle? His side still hurt like a demon, but at least it was bound.

The man and woman came to stand beside him, holding another candle. They had fine, delicate features, long black hair and brown skin. The woman's hair was curly and bound up at the back; a few shorter strands fell about her pretty, round face. The man was a similar age, his face hard and his dark eyes mistrusting. He was tall, maybe as tall as Marakon, and his shoulders were broad and muscular. Marakon wondered if he was a soldier.

Both wore loose fitting, cream-coloured shirts and a knee-length skirt or trousers to match. They stared down at him as they spoke to each other. He felt like an exotic animal being studied. The only words he recognised were "eyes" and "ears." He grimaced, his subtly pointy ears and violet-coloured eye had betrayed him once again. They clearly saw past his human beard.

'Where am I? Why am I bound?' he asked, his voice croaked alarmingly.

He tried to sit up, but the man pushed him back down as easily as if he were a child. He panted as the world spun. The man and woman looked at each other, and something passed between them. The man spoke slowly to Marakon, choosing his words carefully.

'What are you doing here with a sword from the Old World and a wound made by Sea Devil poison?' he challenged, his eyes hard. The woman touched her companion's arm reproachfully and bent to tend Marakon's bandages. It seemed the man had chosen simple words he thought he would understand, though his accent was still difficult. They spoke Frayonesse strangely and seemed very unlike the people of southern Frayon. He began to think he was far from home again.

Being a commander for so long, he was unaccustomed to being spoken to this way, yet he could see no reason not to comply. These people may not trust him, but at least they were helping him; they had tended his wounds. He wouldn't trust a half-naked soldier with a nasty bloody wound and a sword either. He tried to speak, but his throat was too dry. The woman helped him drink some water from a wooden cup, despite the man's frown.

'Thank you,' Marakon said. She nodded. He spoke in short, clipped sentences, shocked at how he struggled to keep his breath.

'We, the Feylint Halanoi, were fighting the Histanatarns while we hunted Maphraxies, the Immortals. My soldiers and I were attacked. I was wounded when the black dragons came. I don't remember much else. I guess I was ship-wrecked and I arrived upon these shores...' he had to stop to catch his breath. 'Where am I?'

'Impossible,' growled the man. 'No one can make it across that ocean, not even if they could get past that white monster.' The woman looked from him to Marakon with a worried frown.

Marakon blinked. "...*Across that ocean...*" Could he have travelled across the Lost Sea? He shrugged. 'I agree. Although now... Where I come from we aren't even sure if there is land beyond the Lost Sea, and certainly not any people. Do you have a map of your land? I have no idea where I am.'

The man narrowed his eyes at him as if measuring him and his words up.

'He does not lie,' the woman said gently, wonderment in her eyes. The man looked at her for a long moment, then relaxed his hard look as if her word was to be trusted completely. He turned back to Marakon.

'And what of these Histan-a-tarns you fought? Are they the sea devils?' he ignored Marakon's question, eyes glittering with hatred.

Marakon wasn't sure how best to explain. 'Small vicious fish-like people on fast boats?'

'Sea devils,' they both nodded, speaking in unison.

'We haven't heard of the other, these Maph-rax-iss,' the man said. 'Unless you mean goblins or Incubi.'

It was his turn to be surprised. Did they not suffer the immortals? Was this truly some remote land free from the tyranny of the Immortal Lord? How far away from home was he? The Maphraxies had not headed west into the Uncharted Lands, was this really where he was now? The man shifted impatiently.

'The Maphraxies are our most reviled enemies. All that lives fight these immortal beasts, for they take everything and leave nothing. They enslave the soul to oblivion, and the lifeless body becomes one of them; a hideous, brainless, immortal beast, mad with a hunger to destroy all life. They take our children and steal their souls,' he stopped for breath. How could he describe in a few sentences those he had fought his entire life? Those who had butchered his family and murdered his friends?

'They gave me this,' he tapped his eyepatch.

The man and woman spoke to each other and Marakon, now a little more familiar with their accents, understood more of what was said. It was like a strange dialect of Frayonesse.

'Can he be trusted?'

'The Elders ... spoken of trouble in the east...'

'…plague so terrible … spreads over the land killing all.'

'…fear it … come here…'

'…they say the white monster is dead…'

'We should not reveal too much,' the man ended and motioned to her to be silent. She scowled at him. They still did not trust Marakon or necessarily even believe him.

'The White Beast is dead?' Marakon said, but the man did not respond.

'We know nothing of these, Maph-raxies… But an enemy of the hated sea devils is surely an ally to us,' the man said to his surprise. 'We will unbind if you swear the oath of peace in our land and against our people.'

He nodded. 'I come in peace. I have no idea how I got here or why I am alive whilst everyone else is surely dead. I am a friend to your people,' he said it almost too quickly, but the pain was returning in excruciating waves.

He passed out with a final thought: they did not know who the Maphraxies were. What a blessing.

Marakon awoke to the sound of birds singing, and bright sunlight fell once more through the leaves. He felt much stronger and with that returned strength came a renewed sense of urgency. He had to find something, something important, if only he could remember what. Perhaps these people knew. They spoke of the Elders; they sounded wise, maybe they could help him.

He sat up, pleased to find he was no longer bound, and the young woman came alone into the room. She passed him a steaming bowl of food that smelt wonderful. He could not remember when he had last eaten. He took the thin, dark-brown bread, and dipped it into the spicy broth. She waited silently while he ate and took his empty bowl when he had finished.

'I'm indebted to you,' he said and noticed his sword had been placed in the corner of the room next to the bed. A measure of their growing trust, or the power of the oath he had sworn.

'So you know of Frayon, of Drax and the… "Old World," ' that is what they had called it.

'Our legends say we lived in a land beside Frayonesse separated by an ocean; long before the Lost Sea and the White Beast came. I guess that is why our language is similar,' she said. 'Our language is sacred to us. We are careful to keep it unchanged since the days of our ancestors.

'Our land was called Unafay, and they say it was a land of abundance, beauty and great people. We were far more advanced than we are now,' she looked into the distance wistfully. 'But then they created Dark Rift and things changed. Then the demons came. Our land was destroyed, and we were forced to flee west. Our land exists no more.'

Memory stirred in Marakon. *"In the Valley of Death terrible things happened."* That strange old man had spoken of a land, the place where Keteth created his Shadowlands. No, that had been a dream.

'I would love to see the Old World,' she said, bringing him back to the present. 'What is it like? We still tell stories about the Old World but... it's not the same as knowing.'

He wondered where to begin. 'It's, well, diverse. Hot and humid in the south with some trees and plants similar to here, though not as big. Atalanph, the furthest southern country is mostly a hot, dry desert.'

'Desert,' she frowned?

He smiled. 'Can you imagine sand, like that next to the sea, and no plants or trees—just endless hills of sand? Trees only exist beside a few rivers.'

She shook her head. 'I can imagine it, but I don't like it. A place without trees seems bad and unnatural. There's a place like that here. An awful place. Cursed. We call it the Drowning Wastes, though we don't know what happened there.'

'The Drowning Wastes,' Marakon mouthed, and a shiver of fear (or was it excitement?) ran down his spine. 'It's cold the further north you go until you reach a frozen desert. Water is also frozen, and the whole place is filled with white mountains where few things can grow. In between, there are many different trees, unlike the ones here.

'There are many lands and many people, or there were. The Maphraxies are destroying us all.' He suddenly felt horribly sad. Sad for his home that was taken from him, even sad for the elves who were forced to leave. It must have shown for she looked sad too as if feeling his pain.

'What happened to your eye?' she asked lightly, changing the subject.

He scratched his eyepatch habitually. 'A Maphraxie bastard took it. Not blind but... changed.' He didn't know what compelled him to do so then, maybe he was keen to prove he was a friend and that he still had an eye, but he lifted up the patch.

She stared at it, stricken. The air around them changed from sunny and light to heavy and cloying. The colour drained from her face, and she fell back against the wall with a gasp, dropping the empty bowl. His eye felt hot and it seemed she stared right through him. A deafening sound of metal grating upon metal filled his head and he struggled to breath the thick air. She tore her eyes away and the noise stopped. With a great effort, he let the eyepatch drop. His heart pounded, and sweat ran down his back. Had she heard that terrible noise as well?

'What happened?' he gasped, gripping the bed to keep from falling off it. She shook her head, trembling.

'Something awful—to do that to you, your eye… You bring danger, yet you don't know it. I don't know what. I can't explain. Never reveal your eye here again, for your own safety and ours.'

'I'm sorry. That has never happened before. I don't understand. I didn't intend to… I didn't know,' he swallowed, desperately trying to understand what had happened. He suddenly felt sick and lay back down. She came closer and spoke quietly.

'I see danger, often before it happens. Just lately I… I see more danger as the days go by. It makes it hard to think straight,' she shook her head.

So, she had the gift of foresight, like the Seers of Myrn, the elven girl in the market, and the old witch in the square. He didn't meet one for years, and then three turn up one after the other.

'You have a rare gift,' he smiled in an effort to ease her worry in spite of his own.

She did not smile. 'Some might say. Though truly I feel cursed.' She fell silent for a long while before she spoke again.

'Your eye. I don't know why, but it brings danger. I see death.'

'I don't know what you saw, but believe me, I come in peace,' he said.

She nodded but said nothing. There was not much else he could say. He swung his legs over the bed and carefully stood up, wobbling a little. At least his wound no longer throbbed so much.

'My name is Marakon. What's yours?'

She frowned as if he had been rude, then smiled as if in forgiveness. 'Jarlain,' she replied.

'Jarlain,' he said it to himself, testing the pronunciation. 'Jarlain, I know nothing about my eye or what it means. But I will never reveal it here again. The one thing I do know is that I'm in sore need of a wash.'

'You can wash through there,' she indicated to the opening on the other side of his bed.

Outside was a small clearing no more than eight feet in diameter and secluded by trees. Water trickled over a rocky wall that had been funnelled deliberately to create a trickling waterfall. A dip in the ground created a pool of water about a foot deep, which then overflowed into another furrow that ran away through the trees.

He slipped off his torn clothes and stood naked in the deliciously cold water. There was a round, pumice-style rock on a ledge, along with orange-coloured soap (he assumed it was soap). He picked them up and soaped and scrubbed himself, working away at the salt, the dirt, the blood—but not the guilt for the soldiers he had led to their deaths, that could never be scrubbed off. That was his curse, a commander's curse. He stepped away from the waterfall and stood in the hot sunlight that came through the trees. It felt good on his wet skin. He closed his eyes. If only sunlight could cleanse his soul.

Bokaard, Lanac, Erylin... Then the Dread Dragon fire. Guilt and memory, all that was left. He blinked back tears.

When he opened his eyes, he noticed clean clothes folded neatly on a stool by the door. His ragged ones were missing. Had the woman left them for him whilst he was washing? Pushing aside his embarrassment, he pulled on the linen tunic and knee-length slacks—the same clothes that they wore, and in this humid heat he understood why. It felt good to be in clean skin and clothes again.

By the time he went back inside the man was there. He was slightly shorter than Marakon but just as well-muscled.

'Thank you,' Marakon said, gesturing to his clothes.

The man gave a half smile, the first Marakon had seen, then turned to leave just as Marakon began to introduce himself.

'Tarn,' the man said from beyond the door. 'The name is Tarn, Marakon,' and then he was gone.

He closed his mouth. The man did not trust him yet, and why should he? He was already sweating from the humid heat despite the cool shower and loose clothes. He couldn't bear lying down any longer, and after a moments thought, decided to leave his sword and follow the man. He bumped into Jarlain in the next room.

'Come, the Elders wish to see you,' she smiled.

He raised his eyebrows and followed her through a small dark room furnished with round wicker stools, rich, red and purple rugs and a low table. The walls were a mix of bamboo and hardened mud. It was lovely and cool inside. They went through another door into a small cooking area. A strange hole in the wall looked like an oven, and various plates and bowls were stacked upon a table. Another door led them outside.

They walked barefoot on sandy, red earth. He squinted in the bright sunlight and took in his surroundings. There were many small, simple houses made of mud and bamboo, bordering the forty-foot or so wide path. Beyond the huts to his left, dense jungle stretched up high, dark and green. To his right was also thick with trees and bushes, but they were not as tall or dense. He could smell the sea and hear the sound of surf coming from the right.

All the houses were decorated brightly with yellow and pink flowering vines cleverly wound around their entrances. There were people everywhere; young and old, male and female—all tall, black-haired and brown-skinned. Some carried big woven baskets on their backs filled with plants he did not recognise. Some had donkeys laden with cloth, others simply stood chatting, the children running around them as they played.

They all looked at him. Some frowned, others smiled uncertainly, some nodded in greeting. He nodded to each of them the same, feeling pale-skinned and out of place. They seemed proud and respectable people. It was a blessing. He could have awoken in the sacrificial cages of Histanatarn.

They came to a stop by a large well surrounded by foot high stones. Intricate pictures of animals and birds were carved into each of them—some animals of which he had never seen before. They looked like huge pigs with long flappy noses. Others were deer-like but with two straight horns rather than antlers. One looked like a bear standing up on two feet, but it had small curved horns, slanted goat-like eyes and a completely flat face that looked unnervingly human. It seemed particularly large. He hoped he wouldn't meet one.

All of the houses had been only one floor except the one closest to the well. It was two storeys high and much larger than the others. Older people emerged from the house. They all had white hair and wrinkled faces. All the men were clean-shaven except for the last who had a long red-dyed beard that reached to his chest. He decided to call him Red Beard. He held an ornately carved staff, though his back was straight and his legs looked strong.

'The Elders?' he queried. Jarlain nodded.

He wondered if Red Beard was a wizard. All the wizards he had known carried staves. Jarlain smiled reassuringly and took his arm, leading him towards the five people who stood staring at him, their long, unbound white hair moving in the wind.

'They don't bite,' Jarlain grinned, and he wondered what sort of expression must have been on his face.

All right, he was apprehensive. Luckily he had decided to leave his sword behind. It showed that he was not afraid and that he came in peace.

The "Elders," as Jarlain called them, watched his approach with solemn expressions and perhaps a hint of wariness. These people had enemies, of course they were wary. Their feet and hands were decorated in swirling blue paint, all similar in design but none exactly the same. They were dressed in loose white linen robes that fell just below the knee.

Other villagers crowded around them. Now they were standing still, he noticed some men and women had long bows slung on their backs that were as tall as they were, and long sheaths of quivers dangling from their leather belts. All those with bows wore wide, foot-long curved blades tied at their waists and held in brightly coloured beaded sheathes.

Not knowing exactly how to greet them, he saluted them in elven, showing them his unarmed upturned palms before bringing them to his heart and bowing as he did so. These people reminded him of elves, the way they lived simply and close to nature, yet were clearly skilled builders, archers and metal-smiths. He sensed the Old Way strong here and not without a pang of loss. He had no qualms revealing his elven heritage to these people who probably did not know what an elf was, let alone seen one before. Their faces did not change and they continued to stare at him solemnly. His palms turned sweaty and he shifted awkwardly under their gaze.

'We have not seen the elven blessing in a long time,' one of the Elder women said in a deep voice that carried easily over the crowd.

'A very long time indeed,' echoed an Elder man, 'and even then only in the Dreaming.'

The others nodded.

'I would not have said you were elven, at first, but now I see more clearly,' the same woman said, squinting.

'My mother was elven, my father, human,' he explained briefly, 'and I carry the burden of guilt of my ancestors,' he added. It was a test, nothing more. How much did these people know of the world? How long had they lived here in isolation? Could this possibly be the Uncharted Lands? It was a crazy idea, but the only one that made any sense so far.

All races in Maioria understood the Elven Burden; the crime in withdrawing from Maioria, leaving her people to a fate worse than death at the hands of the Immortal Lord. It was the burden of guilt those left behind would be forced to carry.

'The Hidden Ones told us of the Elven race fleeing the spreading darkness,' the elder woman said. 'Regardless of the right and wrong of it, the sins of the father are not those of the son, Half-Elf.'

He grimaced at the old label. She said no more as the Elder with the red beard spoke, his thin voice portraying his age, though his clear brown eyes did not. The language he spoke, Marakon did not recognise at all. All the Elders listened and then looked back at Marakon when he had finished. He then spoke in words Marakon understood.

'The Hidden Ones have spoken to me and explained what the Dreaming has been telling me for a full year. Now I understand. The stranger has come to find the Banished Legion. Zanu the dark goddess is calling him to claim back what once was his. The Hidden Ones say Zanu's Chosen walks the land and the dark moon heralds her coming. The same dark moon we have all seen.'

Marakon could not hide the shock on his face as the Elder's words strummed the chords of truth within him. He felt liberated and yet he could not breathe for his constricted throat. It was as if a long-closed door momentarily opened, allowing him access to memories from long ago in which he was another person, in another life, in many lives. The pang of urgency stabbed at him again, the strongest yet, and he fought to slow his racing mind.

He glimpsed his lives like the flickering of a picture book. He had been a soldier of the Feylint Halanoi before, many times before. But he knew that, had felt that anyway. There were lives before those too, though he glimpsed only snapshots of them. He had been everything; a man, a woman, an elf, a dwarf, rich and poor, gifted with magic, and a simpleton—and in them all he had suffered terribly.

Those lives didn't matter now, but they were all leading back to that life he did not want to remember, the time when his soul was cursed to a life of suffering and pain forever. He wanted to turn away from it and begged to be spared from remembering what he had so long forgotten, but who was there to spare him? The world spun and he breathed the air of another land.

Green grass billowed under a clear blue sky. The hooves of his horse pounded into the ground, the metal of his armour shone in the sunlight.

His tabard was white and upon it was adorned a silver star. *Knights of the Shining Star.*

Beside him galloped others; men, women, humans, elves and dwarves. *Our hearts are pure, and we are glorious! We bring freedom. Freedom from the demons. Demons...*

Memories whirled as the visions moved. A battle unfolded. The clang and clash of metal, the roars of hate, the cries of the dying. Huge, hairless beasts flew towards him. They were coming from a swirling black hole in the trees, twenty feet in diameter. Demons from the Murk. His sword rose, a demon fell under his blow with a terrible howling that clawed at his soul.

The battle in the woods became another fought atop a high windy land. Thousands of knights glittered in the darkness against twice as many demons. Cutting, howling, bleeding, dying. An ancient song carried on the air, the song they sang when it was all over.

"We fought them high, we fought them low."

How many battles? How many years? Countless lives lost as decades passed by. The world spun and the demons were gone. He stood staring down at his helmet ringed in a golden crown, the song chanting on the wind.

"We drove them down, deep down below!"

"We fought them high, we fought them low.

"We drove them down, deep down below!"

Astride their white horses, the knights watched the people thronging through the city; all laughing and crying and casting petals upon them. *Victory is ours. We are glorious.* The thought lifted his heart higher than he thought possible.

Clouds darkened the sky, the air, the ground. The sun disappeared, and he was suffocating in a green mist. It came from a broken vial. He tried not to breathe, knew he should not, but a breath forced itself in. The rage came fast. Old faces, young faces, male and female, all whirling before him; crying, bleeding and falling from his bloodied sword.

'No!' he screamed, but he couldn't stop his hands and his killing sword.

Laughter came from behind. He turned and stared in horror at a headless man standing there. The laughter came from the head at his feet. Laughing. Laughing. *I know that face!*

A barren land, a desert. Houses in a rock face. Then skeletons rising out of the dirt. They turned to face him and pointed, then stomped towards him.

'No!' he screamed again. He was falling in that cloying mist, thrashing and choking. A voice echoed around him, the young elf-girl in the market.

"Can you find and restore a long forgotten glory?"

The suffocating receded. Marakon blinked. Sweat ran down his face, and he realised Jarlain was steadying him, a worried look in her eyes. He looked away and breathed deeply, wiped the sweat from his eyes. The memories were true, they did not lie, but he understood none of them.

'The Hidden Ones,' Red Beard continued as if he hadn't noticed Marakon's plight and no time had passed at all, 'see the everlasting truth and the ages pass as seconds to them, but they have deigned it necessary to commune with me at this time.'

'Who are these "Hidden Ones"?' Marakon asked, his voice hoarse, but Red Beard seemed not to hear him and continued without pause. 'Too long have we been apart from the Old World as the darkness rose over it. Perhaps we too should share the Burden.

'The king comes to find his Banished Legion, and his coming signals our time is at an end. The darkness will spread here. He must be led to the Drowning Wastes. There, the Hidden Ones say, is where he will complete his final task, the reason for which the boatman brought him here.' He spread his hands wide. 'I do not understand much of what the Hidden Ones say, I tell you only what they told me.'

The old bearded man turned and started walking back to the house, leaning heavily on his staff as if the effort of speaking had exerted him too much.

'I don't understand,' Marakon started, where the hell did he start? 'What are the Drowning Wastes? Who are the Hidden Ones? I'm not a king. Who are the Banished Legion? Hey!' he called, but the old man did not stop. Marakon started after him, but Jarlain laid a surprisingly strong grip on his arm.

'Our master cannot hear you with his ears,' she said softly. 'He can only hear you with his mind.'

'What? He's deaf?' Marakon said in shock.

'Only in the physical sense. His outer ears are gone so that he might hear with his inner ears. All of our High Elders have had their ears broken so they might hear the Hidden Ones. You have much to learn of our ways, half-elf,' she said.

He grimaced, though her smile was warm. It was the second time in only a few minutes that they had called him that.

'Who are the Hidden Ones?' he asked again. Is that why he had been brought here by the boatman? To find this Banished Legion? No, that had all been a crazy dream, but why didn't it feel like one? How did the old man know more about himself than he did? Jarlain looked at him, her handsome, dark eyes piercing as if she were choosing words that he would understand.

'To us they are the spirits of the forest. They are half in this dimension half in the one above us. Some glimpse them as a light in the forest, gone as soon as seen. Very few people can hear them. We have always had a special relationship with them, but no one knows why or can remember how far back we began communicating. They see the world as it spans the centuries, whereas we can only see the present. That is as much as I know of them. The High Elder mostly keeps the knowledge he receives secret, for it is too much for us all to understand, and it keeps that knowledge from our enemies.'

They walked silently back to Jarlain's dwelling. Unfortunately, her answer only served to create more questions, and his mind was still reeling from the onslaught of memories from his other lives. Lives he couldn't quite let himself believe were real.

'Are you hungry?' she asked when they came to her house.

'No,' he mumbled. 'Thanks. I just need to sleep.'

He certainly did, he was dog-tired. But when he lay down all he could think about were those memories. They went through his mind over and over and over again.

King Marakazian. No, my name is Marakon, I'm no king. King Marakazian of the Banished Legion...

CHAPTER 28

They Call Her the Raven Queen

HAMEKA came to a stop where the dusty road leading from the Castle Elune wound down the hill. The amulet pulsed hot and bright, and within it he saw what the Dromoorai saw; a fair-haired woman fleeing through the woods away from the castle.

'Capture her,' he commanded. 'No one shall escape!'

The Dromoorai silently obeyed and steered the Dread Dragon lower.

'Alive,' he added, grinning like a cat. *We have caught a mouse.*

He held his breath as the Dread Dragon descended upon the woman, tearing trees apart in the chase. She screamed as its giant claws snatched her up in a crushing grip. Hameka lost the woman from view as they soared up into the air.

He let his breath go. Something good had come of today. He waited patiently for the Dromoorai to deliver the prize. Its great black bulk shook the ground as it landed, wings billowing dust and leaves all about them. He shielded his eyes as black wings folded back and the dust settled.

The woman rolled limply from the Dread Dragon's grasp. She wore a nightdress made of fine silk, a thin gold necklace adorned her neck, and a plain gold ring announced her marriage. Not the clothing of a servant, he deduced.

'Lady Eleny, the castle's keeper,' Baelthrom breathed.

His lord's ability to read so much about a person always unnerved him. He could see into the mind and probably into the soul as well. The woman stirred, a groan escaping her throat. He bent over her thoughtfully as she opened her eyes. She tried to sit up. He smacked her across the face, splitting her lip, and flinging her back down on her side. Driven by fury rather than fear, she struggled to sit once more.

Defiance? He grinned, defiance was more fun. Blood flowed freely from her lip and she tried to stem it with a shaking hand. She looked at him with pure hatred and spat the blood at him. He recoiled and wiped his cheek, then grabbed her by the hair and hauled her to her knees. She screamed and kicked at him weakly.

'Where is the dark-haired girl?' he growled, bending her head back.

'I don't know what you mean,' she snarled and struggled to be free of his iron grip.

His amulet flared into a burning ball of red light. He angled her head, forcing her to look into the glow. After a moment or two, she stopped struggling, and her eyes became wide and vacant in the red light. A moment more and her pupils clouded over, turning completely black as Baelthrom locked onto her and began to sift through the contents of her mind.

'They call her the "Raven Queen",' Baelthrom whispered, the sound of wind blowing through leaves.

The Raven Queen... He knew he should have killed that bloody raven.

Ely felt the probing mind as a painful stabbing in her head. She fought desperately to resist, to somehow keep that mind from penetrating hers, but she could no more stop it than she could hold back the tide. So she tried to hide her thoughts, to flee from the corruption that sought to find her secrets and unravel her very being. That too she failed.

The dark mind that entered hers searched for all her memories of Issa, casting aside anything that was not. From the day she arrived half-drowned on the shores of Celene to the time she left to face Keteth. All was seen and taken from her.

I knew they would come for you, Issa, my friend. I've seen this in my nightmares. I could only try to delay them. Thank Zanufey that you are not here now.

She wept as the red light burned into her soul, finding even what she believed the woman to be; Zanufey's chosen Raven Queen of prophecy, the spirit of Zanufey incarnate, the one who could destroy the Immortal Lord and lead Maioria back into the light. She had betrayed Issa, through no will of her own, yet she had betrayed her none-the-less.

Baelthrom released her mind, and she slumped sobbing to the floor. Knowing her betrayal broke her more than anything they could do to her. Her dreams had warned her of now. Her time was near, just as she'd seen it in her dreams. As a priestess of the Great Mother, she would accept her death.

Who'd have thought that now, in her darkest hour, her training as a priestess all those years ago would be of most use. They could and would do what they wanted with her body, now they had already ravished her mind, but they would never have her soul. Already her body felt distant as she closed her eyes and began to detach her consciousness. She was surprised at how easy the old skill came back to her.

In the past, priests and priestesses spent years training their minds to travel free of the body. They were also taught how to sever the silver cord that bound the consciousness to the body should they need to. Such a severing could not be undone. But, as Ely and many others who had left the Temple saw it, the Temple had degraded from spirituality into control and money making. The Order of the Goddess no longer focused on sacred esoterics, preferring instead to study the cold ordinary logic of the mundane.

'Thank you,' the man smiled indulgently, but to Ely's half-closed eyes his face was a blur and his words echoed from far away. 'We have no use for you in our ranks, so you shall be made an example of, to all those who dare to fight against the Immortal Lord; the only true glorious God!'

'We will never stop fighting,' she heard herself say.

She smiled, they were good words, the best words she could have said, maybe even had ever said. It was a shame there was no one there to hear them who could write them on her gravestone. It was a shame they would be her last.

The man gave a cruel smile and motioned to the dark dwarves beside him. To Ely's dimmed consciousness they were little more than greyish blurs with small yellow orbs for eyes. They were growing dimmer by the moment. They lunged for her, gripping her painfully in their thick, strong groping hands, tearing at her clothes.

She snapped the silver cord.

The distant world where her body was, quickly dimmed. She turned her consciousness away from it as soft light surrounded her. Faces, indistinct but somehow familiar, crowded into view, all smiling and beckoning to her. One face became clearer than the rest, and she looked up into the tanned face of her husband, Dargan.

'My love, how I have missed you,' she said, her voice was airy and light. 'So long have I walked this barren world alone. Bring me home, let us be together once more.'

He smiled back at her. The light began to fade, and she no longer remembered she had a body.

Another face formed, hooded. First, only a smooth, luminous chin was visible, but then white hands drew back the hood, revealing a long slender nose and then incredible eyes. Eyes that were beautiful, dark and deep, and within which stars and galaxies swirled. Love flowed from those eyes and she opened herself to it.

Hameka was almost bored by the time they were done with Lady Eleny. The woman seemed to have died before they could torture her, much to his annoyance. The older priestesses and priests were able to depart the body quickly, which is why they were rarely used for the Elixir of Immortality production. *Some revenge that was.*

He ordered her body to be hung, bloodied and naked, from the oak tree that stood in the grounds before the entrance to the castle's courtyard.

'Filthy goddess worshippers,' he spat. With his knife, he carved the symbol of the Maphraxies, the three peaks of Maphrax, upon her chest. Her blood flowed little now her heart no longer pumped it.

'How fitting,' he smiled, for the symbol looked like a crescent moon, a symbol of the goddess, but lying on its back and impaled by the central mountain.

'Lord Baelthrom?' he said into the amulet. 'Our symbol of Maphrax appears to symbolise the death of the goddess, the destroyer of life.' The amulet glowed dark red and a low laugh rumbled from within it.

The Dromoorai that had brought the woman still stood grounded beside the Dread Dragon. Hameka stepped lightly towards it.

'Take to the skies and destroy everything. Anyone not matching the description of the girl or able to wield magic is yours to feed off. Remember to collect the children.'

At his command, the Dromoorai climbed onto the Dread Dragon's back, lifted the heavy chains as easily as if they were rope, and leapt into the sky. The Dread Dragon was so big it appeared to move in slow motion towards the castle.

Red flames bellowed out of its mouth and covered the courtyard. The other Dromoorai closed in, and the castle, the symbol of peace upon the sacred Isle of the Goddess, became a furious battle of flames—a fire so hot that the stones it was built of began to melt. Anyone alive and hiding in there would soon perish.

Hameka split his horde of Maphraxies into three groups. One would move along the north coast, the other the south, and he would take his group through the centre of the island. Burning, killing and capturing.

The first village they encountered was small and in a state of panic. People ran in all directions carrying bundles and loading wagons. They must have seen the smoke from the castle or Dread Dragons in the sky. Not that it mattered, this was a small island, and there was nowhere to go or hide. The village was set ablaze like the castle, and all the inhabitants slain apart from two children.

The Maphraxies moved swiftly through village after village, killing, ravaging and burning as they went; leaving nothing untouched, leaving everything spoiled. But their acts did not go unseen, for throughout it all they were followed by the raven who kept just out of sight; watching, waiting, its intelligent eyes faithfully recording the devastation.

The fog was clearing as the necromancer's magic waned. It would have brightened too had the air not been filled with the smoke of burning villages. But still, they had not found that woman and Hameka's mood was darkening again.

Finally, they reached the last settlement, the glistening white spire of the Temple of Celene reached up through the trees on the east coast. His group was not the first to arrive and already all of the buildings were on fire, even the temple itself.

Bodies of grey, brown and white-robed priests and priestesses littered the ground, ready to be eaten by the Dread Dragons. Terror was rank in the air, as was the smell of burning flesh. The dark dwarves heckled a group of priestesses they had already rounded up, and there was a line of unconscious, bound men, which the harpies were gathering around. One of the young priestesses in grey robes had dark hair to her shoulders.

Hameka pointed at her. 'Bring her to me.'

Two Maphraxies dragged her towards him. She hung limply in their grasp, her head lolling to the side. He grasped her chin and forced her to look at him, but her eyes were dark brown and not the colour of the sea. He snapped her head back viciously and sighed in exasperation.

'Wait,' Baelthrom commanded.

The amulet burst into life once more. Hameka grasped the girl's chin until her eyes locked onto the red glowing amulet. Her eyes were raw with terror as they turned black. Sweat beaded her brow until it ran in rivulets down her face. Blood trickled from her nose, and she began to convulse. The amulet grew dim.

'Not her and no useful memories of her,' Baelthrom's voice was hard with disappointment.

Hameka cursed. They had not found that cursed wizard either. He could not let his lord down. He dropped her head and with a motion of his hand the Maphraxies dropped her. He looked down at the woman. Her body was quivering though her eyes were closed. She was pretty enough, though, and his interrogations needed perfecting for when he found the *real* one.

'Some fun perhaps?' Baelthrom said.

Baelthrom knowing his thoughts unnerved Hameka, but he tried not to let it show.

'Bind her and set her aside,' Hameka ordered. 'No one is to touch her, understand? I'll not have anything touched by filthy dwarves. See to it.'

'Yes Commander,' the two Maphraxies replied, their thick, guttural voices almost unintelligible.

The woman was bound, gagged, set aside and closely guarded. He stalked towards the temple for a final search. Blood splattered up the sides of the once glistening white temple, now mostly blackened and charred from dragon fire. The bodies of those who had tried to fight were strewn about the place, lying where they had fallen. He carefully stepped over bodies, limbs and bloody mud so as not to ruin his clean boots. War and killing was a filthy, messy business.

The temple's entrance was a blackened hole where once the door had been. Hesitantly, he stepped inside. His skin crawled, he hated any place of goddess worship. Their goddess was full of fake promises, useless powers, and death. Who was to say she even existed? There wasn't any proof to speak of. They would wipe away all memory of this goddess in all her guises from Maioria and raise up Baelthrom, a true god who promised life everlasting and powers never seen or felt before.

His footsteps echoed. The temple was still pristine inside, a sharp contrast to its outsides. It was eerily empty and cold. He shivered and pulled his cloak closer about him, hand gripping his crossbow. Somehow he had expected it to be filled with chairs and flowers, rich tapestries and flowing drapes.

Had they been like that when he was a boy? He had a feeling they might have been. But now all memories of his life before Baelthrom were hazy and he had spent years trying to erase them through necromantic black art.

Still, this cold, empty place was a surprise. Perhaps the goddess had also abandoned this world, if she ever really existed at all. The thought made him feel more comfortable, and he walked confidently. He came to a stop in the centre of the great domed hall and the amulet against his chest grew brighter.

'There's an enchantment here,' Baelthrom said.

Hameka looked around but could see nothing out of the ordinary.

'Beneath,' Baelthrom breathed.

He looked down at the black and white marbled floor shaped into a flower with a blood red centre. He shielded his eyes as the amulet grew too bright to look upon. Energy moved. There came a deafening crack as the floor split in two. The crack continued to lengthen across the marble stones in opposite directions and all the way up the white walls. It snaked up into the spire and was lost from view. The weakened floor began to crumble, and the black and white petals collapsed into the crack.

It was not the first time that Baelthrom had used magic through the Key Stone, but it was not a common occurrence. Hameka could feel strong magic, but could not wield much. Each time he tasted the elixir his magical abilities grew.

The magical charge dissipated and the dust began to settle. He made his way to the four-foot wide hole that now severed the marble flower and peered down. A faint, cool breeze came from below, indicating an exit down there somewhere. The petals, though crumbled, were still usable as steps leading down into the darkness.

'Search down there,' Baelthrom said.

The eagerness in his lord's voice was both annoying and worrying. If she was not down there, there was nowhere left to search. Three Maphraxies blundered around the corner, then lowered their weapons.

'There was funder and noith,' one slurred unintelligibly. The others nodded.

A thick wound had slashed part of his top lip in, making it even harder to understand what the numbskull was saying. He probably never even felt the blow to his face.

'The thunder was magic, our Immortal Lord's magic. The noise was the splitting temple,' he explained witheringly, motioning to the great chasm before them. 'Now we go down there. You go first.'

'We go down there, Mafter Commander?'

The hint of uncertainty was odd in the Maphraxie's voice, for they were not given to fear. So, the goddess's temple unnerved everyone, not just him.

'Of course!' he snapped. 'You think we came all this way for fun?'

The Maphraxies actually looked indignant, despite their dim wits. They were getting soft, they had been too long away from the bigger battles. He would send them straight to the front line after this, and starve them too; it always made them fight harder.

The deformed-lipped Maphraxie looked at the other two, then hastily descended into the darkness, black-iron mace swinging loosely in front of it. Hameka went next, the red glow of the Key Stone lighting the way, and the other two followed behind.

The Maphraxie in front stumbled, and Hameka crashed into its armoured back.

'Curse it, what now?' he growled.

'Not enough light,' it mumbled back.

'Let me go in front.' He shoved past into the blackness, hand groping the rock for balance. But even the glow from the amulet seemed dull and weak down here as if Baelthrom himself had been shut out. It was his turn to stumble in the dark.

He walked for what seemed like hours in the dark tunnel, hating every step leading deeper into the lair of the goddess. He began to feel quite alone, despite the immortal presence of the Maphraxies behind him. His mind started to play tricks as he walked, and the ground seemed to squirm beneath his feet as if trying to shake him off. Things brushed past his face, but his wafting hand never hit anything. His breath rattled in his throat and more than once he heard noises ahead.

'Who's there?' he stopped and barked. The Maphraxies crashed into each other.

Only silence replied. There was nothing there. He tore the bandage off his head in irritation. The bleeding had stopped, though the deep welts burned, probably with infection.

The cavern suddenly rumbled and shook violently, flinging him and the Maphraxies against the wall. The tremor was brief. Stillness settled. He steadied himself and wiped the sweat from his forehead, sucking in the cold air, willing his racing heart to slow. The amulet was still dull; it was not Baelthrom's magic that made it shudder. The thought of being crushed or buried alive down here filled him with terror.

The tunnel shook again and with it came the deafening noise of cracking rock. He lurched forwards, half-running, half-falling in the darkness. Finally, he saw a soft light in the distance, too yellow and dim to be daylight, but relief washed over him nonetheless. He slowed as he neared.

'Stay back in the darkness,' he ordered the Maphraxies. 'The mortals can smell your stench a mile off.' He couldn't stand the smell of them either. They shifted behind him, stooped and bent, too big to stand easily within the narrow tunnel.

On silent feet, he crept towards the light, his crossbow at the ready. Half-drawn curtains separated the tunnel from the room. He peered cautiously through the gap, his eyes taking a few moments to adjust to the light. There were candles dotted around a circular room about twenty feet wide and eight feet high, and seemed to be hewn straight out of the rock rather than built with bricks.

There was a human-shaped shadow on the wall on the far side. It moved, and he heard a female voice murmur something. He licked his lips in anticipation. It could be her—and if she was not here, then she was not on the island. It had to be her.

He stepped forward. His foot scraped on a fallen rock. With a strangled cry the person in the room jumped up and fled towards another doorway. He lunged into the room, aimed and fired his crossbow before the figure could disappear through the other curtain. He was deadly accurate, decades of experience with his crossbow had made him so, but with poisoned darts, it didn't matter where you hit on the body, each hit would be a kill. He'd actually had to learn where not to hit to ensure he didn't kill outright.

He cursed again as the fair-haired woman cried out and crumpled to the floor. Not dark-haired and tall, like she should have been. Sighing, he walked over to her, kicking the brightly coloured cushions out of his way.

'Search the place!' he barked to the Maphraxies outside. They shuffled into the room.

He stood over the woman. The dart protruded from her shoulder. Blood darkened her white robes and the poison was already stiffening her limbs in paralysis. He expected her to leave her body quickly, but was surprised when she didn't.

'The High Priestess of Celene,' Baelthrom whispered and the amulet grew a little brighter but his lord's voice sounded far away. 'Keep her alive; she knows much that is of use to us.'

The High Priestess at his feet was slowly dying, but perhaps the poison stopped her snapping her life-cord. That was a good thing to know. She stared up at him in terror; only her blue eyes and mouth able to move as she lay stricken on the floor, her breath coming in gasps. He smiled at her and brushed a few golden strands of hair away from her pretty face.

'Where is the dark-haired girl?' he asked for a third time that day. The priestess's eyes flared in hatred, and she looked away. Her hatred seemed not for him.

'Your temple has been destroyed; your priestesses given to the pleasures of the dark dwarves; your priests given to the pleasures of the harpies. The whole island burns in the fires made by Dread Dragons— and this is how your goddess protects you?' he laughed. 'We want that woman you call the Raven Queen and you will tell us where she is.'

He gripped behind her head and held her face close to the amulet. Her eyes were forced from his, down to the blood-red light. She did not shake and judder like the others had, perhaps the poison prevented her, or perhaps she was simply too afraid to fight. He watched her eyes darken to black. They shone like onyx jewels as Baelthrom's mind locked into hers, and her face contorted in pain. A few seconds more and her eyes clamped shut and she slumped, unconscious.

'She knew the girl and had something to do with that wizard who has the orb,' Baelthrom said. 'She also knows something about a plan to destroy Keteth. She is the one who received the Shadow Stone. This one will be our ally, you will see to it.'

'Yes, my lord,' Hameka replied, wondering what he had seen.

Perhaps finding this High Priestess would placate his lord a little in their failure to find the dark-haired girl. He took a tiny vial of clear green liquid from his pocket. Bending over the now lifeless priestess he opened her mouth and let a single drop between her lips. One drop of antidote gave one more hour of life, but it was not the whole antidote. He wanted her placated and needed time to get back to the ship where he would administer the rest.

The Maphraxies returned. 'There is nothing, Commander. Only a few empty rooms and a collapsed tunnel that may have been a way out,' one rumbled. Hameka nodded.

'Carry this one. She won't give you any trouble.'

The Maphraxie picked up the priestess as easily as if she were a child and slung her over its shoulder. As they left the Mother's Chamber, Hameka snuffed out the candles and darkness fell. He knew that since any temple had been created, often thousands of years ago, candles always lit the Mother's Chamber, never allowed to go out. Now his amulet, the blood-stone of Baelthrom, was the only light.

He led the way back along the tunnel, feeling much better than he had on the way down. He considered what his next tasks were. He would administer the antidote when they were back on the ship, and then questioning would begin.

Once outside the grey skies were showing a hint of blue and sunshine shone down, glinting upon the blood-soaked ground and temple torn asunder from its base to its spire. He laughed aloud, the Maphraxies and dark dwarves looked at him. Despite not finding the sodding girl, today was a victory over the Goddess's Sacred Isle.

'Victory is ours,' he shouted. The dark dwarves and Maphraxies bellowed their cheers and raised their weapons. 'Today we deliver a message to the Feylint Halanoi, the strongest yet! Even their sacred Isle of the Goddess has fallen to us. They may well fight us or die, but if they do not join us *they will die!*'

Hidden deep amongst the branches of an old yew tree beside the temple, the raven watched the Maphraxies. He saw a gull flying strangely and dangerously low above them. It carried something small and dark on its back, and he felt the subtlest magic about it.

The tall, grey-haired man commanding the Maphraxies saw the gull and aimed his weapon. The raven cawed and squawked, distracting the man who hesitated and glared in the raven's direction. The raven nestled deeper into the yew's thick foliage as the gull wheeled away and fled unharmed. The man cursed and turned away.

The raven looked upon the bloodied and bound prisoners that the Maphraxies took with them as they left the temple. The raven followed them silently and unseen as they made their way to the coast, and watched them as they boarded their black ships and disappeared on the horizon.

Movement came from behind. The raven turned and saw the black horse, his master's horse, emerge from the trees and stop. Their eyes met. With a caw, the raven left his perch, circled above the horse, and headed west across Celene and out into the vast expanse of the Lost Sea.

CHAPTER 29

Wizards, Witches and Seers

THERE was a chance he could have made it back from where he had come, even without his staff. No being could stay for long in the astral planes with a physical body. That was why people only travelled to them when they slept. Their minds and souls detached, or extended, from their bodies. Trapped for too long in the astral, the body dematerialises and could no longer return to the physical planes.

Freydel was a Master Wizard, and he knew deeply the peril he was in. As his mind recovered from its link to Baelthrom's, he focused all his will on returning to the place where he had created his portal of projection. Like moving back through a tunnel, he could see the earth, fire, water, and air symbols in the distance. He almost made it.

Black fire flared from the symbols and all around him, immediately destroying his magical portal. He cried out, reached towards the black tongues of flame. His hand burned as he drew close. Ahead he could see his study in his tower beside the Castle Elune. The fire spread all around and within, shattering the windows, setting the curtains alight. He could not get closer without burning. Instead, he watched in horror as his books, scrolls and maps, his magical works and instruments, his vast collection of the prophecies, all burst into flame. The dry old parchment no match against fire that was melting rock.

His soul turned cold. *A lifetime of work... gone!* Another bout of fire came from above, and he saw the beast from which it came. *Dread Dragons? Celene is doomed.*

Freydel watched in suspended terror. He didn't know how to return to the physical world now that his portal was destroyed. Baelthrom would hunt him down in the astral planes, he would never give up searching for the orb.

He may be trapped, but he had to protect the orb with his life. The orb was a physical thing; it belonged to the physical world, and in his wisdom, he knew it would always seek a way to return there. It must never leave his side. He drew his energy close. He would have to hide, however one could hide in the astral planes.

Flying under moody rain clouds, Edarna watched the black smoke rising on the horizon, curling up above the rich, green sliver of land that was Celene. Her heart sank. She was too late, but even if she had got there in time, what could she have done? Baelthrom and his Maphraxies attacking the sacred Isle of the Goddess so far from the frontline was just unheard of. No one would have believed her had she warned them. As they neared she could see the black ships surrounding the island.

'Fly over the island, but not too low!' she shouted to the gull over the wind. It came out a squeal.

Even from this height, the sight of the huge black dragons made her heart shiver. She froze as dragon fear washed over her and felt the gull tremble beneath her. Mr Dubbins meowed, twitched, and hid his head.

From the Castle Elune in the west to the Temple of Celene in the east, there was nothing but smoke and fire and ruin. The harbour on the northern shore was still aflame. No boats were sailing away; no one fled, no one made it out. They didn't know what hit them.

'Goddess bless their souls,' she breathed, the tears clouding her eyes.

There was a concentrated pocket of activity occurring around the blackened and destroyed temple.

'Circle lower if you dare, whilst the Dread Dragons are busy.' *Busy eating the dead!* Her stomach churned. 'If we can get closer I might be able to spy on them.'

The gull hesitated and then dropped lower. She reached into her pocket and pulled out her monocle. She usually used it to read her scrawled spells, but it had other uses. In a witch's hand, with a witch's spell upon it, she doubled how far it could normally see. She put it to her eye and glared down at the ground.

'They have prisoners,' she rasped. Her eye came to rest on the priestess clad in white slung over a huge ugly Maphraxie. 'Ugh, I hate those beasts.'

Though she could make out no specific details, white robes were always worn by High Priestesses. If she could get closer, she would be able to tell blonde hair or a gold sash worn only by the High Priestess of

Celene. It would make sense for them to capture one with such high standing.

'Go lower,' she said. The gull snapped his beak reluctantly but inched lower anyway.

The Maphraxie dumped the priestess on the ground. She spied the gold sash and blonde hair of the High Priestess of Celene just as a tall, gaunt-looking man snapped his head up to glare at her. She squealed and dropped her monocle, luckily it was attached to a chain and it dangled wildly in the air.

'Up!' she screamed as the man raised his hand. Something glinted, but she couldn't see what. A raven squawked loudly from somewhere.

'Turn!' she screamed. The gull needed no telling. It flipped left then right, nearly flinging her off its back. Something small and shiny whipped past, taking a feather or two off the gull's neck.

Gulls could fly fast, but Edarna could not. When the gull took a right angle and went vertically up, she could no longer calm her heaving stomach and vomited. Luckily she was sick over the side, missing herself and the gull's nice white feathers. Hanging on for dear life, they sped away from the Temple northwards.

She took a deep breath as they left the island and flew over open ocean. Gripping feathers in one hand, she glugged from her water canister with the other. She dared not glance behind in case she looked into the horrendous face of a Dread Dragon. Only when the lush green coast of the mainland came into view did her pounding heart slow and she chanced a look behind. The skies were empty; clearly no Dread Dragon could be bothered to follow one scraggly gull.

'Hah,' she squeaked, but the relief she felt was short lived. Celene and her people had been destroyed. Another land ravaged by the Maphraxies, and the most sacred land at that.

'I know, Mr Dubbins,' she reached inside his sling and stroked him. He refused to look up or even meow and instead kept his head buried.

'We should go to the Oracle, straight to the Temple of Frayon in Carvon,' she spoke her thoughts aloud. 'They must be told that Celene has fallen and the High Priestess captured. But it will be an arduous journey, Mr Dubbins, for my shrinking spell will not last that much longer.'

'Hey bird,' she squeaked to the gull, he turned his head and narrowed his eyes at her. 'Head to Carvon. You know, the city with lots of buildings and people. Plenty of garbage there for you, too.'

He seemed to understand, but you could never tell with gulls. You couldn't trust them to stick to the plan either, but the mention of garbage no doubt piqued its interest. They would not make it before her spell wore off, but the gull didn't need to know that. They just needed to get as close as possible. She reckoned she had another good hour of flying left before the potion began to wear off.

The wind was still, and though no breeze sped them, on they travelled swiftly. She looked down at the forest of sub-tropical palm trees, within which were nestled villages and towns. When it was calm like this, she loved flying, but all she could feel in her heart was sorrow.

Soon the sub-tropical palms became speckled with deciduous ones. Their round, small but dense foliage a stark contrast to the tall trunks and large leaves of palms. A lake stretched below them, the sunlight glistening on the clear water.

She was just beginning to enjoy flying when her belly rumbled dangerously. She sat upright, rudely reminded that the potion-wearing-off warning always occurred in her stomach.

'It can't be wearing off so quickly,' she gasped. They were high in the air and above a lake. That realisation was far worse than the sick rumbling feeling that exploded in her stomach.

'Oh dear,' was all she had time to squeak. Mr Dubbins howled.

The unknowing gull gave a startled caw as the load he carried suddenly doubled in size. In one moment Edarna was nestled in the gull's feathers, in the next, she was riding on the back of something the size of a small pony. The gull was forced down from the weight. The drag in the air from her dangling legs disrupted its streamline form, and it rocked wildly from side to side.

Her belly rumbled again, and Mr Dubbins thrashed. There was nothing she could do so she shut her eyes. There came a strangled squawk and then she felt herself spinning. Tiny feathers slipped out of her grasp and then she was falling. Fast. She hit the cold water and all the breath was knocked from her lungs. She flailed, doing everything she could to keep one arm wrapped around her chest and Mr Dubbins in the other.

Edarna was not a slim woman, and after a moment, she felt herself rise swiftly to the surface. She gasped and spluttered and sneezed water out of her mouth and nose. Despite everything she wore (her big boots and two heavy layers of clothes) and carried (Mr Dubbins, the chest, an iron cauldron in her pocket) she bobbed on the surface.

Mr Dubbins wiggled, thrashed, then clawed violently out of his sling.

The bedraggled cat hissed, looked at her in disgust, and swam off towards the nearest shore. She squinted after him.

'What about me?' she called.

The shore had to be at least a hundred yards away, far too far to swim. She shivered then sighed and began awkwardly to swim with one arm after the ungrateful cat. It could have been worse, they could have landed in the trees, or on rocks and died.

By the time she got to the shore the cat was almost dry and the gull stood sleeping on one leg, its beak tucked into the feathers on his back. Clearly it hadn't forgotten the payment, despite dumping them in the lake. She struggled the last few feet out of the lake and up the slippery rocks, gasping and panting while grappling with her travel chest. Only when she plonked herself down on a large smooth rock in the sun did the horrible queasiness start and then the sneezing.

'Goddess curse it,' she gasped between sneezes and lay back exhausted. She hated the potion's aftermath. She couldn't fight the sleep that always came after the shrinking spell, nor ever fend off the awful cold that swiftly descended. She fell asleep beside the cat and gull.

Naksu the Seer had just finished her lunch and was sitting in the warm sunlight smoking her pipe when she noticed a gull flying low overhead. It was a long way from the ocean, but gulls were not uncommon anywhere in the Known World and were especially numerous in the bigger cities where there was lots of food waste. Carvon was still a hundred miles northeast.

The gull was above the lake when an awful sound emerged from it; a squawk followed by a strange high-pitched scream. She squinted up at the bird as it proceeded to plummet towards the water. Then something huge appeared on its back—something with arms and legs that screamed and flailed wildly. She jumped to her feet, unable to believe what she was seeing.

There came a huge splash as the screaming arm and leg thing hit the water and then silence. The gull managed to right itself before it too hit the water and disappeared towards the shore. The arm and leg thing surfaced spluttering and coughing.

'Stay here, I won't be long,' Naksu said to her mule who had stopped eating the grass and was watching the spectacle. She grabbed her bag and knife and ran around the lake towards where the gull had gone and where the person now seemed to be swimming, very badly, towards. By the time she got there, she was greeted with a very strange sight.

A gull sleeping opened one eye, stared at her, seemed to decide it couldn't be bothered and went back to sleep again. A strange, blue-coloured cat stared at her solemnly with big golden eyes. He sat with his tail wrapped around his legs, tail tip flicking. Then he too looked away uninterested and stared across the lake. Beyond them, sprawled on a rock snoring, lay a plump older woman in a soaking wet green shawl.

'Oh dear,' Naksu said, wishing she'd brought her blanket. 'You'll catch your death of a cold.'

She hurried over to the woman who did not even stir at her approach. Prodding her did not wake her either, so she set about prising the woman's arms off the chest she hugged and set it down in the sun to dry. Next, she tried to take off the woman's long shawl, but it was an effort to lift her. In the end, she had to roll her one way and then the next before she managed to get it off. Still, the woman did not wake.

'I think there is more at play here than just colds and sleep,' she said suspiciously as she wrung out the woman's shawl and laid it out flat in the sun. Next, she pulled off her long black boots, emptied the water out of them and laid them out too. She undid her long, pale-blue seer's robe and laid it over her.

She looked down at the sleeping woman, her long grey hair was wet and bedraggled, but her cheeks were round and red, and she looked healthy. She went back to collect her mule, then set about collecting dry wood to make a fire. It wasn't cold, but it would help dry things, and she needed fire to boil water and steep herbs for the old woman to drink when she came round.

It wasn't long before the gull, the blue cat, the sleeping old woman and Naksu were warming themselves before the fire. The cat seemed to think the fire was a great idea and immediately took a liking to Naksu. She stroked him, and he rubbed his head against her leg.

Edarna awoke just as the sun was dipping into the trees.

'Oh my head, my stomach. Argh, my back,' she winced, trying to sit up.

'What's this,' she frowned and fumbled with the soft blue cotton blanket on top of her. She sniffed it. 'Smells strange, don't think it's mine.'

'It's mine. You were soaked through.'

The soft female voice made her jump, and she squinted over the camp fire at the blur in the shape of a woman. 'Blasted eyes, they're not as good as they used to be and that awful *stuff* makes 'em worse than ever.' She reached for her monocle. It was no use for it was all wet and smeary. Instead, the other woman chuckled and came over. Edarna passed her back the blue cloak. Now the younger woman was closer, her eyes focused.

'Oh, a White One,' Edarna said, never able to dislocate her mouth from her brain, and said aloud everything that came into it. She'd learnt to overcome it by refusing to be embarrassed by what came out of her mouth. The albino woman smiled anyway, obviously used to such reactions.

'What "stuff" do you mean?' the White One asked.

Edarna stared at the blue robe in her pale hands. Her eyes travelled over to the white staff by the fire, then back to the blue robes and then into that curious smiling face.

'You're a seer?' she asked.

'Yes.'

'Not a priestess?'

'No.'

Edarna sighed in relief. Witches' magic was detested and scorned by all priests and priestesses, but even then she had to be cautious, not knowing exactly how seers felt about it either.

'What's your name?' she asked.

'Naksu Feyrin and I live on the Isle of Myrn. You?'

'Edarna Higglesworth, the Witch of the Western Isles,' she said proudly. 'Or at least I was called that before the Derobing. Pah!'

Naksu frowned in concern but said nothing as Edarna continued.

'The cat is Mr Dubbins. Don't ask me how or why but he used to be white until the dark moon rose. No idea who the gull is.' The gull opened one eye, stared at the witch and then closed it again.

'Hmmm, I should give him fish... Well, anyway, I made a shrinking potion to get us away from my island in the Lost Sea at the edge of the perilous Shadowlands, to the mainland.' She spread her arm wide for emphasis.

She eyed the seer discreetly, trying to gauge her reaction. However, Naksu only smiled and raised her eyebrows curiously.

'I must have mistimed its duration, or got the strength wrong. The ingredients are rather old, and I'm not as slim as I used to be, hah.

Needless to say, it did the trick as it always does. Leaves me feeling right rotten, though,' her pride faded into a pale-faced grimace.

'Here, drink this,' Naksu passed her a steaming tin mug.

She took it suspiciously. 'What seer's magic is it?'

The other woman laughed. 'It's only ground deven star root and oil of oregano. Simple herbalism.'

'Oh,' Edarna said. 'I've missed oregano on my island. It works does it, this mixture? We witches are the best herbalists in the land, never afraid to experiment with, well, anything,' *even bat's wings*, but she didn't say that out loud. Most folk were squeamish about such things and not cut out to be witches.

'But I don't think I know this mixture,' she ended thoughtfully, staring into the contents of the mug.

'Oregano to kill the cold and settle the stomach. Deven star root to invigorate and quell inflammation,' Naksu explained.

'Of course it does, haha,' Edarna said. She knew that or had known once, surely.

Naksu smiled and sat down beside the fire, crossing her legs neatly as she spoke.

'Lots of knowledge was lost to us when the Ancients split the orbs. Strange things happened that we could not have anticipated. We are just a microcosm of the macrocosm it seems, and when they split the magic, they split everything else too.'

'Uh-huh,' Edarna nodded. She hadn't thought about it in that way before.

'So tell me, Edarna, Witch of the Western Isles, why are you leaving your home?'

The question, along with the surprisingly powerful herbal drink she downed, brought it all unpleasantly rushing back.

'Oh, it's a terrible thing and so much to explain,' she said, wondering whether to mention her involvement with Issa and deciding against it for now. 'Keteth has been slain.'

'Yes, I know as much,' Naksu nodded, 'and a thing to rejoice, for the souls are free, his reign of terror has ended.'

'But yesterday I saw Maphraxie ships, heading south,' Edarna said. 'I found out too that the Maphraxies have colonised the Isles of Kammy. That was how they are able to move so quickly. Those ships were headed to Celene.'

Naksu paled, if that was possible, and looked into the fire. 'I knew something terrible had happened, but I couldn't scry, I couldn't even project my mind into the astral planes.'

Edarna nodded vigorously. 'Neither me. It was like the magic was busy and the Flow couldn't be directed. But there is more, worse. By taking my shrinking potion and flying on the back of a gull, I tried to get to Celene as soon as I could to warn them, but I was too late. There were Dread Dragons, harpies and all manner of awful undead thingies. Smoke and fire covered the island from east to west. It's all gone.' She blinked back tears and continued.

'A man, he looked human but he's in league with Baelthrom, almost caught us. We escaped and made it here. I'm on my way to the Frayon Temple now, to warn them. They took prisoners and amongst them I saw the High Priestess of Celene.'

'High Priestess Cirosa? Oh, what a terrible, terrible thing.' Naksu covered her mouth with her hands. 'Celene is truly lost. I cannot believe it. I knew something awful had happened. I was travelling to Celene seeking the disciple of Zanufey, but now I see why the goddess delayed my path.'

'Well, you're a little late,' Edarna said reproachfully, looking over her glasses. Then realised she'd put her foot in it.

'You've seen her? Know where she is?' Naksu asked, wide-eyed.

'Yes, yes,' she wafted her hand dismissively. 'Issa—that's her name, by the way—is safe for now. She escaped the Isles of Kammy when the Maphraxies came. Only her! She came to my island. I made her well again. She'll be fine, especially with that Dragon Lord of hers.'

Naksu continued to stare at her wide-eyed. 'The Raven Queen and the Dawn Bringer,' she breathed. 'We have seen a Dragon Lord in our visions, the last. We knew that one, and one alone still lives. Oh, the best of news and the worst!'

'Well, glad I can be the bearer,' Edarna sniffed. 'Knowing that the High Priestess has been taken alive; I was on my way to the Temple of Carvon to tell them. Though I don't know why I bother helping that haughty lot. It just seems that they should know what I've seen, there's no one else to tell 'em.

'Then I was going to travel to you lot on the Isles of Tirry, since I wondered why you hadn't bothered to find this Raven Queen of prophecy. Issa's mother was a seer too, don't you know? Issa doesn't know who she is or where she belongs. But I think she has a bit of witch about her,' Edarna nodded at her own conclusion. 'You know that the sacred mound came to her? It actually came to her. We witches spend our lives searching for it in our dreams, and some die without ever having seen it. But it actually *came* to her.'

'We received a letter a long time ago,' Naksu said quietly.

Edarna fell silent. Surprised.

'Well, *they* did. It was before I came to Myrn. Only one letter speaking about an adopted child of a seer, a child who now lived far away in the west on the Isles of Kammy. The girl could heal animals before she could speak and was probably a Daluni like her father. The letter said the seer had come there in secret and her name was not known.

'None of the seers discovered who the mother might be, or at least that is what I was told a long time ago. We replied three times to that one letter, to bring the child to Myrn, but we never heard anything back.

'I have chosen to travel, despite the danger, from Myrn, across Frayon, to Celene and then to Kammy, to see how things are in these places and to discover if this child is indeed a seer. We seers are few now, less than a couple of hundred, and losing more of our number whilst Baelthrom grows stronger. It's too great a risk to let a potential go unchecked. Now it seems this girl is more important than we thought.'

'Uh huh,' Edarna agreed, nodding. 'But the girl is a woman now and she needs help to become the warrior she must be.'

Naksu shook her head. 'She must learn the spiritual side of magic and become adept in it. A seer's training is a must if she is to prevail, and a seer's art is still a powerful force on Maioria. We think it is stronger even than wizards' magic.'

'Hmph,' Edarna said. 'Magic only goes so far, but who's gonna lead the army? She'll need a sword and armour, battle skills and a hard iron will.'

Naksu nodded. 'Magic does only go so far, but it will take more than potions and cold steel to kill the Lord of Immortals. It will take a goddess's hand to stand against a god that came from the sky.'

'Well, whichever it is, she's going to need a lot of help. And it seems like if a seer's magic is so powerful, why then are you *walking* to Celene? Even a wizard can translocate,' Edarna scoffed.

'You forget that the Isles of Tirry are beside Maphrax, right next to the enemies' stronghold, and that—like the elven Land of Mists and the Wizards' Circle—Myrn is shielded by magic from view. Only a seer may enter. We dare not use magic to project from Myrn, for Baelthrom will feel it. The risk is just too great.'

'So you just sit there whilst Maioria falls apart?' Edarna said incredulously.

Naksu looked away. 'It's not how I would have it either, but we must keep our knowledge protected and all the important things hidden and preserved. To lose them would be to lose the world.'

'Pah, it's lost already!' Edarna huffed. Naksu was silent and stared into the fire.

With nothing more to say and the sour thought of Maphraxies on her mind, Edarna got up and gave the gull his fish which she had shrunk and put in a sack in her chest. The sack now stunk, and she ended up throwing it away. Once fed, seeing no reason to leave a warm fire and the protection of humans, the gull settled down close to it for the night. The sun had set, and the sky was darkening.

The witch and the seer ate their own meals from their supplies in silence. After, Naksu filled her pipe and lit it. She turned to sit facing the still starlit lake. The white light of the half-moon Doon shone down upon them.

'You know on Myrn we have a sacred pool,' Naksu said and breathed out smoke.

Edarna stopped fiddling about in her expanded wooden chest and looked up. 'I had heard such things, yes.'

'Well, when we're strong, and many are at the pool we can learn about all the races of Maioria, if they are still on Maioria. That's how we knew that the Dragon Lords were not all gone and that one still remains. It's also how we discovered that pure blood dragons still exist, and not just one but many. There's one other race that has not left us, though we know nothing else about them. The Ancients are still with us. Not many, maybe only one. But they are still here, and it's because of them that it might be possible to recombine the orbs, to make whole what was once broken.'

Edarna blinked in shock.

'Yes, it was a surprise to everyone, but the sacred pool doesn't lie,' Naksu said.

'I think I'd better get to Carvon,' Edarna said, wrapping her shawl tight around her.

'It's a long way, maybe one hundred miles,' Naksu said.

'Urgh, maybe I can make a potion,' Edarna scowled.

'Walking is better for the soul and, by the looks of it, the body as well,' Naksu said, grinning.

'Walking?' Edarna screeched. Mr Dubbins looked at them both, startled.

Naksu chuckled. 'I think I'd better come with you.'

CHAPTER 30

Swordswoman

UNABLE to find Asaph or Coronos, Issa decided to explore the Karalanth village. The day had taken a while to warm up, having been raining most of the night and morning, and the air was fresh and cold. The clouds were clearing, and where sunshine touched the ground it was warm so she walked where it fell. The smell of the wet forest was rich in the air and the pools of rainwater were evaporating quickly, creating clouds of steam above them.

Though Triest'anth said they were a mostly nomadic people, the village had clearly been here some time given the well-worn track between the houses. Perhaps they came here in summer, or perhaps they moved on when attacked, whether by humans or anything else.

All the houses were small and round with conical, thatched roofs, but some had no walls and were open with roofs supported by thick wooden beams. In these were tools or baskets of food and clay ovens, and within each of them the Karalanths worked; young and old, male and female. All had a task to do, whether it was cutting cloth, smoothing wood or preparing food.

Some noticed her passing and smiled at her, inclining their antlered heads in a welcoming gesture. She smiled and waved nervously back, noting how majestic and graceful they people looked. Two Karalanth children hurtled around the corner, screaming and laughing as they chased each other. They narrowly missed her, changing direction so deftly she stood there startled.

'I wish I could run that fast,' she laughed, watching them go.

Outwardly the people seemed happy and content, but Coronos had told her of their tortured past at the hands of the dark dwarves,

Triest'anth embellishing the finer details, and their destruction by all the dwarves both dark and light. She learned of their exile into the great forests of Frayon and how they hoped one day to return to their homeland.

The dark dwarves had for too long gone unpunished for their crimes, crimes they continued to commit against all the peoples of Maioria. But if they were able to be happy and content, then so would she be whilst amongst them. Vengeance lay in the future, not now. She had lived a life of ease and peace up until recently. All her worries back on Little Kammy seemed tiny compared to her life now and all she had suffered and come to know.

She came to the far eastern edge of the village where the last open hut stood. An anvil stood before the forge, proclaiming it as the smithy. She was surprised, for some reason she hadn't expected a smithy here, but then they were warrior people.

The man hard at work inside was huge, his thick muscles bulging on his arms as he hammered upon a glowing metal shard, red sparks flying up around him. He had black fur and long, curly black hair tied back with cord. He looked to be in his late forties, as far as human years went. The walls were lined with blades and arrowheads, some new and some in need of mending, and there was a pile of weapons on one side of the hut. She looked for horseshoes and armour, but there were none. So, he was a weapon's smith, and they didn't seem to need horses or wear any armour.

He was deeply engrossed, and she found herself hypnotised as he worked the metal, hammer clanging upon the red shard. He straightened and stretched, noticing her for the first time, and smiled and beckoned her closer.

'Welcome, there's been much talk in the village about all these strange visitors,' his voice was rich and deep and carried a sense of humour in it. 'We go for years without seeing a human, and when we do it's never a friendly one, then three unusual ones turn up at once.'

He shoved the red-hot blade into a trough of water where it bubbled and hissed, wiped his blackened hands on his apron, and engulfed her hand in a surprisingly gentle shake. He stood two feet taller than she, and that was without antlers.

'You seem to be making a lot of weapons,' she said, glancing at the piles of blades and mountain of arrowheads. His smile faded into a frown as he looked at them.

'We are preparing ourselves. There is change in the winds. The dark moon has risen and now three human strangers have sought our help,' he said.

She looked up into his dark brown eyes but said nothing. She could feel it too, change was coming but how would it come? What was it she was supposed to do? She dropped her gaze and went over to the blades on the wall. One was darker than the rest, almost black, darker than any metal she had seen. She touched it and her skin crawled, a great roaring fire filled her head, and unbearable heat scorched her face. She saw in her mind red eyes within a black three-pointed helmet glaring back at her. She dropped her hand, and the vision went.

'Dark dwarven metal mined from the hellish bowels of the Maphrax Mountains. It was taken in an encounter with a Maphraxie,' the smith spat on the ground in disgust.

'Do you know how to use these as well as make them?' she asked, touching another gingerly, but it was only cold grey metal.

'Of course, all Karalanths learn how to use blade and bow pretty much as soon as they can walk. Which for us is mostly straight after birth,' he jested, a sparkle in his eyes. She snorted but smiled all the same.

'Can you teach me?' she asked hopefully.

He straightened in surprise; clearly, he had not been expecting that question. Asaph had a sword, he could surely teach her, but then she was too shy around him to ask, and it would just be too embarrassing. After a moment, he sighed, eyed her up and down, then took a blade from the wall.

'I used to be a teacher, some years ago now, though only to children,' he said. 'Maybe I could teach you a thing or two, and perhaps I could do with the practice. Hmm. I can teach you what I know, though you'll need to get stronger and fitter. But that will come with time and practice.'

'Teach me everything,' she said. 'I must learn how to fight'.

'Are you really sure? I can teach you a little every day, but you must be disciplined enough to practice on your own, and there will be no substitute for real experience. I can but prepare you, and no more.'

'Anything is better than nothing,' she said.

He nodded. 'True. But the first thing you must know, is who I am,' he grinned.

She flushed and mumbled, 'Sorry.'

'I'm Grast'anth and they're calling you the Raven Queen,' he glanced around at the trees as if looking for ravens, and she wondered where the raven had gone. 'Though I'm not sure I believe in any of that prophecy stuff. Regardless, we are who we are, and all we have is this moment now. I'm sure you have another, more fitting name?' he asked, deftly spinning the blade in his hand and making it flash in the sunlight.

She shifted her feet and smiled at his wise words. He reminded her of Edarna and her quirky sayings.

'Issa,' she said, but the name sounded strange as if it belonged to someone else. It made her uncertain. 'Issalena Kammy,' she said it firmly as if to convince herself.

'Greetings, Issa,' he lifted her hand ceremoniously to his lips and grinned at her with sparkling eyes. He turned back to his weapons. 'We Karalanths prefer the shorter blade; longer ones hinder us when we run.'

She looked at the blade he passed to her and was surprised at its lightness, the simple wooden haft fitted snugly in her hand. She tested its weight with a few amateur swings and thoughts of glory on the battlefield flashed in her mind, her blade glinting in the light as no foe could match her skill. At first seeming light, the blade quickly felt heavy, much to her dismay. She would get fitter and stronger.

'Don't worry,' he reassured, seeing the disappointment on her face. 'It will feel foreign to you at first, it always does. Hmm, you are much older than any I have ever taught,' he added doubtfully, scrubbing his chin.

'I can still learn,' she snapped. 'I have to try. I'll need to use some type of weapon, and these are as good as any,' she waved the sword around, and Grast'anth took a step back with a laugh.

'Easy now, don't kill the teacher.'

She made smaller circles in the air with the end of the blade, testing her wrist against its weight. It would definitely ache after a while, she conceded glumly.

'Well, there's no need to be down about it, you haven't even started yet,' he said, crossing his arms over his chest. 'You'll get stronger if you practice.' He took a larger blade from the wall.

'Shouldn't you have the same size?' she asked fearfully, it could only be fair.

'I'm only going to show you a few things. Besides, the length of the blade matters not,' he said and stepped out of the hut. She followed him to the sandy area in front of the smithy.

'The first lesson, in all of life, in fact, is this. The key to survival is awareness. The more aware you are, the more you are ready to predict an attack and respond accordingly. You must never let your guard down.'

He walked around in a circle, fingering the blade thoughtfully as if recalling his teaching. He stopped and looked at her side on, his tail flicking left and right.

'Stop and listen. Look around you. What can you see, hear and smell? If you can sense magic, how strong is it? From where does it flow, and where to? Who's using it? Awareness, and not just awareness of the things outside of you, awareness of the things inside. What are you thinking? What do you want? What are you choosing? What are you feeling? What are your weaknesses?

'You must know and understand yourself fully. Otherwise the enemy will find and exploit your weaknesses. Focus on increasing your awareness of yourself and everything around you. Try it now. Still the mind and expand your awareness.'

It sounded tiresomely like what Freydel had taught her. *Still the mind…* Hugging her arms, she closed her eyes and focused on her inner self. What was it she desired most now? *To learn the sword, that is what I desire.*

She held the blade in her right hand, felt its cold hard weight—just a piece of metal—waiting to be used. The earth was soft and sandy beneath her bare feet, and warm from the sun. She could feel Grast'anth's presence like a warm glow beside her, and could even sense the birds flittering in the trees around them. She stilled her mind further and felt the trees, green and steadfast, their roots happily moist after the rain. Further still and she could feel the living force of Maioria herself beneath her feet.

'With your increased awareness, seek to understand the land around you in light of the battle before you,' he spoke softly.

She opened her eyes and analysed the terrain, feeling it with her feet and mind. The ground was flat, the village was behind her, and she stood in a wide-open space, a good place to fight. A gentle breeze, carrying the scent of wild apple, eased the heat of the sun, and she could tell from its angle that it was now mid-afternoon. She would have to be careful not to be blinded by it. She shifted her body around until the sun was on the back of her head and Grast'anth was to her left.

'Try to understand your enemy, look for weaknesses physical or mental, but be careful, for the opponent that looks fearful may only be feigning,' he said, beginning to circle her as he spoke.

She focused on Grast'anth, trying to detect any sense of emotion. He was unreadable to her, just a solid object of muscle—a formidable opponent even for a Maphraxie. He was big and long, and that could also be a disadvantage. His back and flanks would be his most vulnerable, if one could avoid those slashing hooves. Those antlers were a worry too, one could be impaled upon them. Caution was clearly necessary with this unknown opponent. She would have to be quick and clever.

'Practice is the key. If you are to survive a fight with a sword, you must practice. Surviving is first, winning is second. Remember this,' he continued his circumambulation. 'Always have your weapon ready; how can you parry a blow when your sword is stuck in its scabbard? You must know when the fight is on and you must have your sword drawn ready for it takes less time to be killed than it does to draw your weapon.'

He stopped and held up his sword, it shone in the sunlight. 'This is a weapon. It's designed to kill. Mercy, honour and chivalry are wonderful words for bards and poets, but when it is kill or be killed, this,' he shook his sword, 'is what will determine whether we speak again. The aim of the fight is survival, not winning, and because of this, all is fair in battle. Be crafty, use whatever tricks you can from within yourself or the environment around you.'

He gestured to the sandy ground. 'An old trick, but throwing that in your opponent's eyes could save your life.' He continued walking and talking, and she listened intently, her mind a sponge soaking up his words. Ma would never believe she'd be a swordsmaster.

'Never ever let your guard slip, and never lose your confidence. The fight to the death will be exhausting, but you cannot afford to let your concentration slip, your muscles fail, or your will to survive diminish. If you do, then the fight is over, you have lost. That is why you must be as fit as you can be, lest your muscles or your lungs fail you, and you must focus your concentration until the end. That is why practice is important, it will make you fit and focused. Some say all battles are a battle of wills; if one's will to survive becomes less than the other, then the end is decided.'

He stopped and faced her. 'Never rush into a fight, but calmly and controllably engage the enemy, lest you impale yourself on his sword. Through calm will your best defences and keenest reactions be at hand. Confidence comes with practice. You'll encounter enemies who will insult you verbally—don't be tempted to insult back. You can insult your enemy, but saving your breath will save you energy. Try to see yourself through their eyes, does he think you are weak? Scared? Use that against him. If you can combine defence and attack, when you dodge or parry a blow, use that momentum and turn the energy into an attack. Oh, and always know the length of your sword. It's no good chopping at air, and it will only tire you out.

'From the looks of you, you will always be fighting somebody bigger and stronger. Therefore you must make sure you have speed and cunning on your side. For a human I would recommend steel armour, but, because of your small size and the bigger size of your opponent, you would do better to wear much lighter armour for speed and agility, rather than chance survival in plate armour under a Maphraxie's crushing axe. At all costs, avoid being hit by the enemy or they will crush you.

'That leads on to another thing. If you can dodge a blow then do so and don't parry it. Parrying will only damage or break your weapon and tire you or, worse, it can break your arm. Remember, the bigger opponent also has weaknesses, less speed, heavy armour, bigger targets and therefore bigger vulnerabilities. It's a sad truth, but the warrior who shows no mercy will be the one still standing at the end of the battle. The Maphraxies show no mercy so why should you?'

'How can anyone have mercy for those monsters,' she growled. Grast'anth looked at her, then nodded slightly.

'There can be no mercy, not while they hold a weapon,' he said. 'Study your enemy as much as you can, know them inside out. What are they wearing? How are they standing? And most importantly, what move will they make next? If you can second-guess his move, then you can chance a killing blow. Now show me your stance,' he said.

Nervously she stepped her feet apart. How the hell were you supposed to stand? She thought about the duelling knights at the Midsummer Celebrations on Celene but still had no clue. She felt her cheeks growing hot. Maybe she should have gone for a simpler weapon like a club, but she so wanted to learn the sword. If Asaph could use a sword, then so could she.

She angled her body slightly to the side, left foot behind right, and her right sword arm extended, tip pointing towards Grast'anth's muscular belly. She licked her lips, suddenly it was very hot. He moved forwards, really quite slowly, and without knowing how it happened, he had grasped her wrist, pulled, and sent her sprawling to the ground, holding her sword arm uselessly above her head.

'Yah,' she puffed for breath, confounded. Great start, she thought indignantly. He helped her up, laughing as she brushed herself down.

'I didn't do that to mock you, but to make you aware of balance. Balance is somewhat easier for a Karalanth,' he said and stomped his four feet.

'Never overreach. Oh, and never jump for you'll have no balance. Keep your moves simple. While spinning may look fancy, death does not, so don't do it. Leave that to the court jesters you humans so love to entertain you. Only use the moves you learned in practice, and don't introduce anything new—any mistakes will prove fatal. If you keep things simple, you'll also conserve energy. Practice as you would fight, because that is how you will fight when it comes to the real thing.'

He took their weapons and carried them back to the smithy.

'Hey, I'm not done yet,' she said.

'Fighting is dangerous. Which is why we'll be using these,' he said, holding up two crude wooden children's swords with a grin. 'Though you are untrained, you can still kill me with that sword. Never underestimate your enemy, no matter how weak or defenceless they may seem,' he winked. He tossed her one of the swords, and she caught the hilt, surprising herself.

'Ya-hah! But there appears to be a lot to learn,' she mused.

'Indeed. But you have to start somewhere. Just enough to protect yourself, or at least know how to swing a sword, will make any attacker think twice. It may be enough to save your life,' he said.

'Hopefully I can be more than that,' she said, and he laughed.

She wanted to be great with a sword. The most feared swordmaster in all the land. The Maphraxies running in terror just from the sight of her. She laughed, now that did sound ridiculous. Was it not bloodthirsty too? Did she really want to be feared? Just able to swing a sword would be good enough.

'Now, prepare yourself for the fight,' he said, grasping the pathetic sword in his meaty hands. It looked so small in his grasp.

She set her chin firm, centred herself, and gripped her sword similarly.

'Your sword tip should be pointing towards your opponent and your body angled towards them so your chest mass is reduced, protecting your vital organs as much as you can. Feel your sword as an extension of yourself; have awareness of your weapon and of your enemy's, but remain relaxed and ready to strike.'

He held his sword towards her. His size was daunting but it would do no good to feel intimidated. She focused on stilling her thoughts and increasing her awareness again. His muscles were taut and coiled tight like a cat ready to leap. He angled his sword slightly and lunged towards her—it was enough to tell her which way his sword would slash.

She stooped, and fell back and to the right as his sword swung left, narrowly missing her. She sprung upright and stabbed before he had finished his swing, but lost her balance and fell forwards straight into him. Her head smacked against his hard chest, and everything spun. He laughed helping to steady her. Nothing could be done for her dignity.

'Maybe this isn't such a good idea,' she said, losing all visions of battle glory, her face hot and annoyingly sweaty.

'Nonsense,' he said, chuckling. He didn't even look hot despite his fur. 'You were quick, and if you'd had a knife in your other hand, I would have been a goner from such close range. You took me by surprise. There was no way I could have hit you with my sword. Remember, use all the tricks. Even mistakes can have hidden blessings. Every part of your sword and body is a weapon, not just the blade. Now, again!'

They took their stances again. Issa attacked first, but he moved with lightning speed. Wasn't she supposed to be the smaller, quicker one? He swiped, forcing her to leap to the left where she stumbled on a rock. She took a gentle slap on her hip from his returning blow.

'Argh, stupid rock!' she kicked it away.

'Again,' he said, unperturbed.

She had to be the worst student he'd ever taught, she thought dismally.

They took their stances again and again, but every time she tried to land a blow he either deflected it or he simply was not there. She lost count how many times she was sent sprawling, but one thing she did have was determination, or stubbornness, and she refused to give up.

He swiped again and she dodged, but he pushed her over with his other hand.

'Is that allowed?' she growled, sitting up and spitting out sand. He only shrugged.

'All's fair. Again!'

She leaped and dodged and swung her sword until sweat poured off her body—which was lucky, she thought, because it hid the tears of absolute frustration on her face. Why couldn't she land just one blow? She wanted to scream and cry and hated herself for her incompetence, and yet her face remained impassive. She would not show her opponent her thoughts; he must not know her emotions and weaknesses. After half an hour her muscles ached and burned.

'We should rest,' he said, frowning. She was panting and drenched in sweat.

'Never,' she growled.

He shrugged and took his stance.

In a final effort she tried to parry his blow, but the force of it sent shock waves up her arms, and she fell exhausted into him. He steadied her again as she got her breath back.

'We should stop, I think. We can do more tomorrow,' he sounded concerned.

She avoided looking into his dark eyes. Leaning on his arm which was the size of a tree trunk, she looked up and was dismayed to find she had collected a bit of an audience. Men, women and children—maybe half the village—had crowded round to watch their duelling. Mortified, she spotted Coronos and Asaph in the crowd. The sun was virtually gone from the sky now, sunk beneath the trees. There was at best only an hour of sunlight left, and the birds and animals were busy scurrying around before the day closed and the creatures of the night came out.

'No, not yet, more,' she said hoarsely. She had to do this. She straightened and moved away from him, forcing her legs not to shake, smoothing her hair back from her wet face, willing her muscles to obey, ignoring as best she could the crowd behind her.

'What you lack in experience, you double in determination, girl,' he laughed, nodding in respect.

'Girl?' she said incredulously and lunged for him once more. She caught him unawares, but he was dismally quick in responding to the unexpected, and again she had to dodge his parry-turned-attack.

She focused on bringing back that centre of calm and awareness that she had somehow lost in her desire to land a blow. She studied him intently, looking for any sign of weakness. They circled each other. He stepped with complete confidence, his eyes sparkling, but face expressionless. Use that then, she thought, turn his confidence into a weakness. Licking her lips, she pondered her move.

She lunged at him, just as she had done so many times before, but this time a fraction slower. Let him think she was very tired. Though she was tired, she still had fight left within her.

He struck. She let him knock her sword down but removed the momentum of his force by pretending to stagger. Instead of regaining her feet, she used the momentum to throw herself forward. She moved with lightning quickness and tucked into a tight roll that sent her between and under his front hooves.

She slashed upwards at his exposed belly before he could rear up out of reach. She hit him hard, knowing the wooden sword would not hurt him, but telling him she had disembowelled him nonetheless. She rolled sideways to her feet. He was laughing loudly. She brushed the dirt from her clothes, smiling sheepishly as the crowd cheered and clapped. He bowed to her and then embraced her in a rough hug.

'I've not had that much fun since I was a pupil myself, and never with a human. We should practice more tomorrow, and the next day. Though today was hard, it will get easier, believe me,' he said. She gave a noisy sigh, relieved it was over so she could rest her aching muscles.

She smiled at the crowd and caught Asaph's handsome face grinning back as he clapped with the others. She looked away shyly, glad he had seen her success.

'Well, I only got in one blow, and it took me many lives to get that far,' she said.

'It's a good start. You must know yourself and learn how you fight; what your style is, what your weaknesses are. And you can only do that with practice.'

With an arm over her shoulder, he led her back to the smithy.

'The final lesson of today is; look after your weapon. If you keep your weapon in good condition it will keep you in good condition,' Grast'anth bent down into a bucket by the anvil and threw a wet cloth at her. The soggy thing hit her shoulder with a slap.

'Ugh!' She laughed as the water slopped down her front. She wiped the sweat off the wooden sword. Grast'anth passed her a mug of water, and they both drank noisily.

'Thank you for training me. I have a few coins. I can pay you for your lessons.'

'No need,' he shrugged. 'It's been an honour to teach again. Maybe I'll take it up again and teach these young rascals how to fight properly,' he gestured at the Karalanth children still chasing each other but now joined by two smaller ones that struggled to keep up. 'Besides, what use is gold to us here?' Grast'anth gestured to the forest. Issa raised her eyebrows with a nod.

'We Karalanths have been too long hidden; we have become soft and weak. I hoped all my life that I would one day see my homeland, but now I doubt I will live to see that day.'

'All things are possible,' Issa murmured, still feeling that hard determination that had kept her fighting for hours.

Grast'anth barked a laugh. 'As you say, missy. I hope you are right.'

Her hard, determined look softened into a smile under his gaze. She felt rather than saw Asaph's approach, a kind of fiery field of energy. For a moment, her eyes had tuned of their own accord into the Flow, and though she did nothing, she could see Asaph exactly as she had felt him; fiery energy—the fire of the sun, of dragons, of the Sun Goddess Feygriene. She wondered what hers looked like since it was difficult to see your own.

'Looks like you need another wash,' Asaph grinned.

Within his blue eyes she glimpsed the dragon as it stirred, no more than a shady image but enough to make her look away. It unnerved her, knowing that he was part dragon part human. She didn't know quite how she felt about it. She remembered only a dreamlike image of a great golden dragon swooping down to lift her from the bloody waters surrounded by Maphraxies. Coronos had told her what happened as she recovered in bed, but most of what he said was a blur in her memories of that day.

She looked down at her filthy sweaty clothes, 'And I'd only just put them on!' she said in dismay.

Dragon spawn. That is what Keteth had called him. Freydel had spoken at length about the great Dragon Lords of Drax, the mighty dragon kingdom of the north, and how Baelthrom crushed it over twenty-five years ago. Asaph was a Draxian, and his parents had been killed by Maphraxies, but other than that she knew nothing of his past or anything about his life, there had not been time to speak of such things.

'And you have recovered well to move like that,' he added, impressed.

'It may have looked like it, but now I feel like I've been trampled by a hundred horses!' She stretched her arms and winced. Her old wounds complained as well and she grimaced. 'Maybe I have overdone it. And another wash is definitely in order,' she smiled up at him.

'Would you like me to accompany you again?' he asked, grinning wolfishly.

'If you can find some soap and carry my towel, then maybe,' she said, her cheeks growing hot.

A female Karalanth came over. She could only have been a few years older than Issa and had light brown hair, golden eyes and a handsome but hard face. She was dressed in a huntress's leather top, a bow slung across her toned torso and a large quiver of arrows strapped horizontally on her back. There was a two-inch scar on her left shoulder. She had the look and hardiness of a warrior.

'I saw you fight. You fought well. Grast'anth was one of the best amongst us once. If you want I can teach you the bow,' she said in a soft voice, belying her tough-looking exterior.

'I'd love to. Anything I can learn between now and...' Issa trailed off, wondering what she meant. They would have to leave this peaceful, safe place one day, probably soon, and she didn't want to go. 'Anything I can learn will be great. But can we try tomorrow? I can barely lift my arms,' she said wearily, wiping a dirty hand across her forehead only to leave a bigger smear of dirt. Grast'anth put an arm around the Karalanth woman's shoulders.

'Rhul'ynth is one of the best shots we've ever had,' he said proudly.

She blushed and immediately looked ten years younger, 'I don't know about that Gra,' she said fingering the string of her bow, 'it was only the other day I missed the rabid boar by a long shot, got it in a right temper too.'

'Bah, you women,' Grast'anth barked humorously, 'you only missed because Dar startled the thing. Your next shot took the beast down in a second!'

Issa wondered at that. She saw them eat no meat but then they had hunters, and killed boars and wore leather and slept on furs. But then deer were herbivores and these were deer-folk.

'Do you eat boars?' she asked tentatively.

'Woetala bless us no!' Rhul'ynth said aghast, her golden eyes wide in horror, 'we kill the sick and lame and sometimes use their skins. Their sicknesses spread to us so we must. That boar was sick and making more like it sick. It was sick because of the foltoy spreading disease.'

She saw the frown on their faces and glanced at Grast'anth who shrugged.

'They are Baelthrom's minions, immortals. They were once some beast or another but now are giant black cat-like bear-like creatures that walk on two legs, or four if they run. They are unnaturally fast, unnatural in every way, really. On two legs they stand higher than a man's antlers. Watch out for them, they kill and eat anything, even if they are not hungry,' she said with a shudder. 'They sometimes come into our village, so we hunt them to keep them away.'

In her mind's eye Issa pictured what Rhul'ynth described; huge slathering beasts with cruel but intelligent eyes and wicked sharp teeth for ripping into flesh. She looked nervously to the woods half expecting them to jump out.

'The immortals take many forms,' Issa murmured, Rhul'ynth snorted and nodded.

'Come, ladies, tonight is a night of celebration, the Feast of Ax'anth, not a time to talk of our foul enemies,' Grast'anth said putting his arms around them both.

Both Issa and Asaph looked at him with raised eyebrows, 'A celebration?' they asked in unison as they all walked back into the village.

'Wow,' they said in unison, staring at all the bright flowers adorning the huts and rows of tables placed either side of the path through the village. Big baskets of forest fruits and flowers and strange brown and orange mushrooms sat beneath the tables ready to be displayed or cooked or something.

'They've done all this since sword training?' Issa gawped.

In only an hour the Karalanths had turned the simple village into a panoply of beautiful colours. Karalanths were hurrying to and fro carrying more baskets of food and flowers. Some hefted great stacks of chopped wood on their backs and were dumping it beside another huge pile. Already a bonfire was being created.

'Aye the Feast of Ax'anth; one of our greatest warriors, though I don't know why we have a feast, he was far too busy fighting to eat, I'm sure,' Grast'anth said, chuckling.

'I'd best get washed and ready,' she said, looking at her dirt-smeared clothes.

'You don't have to worry about those,' Rhul'ynth said taking her hand and swinging it. 'We'll all be naked, anyway.'

She laughed as Issa looked at her in horror. 'Just kidding! Well, sort of,' she grinned impishly.

Issa smiled nervously and carefully avoided looking anywhere in Asaph's direction.

'I think I'll go wash. Alone.' she darted off to the pool to the sound of the other three laughing.

CHAPTER 31

Interrogation

A particularly large Maphraxie hunched under the door frame of Hameka's cabin, grunting and scraping his armour upon it. He dumped the unconscious High Priestess unceremoniously on the floor and left when Hameka waved him away. He turned away from the slumped priestess with disinterest, took his amulet off and hung it on the mirror on his desk.

'My Lord Baelthrom,' he said into the Shadow Key.

The profile of Baelthrom formed within, eyes glowing dark-blue. He was about to speak, but Baelthrom spoke first, a tightness in his inhuman voice.

'I have revisited my communication with this goddess worshipping witch. Within her robes, you will find a Shadow Stone, given to her by the harpy. The girl has not returned to the island after the death of Keteth. This priestess denies the girl's power but is blinded by her own greed and hatred. Such emotions are easy to control, and she might prove useful. She will become one of us. Despite her lack of magic, we shall use the necromantic elixir.'

Hameka hid a grimace. The very thought of serving next to a goddess worshipper turned his stomach. Most magic-less humans were processed to make the elixir itself rather than chosen to consume the elixir. Lately, the elixir was mostly used to turn magic wielders into necromancers. The ranks of their armies were so large now, they didn't need so many Maphraxie grunts, but they could never get enough necromancers.

'My lord, this new power you feel, it could be coming from the dark moon. In fact I—'

Baelthrom cut him off. 'Undoubtedly. But it's also linked to that girl, of that I'm sure. This power is like nothing I have felt here before.' His voice turned ponderous, 'Although, maybe in another time, another place... but not here.'

He fell silent for a moment and then spoke decisively. 'Use the priestess, find the girl. I'm growing exceedingly weary of hunting her.'

Hameka nodded, his request dying in his throat in the face of his lord's anger. 'I will do as you command, my lord.'

The Key Stone turned dark and lifeless. Hameka slumped, feeling weary too now. He got up from his desk with a sigh and looked down at the woman. She might become one of them, but not without a good dose of pain first. The minutes were ticking by, and he wondered how many she had left before the poison worked its grand finale.

He bent down and searched her robes for the Shadow Stone and weapons. He found the stone and a small knife and put them on his desk. As an after-thought, he yanked off her robes, girdle, shoes and small silver bracelet, which he dumped in the corner of the room. It was possible her robes and jewellery were enchanted, and he needed no surprises.

She looked rather weak, pale and puny in her underclothes; slumped unconscious against the door of his cabin and tiptoeing on the edge of death. But then all the goddess's creatures were weak and puny. He took hold of the dart lodged in her shoulder and clicked the pinprick of a button that retracted the barbs. The dart came free with a spurt of bright red blood.

He moved her so that her blood ran onto her underclothes, rather than drip onto his clean cabin floor and make a mess. From his drawer, he picked out a medium-sized bottle of the green antidote and stared thoughtfully down at the woman.

'In a few minutes, you will be dead. But I,' he swung the bottle lazily before her, 'am your saviour. You will be grateful to me for saving your pitiful life.' He grabbed hold of her head and poured the antidote into her mouth. She swallowed in reflex.

'There,' he soothed. 'Enough for a full recovery, just as our lord commanded.'

He let her head flop back. It would take a few minutes to work, and a whole week to recover completely. He noticed a mark on her chest, just showing above her slip. He pulled it down to reveal a faint tattoo—a yellow circle within which were three crescent moons; one white, one orange and one blue. They symbolised Maioria's sun and three moons

'Oh how very interesting,' he mocked, 'the symbol of the Great

Goddess. It's been a while since I've seen that cursed thing. One of those moons should certainly not be there.'

There was a little colour returning to her face.

'So, you worshippers of the pathetic goddess mark yourselves as such. I'm sure we can create for you our own mark,' he smiled indulgently, thinking of the mark of the Maphraxies that he had knifed into the cold dead skin of the other blonde woman.

The priestess suddenly gasped as the antidote took hold. She struggled weakly, trying to sit up, but her hands and legs were bound. She shivered and blinked, her face was deathly pale and dark circles bruised her eyes. Her yellow hair was damp with sweat and plastered to her face. She stared up at Hameka in confused fear, her breathing fast and ragged. She winced and touched her bleeding shoulder, trying to stem the flow with shaking fingers.

He smiled, and she shrank from him. He let the rage and frustration of the past few days swiftly consume him. The blood pounded in his head, and his face grew hot.

'Where is the girl?' He shouted so loudly that she jumped and cowered. When she did not immediately reply, he struck her hard across the face, leaving a bloody welt on her cheek.

'Where is she?' he bellowed again. She seemed too shocked to answer. He reached down and grabbed her shoulders, dragged her to standing and shook her like a doll. She flopped weakly in his grasp and tried to speak, her voice a quivering whisper.

'I don't know, I—' He threw her back against the door, and she slid to the floor gasping. 'I don't know where she is, but I can help you find her.' She spoke rapidly and closed her eyes as if she were about to faint.

'I'm the High Priestess of Celene, I can find those who know her. I can help you destroy her.' He bent close to her, and she cowered.

'Please don't kill me, please don't kill me,' she said over and again.

'Begging is good, especially from a human,' he approved, finding his anger and frustration receding.

'But what is this?' he asked softly, 'what is this? A high priestess turned to begging? Your goddess must have abandoned you, my dear. Otherwise, you would not be here.' He brushed the hair back from her face, enjoying it when she flinched and trembled at his touch. He felt unclean, having touched a goddess worshipper, and wiped his hand on his trousers.

'So you, a worshipper of that whore, would help us, your hated enemy? Why should I believe you?' he asked in a flat voice.

'Because the girl is a fraud and a murderer!' the woman hissed, the hatred in her voice raw, raw to the point of madness. That was good. Baelthrom was right; her hatred could be used to control her.

'You would join us to help find and destroy her?' he said.

'I will do anything to destroy her,' she breathed heavily, her nostrils flared, her face a glistening sheen of sweat. Her eyes were dilated wide, partly from the poison, partly from hatred.

'Either you help us or you die.' He grasped her again by the shoulders, a little less roughly, and lifted her up and pinned her against the door.

'We have ways to bind you to your word,' he whispered, his face inches from hers. 'You will worship the Immortal Lord now, the One True God. You will become one of us, an immortal. Baelthrom will give you powers you cannot fathom.'

The priestess's eyes flared wide as he spoke. So, she was greedy for power too, that was also good.

'I will worship him, the Immortal Lord,' she dropped her eyes from his. He released her, and she slid to the floor. He drew out a knife and cut the cords binding her hands and feet.

Cirosa rubbed her sore wrists where the cords had been and tried to smooth her damp matted hair back from her face. Her hands still shook despite her struggle for composure. She stared dully at the floor where her blood lay drying. She had renounced the goddess, and though she felt gut-wrenching fear for what she had done, it was soon washed away by the thoughts of power that the Immortal Lord would give her. Real power that she had only briefly touched.

Was he not more powerful than the goddess? Was he not winning this war? The goddess was weak, if she was there at all, and no gifts had *she* ever bestowed upon her. This was a new start; a greater power awaited her. She pulled herself unsteadily to her feet.

'You will be irreversibly bound to the Immortal Lord,' the man said matter-of-factly and held before her the amulet that the harpy had given her. The Shadow Stone transfixed her easily in her weakened state, but this time she did not resist and willingly stared into it as it turned dark.

A black cloud as dense as soot, oozed from it and engulfed her. It filled her eyes and nostrils, making her choke as she was forced to breathe it in. She closed her eyes and would have fallen but the black cloud held her up. She felt the amulet pushed onto her chest, atop her mark of initiation into the High Priesthood of the Order of the Great Goddess.

'A new mark,' Hameka hissed from far away. 'The mark of the Maphraxies.'

The smell of burning flesh filled her nostrils moments before the searing agony hit. It felt like a bolt of lightning tearing through her chest. She screamed and arched her back. The black soot from the amulet infiltrated every cell in her body, filling them with the same burning pain until she thought she would explode. The pain receded, and she felt power lingering, she lusted for it.

The amulet was taken away, and the pain stopped. She fell against the door. There was no black soot or any evidence of it. She stared down at the new mark upon her chest. With a shaking finger, she traced the bloody, swollen mark of Maphrax.

'Baelthrom owns you now,' he said.

As soon as he spoke another pain started, only this time it grew from within and it burned cold, deathly cold. Her body was freezing from the inside, each cell turning into ice. She clenched her eyes shut and screamed. Behind closed lids, a huge, black raven watched her, knowing what she had done and condemning her. From far away she heard Hameka speak.

'Now you go for your final trial and your greatest glory. The Elixir of Immortality is a great gift from our lord.'

The door she leant against opened, and massive, cold hands grasped her and dragged her away. There was a horrible dull ache on her chest where the mark of Maphrax was, a pain she would later realise would never go away.

Hameka sat there tapping his chin after she had been taken away to consume the Elixir of Immortality. It was early evening, and he was not tired yet. There was another prisoner he could have fun with this evening. He opened the cabin door and spoke to the remaining Maphraxie outside.

'Bring me the dark-haired one.'

The Maphraxie nodded and lumbered away. It was time to work on some interesting interrogation techniques. He smiled in anticipation.

CHAPTER 32

Sands of Time

MARAKON awoke a little before dawn. The rain pattered on the bamboo and leaf roof, and the air was cooler this morning, blessedly. His wound also hurt less, and he realised now that he would have died of it had he been alone. He should have died on his ship, he should have died from his wound, but he hadn't.

The old boatman came clearly into his mind, and the whole exchange came rushing back to him. He had been whole and uninjured in that strange place. Even his eye was healed. The hourglass and its draining sand flashed through his mind. He tried to reason it through. So, the boatman had brought him here, as far west as one could go, to find something, though Marakon didn't know what. The reasoning sounded ludicrous, yet it felt exactly true.

He looked for his sword in the corner of the room, but it was gone. Either someone had stolen it, which seemed unlikely since there was nowhere to run to and they had plenty of weapons, or they were cleaning it. He laughed at the unlikely thought and swung his legs out of bed. Another cool shower would be most welcome. Perhaps Jarlain would bring it back by then.

Jarlain returned without his sword and not knowing where it had gone, but she did have breakfast—a huge platter of exotic fruits. An orange skinned fruit was so large and full of juice that it was heavier than his sword. She left him to eat and went to speak to the Elders.

He left Jarlain's house after breakfast and a shower, and met a tall and wiry man with a long bow and wide knife at his belt. He was bare-chested and wore light trousers tucked into dark boots. His long black hair was tied back, and his eyes were a rich golden brown. Marakon guessed him to be of a similar age to himself, maybe slightly older. He carried another pair of boots and spoke in a quick voice.

'The Elders have requested that I take you to the Drowning Wastes. You will find your answers there, is all they said. We will go in a group for safety. I must warn you that no one ever goes there. It's a terrible and sad place that will send you mad if you stay too long.'

Questions crowded his mind—he had so many now it seemed pointless to ask any of them, so he simply nodded.

'Jarlain will join us if she wishes,' the man added as she came to stand beside Marakon. She also carried a curved blade at her belt in its brightly beaded sheath.

'Here, you will need these.' Shufen passed him the boots.

'Protection from viper thorns and deadly snakes deep in the jungle,' Jarlain explained.

Marakon swallowed as he slipped them on, they fit good enough. The Drowning Wastes, viper thorns, deadly snakes. Well, it wasn't like he had anything better to do. And always in the back of his mind, he could see the hourglass and its draining sands of time. The pang of urgency struck again, like butterflies in his stomach but far more intense. Would he find what he was looking for in the Drowning Wastes? The cryptic Elders seemed to think so.

'Is it far?' he asked.

'Not really,' was all he got back.

'I'm Marakon. What's your name?' he asked. Didn't anybody introduce themselves around here? Were they so keen to get rid of him that they didn't even want to know his name? But the man looked surprised rather than irritated and glanced at Jarlain. Perhaps they were not in the habit of introductions as if names were somehow not important.

'I'm Shufen, leader of the hunt. Come, we must travel as far as possible while it is light,' he said, and walked away.

Jarlain had seen Marakon's confusion. 'We only ask another's name when we know who they are. When they are friends,' she explained.

'How do you know who someone is without knowing their name first?' he frowned, feeling that the question was somehow stupid. Her laugh confirmed it.

'A name is not who we are,' laughter sparkled in her eyes.

Marakon looked away feeling like an uneducated barbarian.

'I guess not,' he mumbled as they walked to catch up with Shufen.

Two more men joined them as they walked past the central well, running and smiling to catch up. One was surely only a teenager and the other about ten years older than Marakon. Both carried bows and sheathes packed with arrows. They each grasped the other's arm, hand to elbow, in greeting and only nodded to Marakon. He decided not to ask their names this time.

It was still early, so there weren't many people about. But those who were up waved in greeting at them. It seemed that everyone knew everyone and where they were going. Once they entered the dense jungle, the village was quickly lost from view. The younger man came over to him, unwrapped the bundle he carried, and passed him his sword.

'You will need this,' he said with a smile.

'My thanks,' Marakon said, taking the sword suspiciously. It was remarkably shiny and clean.

'We don't allow outsiders to carry weapons in the village,' the boy explained as Marakon tied the sword and belt securely to his waist. He immediately felt comforted by its familiar weight. 'And besides, it was pretty badly notched, someone clearly took a beating. You might find it a little sharper,' he grinned.

Marakon stopped short in his tracks. They had not only cleaned it but sharpened it too.

'Thanks again,' was all he could think to say. The boy shrugged.

Though they walked on level ground, dense foliage made it tiresome as they clambered time and again over thick tree roots and vines. The further they got from the village, the thicker the foliage became. It wasn't long before he was drenched in sweat in the humid heat, whilst the others merely perspired a little. He cursed his human heritage for that; elves did not sweat half as much.

The trees provided protection from the sun, but they also seemed to keep the moisture in. It rose in great curls of mist, soaking everything it touched. The trees were so tall he could not see their tops. Animals and birds rustled around in the undergrowth but darted away before he could get a look at them. Only the monkeys seemed to hang around, laughing at them from the safety of their branches. They lived a life of constant play, swinging through vines, rolling over each other and pulling each other's tails.

The other things that moved were insects. The butterflies were huge with luminous indigo, green and yellow wings the span of his hand. They were so big they flapped their wings like birds. The red ants were almost the size of his finger, and they scurried in long, orderly lines up tree-trunks and under branches, completely oblivious to gravity. He tried to avoid them, but an unfortunate, horrible crunch came underfoot every now, which made him cringe.

What he thought was a dead mouse, on closer inspection, turned out to be a spider. He jumped away in horror. Jarlain looked at him.

'Insects are my least favourite things, after Maphraxies. Probably before Histanatarns,' he said in revulsion, slapping at a fly tickling his neck. 'They shouldn't be allowed to be that big,' he pointed at the spider.

She grinned. 'They get smaller the further north you go, but are far less tasty.'

His stomach lurched. They surely didn't eat them, but Jarlain had turned away, and he decided against asking. Some things were best left unknown. His side was becoming sore with all the clambering, and he picked up a sturdy thick stick to help him, breaking off the smaller branches as they walked. The wound was deep and maybe he would always have a weakness there.

As the day wore on the humidity dropped and the mist clouds dissipated. It would be nice to dry out, but there was no chance given how much he was still sweating. They stopped to eat the food they had brought in their sacks; brown nuts, some kind of chewy bread or maybe dried meat—he didn't ask, if it was spider he didn't want to know. It was tasty, and that was all that mattered. Dessert appeared to be the large pink fruits from the forest floor, the same fruit he had "discovered" a day or so ago.

'Do you have a name for your people?' he asked, between mouthfuls.

'We call ourselves the Gurlanka,' Shufen said scrambling agilely over a huge root. 'It means "people of the forest by the sea".'

'It means all of that?' he said. They laughed.

'The name is how the Elders say it,' Jarlain said smiling at him, the sun dappled through the trees onto her face.

She looked very pretty just then, and he found himself staring at her a bit too long. He dropped his gaze quickly, trying to hide his mistake. It was true he found her attractive, she looked different to women he had seen before, exotic, dark and mysterious. But just then he also sorely missed Rasia. He scolded himself internally for acting like some fool boy. If Jarlain had noticed his staring, she didn't show it and carried on speaking.

'They talk an ancient tongue that the Hidden Ones speak. Only an Elder is able to learn it.'

'Everyone else is too busy,' Shufen snorted.

'Are the Hidden Ones like the goddess?' Marakon asked.

'No, the goddess of the forest is still the same. We call her Woela,' Jarlain said as they packed up their things.

He smiled. 'We call her Woetala. But many where I come from wonder if she still exists, if she ever existed at all. I think the darkness that spreads across our world destroys faith and belief.'

She gave a surprised look and then smiled sadly. 'They say the darkness spreads over all Maioria, blocking out the light of our creator. That it came from the black scar in the night sky and it will consume all.'

He nodded and looked down at his walking stick. 'Then you know of what I speak. But still, we can't give in. Still, we have to fight. What else can we do? Will the Hidden Ones help?'

Jarlain shook her head. 'They don't get involved in human affairs.'

Typical, Marakon thought, but said nothing.

'They have their own problems. The Incubi and Succubi are their adversaries and opposites. Demons that take the life and form of humans. They were once Hidden Ones, but have fallen.'

'Greater demons,' Marakon murmured as memory stirred.

'Demons that came from beyond the Murk,' Jarlain nodded. 'They say they broke through into the Murk and then into Maioria during the Demon Wars millennia ago. The Hidden Ones do what they can to protect us from them, that is the only way they get involved with humans.'

He raised his eyebrows. At least they did something to help.

They walked at a steady pace for several hours with little or no change in the scenery around them. Marakon wondered how they knew the way and how in the world they would be able to retrace their steps home. He couldn't see the sun through the trees, or see anything but a constant wall of green.

After another hour the light slanted through the leaves at more of an angle and was slowly turning golden red. At least that was some indication of what time of day it was. The scenery began to change and now and then they passed large grey boulders, twice the height of a man and five times as wide. There were markings on those rocks, and on closer inspection, he could just make out strange carvings of faces, or maybe just one face.

'What are they?' he asked, but everyone shrugged.

Jarlain nervously glanced around. 'They were already old when we, the Gurlanka, came here, but no one knows who brought them or where they have gone. We think the Drowning Wastes may have something to do with them.'

The light turned red and began to darken as they walked. His whole body ached, but the others didn't seem tired at all.

'Is it sore?' Jarlain asked.

'Yes, but it heals. Thanks to you,' he smiled, noticing how her cheek curved smoothly in the evening light. She smiled back and carried on walking. He did miss Rasia, that was obvious. Would he ever see her again? Well, that was another matter, and he didn't want to think about it. It was less painful to think about Jarlain.

Night fell quickly, but the moons of Doon and Woetala were bright, and enough silver and orange light fell through the canopy to see. There came another light source, yellowish green specs that danced all around them.

'Fairies?' he asked, wide-eyed. He had not seen fairies since he had been a child and had almost forgotten they existed. Jarlain laughed at him again. He pouted indignation.

'Fireflies, silly,' she jested. 'Just another kind of your hated insects.'

'Well, these at least have some use,' he replied.

Shufen slowed his lead. 'We are close to the Drowning Wastes,' he said quietly as if afraid someone, or something, would hear.

'Why is it called that?' Marakon whispered, suddenly wishing he'd asked earlier. He might not have come then.

'Because those who enter drown in misery and are lost forever. The land is cursed, dead, a wasteland of lost hope. You'll feel it the closer we get. We don't know exactly what happens as no one has come out alive to tell us. I've been closest to this place than anyone in the village, though it's not a thing I'm proud of and it happened by accident. I nearly went mad.

'The first feeling is sadness—you see sadness everywhere, in the rocks, in the trees, even in the animals. All your sad memories float before you. If you go closer, it gets worse, much worse. The sadness becomes terror and visions from past lives, or maybe other peoples' lives haunt you; terrible memories of violence and death, plague and famine. The sense of futility and despair consumes you.' Shufen shuddered and looked into the middle distance, his face white.

'Like the Shadowlands,' Marakon mused.

Shufen frowned and then nodded. 'Only you don't have to die to go into the Drowning Wastes. I was hunting a stupid deer. I nearly had it when it jumped away and I fell. I tumbled down forever into that terrible place,' he swallowed. 'It was all I could do to block my ears and shut my eyes from the sound and sight of death. I wandered for three days in the wilderness, trying to find the path out. I was lucky, any further in and... It's a place where all reason for living is taken from you.'

'Why are we going there then? Are you that keen to be rid of me?' he asked even as the memory of the hourglass flashed through his mind.

'No, we go because the Elders told us to,' Shufen shrugged. 'We are to take you as close to that place as we can and let you go your own way. In there you will find whatever it is you seek. That's all they have told us. We risk much even coming this far.'

'How will I know which way to go? How will I survive?' Marakon asked.

Shufen looked at him and then turned away, his face expressionless. He felt like a child, lost and bewildered, caught up in things that were far beyond his understanding. But he knew he could do nothing except keep moving forwards. If he stopped, the faces of his friends and comrades who had died so recently would catch up with him.

'You'll know what you have to do, the Elders have said. They, and the Hidden Ones they speak to, are never wrong,' Jarlain said beside him. 'Like I told you before, I see danger and great changes coming. There's no turning back.'

'We all sense it,' the eldest Gurlanka echoed. He had been silent until now. The youngest nodded.

Marakon had to accept that that was the only answer he was going to receive. He tried to empty his head of the questions that burned inside. Whether that strange old boatman and what he had said had been real or not, he knew the answers lay somewhere in that awful place, it *had* to. Besides, it couldn't be worse than fighting Maphraxies or being captured and becoming one of them. The pang of urgency spurred him on and he could not ignore it any more than he could ignore needing the toilet.

'We'll walk another half an hour from here,' Shufen said sombrely, and they all followed him in a line.

As they made their way through the dark and increasingly silent wood Marakon offered a prayer to the goddess of the forest; mainly for strength, and ultimately to find a way out of this cursed jungle and back home to Rasia. But try as he might he couldn't seem to find the peace he needed. His white eye was hot and sweaty under the patch. He went to lift it, but let his hand drop back down. He didn't want Jarlain to see the things she saw before, whatever they had been.

No bird sang or animal rustled in the undergrowth, and he hadn't seen a monkey for several hours. Tendrils of mist formed again as moisture rose from the warm and pungent jungle floor into the cooler night air. The boulders were more numerous now and stood like ominous, ghostly figures in the moonlight.

How long would it take to reach this cursed place? Marakon thought impatiently. The pressing sense of urgency was annoying him now, it came from within but was not his own. It seemed as if it was placed there. His mind drifted wearily as he stumbled on behind Shufen.

It was inevitable in the boring trudge that his thoughts would turn to that last battle against the Histanatarns. He remembered it clearly now; the strange spinning wheels powering the tiny Histanatarn vessels, the explosion of the harpoons and the violent rock of the ship in the aftermath. The slippery blood covering the decks, the lifeless face of the dwarf woman as she fell dead into the sea below, another to join the thousands in their watery grave. Bokaard, big and powerful, hacking down the enemy. Then the Dread Dragons came.

Did any of them survive? How could they, but hadn't he survived? Why did the Dread Dragons not kill him? Why did nothing make any sense? The frustration annoyed, him and his mood darkened. What about the youngest ones? They could only have been sixteen, maybe even fifteen. It was supposed to be a straightforward mission: sight the enemy. It had had the worst outcome possible, and yet he'd been so sure of success and of victory. It was all his fault; he'd given the order to go west. He deserved everything he got. He didn't deserve to find his way home, of see Rasia and his sons again.

He should have factored in the Histanatarn threat, but they were never supposed to be that far west. Not supposed to… How could he, one of the most experienced commanders of the Feylint Halanoi, ever rely on supposes? The enemy could be anywhere at any time.

He walked deep in dark thoughts, randomly swishing his stick to slice the leaves of bushes and vines away. *Great Mother, pray that Bokaard made it out alive.* He was a strong man, a seasoned fighter, and more than that he was a friend. He forced the lump in his throat back down. Do and die; that's what they did, that's all they were supposed to do.

He rubbed his eyepatch. So many he'd known had fallen in so many battles, it was hard to find friends that lasted long enough. Pointless, sodding, futile war. The enemy was too strong despite the success of the Feylint Halanoi in bringing together all able peoples from across Free Maioria. They weren't enough—it wasn't enough, damn it. It would never be enough. He swiped viciously at a leaf above him and watched the torn part fall to the floor oozing sap.

Ever since his childhood, when the Maphraxies first came, there had been no peace in his life. Had there been peace before the Maphraxies came to Maioria? The elves spoke of constant war between the people even then, and even if there was peace, there was always death. Even dragons died eventually. Did happiness and abundance come with peace or was fighting what all things lived for? Did he even want peace? Maybe he just liked fighting; maybe he was nothing without war.

His mood sank further. Was this the edge of the Drowning Wastes? He hacked at another leaf, but his swipe was weak, driven by futility, and the leaf remained bruised on the bush. He had seen hundreds of men and women, soldiers all of them, die on the battlefield, meaninglessly. Who wanted that? Who wanted to feel like so much worthless grass to be scythed down, their bright light extinguished forever by the immortal Maphraxies? They died for nothing. Nothing! Where was the goddess for those who died? Do and die, and that was it. He didn't know if he was sad or furious.

Abruptly he realised they had stopped. How long had he been wandering in a dark haze? Jarlain leaned against one of the trees away from the group, her shoulders slumped and her back to them. The others sat wearily on the damp forest floor. No one looked at each other. Only Shufen stood up straight and alert, watching the trees.

The air was heavy with the weight of something more than humidity, and it was no longer hot but positively cold. There was an odd light about them as if it were dawn or dusk, and though the moons and stars were gone it was still a long way to dawn. Mist drifted in ghostly ribbons amongst the trees. He shivered, feeling the weight of ages press upon his shoulders.

'I'll take you a little further,' Shufen said in a heavy whisper, 'but the others will wait here, I'll not risk it.'

'Risk what?' Marakon asked, but Shufen stepped away. He was about to follow, but Jarlain laid a hand on his arm making him jump. She had moved so silently he had not heard her.

'Wait,' she said. She looked pale and tired and seemed to be holding back, there was fear in her eyes. 'Take this,' she said, passing him a small woven pouch.

Curiously he took it and emptied the contents onto his hand. A smooth, creamy, opaque pebble fell out, about a third the size of his hand. He turned it over quizzically. On one side a bear was intricately carved and on the other a sun. It was perfectly smooth and cool to the touch.

'It's a gift. It's an old symbol of our people, nothing more. The symbol of hope is the sun that brings the light; the symbol of the bear is the symbol of strength and freedom, which must always be fought for, at least in this world. Funny isn't it that there are no bears here, yet we all remember them clearly.'

He wondered at that. Perhaps it was a memory of their lost land Unafay. Jarlain continued.

'It may help you, in there, but it's only a relic to bring luck and a way for you to remember me, us, when the darkness covers your mind. You'll need something to remember, and this stone holds the encryption of us. In truth, there's nothing that can help you, only yourself,' she gave a smile though it never reached her eyes. He put a hand on hers.

'I'll return, I promise,' he spoke from the heart and his words felt true, but he was unsure if he was trying to reassure her or himself. He put the stone back in its pouch and followed Shufen into the mist. He could not bring himself to look back.

CHAPTER 33

Drowning Wastes

WITH every step, his feet grew heavier, and the air became thicker and harder to breathe as if they walked and breathed in soup. The feeling of sorrow grew within like a knot in the pit of his stomach. Marakon looked at Shufen wondering if he felt it too. The man's face was set and his chin firm—he seemed to be controlling it through sheer will. Marakon decided to do the same.

But his thoughts soon flickered back to the past no matter how hard he tried to control them. Thoughts that became increasingly vivid until they seemed so real he even heard past conversations as if they were happening now. A shout right beside him made him jump and whirl around, but there was nothing there. The forest was empty, except for Shufen and the trees. Shufen was right, even the trees looked sad, grey and wilting as if they had borne witness to awful things.

'This place is always dusk, never reaching the night, never releasing the light to the darkness, as if never releasing the living to their peaceful rest,' Shufen said quietly. 'Another kind of Shadowlands, yet the living can walk here.'

They moved on in silence. Shufen's pale, taut face told Marakon he was fighting his own inner battles too, but knowing that did not comfort him.

The forest began to open up, and an overgrown path was faintly visible. Whoever made that path was long gone and yet the forest was reluctant to reclaim it. A grey figure loomed between the bushes. He jumped, his hand grabbing his sword, but the figure didn't move, and he realised it was a statue.

He gawped at it. A statue? In the middle of the jungle when it should be in some city of the Old World? Beyond it was another and then the grey tip of another lurking up through the mist. Something about them drew him to them at a run. He went to each in turn despite the heavy feeling of trespassing lodging in his gut.

The statues were only slightly taller than he with finely detailed, expertly-chiselled faces. A strange recognition stirred within him as he stared at their disturbing, lifelike expressions. The first was a man with a long moustache hanging below his chin. He wore a short conical helmet, armour and a tabard with the emblem of a star he did not recognise at first. Memory stirred. *A star...* The statue had both hands on the pommel of his sword, the tip resting on the ground before him. His face was drawn in sorrow, and his eyes were shut as if he did not want to see what was happening.

'Who is this?' Marakon hissed, staring at the statue obsessively, but Shufen was out of earshot.

Who was it supposed to be? He desperately wanted to know, *needed* to know, but there was no description on the base or anywhere. Almost every statue in the cities at home spoke of glory and victory and grand status, but this spoke of sorrow and loss and deprecation. He felt sick and walked to the next, though his eyes kept going back to the first.

The next statue was of a boy, not quite a man, unarmed and prone upon the ground, dressed in little more than a loincloth. Arms raised above his head, he was trying to shield himself from whoever was attacking him. His mouth was open in a silent scream that would last forever; a scream that echoed around Marakon's mind. Memory stirred; *unarmed and innocent.*

Marakon pulled himself away and came to the next. A man, dressed once more in armour like the first, but lying on his belly. He was half propped up using his sword in his left hand as he reached with a clawed hand towards something he would never touch. His face contorted in a grimace of pain and loss. What was he reaching for? The desire to know was overwhelming.

He stepped back, staring at the statues with wide eyes. They were so life-like, they filled him with fear. They may as well have been real people turned to stone where they stood. Whoever crafted them was a master in stonework. No moss, lichen or ivy dared to cover them. The dark grey stone had not weathered and looked freshly chiselled—and yet they had to be incredibly old.

He moved faster amongst the statues, feverishly staring up into their faces, willing them to release their secrets, but they did not. Their silence was eternal. Sweat trickled down his forehead, and he heard voices he recognised and those he did not, chattering in his head. Half-remembered conversations from a time long ago. They talked over the top of each other so as he could not make any single word out. He was sure the voices, the memories, were driven by the statues.

The next was of three people. A man in armour, his feet askance and a great sword held aloft just beginning its downward stroke. Under that sword a young woman cowered, unarmoured, unarmed, and terrified; her arms held above her in futile protection and submission. A baby lay face down by her knees in an unnatural, twisted position. The man's face was a mask of rage.

Marakon choked back a sob and tore himself away. Who would make these awful statues? Why?

Lest anyone forget.

He had to stop at every one; they drew him to them as if they wanted to be seen and he could not deny them. A female soldier, long braids hung from under her helmet, her face was full of sorrow and tears were running down her cheeks. She held her sword against her chest, point turned inwards ready to end her own life.

He rushed on, but the statues were many; men, women, children, elves, dwarves, humans... All races of Maioria, fighting, dying, and all with terrible sorrow or rage vivid in their faces. There were no statues of glory or chivalry; none were victorious and none were honourable. He wiped the sweat from his face, his mind spinning, panic rising. He had to get away from them, from the voices.

He whirled around, his face a contorted mirror of theirs. Tears of sorrow and horror blurred his vision. Where was he? What was this awful place? Why did he recognise those faces in the statues? They spoke of something terrible, something awful and the memory was within him, but he did not want to remember, he could not, he must not!

Who am I?

His breath came in ragged gasps as the hundreds of battles in which he had fought flickered through his mind. He felt his head would explode with the rage and sorrow that ravaged him. He clutched his temples and shut his eyes as if he could shut it all out. He fell to his knees screaming.

Suddenly there was silence. He knelt there gulping for air as the images and voices receded. Slowly he opened his eyes. Back by the first statue, he saw Shufen, his face forlorn and sorrowful. He rested with his back against a tree, his attention absorbed with something in his hand.

Marakon staggered towards him and grasped the man's arms. Shufen looked up, surprised and unrecognising for a moment. Slowly he came to his senses, and they embraced roughly. Shufen spoke first.

'Brother, I can go no further. When I last stepped where you did, I wandered for days in madness. The Elders say this place is for you—this is where it all changes, where peace and memory or fear and death will come. Either way, there's release. Take this,' he passed him his small pack containing water and food.

Marakon nodded his thanks and slipped it on to his shoulder.

'You're right. They are right. I don't know what I will find, but here is where I must go. The answers are... all here. Go back to the others, to your home. I hope to see you there.' He turned away, swallowing loudly, the pang of urgency overwhelming his fear. In his mind's, eye he saw the sands of time trickling through the hourglass.

'Time moves differently in this place,' Shufen said, his face pale and drawn. 'Faster or slower, but never the same. If we don't see you again within three days, we shall bless your spirit and pray for safe passage into the light of the One Source.' They grasped each other's arms and met each other's eyes for a long moment, then Shufen turned away.

Marakon watched him walk back the way they had come until the mist and jungle engulfed him. Turning back to the row of statues, he felt the jaws of loneliness open up to swallow him once more. He took Jarlain's stone out of its pouch and gripped it in his hand. He had never been superstitious before, yet he needed something to link him to the normal world as he stepped back down the line of statues. The din of voices grew again, and he started to talk to himself to keep them at bay.

'I am Marakon. I'm not afraid. Here I will find my answers. I am Marakon.'

A seasoned soldier afraid of statues, pah! What an embarrassment. But still, the fear gnawed at him. He tried not to look at them as he passed, but he could feel their eyes heavy upon him, judging him and finding him guilty.

Unnaturally swiftly, the jungle gave way to a rocky mountainside stretching up and away. The sun was high in the sky, but its light was weak and the air hazy, like morning fog, only it was not damp. The plants and trees ended abruptly as if he had stepped between an invisible veil that separated the jungle from a barren desert. When the plants stopped, the statues stopped, much to his relief, and yet that oppressive feeling only deepened.

He walked until the jungle was far behind and lost to the desert. Wind lifted dust from the arid land, making it swirl in eddies before settling it back on the ground once more. The voices in his head were gone, but there were whispers in the wind now, half-heard and never understood. He was certain a female voice spoke right beside him, but there was no one there. Sorrow and hopelessness hung on him like a leaden cloak, heavy and blocking out joy. He steeled his mind and soul against the oppression, trying to deny it entry.

A gust of wind blew sand off a mound of rocks before him, uncovering not stones but worn bones and a skull. He stopped beside it wondering who had fallen here. Then he noticed the other mounds; they were everywhere, littering the ground in all directions as if he walked through some ancient graveyard.

Why was he surprised? There was nothing but death in this hellish place. Not even demons would wander these barren plains. He bent down and laid a finger upon the skull as if bidding a welcome or final farewell, he wasn't sure. Desolation, cold and absolute, exuded from the skull and he watched in horror as it disintegrated to dust.

'*Very* old,' he said to himself. Standing back up, he swallowed and wiped his hand on his tunic. 'Let's not touch anything else.'

He carried on through a ravine, a rocky valley where once a river might have flowed, though now it was long gone. His feet carried him forward, seeming to know the way though his mind did not. Skulls and bones were scattered here and there, some complete skeletons, others mere fragments, and all of different shapes and sizes; child, dwarf, elf—even animals were not spared death for amongst them lay horses and dogs, birds and huge beasts he did not know and small ones he did.

Suddenly the hairs rose on the back of his neck. He was being watched. But how could that be when there was nothing and no one for miles in any direction? The whisperings began again and with every step they grew louder and clearer. A woman sang softly, a sorrowful song that drifted on the wind coming to him from all around so he could not tell from where it came.

He shouldn't listen to it, whatever, whoever, it was. But the voice was beautiful, and the song was a light in this cursed place. He began to drift along with it, his feet wandering left and right depending on where the song was clearest. He could not resist the voice, and he no longer walked purposefully.

Weariness—heavy, eye-drooping, bone-aching weariness descended upon him. He had to rest, to sleep; he'd been walking for hours. He stopped and squatted upon a large rock rising out of the sand. He loosened his sword belt with a yawn, rested his forehead on his hand and drifted. He needed to rest, just for a little while, no harm in that.

He fell asleep listening to that beautiful voice. The further the words carried him to sleep the clearer they became.

> Where do we go when the darkness surrounds us?
> Who will love us when we are damned?
> When will our penance be served?
> Why does the sun never rise for us?
> What is the name of the one who will guide us?

From far away in the distance, it seemed another voice whispered.

> She is the light in the darkness.
> Hers is the love for the damned.
> Our penance is served when she comes for us.
> Now it's the dark moon that rises,
> And she is coming to guide us.

CHAPTER 34

Spear of Light

ISSA stepped out of Triest'anth's house. She was clean and dressed in the clothes given to her by Lys'ynth; a pair of soft blue trousers and a simple linen sleeveless top that reached almost to her knees and tied at the waist with a cord. The night of the Feast of Ax'anth was very warm with little breeze.

In the distance filtering through the mix of oak and pine trees came the glow of a bonfire and the sound of many voices laughing and chatting. Above her, the small, orange moon of Woetala shimmered brightly in a clear night sky.

She stood there for a moment, soaking up the evening, feeling wonderful to be alone just for a little bit, not to think or dream, just to be. They had summer bonfires on Little Kammy. The long summer evenings were always her favourite.

She didn't feel quite ready to face everyone yet, not while she had these moments alone to enjoy her favourite time of year. She slipped into the forest and made it back to the pool she had washed in earlier.

An owl hooted in the distance and was replied by another further away. The only other sound was the tinkling splash of the small waterfall that drowned out the distant voices of Karalanths. The reflection of Woetala's moon danced merrily upon the waters.

She sat down upon a smooth rock that was still warm from the sun and rubbed the mark on her chest. It tingled. She pulled down her top a little. The raven, barely visible in daylight, now shone silver in the moonlight.

Would it be there forever? She doubted she would ever use the spell—who wanted to go to the Shadowlands or any place like it? Although a spell like that could save your life, she only hoped she never had to use it.

She closed her eyes, stilled her mind, and focused on the Flow.

In her mind she could see and feel it around her, flowing gently in all directions, seemingly purposelessly to the untrained mind. She stepped into it so that it flowed around and through her, pastels of purple and blue light. She opened her eyes and could see the Flow as she had seen it in her mind, overlaid upon the physical reality.

She looked down into the pool. It was no longer rippling black water, but swirling with magical energy—the magical life force within and between all things. She focused on creating a lighter circle of energy, about the size of her palm, and the Flow moved to her bidding. She looked down into the pale silvery circle floating upon the surface.

'Freydel. Freydel. Freydel,' she said in her mind, holding a clear vision of the wizard.

He had shown her briefly how to scry, and it was done using a mirror or, better since water was a life force of its own, a pool of water. A clear night with a full moon, any moon, was best and though she hadn't done this before, tonight was as good a time as any to try. She had thought about using the Orb of Water but without knowing anything about it, decided it wise not to try.

"Speak three times with the mind, the mental plane of intention, and three times aloud, the physical plane of intention," Freydel had said. You were also supposed to have a physical object that had belonged to the person or was a gift from them, but she did not have anything of his. It might not work, but there was no harm in trying. She had to let the wizard know she was all right and he could tell Ely and Maeve.

'Freydel, Freydel, Freydel,' she said aloud.

The circle of energy shimmered and shifted, trying to form the connection. After only a few moments, she began to realise how hard it was to focus on just one thing, her mind wanted to jump all over the place. She frowned in concentration, willing Freydel to appear in the circle of light. For a moment, she thought she saw a figure, possibly robed and carrying a staff but the image was so hazy as if surrounded by clouds, and it went as quickly as it had come.

She blinked and tried again, willing the image to appear once more. The energy swirled faster, but nothing became distinct. She thought she heard sounds, people speaking, but it was too distorted to know what was being said. She huffed in frustration; he hadn't said it was difficult. But perhaps it wasn't difficult; maybe he just couldn't be reached right now.

The tuning sound of instruments and laughter broke her attention. She sighed and let go of the Flow, and stared at the black waters of the pool. Her head hurt from the effort, and the magic had drained her unusually quickly. She was clearly still recovering from that awful battle, from the power of the blue moon that had flowed through her. Ely's bracelet may help heal her body, but her magic reserves needed lots of time to rest and heal alone. "Always draining for the novice," Freydel had said, but also that it would get easier. She'd try scrying again tomorrow.

'Maion'artheria,' came a whisper on the wind.

The purity of the voice immediately stilled her world to silence and complete calm and clarity descended upon her. All other thoughts faded away and lost their importance as the eternal voice called to her. The raven mark on her chest became warm and glowed indigo blue above her cleavage. She touched it and closed her eyes.

As she closed her physical eyes, it seemed she opened her inner eyes. So clearly before her stood the sacred mound with its mirror-like entrance and the giant stones standing as ancient protectors. She walked to the liquid mirror surface and, feeling fearless, entered. All weariness and worries, all aches and pains, melted away as the cold engulfed her.

When she emerged on the other side, she stepped not into a dark stone room, but onto an endless desert under a starlit sky. Beside the beautiful twinkling trilithon, the tall robed woman stood, waiting for her. A hot wind blew through Issa's hair, and she breathed deeply. It's so real, she thought, grinding her toes into the warm sand, she had to be here physically and not just in her mind. She looked down and was dressed as she had been before in her clean Karalanth clothes.

The figure beckoned to her with a luminous pale hand, and she forgot all else. She walked towards Zanufey and a sense of infinity flooded through her being. All questions she wanted to ask died on her lips for they seemed so small and unimportant in this being's presence. Instead, awe and humbleness were a tangible thing, and she found herself half-staring up at the shining perfect chin and lips, and half-looking down at her feet. Zanufey spoke, and her pure voice held an angelic harmony as of many beautiful voices singing.

'Remember Edarna.'

Immediately Issa remembered the old witch sitting at her kitchen table, her green eyes and round red cheeks smiling.

'Yes,' she said, looking into Zanufey's robes where stars and galaxies swirled. She half-hoped the black hole sucking everything into it would not be there on her chest, but still it was. Entire galaxies falling into it and their light extinguished.

Zanufey raised a hand. Issa stared as a hazy figure appeared to her left and then many more. The hazy figures became more distinct until a tall man with dark hair and beard stood there. His right eye was covered with an eyepatch, and he was dressed in armour and a tabard with a star upon it. His head hung in sorrow, and his face was a mask of grief. Behind him stood many others dressed the same and their faces drawn and sad.

' "…The raven searches for the Cursed King…" ' Issa said, suddenly remembering Edarna's words, ' "and his Banished Legion." Is that where the raven has gone?'

Zanufey inclined her head in agreement.

'But why? Who is this "Cursed King"? What is it that I'm supposed to do or even can do?' she asked, confusion tinged her voice.

Zanufey held out her hand, palm down, and there came a burst of white light beneath it. The light grew and lengthened into a ten-foot long glowing shard. The light-shard dimmed and became a spear in Zanufey's hand. Its blade was white metal shaped like a leaf and the haft plain.

'It's beautiful,' Issa breathed. It glimmered like the shimmering aura of a star.

The knights turned to stare at the spear in awe. The image changed, and the knights were mounted upon galloping white horses, armour shining in the light. Behind them followed thousands of soldiers bearing the Feylint Halanoi tabard and in front of them she saw herself in black armour atop a huge dark horse.

Duskar.

'Edarna said this king is good, but he also brings disaster,' Issa breathed, focusing on the man with the dark hair and eyepatch. Zanufey inclined her head but said nothing.

'Where is this spear? Why is it important to them?' she asked.

The image changed and she saw upright grey and brown figures. They were all sizes, some as small as cats and others over twelve feet tall. All were hairless, and all were ugly. Their eyes were red or brown or yellow, and some had wings, and some had tails. Their faces were permanently scowled or grimaced. Then she saw the same spear Zanufey held, shining in the darkness and bound in chains.

'Demons,' Issa said. 'The demons have the spear.' A green moon rose above them casting the demons in an eerie light.

'Zorok, the green moon of the Murk,' she said, remembering the images in her childhood picture book, "Fairies and Scaries." She chewed her lip as she pondered what the images meant.

'The Cursed King needs the spear. Maybe it will end his curse?' She chanced. Zanufey was silent.

'Just tell me what I'm supposed to do,' she said, feeling stupid and ignorant.

She dropped her eyes. Perhaps one shouldn't talk to goddesses like that. But Zanufey did not chide her or mock her but stood there patiently and, as always, silent and knowing. The image changed, and a raven flew and landed on the tip of the spear. She stared at the raven and the spear; they seemed important but she did not know why.

'What if I screw up? What if I'm not the Raven Queen,' she said. It was the one question she feared asking the most. If she was the Raven Queen, then the responsibility was too great. If she wasn't, then her life until would seem like a lie.

Only then did Zanufey say the most she had ever said in words that fell softly around her.

'Many things may or may not happen, but above all else, it's through strength and faith of heart and spirit that you will know what needs to be done.'

The spear and the raven began to fade, and Issa felt herself being drawn backwards.

'Wait,' she called. 'Am I supposed to find this spear and the Cursed King too?' she shouted frantically as the desert began to disappear. But all that came was a whispered *'Maion'artheria'* and all was still.

She blinked and looked down at the reflection of Woetala's moon in the pool, suddenly feeling empty in the absence of the divine presence.

Why did everything have to be so cryptic? It wasn't as if anything was being hidden from her, and what had been spoken of was actually quite succinct and straightforward.

'Why can't she just say, "go here to get this" or, "you need to do this, this and this"?' She huffed aloud. It was hard enough just surviving, why did she have to work it all out as well? She couldn't just walk into the Murk anyway.

'Oh, hello, I've just come to collect the Spear of Light,' she scoffed then sighed. It was obvious she was being asked to think for herself and besides, she didn't have to do anything she didn't want to. This Cursed King meant nothing to her anyway. But what else was she going to do? Live a life jumping around with the Karalanths? She doubted the Maphraxies would sit by letting her do that for long.

'But I had wanted to go to the Seers of Myrn,' she whispered. She kind of had. In the few moments she'd had alone, she wondered about her mother, her blood mother, and since she had been a seer going to Myrn seemed to be a logical step if she wanted to find her.

The soft beat of drums and what sounded like a harp started in the distance. A gust of wind brought upon it the enticing smell of wood smoke and something delicious cooking. Her stomach rumbled.

She checked her reflection. She had put on eyeliner borrowed from Rhul'ynth and red on her lips. She smoothed her hair, though she had already brushed it to shining. Would Asaph like how she looked? Hmm, what did it matter what Asaph thought... She barely knew the man, and though he had saved her life and she his, it didn't mean they were suited. She'd always thought she would marry Tarry—Tarry who was dead. She sighed and pushed aside those thoughts. For the foreseeable future, there was no time for relationships, and it would be far safer for everyone that way.

The whole world was at war and she was thinking of a partner... Edarna, Freydel, Ely—all saw a dark path before her, and she knew she had to walk it alone rather than risk another's life, like Rance. Before thoughts of those lost could mar her mood, she turned from the pool and made her way through the trees towards the orange glow of a huge bonfire. She rounded a house so fast she thumped into Coronos.

'Gosh. I'm sorry!' She apologised. Coronos laughed and steadied himself.

'No matter, I was looking for you anyway. I wanted to give you back this.' He passed her a sack with something round and heavy in it. The wrinkles on his brow furrowed deeply. 'I'm sorry I took the orb, but I didn't trust to leave such magical things lying around when you were too sick to protect it. It's bound to you anyway, so I couldn't have stolen it. I had to keep it buried in a hole for my own protection.'

'You were right to take it. Thank you for protecting it,' she said. Coronos was staring at the orb, mesmerised. She too could feel its strange alluring power.

'I know there's much we must discuss, but I don't think there's time tonight,' she eyed him cautiously, could she trust him with the orb? That he already had one made it easier, perhaps, plus he had far more knowledge about it, about things that would take her a lifetime to understand. The orb was vitally important; one key to one power to be kept away from Baelthrom, at all costs. Keteth had already wreaked havoc with it and she could not afford to let it be lost again.

'Coronos?'

He glanced up at her reluctantly, then smiled, though he seemed weary.

'Can I entrust you to guard the Orb of Water until I know what needs to be done with it?'

He looked at her with bated breath. 'I would be glad to be rid of it. One thing of power is quite enough to carry, but two is too much. Half of me wants it, as any greedy human might, but the other half recoils from it. It's quite a burden and not to mention the worry.'

'That's why I know I can trust you,' she smiled, then gave him a pleading look when he did not respond. He looked at her, then slumped his shoulders with a sigh.

'All right, all right. I shall look after it. If you name me as Second Keeper, I'll be able to keep it close without being harmed. Though I'll keep it wrapped up tight, as I have no idea how to use it. In truth, we should take it somewhere safe. Maybe the Wizards' Circle will know what to do.'

She took the orb out of its sack. It was cold and shimmered a beautiful, deep blue colour in the moonlight. She chewed her lip.

'How do I make you Second Keeper?'

Coronos laughed. 'I don't know, I've never named a Second Keeper myself. I only know that it can be done. Usually, it responds to the will of its Keeper. Since you are its Keeper it will respond to your will.'

'Hmm, all right then,' she said, staring at the orb. 'Orb of Water, I name Coronos Avernayis Dragon Rider of Drax your Second Keeper.' She had expected something to happen, some flash of light or tolling of a bell, but there was nothing.

'Did I do it right?' she asked sheepishly.

Coronos laughed again. 'Pass it to me and let me see how it feels.'

He took the orb gingerly, then straightened. 'Well, I no longer feel quite so sick or weak holding it. I assume it worked and all is fine. I shall protect it. You have my word on my life, Issa. Or should I call you the Raven Queen?' he said, putting his hand on his heart and bowing deeply.

She shifted awkwardly, and he took her hand, smiling sympathetically at the consternation on her face.

'I know how hard it has been for you. Losing everyone you know and love, even your homeland. I can only guess at how terrifying the Shadowlands were and what you have been through to be here standing before me. We've all been changed by the enemy and their atrocities. But if we stick together, we can help each other.

'Sometimes I see more clearly than Asaph because he loves you deeply,' he ignored her reddening face. 'There's more in this world and all its dimensions than we can possibly know or understand, but the goddess is always here to guide us.'

She looked up at his smiling face and felt like a girl before a wise old man who made her feel safe and calm.

'I've seen you grow strong since we first met on those grey shores of the Shadowlands. You had almost become a Lost One, forgetting who you are and wandering the realm of the dead. I think you know who you are now. I think you also know where you are going. You may not quite realise it yet, but deep down you know. I believe, we believe, in you, and all that really matters is for you to believe in you,' his grey eyes were piercing as he looked at her.

'I know something of Zanufey's raven. It's a messenger from the night goddess sent to warn us that dark times are coming. You know, in Drax, Zanufey is called the Raven Goddess because she takes the form of a raven to carry the souls of the dead to the light?'

'Really?' she said. 'Well, I guess death must be far away, because the raven's been gone for days without so much as letting me know.'

Coronos grinned. 'Perhaps that's so. Come, let's eat. I'm famished,' he said offering his arm.

'Me too,' she smiled and took it. They made their way to a very crowded and noisy village centre.

CHAPTER 35

The Kiss

ISSA had not seen anything quite like what she was witnessing as she and Coronos slurped down spicy root vegetable soup. The first meal of a very long feast—so they had been told by the old female Karalanth serving the soup from a cooking pot so large Issa was sure she could fit inside it. The tiny local theatrical plays on Little Kammy really didn't come close to the bizarre enactment of dancing, music and acting she was watching.

Karalanth men were dancing dangerously close to the fire, their entire bodies covered in blue and red paint. One of them wore a three-foot round mask coloured in the same paint, with long red feathers sticking out that waved and shook as he moved. He held a large spear in his hand—one that looked real and probably was.

Three other men with smaller masks were laughing and jeering at him in the Karalanth's strange barking and clicking language. She didn't understand a word of it, but whatever they were saying made the crowd laugh raucously.

'It's probably obvious, but the one with the big mask is Ax'anth,' Triest'anth explained to them. He had come up quietly beside them, as most Karalanths seemed to be able to do, cradling a bowl of soup. 'To be honest, I can't remember which battle this is, they all kind of blur into one in the celebrations.'

The dance ended in a mock show of a bloody battle that, for all she could tell, basically turned into a leaping heap of laughing masked men. They looked suspiciously drunk, and when she tasted the contents of the ceramic mug that was shoved graciously into her hands, she understood why. It tasted like some kind of sweet white port; spicy with a heady aftertaste and very strong.

'Made from forest cherries to a secret recipe,' Triest'anth tapped his nose and downed the rest of his mug, wincing and shuddering in the aftermath.

'I don't doubt it,' Issa mumbled and sipped her own. Still, her body shook, whether in enjoyment or revulsion she wasn't quite sure. It didn't stop her from taking a second mug-full, however, and soon she began to find the theatrical displays as funny as everyone else.

There was an endless procession of food trays passed around. Dark green leaves wrapped around mushroom and nut pates, curried tubers, candied acorns, pink, purple and brown tapenades, pumpkin bread and breads of every shape, size and colour that she couldn't even begin to guess what they were. There seemed to be a lot of mushrooms and nut-based dishes, cooked and raw, and arranged in the most imaginative ways.

'Nuts and tubers can be collected in advance,' Triest'anth said, 'and mushrooms are always plentiful.'

'Mmm,' she mumbled through a mouthful. 'I didn't know there were so many types, or how delicious they could be.' She reached for another leaf wrapped thing. The delicious and imaginative food, put her own culinary skills to shame. All she ever bothered to cook was boiled vegetables and fish Tarry had caught.

Despite the huge trays of food being passed around, the food tables lining either side of the path through the village were also heavily laden and bustling. Though her plate was full, her eyes locked on to the dessert table.

There was a huge cake that she thought could only be called Mountain Berry Cake. It was quite literally a cake mountain at least three feet high in the shape of a cone and splattered with wild strawberries, cherries and blackberries. She *had* to leave room for that. But when she looked down at her plate she still had a load of delicious leaf wraps. She decided to finish her plate but stay close to the cake, just in case it disappeared.

The last mouthful and swig of Karalanth wine left her feeling rather dizzy, and she looked around for a place to slump whilst still in sight of her goal; the Mountain Berry Cake.

Between the houses and dotted everywhere were many smaller fires around which huge cushions had been placed. Some were full with four or more Karalanths sat neatly on the cushions with their legs tucked under them, but others still had room.

She found a suitable cushioned slumping place next to two Karalanths chatting to each other, female and male. With a sigh she melted onto the cushion, her eyes never leaving the cake. She could still glimpse it between the moving people.

She turned to the couple beside her, but they had moved closer to each other now, the female Karalanth leaning heavily on the male who was now stroking the soft white fur of her belly. Their red faces and half-filled mugs told her all she needed to know.

When they started kissing, she decided that they, and she, would prefer some privacy, and made her way over to the now fast disappearing Mountain Berry Cake.

'What's it called?' she asked the two giggling young girls cutting the cake. They were probably laughing at a funny two-foot, she mused and grinned.

'Feniserry,' they laughed and gave her a helping. The red berries and gooey white icing slopped deliciously onto her plate.

'Oh, I thought it was Mountain Berry Cake,' she replied in disappointment. For her, it would always be Mountain Berry Cake.

This made the girls cry with laughter. Perhaps they had managed to sneak some wine away from the adults. Grinning, cake in hand, she turned to go and spotted Asaph sitting beside a different fire. She got an extra piece for him and went over.

It was a struggle to carry two plates and her mug of Karalanth wine as well as dodge between the revellers.

As she neared, she suddenly felt ridiculously shy. Asaph was talking to a Karalanth, and his face was turned in profile. His hair was loose about his broad shoulders and shone golden red in the firelight. Perhaps she had drunk too much already to talk to him and eating both pieces of cake herself wasn't outrageous really.

Actually, it sounded like a great idea, she thought, looking down at the cake. She was about to turn away when he saw her and waved. *Damn!*

She made her way over and sat down awkwardly.

'Oh no!' she cried as the cakes began to slide. She would have lost the lot had he not caught everything. He laughed as he grappled with both plates and her mug.

'Cake?' she asked, unable to stop a giggle escape her throat. She'd definitely had too much wine.

He grinned. 'Uh, why not? I'm sure I can squeeze it in.' He took the cake and began eating. 'Great cake *and* wine,' he said between mouthfuls.

She nodded. 'The best cake I've had since I was on Celene.'

'The wine reminds me of the fire wine we had back home with the

Kuapoh, on the Uncharted Lands,' Asaph said. 'Wild and strong. But at least it gives us a good excuse to avoid dancing. I think we'd stand out like a sore thumb,' he motioned to the dancing Karalanths. 'They have four legs and *never* lose their balance.'

She giggled again, and he grinned at her.

'You look beautiful,' he said, his blue eyes flashing in the firelight.

'Oh, it's amazing what kohl, clothes and wine will do,' she said dismissively, hoping the firelight hid her blushing.

'You look, er, clean,' she added, blushing deeper. 'Er, strong, uh.' How on earth did you compliment a man?

For a moment, she was sure she must look like a goldfish, mouth opening and closing as she tried to find the right words. She gave up with a sigh when he burst out laughing. Luckily another jug of Karalanth wine made it their way, and she hastily refilled her mug, glad for the distraction.

She had no idea what to say to him or why she always got so flustered when he was near. To make it worse, he just sat there grinning and sipping his wine. He always seemed to know what to say and when to say it. He probably had lots of girlfriends anyway.

'It's the wine, uh, it makes me say funny things,' she said. She couldn't tell him he looked handsome and his hair matches the colour of the fire— that would be flirting.

'Do you have a girlfriend? A wife?' she asked, trying to sound conversational, but it actually came out sounding confrontational. He chuckled and she coughed. 'Of course, it's none of my business...' she wafted a hand.

'No, I don't,' was all he said.

He drank his wine but his eyes never left hers. She looked away first, feeling very hot. Wasn't he going to ask her the same? Clearly he wasn't. It probably wouldn't matter to him if she were married anyway!

'Oh no,' Asaph said, his face horrified.

'What?' She turned to see what he was looking at and to her dismay saw four Karalanths approaching with wicked grins on their faces. 'Oh no,' she whispered.

The thick arm of a male Karalanth scooped around her waist, easily lifting her bodily and, ignoring her squeals, carried her into the dance. From the yelps behind it sounded like Asaph was in a similar predicament.

'All must dance at the feast of Ax'anth,' the Karalanth holding her said, and those closest roared with laughter.

'But I don't have four legs,' she squeaked, but it only made them laugh harder.

'Even funny two-feet,' he replied as he dumped her into the foray of dancing, rearing Karalanths.

She looked at him shyly. He had a short fair beard and a warm smile. There were distinctive dappled white spots on his fur. She tried to see Asaph, but he was lost in the swirling mass of Karalanths.

The Karalanth danced with her—if you could call it dancing. It seemed more like spinning and stamping to the drum beats. The drums were played by Karalanths seated around the dancing ring and small delicate harp type instruments were played further back, protected from the rearing dancers. The music was a bizarre symphony of heavy drums and beautiful tinkling sounds that she began to really enjoy.

Dancing turned out to be fun, and she laughed so much she thought her sides would burst. When the song changed, everyone swapped partners. The Karalanth she danced with winked at her, and as she turned away, slapped her on the bum. With a shocked squeak, she fell into Asaph. He laughed, but the surprised expression on his face said something about his own encounter.

'Ugh, maybe we shouldn't have had that cake,' she said, feeling dizzy.

'You and me both,' he nodded. 'Let's find somewhere to rest.'

They cleverly spun to the edge of the ring and slipped out of the firelight. Further away from the commotion than the rest was another small fire surrounded by cushions which were blessedly empty.

'Phew,' she sighed, as they sunk onto cushions again. She lay back and stretched.

'Alone at last,' he said, perched up on one elbow beside her.

She looked up at him. He was looking at her oddly. His deep blue eyes were captivating and her pulse quickened. No one had really looked at her like that before, not even Tarry, and she was suddenly nervous with no idea what to do.

Everything moved in slow motion as he bent his head towards her. His warm lips touched hers, and it seemed fire ignited there. A knot of butterflies fluttered in her stomach. She opened her lips, and he kissed her harder.

The knot in her belly burst into passion that flooded through her veins to her lips and throughout her whole body. Her head swam, and she found herself looking into the Flow. It was alive with swirling orange and red waves or flames, like firelight. It mingled with an endless stream of indigo blue flowing like the ocean.

She opened her eyes and was shocked to find that she could see the Flow clearly, flowing all around and through Asaph and her own body. She closed her eyes and could do nothing but return the passion. It would be up to him to release her. When he finally pulled back, it took some time to regain her senses and the Flow to calm.

She blinked in shock. She had been easily and completely disarmed, stripped naked and quivering with a desire she had never known before. Slowly her breathing calmed, and her senses returned. He was still looking at her, a soft sheen of perspiration on his flushed face. There was both fear and raw longing etched in his eyes, and something bordering on guilt.

'I'm sorry,' he said, seeing the shock on her face. 'It's just you looked so beautiful lying there and I…'

She didn't know what to say. She wanted more but thought she shouldn't.

'Uh, it's all right. I drank too much wine, uh, maybe I should go and sleep it off.' Her voice was shaking, partly from fear and partly from the desire that still sung in her veins. Damn it, she wanted another kiss! Right now she felt more afraid of herself and her emotions than she had of Keteth.

'Or maybe we should have more wine,' Asaph said, seemingly equally disarmed.

She giggled, and he grinned down at her. They found some more wine and sat with their arms around each other, watching the dancing. Over the next hour, the feast began to quieten as people made their way to bed, or suspiciously into the forest.

By the time they had finished their wine, it was very late, and there was no sign of Coronos or Triest'anth. Only the drunkest Karalanths were still up, joking amongst themselves. The dancing had stopped, but a woman and man played a softer tune on their harps by the much-reduced bonfire.

'Let's help each other to bed,' Asaph said, lugging himself up and swaying a little.

She nodded, but when he pulled her up, the whole world rocked. She squealed when he heaved her into his arms. The Karalanths turned to look at them and grinned. One made a rude joke from the sounds of it, which she was glad she didn't quite catch.

'I can walk you know,' she slurred, 'sort of.'

'I'm sure you can. But I can't, I need your weight to balance me,' he replied, equally slurry, and staggered towards Triest'anth's house.

Surprisingly, the house was empty.

'Poor Triest'anth', she said. 'He must long to have his house to himself.'

Asaph grunted in agreement and set her down on her bed. Someone had thought ahead and left large pitchers of water by the hearth ready for the morning headache.

She wondered if he would kiss her again, but stifled a yawn. He kissed her on the cheek and sat down on his bed opposite. Maybe it was best if they just went to sleep.

'Goodnight,' she said and drew the curtain around her bed.

'Goodnight,' he replied.

She didn't think she would sleep for a long while as she wondered whether to creep into his bed or not, but sleep came fast.

CHAPTER 36

Knights of the Shining Star

MARAKON awoke to find a crown in his hand—a simple golden band, inlaid with a shining white crystal. He placed it on his head and knelt upon the red carpet flowing over a wooden stage. A stunning lady with long straw-coloured hair and clear blue eyes stood before him. She also had a golden circlet upon her head, and he felt a deep love for her.

'Today is a great day,' the woman's voice carried well and was rich, like a singer's voice. 'Today we celebrate a great victory. The Knights of the Shining Star, lead by our beloved King Marakazian, have defeated the hated demons that have plagued our lands and murdered our people for years.'

She smiled at him, and he felt giddy under her gaze and the gaze of the adoring crowd. She called him Marakazian, but he was Marakon. The thought was vague under the weight of the crowd's eyes and her voice as she spoke.

'Long ago, these evil demons led by the demon wizard Karhlusus rose up from the Murk deep beneath Maioria. This depraved wizard found a way to unlock the gate to the underworld where the demons reside, and let them loose.

'But the goddess will not let such a despicable act go unpunished. She blessed our King Marakazian to find the most honourable and courageous men and women to become the Knights of the Shining Star.'

The crowd cheered and whistled behind him. He gave a sideways glance at them and smiled, trying not to shake under the pressure.

'They fought valiantly—for our lives and the freedom of all Maioria—against the demons. Many have fallen, but they did not falter, such was their love, such was their determination to end the darkness that

Karhlusus has wrought upon us.

'Now, after so many years of struggle, we've triumphed and driven the demons back into the Murk and beyond from whence they came. Behold King Marakazian. Behold the Knights of the Shining Star!'

The crowd roared and chanted, "Knights of The Shining Star! King Marakazian!" and showered flowers upon the stage. They fell around him as he stood up and took the shining sword she passed to him. He paused, glimpsing his reflection in the polished blade. A middle-aged man with blue eyes, short black hair and black stubble. King Marakazian—not so different looking to Marakon. He smiled and turned to face his knights.

There were several hundred mounted before the stage, beyond which a cheering crowd stretched out past the city walls. The knights were smiling and dressed as he, polished armour shining, white tabards ablaze with a silver star. Some knights held poles with long banners and battle standards, each with a star embroidered. Their horses snorted and tossed their heads. The sky was a clear blue, and the whole city was decorated in ribbons and flags that billowed in the breeze. Beyond the red and brown roofs was a glistening lake, around which bustled green hills and forests.

He looked at his knights with such pride he thought his chest would burst. These were chosen men and women from all nations and all races, with only the purest of heart, the greatest valour and the strongest courage—all the things that were needed to fight the darkness of a demonic force.

'Hail to our saviours, the Knights of the Shining Star!' The people chanted over and again.

He stepped down the wooden steps leading off the stage and took the reins from the young steward holding his horse. He mounted and turned towards the crowd. His knights followed, and the crowd parted before them, hands reaching to touch their horses, feet and legs as they passed. Petals fell like snow, and the people adored them.

Then the darkness came.

It grew within Marakazian's own heart and mind, and nothing could save him from it—perhaps the demons put it there. It was said one could never truly defeat a demon, that the worst demon lived always within.

The victories over the demons had fed his invincibility. Now they were gone, he wanted more. His honour had turned into arrogance and abundance became greed. He had defeated the undefeatable, and the people loved him as they did the goddess. He was blessed, a king becoming a god, and the world belonged to him. He had riches greater than any man, had lands abundant, yet he wanted more. His kingdom would grow, and if the people resisted, he would take their lands by force, so his thoughts went.

Marakon understood Marakazian's thoughts clearly; he sought dominion over the people he had freed.

'Get rid of Karhlusus,' his knights had warned him, and not for the first time.

Their faces were pale and drawn as they looked at him now. They were clustered around the long wooden table beside a great fire. The room was dark save for the fire in the hearth and candles dripping wax upon the walls. He couldn't stand their gazes and dropped his own to look at the floor.

'Great King Marakazian,' Azon began, black hair short, brown eyes searching, beard trimmed and shaved into thin lines about his jaw and lip. Marakazian could barely hold his gaze, anger and something else that plagued and twisted his mind warred within him. 'Send him back to the Murk forever. Whatever you do, do not keep him near; he's a poison in your mind, in all our minds. His magic is dirty and evil and worse than that, he is still strong in demonic magic.'

'You would dare question your king?' he challenged. *How dare they question me, how dare they tell me what to do. It is I who rule and none other!*

Azon held his gaze for a moment, searching.

Always they look at me with their damn searching eyes!

Worry clouded Azon's gaze, and he looked away. 'No,' Azon breathed, 'but he's a sickness in all our minds, in all our hearts. With him here the darkness is close. Who knows what evil he spreads.'

'As the old saying goes, Azon, I will keep my enemies close. Karhlusus is chained deep underground within our strongest dungeon. His body is bound in iron chains and enchantments seal his door. Do you really think he can harm us still?' Marakazian chuckled in disbelief. He was not about to give up his trophy of war either. 'Do you really think Karhlusus deserves such leniency as to be returned to his home in the Murk? You have grown soft, Azon, or forgotten the horror this bastard has wrought upon us. No, I shall keep him there—forever if I must. Imprisoned as a trophy of war, and of unending punishment.'

'My king, it's not the demon wizard's body I fear but his mind,' Azon said wearily. 'No one can bind a wizard's mind, and a mind that has been possessed by a demon lord at that. That cancer you hold deep within those dungeons will act according to its nature, it knows only to feed on life and destroy. It is our fear that whilst the leader of the Grazen remains alive, he will always seek revenge.'

'How dare you disagree with me,' Marakazian seethed, his anger boiled up and spewed out, fury he did not know he possessed.

Azon's cheeks turned red. 'I express only what we all fear, out of concern for you, for the Knights of the Shining Star, for the people…'

But Marakazian's anger was a torrent he could not reason with or control.

'Call yourself a Knight of the Shining Star? Well, you are no longer! Always you disagree with me, Azon, always. You disagree with your king! Now get out of here before I have you hanged for treason.'

Fury and disbelief flashed in Azon's eyes. The others looked on in shock too, but Marakazian forced himself to not look at them, struggling to maintain the fury that would draw the sword from his scabbard.

'All of you go, leave me,' he wafted them away. They hurried out of the door, and he slumped in his red velvet-draped throne. He sat there alone with his anger and befuddled thoughts. Dust flies swirled in the mottled sunlight that seeped through the windows.

Azon had been right, Marakon thought as the image faded. *They had all been right. How can a mad man see past his own madness? Greed and glory, a human's blight. Karhlusus knew it well, used it well. Now that I think of it, I could feel the darkness growing in my heart even then. But I learned to ignore it, I wanted to ignore it. I was invincible. I wanted to become a god, greater than all things. Those were the lies the Demon King whispered to me. I had destroyed him and taken his power, and now he would destroy me.*

Nay, the sayings were all wrong; you should not keep your enemies close, but far, far away. Karhlusus would ever be our undoing.

CHAPTER 37

Demon Wizard

DEEP underground in the pitch-black of his small, stale prison, Karhlusus plotted his escape. His hands were bound in chains above his head so he could not sit down, and his feet were chained splayed to the wall so he could not move them. He had been bound for years, or so he thought, in the darkness there was no way to tell.

His hair and beard had grown long and straggly and hung in unwashed clumps to his scrawny chest. Beside him lay rotting chicken bones from the scraps of food they gave him. Most prisoners would be disgusted by them, the putrefying clumps of flesh, the reminder of death waiting just around the corner, but he kept them close, bones were useful. It was a poor man's magic that used bones, for sure, but useful nonetheless.

The air stank of those rotting bones, dried sweat, the waste and urine on his body and feet. But he did not mind the stench either, for demon magic required the use of rotting things, the fetid and the slime, the bodily fluids and excrements of all types and from all things.

He wore nothing but a rag in the cold and frigid darkness, yet he did not suffer the cold or dark—in fact, he thrived in them. Such was a demon wizard's disposition. For he was not possessed by just any demon; he was the ancient demon King Kull and a powerful human wizard in one body. Kull was a Demon Lord and a greater demon from beyond the Murk.

Alone in the darkness with all the time in the world, he slowly connected to the fat and lazy king while he slept. It was easy to reach King Marakazian when he dreamed, and Karhlusus could take any form and be anything he wanted to be. The stupid, arrogant king believed he could be a god, and Karhlusus nurtured that belief. Whilst the king's idiots could bind his body, a demon wizard's mind was always free and always connected to demons. With his magic he could still reach the Murk, he could still reach the lesser Grazen demons.

'Make the potion,' he whispered to the Grazen. Their yellow eyes flashed in the blackness before him, red mouths opened then closed; grinning, grimacing, hissing and chattering.

'Make the potion, and we will have our revenge.'

The demonic potion would be a gift to make the king invincible, just as he desired, but it would take time to make and longer still to transport the physical object through the veils between the Murk and Maioria. But Karhlusus was adept at demon magic, and he had plenty of time.

'Shadows, come to me,' Karhlusus whispered in Demonic when the potion was ready.

In the darkness a luminous green shape flashed before him, startling a rat chewing on a chicken bone. It ran away screeching into the darkness. More shapes flashed as he whispered the demonic words, his voice sometimes low and growling—the voice of King Kull within him.

Some shapes were simple, such as the outline of a square or triangle, others were highly intricate lines and dashes. Each one flashed on the cold stone floor before him, one after the other. They formed slowly at first, but as he spoke faster the shapes came quicker, and as he spoke louder the shapes flashed brighter. Soon, the shapes were so bright they blinded him every time they appeared, and his voice was so loud it boomed around him, rattling his chains and shaking the walls. But there was no one to hear him down here in the deepest, darkest dungeon.

Sweat rolled down his skin as the demon magic flowed around him. They called the magic of Maioria the Flow but this was not the Flow, this was demon magic from the Murk, dark and shadowy—the opposite of light—and his prison chamber was thick with it. He strained against the chains, feeling his muscles bulge as the demon King Kull tried to come through him and then receded. The shadow magic flared and screeched as it built.

'NOW!' he cried, his voice a mix of King Kull's and his own.

Bright light flashed, and the chamber shook. Shadows thickened and swirled. He collapsed and flopped in his chains against the wall.

It was several hours later when he came around again and the chamber was still thick with demon shadows and magic. He feverishly peered through the strands of grey hair that were plastered to his sweaty face, and his gaze fell upon the small vial on the floor. The last symbol he had cast, a square inlaid with demon lettering, still pulsed red beneath it and shadows swirled around it.

'It worked,' he hissed, his voice broken and hoarse from the demon tongue. 'It worked!' He laughed long and loud.

'King Marakazian, I have before me your utter destruction.'

Now it was time to sprout the seeds he had sown in the king's mind, now it was time for revenge.

'Lord Marakazian, Lord Marakazian, I have what you most desire,' he whispered in the mind of the sleeping king. 'You can be so powerful, so rich, if you take what I have to offer. I have what will make you a god, if only you release me.'

Night after night, over and again, he whispered of what the king could be, of the greatest powers that could be his, of the world that he would rule, until the king's blood ran hot with greed and desire.

King Marakazian could resist the torment of power, the desire to rule others, and the kingdoms that would be his, no more. Was Karhlusus infecting his mind? Did the demon wizard really have what he most desired? He had to find out, he had to end the torment in his dreams. In the dead of night, he left his bed and descended into the bowels of his castle.

'Open up the prison,' he demanded of the sleeping guards.

They looked at each other with a worried frown, but knew better than to try their king's short patience. They opened the heavy door that led to the dungeons far below and, holding braziers, descended until they came to the last cell—Karhlusus' cell. The guards' faces were fearful as they opened the iron door. The bolts were rusty and stiff, and the key took several minutes to grind through the lock, the noise echoing loudly in the otherwise empty dungeon.

'The door has not been opened since it was shut over a decade a go,' the sweating guard said as he hefted the final wooden bolt off its slot. Only the small spy-hole was ever opened to shove food scraps in.

'The bastard just won't die,' the other guard muttered.

'No one possessed by a demon can die without being killed deliberately,' Marakazian said between gritted teeth. 'Perhaps it's time the bastard was put to death.' He stepped down the stone steps into the darkness. 'Bring the torches.'

The guards obeyed and shuffled down beside him.

Marakazian unsheathed his sword with a loud ring, making sure the demon wizard knew he was armed and ready to kill him.

'Ugh,' he gagged at the stench of the chamber and held a handkerchief over his nose and mouth. A mad cackle came from somewhere in the darkness. The guards stepped back afraid.

'Give me the torch, coward,' Marakazian snarled and snatched it from the nearest guard. He stepped forwards, and the light fell upon the filthy demon wizard.

'You,' Marakazian growled and shook his sword tip at the wizard. He had not seen the disgusting man since the final vicious battle against the demons. Karhlusus had been dragged screaming from the back of his demon mount. Marakazian hated him now as he had then.

'You plague my mind, wizard. They were right, you are a cancer that festers and grows. It's time you were done away with.' Marakazian swallowed, he wanted desperately to be gone from this stinking place, from the skin-crawling feel of demons close by.

The wizard chuckled fearlessly. 'Oh, powerful King Marakazian, we both know why you really came here to see me,' the wizard's voice was hoarse from lack of use. 'Kill me you may wish, but that isn't why you came here, is it.'

'You lie. All demons lie. There's nothing you have that I want,' Marakazian growled.

'Ah, what about magic, power and rule? I have a potion that would make you a god.' The wizard laughed. Again fearless, again confident— and this unnerved Marakazian.

It couldn't be true, could it? He had seen in his dreams a vial containing power that could be his. No, he was a liar, and could never to be trusted.

'Give it to me then, this potion of which you speak and dangle like a carrot in my dreams,' he snarled. 'I know it's you infecting my mind. There *is* no potion. This is a trick.'

The shadows moved close and hugged him, settling cold and wet against his skin. He shivered, heard the guards shuffle further away. He should have killed him years ago. Even here he could work his evil magic, for the most powerful wizards could not bind a wizard possessed by a demon. His human body could be bound and chained with iron and magic, but not the demon within.

Marakazian stepped closer until his sword was less than a foot away from the hated wizard's throat. Karhlusus grinned at him, stained and broken teeth between bloodless lips. A luminous symbol flashed briefly in the wizard's hand, and Marakazian saw he held a vial.

'Woo-hoo,' Karhlusus laughed insanely, dangling the vial back and forth.

Marakazian took a subconscious step forwards. 'The vial?' he breathed. 'No, a trick!'

But clear as day, there the vial was, he could hear the liquid sloshing inside. Karhlusus grinned, eyes gleaming in the dark. Marakazian could not help himself; he had to have that vial. It was like a sickness of desperate need within him. He lunged forwards, but with a flick of the demon wizard's chained wrist, the vial disappeared.

'What? Where is it?' he glanced about the chamber feverishly. 'I knew it was a trick!'

He whirled and sliced his sword through the air, bringing it to a dead stop an inch from the demon wizard's throat. But again Karhlusus only smiled. He was not afraid of death, something that Marakazian grudgingly respected.

'If you kill me, there's no vial. If you release me, you will have the vial. I'm not a fool,' Karhlusus said flatly.

Marakazian considered this, the greed for power battling against his conscience. He knew he should refuse, should kill Karhlusus there and then, but his mind was sick with the need for that power.

'You shall be released from your prison, but your hands will remain bound. If you even so much as look at a weapon, I will chop off your head in an instant. If you so much as mutter a demonic word or attempt to use magic, I will cut you down and my wizards will destroy you where you stand. When the vial is mine, you will be returned to the Murk where you belong,' he growled.

He expected the demon wizard to protest, but Karhlusus only bowed his head in acquiescence.

'As your great Lordship wishes,' Karhlusus snivelled in laughter.

He never for an instant trusted the demon wizard to keep his word and he kept his hand ever at his sword. When the vial was his, he would kill the wizard. When he was that powerful, the wizard would be no match for him—something Karhlusus had foolishly overlooked.

Half a day later the demon wizard sat manacled in a chamber. He was cleaner, having been dunked in the moat before dawn, and clad in a simple woollen robe. Two guards and two wizards stood beside him, nervously watching the hated man's every move. Six more guards stood outside the door. Candles flickered around the dim room. Bright sunlight pierced through every gap in the closed shutters and every hole in the drawn curtains. The demon wizard could not abide the light.

Karhlusus showed him the vial, and again Marakazian forgot all reason. He lunged for it, desperately wanting the power, desperately wanting to be rid of this hideous man and the awful crawling feeling of demons nearby.

'Give it to me or lose your head,' his sword hovered once more at the demon wizard's throat.

'Patience, King Marakazian,' Karhlusus grovelled. 'I'm not without reason.'

Marakazian snorted.

'All you have to do is unstopper the vial and smell its power-giving contents. But it must be done in my presence because the vial is linked to me. If it leaves my company too far, it will disappear and return to the Murk. But what better way to show your new god-state than to transform into it before your knights? Before your entire kingdom? With so many near you, how can you not trust me? If I should do something, you can easily kill me,' he held out his skinny, purple-veined and manacled hands helplessly.

Marakazian twitched. Never trust a demon, he may look like a man, but inside the demon lives. But then, how harmful could it be? His desire for adulation overcame his suspicion. All *should* watch their beloved king in his transformation, then they would cheer when he killed the demon wizard in front of them. As soon as he unstoppered the vial, he would signal his guards to kill him. There was no way Karhlusus could escape. Marakazian smiled. Karhlusus was a fool. He expected more from the demon lord King Kull.

'So be it,' Marakazian grinned. The demon wizard inclined his head.

'Get this bastard out of here,' he motioned to the guards. 'I'll gather the Knights of the Shining Star and tomorrow... Tomorrow will be a great day.'

A sunny day dawned on the hilltop City of the Star. King Marakazian addressed his Knights of the Shining Star when the sun was highest. The city dwellers and nearby villagers had flocked to see their king and the hated Karhlusus. Today would be a day to go down in history, and it reminded him, as he knew it did his knights, of their days of glory, when the crowd hurled flowers upon them and chanted their name aloud. All stood proudly in their shining armour and star-embroidered tabards, their white horses clean and brushed.

The crowd was shifty, nervous smiles on their faces as they fidgeted and murmured amongst themselves. They detested being so close to the demon wizard, despite the chains about him.

Standing beside the bound and gagged Karhlusus, Marakazian delivered his speech to the people.

'Beloved people of the City of the Star, and those from beyond. We are gathered here today to remember our victories over the demons, and to remember our glorious Knights of the Shining Star.'

The crowd cheered. He glimpsed Karhlusus smirk and then hide his face under strands of grey hair. He shuddered now and again in the sunlight, even though a canopy had been drawn over his head.

'Our most hated enemy stands before us in chains!' He gestured to the demon wizard and the crowd screamed and booed. Some punched the air, others had tears in their eyes, perhaps for loved ones who had been slaughtered by demons. 'We have kept the demon wizard Karhlusus imprisoned for years as a reminder of how close we came to complete annihilation.'

Karhlusus seemed to be laughing to himself, but Marakazian ignored him.

'But for his murderous actions and the hell the demons wrought upon us all, for all those who were slain, possessed, and turned mad so that they killed their own and themselves. Oh, we'll never forget the bloodshed, the pain and the torture. No longer do we want our enemy close. We have magnanimously shown mercy, something which demons cannot do, and will soon be sending him back to the hell from whence he came.'

The crowd cheered again, and shouts of, 'Get rid of him,' 'Send him back to the Murk,' 'Kill him!' echoed across the open square. He held his hands up for calm.

'In return for this gesture, the demon wizard has made a potion, a potion so powerful it will make our city rise to become the greatest Maioria has ever seen. I have seen that we will become the most advanced, the most civilised, the most prosperous nation in the world.'

The crowd was a mix of smiling, frowning and confused faces. Was this not what they wanted? Didn't the fools know how grand it would be? How rich they would be? Perhaps they needed some help.

'Imagine having no enemies; no demons, not even goblins, for they would not dare attack so mighty a race. Imagine a life without sickness and one day no death. Imagine your children never getting sick and dying, imagine all physical ailments healed, imagine not even ageing. Imagine having all the wealth you could ever want.' The crowd smiled and nodded at each other. 'I can bring all this to us, through my power and will… and this vial!'

The crowd squinted at the small, green bottle in his hand. Some looked nervous, but most looked on in awe. He did not lie, he had seen that such a reality could be theirs, he only had to bring it to them, he only had to become their god. Any remaining doubt he may have had about the vial and its contents were forgotten before the adulating crowd.

Hushed anticipation silenced the people as their king turned his attention the to vial. The guards and knights surrounding him shuffled closer, ready. Some had had their swords drawn right from the start. Others glared at the demon wizard with hands on their pommels. His wizards were dotted all over the place; two stood close by and he felt their magic tingling his skin.

He glanced sideways at the chained demon wizard. Karhlusus smiled and took a step forward, as far as his chains would allow him. His eyes were wide and staring, red tongue licking bloodless lips.

Bastard, your time has come. You really thought you would see the Murk again? Well, I hope your demon comes for you!

Karhlusus blinked. He couldn't believe it was happening, was the fool really going to do it? He could feel the demon lord King Kull squirm within.

'*Not yet my lovely,*' he soothed, '*not yet. Soon we will be free again.*'

Even he did not know exactly how the potion would work when opened. Demon magic had a will of its own. The shadow energy from the Murk answered to no man and seldom even to demons. It was a barely controllable demonic force. He giggled quietly, how easy it was to make the greedy dance to his tune.

Marakazian unstoppered the bottle. Karhlusus breathed in sharply. All eyes were on the king.

Nothing happened.

People shifted. Seconds passed. Nothing happened.

Marakazian glared at Karhlusus dangerously. The demon wizard nodded and smiled that insane smile in encouragement.

Marakazian tipped the vial to his lips. The liquid, if you could call it that, was so thin and light he could barely drink it. The liquid gas was tasteless. He pulled the empty bottle away with a gasp.

'Behold your god-king!' Marakazian cried aloud.

Karhlusus chuckled quietly, but he ignored him. A pale orange gas spilled forth from the bottle as the remaining liquid evaporated. It seemed a lot of gas, for so small a bottle. Marakazian lifted his arm to give the signal to his guards and knights to kill Karhlusus. And then it began.

All Marakazian knew was pain; in his eyes, his head, his feet—his entire body screamed out in agony, and he fell to the floor retching the foul liquid. Everyone looked on aghast as the orange gas spewed in thick bouts that spread and engulfed all. The knights and guards lunged towards Karhlusus but he had moved into the gas.

Marakazian strained to see where the screaming came from through the orange fog, but he retched again, and his eyes streamed. Then the demonic madness came, and rage built behind his eyes.

'You!' he choked as the demon wizard appeared before him. All about him his knights and guards clutched their heads, vomiting, their noses streaming foul, black slim, their eyes red raw and unseeing. He forced his body forwards, but it convulsed and he fell again.

'You!' he choked, fumbling for his sword. 'Kill him!' he screamed. 'Kill him!' But his knights did not obey, could not obey. Perhaps they could no longer even hear him.

Karhlusus grinned down at him. His eyes flashed from washed-out blue to all black demonic eyes with red slits down the middle. Marakazian blinked, trying to blot out the madness, trying to blot out those demon eyes he had long thought he would never see again. He screamed, and Karhlusus roared deep demonic laughter.

Marakazian's clumsy fingers pulled on his pommel. The sword slid free, cutting his own side as it did. He gripped it and roared, jumping up and swinging his sword in the same motion. He barely felt it strike through flesh and bone. In a spray of blood, Karhlusus' head flew from his shoulders.

Marakazian staggered from the momentum of his blow. He glanced up, choking and snotting black foulness. The body of Karhlusus still stood, the mist wafting around him, but his head rolled towards him. The horrid thing still laughed, the lips moved, the demonic eyes blinked, yet even without lungs the laugh still came, came from the demon lord King Kull. Then those awful eyes dimmed, and the face of Karhlusus stared back at him; empty, mouth in a permanent howl of laughter.

Marakazian fought against the murderous rage that infected him but failed. He could not fight demon magic, no one could, and the mist spread far, it spread wide. How far he would never know, but all whom it touched succumbed to it. He tried to close his eyes against the scene of spreading slaughter, but could not.

His knights, the best trained, the most heavily armed, the most honourable people he had ever met, turned upon his guards, upon each other, and upon the men, women, and children who had gathered to see their beloved king today. Lips snarled and spat, voices cursed, and teeth gnashed as they fought each other with a rage and hatred never witnessed before. Even the animals were not immune to demon rage, and horses bucked and dogs bit.

The poison dictated that it didn't matter who you fought, only that you killed them, all of them—man, woman, child, dog, horse. But only he and his knights and his guards had swords. Their swords rose and fell in the orange gloom, and it seemed they could not tire.

Two of his knights turned upon him, their faces contorted in rage beneath their helmets. He raised his shield, blocked a sword and swiped his own. One knight fell, blood spurting from his neck. Raise shield and stab. The other screamed as the force of his blow, made stronger by the poison, pierced through steel breastplate.

He hacked again with a strength he did not know he possessed. His sword smashed through gauntlet, pauldron and shield. Rage seethed, blood showered. It ran down his face, it stung his eyes and drenched his tabard. He howled in victory as the two knights fell.

Ahead there was another knight with his back to him, fighting two guards. He lunged forwards. There, under his raised arm where the chain mail was loose, he plunged his sword with all his weight. His sword sliced easily, and still he thrust until it pierced the chest of the guard as well.

He wrenched violently left then right, blood coursing over his sword and arms. So much blood it soaked his legs and pooled into his boots. He screamed and pulled back. The guard and knight slumped with a gasp at his feet.

The other guard snarled at him, fearless and mad. Marakazian hacked his sword down in a movement so fast it was a blur. The guard's helmet fell in two pieces, his face split in half as he collapsed. Marakazian moved on grinning, stepping over the bodies.

Two villagers were fighting each other ahead. An old man and a woman punching each other pathetically. He struck them both down with one blow of his sword. Something jumped on his back, snarling, blunt teeth tearing into his exposed ear. He grabbed and wrenched them off his back, and flung the young woman to the floor. Stab and trample and move on, the broken body forgotten. All must die.

The cobbled streets pooled dark red. Those who had not been touched by the mist tried to flee, but they could not escape, and it seemed very important not to let them. He was not alone in this feeling, and all those infected surged towards those who were not. But it was the armoured, trained and experienced Knights of the Shining Star and their king who killed all in the end. And the potion made him strong and powerful, just as Karhlusus promised. Death came where he passed.

The mist cleared a little. Dimly Marakazian watched his sword rise, a flicker of silver in the sunlight, followed by red droplets falling like rain. On and on he struck, he could not stop. The carnage endured until everything—the castle walls, the cobbled streets, the fallen bodies—was painted with blood. But no one could kill the king for he had what he wanted, he was invincible, and all must die.

The orange gas dissipated, the toxic potion weakened as its evil magic was spent. Slowly, Marakazian's senses returned and with it horror, despair and that terrible, terrible guilt—guilt he would be cursed to carry through all his future lives.

When it was done, all were dead except him and twenty of his knights. Nobody could tell how many lay slain; the place was awash with blood and limbs entangled. The sun shone down, but no bird sang or even flew in the air.

The knights all stood there swaying like drunkards, twitching and shaking and covered in blood that was not their own. They turned to look at him, and all he saw was his own horror reflected back.

'How did we become this?' he gasped.

Some staggered towards him, bloodied and horrific, wild terror in their eyes.

A blond, bearded man stood swaying. Marakazian did not recognise him for the blood covering his face. At his feet lay bodies and limbs Marakazian did not want to see.

'No.' Marakazian reached forwards as the knight lifted his sword to his chest and fell upon it. Together they gasped, and Marakazian watched the man collapse. Who was he to say no? Perhaps he should have taken his own life then too.

It was like watching dominos fall then, for eight more followed suit, thrusting their own swords into themselves and dropping beside each other atop those they had slain.

'We are damned, damned for all eternity,' he fell to his knees. 'I have damned us all.'

In silence, they searched the carnage for survivors, but there were none. All about the place were the tabards, flags and banners of the Knights of the Shining Star stained red with the blood of the innocent.

'What do we do? Where do we go?' A young woman's bloody face looked to him for answers, but he had none. Oria, that was her name. The pain was a tangible thing in her bright green eyes. Eyes longing for this to be just a nightmare that they would awaken from. But there was no waking up.

'This place is now cursed. We cannot bury so many, we cannot stay,' was all he could think to say. 'We shall cremate their bodies so their souls might find freedom, that's the least we can do.'

They torched the City of the Star and left, turning only once to look at the inferno on the hillside of a once beautiful city. But he knew that the fire could not cleanse the earth of the demon curse, and that the land itself would die and become barren. Nothing would grow, and only the sorrow of those slain would sing through the bones of their own skeletons.

He learned later that those who had escaped, those few who had been closest to the gates, fled to the villages, towns and cities spreading word of the massacre at the City of the Star by the hand of King Marakazian and his Knights of the Shining Star.

He and his eleven knights wandered cursed and banished with the memories and the pain of what they had done, for they had no loved ones to run to, all had been slain. It was decreed that the great deeds of King Marakazian and his knights were to be erased from the books and the scrolls in every library, in every village, in every house. All their statues were destroyed, all their banners burned, and the world sought to erase even their very memory.

Once glorious and valiant, the knights and their king became known only for their evil slaughter of thousands. The truth about the demon wizard Karhlusus and his trickery was lost. No longer were they called Knights of the Shining Star, but the Cursed King and his Banished Legion.

Marakazian and his knights fled south then east across an unknown ocean, far from their homes and from anyone who would ever know them, until human civilisation was a long way away.

Finally, they came to another cursed, hot and barren land. The bones of people and animals lay on the ground, and the valley whispered of another terrible thing done eons ago. There the knights died, but their souls were cursed to relive endlessly the slaughter of that terrible day.

As the memory returned to Marakon, he understood then that Marakazian's penance was greater than the knights, for he was bound to be reborn again and again, never finding the light of Feygriene, never finding peace—always to live a life of pain and suffering and guilt.

He remembered the dreams of glory and the power Karhlusus showed him. It seemed so real and attainable then, but now he didn't want those things. How funny the soul was moulded through many lifetimes. All his life he carried the feeling of terrible guilt and of searching for something he could not find. He had thought it was the Elven Burden, had thought it was a commander's guilt, but now he'd found its bloody roots.

CHAPTER 38

Mark of Woetala

ISSA was awoken by the smell of something cooking. She sat up and held her throbbing head in her hands, a groan escaping her lips as she remembered the night before. She considered pretending to sleep until everyone had gone.

Peeking through the curtains, she could see Asaph eating breakfast by the fire with Coronos. On seeing movement, Coronos stood up and came over with a smile, passing her a hot steaming mug through the curtains.

'Purple nettle tea. It's really good stuff for times such as these,' he said.

'Thanks,' she mumbled. 'Though it might take more than tea to fix it.' She smiled weakly, knowing without looking that her hair was probably in the shape of a hedgehog. How come he wasn't hungover? He was as perky as ever.

'I used to drink more in my youth. Back then I loved the celebrations just as much you young people do now. Luckily I've learned my limits,' he winked. She groaned.

He went back to his breakfast, and she sat sipping the hot, bitter tea, praying it would work. Maybe, some fresh air would help too.

She dressed slowly, buying as much time as possible before she would have to pull the curtain back.

'Morning,' she said airily as she emerged through the curtains.

Asaph turned and smiled. He looked tired and hungover too. 'I put a plate of food together for you,' he motioned to the ceramic plate of apples, jam and bread.

She nodded her thanks and sat down beside him, unable to look him in the eye for long. They shouldn't have kissed. It had made everything difficult. Did he feel embarrassed? But from what her glances could decipher he didn't seem to. She tucked into the warm bread and jam; filling her mouth so she couldn't speak.

A few minutes later there came a knock, and Rhul'ynth stood in the doorway. Her long brown hair was plaited, and her majestic antlers had flowers interwoven in them.

'Fancy joining us on the hunt today?' she asked Issa, the gleam in her eyes suggesting it would be adventurous.

'Mm-hmm, absolutely,' she said over a mouthful. Hunting? What could they be hunting if they don't eat meat? Sounds like an interesting adventure.

'I wish I could, but I promised to help Coronos and Triest'anth,' Asaph said, clearly disappointed.

Issa hid her relief. Though she felt rough, she was desperate to get away and to try to clear her head. Her emotions were in turmoil. She stood up and brushed the crumbs off her lap, catching Asaph's eye as she did so. He was still grinning at her and, embarrassingly, she felt herself blush.

'Thanks for breakfast. Bye.' She hurried out of the house with Rhul'ynth. Rhul'ynth was also grinning at her in some knowing way. Had she been watching last night?

'Nothing happened,' Issa sighed.

Rhul'ynth laughed. 'Looked like you had fun, though,' she said with a wicked grin.

Issa rolled her eyes. 'Far too much evil wine. Anyway, where are we going?'

'We're doing the usual, hunting for Life Seekers, Ogres, or any sick beasts that have been infected by the Life Seekers. The war may be in the north, but no sword can stop the sickness of the immortals.'

'Tell me about the Life Seekers,' Issa said. Freydel had mentioned them before.

'They're formless, undead essences always searching for a living body to take over, and they never seem to be far away. But don't worry, we probably won't see anything after last night's partying.'

They chatted about the food, dancing and music as they left the village. Though older than Issa, Rhul'ynth was in her mid-twenties and much closer in age to her than Ely had been. She felt a pang of worry thinking about Ely and resolved to try scrying for Freydel again. They came to a stop in a clearing between the oaks and pines away from the village.

'The others aren't here yet, so let's practice while we wait.' Rhul'ynth passed her the smaller of the two bows she was carrying and a thick belt, attached to which was a small quiver. The arrows were also smaller than the ones Rhul'ynth carried.

'It's for a child, but easier to learn with and it can still kill,' she explained. 'And to be honest, for you funny two-feet, it's not too small after all,' she laughed.

Issa stuck her tongue out. She awkwardly strapped the quiver around her waist over her blacksmith's belt. The quiver was surprisingly light.

'You may prefer to attach it to your back, but try it like that for now,' Rhul'ynth said, adjusting the straps. 'Hitting a target takes practice, practice, practice. See that tree stump over there?' she pointed to a three-foot high mossy old stump about ten yards away. 'I want you to try to hit it.'

Issa nodded and fumbled one of the arrows out of the quiver. She adjusted her stance, and Rhul'ynth showed her how to notch an arrow.

'Now, raise the bow, so the arrow points at the target, then lift it a little above. The idea is to get your arrows in roughly the same area, rather than to hit the same spot every time. Your left arm should be straight and elbow a little rotated but not locked. Otherwise the string will strike it.

'Now, draw the bowstring so that you are looking straight down the arrow shaft toward the target. You want your elbow a little higher than your shoulder and out a way from your body.'

She drew the bowstring until she could pull it back no more, even though it was a child's bow it seemed rather stiff.

'Because this is a child's bow, you don't want to pull it back too far otherwise the arrow spine may snap when released. Don't worry about the technicals right now, we'll study them later,' she added on seeing Issa's frown.

'It's up to you where you draw the bow to. That preference comes with time. I draw to my cheek, others draw to their ears or mouth and nose. Once you find what you prefer, then consistency is key. Think about which way the wind is blowing, and most of all focus.'

She focused on the tree stump. There was a slight breeze blowing from the left, carrying the smell of the bonfire from the night before. She angled the bow a fraction to the left and let the arrow go. She forgot to unlock her elbow and smarted when the string smacked hard against her forearm, leaving a red mark. Through the pain, a delighted squeal from Rhul'ynth told her she'd hit the target.

'Beginner's luck I guess,' she grinned, rubbing her arm and looking at the arrow that had only just made it to the base of the stump.

'Are you sure you haven't done this before? Your stance and judgement were perfect,' Rhul'ynth said slapping her on the back.

'Your direction and Grast'anth's teachings helped somewhat,' she replied. 'I remember not doing so well then.'

Rhul'ynth looked at her reddening arm and held up her own bound one. 'It's a beginner's bane, though I still wear one even now.' She took out a similar strip of cloth from her belt and tied it around the red welt.

Issa loosed two more arrows. One hit just above the first and the other just missed. Hitting the target from afar was far less frightening and strenuous, and far more rewarding than close-combat sword fighting. But then it was only a tree stump and not a moving, intelligent being.

'Just in case, you should have this,' Rhul'ynth attached a small dagger to her belt. 'An extra weapon never goes amiss, and a dagger is useful tool.'

They turned to the noise of laughing and were joined by three more Karalanths, two men and a woman. The other woman was young and slender with dark hair and fur and even darker antlers. She was a stark contrast to Rhul'ynth's tall and muscular build.

One man was short, but stocky and heavily muscled, with fair hair and a short, trimmed beard. He had dappled white spots along his back, and Rhul'ynth introduced him as Palu'anth. He grinned at her and she wondered if he was the one who had carried her into the dance. She looked away blushing.

Fris'anth was a stern-faced, quiet Karalanth, tanned and mahogany brown. They all had bows and quivers slung across their chests and backs, as well as thick hunting knives tied at their waists.

'We have Diarc'ynth with us as well, making two willing students. She has come of age to join us now,' Rhul'ynth said putting her arm around the young woman.

'I've been using the bow for years now, Rhu,' she said shyly.

'I know, and soon you'll be better than me. Now then, let's get you ready,' Rhul'ynth said and took out a small wooden pot from her belt pocket. She popped the top off and scooped out the dark green paste. With her finger she drew swift yet precise and delicate lines on Diarc'ynth's face and arms, careful to be symmetrical on either side.

'This is the mark of Woetala; a new huntress has come to the hunt,' she said as she worked. 'It's a tradition that we mark the new initiate for all to see as well as give them the blessing of Woetala; the supreme huntress and provider. We can take nothing from the forest that she does not give to us.'

Minutes later, she stepped back to look at her work. 'Perfect,' she said satisfactorily. Diarc'ynth grinned, looking at the green swirls on her arms. The men cheered.

'You're next,' she said, coming over to Issa.

'Oh no, are you sure? I surely don't count. I still don't have four legs,' she backed away.

Palu'anth laughed loudly and muttered to Fris'anth who broke into a rare smile.

'Nonsense,' Rhul'ynth said. 'One blessed by Zanufey is surely blessed by Woetala, for really they are just different aspects of the same goddess, the Great Mother.'

Issa knew there was no getting out of it then.

'You have a pretty face,' Rhul'ynth said as her deft fingers smoothed on the paste. 'For a human.' Issa gasped in feigned indignation.

'Tanned and fair hair is surely prettier,' she replied.

Rhul'ynth guffawed. 'I don't think it matters. I think men take whatever they can get.' She looked slyly over to Fris'anth and winked. The dark-haired Karalanth stamped his foot and tossed his antlers, a wicked grin spreading across his face.

'What exactly happened last night?' Issa asked as she twiddled the flowers in Rhul'ynth's hair. It was the Karalanth's turn to blush.

'Oh uh, nothing unnatural.'

'Oh really?' Issa burst out laughing. 'I don't think I want to know!'

Rhul'ynth smiled then looked more thoughtful. 'You know, when you first arrived you looked pale and gaunt, but now you're stronger. There's colour in your face, and you glow from within. I can't imagine what facing that awful beast must have been like. But that aside, Asaph really must know what he is doing,' she teased.

'Nothing happened. We went to bed. Alone!' Issa yelped. She turned her attention to cleaning her nails.

'You're right, though,' she admonished. 'I'm not the same person I was before Keteth. Something has changed. I feel stronger. It's funny, but I do feel more... me, somehow.'

'The goddess is with you, it's plain for all to see,' Rhul'ynth said. 'Quite a feat to slay that beast. You're already a hero and will be remembered in ages to come. We're honoured to be in a hero's company.'

'Nonsense, it was the power of the dark moon and Zanufey that did it.

I couldn't have done it alone. And anyway, it's I who honour you. I would have died had you not cared for me. You treat me as one of your own and share all that you have. That's surely the greatest honour.'

Rhul'ynth smiled and squeezed her shoulder. 'Come, let us hunt!'

She took the lead and Palu'anth took the rear. Issa had to run to catch up with them. It felt so good to be wild and free in the forest with the Karalanths; jumping over roots, ducking under boughs at break-neck speed. How they managed to avoid getting their antlers caught, she didn't know.

She ran as fast as she could, but had no chance against her four-legged friends and swiftly fell behind. They tempered their speed accordingly, and though running was easy at first, it wasn't long before she was sweating profusely.

They must have massive lungs, she thought. She refused to be a "weak two-foot" but there was no way she could run faster, her muscles were already burning. They all turned to see where she was without so much as slowing their speed.

'Don't let me hold you back. I can catch up,' she gasped.

Palu'anth circled back and hoisted her squealing into the air with those same tree trunk arms, laughing again as she squirmed. He moved his quiver onto his upper back and shoved her in its place.

'Just hold on,' he said with a wink, and they all leapt into a gallop.

Her scream was lost in the rushing air as she clung to his torso for life. Now they raced through the forest at twice the speed. It wasn't easy riding bareback, nor the most comfortable, everything kept jolting and banging, and she hoped Palu'anth wasn't being bruised under her weight. If he was, he didn't show it and didn't even seem to notice he carried a heavy passenger on his back. Despite the discomfort, her aching legs were relieved.

The forest was mainly deciduous trees, some so densely packed together that little light hit the floor. Vivid green ferns splayed their delicate fronds, and between these, they ran upon dark earth. The air was cool in the thick forest and glimpses above told her the day was cloudy.

They must have been running for about an hour when Issa first felt something wrong. She closed her eyes and focused on the Flow. She opened them and saw the pretty, lush forest suddenly shot through with black, with wrongness.

An icy wind rushed past her, and the forest darkened. She closed her eyes and swallowed down a wave of nausea. It wasn't the bouncy ride, something was wrong. Where was the raven? She suddenly felt vulnerable without her friend. She hadn't seen him since they'd left the Land of Mists.

"Even as we speak, the raven searches for the 'Cursed King,' and Murlonius waits to take him to his Banished Legion."

She remembered Edarna's words and her chest tingled where the raven mark was. Perhaps it was warning her that danger was near, or perhaps it was reassuring her that the raven was with her in spirit.

A sharp headache came, warning her of an impending vision. Always the animal communion, the gift of the Daluni, hurt more the longer she ignored it. She opened her mind to it. It was not coming from the raven.

In her mind she saw the fleeting image of a large cat, black as midnight cowering in the shadows, its green eyes wide and gleaming. It hissed and bared white fangs. It was afraid, but of what? The vision went. Adrenaline hummed in her veins and the hairs on her neck prickled. She glanced around, looking and feeling for the source of danger and where the cat was, but there was nothing. It was safer not to enter the Flow when an unknown threat was near.

'Danger,' she hissed into Palu'anth's ear.

'Danger?' he said and dropped to a trot.

The others slowed; they had amazing ears to hear him over the pounding of their hooves. They walked and then stopped, nodding as if feeling it too. Bows and arrows were readied, and Isaa slipped off Palu'anth's back.

'I felt it briefly, but now nothing. Perhaps it's gone,' Issa said.

As soon as she finished speaking, the dark, twisted feeling came again, but twice as strong. She grasped her bow, fear rising in her stomach knowing that she wasn't ready to face a real enemy with her new weapon.

She looked around, the roots of the trees entwined around each other like lovers. Nothing there. She looked up at the leaves blowing in the breeze, no danger there either.

'The forest is silent,' Rhul'ynth said, also looking about her nervously.

Pressure on her mind. Issa closed her eyes. The black cat hissed its warning again, and she saw through its eyes. Three huge, ugly cat-like beasts exploded out of the forest. She blinked.

Within seconds, those same three beasts bounded out of the undergrowth towards them.

'Foltoy!' the others screamed.

With trembling hands, she fumbled for an arrow, dropped it and knew it was too late. She stood the furthest from the group and closest to the three beasts hurtling towards her. They were slightly smaller than Karalanths but long and skinny. They had massive feline heads with pointy ears, yellow fangs, flaring green eyes and slick, furless skin. They made a terrible snarling sound as they closed in.

Everything slowed down and yet so much was happening. Calm stilled Issa's shaking hands even though her body screamed at her to flee. The last moments inched by, but there was so much to be done.

Above her was a thick branch. There was no way she could reach it even if she jumped. The foltoy were only a few feet from her.

She bent her knees, all so slow, reached her arms wide, and leapt. She swiped her arms down feeling their undersides fill with air. She didn't think, she only did. Her feet became black-taloned claws as they rose above the foltoys' ugly heads. She blinked and beat her wings again. Twelve feet above the ground and the tree branch loomed into view. She plopped onto it, her talons gripping it easily. Time speeded up.

She looked down upon the foltoy as they fell upon the empty space where she had been seconds before. *My arms are wings!* She stared at them astonishment. She had not even entered the Flow. She laughed down at the howling foltoy, and it came out a raucous cackling. She had become a raven completely, as she had once before, and yet she still didn't know how.

Her awe was soon forgotten as the battle unfolded below her. She had bought enough time for the Karalanths to draw their bows and loose their arrows, but they were now locked in a close-quartered battle as the foltoy turned to face them.

With little more than a semi-conscious thought, she swooped down behind the beasts and became her human form once more. The foltoy had their backs to her. She found her dropped bow and arrow, notched it and let it loose, but her hands trembled too much. The arrow glanced off the back of a foltoy's head and whizzed away harmlessly. It was enough to make it turn towards her.

She drew and loosed another arrow. It sank deep into the foltoy's shoulder, but it seemed not to notice and bounded towards her. She fired another arrow as fast as her novice hands would let her, striking it in the chest. This time it slowed.

The sweat dripped down her face, and her breath came in painful lumps in her throat as she stared into awful intelligent eyes. She suddenly desperately needed the toilet and stepped backwards as it came on.

"The warrior who shows no mercy will be the one still standing at the end of the battle," Grast'anth's words echoed in her mind.

The foltoy leapt. Abandoning her bow, Issa rolled away and under the beast, drawing her knife as she did so. She was terrified, she did not deny it, but her will would be unbreakable.

'My will is greater,' she snarled as the foltoy spun to face her, its eyes dropping to her knife. It snuffled a strange sound, almost like a laugh as if it understood what she said. And then, to her shock, it hissed and spoke in words she could just about make out.

'They're all coming for you.'

She laughed a loud, cold laugh filled with a confidence she did not quite feel. She glanced past the foltoy to the Karalanths, but they could offer her no help, they were fighting for their lives against the other foltoy.

She turned her gaze back to the beast, licked her lips and tasted blood. For one bizarre moment, a part of her was enjoying this, she felt alive. This was her chance to get back at the bastards for all they had taken from her.

'Ma and Tarry died, they didn't stand a chance. But I'll fight you and take you with me before I die!'

A raging fire ignited in her heart, and a savage passion overcame her. She screamed and attacked first, running at the beast, slashing viciously with the knife. Such was her fury that the foltoy hesitated, but only for a second and then it bounded to meet her. She could smell its rotting breath as it neared. It was three times her size, and the goddess only knew how much stronger, but those things were meaningless in the face of her fury.

On the borders of her awareness, she felt the presence of something else moving through trees. She was too focused on the foltoy to think about it.

She sidestepped and slashed, but the foltoy was ready, and its claws struck a crushing blow to her side. As it did so, she struck upwards and drove her blade deep into its neck even as the force of its blow sent her backwards. She smacked into a tree, feeling ribs crack as the wind was knocked from her lungs. Pain flared in her side as she fell to the floor and lay there dazed and gulping.

The foltoy still came on, despite the blood gushing from its neck. She struggled sluggishly to her feet, breathing hard against the pain. Her legs gave way as it bore down upon her, and then out of the trees another dark shape leapt.

She glimpsed a large black leopard with orange stripes upon its legs and tail hurtling into the foltoy. It tried to turn, but the leopard was quicker. Claws sunk into the foltoy's back and the leopard clung there. Now was her chance.

She staggered upwards and forwards. The foltoy had its head turned back towards the leopard exposing its throat. She plunged her knife, expected it to be easy, but it still took all of her weight to sink the killing blow through unnaturally tough flesh.

The foltoy gave a gurgled howl and blackish blood oozed over her hand. She pulled the knife free, gagging in revulsion, both at the foul beast and what she had done. She watched horrified as it fell twitching to the floor. The forest leopard slid to the ground unharmed, foltoy blood matting its coat. Its orange eyes looked at her, and she felt its feline mind touch hers.

'Embrace your fear, it teaches courage, sister,' it said.

'Woetala protect you, sister,' was all she could think to say.

In stunned awe, she watched the leopard pad back into the forest.

Thank the goddess you came. There's still no sign of that bloody raven. I thought it was supposed to be protecting me. She wondered if the leopard had heard her thoughts.

Her pulse slowed, and adrenaline dropped, but now the pain in her side began with a vengeance. The Karalanths came bounding over, the other two bodies of the foltoy twitching behind them. They seemed unharmed as they circled around her, worry and awe in their faces. A barrage of questions followed a short silence.

'Are you all right?' 'How did you do that?' 'How did you sense them?' They looked at each other then fell silent again.

'Somehow I felt danger before it arrived. I don't know how, but I think the leopard warned me,' she said.

They nodded.

'Animals always warn us of the immortals if we are open enough to hear them. The foltoy are masters of stealth though, even for us Karalanths,' Fris'anth said.

'The Daluni talent can be weak or strong. It's strong in Karalanths, but that cat must have spoken only to you,' Diarc'ynth said thoughtfully.

Issa didn't add that she could see through its eyes and talk with it. It was enough that they understood what she meant.

'But never have they fought for us,' Fris'anth said, his face a mix of frowns and wonder.

'If it had not come, I doubt I would be standing here now,' she said. Now the fighting was over, fatigue crept in. 'That was close, too close.'

'They were after you only, and I don't think they wanted to kill you until you maimed one. Look at what they carry,' Fris'anth said, inspecting the foltoy she had slain.

Around its thin waist was tied a net and a curved knife. 'The others have the same. They didn't attack from the front either like they usually do, but from the side, where you were,' he added.

'It spoke too. I didn't know they could speak. It said "they" were coming for me,' Issa said.

'It spoke?' Rhul'ynth said incredulously.

'We've not heard them speak before,' Palu'anth said. 'They were the biggest I've seen. Stronger and sort of crazed. Maphraxie filth,' he spat on the body.

'How did you do that?' Diarc'ynth asked, eyes wide with wonder.

'Do what?' Issa frowned.

'Change into that bird, a raven.'

'Oh,' she had forgotten that bit. One moment she faced three hideous beasts hurtling towards her and the next she had leapt into the air spreading her arms wide, and they had become wings without her even entering the Flow. How had it happened? What did it mean? She rubbed her chest above her breasts where the raven mark was.

'I... don't know,' she said. 'It just kind of happened. I needed to get out of there and I, I don't know, suddenly I was flying. Perhaps I can only do it when in danger.' Was she becoming more and more the Raven Queen as each day passed? The pain in her side made itself known fiercely, and she sat down gasping.

'You're hurt. You could have killed yourself taking it alone like that,' Palu'anth said, but there was kindness in his voice.

'I didn't have much choice,' she groaned. He laughed and settled on the ground next to her.

'Lie back and let me look,' he ordered, pushing her firmly to the earth. 'I can set a broken bone, and the sooner, the better.'

'Palu'anth is a healer,' Rhul'ynth reassured.

'I am too, but mainly horses, and it never works on myself,' she mumbled and winced, waiting for Palu'anth's touch to hurt.

'A healer's curse; the inability to heal oneself,' Palu'anth nodded.

He pulled aside her top to reveal angry purple bruises. They covered her right side from hip to shoulder where its claws had hit.

'Oddly, the skin is not broken—its claws should have ripped you in two,' he said. 'Clearly it wanted you alive.'

'Thank the goddess,' she said, a little sarcastically. 'It got what it deserved.'

She readied herself for pain as he laid a warm hand on her, touching lightly. He closed his eyes and frowned in concentration.

'Not broken. One rib, a small fracture, the others are badly bruised. Still intact.' He sounded pleased. 'Not as bad as I feared.'

'It still hurts like hell,' she said and closed her eyes.

He moved his hands slowly over her side. She felt no pain only warmth verging on hot. The Flow moved a little, barely detectable, and it carried the feel of the forest. An earthy magic, a little like Edarna's witching magic, but more natural and pure. The gentle magic surrounded her and there came an intense unscratchable itch within her side. The air turned warm and heady, her head swam, and then a fresh breeze blew once more. He took his hands away, and she opened one eye.

'Is it done?' she asked, unsure what "done" meant. He laughed at her fearful expression.

'Aye, it's done,' he nodded. 'The fracture is sealed, but you'll have to be careful for a few days whilst the bone knits together. Then they will be as they were before. As for the bruising, I can only help reduce the swelling. Bruising is the body's healing process, and we'll never interfere with the more powerful healing force of nature.' He helped her to her feet and looked paler than before as if the healing had taken something from him. Using the Flow always carried a cost.

'My thanks. Maybe you can tell me how you did it later. There's much I need to learn,' she said and touched her side gingerly; it was tender and hot.

'Right, where to next?' she asked breezily, wincing as she picked up her discarded bow.

They laughed.

'I think three foltoy in one day is more than enough,' Rhul'ynth chuckled. 'Killing one of those beasts is taxing, but three at once? It took four of us to bring two down, but you took one on your own,' her face was incredulous.

'I had help; the leopard,' she reminded her, but Rhul'ynth shook her head.

'You had the courage of two warriors to face it, and I think you would have won without the leopard. You've only had one or two days training with a weapon. It comes naturally to you. I think with time and training you might become a great warrior,' she said, her face serious.

Issa smiled, but stayed silent. Even she wasn't sure what had happened. She looked back at the black and bloodied bodies of the foltoy. She had been so furious and vengeful, she'd wanted to kill them all. She could never forgive them for Little Kammy, but she worried about the murderous fury she'd felt. Something she would have to think about later when she was alone.

'Should we leave them there?' she nodded to the three bodies.

'Yes. Those *things* stink of corruption like all Maphraxies stink,' Fris'anth said. 'We won't touch them and neither will the forest, not even the flies. Nothing that lives can abide the immortals; their bodies will soon shrivel into dust and blow away. Look, you can even see them crumpling now. Hideous things.'

He was right. The dead foltoy seemed to be sinking slowly in on themselves.

'Ugh,' she scowled and looked away. 'Let's get away from them. They stink worse now.'

The others nodded and sheathed their knives.

'We must tell everyone as soon as we get back. The foltoy are bigger, cleverer, and attack in numbers now,' Rhul'ynth said with a worried frown.

Palu'anth helped Issa onto his back, and they walked back the way they had come, this time bunched closely together. It would take a while to get back at this pace, but he said riding fast would hurt her and undo his healing. No one agreed to go on ahead, they all felt safer travelling together.

She reflected on the battle as they walked. The ferocity with which she had fought frightened her. It was as if a cold rage had descended upon her and she forgot all fear for her own life, whether or not it was in proportion to her ability. How many would she have taken on alone? Three? Ten? An army?

She'd lost all sense of reason and would have fought them all to the death, even her own, and done so willingly. Could she have killed one alone? Possibly, she couldn't be sure, but possibly. She certainly felt like she could, misguided or not. She had wanted to draw blood, had wanted to maim and kill the hated immortals, and that realisation made her afraid.

"Embrace your fear, it teaches courage," the leopard had said. Was ferocity the same as courage? Maybe. Was this what blood lust was? Perhaps it was revenge she lusted after—revenge for all those the Maphraxies had taken from her.

'Come, hunters,' Palu'anth broke their subdued silence. 'Today is a great day. Not only have we slain the hated foltoy, but three of them at that. We should celebrate and honour our new warriors; Diarc'ynth and Issa, Queen of Ravens.'

Everyone cheered making her blush.

CHAPTER 39

The Final Price

MARAKON stood up. A terrible fear knotting his stomach as he swayed between remembering his previous life as King Marakazian and his current one as Marakon.

'Who am I? What is my *real* name? Marakazian,' he gasped and sank to his knees, the name echoed tauntingly around him. He wiped the sweat from his forehead with a shaking hand. In his other, he held his sword, and saw the faces of those he'd slain. Madness crept at the edges of his mind.

'Follower of the dark moon.' The voice was nothing more than a mocking whisper that caressed his ear.

'Who said that?' he shouted and stood up, his sword high and ready to strike. 'Who's there? Coward, show your face to me. What is this madness? What games are these? Tell me why I'm here, damn you!'

A voice chuckled and then became the wind.

'You still deny who you are? Murderer.' The voice seemed to come from everywhere at once, but the valley was empty, nothing but dust and bones.

'Wait,' Marakon breathed to himself, blinking against the sand he had kicked up. 'Wait,' he tried to be calm and rational. He stood still and spoke loudly to the voice, to himself, to the wind and the dust and the bones at his feet.

'I am Marakon Si Hara half-elven, Commander of the Second Fleet in the war against the Maphraxies. And I know who I am!'

The voice chuckled, its echo resounded around him. Without his armour, he felt very vulnerable.

'You are who you've always been, King Marakazian, slaughterer of innocents. Leader of the Banished Legion and cursed to live a life of suffering forever!'

The voice raked through his head and memories of that terrible day flooded through his mind until he thought it would burst. The rage, the screams, the endless pools of blood. He fell to his knees unable to hold back the tide of grief and pain. He clung to the pommel of his sword as he sobbed, grinding the tip into the sand.

'The price has been paid. We have suffered enough. The price has been paid.' He laid his head against his sword, unable to deny the past any longer. He remembered it all as if it were yesterday. It was him, it had always been him. The darkness, the guilt, had been with him his whole life like a black hole, a void he could never fill.

'We were glorious once,' he whispered and closed his eyes. 'We were the Knights of the Shining Star—of the light and the truth once.' He breathed heavily trying to regain himself in the silence. Anger seeped into his heart, and he lifted his head.

'We were tricked,' he shouted, staring up at the cliffs towering above him, looking for the owner of the voice in the wind. 'We have suffered enough, suffered far beyond any curse could dictate, and the price has been paid.'

He stood up. There came a great cracking sound of rocks breaking and the ground trembled beneath his feet.

'The price will never be paid!' the voice howled so loudly that he dropped his sword and clasped his hands to his ears, cowering.

The ground shook violently, and boulders tumbled down the cliffs either side of the barren valley. He swayed as the ground rocked, and staggered out of the way of the crashing boulders. Dodging one brought him into the path of another, then another. Bones and sand spewed into the air in billowing clouds that choked him and filled his eyes and ears. Something moved in the sandstorm. In the haze, a huge shape taller than any boulder moved towards him with a heavy, lumbering gait.

He wiped the sand from his eyes and picked up his sword. A break in the dust cloud revealed a beast that filled him with terror. He stared incredulously as a human skeleton twice his size came striding towards him, huge rusted sword raised above its head, upon which sat askew a rusting metal helmet with a twisted nose guard and a dull gold band. A torn chainmail shirt hung loosely on its shoulders and an old scabbard and sword belt dangled around its fleshless hips. Though the skeleton had no face, its eyeless sockets burned red, and its lipless mouth was twisted open in a howl.

He had no idea how to fight something that had no flesh and was already dead. Was this beast from the ancient curse upon this land or did he face himself? He could not know; did not want to know. He would be forced to fight it anyway. He licked his lips with a parched tongue.

The skeleton was upon him, and the smell of something long dead made his stomach revolt. He dodged the first swing of the skeleton's sword but misjudged its massive length. He ducked down and went sprawling as the flat of it hit him. The blow was painful upon his unarmoured flesh, and he could feel a bloody bruise welling on his back.

He rolled to his feet in time to dodge another swing. The thing was not only big but lightning quick, and his hopes sank. This was no Maphraxie—though immortal they could be killed—and it certainly was no Histanatarn. He dodged left and right, falling back at every strike from that massive sword, unable to even reach the skeleton for the length of its weapon.

He was exhausted before the fight had even begun, and now drew upon every ounce of strength and skill just to avoid those crushing blows. There was no time to think about attacking, and he dared not parry those pounding strikes for they would surely shatter his arm. Nothing about the warrior skeleton suggested it would ever tire, for what muscles did it have to weaken? What air did it breathe to keep moving? He couldn't flee either because it was faster.

Sweat poured down his face as he dodged and jumped and rolled. His heart felt as if it would burst with the exertion. He slashed where he could, but mostly it was dodge, jump, roll, and repeat until his arms became leaden, and his legs stiff. The sand billowed around them making it harder to see, but the skeleton did not even notice as it tirelessly swung its dull, rusty blade.

He dodged another whistling blow and with a quick step leapt forward past its sword and smashed his own upon its arm with all his strength. The skeleton's arm crunched and fell twitching to the sand. His arm shuddered from the force of the blow.

The skeleton lunged forwards unfazed as if not noticing its missing arm. Marakon was forced to roll again from the jabbing sword. He reached deeper into his energy reserves, knowing he couldn't fight like this for much longer.

In the flicker of their swords flashed the faces of those he had slain. A knight in a bloodied tabard, the silver star turned red; the blonde curls of a woman he had loved now matted with blood. If he died, would his curse end? That bastard Karhlusus did it all. He cursed them. They were tricked, damn it! He railed against the injustice of that day, the anger giving him strength, and the voices of those slain clamouring in his head.

He dodged a left swing, only to have to dive on the ground as the sword whipped back low with ferocious speed. He rolled again and staggered to his feet, the hopelessness closing in. Why carry on? He couldn't fight this abomination. He couldn't win. The skeleton advanced, and he fell back. A rasping voice came from somewhere within it.

'King Marakazian has not returned to find his Banished Legion, but to pay for a crime, the final price paid in full. I have come to claim it. Your life for the life of the thousands you slaughtered.'

'We were tricked. I was poisoned,' Marakon said. 'We killed against our will. We were not ourselves, and for that, I have paid a thousand times, a thousand times a thousand.' He dodged another crushing blow as the skeleton advanced, unheeding.

He would die here, again, and what then? A lifetime wandering this barren plain as a wraith? Or another lifetime spent at war, in pain and suffering, carrying that awful guilt like a cancer in his mind? His death flashed before him in that skeleton's rusty sword, but it was not fear for his life that came to him, it was anger—cold, pure, sweet anger. It washed away the hopelessness and the fatigue that burned in his body. It focused his mind on not the past or his impending death, but in the present.

Anger for the injustice of thousands of years of torment for a deed he did not knowingly commit or condone. It was the same anger that led him to victory against the Maphraxies again and again, driving him up through the ranks of the Feylint Halanoi. He may have suffered a thousand lifetimes of pain, but he got what he wanted, he had become invincible.

With a roar that ripped itself from his very soul, he leapt forwards thrusting his sword, following it with all his weight. It smashed through the skeleton's other arm and cracked down, splintering ribs. The massive sword still held by bony fingers fell useless to the floor as both he and the skeleton fell. The skeleton's bones cracked under his weight, and he lay there atop it for a moment, shaking with exertion.

'Ugh,' he rolled off it in disgust.

A strange flicker of surprise worked its way across the skeleton's face, and then it crumpled into dust, joining the bones of countless others who lay there.

Marakon stood up swaying, staring at the pile of dust and bones. He shook his head. His death was not the final price to pay, it had been paid already. He slumped to the ground and drained the last of the water from his pack. *It is done.*

Sorrow welled up, and his eyes blurred with tears. He remembered the faces of all of his knights better than he remembered his wife Rasia, so clearly he could see them. Every wrinkle, every scar, every smile and flick of hair. It was as if he was looking at a painting of each of them in his mind. They had all fought for freedom against the dreaded greater demons. Over the years and countless battles, many died, but they braved all, and in the end, they triumphed. They had been loved by all until their great deeds were crushed, erased and forgotten. The bones of his knights lay here, in unmarked graves in this distant land far from their homes.

The dust was settling now the battle had ended, and the quaking earth and rolling boulders lay still. The air cleared, but rather than getting brighter it seemed to be getting darker, and quickly too. Like the sun going behind thick clouds, *or Dread Dragons passing over the sun.* His eyes darted upwards, but there were no dragons or clouds.

He rubbed his eyes and blinked in awe at the huge dark round orb rising slowly above the cliffs. He had seen the dark moon before, it must only have been weeks ago, but it felt like a lifetime. He had felt unsettled, not knowing what to make of it and always thinking anything new was bad, but now it seemed it rose for him, now it seemed not bad but good.

The land turned dark as the blue moon passed in front of the sun. The temperature dropped, and the wind stilled. All was silent and bathed in the blue of the dark moon. He stared at it wondering what it meant, it made him feel defiant.

His death was not the final price for the sin they committed. The sin was in the trickery; the sin was in remembering only the evil and not the good that was done before. The final price to pay was to remember the values they strove for; justice and freedom, lest they be lost and forgotten forever from the world. The greatest crime was that the knights and all they stood for would be forgotten and consigned to the realm of oblivion—and that would mean the demons had won. He would bring their memories back; he would remind the world of their deeds and glory once more.

'I am King Marakazian. No longer leader of the Banished Legion, king of those cursed. I come to claim what is rightfully mine. I am king of the Knights of the Shining Star, and I call my knights to me. Knights of the

Shining Star, rise, heed your king. Look up, see the dark moon rising. It heralds our glory. It calls upon us to right a wrong and end our curse. Come to me, your king.'

A great weight seemed to lift itself from his shoulders, and the wind sighed around him as if in relief. Dust began to swirl and became great eddies. Skulls and bones were dragged into the growing maelstrom. In the dense clouds formed human, skeletal shapes until eleven skeletons stood in the sandstorm, each carrying an ancient sword and wearing rusted armour that hung off their bones. They watched him with eyeless sockets, their ragged armour rattling in the wind.

His smile turned to dismay. 'So few?' he whispered sadly, remembering his knights had once numbered in the thousands. 'I have returned to unite the Banished Legion. No longer will we walk the world in a living hell for a heinous crime committed against us. We will reclaim the glory that should have been ours.' He looked at each of them in turn as he spoke, his passionate voice cracking with fatigue.

'We'll tell the world the truth of that day, and remind them what we were, what we stood for. Once more a plague blights Maioria and the dark moon calls us to do our duty,' he pointed to the huge blue moon. 'The Night Goddess calls to us, and we will heed her call. Return to me my knights, I am Marakon, I am King Marakazian, and I call you to your duty.'

With a roar he lifted his sword high and the skeletons mirrored him, shouting, their rasping voices filling the valley. Light began to glow in their empty eye sockets as their imprisoned souls returned. Their bones disappeared beneath flesh, and their rasping roar became more human as their throats became whole once more. Their armour became solid and clean and shining like once before. Tears blurred his vision as their faces turned into those he knew and loved.

'Forgive me, my knights, my mind was poisoned,' his voice cracked. 'Demonic greed can never possess me again.'

His eyes rested upon two elves, female and male—Ghenath and Hylion, he remembered their names. They stood there blinking at him with clear and sparkling eyes as if they had never died. Blessed Woetala, did they even know of the elven Land of Mists and what had happened?

He looked at the dwarves; Ironbeard, Konnen, Cormak and Drenden, then the humans; Lan, Meyer, Nemeron, Oria and Hally. Eleven knights who were his best. The fastest, or the strongest, or the most skilled. And it was because of those things that they still remained. But their curse and their burden were the greatest. They killed the most, and they suffered the most. There was nothing but sorrow in their story.

Seeing them again, knowing all they had suffered; the bloody battles they had fought together to keep the demons out of Maioria, only to be banished to a foreign, barren place to die in the dust, hated and forgotten. Tears ran down his cheeks as their armour shone in the blue light; they looked glorious once more. Pride for what they once were and could be again rose as a lump in his throat and he smiled.

'Are we free?' Hally asked, her voice weak and disbelieving. What horrors had she suffered wandering this evil place?'

'I think so,' Marakon nodded.

'It's been so long,' Cormak's voice was gruff as always.

'We are whole once more,' Hylion said, looking down in awe at his hands.

'This place was cursed long before we ever came here,' Ghenath said staring out across the barren valley. 'But now we can leave it. How I longed to be free,' she breathed and closed her eyes.

'We have a chance to make things right. To restore our former glory,' Marakon said. 'Deep in the Murk I know Karhlusus still lives, and he will be made to pay for what he has done. But now a greater enemy, more dangerous and deadly even than the greater demons from beyond the Murk, plagues this land. That's why we've been given a second chance; we've been called to serve the light once more to redeem our souls.'

He took a step towards them with a clinking sound, suddenly feeling heavy and strange. He looked down shocked to find that he was no longer dressed in torn linen but wore polished armour like his knights. His sword was his own, but now it was polished and sharp like new. No evidence of his battle with the skeleton marred its shining surface. He took his helmet off and traced in wonder the golden circlet upon it, the circlet of a good king who had once been loved.

There came a rumbling in the distance. It grew louder and louder until thunder filled the valley. A huge billowing dust cloud moved towards them led by a dark shape. He lifted up his eyepatch and saw it was a raven. *The messenger of the Night Goddess.* Behind it followed twelve white horses, each with gleaming armour and saddles.

The horses slowed as they neared and pranced around the knights, stomping the ground and tossing their majestic heads. The knights laughed, wonder in their eyes as they reached for the reins. The raven circled down and landed beside Marakon, cocking its head to look at him.

He looked down at it thoughtfully. All elves, even half-elves, knew Zanufey's messenger when they saw it. What it meant he did not know and found himself rather wary of it. From the way the raven shifted as it looked at him, the feeling was mutual.

He turned and mounted his horse, and his knights followed.

'You look funny,' Hylion said to Marakon as he settled down in his saddle, 'but somehow the same.'

Marakon gave a sour smile. 'My fate was much more fun than yours. I had to live out my agonies, not wander around for thousands of years moaning like a banshee.'

The knights laughed and he joined them. It felt good to laugh with them once more, especially then, and about that.

'Wait until you hear about the elves,' he added as he turned his prancing horse. 'You might find yourselves in rather a quiet world when it comes to elves. This time I'm half-elven, so you can't mock me any longer,' he winked.

The raven launched into the air and headed off slowly as if waiting for them to follow.

'Knights of the Shining Star,' he shouted, 'we ride to restore our former glory. The world has need of us again, and they will remember who once we were; they will remember honour, justice and freedom!'

He spurred his horse forwards after the raven, and together he and his knights galloped across the Drowning Wastes into the world once more.

CHAPTER 40

Lovesick

ASAPH watched her leave the hut. It was obvious she was trying to avoid him and wouldn't look him in the eye. She looked lovely as always, even after last night's over-indulgence. Her tangled hair cascading down her back and her lips, albeit a little smeared with the red stuff she'd put on them, he longed to kiss again.

He hadn't meant to kiss her at all, but she'd looked so beautiful lying there, smiling up at him, drowning him in her sea green eyes. It was as if a spell woven of the most potent magic had been cast upon him—she had looked vulnerable and delicate, and yet the spell she'd cast had been deadly.

She responded hungrily—just remembering it sent his blood racing, and now his sore head pounding. But this morning, now the wine had worn off, she was too embarrassed to look at him or even speak to him. Did she regret what had happened? He hoped she didn't. But then he didn't even know if she liked him, and why should she? He was just a stranger to her. He sipped his tea sullenly.

He'd dreamed of her ever since he could remember, and today she wouldn't even look at him. He stared sadly into the bottom of his empty cup. He would die for her—he knew that when he first saw her standing forsaken on the edge of the Shadowlands.

Watching her leave on this dangerous hunt filled him with fear. He would have tried to talk her out of it, would have gone with them had he not promised to help Coronos. He would have gone anyway if didn't feel so guilty about kissing her. So he let her go, though now she was gone he couldn't stop thinking about her. He was hopelessly besotted, and it was hard to focus on his own direction right now. He set his cup down and looked around for something to do.

Not wanting to speak to anyone yet, and since Coronos was nowhere to be seen, he set about cleaning and sharpening his sword. He found a quiet, sunny patch of grass between the trees not far from Triest'anth's house, settled down on the warm ground and removed his sword from its scabbard. It glinted in the sunlight and didn't really need cleaning or sharpening, but it was something he could do whilst trying to take his mind off her.

He quickly found that when he managed to turn his mind off Issa, and it was quite difficult to do, he heard another voice calling him. It whispered of snow-covered peaks, of clean icy winds and clear blue skies. Drax. If all else failed, he *would* see his homeland, and he didn't care if he died trying. He had to find the dragons if any still lived, and he was sure they did, sleeping deep in their lairs. He even had notions of finding the Sword of Binding—his sword, as it was his mother's sword before him— but he dared not mention that to Coronos, or anyone else, in case they thought he was insane.

They would need to leave here soon. The enemy would be hunting for them; a Dragon Lord and the one who had killed Keteth. They would leave together, they were safer in numbers. Maybe they had stayed here too long already, enjoying the company and peace of these new found friends. The Karalanths would be valuable allies against the Maphraxies if the war ever came here. *When* the war came, he corrected himself. He would need some armour, maybe even a shield. Perhaps they had something useful here, though a search through Grast'anth's smithy had revealed only weapons.

His thoughts soon turned back to Issa. Maybe he could make it up to her if she was cross with him. He could help her practice with the sword, could teach her everything Coronos had taught him. He had enjoyed watching her fight, she picked it up quickly and fought with passion. Watching how Grast'anth moved, remembering his own skirmish with Cusap'anth and his band when they had first encountered the Karalanths, he knew the deer-people made formidable opponents. For a moment, he was glad they were fighting on the same side.

Yet she had defeated Grast'anth with quick and clever decisions, fearless actions and a stamina he doubted even he had, despite all his years of training with the Kuapoh. Her passionate determination was impressive. Was it driven by revenge like his was? It made them fearless, but perhaps also foolish. Two determined fools, he laughed aloud at the thought. Both of them lost in the world, their homes and loved ones taken away by the Maphraxies.

He wondered what her home had been like. There was so little they knew of each other, he didn't even know her family name. And yet none of that seemed to matter. Ever since the raven had stolen his mother's ring, ever since Feygriene herself had come to him, he knew they were being called to a higher purpose. One in which he must help and protect her, just as she had helped him and saved his life. It was a purpose that would one day lead them against Baelthrom, and so he didn't dare think about it too much, for who could stand against the Immortal Lord and triumph?

If he stood by her side, no harm could come to her. He was a Dragon Lord, the last, so Coronos said, and he would not go without a fight. He only had to master the dragon within. But how could he master it when there was no other Dragon Lord to teach him? He thought of Faelsun, the Guardian of the Dragon Dream. Maybe Faelsun could train him if he entered the Dragon Dream again. Something which, even now, he wasn't sure how to do at will. All these things would be easy, he mused, if he had been trained properly like every other Dragon Lord before him.

She had been chosen by the Night Goddess to walk a dark path no matter how hard it became. He could not change that, but he was determined to walk it with her. They were not simply pawns in this life to be moved around at a deity's whim. They were dynamic, interactive souls driven by a desire to be free, to live in peace. Just as the One Source of All intended, to be free.

They called her the Raven Queen, and it seemed a fearful term, a dark and deathly aspect of the Great Goddess. But she was not so frightening or fearsome as the texts led one to believe. Elegant, beautiful, regal like a queen, yes, but not that foreboding warrior aspect of the Great Goddess. He remembered the ominous Annals of Deeatrice that Coronos had quoted a long time ago.

"Fear the Raven Queen when she comes, but bless her too for she will come in the direst moment to lead us through death and darkness and destruction. Terrible is her will and her determination unstoppable, but come she must, or all is lost..."

That was how the prophecy started, and despite not being able to sleep much afterwards, he had since paid such scriptures scant attention, dismissing them as flights of fanciful imaginations. He was a Dragon Lord after all, and not given to fancy poetry. But now it seemed he should have listened to Coronos' reciting more carefully.

It's not like he'd had any books to study, they were all left in Drax and probably destroyed. The Kuapoh did not have books. They told stories of history from memory. Funny then, it seemed, that all of his lessons on history were also word of mouth from the memory of Coronos, and the orb that was an endless source of information.

He did not want to link the Raven Queen to Issa. It seemed too much responsibility, too much to understand. Raven Queen or not, Zanufey's chosen or not, she was precious to him, and he refused to leave her side regardless of her mission. All his life he had seen the Kuapoh women choose another over him, a foreigner, and he was not about to see another chance pass him by.

'Urgh, I'm hopeless,' he huffed. No matter how hard he tried, his thoughts always returned to her. He shoved his sword back in its scabbard with a loud smack. This was no time to be thinking about love, not when they were being hunted and the whole world was at war, and yet think about love was all he wanted to do.

'Hopeless?' He jumped at Cusap'anth's voice. 'Nothing I've seen about you could possibly be called hopeless,' Cusap'anth said, his stern face regarding him, then softening into a smile. 'Unless of course, you are talking about matters of the heart.'

Asaph snorted. The proud Karalanth leader had become a friend since they had forgiven each other for their aggressive first encounter. Cusap'anth had saved his life in the end, and for that he was grateful.

Asaph groaned and stood up. 'Am I so easy to read?'

'Only about the dark-haired one. It's hard to tell what you're thinking at the best of times. But then again, Dragon Lords were ever mysterious beings,' Cusap'anth said. 'It's high time you should have a mate, and for all the darkness and heaviness of the world around us, she is still just a woman, and you are just a man.'

'You're right,' Asaph nodded, the Karalanth's words lightened his load a little. 'But I don't even know if she likes me,' he sighed, feeling like a pathetic, lovesick teenager.

'Give her time. It must be hard for her with so many things going on. From what I've heard, her pain and loss are still raw, whereas ours are old,' he gave a half smile. 'And besides, I didn't exactly see her run away from you last night,' he winked.

Cusap'anth was right. He was being impatient. 'Maybe I should leave her alone. I only wish she would leave my head alone.'

'I think she needs you more than she realises,' Cusap'anth said, and after a pause added, 'Come, there's something I must show you.' He motioned him to follow, but Asaph saw a frown pass across his face as he turned to go. He grabbed his sword and cleaning cloth and followed the Karalanth, the deer-man's tail flicking to and fro they walked through the village.

'My father thinks you should know the truth. We never thought to see another Dragon Lord again after Drax fell,' Cusap'anth said quietly as they entered his house. He opened the door of a cupboard and dragged out an old wooden chest sealed with a large iron lock. He took a key from one of the jars on a shelf and hesitated.

'As much as you might try to you cannot hide your identity from me, Prince Asaph, or should I say King Asaph? A Dragon Lord when no other Dragon Lord still exists. An old Draxian carrying the Orb of Air. The few Draxians who managed to flee Drax speak of a hunt for a missing baby, the queen's baby, yet none was found. There came rumours of people escaping on a ship heading west. Then decades later, two people arrive in our lands from the shores of the Uncharted World, when none has ever travelled those seas and returned to tell of what they found. There are too many coincidences for you not to be the heir to the Draxian throne.'

Asaph was stricken, his hand instinctively went to his sword. His heart pounded in his chest so hard he was sure Cusap'anth could hear it. He was certainly getting to know the Karalanths' direct manner and demand for the truth.

'King of what?' he challenged, the bitter gruffness in his voice surprised him. 'King of a wasted land? King of a destroyed people, few of which now live? What kind of king is that?' He couldn't keep the bitterness from his voice. His anger stirred the dragon within.

'I don't want to be king of anything. All I want is to see Drax again and avenge my people, avenge my mother for what that bastard did to her. Being king means nothing to me, I'd sooner forget about it.' His mother's face floated in his mind, her flame red hair matched by her fiery spirit, then her body and soul ravaged and destroyed by Baelthrom. The pity in Cusap'anth's face angered him further, and he closed his eyes, trying to control the awakening dragon.

'We both have lost our lands to that enemy, my friend. Don't forget that. Though few of us remain, we will fight to the death to take back what was ours. One day Karalanths will rule the west of Venosia, and it will be called Karalanthia once more. We don't care if the dwarves are on our side or not. The lands west of the Eryvin Hills will be ours again!' Passion flared in Cusap'anth's eyes, softening Asaph's anger.

'Yes, you're right,' he sighed. 'Ours is a similar story. For me, it still feels raw. I doubt if I will ever know peace.' He let go of his pommel and the dragon closed its eyes. 'All the hating and anger won't change anything unless we act on it. We must all take back what is rightfully ours.'

Cusap'anth said nothing, only nodded. He turned back to the chest and unlocked it with a loud click. The lid was heavy as he lifted it and he pulled out a dark, leather-bound book. He blew the dust off and looked at it for a long moment before speaking.

'Many years ago, when we were five times our number and before the Great Divide, our people frequently raided the dark dwarves' strongholds on Venosia.'

'The Great Divide?' Asaph frowned.

'Such was our persecution that my ancestors decided to split the Karalanth people into eight groups. Those eight groups would go in different directions and find homes where they could to give our people a chance to survive. There they remain, more or less, to this day.' Cusap'anth explained.

'To stay in contact both socially and by blood, every now and again we send our young to join our cousins' clans and they with us, so we always remain blood-bound and connected. After the Great Divide we no longer raided the dark dwarven territories, for it was too far and too costly and, in the end, it gained us nothing. However, it was decided that the young would-be-leader of the tribe should see their homeland and the enemy who had stolen it from us.

'I was one of them, for I was the next appointed leader after my father Triest'anth. I was taken by my father into a raiding party so that I might see the land that was once my home,' Cusap'anth stared into space. 'Unlike you, I have indeed seen my homeland, what was left of it. It's all barren, and the trees are sick if they stand at all. The life force has been sucked out of the land and everything upon it. Such is as the Immortal Lord wants. He cares nothing for life, for beauty.

'It was a long journey to Venosia only travelling at night. When we got there, we saw dark dwarves. Evil twisted beings. I was young and very afraid and stuck close to my father. We lost half our raid in the battle, including my grandfather, but slaughtered forty of our foe before they fled the encampment. It was bloody, but I became a man that day for I took my first kill.' Cusap'anth stood proud and grim.

'We searched through the camp before we burned it to the ground. It was there that we discovered that Drax had fallen only a week before, for we came across this log,' he tapped the book. 'Mostly it's a record of certain events—some important, some not, and most known as history to the rest of Maioria. Other sections are simply lists of supplies. A bit like a diary I suppose. But there's a section at the end detailing an event of such awfulness it took me a week to read it all,' his voice wavered, and he looked at Asaph oddly.

Slowly he passed Asaph the logbook, and he found he really did not want to take it. But take it, in the end, he did.

'There are things you should know about Drax, though you won't want to read it,' Cusap'anth said.

'I already know the story of the fall of Drax, Coronos has told me many times,' Asaph said. 'But I have also seen awful things in the Recollection, the shared memory of dragons and Dragon Lords. My hatred and anger are great because I saw my mother's end through her own eyes.' His voice had dropped to almost a whisper as he stared down at the journal. He hated even looking at it, wanted to throw it into a fire and watch it burn.

'Then perhaps you already know all there is to know. Still, it's your right to read the accounts as seen by our enemies. Maybe it will shed new light on things,' Cusap'anth said. 'My friend, I fear the days are darker than we would have liked, for even our allies betray us in their lust to taste Maphraxian immortality.'

The last comment jolted Asaph. *Betrayed, as Coronos suspected. But by whom?* Cusap'anth placed a firm hand on his shoulder and left him alone with the journal.

CHAPTER 41

Vornus the Betrayer

ASAPH stared at the leather-bound book, willing it to tell him what was inside so he wouldn't have to read it for himself. Finally, he seated himself on a cushion beside the cold hearth and opened the book.

He flicked through the pages. Most were notes; details of food and rations, numbers of ships and weapons and their locations in various places. Now and again there were snippets of events, mostly unimportant such as the loss of weapons or food gone rotten.

He was surprised and disheartened to find the dark dwarf who wrote it showed a good level of literacy in Frayonesse, with only the odd dark dwarven runic symbols thrown in. He'd assumed they lacked some fundamental intelligence and could only speak dark dwarven.

That they spoke Frayonesse at all suggested all their logbooks and shared documents were written in that language—which suggested they had far more allies than just dark dwarves and Maphraxies. Humans, elves, and of course harpies, were all traitors to freedom.

He was over two thirds through when he came to a section titled in scrawling letters:

Age of Immortals; day 45 of Masuma Month. Concerning Drax.
A Brief Account.

Coronos had told him that the dark dwarves followed their own calendar, which started when Baelthrom broke free from his prison. It was called the Lost Age to the free peoples of Maioria; marking the arrival of Baelthrom and the departure from the Age of the Ancients. He squinted down at the words.

"We approached the city of Draxa under cover of the necromancers' fog. The city was quiet, and there were few lights. The fools still slept, unaware, unprepared. We were virtually at the enemies' gate before the first alarm bellowed out across the city. By then it was too late for them, though they were swift to answer that call. Within minutes Dragons and Dragon Lords had taken to the air. Their fire and fury were devastating, but we outnumbered them some three to one.

Our full force attacked the eastern gate. The gates-men were slain and the archers destroyed by necromantic fire. By magic, the eastern gate exploded, and through it we poured into the city. There we met the king, mounted, along with many knights. He charged first and last for only death met him. Our superior black axes felled him through his armoured body and his horse's armoured body. He did not even take one of our own before he fell."

Asaph closed his eyes. Maybe he couldn't read this. But he had to know, for the sake of his people, for his mother and father, he had to know what had happened. He forced himself to read on.

"Having slain the king, his body was lost and forgotten under the stamping boots of the victorious Immortals, for it was not the king Baelthrom hunted. To utterly destroy the Dragon People, he had to take their dragon queen and then the rest would fall. It was all too easy..."

There came a pause in the writing, and some meaningless scribbles and ink blobs splattered the page. The next writing was in darker ink as if a new ink bottle had been opened, and the quill was thicker than before, but the handwriting itself was still the same.

"The ease with which the city of Draxa was invaded and taken would not have occurred had the powers of our Exalted One not been so desired by humans. Humans are by nature weak-willed and weak-minded. The barest sniff of power found a traitor running to our door.

Vornus proved himself to be a trustworthy ally, though Hameka kept the human on a tight leash, for once a traitor always a traitor. It still took many months to create our plan of attack, even with Vornus's aid. The consumption of the elixir served to render his soul most fully to the Exalted One, and he is more trustworthy now than ever he was as a human. Such is the power of the Exalted One's marvellous gifts."

Asaph felt sick. Vornus had been second-in-command to his mother for the Draxian armies. Coronos always talked so highly of Vornus, "a strong and courageous man, though quiet and calculating," he had said. Had Coronos had any clue about Vornus, any clue at all? Asaph doubted it, they would never have suspected.

He turned back to the book with fervour. On he read, faster and faster, gripping the pages so tightly his fingers hurt as he learned how Vornus had betrayed them.

"The man lied easily and frequently to his king and queen. Such was their foolish trust, they never suspected that a disciple of Lord Baelthrom now walked amongst them. They did not even know when the Maphraxies stepped upon their southern shores. When Draxa fell, Vornus made his escape before his people could discover his treachery. Without weakening them from within, Drax could not have fallen."

The words misted over as he fought back the tears. *"Drax could not have fallen."* Would not have fallen. He forced himself to read on, squinting through the blur.

"We hunted down and slaughtered all the mortal vermin. None could escape our mighty blades, none could escape the black magic of our necromancers. But there was one we sought above all else, the dragon bitch who led them. In the darkened halls of their crumbling fortress, we searched for her lair.

From Vornus's list, we hunted, enslaved and killed all upon it. No Dragon Lord blood could be left alive to take the throne of Drax ever again. Deep in the castle, we found the wretched Dragon Queen Pheonis. Baelthrom, hungry for his prize, took her. It was not difficult to break her, weak from childbirth such as she was ..."

He only just made it outside before he vomited, retching until his stomach hurt and his knees trembled. Weak-legged, he found shaded patch behind the house, away from watching eyes, and forced himself to read the last paragraphs. He would not let his mother suffer alone and in silence, he would bear this burden with her.

"It was more than sport for our Exalted One as he ravaged and crushed the Dragon Queen. The Dragon People must be punished for their insolence, too long have they resisted us. Now they must know they are defeated utterly, and never will they rise again. Her cries echoed even beyond this dimension, and her soul was ripped to shreds.

Our Exalted One did not hurry. Indeed, we have much to learn how our Exalted One keeps the body alive so long under such forces. His blackness seeped into her, forcing her life blood to seep into him—feeding him her power, feeding him her life force in a beautiful exchange.

Her babe was certainly slaughtered as all the newborns were. We were all rewarded well that day…"

Though Asaph had already seen glimpses of his mother's death, it broke him to read it in his enemies' joyous prose. He crouched beside the house, sweat and tears covered his face.

'Vornus still lives. I'll find him and kill him, or die trying!' he vowed. It was something, but it could never right the wrongs that had been done. He could not bring her back, he could not change the past. His soul felt ravaged as her body had been and silent sobs shook his body as Baelthrom had shaken hers.

He thought the pain would never go, but eventually, it receded, leaving him in a terrible silence. In that unbroken stillness where thought was clear and true, the actions he decided then were absolute and unstoppable.

His dragon-self, fully awakened by his anger, indulged in wild thoughts of vengeance wrought in dragon form; of terror and power and fire consuming, burning and destroying the world. He was deeply restless and did not hear Cusap'anth arrive, nor see the terrible look upon the Karalanth's face. He did not even blink when the deer-man's shadow fell upon him, his eyes stared into some other time and place.

'I'm sorry, brother, truly I am. I just hope we live long enough to see the day when we can all take our vengeance, or at least get back what is rightfully ours,' the Karalanth said. Asaph did not look at him, only stared, unseeing, straight ahead.

'I had to know the truth. Maioria has to know the truth. If we weren't betrayed, Drax would not have fallen. We might have had a chance. Might have.'

'Perhaps…' Cusap'anth said sadly. 'I think it would only have delayed the inevitable. We cannot change what's happened. Pray that Woetala fights for us,' he added softly and passed Asaph a flask of water. He took it and drank, but refused the offer of food.

'I cannot eat,' he said and passed back the journal. 'I think I need to be alone.'

Cusap'anth nodded respectfully and left him to his emotions. But Asaph did not sit there for long and instead got up and left the village, neither knowing where he went or caring. Thoughts of Issa were now far from his beleaguered mind, and instead, he sought the Dragon Dream.

Triest'anth watched the young men talking from afar; a Dragon Lord and a Karalanth leader—an unlikely friendship, a powerful friendship.

Cusap'anth turned and walked towards him, his face grim, shoulders sagged. He passed him the journal without saying a word. Triest'anth took it from his son in silence. It was time to destroy someone else, he thought sadly. He turned and began searching for Coronos.

Asaph made his way through the pathless forest, hoping to lose himself in it. It was mid-afternoon and hot and humid. Every now and then, he clenched his jaw, and his hand went to his sword, grasping it until his knuckles turned white and ached. His hard face softened only when tears blurred his vision.

He walked for hours, but heard nothing, saw nothing—not the wind through the leaves, the birds singing in the trees, not even the herd of deer who bounded away, startled by his silent approach. And yet he felt everything; grief, anger, hatred, hopelessness—each emotion scouring him before giving way to the next in a relentless torrent. The only relief he could find was in thoughts of vengeance.

He was forced to stop his mindless walking when the trees gave way to rocks and revealed a deep ravine that fell several hundred feet below. He leant on one leg and peered over the edge, dislodging a rock as he did so, and watched it tumble into the depths. An eagle soared above, searching the rocky ravine and forest for a meal.

Watching it fly made him want to do the same. *I need to fly. I need to be a dragon.* When he was a dragon, things were different. In some ways, he saw more clearly, and grief became fury.

He closed his eyes. The dragon within was not asleep, it was awake and awaiting his command. In his raw state the dragon form came so easily and naturally, he wondered how he had ever had difficulty calling it.

It filled him with music, beautiful and natural. He felt his small human self grow large and powerful. It was in the change, where man and dragon stood in equal measure, that he felt most complete, that he knew many things. The knowledge of humans and the knowledge of dragons combined.

He felt his great size behind closed lizard lids, could feel the enormous strength latent in his muscles, the hot sun warming his iron-strong scales, the rumble of fire in his belly and the smoky air in his nostrils. Now he was alive. Now he was free.

Though young for a Dragon Lord, he felt truly ancient as the blood of his ancestors coursed through his veins. His mind was released from the confines of human thoughts, but the unbreakable bond with his Dragon Lord mother remained. Her face comforted him and soothed his aching heart and mind. She could have taught him so much. At least they could not hurt her anymore.

Were all the Dragon Lords truly gone? The thought disturbed him, particularly in his dragon form. If the Maphraxies could destroy them so easily, was there ever really any hope? The eagle cried a long forlorn cry as if saddened that the golden dragon beneath it had scared off all the food. He didn't need to open his eyes to see it; he could sense its beating heart within his dragon mind.

He opened his eyes and did not blink in the bright sunlight. Unlike humans, dragons could look straight at the sun without being harmed by its rays. He stretched his wings, felt the breeze fill them like a ship's sails, and leapt powerfully into the air. His great bulk lifted easily.

Glorious! That was the only way to describe how he felt when he flew. Barely moving his wings, he circled higher and higher until the air grew thin and he could see the curve of Maioria, the seas to the east, south and west. Higher he circled until he could just glimpse the northern sea, and beyond it the tiniest sliver of a dark landmass. Could it be Drax? It would be home again, one day.

Still higher he climbed until there was no air to lift him and there he hung, breathing the thin air on the edge of the atmosphere, looking at a world that was falling into darkness. In this near airless orbit he closed his eyes, his ancient dragon mind turned inwards, pulling away from the outside world, and he wandered its cavernous corridors until the majestic dragon door stood before him. At his will, it opened, and the light engulfed him.

Joy filled Asaph like a physical thing; hugging him and pushing the darkness away. He breathed in the fresh air and opened his eyes. Lush green hills rolled away into the distance under a blue sky. White mountains towered beyond, and two golden suns shone down. He walked upon the grass in lumbering footsteps, his gigantic tail swinging out behind him. Perhaps the Dragon Dream was truly home, the home of the soul, and he longed to stay here forever.

'Faelsun,' he called aloud and silently with his mind. Only moments had passed when a deep dragon voice came from behind.

'Welcome again, my son. I see a man before me where once there stood a boy.'

He turned and looked at the serene white dragon. The sun shone brightly off his pristine scales, and his eyes were glistening sapphires, much like his own, only lighter.

'I've seen the truth of what happened to my home, to Drax. I want a way to make amends to what was done and take our land back, but I don't know how and I don't think I can do it alone. Can you help me?' he said, unable to stop the raw need surfacing in his voice.

Faelsun's face was sad, as much as a dragon's face could be sad, and this disturbed him for they were in a place where sadness should not exist. They were home and far from the darkness; sorrow did not belong here.

'Maybe the time for us has passed, my son. Perhaps Feygriene calls all her dragons home from the mortal, material worlds. Perhaps we should rest and be thankful that we still have the Dragon Dream, young prince.'

'Our time cannot be over, it has only just begun,' Asaph said, his deep voice rumbling. 'Feygriene came to me; I undertook the Trial by Fire and survived. She would not have done that if there was no hope. Even her sister Zanufey came to me and led me to the Raven Queen. Why would she do that if our time is at an end?'

'For you, life has just begun, and there is much for you to learn,' Faelsun said. 'You have all the vigour and passion of youth; death for you is far away. But I am ancient, and I see a world that is failing like it never has before.

'Think on why Drax was betrayed. Vornus was no different to any other. In this world, the desire to live forever in our current form is the most seductive potion you will ever live to witness, but it is destroying the very essence of life, true eternal life as it was meant to be. For a long time now beings have lived and died upon Maioria because of the Great Rift. Death is unnatural, and they have long forgotten what it's like to be eternal.

'It's every being's innermost desire to live forever, to never experience the horror of ageing and death, of themselves or their loved ones. Baelthrom has this gift, the gift of immortality. Do you think you can fight your, and everyone else's, inner most desire? Can you stand the thought of dying when there's a chance to live forever? Baelthrom knows this, and he is infinitely clever and infinitely powerful, for he would lock us all into physical form and deny our spirit freedom.

'The truth is we do not die; we only change form. The problem is no one remembers this. Few know what I know, few see what I see, Asaph. The path back to the goddess, to the Source of All, is fading away. The Immortal Lord works his unholy magic in potent ways. Soon our bodies and souls will be trapped here eternally, under Baelthrom's dominion. He will become our new god and the beings upon Maioria will forget that the goddess ever existed. And none could say otherwise, for when that happens the goddess, in any of her guises, will not be able to reach us— we will have fallen too far.'

'It cannot be,' Asaph began, struggling to find the words to describe what his spirit knew to be true. 'The goddess, the Source of All, is eternal, is all around us; we can never not be a part of it,' but even as he spoke; the wise and ancient Faelsun instilled doubt in his heart.

'What you say is right, Asaph, but you can forget that you are part of the divine, and that is as good as being so. It's hard for you to understand, and that's all right. To live and die and live again is the way of life here. But what if one did not die? If one being lives trapped forever in their current form, then how do they ever return to Source of All; the point of joyous unity from which we all came? To be eternal, we must be able to grow our current form, to be more of who we are until we have expanded the all of us back into that single point of unity.

'We, all of us, are becoming trapped in an immortal body so that we can never ascend back to the One Source. Do you not see, my son? The old world is crumbling, and the new age looms before us, one which will undo the very fabric of our being,' Faelsun said.

Asaph could not believe what he was hearing from the one being he thought would know what to do. 'We have a chance. We can defeat Baelthrom and his Maphraxies, we have to!'

What Faelsun spoke of was far beyond him; he had never even considered the greater future of Maioria, but he knew that Faelsun was correct. The wise dragon's words had taken his world and shredded it with knives of truth so it lay in fragments at his feet. He'd come here for solace, for help, but all he found was more sorrow.

He shook his great head in denial and the sadness somehow brought on his human form. He wanted to run, to scream, to beat his chest and tear out his hair. He could not believe there wasn't a chance or a future, he would not believe it. But all the denying of it did not make it untrue. His eyes wandered over the landscape, and he noticed that the grass was turning brown and patchy, the sky grey and the suns dull and lacking heat. Was the Dragon Dream fading?

'I cannot let this be,' he said, shaking his head.

'My son, you must understand that what is so is what must be.'

He knew Faelsun was trying to help him, to comfort him, to ease the pain of the truth that stabbed at him. Anger flared.

'She showed me the way to Issa, and I found her,' Asaph said firmly. 'She is the Night Goddess's chosen. She *is* the Raven Queen; the one who can unite us and lead us against the Maphraxies. The dark moon *has* risen. Why would the goddess do that if our world is ending?'

'Asaph, the Night Goddess comes not only to fight the enemy but to find her children. She comes to lead those who remain free of Baelthrom's immortality along the path of the dead. A mercy mission to save those who can still be saved and return them back to the loving fold of the Great Mother before they are lost forever. There is much you do not know, cannot know, even I can only grasp but a small part of her grand design.'

'No, I refuse to believe this,' Asaph clenched his fists. 'I won't lie down and die, I cannot. I will have my revenge. I must. It cannot be this way, Feygriene curse it, it cannot! Faelsun, I will tear myself apart to see the fall of the Maphraxies, to see Maioria free and alive once more. Issa and I are destined to do this, of that I am certain. Together we have a chance, greater than any chance Maioria has ever had before.' He blurted the words out, desperately clinging on to the remnants of hope.

Faelsun watched as the young Dragon Lord let the force of his emotions work through him like a tornado, and who was he to tell the last remaining Dragon Lord that all hope was lost? Would he have been any different? He doubted it.

'I will wait here for you, young Asaph. I will wait and watch and welcome you home. You have a strength rarely seen amongst our half dragon, half human kin. You will need that strength to survive these dark times. You need be taught nothing other than that which you already know. The teachings of the old Dragon Lords are part of yesterday, of what went before; they will not help you now.

'All I can say to you now is this; do not look for counsel outside of yourself, but seek the answers from within. Listen to the voices of your ancestors in the dragon memory, but do not blindly follow what they say. Be your own master. This is the greatest advice I can give you, the only armour I can place upon your body.'

'I will prove to you that this is not the end. You will see Maioria free and shining once more,' Asaph's eyes were alight with the fire of life, and with that he bowed and turned away.

Faelsun watched the passionate Dragon Lord disappear back through the Dragon Door to be alone again in his airless orbit above a dying planet. It had been ten years or more since he had seen him last in the Dragon Dream. Ten years to less than a month in his world. Ten years too long and much had changed. Between the realm of the Dragon Dream and Maioria, time flowed very differently. Evolution was very slow in the mortal worlds compared to the ethereal ones.

'The end is drawing near, and it becomes harder to see the other worlds as the mist draws thicker around us,' Faelsun said softly, talking to Feygriene if she was listening. 'The Immortal Lord sucks the life and power from the universe itself. Blessed Feygriene, lead us home before we are lost forever.'

He spoke his prayer aloud and afterwards, he felt old, terribly old and tired. But there was still work to be done; his soul could not rest yet. Perhaps there was hope. Perhaps the Dragon Lord was right. He had seen the love in his eyes when he spoke of her, the Raven Queen, a love that just might be strong enough to face the darkness.

Had he, Guardian of the Dragon Dream, somehow lost his faith? A tear formed in his eye—a tear! He wondered at that. In how many thousands of years had it been since the last? Dragons do not cry.

He watched the silver drop fall to the ground, twinkling in the sunlight. A tear of hope, a tear of love. *Pray please not a tear of sorrow.* The tear was lost in the grass, but it was not gone; a silver crystal shining alone in the waning sunlight of the Dragon Dream.

CHAPTER 42

Life Seeker

ISSA and the Karalanths arrived home by mid-afternoon, exhausted and hungry. But they shouted and laughed jubilantly, stomping and yelling to announce their triumphant return. They passed through the village picking up a large number of curious and excited followers and came to a stop in the clearing by the smithy where Issa had had her first sword fight. The enthralled crowd clustered around them, eager to hear the news as Rhul'ynth's rich voice rang out.

'Today we have won a great victory.' The crowd murmured amongst themselves, and then hushed as Rhul'ynth continued. 'Today we slew not just one of the hated foltoy, but three.'

A huge cheer exploded from the crowd.

Rhul'ynth waited until the noise quietened, then spoke again. 'Though today has been a great victory, it's also been one which will instil fear into the heart of you as it did in us.'

Issa scanned the crowd for Asaph, only to be disappointed when she could not find him. The embarrassment she had felt earlier about their kiss no longer seemed quite so important. She wanted him to hear about their victory, wanted to make him proud of her, though part of her wished she didn't care quite so much.

Her eyes settled on the tall figure of Coronos as he leant upon his staff. He looked pale and, though he was smiling at her, there seemed to be a terrible sadness in his eyes. She smiled back exuberantly anyway. Where on earth was Asaph? Maybe they'd had an argument, though she had never seen them argue before, not seriously. Sighing, she turned her attention back to Rhul'ynth.

'Three foltoy of a different sort attacked us in an organised ambush, and they could speak!' Rhul'ynth was silent for a moment, letting the news sink into the shocked crowd.

Triest'anth came to stand beside Coronos, and both looked worried.

'Today we witnessed what we all have suspected,' Rhul'ynth continued. 'The enemy has grown stronger, smarter, quicker and more numerous.' The crowd spoke in worried tones amongst themselves, and Rhul'ynth held up her hands to quieten them.

'We all knew it was just a matter of time before the enemy would come to us—we cannot hide away forever. We know the Maphraxie method is to infiltrate us through their Life Seekers and any evil means they can. Baelthrom's spies are everywhere, both seen and unseen. Our cousins in the Northeast have sorely witnessed this. It wouldn't be long before the evil Life Seekers of Baelthrom reached here.' There came murmurs of agreement.

'We must be strong. We are Karalanths. When have we ever turned away from our enemies?'

Some cheered amongst shouts of "never," and others just looked worried. 'Today we defeated those Maphraxie bastards. We are strong. We can beat them!' She held up her arm, fist clenched and the roar from the crowd was deafening.

Out of nowhere a needle-sharp pain struck through Issa's mind making her wince, then was gone. She looked up hoping no one had seen her flinch; she didn't want to ruin the moment. Luckily all eyes were upon Rhul'ynth stood in front of her.

'We have two new huntresses amongst our ranks,' Rhul'ynth said, making Issa, now sensitive to sound in her alert awareness, wince again. Rhul'ynth took hold of her and Diarc'ynth's arms. She smiled up at the Karalanth despite the tight knot of worry forming in her belly.

'Today I saw this woman become truly the Raven Queen.'

Everyone was looking at her, and her legs quivered under the weight of their stares. She smiled weakly feeling her cheeks grow hot.

'This day Zanufey's chosen single-handily slew a foltoy of immense proportions.' Sounds of awe and respect for the two-foot drifted around the Karalanths. 'Praise the huntress, Issa the Raven Queen.'

Cheers exploded from a crowd. Issa cringed, wishing the speech was over. She realised then how much she hated being the centre of attention, all those eyes watching her, it was exhausting. She prayed she wouldn't mention that she'd turned into a raven. Rhul'ynth smiled indulgently down at her, and she managed a weak smile back as her arm was released.

The cheering died down, and Rhul'ynth continued. The Karalanth's voice floated down to her, suddenly seeming very far away. The pain came again, so sharp it blocked out all else, and she tried not to cry out and double over. Danger, terrible danger—that was all she could describe the feeling as. It made her want to run away screaming. Then it was gone, and all was still and calm except her.

Fear slithered down her back. Her eyes darted to the houses and then to the forest beyond. Nothing was out of the ordinary; the trees, the houses, the animals and birds were as they were before. Nothing had changed. What, then, was wrong? What was the pain in her head telling her? If that bloody raven was here, she'd know what was wrong. But wherever her supposed protector and companion was, he was not here, and neither was Asaph. She suddenly felt very alone and, if she was honest, frightened.

She quelled the fear as best she could. Rhul'ynth didn't seem to sense anything wrong, and there was no point causing panic without knowing what the problem was. With the crowd focusing on the Karalanth woman, she closed her eyes, stilled her mind and observed the Flow, using it to reach outwards.

She touched the mind of a sparrow far away and there she rested, seeing through its eyes. She saw the creature then and felt the sparrow's fear as her own. A shudder shook her as she stared down at the slathering beast lumbering through the bushes below, drool hanging like glue from its muzzle and its face contorted in a permanent snarl such as only a hideous Maphraxie could display. The sickly-sweet, yet rotten stench of immortality exuded from its oily pelt. *The smell of the Black Drink.*

The beast stopped and sniffed the air as if wondering where to go next. She pulled away from the sparrow, letting it fly away to seek shelter. Opening her eyes, she swallowed. How far away was that beast?

Coronos was watching her now, a frown of concern on his face. Could he sense something wrong? What the hell should she do? She didn't want to cause alarm, and if she caused panic, the beast would hear it and come straight for them. The crowd cheered for Diarc'ynth.

'Not quite so loud,' she whispered, pleading as she stared about the forest. Her worried looks had not gone unnoticed, and the most observant Karalanths were beginning to wonder what she was looking for. She could hold her silence no longer.

'Rhul'ynth, something is wrong,' she said as calmly as she could, but her words were lost in the din as the less observant Karalanths cheered again. *I must not be afraid*, she thought, fingering the blade at her side as the blood quickened in her veins. She scanned the trees again and again, her awareness sharpened to a knifepoint. It would be here soon, she was sure of it.

'Rhul'ynth, there's danger,' she said louder. Rhul'ynth finished her sentence and turned to her.

'Nonsense, we have slain the only danger for fifty miles around or more,' she said.

Issa ignored her, took her bow and notched an arrow. Rhul'ynth must have seen the deadly look in her eyes as she scanned the forest, for she shifted uneasily.

'Karalanths and two-feet, the Raven Queen senses danger,' Rhul'ynth said to the crowd.

The Karalanths immediately took heed. All who carried weapons had them in their hands in a blink. Laughing children, unaware of the imminent danger, were rounded up and dragged away.

Issa felt something moving in the distance. It paused, recalculated and changed its course. She lost it again. The sun was dipping into the trees and its heat weakened as the afternoon turned into evening.

Their cries of triumph echoed through the forest like a beacon. She saw it again clearly in her mind; that abomination of nature running and growling in a maddened frenzy as it hurtled towards the noise.

Like an unseen wave the forest fell silent before the Life Seeker—the size of a buffalo and twice as fast. It was more doglike in its appearance than a foltoy, short ears, long snout, large canines, oily matted pelt that was neither scales nor fur, but something in between. Issa felt that it lacked the intelligence of a foltoy. Baelthrom must know she was here; the forest was filled with his immortals today. Cold fury flowed through her veins.

'Rhul'ynth, get ready,' she spoke quietly, yet her voice cut through the air like a knife.

Rhul'ynth's face was filled with worry, and she shifted her feet, gripping her bow tightly. 'We must get the most vulnerable away!' she shouted, fingering her notched arrow.

The crowd hurried faster, mothers and fathers dragged their children away, panic building in their eyes. Issa knew they now sensed what she felt, what the whole forest felt. She looked down at her small bow and arrow—she needed something better than those. She darted back to the smithy and grabbed a sharp steel short sword from the wall. This time she would not be using a wooden one. She stuffed it into her blacksmith's belt next to her hunting knife.

The other villagers, seeing her grab the sword, also grabbed extra weapons from the smithy. Coronos joined the hunting party behind her, and they drew close together. Calmly, quickly, they all notched arrows.

'Almost upon us,' she whispered, a strange excited fear tinged her voice.

She gathered the flows of magic, reaching deep into the earth and pulling them to her. She fed the magic into a single stream that flowed through her, so that it seemed she stood in the Flow like a great tree made of magic; the energy flowing up from her roots and spreading out through her branches.

The forest's magic was strong here amongst the Karalanths blessed by Woetala. The energy came to her in earthy waves of golden brown and emerald green flecked through with silver. The sound it made was at first like the rushing wind and then the faintest tinkle, like that made with pipes.

She focused on drawing more. Soon the stream became a river and then a great torrent that roared and surged through her. Exhilarating! Like swimming in a raging tide or flying in a thundering storm. She should be afraid but she was not. It seemed the most natural thing, the most enlivening thing, in all the world.

Through the torrent of the Flow, she felt another stream move. It was Coronos channelling his magic close behind her; it came from a glowing ball of light about three feet in diameter. *The Orb of Air.* It comforted her that he was beside her in the Flow, but she also worried for his safety. If the Life Seekers were hunting only her, she had put them all in danger by staying here. She held the Flow firm and turned her attention back to the trees ahead.

'Almost upon us,' she whispered again, licking her lips, feeling that same excited fear. She was certain she could feel the earth shudder from the pounding of the beast's feet. Calm and focused, she pulled back her bow. It surely came for her, but why? Baelthrom must know Keteth was dead, must have felt the power of the two orbs combining. That he could act so quickly was frightening. She remembered her dream of Duskar screaming and rearing, and shivered. Something had happened, something terrible, and they knew where to search for her.

The sound of splintering rock echoed through the forest, and the tops of the trees quivered. She could hear other beasts following, how many she could not be sure. A blood-curdling baying ripped out across the forest, as of crazed, wild dogs in some terrible hunt.

'How many are there?' Grast'anth breathed. He had come to stand next to Rhul'ynth. Issa was glad he was there. Rhul'ynth shook her head, eyes wide.

'I smell death hounds, lots of them,' Palu'anth spat in disgust.

'This is going to be a tough fight,' Issa said.

Rhul'ynth drew her bow, a fierce look in her eyes. 'Let them come. We are ready.'

The huge dark shape of the Life Seeker paused within the trees out of range. Ten large death hounds with smouldering yellow eyes burst from the woods. She grimaced from the sight and smell of the immortal corruption exuding from them. They were the size of wolves yet wholly vicious and with half a wolf's wit.

She loosed her arrow and drew another whilst it was in mid-flight. It fell short, but the second struck the paw of a death hound. It screamed and rolled and was taken down by another arrow not her own. Five more were struck dead by Karalanth arrows in seconds. The other hounds jumped, unfazed, over their dead and streamed out of the woods, baying. The Karalanths around her spread out to sight and loose their arrows more effectively.

She reached out to the death hounds' minds, searching for a connection as she did with horses. She struggled to find their minds at first, but when she did they were blank. She blinked in surprise. Blank with a single desire to kill and feed upon the living. Living blood gave them energy; they had no life of their own. That realisation came as a shock, and she stood there dumbly whilst the others fired their arrows. She wished she hadn't looked.

A death hound dodged two arrows and veered straight towards her. Too late to notch and draw an arrow, she dropped her bow and freed her sword. She raised her blade, but the death hound never came within reach and instead ran right past her without a glance. Her sword sliced uselessly through the air.

'Huh?' She turned in surprised disappointment as it went for Grast'anth instead. He swung his sword, lifting it bodily into the air and severing it in two. It thudded to the ground dead and twitching, dripping blood so dark it was almost black as it oozed over its matted fur. She grimaced.

A screaming howl ripped through the air, and her attention whipped back to the forest. The Life Seeker all but exploded out of the trees, roots and earth flying up around it as it surged towards her. Surrounding it was a dense pack of death hounds. Her blood ran cold. It looked like a demon flying straight out of the gates of the Murk in the old picture books. And it was coming straight for her.

Refusing to put others in danger, she pushed past the Karalanths, and ran to the right, hoping the beast would follow her. She ignored their horrified shouts of, "What are you doing?" "Where are you going?" Like the foltoy earlier, it wanted only her, and she would not let them die to protect her.

A glance behind told her they had their work cut out, and were beleaguered by death hounds that ran straight past her.

'Are you coming for me, you bastard?' she growled lifting her sword, eyes never leaving the slavering beast that angled towards her. 'Or is it I that come for you?'

It remained out of the range of arrows, and she ran towards it. The stench of rotting flesh made her gag. She took her sword in her left hand and raised her right, fingers splayed wide. The Flow was ready and waiting.

'Fire,' she howled. The voice always gave greater weight to any magical command.

A flaring ball of fire exploded from her outstretched hand, scorching the grass black beneath it as it smacked into the beast. It screamed a sound that rang painfully in her ears, its momentum halted as the fire burned ferociously.

A slick dark flow of magic moved around her then, quite apart from the Flow she could see in her mind. It had magic… But magic she'd never seen before, not even from Keteth.

The thought was a game changer, and her mouth went dry as the Life Seeker drew upon its black force. This magic was from another source, a source of power that did not connect to and bind all things, a power she did not understand. The Under Flow, that was what Freydel called Baelthrom's dark magic. Is that what his beasts use too?

She hesitated. Her fire dissipated, extinguished by a black cloud, but smoke still smouldered from patches of charred flesh. Its eyes were all pupil and completely grey, so it seemed that it was never looking at her, but she could feel its dead, soulless gaze. It snarled, revealing long yellow fangs, and crouched low as it walked towards her in a snaking movement.

She gripped her blade in her right hand and measured up her opponent, taking in the slightest movement. More death hounds streamed past her, doing away with any hope she might have had for assistance from the struggling Karalanths.

Behind her came the screams and shouts of a vicious battle being fought, but she dared not take her eyes off the beast in front of her. She didn't need to see to know the Karalanths were outnumbered. She had to defeat this beast alone, or not.

The Life Seeker stepped left, and she stepped right. They circled each other. Her fire had left five bloody burns across its face that oozed black-red blood—immortal blood, thick and dark and dead. Its ears flickered back and forth, and its matted pelt was stiff and looked as hard as steel. Dead eyes calculated her every move. Fear gnawed at her.

The beast seemed to grin and then it leapt so fast it was a blur. Instinctively she rolled and sliced at its claws, slashing the air above her. Dark blood splattered down upon her face, and the beast howled once more. She jumped up and spun to face it, licking a drop of the beast's blood from her lips as the battle fury surged within. The immortal blood was acrid and powerful, and she spat it out quickly. The beast laughed an awful rasping chuckle.

She snarled and charged, but it moved fast, too fast for a thing that size, and her sword struck only air. Dimly she was aware of her bruised and aching ribs as her body rebelled against two battles fought in one day. She staggered and reached for the Flow—she could not fight this battle with strength or speed. Magic flooded into her willingly, filling her with renewed energy and resolve.

If the dark moon were with her, the fight would already be won. But it was not, and now she had to rely on her skill with magic and sword. With a flick of her hand and a whisper of her intention, lightning snaked forth and struck the beast, flinging it backwards. It hurtled head over tail into a tree, splintering it in a shower of bark and branches.

Magic could buy her time, could rest her body, but even with magic she was still a novice, and without having recovered from the earlier fight, her reserves were pitifully low. Though the earth-based magic came to her willingly, and with each use, she understood more, her ability to command, direct and wield the Flow was sorely weakened by fatigue and inexperience.

The Life Seeker clawed to its feet and laughed, its flesh flickering with static.

'The Immortal Lord will be pleased to know you have been found,' the beast spoke with difficulty in a growling voice through vocal chords never meant for human words. 'I shall be well rewarded for this day.'

She laughed back, ignoring the unnerving fact that it could speak. Her voice was strong, belying her fear and fatigue. 'Let him come, let them all come—come to their deaths as you will soon meet yours, you pathetic rabid beast,' she snarled.

The beast leapt before she finished her sentence, claws spread wide. She sidestepped, but not quite far enough for its massive reach. A claw caught her, sending her with crushing force to the ground. The breath exploded out of lungs, and her injured ribs made her scream in pain. She rolled as much as she could, her clothes tearing under its claws as she tried to get away.

She struck upwards sinking her sword deep into its shoulder, pushing with all her might. Its howl close to her ear was deafening. Dark blood spilled down her sword making it slippery. She tried to pull it away, but her grip slipped, leaving the sword embedded in its shoulder as it reared.

She grappled for her knife while reaching frantically for the Flow. In the next few moments, the exhausting fight unfolded into a dance of flashing magic and slashing teeth and claws. The beast fell back from her wall of flames. It reached up and wrenched her sword from its shoulder, tossing it aside as its black blood splattered the ground.

The beast growled. 'What's the point in fighting? You cannot win. You want to stay like this forever; a weak, pathetic pawn to an absent goddess? The Immortal Lord gives so much more, foolish human.'

'You are dead. You cannot feel the living force within all things. Stupid immortal,' she snarled.

Fury made her lunge through the wall of fire to her sword, but the beast pounced to meet her. Dark magic moved beneath her, and a pool of black water sloshed around her ankles. Energy drained from her body and the Flow drained from her grasp into that pool. She slumped to her knees in the black. Paws swiped at her but she could not dodge them and was flung high.

She twisted in mid-air, trying to control her fall, but the ground spun too fast. She smashed into the earth and rolled limply, all breath knocked from her. Through the agony of her ribs and her gasping breath, she opened herself fully to the Flow, uncaring of the danger if she pulled upon more than she could hold. It would be over soon anyway and she would rather die at her own hands than let this slavering beast have her.

The Flow flooded back now she was out of the black pool. She called to the blue moon and prayed to Zanufey to give her strength, but they seemed far away, and the moon could give her none of its power. She pulled harder on the Flow, thinking she could hold no more and yet a little more came. Through half-lidded eyes she saw the Flow fully—a world ablaze in a maelstrom of earth, fire and lightning as the magic followed her intent, a torrent of destructive power.

She struck the beast with it again and again, driving it back. Lightning and fire flared between them, draining her resources at an alarming rate. It staggered, bleeding and breathless under her onslaught, but slowly formed a shimmering protective shield around it that rendered her attacks useless. She couldn't fight for control of the Flow when the beast's magic came from somewhere else entirely.

She paused her assault for rest and became aware of her blood trickling down her arms and legs from jagged wounds. Her whole body trembled from physical and mental exhaustion. The Life Seeker shuddered too, but even as she watched the magic surrounding fed it and made it stronger.

She gripped her last weapon, the hunting knife, and pulled it from its sheathe grimacing, willing her muscles to obey. The beast leapt, she rolled, deflecting claws with the knife, buying time. It leapt again, and back she rolled, deflecting again.

She moved in desperation and pure survival for the beast moved too fast for her to think and form control over the Flow. Each time she rolled she managed to slice small wounds upon claws and legs, but never enough to maim or injure. She staggered up too slowly and heavy claws dragged and pinned her to the ground. She screamed as they pierced her shoulder, and struggled to draw breath into her crushed lungs. The beast laughed triumphantly.

'Too easy... Why the Immortal Lord hunts you, I do not know,' it mocked.

She couldn't speak, she couldn't even breathe. And then the crushing weight was gone as it lifted off her. Instead, rope made of black magic slithered around her, binding her tightly. She gasped, her mind reeling from exertion, terror making her shake. Where was Asaph? She was trapped. She tried to think, there had to be a way out. She closed her eyes not wanting to see the hideous beast above her, but its rancid breath made her retch, made her woefully aware of its presence. Her magic seemed useless against the rope, and her mind was too weak to command it.

She closed her eyes to see the Flow more clearly and there, bigger than a horse, stood an image of a raven. This raven was made of indigo and silver magical energy. It looked at her. A bolt of understanding shot through her, and she wondered why she had not thought of it before.

'Raven,' she gasped, asking the Flow rather than commanding it.

She felt her form shifting. The rope restraining her changing body could not hold her. She cawed, beat her wings and lifted. The beast howled and leapt to catch her, but its frothing mouth snapped on empty air. Her wings were bleeding just as her arms had been, and the change took her to the edge of her reserves. Her consciousness wavered, and she floundered in the air, dazed.

She glanced back at the village. The battle had taken her a long way away. In her glimpse, it seemed the Karalanths were finally overcoming the enemy, but amongst the black and twisted bodies of death hounds lay many fallen. She prayed to Zanufey to come for them.

She turned in the air. The sun was sinking in the west turning the sky blood-red. She looked down at the beast staring up at her. Her blood fell in drops around it, splattering on its fur and its muzzle that he licked hungrily. She had to finish this, she could not let it live. She calmed her exhausted mind, flew in a high arc and then dropped like a stone towards it.

In the last instance, she let what she could hold of the Flow fill her as the beast reared up to meet her. In her raven form, she released the last of her magic and engulfed them both in indigo fire. In the same moment, she let her raven form go and drove her blade through the Life Seekers open jaws, embedding the blade through its throat and deep into its skull.

Together they fell to the floor, her hand still holding the knife now stuck in the beast's throat. She struggled to keep herself on top of it as they rolled, trying to avoid being crushed by its weight. The indigo fire receded, leaving behind it the smell of burning Life Seeker flesh. It lay still, did not even twitch as she flopped beside it. She could not free her arm, had not the strength to try, and stayed on her back in the gore, spent.

Her mind was burned, drained into negative. She could not think clearly as if the neural pathways of her thoughts had been disrupted and confused by overuse of magic. She tried to think of where she was but struggled to remember even that. She'd used too much. Freydel warned her never to use too much too soon, but she'd had no choice

A shadow blotted out the light of the setting sun. It was so big she thought night had come. She blinked up. and her heart lurched in her chest.

'No,' she shivered in horror, refusing to believe what her eyes were telling her; that there was a huge dragon, black as midnight, eyes the colour of burning coals, circling above her. Her blood ran cold, and her bladder emptied itself. She could not run, she was trapped by her arm in the stinking Life Seeker. Dragon fear trembled through her, and she closed her eyes, but the Dread Dragon came even there, red eyes burning into her soul.

She heard the cries of terror from the Karalanths somewhere beyond the mass of the dead Life Seeker as the dragon fear engulfed them too. Dromoorai; the hated name of those who had destroyed her entire world and all she loved. The Flow drained away as the Dromoorai began to weave a spell. She shivered uncontrollably and sweat rolled off her face and body. She couldn't fight. She should have known the Life Seeker was not alone. The Dromoorai touched her mind, and she shrank from it.

Her eyes flew open and stared at Dromoorai hovering very close. Its pupil-less eyes glowed dark green within its three-pointed helmet. Black armour encased it in an impenetrable shell. Her gaze was drawn down to the burning red amulet upon its chest. She forced them shut against the thing that was trying to get inside her mind. Black clouds filled her head, and her consciousness flickered out.

CHAPTER 43

Asaph's Dark Brethren

ASAPH was lost deep in his thoughts as he drifted in the near-airless part of the atmosphere. He was surrounded by blue that changed from light beneath him to dark above. The world far below was a distant, hazy land of smudged azure, greys and greens.

He did not need to think about flying, drifting was easy up here and his wings seemed to instinctively know what to do. Up here the air currents were much more stable, flowing in predictable and unchanging directions. He wondered if this is what the dragons of old liked to do before Baelthrom came.

Something important tugged at his consciousness, something he had forgotten about but shouldn't have. He pushed it away. He needed to think, to plan, to find answers. That he must tell Coronos about Vornus was obvious, though he didn't want to tell his father about the betrayal of someone he trusted. Telling him would change nothing, however, for the past could not be changed, the dead could not be brought back, and all that mattered is what they did now.

They should raise an army. But how could they do any better than the Feylint Halanoi who had been fighting against the Maphraxies for hundreds of years? Nothing had been in their favour, but now, perhaps, the tide was turning. There were many things on their side; the dark moon of Zanufey rising, the Raven Queen, the death of Keteth, the return of the last Dragon Lord and heir to the throne of Drax. He could find the sleeping dragons and bring them back to the world. All those things were on their side.

They could join the Feylint Halanoi and rally a greater army than they ever had before. Unite the whole of Maioria in one massive assault upon

Drax and push the enemy out. After Drax had been purged, why not Intolana? Maybe then the elves would return. They could scour the world to find the numbers needed to fight them. They had the Karalanths on their side already. The Kuapoh would certainly fight that which threatened the whole of Maioria. They could build boats, and now Keteth was gone, the seas were free.

A ring of silver surrounded by flames flared before him in the Flow. The flame ring, he recognised it instantly. There came an echoing scream that cut through his thoughts like a knife. The world stopped turning and time stood still. *Issa!*

In a panic, he almost changed back into his human form and plummeted. He struggled to regain his senses and control of his wings. He was an idiot for leaving her alone when danger was near. He drew his wings together and shot down through the sky. The world was a blur of blue and green, and the air became rich and thick. He drew his wings closer and half-flew, half-fell at great speed. The wind was a howling banshee in his ears as it screamed past. He was sure the slightest twitch of his wings would rip a hole in them at this speed, but he didn't care.

The flame ring called to him, a burning circle of fire pulsing below him in the Flow, telling him where she was. Magic flared a brilliant light that dimmed to dark blue. The magic was earth-based, and yet it was moved by a force beyond it, a force that could command all the elements. Issa's pre-elemental magic, he would never forget the feel of it.

The great forests of Frayon came into view. He opened his wings a little and took a less vertical angle. An explosion of magic flared in the distance. That was not Issa's magic, it carried the feel of something dark and corrupt, and it did not come from within the Flow. *Immortal magic; the Under Flow.* The thought made his reptilian blood run colder.

By Feygriene's fire, not magic wielders too. Issa, wait for me. Hold on! He suddenly sensed the presence of another dragon and slowed in surprise.

Brother? Sister? He reached out with his mind only to recoil when he touched the dead mind of his kin, the mind of a Dread Dragon. He could not understand that mind; it was dark, alien and instilled with life of a different kind, or maybe the absence of life. He doubted if the Dread Dragon had felt his greeting.

Attached to it was another mind, like a conjoined twin. Dromoorai, he shuddered, and dared not even try to reach that mind. It was impossible to believe they had been Dragon Lords once. He spotted the huge snaking black shape of the Dread Dragon just above the tree line. Utter hatred for the thing that had once been a Dragon Lord made his belly rumble with fire. It was facing him as he closed in but was so intent upon the ground that it did not notice him. He glimpsed a small pale shape trapped and unmoving beside the body of a Life Seeker.

'Issa,' he growled. He was not afraid, he was furious.

The Dromoorai dropped low, the gusting air from its wings billowed the trees violently around it. It reached out a claw to grasp her. Asaph roared in rage. The Dromoorai's helmeted head whipped up just as a fountain of yellow flame spewed from Asaph's mouth and engulfed it. It yanked hard on the reins, hauling the Dread Dragon upwards. Fire flickered all over them as it took a steep angle up, trying to extinguish the flames in the rushing air.

Without pause, Asaph followed them skyward and released another torrent of hotter, whiter flames. Careless of his own fire, he hurtled into the underside of the Dread Dragon, golden talons slicing into black scales.

The Dread Dragon could not fly with the weight of Asaph clinging to him, and together they spun in the air, golden dragon entwined with black in a deadly embrace. Down they tumbled, clawing and gnashing, each trying to find the other's throat as the Dromoorai struggled to stay mounted. They smashed through the trees and hit the ground making it shudder. The force of the impact tore them apart. A splintered pine pierced the Dread Dragon's wing, and black blood splashed around them.

Asaph rolled onto his feet and stood dazed, panting smoke. He glared at the equally disorientated Dread Dragon. The Dromoorai rider had managed to remain on its back unscathed. The sun had gone completely now. His blood slowed with the loss of the sun's heat, but the fire in his belly and hatred of the beast fuelled his strength.

The two dragons faced each other amidst the debris of smashed trees and gullies of raked earth. The Dread Dragon flicked its bleeding wing at him, spraying him with black blood. Though torn, it was not enough to stop it flying. He shook off the immortal blood and regarded his foe, this abomination of nature. Dragon Lords were filled with life, enough life for two beings; dragon and human. He couldn't imagine being severed from his dragon or human self. The very thought sent chills through his body. Only Baelthrom could think up such a sick thing. Despite his disgust of the Dromoorai, a part of him felt sorrow for the Dragon Lord it once was.

'I shall put your soul to rest, brother,' he said in a voice low and rumbling like thunder. 'Whatever is left of it.' Maybe there was nothing to be saved or set free within this Dread Dragon or its Dromoorai rider. If there was, he could not feel it.

The Dread Dragon narrowed its eyes, and they turned smouldering red. Its huge muscles bunched, then it lunged, claws flinging up clods of earth. Asaph stayed his ground, the claws on his hind legs splayed and digging deep for grip. The Dread Dragon ploughed into him, trying to topple him over, but he stayed grounded and instead was shunted backwards.

He sunk his claws through scales as tough as metal and hugged the Dread Dragon close to prevent it finding his throat. But that brought him close to the Dromoorai on its back. The man-beast raised his claymore and thrust down. He expected it to clang off his own thick scales, but instead searing pain exploded in his back. The blade was enchanted with Baelthrom's immortal magic.

He opened his mouth and bellowed yellow fire, emptying all that he had until the yellow flames became red and then smoke. He felt the blade pull free and blood trickle down his side. The enchantment stung more than the wound made by the blade. It wasn't deep, but the stinging pain enraged him more.

The Dread Dragon sprayed dark red fire down his back. He could smell his own resilient flesh begin to char in the unholy flames long before he felt the pain. Dragons retained some immunity to fire, but eventually, it would kill them too, though they could not be set alight.

He released his grip, pulled away, and struck fast through the Dread Dragon's fire so that it did not see him coming. He went straight for the neck, and this time his teeth found what he was looking for. His jaws closed around the beast's throat in a crushing vice. He twisted and lunged, throwing the surprised Dromoorai from its back. He whipped his tail around and struck the Dromoorai, flinging it back into the trees and buying him time to fight each foe alone.

The Dread Dragon writhed furiously in his death grip, lifting him bodily off the floor and then smacking him back down, but he did not let go. Its claws pierced his shoulders and belly. He struggled to push the Dread Dragon beneath him, trying to hold the bigger dragon down with all his weight. Its tail whipped up and smashed him on the head, the three horns upon it were sharp enough to pierce his scales. Blood trickled down his forehead and into his eyes. He blinked it away and snarled.

He bit harder, through the smaller scales of the neck and down into softer flesh and sinew. He bit so hard he thought his teeth would break.

Cold, syrupy blood filled his mouth making him gag. He closed his throat so as not to swallow any—drinking the blood of immortals was akin to drinking a drop of the Black Drink. His teeth finally met bone and could go no further. Dragon bones were harder than rock and impossible to break.

The Dread Dragon jerked and writhed violently before crumpling under him.

He held the still Dread Dragon for a moment more, staring into its dimming red eyes, wondering if, and hoping that, something had found release. Slowly, tenderly almost, he released its throat, letting it flop to lie still on the ground. It had once been his brother or sister, one he would never know.

What have they done to you, to us all?

He heard the sliding sound of a sword being drawn and whirled to face the Dromoorai he'd forgotten about. It was huge, twice the size of a human, though still dwarfed by his dragon self. He lifted away from its massive swinging claymore, which it swung as easily as if it were made of balsa wood. The wound on his back was already festering from that blade, and he didn't want another one to add to it.

His fearless foe was unreadable. It seemed to be made of solid armour, from its black metal boots to its gauntlets, even its three-pointed helmet seemed to be part of its face. He snaked to the left, eyes never leaving the Dromoorai's that changed from dark green to red—red to match the amulet glowing upon its chest. He tried not to look at that amulet, his soul screamed at him not to, but then it flashed and forced his eyes upon it.

In the Flow, he could see a red line stretching from the amulet, through the Dromoorai and back beyond it. Did it link back to Baelthrom? The thought unnerved him, and he forced himself to look at the Dromoorai's claymore.

They circled each other. The Dromoorai's black cloak billowed as it advanced, completely impervious to the dragon fear Asaph exuded. Even without its Dread Dragon, the Karalanths had said a Dromoorai was notoriously difficult to kill. It lunged with lightning speed; the black claymore rose and fell. He drew back at the last second and spewed white flames onto it, turning the sword into a shard of red-hot metal. It crackled and buckled and weakened in the intense heat, but the Dromoorai seemed immune to his fire and the burning sword in its hand, and pressed forwards.

Asaph stepped back, resumed his human form, and drew his sword in one swift moment. If his flames did not burn it, then perhaps it would be better to fight with his sword.

'Let us fight, man to man,' Asaph growled. It somehow seemed more honourable. *I'll kill this abomination as a human!*

The Dromoorai said nothing and reacted to nothing; only coming on fearless and unreadable. It raised its sword and Asaph raised his. Sword struck sword in a clash of metal. He staggered under the Dromoorai's blow, its strength was frightening, but his fury and victory over the Dread Dragon gave him confidence and strength. He shoved the claymore back and stepped away, scanning his opponent's armour, looking for any weakness. It *had* to be weaker without its dragon, but weaknesses seemed woefully absent.

Their swords rose and fell. Asaph deflected another crushing blow with a slice and duck, recovering his lighter weapon swiftly. He stabbed at the Dromoorai's side where he thought the armour might be weaker and ground between the plates. The Dromoorai grunted in surprise, its eyes turned black, and it pulled back.

Unlike the Dread Dragon, the Dromoorai's blood was watery and grey, and it gushed over Asaph's sword as he yanked it free. The man-beast was only half a being, its blood weak like water, and yet it was as strong as a bear.

'Give yourself to me. The Immortal Lord owns you and us all,' the Dromoorai's voice was gravelly. That it spoke was a surprise.

Asaph laughed, but as he did so, the amulet whispered to him.

'Join your brothers and sisters. Great power and a life untouched by death awaits you.' The words wrapped around him and he instinctively strained to hear more. 'Come to us. You will be king.'

He felt weak as he listened. The glowing amulet was draining his strength; he mustn't look at it or listen to it. He tore his eyes away and lunged left then right, driving the Dromoorai back. But it was strong and deflected many of his blows without tiring.

Its claymore swung fast, and he narrowly dodged the blow. He glanced down at his woven breeches and linen shirt, and then ruefully back at the metal encasing the Dromoorai. If it landed a blow, he was finished. He felt fuzziness in the air, charged like static. *Magic!*

Without his dragon's abilities to see magic, he was at another disadvantage. There came a clap like thunder and without moving, the Dromoorai was inches from him and knocking him to the ground. It towered over him, crushing his sword arm beneath its metal-encased foot. The other foot crushed down upon his chest.

He tried to keep a grip on his sword, but it was agony, and he was forced to let go. He punched at the boot on his chest, but attempts to dislodge it were useless; it was like trying to move solid rock. He gasped for breath and kicked, but his soft boots thumped uselessly into iron armour and hurt his own feet instead. He was doing more damage to himself than to the thing that was about to kill him.

The metal boot crushed harder on his arm. He bit back a cry of pain. He would show no pain to this bastard. Red amulet and eyes burned into his own. Something corrupt and awful pressed upon his mind, and he fought to keep it out.

'The last of the Dragon Lords struggles before me, as they all have,' the Dromoorai growled. His voice was low and airy, like the wind blowing through dead leaves.

'You killed your own kin, you bastard,' Asaph roared. 'I'm going to avenge them.'

He looked to his sword, but there was no way of reaching it. He knew the Dromoorai wanted him alive, to be turned into one of them. He would die rather than let that happen. It seemed the Dromoorai was waiting for instructions from whatever that evil red stone was connected to.

He considered his limited options rapidly. He had a knife tucked away inside a pocket on his thigh, but it was tiny and only used as a cutting tool. It had been a long time since he'd sharpened it too.

'We were betrayed,' he gasped through the pain of his crushed arm. The claymore wound on his back began to throb as well. 'You are slaves to a greedy, vengeful bastard who has enslaved your soul and cares nothing for you.' He struggled to free his trapped arm again, using the movement as a distraction whilst his other hand fumbled for the knife.

The Dromoorai laughed, a hollow sound that made him shudder. 'We were saved from our pitiful existence. Your deceiving goddess denied us our true power. The Immortal Lord has set us free and given us powers beyond anything thought possible in this world.'

'You murdered my people, our people. Traitor!' Asaph screamed.

The knife was at his fingertips, but then it shifted and fell from his grasp. He fumbled for it again as the Dromoorai bent closer; soulless eyes inches from his face. He could feel the amulet burning into his chest, leaching the life from him, making his head pound with its awful red light.

'You will become one of us. Even the Dragon Queen herself begged to be made one of us as our Lord destroyed her.'

The knife fell into his grasp. He pulled it free and in one swift motion plunged it through the dangling amulet, the only part of the Dromoorai he could reach. The knife buckled under the blow, and there came a cracking sound. The Dromoorai lurched backwards off his arm and chest. The amulet exploded as latent magic was released. Asaph grabbed his sword with his good arm and staggered to his feet, falling towards the Dromoorai as it fell back in shock. He thrust his sword into its burning eyes and drove forwards hard.

The Dromoorai gasped—an awful sucking sound—and stumbled onto its back, pulling him down with it. The gasping turned to a high-pitched wail so piercing he let go of his sword and rolled away covering his ears. It thrashed on the ground, its watery grey blood gushing. The screams stopped abruptly, and it lay still.

Asaph staggered to his feet cradling his crushed arm. It was still whole, but bloody and bruised, maybe even fractured. He felt his back. There was a long shallow cut stinging with unholy magic. Luckily he had been in dragon form when he took it. Otherwise, the blow would have severed his soft human spine.

In the stunned silent aftermath of the ferocious battle, he looked upon his dead enemies; two black shapes in the growing darkness. Steam still rose from them, and they were beginning to collapse as if melting into the ground. They were decaying swiftly because they were long dead, mere walking shells instilled with unholy life. *Some idea of immortality,* he snorted.

He reached down to the Dromoorai and pulled the shattered amulet free. The broken stone was now pitch black and so cold to the touch it burned. It still felt as if it were sucking the life out of him. He wrapped it in his sword's polishing cloth and stuffed it into his pocket to study later.

As his pulse finally ceased pounding, calm returned.

Issa!

CHAPTER 44

The Warrior Within

ASAPH reached Issa at the same time as the bloodied and bewildered Karalanths did. He sunk down beside her. She was barely conscious, and her hand was trapped in the decaying stinking skull of a Life Seeker. He cradled her head in his hands.

'I'm so sorry I wasn't here,' he whispered, stroking the hair from her face.

Her eyes flickered open and she smiled up at him, too weak to speak. Coronos knelt beside him, the Orb of Air in his trembling hand, milky white in the darkness. The older man took hold of her trapped arm and whispered words he did not understand in his human form. The orb grew brighter and magic sparkled in the air. The Life Seeker's skull gave a sickening crack, and her hand fell free, together with a knife she still grasped and black gore. The Karalanths poured water from their flasks to wash it away, grimaces on their faces.

'You came just in time,' she whispered.' Her eyes were a strange, brilliant turquoise. He looked at Coronos worriedly.

'She has used too much of the Flow,' Triest'anth explained, peering over Coronos' shoulder.

Coronos agreed, a frown creasing his forehead. 'Through the orb, I can feel her life force stronger in the Flow than in the physical world, but there's nothing I can do to help her.'

'If she did not have Zanufey on her side, I would doubt she could recover from such overuse of magic,' said Triest'anth. 'Don't worry, friend, the Night Goddess is with her. I'm certain she will be all right.'

Issa looked at her bruised and bloodied arm and winced. He grinned and held up his own crushed and bloody arm.

'Snap,' he said.

She laughed and passed out. Asaph tried to pick her up, but his arm was not strong enough.

'Let me,' Grast'anth insisted, and picked her up easily. She looked so small and fragile in his arms.

'Come, we must tend to your wounds also,' Coronos said solemnly, putting an arm around his shoulders. 'She needs rest, that's all.' Asaph nodded, suddenly feeling horribly weary.

'Many Karalanths lost their lives today,' Coronos said quietly as they made their way back to the village.

Asaph looked away, not knowing what to say and feeling horror settle in his belly. He should have been here.

Those who lived were solemn-faced and busy covering their dead with blankets. There was already a pile of rotting death hounds, far outnumbering the blanketed bodies of the fallen Karalanths. It offered some respite.

Many houses were damaged and had holes in their soft mud-based walls. Food and crockery were strewn everywhere, and over everything were splashes of red and black blood. No one spoke as the Karalanths quickly restored order to their village. No one was idle, not even the children as they helped their parents in silence. The blanketed covered bodies were then carried and laid around a hastily constructed pyre in the village centre. Asaph hung his head. He would certainly know at least some of the fallen.

'I have brought nothing but death here,' he sighed heavily. He had not meant for this to happen.

'That's nonsense,' Triest'anth said. 'This was coming whether or not you were here; it only came sooner rather than later. The foltoy have been sniffing around us for months now, and their numbers are growing. If it weren't for you and her, we wouldn't have survived such an attack.'

'It's us that brought them here,' Asaph said, staring at the ground.

'The Maphraxies won't stop attacking all who live even if they capture the last Dragon Lord and the Raven Queen herself,' Triest'anth said. 'They won't stop until all of us have fallen to them and the great Source of All is crushed beneath the Immortal Lord's feet. Many times we have seen Baelthrom's death hounds and foltoy sneaking through the forest and reporting back to their master. Even the harpies grow more daring and fly low over our lands—unheard of this far into Frayon.'

'Triest'anth is right, Asaph. The Maphraxies will plague all nations and none are safe from them. You cannot blame yourself,' Coronos said, squeezing his shoulder. 'And yet, perhaps it *is* time we left. They are hunting us and we can draw them away from here whilst you rebuild your homes,' he said to Triest'anth.

'This was just one small battle today, no doubt the first of many. They will come again, of that we can be sure,' Triest'anth said. 'I think the time has come for all of us Karalanths to re-unite—that way we'll be stronger. Maybe we should even join with the Feylint Halanoi, for in unity there is power. But I severely doubt any Karalanth will ever willingly join forces with the dwarves amongst the Feylint Halanoi. Yet if we do not, then I think we are doomed.' Triest'anth spoke quietly as if he didn't want his musings to be overheard by other Karalanths.

'But on a lighter note,' the old Karalanth glanced at Asaph, his greying beard and pale antlers catching the light of the bonfire, 'the last Dragon Lord has returned to the world, so there is hope again. The dark moon rising proves that the goddess is with us. Perhaps under the heir to the throne of Drax and the Queen of Ravens we could all unite, unite the Free Peoples of Maioria.'

The look in Triest'anth's eyes and the weight he suddenly placed upon his shoulders felt enough to break him. All the thoughts he'd had earlier about uniting the people with the Feylint Halanoi now seemed a huge, impossible task.

'That's what we all need, to be united, but how it can be done I have no idea. We were lucky to survive this attack. We only barely did so,' Asaph said wiping his eyes with his good hand.

'With the Raven Queen at your side, you'll find a way,' Triest'anth said. 'I've never been so sure about anything than I am about this. The world needs a powerful symbol to unite under. A Dragon Lord returns, the dark moon rises and the Raven Queen is chosen by Zanufey... This is exactly what the people need to rise up under. You bring a bright dawn, Asaph the Dawn Bringer.'

He coloured, and Triest'anth smiled at him in a fatherly way. Perhaps it was the thrill and near death experience of the fighting that made the old Karalanth speak so profoundly. The vicious battle had certainly made them all aware of how perilous their lives were now.

'There will be many more battles and dark times ahead, but stay close to her and she to you. We have a chance to end the immortal bastard's reign over us,' Triest'anth said. He must have glimpsed his worried frown for his solemn face broke again into a warm smile. Asaph nodded but said nothing. He was tired, far too tired to think anymore.

The last of the dead were still being brought to the now smouldering pyre and laid gently upon it. Triest'anth went to help a Karalanth struggling under the weight of a large deer-man. Asaph didn't know who it was, didn't want to know. He only hoped that whoever it was, took many death hounds with him before he died. He came to a stop a few paces from the pyre, feeling at a loss at what to do.

'We will pray to Zanufey to lead our dead into Woetala's peaceful, endless forests. They died a warrior's death, and there's no greater glory than that,' Grast'anth said gruffly, blinking back tears. 'Finally, the war has come to us and we must strengthen our minds, our bodies and our hearts.'

There was nothing Asaph could say. Seeing the dead washed away any sense of victory from his mind and replaced it with a horrible, gut-wrenching sadness. Victory wasn't supposed to feel like this. Not only had he fought and killed one of his brethren—killing a Dromoorai and its Dread Dragon was not something he thought he would ever be able to do—many Karalanths had lost their lives in a battle that they shouldn't have had to fight. Maybe Coronos sensed what he was feeling, or maybe it was just coincidence, but his father tried to ease his sadness.

'Dromoorai are not one of us, Asaph. Their souls are long gone and whatever inhabits those two bodies is not human or dragon. The goddess only knows what it is. Don't think you killed your own today. Think of it as setting them free, free from a life of slavery serving Baelthrom and killing countless innocents. I saw you fight magnificently today and would have helped if I could.' Coronos showed him his own bound arm that had seeped blood through the bandage.

Asaph smiled and blinked back tears.

Issa was aware that someone was carrying her, but her eyes were so blurred with fatigue she could not see who it was. She drifted somewhere between reality and the swirling energies of the Flow. It was as if she had used so much of the Flow that she was somehow trapped in it, floating on a sea of purple and blue with no ability to control her direction or her thoughts.

She focused on the recent battle as a way to somehow anchor herself in reality. The Dromoorai had come. She'd seen Baelthrom in that awful red amulet. Then a ball of golden fire took it away. Asaph was the fire—a golden dragon who fought with such passion and fury that no lifeless immortal could match him.

The Karalanths were dying. Issa's subconscious mind had felt their souls leaving; each soul, a star shooting across a night sky, leaving the mortal world to return once more to the One Source. *Beloved Zanufey lead your children home.*

In the Flow, dark blue swirled and formed into an indistinct figure. She turned her focus upon it, felt herself smile as a feeling of love surrounded her. She seemed to move above the Flow then and everything fell away, including the pain of her physical body.

She sat cross-legged in darkness. Her head was clear and her body pain-free. The air was cool, and she realised it wasn't totally dark. The night sky above was filled with twinkling stars. A desert stretched out in all directions, and the huge trilithon was before her. A figure robed in stars stood in front of it.

Was it really Zanufey? She wondered as she did every time. It seemed too much to be real, that the Night Goddess was stood before her now, communing with her as if they were both ordinary people. The figure stepped lightly towards her, alabaster chin and pale pink lips all that was visible beneath her cloak. She smiled warmly down at Issa, and she found herself smiling up, filled with love and awe.

'If it weren't for me they would not have died,' she said. It seemed the most important thing to say.

Zanufey spoke, her voice echoing in Issa's mind. 'They chose their lives and their deaths before they came into the mortal worlds. Your presence and connection to me ensured their souls did not get ensnared by the immortal web surrounding Maioria.'

Issa considered this. The implications were too deep for her to understand easily. She helped them get free? They chose how they would die? Had this all been decided before? She looked up questioningly at Zanufey, sensing she could read her thoughts. Those pale lips only smiled.

'Many souls will choose to leave their bodies in the coming years. Your gifts help set them free, so they do not become trapped.'

'How do I assist them?' Issa asked.

'By being,' Zanufey said.

Issa frowned, struggling to understand. 'I'm here to help them get free? Even if Baelthrom destroys us all and takes Maioria?'

'The future has not been decided,' Zanufey said, retaining that same wise, enigmatic smile.

'Are you worried?' Issa asked.

'No.'

'Do you care?' she felt bad for asking the question.

'Endlessly. Worry cannot exist when there is only love,' Zanufey said.

Issa found the reply even more confusing and thought her mind and consciousness must be very small. She felt tired and found herself drifting back down into the swirling energies of the Flow once more.

They tried to carry Issa to her bed, but she awoke suddenly and protested so loudly that Grast'anth was forced to return her to where the Karalanths stood beside the funeral pyre. Asaph helped her sit on his lap and held her close as Grast'anth led the funeral rites. He had expected Triest'anth to do it, or Cusap'anth, being the leader, but the grief on Cusap'anth's face told him everything. He blinked back his own tears.

'Blessed Woetala, today many of our people have left their mortal bodies behind and are with Zanufey on their way to you. They are all heroes and must be honoured as such,' Grast'anth spoke strong and firm, though tears filled his eyes.

The tears would not come to Issa, and instead, she said a silent prayer to Zanufey as Grast'anth continued.

Beloved Zanufey, I won't cry for those who released their mortal bodies today for you have told me they are free. If I cry for them, it defeats their purpose, and mine. If I cry, I think I will never stop.

Brave, courageous warriors loved by Woetala. You died a hero's death fighting for freedom. Zanufey will lead you home, into the eternal light from which we all came.

Grast'anth finished speaking, and silence descended on the grieving Karalanths. Tears glistened on everyone's faces as flaming torches were thrown upon the bodies and the pyre became a roaring blaze.

'Come, let us celebrate the deaths of these mighty warriors,' Cusap'anth boomed. Despite the sorrow in his face, he raised his arms wide as if to lift everyone from their gloom. One by one they began to cheer, louder and louder until the whole forest echoed with their voices

Issa allowed the exuberant feeling of victory to wash over her for the first time. Today she had proven to herself her own worth as a warrior and something more. Understanding the power of her magic had saved her as much as quick thinking and use of her sword. She felt the warrior within truly awakening. She looked up at Asaph cradling her with his good arm. He looked down at her.

'You feel it?' she asked. She wasn't sure if she meant their victory or the powers within them awakening. Perhaps she meant both.

He smiled a smile that she would never forget, one mixed with grief and loss, and yet filled with awe and an unbreakable resolve.

'I feel it,' he said, and she reflected his smile back.

CHAPTER 45

Baelthrom's Determination

HAMEKA sat bolt upright in his bed, his face covered in sweat and the sheets twisted around him. *Sodding ravens!* They had been attacking him, hundreds of them, all scratching at his face and pecking at his eyes. Then *she'd* stood before him, dressed in Dread Dragon armour, crowned in black feathers, blue-green eyes glaring.

He couldn't get rid of her cold, knowing and infinitely aggravating face from his mind. She'd looked right into his soul, and he'd seen his death in her eyes. Breathing deeply, he wiped the sweat from his forehead with the back of his equally damp hand. His throat felt as if it had been strangled and his eyes watered from the memory of those awful pecking beaks.

The girl that had entertained him last night lay slumped unconscious on the floor, a few spots of blood on her torn shirt and nothing more to indicate his experimental tortures. Techniques he had been exploring intended for the woman whose face he could not now banish from his mind. Strangely, seeing the unconscious woman calmed him. Odd that a human could make him feel better knowing how much he despised them.

He stood up, poured a glass of water and sucked the lukewarm liquid down his parched throat, pressing the cooler glass against his forehead once he was done. He had to get off this bloody ship. He hated being at sea, but at least it gave him time to think and plan. He liked to think and plan, it was what he was good at. Well, it was either this or fly upon one of those horrendous dragons. He preferred feeling something solid beneath his feet, even if it was floating on an endless ocean.

The girl on the floor moaned. Her dark hair was plastered in sweat to her red-blotched face. He'd liked this one, she'd shown spirit, so he had decided to let her recover a little before resuming. He trickled some water into her bruised mouth, and she spluttered, one brown eye flickered open, the other was swollen shut.

'Clean yourself up,' he said, tossing her a rag.

With some amusement, he watched her struggle to sit up, then pulled on his own clothes while she covered herself with the tatters of her shirt. He peered out of the porthole. Rain or seawater splattered the glass, marring his view, but the grey light told him it was past dawn.

'Damn.' It was later than he thought, and there was no more time to perfect his torture techniques.

'Guards,' he yelled.

The two Maphraxies guarding his door struggled into the small room. They were barely able to stand upright under the doorway, armour clanking and scraping against each other and the door. The girl shivered and moved groggily away.

'Take her down with the rest,' he said dismissively.

They grasped her arms and dragged her up. She turned her head and spat at him.

'Zanufey damn you,' she snarled, hatred bright in her one good eye.

Impressive. She still had the energy to hate and not fear him. He smiled sweetly back at her, but could not suppress the shiver that ran down his spine as the door shut. He would double the pain on her next time, he thought as he combed his hair. She would fear him in the end, just before he killed her.

He sighed. The cursed dark-haired woman he hunted was not on Celene. That traitorous High Priestess Cirosa knew nothing of her whereabouts and Baelthrom had ordered the Dromoorai to sweep the coasts for her. His other Maphraxie beasts had been sent into the forests of Frayon, likely never to be seen again. What a loss. That girl was his master's obsession. She needed to be found and eliminated quickly. The more Baelthrom focused on the wench, the more it drew his attention away from this war and Hameka's own victories.

As if in response to his thoughts, the Shadow Key at his chest grew warm, its all-absorbing red light began to glow. It was not Baelthrom this time—the amulet always glowed brighter when it was. It was waiting for his acceptance of the communication request. He looked expectantly into it.

'Yes? Where are you?'

'Western Frayon,' the Dromoorai's low and toneless voice replied.

Through the Dromoorai's Shadow Stone Hameka saw her, the dark-haired bitch, trapped beneath the body of a Life Seeker. Alabaster face, sea-green eyes. He could barely contain his excitement. He grasped the amulet.

'Take her. Take her now!' he shouted.

The Dread Dragon angled downwards and reached a giant claw towards her. His eyes bore into hers through the amulet, but he could not penetrate her mind or take control of her. She somehow managed to block him with the Flow. Frustrated, he searched for a way in, looking for any weakness in her mind shield. There was none. He pushed harder, scratching and smashing, but her mind barred him like a wall of impenetrable metal.

Suddenly the world he looked upon lurched and his probing mind was ripped painfully from hers. He clutched the amulet so hard his knuckles cracked, and the gold frame pierced his palm. He closed his eyes against the rising nausea. The world slowly ceased its tumbling, and he opened them again to catch glimpses of another dragon made of gold. He stared dumbly as the aerial battle unfolded. The golden dragon wrapped around the Dread Dragon in a crushing embrace.

'Kill it and get the girl!' Hameka screamed, his voice shaking with fury and desperation. But he watched in disbelief as the girl was largely forgotten and all the Dromoorai could do was try to stay mounted upon his spinning, writhing mount.

There should be no more dragons. They were dead or asleep, permanently. Baelthrom saw to that. But now he watched a massive golden dragon fighting Baelthrom's most prized possessions. They crashed to the ground and the world stopped spinning. The dragons lunged at each other. In the struggling blur, the Dromoorai was flung from its mount, and he lost sight of the battle.

'Get up and kill it. Get the girl,' he screamed again.

The Dromoorai got up and went towards the battling dragons. The golden one wrenched and dropped the Dread Dragon's shredded, lifeless throat.

'No!' Hameka yelled.

The Dromoorai swung his claymore, but the golden dragon was no match for it and easily dodged. The air shimmered and the dragon began to change. He watched the dragon transform into a man like some awful play created to mock him. His blood turned cold. There *were* no Dragon Lords. This had to be a trick; magic or enchantments. Regardless of what he thought, there the tall reddish-blond man stood, and looked every bit as Draxian as the people he had fought and destroyed so many years ago—as tall and proud as the people still imprisoned in his dungeons in Draxa.

'Kill him now, quickly while he's a man,' he growled, nervous excitement kept him clutching the amulet to his face. Dromoorai were powerful, even without their dragons, and they could wield magic. But this was no ordinary man, this was a Dragon Lord, and deep down he feared the Dromoorai would be no match for him.

'This one cannot be a trained Dragon Lord. He is young,' he said through the amulet. 'He won't be that powerful.'

His assumption turned out to be correct. The blond man was not as fast as the Dragon Lords he had fought against nearly three decades ago. He moved a little too slowly and nervously, and twice he hesitated as if he had never faced a foe like the Dromoorai. Hameka's luck had changed, and now the Dragon Lord was pinned beneath the boot of the Dromoorai.

'Take him to the brink of death and keep him there. We need to replace our missing Dread Dragon,' he commanded with a smile. The Dromoorai moved to obey.

Thinking the battle was done, he was about to look away, but there came a blinding flash. It burned through his eyes making him cry out and drop the amulet. The pain went quickly, but his vision did not return immediately. Cursing, he searched the floor for the amulet, found it and blinked into the bloodstone. The image and the connection were gone. He tried to reconnect, but it seemed as if there was nothing to connect to. He rubbed the amulet and shook it, willing the images to reappear, but again, nothing. The stone remained empty and dull.

He sat back, blinking in disbelief. With a howl, he hurled it across the room where it bounced off the wall unharmed. He smashed his fists down upon the desk, the wood creaking under the assault. Breathing deeply for several moments, he forced composure on himself, refusing to let his emotions take control of him. He smoothed back his hair and went to retrieve the stone.

So, the Dromoorai had been in Western Frayon. No doubt the girl and that cursed dragon would be on the move soon. The blasted Feylint Halanoi were still concentrated in the north, but in a few months, the Maphraxies could attack the relatively undefended west coast before the Halanoi had a chance to even organise themselves. If Lord Baelthrom was not obsessed with this stupid girl, they could be planning their attacks this very moment.

'We'll hunt them down,' he said aloud. No Dragon Lord could remain hidden for long. Lord Baelthrom would be pleased to hear of another to add to his Dromoorai if he managed to gloss over the one they'd just lost.

With calm and some hope restored, he looked into the Shadow Stone again, seeking counsel with his Lord.

'Tell me, Hameka, something I want to hear,' his lord's voice echoed around the room before his image fully materialised, and he did not sound happy. Hameka suppressed a weary sigh.

'The girl, my lord, is somewhere in the forests of Western Frayon. A Life Seeker and Dromoorai found her but then... something happened.'

Baelthrom's eyes glowered blood red, but he said nothing. Hameka continued.

'It appears there is another Dragon Lord loose in the world... From where he came I do not know, but together they destroyed the Life Seeker and the Dromoorai, my lord.'

The silence that followed was crushing. Hameka's heart pounded until he was sure it had moved from his chest into his brain.

'Hameka, get the girl and bring her to me. Get the Dragon Lord. You have your orders. I do not see what is taking so long. Get her before she becomes a bigger threat than she already is. Our spies speak of the Raven Queen of prophecy, and there are those rallying to her cause. You know how much trouble the rising dark moon has caused, how much harder the humans have been fighting since. If she's not captured soon, I foresee a greater uprising against us than we have ever had before!' Baelthrom's voice boomed so loudly the cabin shook.

He was taken aback by his lord's determination. Yes, the Feylint Halanoi had been fighting harder since the strange dark moon had risen. Yes, it seemed their ranks were more numerous. Yes, they had lost some ground, but not as much as they had gained. Did his Lord really think this girl was such a threat that she could threaten their control of Maioria? He almost laughed aloud, almost. It was clear his Lord was deadly serious about this. and he dared not displease him further, so he managed to keep his mouth shut.

'Never forget, Hameka, that I can see far more than you can with your *human* eyes.'

The comment stung, but he kept his face blank.

'I don't think you quite fathom the threat of the magic that is moving through Maioria of late. It is powerful and dangerous, far beyond anything Keteth ever was. I don't even think our enemies know how powerful this magic is and it's possibly linked to the dark moon, and it's possibly linked to that girl. I want to crush our enemies before they have hope again. This must be done swiftly and it must be done now.'

'Yes, my lord,' he said tightly, but Baelthrom was already gone and the amulet cold and dull. It was the first time his Lord had ever spoken to him in such a displeased manner, and it unnerved him completely. He bit his lip until blood flowed, enjoying the pain that took his mind off his fury.

Baelthrom moved away from the Shadow Master and breathed the cold, damp air of the dark chamber. She was getting stronger with each passing day, and each day he could feel the shift in the energy of the world towards her. It was a power he did not have access to, and yet he could feel the strength of it—magic drawn from the dark moon and from within the earth itself. It was as if Maioria was a living thing, willingly giving her energy to the power of this woman.

His power came from beyond Maioria, beyond the universe of change, beyond life. The more beings he made immortal, the greater his power grew. The balance in the universe had slowly been shifting in his favour, but now, after millennia, the tide was changing.

If only he had her, he could control her. If he controlled her, he could find a way to access the power that was hers, use it for his own and ensure it could never be used against him. Hameka must be growing weak; she should not have escaped so easily.

'I will have her,' he growled, clenching his fists.

He had watched the battle unfold through the Dromoorai's amulet but, he could not break the barrier that she managed to put up. He could have done it, in time, but then the Dragon Lord had come. In his frustration, he had very nearly smashed the Shadow Master.

So, a Dragon Lord returns. The last one. The heir to the throne of Drax. He knew it was the heir, recognised the Dragon Queen's features in his face. What he had to do with the girl, he had no idea, but somehow he was with her, the one they were beginning to call the Raven Queen.

'I always knew the Dragon Queen's child had never been found. It must be him. All other Dragon Lords fell to me decades ago. Now he returns and seeks his vengeance,' Baelthrom breathed aloud, staring into the darkness.

'We will crush them, my lord,' Kilkarn snivelled from behind. 'He will be no trouble, just like the others were no trouble. He will be brought to heel like a dog on a leash and replace the Dromoorai he has slain.'

'Yes, that is true. He will be no trouble,' Baelthrom said. 'But an heir to the Draxian throne is dangerous and could spark an unfortunate uprising.'

'We'll capture him quickly, my lord,' Kilkarn said.

Baelthrom turned to his thoughts. It would not be long now, soon she would be in his grasp, the Dragon Lord would be in chains, and the uprising would fizzle out with a whimper before it had even begun. Then all would crumble and fall to him as the last dregs of hope were finally crushed. Then would his power be complete. He had already waited thousands of years; a few more would not hurt.

She fascinated him in ways he had not felt before. He feared and desired equally the power she possessed, and she barely knew how strong she was. She could not be allowed to know her own power, that was certain.

He stretched his wings, flexed his clenched fists and turned to the iron ring. It burst into a cold blue light. Within its watery surface, he began to map out his plans and view their potential outcomes.

CHAPTER 46

An Untrained Dragon

BEFORE dawn, the dreams came to Issa, and in them a horse made of the night tore across a smoke-filled landscape, his flanks lathered with sweat and foam dripped from his mouth.

'Duskar,' she whispered.

He stumbled in exhaustion but on he galloped, running from something she could not see. He was looking for her; she could feel his thoughts, see her image in his mind. The stench of death and immortals filled the air, cloying and sickly.

She cried out his name but green fog filled the world and made her choke.

She jerked awake. The soft light of dawn filtered through the shuttered window behind her. Coronos and Asaph were still sound asleep. Her racing heart calmed, but the sense of panic remained. She was wide-awake and desperate for fresh air as if her lungs were still filled with that choking green fog.

The dawn light told her she'd slept at least half a day—and that's after sleeping a whole day before. Asaph had also slept for a day, so Rhul'ynth had told her. She still felt weak and weary, despite keeping Ely's healing bracelet on her wrist, and the very thought of using magic made her dizzy. She pulled on her clothes, ignoring her aching arm and ribs, and left the hut.

Grey clouds concealed the sun, and a soft breeze whispered of rain. The smell of the bonfire hung in the air to remind the living of those who had died. The raven was perched on the thatched roof above the doorway as if he had been waiting for her all this time.

'Where have you been?' she scolded. 'I nearly died. Twice!'

The raven ruffled his feathers and stared down at her wide-eyed, seeking forgiveness. She spluttered a laugh at him; all fluffed up and guilty looking.

'Some fearsome bird you are, and you haven't even told me your name yet so it's not like I can call to you.'

Despite the comfort of her companion's presence, the sense of unease remained. She wondered if it had ever really left her since she had tried and failed to scry for Freydel. And now nightmares about Duskar set her on edge. Why was she dreaming of Duskar? Why hadn't Freydel scryed for her?

Her worry deepened. She sighed and slumped her shoulders. Could she not have a day off? She needed a week off at least, and even then she might never be able to use magic again. Imagine that, a day to feel normal again, a day simply to be ordinary. She didn't even know what normal was anymore.

The raven left his perch and landed at her feet, his shiny black head reaching up to her knees. He stumbled as he did so and his wings drooped with fatigue.

'Where in Maioria have you been? Did you find the Cursed King?' she said with a half-smile, only half believing it, but then Zanufey did not lie.

He cawed, and she hushed him to be quiet, not wanting to wake the others. He stopped squawking and hopped about in frustration. It was obvious he wanted to tell her something, but she dreaded what it was. She sighed again. She couldn't ignore his messages, not when he risked life and limb to bring them to her. She hunched down onto her heels.

'All right. Tell me what's up.'

She stroked his feathers, feeling him relax. His intelligent avian mind touched hers and they connected.

A green fog swamped all, dense and thick as in her dream. Dark shapes moved within it; short, squat figures with darting yellow eyes and grey skin. Dark dwarves. She shuddered. Beside them lumbered huge, deformed beasts holding the chains of death hounds. Maphraxies, she thought in disgust. Above them, things flew. Harpies and Dromoorai. Her blood ran cold, and dragon fear knotted her stomach.

There were many Maphraxies, all marching along a path she wished she didn't recognise. She shook her head, not wanting to believe it. It couldn't be Celene, not her new home. The vision rolled on, and Castle Elune came into view, dissipating all doubt. The vision moved fast then as if to spare her the details, but she still glimpsed the horror of black weapons rising and falling upon those who had become her friends.

She sank to the ground, tears of pain and anger rolling down her face. The vision changed.

Duskar's black hooves pounded on the ground in time to the beat of her heart. He fled in from the green fog.

'Duskar…'

The vision changed again. Ely's bloodied, lifeless face. The vision dissipated. She felt numb.

The raven looked downcast and climbed onto her lap where he nestled and tried to comfort her. She stroked his feathers and let fall the tears she had not been able to shed for days.

'Thank you, my friend, for bringing me the truth,' she whispered. He croaked.

Having been awoken by the noisy bird and seeing Issa was missing from her bed, Asaph ran outside, followed by Coronos and Triest'anth.

'Issa, what's wrong?' He knelt before her and pushed back the hair falling around her face. She looked up at him, and he smarted at the terrible sorrow in her eyes.

'Celene was attacked. They're all dead.' She was clearly trying to keep her voice steady, but the sobs broke through. She shook her head. 'I cannot do this. I cannot be this. Whatever is expected of me, it's too painful, too much.'

'Hey,' he hugged her. The raven stayed firmly in her lap eyeing him shrewdly, but he ignored it. 'I know it's hard, I know. But we have to go on. We don't know for sure what's happened.'

He took her face in his hands and smoothed back her hair. Her eyes were wide and lost, filled with pain and still luminous turquoise from overuse of the Flow. 'We can do this. Together. You and I, and Coronos and the Karalanths. We have all suffered great losses, but we're all in this together, we're all on your side.' He spoke these things, and all the while knew he was reassuring himself as well as her. It was painful, by Feygriene's fire it was painful, but they had to carry on.

She nodded and sniffed. 'I must go. Now. I have to get to Celene, somehow. Something terrible has happened.'

'Then I'll go too. We'll go together,' he said firmly.

'I must go as soon as possible, though it's already too late,' she said.

He nodded and turned to Triest'anth. 'I think it would be wise to move the Karalanths far from here. It's no longer safe. I'm certain they'll be back and more of them.'

'Friend, we're already packing. We started yesterday while you were sleeping,' Triest'anth said with a weak smile.

'Come, let us pack too and go,' Coronos said, breaking his worried silence. He disappeared back into the hut.

They worked swiftly and silently. Food and water and the few clothes they had were soon donned or packed. When they left Triest'anth's house for the last time, the whole village was up and about and busy packing their belongings in a similar silence.

Even the day seemed grey and grim to match everyone's mood. When the rain came, it thankfully fell in only a light mist, rather than a downpour to soak them all.

Rhul'ynth and Palu'anth came up to her, both eyeing the raven curiously as they passed. Palu'anth looked drained as Issa embraced him.

She turned to Rhul'ynth, saw the dark circles under her red eyes and didn't need to ask about Fris'anth. A lump rose in her throat preventing her from speaking. Instead, she opened her arms and hugged the deer-woman. The woman hugged her fiercely back.

'I'm so sorry,' Issa whispered.

'It's not your fault,' Rhul'ynth said, softly but firmly. 'Never think that it is. I will avenge him. A fire has ignited in my heart that will not be quenched until I'm dead.'

Rhul'ynth pulled away to look into her eyes. 'Besides, he isn't lost to me, I carry him in my heart and,' she gestured up at a pink and blue jay watching them from the trees, 'his spirit animal is with me now. Life cannot be destroyed,' she smiled.

Issa's eyes filled with tears as she smiled and cried at the same time, her admiration of the deer-woman deepening. 'Your words give me strength, but I fear that even more of my friends have been killed in the hunt for me,' she looked off into the forest.

'The immortals will be coming for everyone, eventually,' Rhul'ynth said. 'Now is the time for us to stand and fight. Which is why we are coming with you, for a little way.'

'No, it's too dangerous. I cannot bear to risk any more lives,' said Issa.

'It's not for you to decide what we do with our lives,' Rhul'ynth replied, smiling, 'and you are not responsible for the choices of others.'

She was struck with the memory of similar words Zanufey had once spoken. 'It's just… You have lost so many already,' she said, knowing that she could not reign in Rhul'ynth's wild spirit, and who was she to say what the Karalanth woman should do anyway?

'We'll come with you as far as we can,' Cusap'anth said, stepping beside them.

'You cannot come,' Asaph said, echoing Issa's words and her worries. He buckled on his sword. 'To get to Celene quickly we must fly, and I can't carry all of us.'

Issa stared at him. She had not ever considered she would be flying on a dragon, but then it would be the quickest way by far.

'True that the forests are infested with death hounds and foltoy and other abominable things,' Cusap'anth agreed, 'but what if you meet another Dromoorai? You'll be much faster than us in the air, but we can move quickly through the forests in the direction you are heading. If you get into trouble, we'll be on the same route and can help.

'Wait, listen to me. There's more to our plan. We intend to rendezvous with our cousin's clan and rally them to our cause; to the Raven Queen, to the Dawn Bringer, to the dark moon, to Karalanthia—maybe even to the Feylint Halanoi.' She saw Triest'anth raise his eyebrows at that, but he said nothing as his son continued. 'From there we'll head south until we reach the shore, and await your return.'

Asaph looked doubtful, but she began to see the importance of it. 'He's right. We're safer if we look out for each other. We need as many people as we can get. If we can't do this, how else can we unite the whole of Maioria against the Maphraxies?'

Asaph sighed then nodded. 'Karalanths really are stubborn,' he muttered. 'All right, we'll meet you on the shores closest to the Isle, but I don't know how long we'll be.'

'Don't worry, I have my owl who will follow you and us,' Cusap'anth added. Asaph frowned.

'They have spirit animals, a bit like that raven of Issa's,' Coronos explained. Everyone smiled and nodded.

Grast'anth approached her. He looked tired but dry-eyed, and she wondered how many battles he had fought in his lifetime, he seemed a hardened warrior. He was followed by Diarc'ynth, a sorrowful smile on her young face as she watched her friends get ready to leave. Issa was relieved to see her alive and squeezed her arm.

'I thought you'd better have one of these,' Grast'anth said, holding out a wickedly sharp short sword. He sheathed it and passed it to her grinning. 'For my favourite student.'

'I'm your only student,' she chuckled, taking the sword and gasping when he embraced her roughly.

'Remember everything I've taught you. You may be the Raven Queen to others, but to me, you are still my student.'

She hugged the big Karalanth, blinking back the tears that threatened overwhelm her again and wishing for all the world that she was indeed just his pupil. She looked up into his wise brown eyes. 'You've done so much for us, words cannot really express my thanks.'

He simply nodded and took her hands. 'We will meet again, Queen of Ravens,' he said and bowed.

Issa picked up her sack and began walking away from the village with the others, the raven circling them close. At the edge of the forest, they waved goodbye and headed towards the clearing where Asaph could change form and take off easily without spreading dragon fear through the village.

It was an awesome moment as the air around him shimmered. In the Flow, it was a golden mist sparkling in the shape of a dragon surrounding the man. The magic that flowed around him felt ancient, wild and free. The Flow surged and there stood before her was a huge dragon, scales gleaming in the rain, huge tail curled gracefully around equally huge legs. His talons were as thick as her arms and deadly sharp, his wings were folded neatly on his back. Golden horns curved up beside his long ears, and his sapphire eyes blinked as he considered his new form.

Awe gave way to fear. She shivered and sweat rolled down her back. She tried to pretend she was calm and unaffected by the dragon fear, but she was frozen in terror. The raven hopped madly around her feet, squawking. All she could do was move her eyes a little to side-glance at the others.

Coronos gripped his staff in one white-knuckled hand and looked about to pull out his beard in the other, but his face was otherwise unreadable. Cusap'anth's legs trembled uncontrollably, and he was trying to look everywhere but at the massive winged serpent in front of him.

Palu'anth had an arrow in one hand and a knife in the other, looking at each in confusion as if he didn't know what they were for. His face was a mask of sweat. Rhul'ynth was so white she looked ready to faint. Diarc'ynth's mouth hung uselessly open, and her eyes seemed about to pop out of her head. The raven stopped squawking, lodged its head between her feet and pretended to be dead.

Only when her heart pounded less could she bring herself to look at Asaph again. There was still a shimmer in the air as if he kept some magic around him, and he had curled up tighter and sat lower on his haunches as if trying to make himself as small as possible. He avoided looking at anyone directly and held a remarkably placid and sleepy look on his otherwise expressionless face.

Was he trying to protect them from the dragon fear by trying to make himself seem small and harmless? A small, high-pitched laugh escaped her lips. People began to twitch and come back to life. She wiped a shaky hand across her sweaty brow.

'Phew, glad that's over,' she said, breaking the silence. There came a few nervous laughs from the others. The fear didn't go completely, and she was certain that he sensed it as all animals could. He turned his head to look at her, but she could not meet those massive eyes and pretended to be busy with her bag.

'Please don't fear me,' he said in a surprisingly soothing voice for a dragon.

Issa swallowed. 'I'm, uh, not scared, heh,' she smiled back and darted her eyes away.

Asaph gave a low sigh as if saddened. Maybe he wanted her to feel safe and protected in his company, not afraid. He tried to smile, perhaps in reassurance, but ended up baring his huge teeth in what looked more like a growl. Her eyes widened, and her heart pounded. He immediately stopped smiling.

'Dragons cannot smile,' he rumbled and looked away.

'It makes me sad knowing you fear me.' A deep, soft voice said, carrying with it ancient wisdom.

Issa jumped and dropped her bag. He had spoken to her with his mind, just like the Wykiry had, and Keteth.

'I didn't know you could mind-speak,' she said, awkward and rusty with the skill.

'It seems to be a natural part of being a dragon. It seems all magical creatures can. And yet I cannot commune with you like this as a man.'

'No, well, I guess we'll have to make do with spoken words then,' said Issa.

'I'll never harm you. I want you to feel protected by my dragon self,' he said, the tenderness in his voice surprising her.

'I'll try, but it's pure instinct and I—' she was cut off by Coronos.

'You two may be able to speak with your minds, but we all know you are doing it,' Coronos grinned. They stared back at him. The Karalanths were also grinning knowingly with arms folded. Asaph snorted.

'Oh,' she said, her cheeks growing hot. 'Sorry. I didn't know we could commune like this. Perhaps it's rude. Only the Wykiry and Keteth have spoken to me this way. I can commune with some animals too, but they talk in pictures, and only sometimes.'

'All Karalanths are what you humans call Daluni,' Cusap'anth said. 'That's how we communicate to our spirit animals. But, as you say, only when they will it' he huffed.

Coronos set about arranging his makeshift harness of ropes and blankets with as much aid as Asaph could offer, and inched himself up onto his back. Asaph didn't seem too impressed.

'We should get something safer and more secure made,' Asaph grumbled.

'Indeed. Which village shall we stop in to place our order for a dragon harness? Who would you like to take your measurements? Which smithy would you prefer to test that it's fireproof?' Coronos asked lightly. Asaph snorted a cloud of smoke that made his father cough.

'The best harnesses were made to a design probably long since destroyed in Drax. But in saying that, perhaps with the help of the orb, I could sketch out what I remember. It took a lot of dragon scales and iron rings as far as I could work out,' Coronos scratched his head thoughtfully. He turned and pulled a rope tight.

'There, we're all set and ready to go,' he looked proudly at the mess of ropes around Asaph's neck and back and began climbing up them. He turned and his gaze settled on her. This was the part she had been dreading.

'I've been thinking,' she began, 'that I'll probably be of more use down here with the Karalanths.' It was lame, but the thought of jumping on the dragon's back, much less flying on it, made her sick.

'Nonsense. Get up here, Raven Queen, before I come down there and carry you,' Coronos said firmly, amusement dancing in his eyes.

Before she knew what was happening, Cusap'anth had grabbed her waist and Rhul'ynth her legs. She squirmed as they carried her to the amused-looking dragon.

'All right, set me down! Will you quit hoisting me about all the time,' she squealed.

They laughed and plonked her onto a massive golden paw. With a loud sigh, she took Coronos' out-stretched hand and with some difficulty clambered up Asaph's shoulder.

'We'll head off now,' Cusap'anth said. 'See you soon,' he winked, and with a short wave goodbye, the Karalanths bounded off into the forest.

'Flying is a cold business,' Coronos explained as he settled down in front of her and secured the ropes and blankets. 'I'll be flying and controlling the dragon, having been a Dragon Rider,' he added.

Asaph seemed remarkably deaf to anything his rider was saying and, despite Coronos pulling on the ropes to go one way, he ignored him and turned in the opposite direction.

'This is an untrained dragon,' Coronos cautioned over his shoulder with a chuckle. Asaph snorted smoke again and made them both cough.

She clung to Coronos' waist as Asaph stood up and spread his wings. Flying as a raven was a far different game to flying on the back of something else. She closed her eyes as he bunched his legs, then squealed in terror as they launched violently into the air. The air whooshed past, but she couldn't bring herself to open her eyes. The make-do harness seemed remarkably weak and flimsy, but Coronos laughed in delight, clearly loving the take-off part of the journey.

Only when they began to level out did she open one eye and peek under his' arm. The green forest was a blur below. Every now and then, she glimpsed the brown form of a Karalanth galloping between the trees, but they were slowly dropping behind. She prayed to Zanufey that they would be all right. She sat relatively comfortably behind Coronos, still gripping his waist, though the rain had soaked them through, somewhat diminishing the glory of flying on a dragon.

'Aren't you scared?' she shouted over the rushing wind. Coronos laughed.

'No. I used to ride dragons all day, every day when I was a commander in the Draxian army. They're smaller than Dragon Lords though, and it was a long time ago. You just have to hang on tight,' he shouted over his shoulder.

His words did little to reassure her. She would have preferred to fly as a raven and join her companion following behind if she hadn't felt so weak and exhausted. Flying as a raven seemed so natural; a human riding atop a dragon was definitely not natural. She closed her eyes and tried not to think about it.

'Can he fly at night?' she asked a few hours later as the grey day darkened.

'Yes, though it's not preferred. Dragons can see well in the dark, but flying at night is more dangerous—it's harder to see the enemy,' Coronos said.

'How long will it take to get to Celene?' she said.

He shrugged. 'I've never flown this path before. It depends on the wind currents mostly. Though I would say all night. Asaph may have to rest depending on how tired he is.'

Issa nodded and settled back into her harness. For the next few hours as darkness fell and the rain blessedly stopped, she thought of Ely. She had been too busy to think about her friend, but now there was nothing to do, worry clamped around her stomach and the raven's visions plagued her.

Why had Freydel not sent her a warning? Could the raven's message be about the future? Though she wanted to believe it, the vision was simply too clear to be so. How long had it taken the raven to find her? And then there was that dream about Duskar—how many nights ago was that? Two? But before that, there had been another dream where he was trapped in his stable. Despite the knots of worry in her stomach, she found herself drifting in and out of an exhausted slumber.

She roused when a warm breeze blew through her hair. She blinked and rubbed her eyes. Either they were descending where it was warmer or the dawn was coming. It turned out to be a mixture of both as they burst through a cloud. She looked to the horizon where the brightness was growing. The rain had stopped a while ago, but they were still soaked through.

Far below, the forest had been replaced by a calm sea and many islands of various shapes and sizes. Some were just rocks that white waves pounded against, others were big enough to have tiny coves with turquoise waters and palm trees. The palms reminded her of Celene, and for a moment—for the first time in a long time—she actually felt like she was returning home.

Everything would be fine, she tried to convince herself. The raven had only delivered a warning, and they had come in time to stop it. She breathed the warm air filled with the scent of the sea and allowed the relief wash over her. She would have a long hot bath and chat to Maeve about everything that had happened. She would wear that dress Ely had given her and they would have a banquet.

Asaph and Coronos could meet Freydel, and she would take them to see Duskar. It was going to be wonderful. Asaph would love Celene, she was sure of it. Perhaps they could build a house there together to be their new home. The wonderful thoughts filled her with such relief and joy that she felt tears come to her eyes. They could even fly to see Edarna. Maybe they could convince her to come to Celene as well. The villagers could do with a witch. How wonderful it would be to have everyone together.

CHAPTER 47

The White Owl

IN the weak candlelit gloom of her cell, Cirosa blearily watched the dark dwarf. He opened a black box and drew out a small, conical-shaped flask made of thick blue glass. She lay on the cold hard floor in only her undergarments. She loathed the way the dark dwarf's yellow eyes stared lustfully at her bare legs and imagined the satisfaction of sinking a knife into him.

But the light in the bottle lifted her horror and filled her with wonder. Within the blue glass danced the most brilliant white light she had ever seen as if a firefly were captured therein. It filled the cell with beautiful rays, suddenly illuminating the tall, black-cloaked figures huddling around her.

She shrank from the necromancers, the beauty of the light forgotten. Her heart began to pound. She tried to sit up but found her arms and legs were bound. She tried to think, but her mind was hazy and when she moved her head everything lurched. She'd been drugged. What were they doing to her? She tried to remember how she'd got here, but could not.

The rising panic could find no outlet as she lay there unable to move and the black figures crowded closer. Their cold breath on her skin made it crawl, and the staleness of it made her gag and long for fresh air. She tried to see their faces, but they were hidden in the hoods of their black robes. Her body trembled, and sweat prickled all over.

Pale, icy hands grasped her mouth and forced it open. She was too weak from the drugging to resist. A metal funnel was shoved in place, forcing her jaws apart. She stared in horror up at the dark dwarf as he unstopped the flask, lifted it to his fat, squashed nose and closed his eyes, revelling in the smell of it.

Her soul shrank from it. *It is not the Black Drink, it is not!* But the light dancing inside was enchanting. She caught the barest whiff of sweetness, and her mind reeled with desire. Whatever was in that bottle was beautiful and divine, purity encapsulated, and she wanted nothing more than to stare at it forever—to smell its holiness, to taste its divinity. And all the while her soul trembled in terror.

The dark dwarf lifted the elixir and poured it into the metal funnel held down her throat. Moments later, he snatched the bottle up to his lips and slurped up the drips, snorting any essence that remained within the bottle.

The funnel was pulled out, and her mouth clamped tightly shut by those deathly cold hands. Other hands stroked her throat, almost tenderly, as they made her swallow the strange liquid.

The Sirin Derenax was so cold it burned. With it being poured straight into her throat, she couldn't tell exactly what it tasted of, but she caught the faintest sickly sweet smell-taste. It was how the Maphraxies smelled. It was the Black Drink, and yet it didn't seem so bad. It felt almost wonderful, and she wanted to taste it again. Then she forgot about the dark dwarf and the necromancers.

The cool liquid slipped into her stomach, and it felt as if she had swallowed ice. Her body convulsed once and then began to shake with the cold. She was freezing from within. She tried to scream for help, but all that came out was a weak moan. The convulsions came again, one after the other, shaking her so violently the necromancers had to hold her down. The cords restraining her wrists and ankles dug deeply into her skin.

The coldness was spreading through her veins and grasping her lungs. She tried to gasp but couldn't breathe. She began choking. Pain like nothing else exploded through her body and felt as if each cell had been set on fire.

'Your weak, mortal body is dying,' the dark dwarf said in an excited voice as he leaned close. His feverish yellow eyes burned into hers and his breath was different from the necromancers, hot and stinking of rotting meat. 'You cannot fight it. Your soul will soon belong to Baelthrom. The Elixir of Immortality kills from within, replacing all inferior living cells with immortal ones.

'You are most fortunate indeed. Our Great One requested the finest elixir be given to you,' the dark dwarf's eyes were wide with reverent wonder.

Cirosa could say nothing; her whole being was taken up with what was happening inside of her and the immense agony. It seemed each cell froze and then burst into flame again and again. Her heart beat loud and so fast she thought it would burst, and then it would drop to nothing and was so weak she began to pass out. Her body was being cleansed of its life force, and there was nothing she could do.

She silently begged for unconsciousness, even for death, anything to release her from this unbearable pain. But consciousness would not let her go, it was the last thing clinging to her dying body.

An eternity must have passed when her mind finally fled from her body into a world of nightmares. She ran in darkness from a monster that thundered after her. The ground shook, and there came the snapping sound of a hundred jaws as the beast closed in. She glanced behind and screamed.

A huge, dragon-like beast with a hundred heads snaked towards her. Those heads turned into her own, mirroring her howls of horror a hundred-fold. Their eyes cried blood, and their teeth were rows of gleaming fangs. They descended upon her, and she screamed again as their teeth ripped into her flesh and began devouring her.

Then the beast vanished, and she lay bleeding on the ground. The Immortal Lord materialised out of the darkness, his armour clanking as he stepped towards her; his clawed feet scraping, tail swinging and black cloak billowing. Triangular eyes hidden beneath a tripartite helmet smouldered the darkest blue. He held a gauntleted hand forward, and from it white light came and surrounded her, lifting her from the floor. She looked down and found her bloodied body healed and whole.

'Thank you,' she sobbed.

The light continued to spread from his hand filling everything, even himself until he appeared to be made of white light. Only his eyes shone black in the whiteness. The energy began to fill her, and she moaned in the ecstasy and omnipotence that came with it. She could be anything, do anything, have anything with this power. She breathed it in with all her being.

'More,' she gasped and was not denied. More came and yet still more she wanted. It caressed her body and her whole being, filling her with euphoria, giving her all the power she had ever desired.

'See the things that I can give you?' his voice vibrated through her, a beautiful, harmonious sound that made her tremble.

She nodded reverently. 'Yes, my lord.'

'The goddess has abandoned this world. Now it's time for a real, worthier god. I am that God, and I give you a life of power and magic, a life without end. Do you serve me?' His last words boomed around her, shaking her body.

She nodded. 'With everything that I am, I will serve you.'

He laughed a deep, rich, triumphant laugh. It pleased her immensely that she had pleased him and she laughed softly in ecstasy.

'Go. Enjoy the gifts that I, your Immortal Lord, have bestowed upon you and upon all my faithful servants. Bring others to me to bend to my will. Bring them so that we may all be free. Free from the goddess forever.'

'The goddess is dead. I embrace you, my Lord,' she said in adulation, glorying in the power that coursed through her. True power, real power, power the silent goddess had never bestowed upon her.

Yet deep within her mind, sadness pooled like clotting, lifeless blood. In that dying blood, knowledge and grief mingled, whispering their secrets over and over; *"There is no life without love."*

The Sirin Derenax stilled those voices until they were gone forever as the light of Cirosa's life force went out, and consciousness faded. She had no use for love now, her soul had embraced oblivion.

Hameka stormed up the wooden stairs and thrust open the door to the main deck. He was met with battering wind and sheets of rain that made him gasp.

The Maphraxie captain watched him approach and shuffled nervously. Already three of the crew had been thrown overboard this day for failing to increase their speed, despite the terrible wind that blew them in every direction but forwards.

Hameka stared at the captain's ugly face. He was sure excessive consumption of the Sirin Derenax made Maphraxies stupider in the same measure that it made them stronger.

'How long until we reach West Frayon?' he barked.

'Commander, the answer is still two days,' the captain said meekly, grovelling so low his great bulk almost toppled forwards. Hameka smashed his fist down on the railing. The crew hastily busied themselves with the rigging, and no one looked in his direction.

'We are running out of time. Whatever it takes to get there sooner, do it,' Hameka shouted. 'Even if it means abandoning all supplies and losing half the crew!'

He turned and stormed back inside, not waiting for the captain's response. If he had not left then, he would have thrown the captain overboard, and he needed the captain to get them to their destination.

He had to get off this cursed ship, it was all he could do to keep himself entertained with his prisoners. He stood there for a moment, breathing hard, soaking wet but glad to be out of the wind and rain. He had to get a grip on his emotions, they were destroying his logic. An idea came to him, and he stalked towards Cirosa's prison cell down in the hull of the ship.

Unlocking the steel-enforced wooden door, he entered the pitch-black cell. The air was stale and sweaty and clung to him. He clicked an oil lamp alight, casting the cell in a pale yellow glow. The woman on the floor had her hands manacled behind her back, and she was chained by the throat to the wooden beams above her. There was just enough chain to let her lie on the floor. Two days had passed since she had taken the Sirin Derenax and the changes were nearly complete.

She got unsteadily to her feet and squinted at him in the light. She had been kept in isolated darkness all this time. Her yellow hair was now platinum white and her skin pale and bloodless. Her blue eyes were much paler than before; blue like ice. Only her lips retained any colour, more than they had before. Now they were almost blood red. Those lips formed into a tentative smile that did not reach her cold eyes.

So, she had gone more the way the necromancers go; all the colour sucked out of her. She would probably then have some ability to command the black magic of the Under Flow, if only a little at first.

She was sharply beautiful, more so than she had been before, but he found it a frigid, deadly and alien beauty. Maybe now she was no longer human he could muster up a small amount of respect for her. But that, of course, depended on how well she served him. She stared up at him now unblinking, still as a statue, and the room grew colder under her gaze. She hated him, it was tangible, and that was good, hate was useful. He smiled equally coldly back at her.

'It's time for you to prove your usefulness to us,' he said matter-of-factly, eyeing her up and down as he circled her. Her chains rattled as she shifted her weight. Was she nervous? It was impossible to tell. She would not be cold. Immortals never felt the cold. She could be hungry. Some still needed to eat food as well as sip the elixir to keep their bodies functional. Some needed only the elixir. If they needed food then liquids were best—blood from the living was best, human blood was better. If she needed food, she would have to go without. It was not his job to feed anything.

'It seems that the dark-haired bitch is aided by a Dragon Lord. It turns out that she has escaped our clutches a second time!' He barked the last and stopped in front of her, his voice echoing off the walls. For all the immortal changes brought about by the Elixir of Immortality—such as removing the lesser emotions of empathy and compassion—the elixir made hatred and fury burn brighter. She continued to glare at him, seemingly completely unafraid.

'I'm sure a woman with your... attributes can find and ensnare this Dragon Lord,' he said suggestively. She smiled again, her lips becoming a thin red line.

'With this precious gift the Immortal Lord has given me, I'm sure such things are feasible. Besides, this Dragon Lord is just a man,' she said acidly, 'and all men are weak.'

He smiled, unaffected by her venom, and grabbed hold of her metal collar. He jerked her to her feet, inserted a key into the lock and let the collar drop from her throat. He spun her around roughly and unlocked her manacles. They fell to the floor with a clang, and she rubbed her wrists. He grabbed her chin and pushed his face close to hers.

'If you fail at this, I will kill you,' he said simply. Her face remained cool and expressionless. 'Take this but hide it from them, they may have discovered its importance,' he shoved into her hands a Shadow Stone. She looked at it, then hung it around her neck and tucked it under her robes. He stalked out of her cell leaving the door open.

Cirosa watched Hameka go, glad to be alone again. So, he was the Immortal Lord's favourite. It was a pity, her lord could do so much better.

'When I'm done with her, I'll come for you,' she rasped after him.

She breathed deeply and stretched her arms. Her body felt different; strong like iron but heavy like death, and now she could feel magic all around her like she never had before. The Immortal Lord's black magic she felt as a subtle hum in the ear, a shade of blackness in the corner of her eye.

She stroked her arms; her skin was ice to the touch and hard where once it had been soft. She lusted with an insatiable desire for more of the

Sirin Derenax, it was a fire that burned within. She had been terrified of becoming one of those brain dead monsters, but the dark dwarf said they had given her a stronger purer elixir.

Now that she was free of the goddess, and no longer gripped by gut-wrenching guilt for betraying her, she found she despised the goddess in all her forms. The goddess had imprisoned her in a weak body and denied her any power.

'Look at me now, *Great Mother*,' she hissed into the darkness. 'Powerful gifts I deserved for so long are finally mine. Gifts that even you can not imagine.'

'Cirosa,' she tongued her name as if for the first time. Yes, that had been her name. The memories of who she had been before felt foreign as if they belonged to someone else, a lesser being. *One day I will be stronger than Hameka, and then I will remove him and bask in the favoured light of the Lord.*

She stepped out of her cell, feeling power fill her body with energy. She turned right to where the stairs led up and eventually found her way out onto the deck.

The wind and rain tore at her body, yet it could not so much as shift her. She was solid, like a rock. Even in only her undergarments, she did not feel the cold. Her dead body was immune to the physical elements. The dark dwarves stared hungrily at her white legs. She looked at them each in turn, projecting into their minds images of how they would die. She smiled as she watched the colour drain from their faces. One collapsed onto the deck shaking and then lay still. Hopefully dead, she thought, feeling nothing for the pathetic dwarves.

She came to the starboard and jumped easily onto the wooden railings, balancing perfectly despite the ships pitch and roll in the lashing waves. Turning her gaze eastward she stared at the rain clouds and after a moment raised her arms. Wind and rain gathered in billows around her as she pulled upon the Under Flow, marvelling at how easily it came to do her bidding.

Her whole pathetic life she had watched that idiot wizard Freydel use magic and never been able to touch it herself. Now that power was hers. She focused inwards and two faces formed in her mind; one female, pale-skinned, green-eyed and dark-haired; the other male, tanned, with fair hair and blue eyes. She laughed aloud, not caring who heard her or what they thought. She was more powerful than they anyhow.

She crouched and leapt off the railings. Dark magic flared around her. Her arms sprouted white feathers, her nose curved and hardened and her feet lengthened into talons. The wind filled her wings, lifting her high into the air. Upwards she circled until she was above the soaking rain.

East Cirosa flew in her white owl form. East to hunt down her prey.

CHAPTER 48

Mark of Maphrax

THE sun broke over the sea and spread its warm rays over them. Issa closed her eyes, and let light fall upon her face. Perhaps the clouds would all dissipate, and it would be a lovely day.

There was nothing but sea below for a time and then she glimpsed the shores of Celene. They were approaching from the east side and though she strained to see the white spire of the temple, she couldn't find it. Perhaps it was hidden by trees.

'We need to be on the west side of the island. There's a red brick castle with a single turret,' she said. Coronos nodded and yelled to Asaph.

As they drew closer, the joy in her heart was crushed by horror. Even from this great height, it seemed that the whole island was blackened and charred. Plumes of smoke billowed up through broken trees where villages once stood. The fields where crops once grew were now blotched by fire, empty and barren. She looked for the temple but couldn't find it. She began to tremble with sorrow and a horrible anger.

'They did this to Little Kammy, to my home. How long ago did this happen?' she said, half to herself, half to Coronos.

'At least a day ago, probably more,' Coronos' voice was low and sombre. 'If there's been no rain, some things can smoulder and burn for a week. Depending, also, on whether magic was involved.'

'Keep going west, to Castle Elune' she said, her voice hoarse.

Asaph glanced back at her, a strange look in his reptilian eyes, and then looked down, scanning the ground for enemies. They were long gone now, though, leaving nothing but destruction in their wake. Seeing no danger, he dropped lower.

More trails of smoke appeared above a section of green forest. Any stupid hope she might have had for the castle being unscathed was quickly dashed as a ruin came into view. Its red walls were black and crumbling, and most of the slate roofing was missing. Half the castle had collapsed, and though the turret still remained, it was on an angle and looked about to topple down at any moment. Freydel's prized stargazing windows were all smashed, and his room was now an empty blackened shell.

Asaph circled down and landed on the scorched grass in the castle grounds, close to where they had celebrated midsummer, though it seemed so long ago. She saw Rance's face laughing before her as she looked upon where they had danced. He was dead because he tried to save her. She swallowed back the tears.

The raven landed messily and nearly rolled over from exhaustion. He righted himself and sat there ruffling his feathers. As soon as Asaph folded his wings, she struggled out of the harness and slid down his scales to the ground. She ran as fast as she could on stiff legs towards the castle.

'No wait,' Asaph cried out after her in his human form, but she did not stop. He was wobbly from flying for so long and standing up suddenly made him dizzy. The sun struggled to break through the clouds, and the air was sticky and uncomfortable. He ran awkwardly to catch up with her and glanced behind. Coronos followed more cautiously, the Orb of Air already in his hand.

Half the castle still stood, whilst the other half had crumbled away as if a giant had stamped upon it. All the windows were smashed, and many still had tendrils of smoke wafting out from them. It was impossible to tell where any door might have been given the gaping holes in the walls.

He caught up with her as she reached the castle, grasped hold of her shoulders and turned her to face him. She did not look at him and instead stared at the ground. His eyes followed hers to the blood-soaked flagstones, linen and clothes. Blood was splattered everywhere like some hideous painting, all that was left of someone who had died horribly.

He tore his eyes away and gently lifted her chin. She did not see him at first, and for a moment, he was lost in her eyes. She looked very young just then, and his heart lurched.

'Issa, my love, the Maphraxies who did this may still be here. We must go carefully and prepare ourselves for more horrors. We must be strong.'

She nodded dumbly. 'I don't think anything alive remains...' her voice cracked.

'Most of our enemies are not alive,' he smiled wanly, knowing that was not what she meant.

'Oh Ely, please tell me you're safe,' she whispered, pulling away. She ran through a hole in the wall that may have once been a door.

The place was a mess. Everything was broken and splintered; from the pictures on the wall to every ornament, table and chair—and those were just the things that had escaped the fire. Splashes of blood and chewed bones littered the floor. The stench of death dripped from the walls, and mingled with it was the sickly smell of immortals that made his stomach heave.

He followed Issa, watching and feeling her panic as she searched each room whispering to herself like a mad woman. He had to keep her close and laid a hand on his sword hilt, ready.

Every room she looked in was empty. Where on earth was Ely? The once happy, vibrant castle was nothing more than a giant tomb; empty of life, the domain of the dead. As much as she had been desperate to get in, now she was desperate to get out. She ran down the blackened halls wanting to be away from the death and corruption that reeked around her. If she listened, she could hear the wails of those who had been slain, the gnashing teeth of death hounds and the screams of Dread Dragons.

She stumbled into the front courtyard, gasping. The raven met her there, he had not wanted to go inside. Her head pounded. She clasped her hands over her ears willing the din in her mind to stop, fighting the madness and sorrow that threatened to consume her. She closed her eyes and sought sanctuary amongst the ancient stones and sacred mound of the goddess. She hungered for the peace that lay upon the surface of the sacred pond. She sank to her knees, clinging to that vision just for a moment, but it would not stay.

The raven's caw forced her back to the present, her unwilling mind unable to ignore her companion's call. Opening her eyes, the black bird filled her vision, and suddenly she was looking back at herself. It turned and flew to a tree. Again she looked back at herself from the raven's perspective. She stood up reluctantly. Asaph came to her side and put his arm around her, but she pushed it away.

'You must wait here,' she said coldly in a tone that made him freeze and stilled the protest on his lips. 'Stay with Coronos,' she said without looking at him, but could feel his confused fear, fear of her. She heard him turn away and call for Coronos.

Her feet moved against the will of her protesting mind. She felt detached from her body as she walked alone towards where the raven had gone. She didn't want to see, but she could not turn away. There was something pale hanging from an old gnarled oak tree; it swayed slightly in the breeze. She walked in a silent timeless world towards it. Her soul drifted far away as she stood, unseeing at first, before the hanging thing.

Dimly she recognised the face of her friend. Her friend had gone now. The bruised and bloodied body before her was not her friend but a lifeless corpse. Its face was a mask of death, a face she had seen too many times before upon those dearest to her. It was the face she ran from, the face she denied. *I have returned home only to see the face of death again.*

'I know you,' she whispered. *I know you, Death.* She blinked the tears away and swallowed the lump in her throat. 'Why will all that I love be taken from me?' she demanded aloud.

The question burned in the pit of her stomach, demanding answers she could not provide. Her fists clenched so hard her nails dug into flesh. Where was the goddess when Ely needed her? Was this what Zanufey wanted? Who of her friends was next to die? What lesson was she supposed to learn here?

'How can you let this be?' she cried, shaking her fists up at the sky as tears coursed unchecked down her cheeks. It began to rain. There came no answer to her questions, only silence and the cold pattering drops. No goddess was here, in this place of desecration and sorrow.

The wind gusted through the trees, and the drizzle turned the burnt earth beneath her feet into black sludge. She lifted a hand towards the body, hesitated, and let it drop. The tears came, and she buried her head in her shaking hands.

'Ely, don't leave me. I'm afraid. I'm lost in a world of chaos and loss,' she choked. 'I cannot do this. I cannot be who you all want me to be. I cannot be the Raven Queen. Zanufey, I'm afraid. So afraid,' she shuddered.

There was no comfort, only the wind and the rain and the horrible sorrow. She wished the world would end so she wouldn't have to suffer it anymore. It was foolish to think she could fight the immortals and it was foolish to think even the Raven Queen could. The price of loss was too much, the pain too great. Maybe she should give herself up to the Immortal Lord and end this whole sorry thing.

The tears sobbed themselves out, and stillness settled her churning emotions. She looked up at the face of her dead friend. She had to force herself to notice the grey flesh and those dead eyes that had once been blue and so full of life. It was then she saw something stuffed in her mouth, a gag or something. It was horrible, unnatural, and with a shaking hand she pulled it out.

Her empty stomach heaved as the rag came free and a piece of bloody paper fell out. She reached to pick it up, her hands shaking so much she had trouble unfolding it. Through the bloody grime, the words were clearly visible.

"Those who do not serve the Immortal Lord are his enemies."

Fury surged within her, driving away the sorrow. The cold hard anger was enough to pull her forwards, enough to give her strength to go on, if only for a little while.

'I will spend my life hunting down the bastards who did this to her, to Mother, to us all. I will destroy the Maphraxies until either nothing remains of them or nothing remains of me,' she made her hands into fists and stared at the black mud.

'Maioria must be cleansed of the immortals. Only then can we be free.'

Gusts of cold wind swept over the grounds and seemed to blow through her empty heart. This once beautiful place, her home and the goddess's sacred isle, had been ravaged and desecrated. The raven at her side sat silent and unmoving.

'They say that ravens move between two worlds, the living and the dead. Then so too must the Queen of Ravens. But how?' She spoke softly to the raven, to Ely's dead body, to Zanufey, to anything that might be listening. 'Keteth passed on to me his ability to walk in the realm of the dead. If these things are so then, of all my *gifts,* show me, Ely, how you passed from the living into the dead.'

She put her hands upon her friend's cold face. For all that had been said and done, surely she could see those last moments of her friend's life and those bastards who murdered her. She was not afraid of what she might see. She just had to know.

Closing her eyes, she focused on the Flow, a vivid mass of swirling turquoise that hurt to look upon. She called it to her, shocked at how little she could pull and control, and how it made her dizzy. She persevered and urged it to show her what had happened to her friend.

The Flow faded, turning dark and hazy. The world around her dulled until she could no longer feel the wind or rain on her skin. It felt as if she had moved into a different time and space entirely.

The last moments of Ely's life formed before her, devoid of any colour, like black and white drawings. They were weak and faint, maybe because they happened some time ago.

She flinched from what she saw, her heart hammering in her chest. It took all of her courage not to turn away from the terrible scenes as the Dread Dragon caught her friend and the dark dwarves ravaged her. But in the end, only one face laid its imprint in her mind; a tall man with a gaunt face and grey hair that matched grey eyes filled with a cruel intelligence. He forced his way into Ely's mind just as Keteth had into hers; taking, breaking, scouring—a ravaging of the soul. Ely was powerless to fight him. Through her mind, he found her, Issa, and discovered that she might be the Raven Queen of prophecy. She felt Ely's miserable sorrow of unwilling betrayal as her own; it stung like an open wound.

'Oh Ely, you did not betray me, you could never betray me,' she breathed. 'It's I who have betrayed you. I'll find him. He will pay for what he's done.'

She opened her eyes breathing hard. She drew her sword with trembling hands and in one stroke cut Ely's body down from the tree. She tore off her cloak and, though it was soaking, draped it over her friend. She sunk on her heels in the mud beside her. The anger and injustice she had felt earlier began to drain away and leaving her empty.

'Zanufey, take my friend into the light,' she whispered and closed her eyes against the tears.

She was surprised to see behind her weary eyelids the desert plain stretching out under a night sky. She had not intended it to be there, almost did not want it to be. Zanufey stood before her, and she felt bad for feeling angry. She wanted answers but looked away from the goddess, feeling too sad to ask for any.

Issa opened her eyes, but everything as it was before. She sat alone, with only the raven and Ely beside her. She closed them again, and the desert slid into view.

'I deny death,' she said. The anger made her want to turn and run away. But she stayed, and calm and peace spread over her from Zanufey.

'*Call to her,*' the soft, gentle voice of Zanufey spoke in her mind.

'What's the point? She's gone, her soul probably enslaved by the immortals,' Issa said, keeping her eyes closed and looking out hopelessly across the midnight dunes.

'*She's waiting to be set free,*' Zanufey said.

'How is she still here?' Issa asked in surprise.

Zanufey lifted her hand and in the air before her a blue and green planet formed. There seemed to be a black web-work or netting surrounding it. It looked unnatural and wrong. Issa peered closer and saw little lights struggling in the web.

'Are they souls?' she breathed. 'They're trapped. By Baelthrom's magic?'

Zanufey did not reply, and Issa felt she was being guided to answer her questions herself.

'Is that why I'm here? To set them free? Is that what the Raven Queen is supposed to do?'

But again Zanufey remained silent, only that subtle smile on her pale lips. Issa frowned, but she would do anything to help her friend.

'Ely? Are you there? Zanufey is calling you,' she said, feeling silly.

Nothing happened at first, then there came a warm glow, and she could feel her friend Ely beside her—a familiar presence. She flicked her eyes open. There was nothing but the rain, the mud and the raven. She closed them again, and the warm glow was there. Issa smiled, joy and sorrow catching in her throat.

'Ely, be free. Go into the light,' she said.

The soft glow grew brighter, as did Zanufey and the desert until it was so bright that she had to open her eyes to avoid being blinded. She blinked and closed them again, but Zanufey was gone, as was the soft glow of Ely and there was only darkness. She sat alone again in the mud.

'Go home, my friend. One day I'll see you there,' she whispered.

She smoothed the blonde strands back from Ely's face. She looked serene now, like a face of Feygriene. She noticed then the strange markings cut into her chest; three triangles in a row, the outer two curved inwards to the first. The symbol of the Maphraxies. She would recognise that symbol anywhere, ever since Freydel had shown it to her in one of his books.

'Bastards,' she growled.

She placed her hands over the mark of Maphrax on Ely's chest and poured the Flow through her palms. The mark began to glow dark blue then burst into brilliant azure. She pulled her hands away. The mark of Maphrax was gone and in its place now shone Zanufey's raven, like that upon her own chest.

She glimpsed Coronos and Asaph pointing to her in the distance. They came running over, but she didn't look up. Coronos gasped and sank down beside her.

'Fly, Ely, fly on the wings of the raven back to the One Source,' she said, her attention fully absorbed upon her friend. She released the Flow. The raven symbol of Zanufey flared into blue fire and spread rapidly, consuming her friend's body. She stood up and looked at the others. Coronos' face was a mask of grief and Asaph was deathly pale.

'Some time alone,' she whispered.

Asaph nodded. From the look upon his father's face, it seemed Coronos needed comforting the most right now. Coronos knew Freydel, so he probably knew many people on the Isle of Celene, people that were all dead now.

Asaph reached down to his father, and she turned away. She had intended to go and sit alone somewhere but instead, she carried on walking, away from the castle, the raven following above. She felt strange. Part of her was so upset and angry that she lusted for bloody revenge. The other part was serene and calm and filled with a deeper understanding. She needed time alone to work through them both. Uncaring for her own safety, she began the long walk east to the Temple of Celene.

CHAPTER 49

The Talisman

ELY'S journey may have ended but mine has not. I must go on without her.

Issa felt her heart hardening which each step, along with her resolve. If she did not fight, then the Maphraxies had already won. She had to be strong even though she didn't know how. Perhaps the Raven Queen could give her that strength.

'Zanufey, show me the way when I understand the least. The darkness is upon me now, and my heart is turning to stone,' she whispered aloud.

A cold wind blew making her shiver, and she thought she heard it whisper 'Maion'artheria.' She smiled—a sad smile, but a smile nevertheless.

The rain fell heavier and ran in rivulets down her face. She sneezed, feeling a cold coming on through the exhaustion. The raven circled above, comforting her with his presence. She lost herself in thoughts as she walked the road she had first travelled with Freydel, what felt like a decade ago. Once it had been green and lush, and children played alongside it. Now it was charred and deserted.

She came to a rocky point that marked the highest part of the isle. From here she could see every coast and all the smouldering villages that lay between. Great claws of charred earth, the tell-tale signs of Dromoorai and Maphraxies, marred the land, just like they had on Little Kammy. From here she should have been able to see the shining white spire of the temple, but instead, she saw a short blackened shard sticking up between broken trees.

What about Freydel and Cirosa? What about Arla? She shook her head, she dared not hope. But what about her dream? Her heart beat faster in her chest. Duskar had to be alive, why else did she have those dreams?

'Duskar,' she called out. 'Duskar!' she cried louder, her voice ringing in the silence.

Duskar, come to me,' she called with her mind and stood there waiting fearfully, this time daring to hope. Time ticked by and then, there in the trees, a dark shape appeared and a big black horse stepped cautiously into the clearing.

'Duskar!' she cried and ran to him. He stood there for a moment, sniffing the air, and then trotted towards her, ears pricked forward and tail raised high. His hair shone with sweat and rain, and he whinnied. She hugged his neck, and he bent his head down to nibble her thigh as he always used to. He trembled and looked thin, but he was alive and strong.

'Hey, old friend. It's all right, I'm here now,' she soothed and smiled. 'They haven't destroyed everything then, and I'll bet you gave them hell. Come with me to the temple to look for Freydel. Are you strong enough to let me ride you?'

He snorted and seemed to be pleased with the thought. She eased her sore body onto his back and nudged him into a walk towards the temple.

The Temple of Celene and its surrounding buildings were much as the villages had been, burnt and crumbling. The pristine white spire was sundered in two by a huge chasm that ran through its middle, slicing through to the sacred womb of the Mother's Chamber deep below. The Maphraxian symbol was scrawled in blood on parts of the wall where there was still white showing through. She slid off Duskar's back and looked at them.

'They left all these signs for me?' she laughed—a hollow sound that echoed loudly in the emptiness of the temple.

'Do you fear me so much already?' she shouted and laughed again. 'This temple was corrupt long before you ever came,' she mocked, thinking of Cirosa and her greed.

She looked around. There was no one here, not even Cirosa or Arla. The place was destroyed, and everyone was dead, but she had to be sure. Maybe Arla was hiding in the Mother's Chamber, what was left of it. The girl was adept at disappearing. She refused to think that she'd been taken or killed. She had a feeling she'd find something here, but what or who she did not know.

With her sword drawn, she tiptoed after the huge, booted footprints that led into the temple. Padding silently across the trashed and broken marble floor, she came to a huge hole in the ground where the secret staircase to the Mother's Chamber had been. She grabbed the smashed lantern lying in the rubble and clicked the knob. Amazingly, it flared into life.

Some stairs were completely missing, and all the others were crumbling. The spell that had once sealed the entrance was now broken for good. She followed the footprints down into the darkness, the heavy smell of Maphraxie burned in her nostrils like sickly sweet sulphur.

What had happened to Cirosa? Would they have taken her captive? It seemed they only wanted magic wielders and children. For a follower of the goddess, wouldn't they have left her body broken, and hanging and marked like Ely's? Or maybe they had captured her, and she would soon be one of them. She might have escaped, though it was doubtful. With a shiver, she steeled herself for horrible sights.

In the first chamber, the cushions were flung everywhere, but there had been no fire. In this moment, there was less fire here than there normally was for the candles no longer burned—candles that had been kept alight since the temple had been consecrated hundreds of years ago were now cold and dead. Like Celene herself, she thought sourly.

With her broken lantern, she lit the candles once more. It seemed like the right thing to do; return the light back into the darkness. She stood there listening to the silence and closed her eyes. She entered the Flow to see if there was anything more to the room that she could not see with her inner vision. Beyond the walls, a soft light glimmered. She couldn't feel danger and opened her eyes.

'Arla?' she called out. 'Arla, are you here hiding somewhere. Is it you I can see in the Flow?'

Nothing moved. She closed her eyes again. Beyond the walls there came a magical shimmer of light, but it did not move. Perhaps it had always been there; she had never looked through the Flow at the Mother's Chamber before.

'Cirosa? Freydel? Anyone?' but nothing moved, and there was no sound except her voice echoing.

She let her breath go and walked into the passage adjoining the room where the glowing object was. In the Flow, the object was shining white, about a foot square wide, but it seemed to be behind the rock wall, and there was no way she could get to it. Did an outside tunnel lead to a secret chamber?

She headed to the sacred garden. The big stone door that usually blocked the way was broken in two, but she managed to squeeze between the two halves. The garden was as it had been when she left it; unscathed, beautiful and green. Mist hung in the air now the rain had stopped. The old willow tree still stood there, its delicate leaves moving gently in the breeze. A strange last place of serenity when all around was blood and murder.

The raven cawed and landed on the stone bowl, making her jump. She went over to it, surprised to find it still full of water.

'The rain has filled it.'

The raven croaked and shook his head in disagreement.

She stared at her reflection in the water and was shocked to see her luminous, turquoise-green eyes. Overuse of the Flow. How close had she come to losing herself completely? But if she had not, the Life Seeker would have captured or killed her. Her eyes were red from tiredness and tears, and there were dark circles under them, but her face was hard and determined—as hard as the warrior woman with the raven-feathered crown.

There was a piece of paper stuffed in the ivy. It was only visible in the water's reflection, having been tucked up under the leaves. She pulled it out and, setting her lantern down, unrolled it. It was a note scrawled in childish writing.

They came, and I hid. Freydel went to the Wizards' Circle but has not returned. They took Cirosa. She has betrayed us and agreed to help them find you. She blames you for Rance's death and believes you are a threat to the Order of the Goddess.

It took so much out of me to find and take the talisman that I cannot return for a while. Baelthrom knows I have returned and so I must hide.

Speak the name of the raven into the R-shaped crack, and it will open. The talisman will give you strength. There is much that has not been explained for our safety. Know that I'm safe and I shall find you when I return.

- Arla

She frowned. The writing was childish, but the words were those of an adult. The girl was strange. Where in Maioria had she gone that no one could find her? She stuffed the note into her pocket, relieved that Arla and Freydel were still alive.

Half sceptical, she began searching the cliff face for the R-shaped crack. There, to the right of the entrance, she found a jagged crack that looked faintly like an "R". She traced it with her fingers.

'But I don't know the name of the raven,' she said and looked at the bird. He came hopping over. She knelt down and focused on his dark brown eyes, opening her mind to him in the Daluni way.

'What's your name, my friend?' she asked and directed the thought towards him. The subtle pressure came again, and she looked out across a swirling mist of indigo. She blinked.

'But that has no word in Frayonesse.' She closed her eyes again and asked the same question mentally. But again all she saw was a sea of indigo mist swirling and flowing gently in all directions. She stood up and put her hands on her hips.

'How can I speak that name if it has no translatable word or even a sound tone?' She chewed her lip and at the raven. 'On Little Kammy, we have a tiny wispy flower that comes out only at night and in the moonlight. When they bloom, they are like a carpet of mist. They are called "ehkas," a sea of ehkas. Ehka is a Kammy word for indigo. Do you think Ehka is a good name for you?'

The raven cawed, ducked his head, and turned back to examine the R-shaped crack. She laughed and shook her head. How did Arla know his name? Or perhaps she didn't, and all that mattered was she gave him a name he accepted.

She bent close to the crack and spoke, 'Ehka.'

The "R" shimmered, the rock began to dissipate, and a hole appeared. The hole grew bigger and deeper as she peered through it into darkness. The hole stopped growing when it was big enough for her to squeeze in crawling. Grabbing her lantern, she got on her hands and knees and crawled forwards. Getting her hips through was the hardest part, but once she had squeezed inside, the tunnel widened, and it was easier to move.

The lantern light fell upon a flat rag-bound object about the size of a saucer. She could feel magic emanating from it, and the raven mark on her chest began to tingle. She stopped in surprise. The magic felt uncannily like dark moon magic, only less powerful.

She set the lantern down and picked the object. It was incredibly heavy for something so small, and as soon as she touched it, even through the rag, she felt the weight of ages exuding from it. She gripped it, enchanted by what she was feeling. It was powerful, like an orb, only more so, and certainly purer. The orbs were divided magic, but this felt whole and complete. It was filled with the same ancient magic as the dark moon, and yet it felt empty, like the space before thought and before creation; the void-place where anything could be created, and from which all things emerged and took form. It was magic in its purest form, so what on Maioria was it?

She tore off the cloth and stared at it. It was shimmered black like onyx and was fashioned into the shape of a flying raven, like the mark upon her chest, only far more detailed. Each feather was intricately carved; the curve of its beak and the shape of its eye were perfect, exquisite craftsmanship. It was as solid as iron and as heavy.

The raven mark upon her chest began to pulse in time to her heartbeat. She pulled her shirt down, and the mark filled the chamber with pulsing silver-blue light. She looked back at the object and noticed it wasn't solid black stone at all, it only seemed like that in the dark tunnel. The black stone was filled with twinkling lights, like stars captured within it. The stars were all different sizes, and some were close to the surface whilst were others far away. It was like looking up at a night sky, or at the stars on Zanufey's robe, or at the trilithon in the desert. Yes, they were made of the same black stone, flecked through with silver and gold and all the colours of the spectrum.

'It's beautiful,' she breathed and gasped. The stars were moving, like they did on Zanufey's robe, but this time they were moving naturally in gentle arcs and beautiful orbits and not being sucked into a black hole. Was this a hologram of the universe as it was supposed to be?

She watched them in wonder, there were so many. Some clustered together, others formed into delicate swirls. She felt herself drawing towards them until she became one, a star moving through endless space, surrounded by hundreds of planets and their moons, a thousand suns twinkling in the darkness, an entire universe stretching out into infinity. All was serene and eternal, here amongst the stars.

She pressed the talisman against the raven mark. Even with closed eyes, she could see the blue flare as the two connected. The talisman became light in her hands, just as she felt her own body lighten and become less dense. She opened her eyes. Around her was a world of light and shadow devoid of any colour. It was just like the Shadowlands only not as dark and not as threatening. It felt still, mysterious and expecting, but just as strange.

There were twelve ghostlike figures before her, and she jumped in alarm. But they were not threatening, and their faces were smiling faintly. They were dressed in armour, and one had a helmet with a circlet upon it. Their visors were up and immediately she recognised the one with the eyepatch, the one with the circlet. *The Cursed King and his Banished Knights.*

She pulled the talisman away and in a blink the shadowy world was gone. The talisman remained light in her hands and her mark no longer glowed. She turned the talisman around and noticed at the base there was a thick hole as if it fitted on top of something.

'There is another part to this,' she murmured, tracing the hole with her finger. A vision flashed in her mind of the shining white spear and then was gone.

Feeling hot and claustrophobic, she tucked the talisman into her blacksmith's belt, grabbed her lantern, and crawled backwards out of the stifling tunnel. Once outside, she breathed in the fresh air and stretched.

A shadow fell upon her making her skin crawl. She peered up at the sky. Another shadow passed, and she glimpsed dark wings, the shape of a head, the curve of a breast.

'The harpies have returned,' she said in a low and deadly voice to Ehka. He croaked, watching the sky. 'If they think this land is theirs for the taking, then they have a fight to the death on their hands.' Thoughts of vengeance filled her mind, and her pulse quickened.

CHAPTER 50

The Ravens of Zanufey

AS soon as Issa saw the harpies, she worried for Asaph and Coronos. A whole brood would be no match for a dragon, but if Asaph were caught unawares in his human form, it would be the death of him. She needed to capture the bird women's attention.

'They will not lay a dirty claw on him, on the sacred garden, or the Mother's Chamber, even if it is desecrated and empty,' she said to Ehka.

She gathered the Flow to her fearfully. It came, but her grasp on it was weak. She knew she did not have the strength to fight them, but her need for vengeance was overpowering, and there was no way on Maioria she would let them take Asaph.

'Destruction,' she breathed and formed a flickering ball of pale blue lightning. Tighter and tighter she made the ball until it was smaller than an egg. The dense ball of wildly flickering electrical power hummed.

'Let's go,' she said.

Ehka launched into the air. She spread her arms, willed the raven form to come, and leapt. Her arms grew long and sprouted feathers, and before she lost her human vocal cords she shouted, 'Now!'

The flickering ball fell to the ground, flared and then exploded. The shock waves shoved her high into the sky where she joined Ehka. The explosion was brief, but the devastation great. Rocks tumbled down, crushing the sacred bowl and filling the entrance to the Mother's Chamber, sealing it forever. The entire cliff side began to crumble away with the deafening noise of falling rock. Only the willow tree and a small patch of grass surrounding it remained, still and serene.

Her extravagant idea had the intended effect. The harpies screamed, turned and headed towards her. She flew south, a little beyond the destroyed temple to where the cliff rose highest. It was a sandy, rocky place where no trees grew, and from here she could see the rest of the island stretching out ahead, and the ragged drop behind to the sparkling sea below.

She landed and resumed her human form. Her heart thudded excitedly in her chest, and she clenched and released her sweaty hands. Fighting and killing harpies would give her release, would drive back the sorrow of loss, would help slake her furious desire for revenge.

She closed her eyes, searching for the dark moon. It was out there somewhere but far away. It could not help her. Her hand brushed the raven talisman in her belt. The magic felt dark and mysterious, soothing and powerful—the power of the Night Goddess and the creative force that could restore the divine order of things. She wondered if the talisman drew its power directly from the dark moon.

High in the sky black shapes circled. There were many harpies now, too many to count. Even from this distance, Issa could feel their eyes upon her. Freydel feared even one harpy, how could she face so many and survive? She could feel the magical exhaustion as a physical thing making her light-headed, ethereal and weak. Freydel had warned her that overusing magic was a great danger, and those who did ended up becoming the Flow, unable to return to the world as their bodies transmuted into pure magical energy. He was right. Even now when she entered the Flow, she felt more real there than she did in the physical world.

Was it really possible to disappear into the Flow completely? If she did not face the harpies, they would torture and kill them anyway. She had no choice but to stand and fight. She laid a hand upon the talisman. If the talisman was like an orb, she could use it to command the Flow.

The harpies were closer now, and they began to scream for her blood.

Wondering if this would be her last battle in her short life as a warrior, she closed her eyes and immersed herself in the rush of the Flow, letting all worries of Asaph and Coronos go, forgetting all fears for her own life, even if she lost herself to the Flow. As Grast'anth had told her, survival depended on her being focused, single-minded, free from doubt and filled with absolute faith. Somewhere, far out there in space, the dark moon moved, and though it was far away and its power weak it was not gone from her completely. She whispered a short prayer.

'Beloved Zanufey. My body is drained and my command of the Flow the weakest it's ever been, but my will is strong and my determination absolute. I will not shy away from those who murdered my friends and destroyed my home. Vengeance will be mine. But if it's my time to die, I'm not afraid.'

The words made her feel good, but they weren't completely true. She *was* afraid. Her legs trembled, and her bladder threatened to empty itself, as it always seemed to want to do before a fight. She gripped the cool surface of the raven talisman. 'Show me how to use you,' she asked.

Just as the Orb of Water had responded to her barely conscious touch when faced with the Maphraxies, the talisman pulsed in her hand and opened to her. At her touch was a vessel of ancient and forgotten magic that had lain latent for a long time. The raven mark upon her chest tingled in response to it. With the raven talisman she had a chance at fully controlling the Flow once more.

The talisman flooded her with power. There came a lull in the magical tide as if she had filled her lungs with air and was ready to exhale. She looked out through the Flow, and the magical world and the physical world were one.

Everything around her including her body was not solid matter but made of light in all colours and hues and moving in all directions. Each colour had a sound tone, and the music the magic made was a harmony purer than any instrument or voice. The magic made her feel that anything was possible.

The raven cawed. She blinked out of the Flow and focused upon him. He flew above trees towards the temple. She spotted Asaph and Coronos running below him, just before the trees gave way into the temple grounds and to where Duskar paced nervously.

She glanced up at the harpies. They flew in a dense flock that was dropping towards her. They were not interested in the raven or the horse, and luckily they had not yet spotted the two men. She had to act fast, as soon as they burst through the trees, the harpies would see them. She held her arms wide.

'Fire. Up,' she said quietly but firmly and exhaled as she brought her arms up above her head. Roaring fire flared from her arms upwards towards the harpies. She struggled to stand upright from the force of the power pushing down on her. The roaring receded, and all she could hear was the symphony of the Flow as it moved through her.

Above her harpies screamed and their flaming bodies fell from the sky. They rolled and screeched on the ground, the stench of burning flesh and feathers filling the air. She drew her sword upon the closest stinking bird-woman and with a cry she sliced down and ended her horrible squawks.

The ground shuddered beneath her feet, but not because of her magic. She steadied herself and moved away from the cliff-edge. There came the thunderous sound of cracking rock and another shudder sent her to her knees.

In the Flow the ground looked like an angry sea of purple. To her right the temple shook, then what remained of the blackened broken building collapsed and sank into the land. A snaking crack a foot wide whipped across the earth in front of her and disappeared into the forest far to her left. Trees plunged into the crack as it split the forest apart.

There was a moment's stillness, then the earth quaked again. The splitting land tore apart another foot and then another until a great chasm gaped in front of her, stretching from the temple to her right and all the way into the forest where it was lost from view. There came a strange hissing, thundering noise that took her a while to work out what it was until she saw seawater gushing into the chasm. Steam and dirt churned up into the air in great billows.

The shaking earth, billowing dust and steam created enough confusion to give her time to rest and recharge her reserves of the Flow. Her hands that had dug fearfully into the earth now relaxed as the earthquake subsided. The severed land was trembling, but each tremor shuddered less. The desecrated island seemed like it was trying to destroy itself.

She let out a deep breath she hadn't realised she held, inched onto her feet and held her sword at the ready. The airborne harpies were reorganising themselves and searching for her in the settling dust.

'Slow. Calm. Balance,' she breathed, barely audible but the magic willingly obeyed and sought to calm the shuddering ground. Through half-closed lids, she viewed the Flow. The whole island had been sundered apart and seawater, bright turquoise in the Flow, white in the physical, was a frothing torrent surging into the chasm some fifty feet below.

The dust cleared. She looked up at the bird women.

'I have their attention now,' she murmured with a grin and readied herself to face the brood of a hundred screaming harpies.

Ehka squawked and landed beside her, huddling close. The harpies descended, screeching their hatred in a strange language that was halfway between human words and the noise of screaming gulls.

Her sword flickered, and she slashed back talons that sought to rip and tear her flesh. She gripped the raven talisman in her other hand and it waited patiently for her command. Her sword arm ached already from her battle against the Life Seeker and every time she struck a talon or speared through feathers, pain shot up her arm.

Whenever he could, Ehka pecked and clawed at them, but against so many his efforts were mostly useless, and she worried more for his safety than her own.

The harpies wheeled away as one flock and then two came at once, one black-feathered, the other brown. Their faces were beautiful from a distance, with their smooth skin, arched eyebrows, full lips and flowing feathery hair. But as they neared their eyes shone black and their mouths snarled fangs.

She squeezed the talisman. As long as she held it in her hand, she knew she could harness the Flow. But how much could the talisman assist her before it too burnt out? It was a risk she had to take. Her revenge still burned hot inside her, overriding the logic that told her she was vastly outnumbered. She would fight until her revenge was spent or she died.

'Fire. Now!' she barked as the harpies neared.

A line of indigo fire snaked from the talisman, exploding upon contact with the nearest two harpies. They fell writhing in balls of flames that burned hard and short. In seconds all that remained of them was smoking feathers and lumps of charred flesh.

Ehka pecked at the carrion that rolled passed him.

'How can you eat that and at a time like this?' she said in disgust, but he completely ignored her.

She looked up at her enemies. They did not retaliate immediately and instead circled above their magic-wielding enemy more cautiously, swarming like wasps as they screamed in their ear-grating language.

'Traitors!' she shouted. 'You turned your back on the goddess. You turned your back on Maioria.' The harpies laughed, and one after the other dropped towards her, talons shining, their magic shimmering around them.

'There is no goddess here. The Immortal Lord claims all,' one screamed in Frayonesse as it tried to reach past her slicing sword. Its talons glanced off metal with a clang.

Harpy fire hurtled towards her, but the talisman responded as quick as she thought it. Blue fire surged and engulfed the enemy's red flames.

'We'll kill you, eat your flesh and suck your bones,' another screeched in her face.

Her blade moved faster than the harpy could dodge and she struck with such force that its body was severed almost in two from its shoulder down to its feathered hip. Bright blood sprayed over her face, stinging her eyes. She blinked it away to see the harpy tumble into the chasm and barely had time for the next attack.

She stepped sideways, coming dangerously close to the edge of the chasm, and ducked as the harpy came low. At the last moment, she thrust up to meet it, sinking her sword into its belly. In horrified death throes, the harpy flailed, her talons scraping painfully into Issa's arm.

Adrenaline numbing the pain, she wrenched her sword free, glimpsed the next harpy coming from behind in the bloodied reflection of her blade, and spun to meet it, slicing desperately in the air. Wing severed, it fell with a surprised expression, following its comrade into the chasm. She swung again and another tumbled after them.

'You told me to practice, Grast'anth, but I never thought practice would always be for real,' she whispered grimly.

Blood ran down her arms and soaked her clothes. Her blacksmith's belt protected her midriff, and not for the first time she gave thanks for that. But the harpies were many, and each one of them that fell only seemed to make their fury burn brighter, their attacks more reckless and unpredictable. They dived at her faster, despite her deadly blade, as if they no longer feared death. The furious brood screamed and cackled—a terrible sound that raked at her ears just as their talons raked her flesh.

She slashed and stabbed, driving them back, using the talisman to block their red fire with her blue. The red fire stopped coming, and for a moment they stopped attacking. The hilt of her sword was slippery with blood and her grip on it ached. She gasped for breath in the welcome pause, wanting nothing more than to rest.

Their screeching changed and rather than unordered threats, it began to sound more like ordered noise as they spoke their strange words in unison. It took on the sound of ominous chanting, a hundred banshees wailing their dread-filled song.

The Flow moved in a way that made her feel sick. Dark magic flowed beneath the pastel hues distorting it, turning dirty and viscous. The Flow faltered in the talisman, and she couldn't draw it easily to her.

The rise and fall of their voices made her heart thud in her chest. She felt heavy and slow as if every ounce of energy had left her. Her eyelids wanted to close, and a desperate tiredness came over her. More than anything she wanted to lie down and sleep.

So this was harpy magic. With no experience fighting this enemy, she was at a disadvantage. Harpy magic closed in around her, blocking her view and feel of the Flow.

'Barrier,' she gasped, struggling to breathe the air that was thick as soup.

The talisman pulsed. A field of indigo light shimmered close to her body, protecting her before the harpy magic could cut her off from the Flow completely. They circled as one towards her, then ten or more splintered from the rest and descended upon her from every side.

'Eat your bones,' they screeched. 'Take your man and devour him too.'

'Protection!' she screamed.

There came a clap of magic, momentarily stunning her. She drew the Flow close, feeling like she was about to vomit from using it. White flared around her as everything burst into pale fire apart from herself. Harpies screamed as she swayed. The Flow seemed to be moving her this way and that, but her physical feet stayed put.

She was falling into the Flow.

She blinked, struggling to see the physical world, and saw the flaring white bodies of the harpies writhing around her, the smell of burning flesh and feathers seared her nostrils.

A harpy descended upon her, struck and wheeled away. Stinging pain exploded in her shoulders and hot blood trickled down her arms. She vomited, swaying sickeningly somewhere between the Flow and the physical world, burning any energy she had left to stay anchored in the present.

The harpies saw their flagging enemy and attacked. Again her white fire flared but weaker than before. She swayed dangerously close to the chasm's edge, barely able to distinguish it from the rush of the Flow around her. It was the form of Ehka beside her, dark blue in the Flow, that helped her know where she should stand.

With great effort, she forced herself out of the Flow and raised her sword. She dared not use magic for the next attack. She sliced at the harpies in a big arc, her arms burning with the effort. Red blood, both hers and the harpy's, splattered the ground. She stumbled. Talons gripped her shoulders, lifting her momentarily off the ground. She stabbed at the talons and fell hard, rolling away from the edge.

Dragging herself to her feet, she glimpsed Coronos and Asaph engaged in battle. They stood beside the broken temple, hugging the black and bloodied walls for protection from the harpies aerial attacks as best they could. From what she could make amongst the blur of harpies, Asaph swung his sword ceaselessly whilst Coronos held his orb aloft. Dead and dying harpies littered the ground but still they came on.

She understood then why Asaph was not in his dragon form. To leave Coronos' side for a moment would be the last time he saw his father. The harpies would stop at nothing to steal a man, even if it meant leaving their brood in the middle of a fight.

There were so many harpies it seemed the entire race had come. Why had so many come to Celene now? Had they been promised this sacred land for their new breeding ground? The thought made her furious, and the fury made her want to fight more.

The harpies were gathering for another assault, their chanting growing loud. The talisman was hot and heavy in her hand, and she longed to put it down. She glanced down at the raven. He had bald patches on his back and blood dripped from a wing. He stared up at her. She looked at her weak and bloodied arms. She couldn't fly, and even if she could, she could never outfly a harpy. And besides, where would she flee? Would she leave Asaph and Coronos to their fate?

The situation was desperate. She wanted to cry. More than cry, she wanted to curl up and die as the utter devastation of failure sunk in. She had failed—failed Ely and failed Asaph. Her need for vengeance would be the death of them all.

She blinked, seeing the Flow in one moment and the blurry physical world in the next, no longer able to control which she looked upon. The brood of harpies was getting ready for another assault.

She tried to focus on the talisman, tried to think of some command it would respond to, but its power was also spent. She thought of Arla and tried to remember if she had written anything about the talisman, but nothing came to mind. She probably knew more about the talisman now than anyone else on Maioria.

'Issa.'

The word was a strange drawn out calling that came from far away. She blinked as a faint light formed, taller and wider than a human, and whether in the Flow or the physical world, she could no longer determine. She tried to focus on the light, but it seemed to struggle to stay there, fading in and out.

'Issa, remember Karshur,' the words were barely distinguishable, so long and drawn out were they. The voice was female. It sounded familiar, like the voice that had called to her in the storehouses of Little Kammy.

'Karshur was returned to the elves. Karshur is gone,' she croaked, feeling stupid. But as soon as she said it she remembered her gift. She squared her shoulders and glared at the descending harpies. It had to work, it was all she had left.

'A'farion, A'farion, A'farion,' she cried aloud and thrust the talisman against her bloodied chest and the mark of the raven.

The world flashed, and she fell forwards into silver light.

The light faded to a dull grey, and she found herself in a world of shade. The ground beneath her feet felt hard and rocky, only it looked grey and insubstantial as if she could push her hand through it if she wanted. The sky above was a lighter shade of grey.

Everything around her was a ghostly copy of the physical world in which she had just stood. The trees and the cliffs were all as they were before, and yet she knew she wasn't quite in Maioria anymore. For a moment, the awful memories of the Shadowlands rushed back, and she wished she were back fighting the harpies.

She looked down at her hands, even they seemed shadowy, though more real than anything else here. She turned and saw the spire of the Temple of Celene in the distance. It was not destroyed and still stood whole and tall, but it lacked beauty in its muted shade of grey. She glimpsed figures moving beside the temple and swallowed. She did not want to meet anything here, especially not the dead.

Ehka cawed and landed beside her, making her jump. He was black and solid.

'You are real here,' she said in surprise, more of a statement than a question.

He dipped his beak, and she noticed his body was smooth and sleek, not bald and bleeding as it had been in the real world. She looked at her arms. They weren't injured or bleeding either, and her shoulders were whole and unharmed. Instead, she ached all over. Extreme tiredness nagged her, and she sorely wanted to lie down and sleep. That seemed like a very dangerous thing to do in this ghost world.

'Now I'm here, what am I supposed to do? The harpies won't simply fly away,' she said to the raven. 'They'll kill Asaph and Coronos.' The very thought made her panic.

She looked at the talisman. It too was black and solid and real. She tried to enter the Flow, if only to feel it, but even in the ghost world, the attempt made her feel sick and weak. What could she do when they were outnumbered? A thought came to her so suddenly, she wondered if the talisman had placed it there. The thought was a picture; a sky filled with ravens.

'I know what to do,' she said. Ehka cocked his head. 'I will call your brothers and sisters. Surely *all* ravens fly between the living world and the dead. After all, what's the point of the raven talisman? What's the point of being the Raven Queen if I can't even call ravens to me?'

She focused on the talisman. 'I call the ravens of Zanufey to me. Bring to me our brothers and sisters. Call to me my ravens.'

Nothing visually happened, but she felt a pulse of energy flow out from the talisman in a circular wave. It pulsed several times and then was still. They stared up at the sky expectantly.

'There look,' she pointed to a small black shape flying fast towards them. Just as she said it, two more came into view. 'Hah. I knew they would come.'

The first one landed at her feet. It was smaller and younger than Ehka. Two more landed, one was bigger and the other older and more scraggly.

'But how will I be able to tell you apart from the others?' she asked Ehka.

He gave a low reproachful caw, and she felt wild magic move. A faint aura of indigo blue, the colour of the dark moon, shimmered around him.

'I forget you can use magic of your own,' she laughed.

More ravens landed, crowding around her as still more filled the sky. She willed them to hurry, feeling more anxious by the second. How time passed in this place, she could not be sure, but one thing was certain, Asaph and Coronos were running out of time.

'We must return to the living and fight the harpies,' she addressed the ravens. They were all looking up at her, hundreds of shining, dark brown eyes. But how did she do that? Karshur had not told her how to return. She held the talisman to her chest.

'Return us to the living?' she chanced.

The world flashed, and she fell forward into silver light.

Whatever respite she'd had in the ghost world was swept away in moments. She felt like death, swaying like a drunkard with exhaustion on the edge of a sundered land. Harpies still wheeled above, and it seemed she had only been gone seconds. Seeing her return they screeched excitedly and came towards her.

She held the talisman high in one hand and her sword in the other. 'Ravens, come to me,' she cried.

The talisman pulsed once, the air shimmered silver around her and then hundreds of ravens burst into the air around her. From where they emerged, the air shimmered and rippled like water. All around her, they circled and then as one they flew at the harpies. Despite their far greater size, the harpies were vastly outnumbered by the ravens.

The air filled with screams, screeches and caws. Talons clawed, beaks flashed, feathers and blood fell from the sky. Now engaged in an aerial battle, the harpies forgot about the humans.

Ravens and harpies tumbled from the sky, and each small black body filled her with sorrow. They fought and died for her, their Raven Queen. She'd called them to their deaths.

The harpies, already weary from battle, began to retreat. There came one last blood-curdling scream and the bird women fled, the ravens in pursuit.

'Go back to where you came from. Celene will never be yours,' Issa screamed at them.

She watched the ravens chase them until the fast fleeing harpies were lost from view. Unable to keep up with the bird-women, the ravens began to turn back.

She raised her arms up to the ravens as they circled above her. 'Brothers and sisters, messengers of Zanufey, return to your homes across Maioria. Speak to all the Daluni that you find. Tell them Baelthrom and his Maphraxies have destroyed the goddess's most sacred isle. Tell them about the fall of Celene. Then tell them that Zanufey is with us and that we must unite all against the immortals and drive them from Maioria for ever.'

The ravens cawed and disappeared back into the invisible veil that separated the land of the living from the dead. Only one raven did not follow and Ehka, with his indigo aura, landed wearily at her feet.

CHAPTER 51

The Fall of Celene

ISSA stepped back from the edge of the chasm and became aware of the others on the opposite side. Asaph's face was bloody and pale, his shirt was in shreds, and he still gripped his sword. Coronos leaned heavily on his staff clutching the Orb of Air, his face a mask of fear and wonder, his cloak ripped and stained with blood. Duskar paced frantically backwards and forwards, desperate to get to her.

Asaph beckoned to her but, she could neither hear what he said nor felt like moving just yet. If she could see the blood that fell from the gashes on her arms and back, she might have felt compelled to move. Right now, she stood in a strange silent world empty of thought, feeling and everything but the sense of calm.

She felt her knees buckle and sank to the floor. The air began to rush around her, and magic flowed but she was beyond the ability to read it anymore. The ground moved away from her—or perhaps it was she that moved away from it—and below her the great chasm gaped, filled with frothing sea.

Solid earth slid beneath her as the rushing air stopped and she lay blissfully on the soft grass. The Orb of Air dimmed in Coronos' hand.

'Why didn't you wait for us?' Asaph's worried face filled her vision.

Cloth was torn and wrapped around her shoulders. Beyond Asaph, the long black face of Duskar peered over. She began to laugh weakly. Suddenly it was all very funny.

'Wait for what?' she whispered. 'I couldn't stop them, they were already here. I don't think they'll be coming back anytime soon, though,' she laughed, but Asaph's face was like stone.

'You should never have faced so many, you could have died. They'll be back and more of them, and who knows what else.' He pulled a strip of cloth too tight, and she cried out in pain.

'Sorry,' he mumbled, guilt softening his features.

'Let them come,' she challenged. 'We can't run and hide forever.'

He let out a sigh and wrapped more cloth around her.

'Some of your wounds are deep. Let's hope that they don't get infected. Come on, let's move from here before anything else turns up.' He helped her onto her feet, but her legs were like jelly, so he lifted her into his arms.

'If you insist on fighting these beasts, you'll need more than this,' he said, tugging on what was left of her tunic that now revealed more flesh than it concealed.

'And at least wait for me to help,' he added indignantly. 'Who knows, you might need a dragon one day.'

She suppressed a giggle but caught the glint in his eye.

'I'll always need a dragon, Asaph,' she said seriously, liking it when he blushed.

'Let's get somewhere safe where we can better tend our wounds,' Coronos said. 'We haven't eaten breakfast yet and I'm famished.'

'There's a small cave in a sheltered cove not far from the temple. We could go there,' she said, feeling sick but also famished.

Asaph tried to put her on Duskar's back so he could support Coronos, but she refused and tried to stand.

'If my feet can no longer carry me, then I may as well be dead.'

'But you're injured, worse than you know,' Asaph said. 'Besides, if I hadn't suggested it you would have sat on the horse anyway.'

'I'm fine,' she replied and winced, feeling not fine at all.

'Curse her,' he grumbled. Coronos chuckled.

With quick hands, Asaph hoisted her into the air, ignoring her yelps, and plonked her on Duskar's back.

Duskar whickered and looked at her as if delighted to have her on his back. She stopped moaning and sat there indignant. She smiled at Duskar and stroked his neck, suddenly relieved not to have to walk anywhere, anyway.

Asaph smiled triumphantly and turned to help Coronos. His father looked terribly old and worn, and there was deep anguish in his eyes. His smile faded.

'Is everything all right?' he asked, worry twisting his stomach. Was he injured? But Coronos just shook his head and remained silent.

'Some food and rest will help everyone,' Asaph smiled, trying to be reassuring though not feeling it. He held Coronos' arm and helped him walk as they followed Issa and Duskar.

They walked in silence through the rubble, dead harpies and ravens, down a path leading to the ocean. It began to drizzle again, dampening the mood further, and the earth turned into rain-drenched sand as they neared the beach.

Issa's cave loomed in the distance, and they huddled into the welcome shelter. The cave was shallow but big enough for them to fit, horse and all. They made a fire from a pile of dry wood that someone had collected there. Someone who was probably dead now, Asaph thought sombrely. At least they wouldn't be needing the wood anymore. From their packs, they took strips of cloth and poultice and set about cleaning and wrapping each other's wounds.

Issa's were awful. The bloody claws of the harpies had sunk viciously deep. She was pale and exhausted, and her eyes were frighteningly more luminous than they had ever been, but there was a small smile of triumph on her face. He felt it too; they had faced another enemy and survived—just.

Once they had tended each other's wounds, they ate the food the Karalanths had given them. Devouring bread, fruit, nuts, and jam in famished silence.

Asaph thought about Celene as he ate. From the remains he had seen, Celene had once been a nice place. The white sandy beaches reminded him of his home with the Kuapoh in the Uncharted Lands. He wondered how they were and if he and Coronos were missed. The Fearsome Four probably missed him. Gurapoha missed Coronos for sure—who else would he be able to talk with late into the night? But he didn't want to return. Not now Issa was by his side.

He was about to mention the Kuapoh to Coronos, hoping to lift the silence and speak of happier things, but the awful sorrow on his father's face caused the words on his lips to die silently. He looked at Issa. She was trying to clean the dried blood from her fingernails. She caught his eye and gave a weak smile.

'There used to be a wet room in Castle Elune with a big iron bath. I long for a hot bath, the only thing that can wash away this dirt,' she reminisced mournfully.

'The Kuapoh, our family on the Uncharted Lands, used to visit the hot springs, about an hour's walk inland,' he said, feeling very much like he would love to go there right now. Especially with Issa. Naked of course.

'I should like to visit it, one day,' she said.

'The Kuapoh have no books or maps, everything is from memory. So my father, or rather, my adopted father...' Asaph smiled at Coronos, but he was lost deep in thought and staring into the fire, '...drew for me where the Isles of Kammy were. Apparently, in Draxa, the capital of Drax, there were vast libraries filled with books, maps and scrolls. I guess they must all be gone now. But luckily for us, the Orb of Air was often used to record all books and scriptures. If Coronos can remember the book or the name of the author, we can access it through the orb.'

Issa listened in fascination. 'Freydel, the wizard who taught me magic, said crystals had memories and could be used to store information. Orbs were the most powerful of all.

'My home, Little Kammy in the Isles of Kammy, is much like the mainland of Frayon, only tiny and surrounded by sea. Like here but colder.' She seemed about to say more but stayed silent.

It was a difficult question, but he thought he'd ask anyway.

'Is there a chance you might have family left, any at all, on Frayon or elsewhere?'

She shook her head then stopped. 'It's possible, but I think unlikely. My father died when I was born, and to protect me my blood mother gave me to Fraya, my adopted mother. It's possible my blood mother lives. She was a seer.'

Asaph considered this for a while before speaking. 'If you knew her last name, perhaps we could search for her. All seers are trained on the Isle of Myrn, where they live, or at least that's what Cusap'anth said.'

Issa shook her head and looked down at the floor as if she had already considered such things. 'The only last name I have is Kammy, Fraya's last name. Issalena Kammy,' she said her full name aloud. Asaph liked the sound of it. 'But even Kammy is not Fraya's real name. She changed her old one to Kammy when she moved to the Isles, and I can't remember what she said her old name was. Fraya never told me my blood mother's name because she didn't even know it herself. Do you have a family name?'

The question caught him off guard. He shook his head with a frown, trying to remember something Coronos had once said long ago.

'It would have been Dragon Born,' Coronos said, his eyes never leaving the fire as they both turned to look at him. 'All those born of Dragon Lords are called Dragon Born. But since you have the gift as well, you are called Dragon Lord, Asaph Dragon Lord, belonging to the family of Dragon Lords.

'I was called Coronos Avernayis Dragon Rider, since that was the profession to which I was called. Before my time as a Dragon Rider I was simply Coronos Avernayis, after the name of a small coastal town in South East Drax. That is how things work in Drax, or at least it used too...' he trailed off and said no more, losing himself once more in his thoughts.

'Asaph Dragon Lord.' She spoke his name, and he liked it, having only heard his full name spoken for the second time in his life, and never from her lips.

Somehow it made him feel as if he had a place in the world. He had always been an outsider with the Kuapoh, but now he felt his home was part of his name, his home was Drax. He glanced back at Coronos and sighed, wondering what, if anything, he could do to help. When in this mood, his father was unreachable. Asaph changed the subject.

'This place looks nice,' he indicated about him, meaning Celene. 'Plentiful land, clear running rivers, calm seas and a warm climate. Or at least it was before they came and destroyed everything.'

Issa nodded, her smile dropping. 'I'd just begun to consider it my new home. I was looking forward to seeing... my friends again. I had even thought you and Coronos might like to live here. We could start a new life, together.'

Seeing the dashed hope on her face, he looked down into the fire. He too felt like giving up hope of ever finding peace, of ever leading a normal happy life. He gave up on trying to cheer anyone up, including himself.

'It seems such a pleasant life is not meant for us,' he said quietly and glanced at her.

She gave a wry smile and nodded. Tears glistened in her eyes, and she looked away to the entrance where Duskar stood dozing. It had begun to rain harder.

Issa lay down on her blanket and willed for Coronos' poultice to calm her painful shoulders.

Asaph busied himself cleaning his sword and then her sword and anything else that looked grubby, which was most things. Coronos continued to stare into the fire, and she thought it best to leave him to his thoughts.

She thought of Arla and wondered where she had gone and when she would return. She didn't doubt the girl could look after herself, surviving Cirosa this long was no easy feat, but what if something had gone wrong? Worry for Arla kept her from thinking of Ely for a time but then, when the tiredness weakened her mind, thoughts of her friend plagued her.

She traced the silver leaves entwined around her wrist and glinting in the firelight. Ely's gift now made more precious with her death. She felt eyes upon her and looked up. Coronos was staring at the bracelet as well. The realisation suddenly hit her, and she sat up.

'You knew her didn't you,' she said, breaking the silence.

Asaph stopped cleaning her scabbard and stared at his father. Coronos did not break his gaze upon the bracelet and took so long to answer she thought he would not.

'I did,' he sighed eventually, then pulled out his long pipe from his pack. He tapped out the old ash, refilled it with lintel weed and lit it with a smouldering stick from the fire, puffing on the pipe until it was smoking. Only when he had placed the stick back in the fire did he say anymore.

'I had not seen her for nearly thirty years, certainly not since we fled Drax. It was really her mother I knew well,' he said, looking far away into the past, his eyes filled with sadness. He indicated to the silver leaves on her wrist. 'And that was her bracelet. It symbolises the Tree of Life and is a thing of beauty and healing power. I know these things because I watched her make it, and with the Orb of Air I helped her enchant it.'

Her mouth fell open and she caught Asaph's glance. The shock on his face mirrored her own.

'Ely gave it to me as a gift... I refused to take it, but she insisted,' Issa said. 'She told me only that her mother was a gifted healer priestess and that she wanted another with the gift to have it.'

'I know,' Coronos said with a knowing smile. 'I've seen it on your wrist before and recognised it instantly. It gave me hope that I would...' he hesitated for a moment as if wondering what to say then continued. 'Her mother was called Harianna, and she and I were lovers once.'

Issa and Asaph looked at each other again, then back at Coronos. He looked at them amused.

'What's wrong? Am I too old to have loved?' But the amusement swiftly left, and his face darkened once more. 'As a high priestess and healer, she was required to travel all of known Maioria visiting the

Goddess's Temples and teaching her healing to others. No matter what the danger, as a healer in a time of war, her skills were very much needed.

'I met her when she came to Draxa. I was a soldier in the Draxian army. To me, she was beautiful, fair and regal with blue eyes like the sky. I couldn't stop looking at her until she scowled at me for staring,' he laughed.

'But our love was fated. Though we shared our nights together, our days were spent apart because of our commitments. My position as second-in-command to the king and queen of Drax, and her duties healing the sick and injured made our lives impossible. We were sorely needed by others and were oath-bound to honour those duties. Though we loved each other deeply, and every moment we could find we spent together, in the end, we could not be together.

'Eventually, the Temple called her elsewhere. The years passed and then we were brought together again. Those times together were the happiest years of my life. Again we were called apart and after a year or so I received a letter from her telling me she had given birth to a beautiful child, our daughter. I wrote a letter in response, telling her that I would come to her on the Isle of Celene as soon as I could leave the king and queen's side.

'It would be two years before the relentless attacks of the Maphraxies would wane just enough for me to visit her. For one wonderful month, I spent my time here with Harianna and little Ely. I got to know our beautiful precious daughter.'

Issa held back the tears that welled within. Tears would not change anything; tears would not bring Ely back. She thought it ironic, then, that she knew more about Ely's parents than about her own. She would never in all the world have guessed Coronos was Ely's father, and now she knew it, she could see the similarities in their features; the arch of their eyes and the shape of their faces.

'The years passed and Harianna died, as people do. Sadly, non-Draxians do not live as long as we do,' he said, a tear made its way down his wrinkled face, and he wiped it away in surprise.

'Time does not heal everything,' he said softly, 'not everything, Hari.'

He sighed and wafted his hand. 'Anyway, all this happened so long ago, and many, many lives have been lost in this unending war. Now little Ely has been taken away from us by them too. I had only one last wish; to see her again, alive.'

'I'm sorry. I wish I could have stopped this,' she said, blinking back tears.

'We all do,' he breathed.

'Zanufey spoke to me back there,' she said, daring to admit the goddess spoke to her. She never liked talking about it to anyone, but now it seemed important. 'We can all find peace knowing that Ely is free from here and on her journey back into the light.'

Coronos swallowed and gave a sad smile. 'I wish I could have known the woman she had become.'

'She was kind and caring and giving to a fault,' Issa said fiercely through the tears. 'She was strong, like you, and regal like a queen. She had honour and determination, and she was my friend...' she couldn't go on and looked at the ground, fighting the sobs in her throat.

There was silence for a time and when Coronos spoke, his voice hoarse. 'We should try to get some sleep. Sorrow is exhausting, and we sorely need our strength. We must leave as soon as dawn breaks. It's not safe here.'

Issa was dragged up from a deep sleep born of magical exhaustion to the nudging of her sore shoulder. Duskar snorted in her ear.

'Duskar stop,' she groaned and tried to slip back to sleep. He nibbled her ear making her laugh but couldn't open her heavy eyes. She heard the others shifting at the sound of her voice, and looked up blearily into Duskar's big brown eyes. She yawned and stretched, feeling in sore need of more sleep.

'It can't be time to go. I've only been asleep five minutes.'

The embers of the fire gave a small amount of light, and the barest hint of grey came from the cave entrance, speaking of the coming dawn. Ehka had found a perch in the rock just before the entrance and still slept. The rain had thankfully stopped.

'Do you want some food?' she sat up and rummaged in her pack. She pulled out an apple, took a bite, and gave the rest to him. He munched on it noisily.

She stood up slowly, wincing from new wounds and aches that overlaid her old ones. If this was what getting old was like, she hoped she died young. The thought made her smile. As a warrior, she appeared to have chosen the right profession in order to die young.

Coronos and Asaph sat up, both looking tired and clearly wanting a lot more sleep. She hugged her shoulders, feeling danger like a feather brushing past. Duskar lifted his head and twitched nervously. Ehka awoke and looked out of the cave. The men got to their feet. There was only the noise of the surf in the distance, yet still, the uneasy feeling remained.

In silence they stuffed a bland breakfast of bread and water down their throats, packed away their few belongings and stamped out the fire.

'I'm thinking that, after we rendezvous with the Karalanths on the mainland, we should head for the city port Corsolon,' Coronos said, as they left the cave. 'We can buy horses for Asaph and I, and maybe even some armour. Although perhaps we'd better get to Carvon for that, where it's possible I may still have a friend or two there who can help us. Newcomers buying armour in a city might not go down too well with the locals.'

She and Asaph nodded. She hoped he still had some old acquaintances somewhere who could help them.

The air was still damp from the rain overnight, but at least it had stopped raining. The uneasy feeling grew, making her keen to be far away from this place.

'Are you both all right to ride?' Asaph asked.

Coronos nodded as he pulled his cloak closer around him. Issa paled at the thought of riding on a dragon's back again but nodded anyway.

Asaph touched the bandages about her shoulders and waist. There was no blood on them, which meant the bleeding had finally stemmed some time in the night. She shifted shyly, but let him pull them aside to see. His face turned to shock, and he began to pull them loose. She felt the blood rush back into her face as his hands touched her bare skin and he gave a wicked grin.

'By Feygriene's fire, they healed quick. Look, there are only red slashes where great welts had been,' he said in astonishment, gently touching the skin on her stomach and shoulders.

'The healer's bracelet—the Tree of Life is no myth,' Coronos said over his shoulder.

Asaph's fingers lingered on her belly causing butterflies to flutter there. She pulled away.

'Does it hurt?' he asked worriedly.

'No, it's fine,' she blushed. 'I'm glad it heals quickly. Here on Celene I think the bracelet's power is stronger, and maybe Ely's spirit is close...' she said touching the silver leaves. 'My ability to use the Flow has not healed at all, though.'

'The Tree of Life,' Asaph said thoughtfully. 'Though I doubt it will stop you getting killed. You'll need a dragon for that,' he winked.

'Really,' she said and put her hands on her hips.

He only smiled at her more. 'I'll try to protect you, whether or not you want me to.'

A rumble within the earth shook the ground, violent enough to make them stagger. The sea in the distance began to surge and the wind gusted. Duskar stomped his feet and Ehka flew squawking into the air.

'We should go,' she said, but the men were already running away from the cliff as rocks began to crash to the ground.

Quick as a flash, Asaph shifted into his dragon form, spreading dragon fear just as fast. Duskar bolted, Ehka darted back into the cave, and Coronos dropped then fell over the rope harness he had been carrying. All she could do was stand frozen to the ground.

'Sorry,' Asaph rumbled and tried to make himself smaller by curling up.

'The d-danger we f-felt is c-coming from the quaking earth, not M-Maphraxies,' she stammered.

The thought was not much consolation, though, even when the dragon fear began to subside. When she could move, she helped Coronos to his feet. Another rumble sent more rocks crashing down the cliff. The raven darted back out of the crumbling cave, and they all scrambled towards Asaph, suddenly unafraid of the golden dragon. Coronos was quick with the harness, and soon they were both clambering into it.

'What about Duskar? I'll not leave him,' she said, watching the horse pace nervously at the ocean's edge. He hadn't gone far, clearly not wanting to leave her side again, but terrified of the dragon.

'I don't know, I've never carried a horse before,' Asaph shouted over the wind, his massive teeth flashing in the darkness. 'Maybe I can reach his mind.'

After a moment, he shook his head. 'It's not like touching the mind of a dragon or human, or even a Wykiry. The horse's thoughts are scattered and wild. Full of energy.'

Splitting granite boomed making her squeal, and the earth quaked beneath her feet. The sea frothed and boiled, and Duskar reared, neighing as cracks snaked across the sand.

'Asaph hurry, the island is breaking,' she screamed. As she spoke he spread his wings wide and leapt into the air, making her squeal again.

He turned in a tight circle and glided low. At the last moment, he reached down massive claws and grasped the horse gently. Duskar whinnied and bucked, but Asaph held him firm as he soared into the air. The raven flew beside the bucking horse as if to calm him.

The ground below cracked apart, revealing a thick, blood red chasm like a vein. Hot lava spewed out, and seawater surged in, hissing and spitting violently. The red lava poured from the earth like blood, lighting up the darkness.

She looked back at the crumbling, steaming land that had been her home. Her eyes settled upon the blackened remains of the temple, half of which had disappeared into the great chasm. The other half was all that remained of the beautiful and shining Temple of Celene—once a symbol of peace and unity between dwarves, elves and humans, now a desecrated ruin. More lava chasms appeared, and the whole island shuddered.

'Why is it happening?' Asaph's voice boomed.

It was a good question for none of the other smaller islands seemed to be suffering the same fate as Celene.

'I don't know,' she said. 'Maybe Maioria herself is cleansing a desecrated holy land. In a way I'm glad. It's better to destroy it than leave it to the Maphraxies. Perhaps this should be our rallying call. News of the destruction of the Goddess's Sacred Isle will spread to every corner of Maioria, and who will not be enraged by that? Maybe the fall of Celene will unite the free people and renew their strength. Maybe they will then heed the call of Zanufey and stand as one against the immortals.'

Only when the red lava light of Celene was lost from view did Issa turn to face north where they were headed. The light of the sun broke once more upon the horizon, and once again she wondered where next she would find a place to call home. But for all the loss she found a little warmth in her heart, for this time she was not alone and her friends were with her.

Continued in *Storm Holt*

STORM HOLT

The Goddess Prophecies

Book 3

Araya Evermore

Would you sell your soul to save the world?

"How can I run? How can I turn away and leave them all to their fate? I will stay with them. I will die with them." ~ Issa

The Storm Holt—the ultimate Wizard's Reckoning, where all who enter must face their greatest demons. No woman has entered and survived since the Ancients split the magic apart eons ago. Plagued by demons and visions of a strange white spear, Issa must take the Reckoning to find her answers and fight for her soul to prove her worth to the most powerful magic wielders upon Maioria.

Rejected by Issa, Asaph lusts after the enchanting pale woman who stalks him, but her allure is foreboding and her power deadly. The Cursed King and his Banished Legion return to end their curse, but all around them is bloody chaos and sorrow and all seems hopeless.

Without the help of the Shadow Demons, Issa cannot hope to survive the Storm Holt—and without the help of the Raven Queen, the Shadow Demons will be destroyed. If Issa does not make a pact with the demons, then both Maioria and the Murk are doomed.

ALSO BY ARAYA EVERMORE

The Goddess Prophecies series:

Goddess Awakening ~ A Prequel

When darkness falls, a heroine will rise.

The Dread Dragons came with the dawn. On dark wings of death they slaughtered every seer and turned their sacred lands to ruin...

Night Goddess ~ Book 1

A world plunging into darkness. An exiled Dragon Lord struggling with his destiny. A young woman terrified of an ancient prophecy she has set in motion.

He came through the Dark Rift hunting for those who had escaped his wrath. Unchecked, his evil spread. Now, the world hangs on a knife-edge and all seems destined to fall. But when the dark moon rises, a goddess awakens, and nothing can stop the prophecy unfolding...

The Fall of Celene ~ Book 2

Impossible Odds, Terrifying Powers

"My name is Issa and I am hunted. I hold a power that I neither understand nor can barely control..."

The battle for Maioria has begun. Issa faces a deadly enemy as the Immortal Lord's attention turns fully in her direction. Nothing will stand in Baelthrom's way—he must destroy this new power that grows with the rising dark moon...

Storm Holt ~ Book 3

Would you sell your soul to save the world?

The Storm Holt... The ultimate Wizard's Reckoning, where all who enter must face their greatest demons. No woman has entered and survived since the Ancients split the magic apart eons ago. Plagued by demons and visions of a strange white spear, Issa must take the Reckoning to find her answers and fight for her soul to prove her worth to the most powerful magic wielders upon Maioria...

Demon Spear ~ Book 4

Demons. Death. Deliverance.

All these Issa must face as darkness strikes into the heart of their last stronghold. Greater demons are rising from the Pit, Carvon is brutally attacked, and a horrifying murder forces Issa and her companions to flee. But despite the devastating loss, she must keep her oath to the Shadow Demons and alone reclaim the spear that can save them all...

Dragons of the Dawn Bringer ~ Book 5

An Exiled King. A Broken Dream. A Sword Forged for Forever.

Issa can trust no one. Her closest allies betray her and nobody is as they seem. When a Dromoorai captures her and a black vortex to another dimension rips into her room, she realises the attacks will never stop and there is far worse than Baelthrom reaching for her out of the Dark Rift...

"Be the light unto the darkness…Be the last light in a falling world."

They had both been chosen: he to save another race; she to save her own from what he had become. Now, both must enter Oblivion and therein decide the fate of all…

BOOKS BY JOANNA STARR

Farseeker

Enlightened. Enslaved. Erased.

Earth, 50,000 years ago before the magic vanished. Invaded by aliens posing as gods, advanced civilisations crumbled. Now, these powerful off-worlders war for control of the planet, and the people who remain no longer remember what they once were. Seduced then enslaved, humanity has fallen…

Free Starter Library

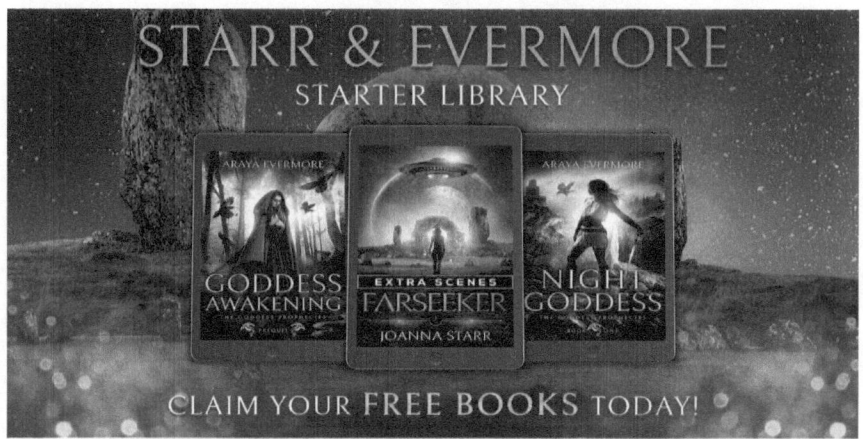

Join the mailing list and get your FREE Starr & Evermore Starter Library available only to subscribers. You'll discover Issa's origin story in my prequel, *Goddess Awakening*, which is not available anywhere else. You'll also get a taster of my latest *Farseeker* series with extra scenes not included in the main story.

To receive this epic free gift, please go to my website below. As a subscriber, you'll also be the first to hear about my latest novels, and lots more exclusive content.

www.joannastarr.com

About the Author

Araya Evermore is the pen name of Joanna Starr - a half-elf and author of the best-selling epic fantasy series, *The Goddess Prophecies*.

Joanna has been exploring other worlds and writing fantasy stories ever since she came to Planet Earth. Finding herself struggling in a world in which she didn't quite fit, escaping into fantasy novels gave her the magic and wonder she craved. Despite majoring in Philosophy & Religion, then Computer Science, she left her career in The City to return to her first love; writing Epic Fantasy.

Originally from the West Country, she's been travelling the world since 2011, and has been on the road so long she no longer comes from any place in particular. So far, she's resided in the Caribbean, United States, Canada, Australia, New Zealand, Spain, Andorra and Malta. Despite loving the mountains, she's actually a sea-based creature and currently resides by the ocean in Ireland.

Aside from writing and working, she spends time talking to trees, swimming with fish, gaming, and playing with swords.

Connect with Joanna online:
www.joannastarr.com
author@joannastarr.com

Enjoyed this book? You can make a big difference…

If you love fantasy books and would like to bring this series to the attention of other fantasy readers, the best thing you can do to reach them is to leave a review.

If you've enjoyed this book, I would be very grateful if you could spend just a minute leaving a review, (it can be as long or as short as you like) on the book's Amazon page.

A heartfelt Thank You in advance.